GARGANTUA AND PANTAGRUEL

GARGANTUA
A N D
PANTAGRUEL

François Rabelais

Translated by Burton Raffel

W·W·Norton & Company ⁄⁄ New York London

First Edition

Library of Congress Cataloging-in-Publication Data

Rabelais, François, ca. 1490–1553?
[Gargantua et Pantagruel. English]
Gargantua and Pantagruel / François Rabelais; translated by
Burton Raffel.
p. cm.
Translation of: Gargantua et Pantagruel.
I. Raffel, Burton.   II. Title.
PQ1685.E5R34   1990

843'.3—dc20   89-25595

ISBN 0-393-02843-7

W. W. Norton & Company, Inc.
500 Fifth Avenue, New York, N. Y. 10110
W. W. Norton & Company Ltd.
37 Great Russell Street, London WC1B 3NU
1 2 3 4 5 6 7 8 9 0

For KEZIA BETH RAFFEL

CONTENTS

TRANSLATOR'S PREFACE

FRANÇOIS RABELAIS was probably born in 1483. The son of a successful lawyer and property owner in Touraine, he became first a Franciscan friar and then a priest. He also became a remarkably well-schooled linguist, theologian, and classical scholar, a lawyer and diplomatist and, finally, a university-trained practicing doctor. Although he was never formally married, by papal dispensation the children born to him out of wedlock were permitted to bear their father's name. He edited learned texts, did a fair amount of translating, and lived a literally far-ranging life among the high and mighty of his time. Much influenced by the great Humanist Erasmus, who was fifteen years his senior, Rabelais was exactly the same age as Martin Luther and sixteen years older than John Calvin. He lived in stormy, fast-changing times, when one could be burned at the stake for an idea—as at least one of his close friends was. And from 1534 to the probable year of his death, 1554, he also wrote, in brilliant, sharp-edged prose, the first great novel in French literature, the sprawling, large-hearted comic chronicles of Gargantua and Pantagruel.

The immediate inspiration for his fiction was the great success in 1532 of a casual tale about the giant Gargantua. Piggybacking on this enormously popular and immensely forgettable book, Rabelais published what appeared to be a "continuation," recounting the adventures of Gargantua's son, to whom he gave the name Pantagruel. The success of this first volume led Rabelais to quickly write his own version of Gargantua's life: all later editions and translations print this second book as if it were the first, since in the fiction's chronological order it clearly takes precedence. The third book, entitled *Le Tiers Livre de Pantagruel*, The Third Book of Pantagruel, appeared in 1546, and the fourth in 1552. Two years after Rabelais' death the fifth book was published. Its authenticity has been much questioned from that day to this: it is my own view that, although much and perhaps even all of it was indeed written by Rabelais, the inferior quality of virtually the entire volume indicates that it is mostly either early draft material or else canceled fragments, which Rabelais left incompletely worked up or had expressly rejected.

The greatest of living Rabelaisians, Professor M. A. Screech, says flatly, "Scholarly and literary Frenchmen have been known to classify Rabelais as the most difficult author of any period writing in French." It may help explain this judgment to observe that Rabelais is something like a cross between James Joyce and Laurence Sterne (the latter, like Rabelais, an ordained clergyman), blessed in addition with profound classical and theological learning, proficient in many languages, deeply involved in matters scientific and medical, continuously active in issues legal and diplomatic, passionately curious about the lore of the folk, fascinated by the details of almost every occupation, trade, and profession known in his day, and on top of all this, a perpetual punster and prankster with his time's typical openmindedness and candor. All the obscenity, all the scatology, in these five volumes is Rabelais', but in his time he was not exceptional. Says Professor Screech, "A Renaissance author lived among fetid odours and ghastly stenches. He was at home with pain, deformity, illness, starvation and death. He did not like them, but he was not averse to referring to them." Erich Auerbach's study of two thousand years of European literature, *Mimesis,* beautifully sums up:

> Almost all the elements which are united in Rabelais' style are known from the later Middle Ages. The coarse jokes, the creatural concept of the human body, the lack of modesty and reserve in sexual matters, the mixture of such a realism with a satiric or didactic content, the immense fund of unwieldy and sometimes abstruse erudition, the employment of allegorical figures in the later books—all these and much else are to be found in the later Middle Ages. . . . But Rabelais' entire effort is directed toward playing with things and with the multiplicity of their possible aspects; upon tempting the reader out of his customary and definite way of regarding things, by showing him phenomena in utter confusion; upon tempting him out into the great ocean of the world, in which he can swim freely, though it be at his own peril. . . . The revolutionary thing about his way of thinking is not his opposition to Christianity, but the freedom of vision, feeling, and thought which his perpetual playing with things produces, and which invites the reader to deal directly with the world and its wealth of phenomena.

Plainly, translating Rabelais is extraordinarily difficult. I have tried to devise a flexible and responsive contemporary English prose equivalent, while trying at the same time to capture as much as I possibly could of the sweep and slash of Rabelais' writing. I have worked hard to keep his long, gorgeously piled-up sentences—not always easy to follow, even in the original Middle French. Chopping him into neatly logical short sentences makes Rabelais superficially more comprehensible, but infinitely less interesting. Similarly, I have sometimes briefly and I hope unobtrusively cued the curious reader to the books, personages, and events behind Rabelais' many erudite references, but unlike Jacques LeClerc, whose translation is in many ways an encyclopedia in disguise, I have not sought to explain in detail each and every such reference. Nor have I relied on footnotes, which seem to me out of place in a work meant to be read as literature and, as its author intended, for enjoyment as well as enlightenment. Neither, of course, have I suppressed or consciously altered anything, re-assigned speeches, or taken the other liberties so freely exercised by earlier translators. In spite of all the cross-checking and repeated reviewing by myself and a number of anonymous scholarly reviewers (to all of whom I am grateful, though I have not always accepted their suggestions), there are bound to be missed opportunities and even outright errors. But there has been no trifling with Rabelais' text.

That text has, to be sure, a long and tangled history. Rabelais wrote and then rewrote; he amended and enlarged; he suppressed and cut. For books one through four I have relied on two principal textual sources: the four volumes in the Droz series, *Textes Littéraires Français,* edited (from *Gargantua* to *Le Quart Livre*) by Ruth Calder and M. A. Screech (1970), V. L. Saulnier (1965), M. A. Screech (1974), and Robert Marichal (1947), and also the comprehensive Pléiade edition, edited by Jacques Boulenger and Lucien Scheler (1955). For the fifth book, I have relied on the Boulenger and Scheler as well as Guy Demerson's comprehensive *Editions du Seuil* volume (1973), though ignoring the loose and sometimes cavalierly inaccurate modern French translation that Demerson prints in parallel columns.

My preparatory reading was guided by Professor Joseph Duggan of the University of California at Berkeley, who has been as generously helpful with this translation as he was, not too many years earlier, with my version of Chrétien de Troyes' *Yvain.* Any sort of complete bibliography would be out of place, but I have drawn heavily on Christiane Marchello-Nizia, *Histoire de la langue française aux XIVe et XVe siècles* (1979); the fine, concise introduction to Peter Rickard, *Chrestomathie de la langue française au quinzième siècle* (1976); Lazare Sainéan, *La Langue de Rabelais* (1922–23); and, among books available in English, Mikhail Bakhtin, *Rabelais and His World* (1965); Florence M. Weinberg, *The Wine and the Will: Rabelais's Bacchic Christianity* (1972); and—to my mind the best critical study of Rabelais in any language—M. A. Screech, *Rabelais* (1979).

Among all the other debts left unrecorded, I should like, finally, to specify that to Barry K. Wade, whose enthusiasm for earlier translations of mine led him to commission this one.

Lafayette, Louisiana
November 1989

The Truly
Hair-raising Life
of the Great Gargantua
Father of Pantagruel

Written Many Years Ago by

Maître Alcofribas

Extractor of the Fifth,

or Celestial, Essence

A BOOK FULL
OF PANTAGRUELISM

To My Readers

Readers, friends, if you turn these pages
Put your prejudice aside,
For, really, there's nothing here that's outrageous,
Nothing sick, or bad—or contagious.
Not that I sit here glowing with pride
For my book: all you'll find is laughter:
That's all the glory my heart is after,
Seeing how sorrow eats you, defeats you.
I'd rather write about laughing than crying,
For laughter makes men human, and courageous.

BE HAPPY!

GARGANTUA AND PANTAGRUEL

THE AUTHOR'S PROLOGUE

HIGH and mighty guzzlers! And you, O all you precious pox-ridden—I dedicate my writings to you, not to anyone else—

In Plato's dialogue *The Banquet,* Alcibiades praises his teacher, Socrates—without any argument the prince of philosophers—saying among other things that Socrates seemed like a Silenus.

A Silenus: those used to be little boxes, the kind you see, today, in drugstores, painted all around with light and happy figures, like harpies, satyrs, bridled geese, hares with horns, saddled ducks, flying goats, stags in harness, and all sorts of such images, invented in good fun, just to make the world laugh (exactly as Silenus used to do, honest Bacchus' master). But what they used to keep inside these boxes were rare medicines like balsam and ambergris, cardamom and melegueta pepper, musk, civet, gemstones, and all kinds of precious stuff.

And that was what Socrates was like, Alcibiades said, because just looking at him, trying to weigh him from the outside, you wouldn't give a bite of onion for him—his body was so ugly and he walked so clumsily, with a pointed nose, the eyes of a bull, the face of an idiot, the simplest, plainest manners, a peasant's clothes, poor as a church mouse, unlucky in love, incapable of holding down any office, always laughing, always chugging down glass after glass with anyone who came along, always making fun of himself, always hiding his divine wisdom. But just open that box and you'd find heavenly, priceless medicines: an understanding more than human, miraculous virtue, invincible courage, unmatchable sobriety, unshakable peace, perfect confidence, and an unbelievable contempt toward everything that makes human beings peel their eyes, everything they chase after and work for, and sail the seas to find, and fight wars over.

And what's the point, do you suppose, of all this preliminary stuff, this warning flourish? So that you, my good disciples—and other fools with too much time on their hands—reading the cheerful titles of some of my books, like *Gargantua, Pantagruel, Guzzlepot, The High Importance of Codpieces, Peas in Lard (With Commentary),* etc., can more easily perceive that they're not just about mocking and scoffing, full of silliness and pleasant lies—having seen, without having to look any harder, that their outer image (that is, their titles) is usually received with mocking laughter and jokes. But it's wrong to be so superficial when you're weighing men's work in the balance. Wouldn't you yourself say that the monk's robes hardly determine who the monk is? Or that there are some wearing monk's robes who, on the inside, couldn't be less monkish? Or that there are people wearing Spanish capes who, when it comes to courage, couldn't have less of the fearless Spanish in them? And that's why you have to actually open a book and carefully weigh what's written there. Then you'll understand that the medicine inside is worth more than the whole box seemed to be worth—which is just another way of saying, of course, that what you'll meet in these pages isn't as flighty as the title you find printed on the outside.

Anyway, let's suppose you really do find the words as gay and bright as the title—well, are you supposed to stop at that, as if you'd gotten yourself trapped in the bewitching song of the Sirens? Aren't you supposed to bring a higher level of understanding to a book—even if, at first, you thought it was written simply in fun?

Have you ever stolen a bottle? Oh, you dog, you dog! Remember how you looked. And have you ever seen a dog find a marrowbone? (In book two of the *Republic,* mind you, Plato says the dog is the most philosophical beast in the world.) If you have, you saw with what devotion he guards it, with what passion he holds it, with what care and judiciousness he takes the first bite, with what love he cracks it open, and with what care he sucks it dry. What impels him? What does he expect from such zeal? What benefit does he expect? Just a bit of marrow, that's all. To be sure, this tiny reward is more delicious than a vast quantity of other things: as Galen explains, in the third part of *On the Natural Faculties* and in the eleventh part of *On the Use of the Various Parts of the Human Body,* marrow is nature's perfect food.

Just like the dog, you ought to be running with your educated nose to the wind, sniffing out and appreciating such magnificent volumes—you should be light on your feet, swift in the chase, bold in the hunt. Then, by hard reading and constant reflection, you ought to crack the bone and suck the nourishing marrow—or, in plainer words, you should get to the sense of these Pythagorean symbols, hoping—no, *knowing*—you'll be wiser and more far-seeing for your labor. Because you'll find all sorts of flavors here in this book, and secret learning, which will open in front of you the highest sacraments and the most hair-raising mysteries, not only concerning our religion but also politics, even economics.

Do you actually believe in the bottom of your heart that Homer, writing the *Iliad* and the *Odyssey,* ever thought of the allegories pulled and tickled out of him by Plutarch and Heraclides Ponticus and Eustachius and Cornutus the Stoic—or by Politian, who stole his arguments from all the rest of them? If you do, you don't come within a step—no, not even a hand's breadth—of my opinion, because I solemnly swear that Homer no more dreamed of them than Ovid's *Metamorphoses* are all about the mysteries of the Gospel, which that idiot Friar Lubin (a true parasite) has tried to prove. Maybe he thinks he'll meet someone as stupid as he is, someday—as the proverbs says, another lid for the same pot.

But if you don't believe it, why don't you do as much for these merry new tales of mine—because, writing them, I never once thought of stuff like that any more than you did, probably drinking your wine, just as I was. In fact, while working away at this noble book, I never spent (or lost) time over it except when I was also working away at my bodily refreshment, drinking and eating. Which is the right time for writing about such exalted matters, such profound truths, as Homer knew perfectly well—he, the very model for all our learned literary people—and Ennius, too, father of Latin poets, as Horace bears witness, though some swine has said that *his* poems had more to do with lamp oil than wine.

Some scabby beggar said the same thing about my books, but shit to him!—But the bouquet of good wine—ah, how sweet, neat—what a happy treat—incredibly more delicious, more heavenly, than oil! When they say of me that I've spent more on wine than on oil, I'll be as proud as Demosthenes, when they said of him that he spent more on oil than on wine. To be a jolly man, a good friend, a good boozer—to me, that spells honor and glory. And that well-deserved reputation makes me welcome anytime Pantagruelists sit down together. A peevish bore scolded Demosthenes that his *Orations* smelled like the filthy, dirty apron of a peddling oil seller. Nevertheless, interpret everything I do and say in the most gracious light; show proper respect for this cheesy brain, which pleases you with all this charming nonsense; and—as much as you can—always think of me as happy.

Now have fun, my lovely friends, and read all the rest of this gaily, because it's good for your body (and not bad for your kidneys, either). But listen, you old donkey pricks—may the sores on your legs turn you lame!—you'd better not forget to drink to me, in return, and I'll do the same for you without wasting a second.

Chapter One ⁄⁄ All about Gargantua's Genealogy and Antiquity

Let me remind you how the great chronicle of Pantagruel told all about Gargantua's genealogy and the antiquity of his family. There you can find, set out at much greater length, how the giants were born into this world, and how Gargantua, Pantagruel's father, is their descendant in a direct line. So don't be angry if, at least for now, I don't repeat it all, though it's a story that couldn't help pleasing Your Lordships even more, every time it was told. Don't we have the authority of Plato, in his *Philebus* and his *Gorgias,* and that of Horace, too, who says there are some things—and these among them, without the slightest doubt—that become more delightful the more they're retold?

Would to God everyone could know as much about his genealogy, from Noah's ark down to today! I think there are lots of emperors walking the earth, these days, and kings and dukes and princes and popes, too, who are descended from peddlers of indulgences and grape baskets, just as, the other way around, there are lots of people down at the heel, suffering and miserable, who are descended by blood in a direct line from the greatest kings and emperors. Just consider the wonderful succession of kingdoms and empires:

> from the Assyrians to the Medes,
> from the Medes to the Persians,
> from the Persians to the Macedonians,
> from the Macedonians to the Romans,
> from the Romans to the Greeks,
> from the Greeks to the French.

And to tell you about the man who's speaking to you, I suspect I might be descended from some rich king or prince of olden times—because you'll never see anyone who'd rather be a king, and rich, than me, so I could spread good cheer everywhere, and never work, and never worry about anything, and pour down gold on my friends and all good and learned men. But I console myself that in the next world I'll be grander than in this one—grander than I dare dream. Drown your own bad luck in such a thought, or a better one, and drink as much as you can, if you can.

Getting back to our mutton chops, let me explain that by a sovereign gift straight from heaven we've been given Gargantua's genealogy, right from the beginning of time, more complete than that of any man but the Messiah, of whom I say nothing, because it's none of my business. Also, the devils (by which I mean slanderers and hypocrites) don't want me to. Gargantua's genealogy was found by Jean Audeau in a meadow he owns, near the Gualeau arch, down past l'Olive, getting close to Narsay. He was cleaning out the ditches, and one of the workmen's hoes hit a great bronze tomb, huge beyond measuring—no one could find the end, because before they got to it they ran into the Vienne sluice gates. Opening it where they saw a special mark, the sign of a goblet, written all around in Etruscan lettering, DRINK HERE, they found nine tall drinking flasks, lined up in three parallel rows, the way they set ninepins in Gascony. And in the middle row they saw a fat, greasy, thick, gray, pretty, tiny, moldy little book, which smelled more—but not better—than roses.

And here's where they found the genealogy, all carefully written out in a chancery hand, not on paper, not on parchment, not cut into wax or chiseled in stone, but on thin elm bark, so worn, so decayed, that you could barely make out three letters in a row.

I did not deserve the honor, but I was called there and, relying heavily on my spectacles, practicing that art by which one reads invisible letters (as Aristotle teaches), I translated it, as you can see when you're pantagruelizing, that is, as you're drinking your fill and reading these hair-raising stories of Pantagruel.

Now, at the end of the little book was a small treatise, entitled *Antidotal Jokes*. Rats and moths—or, more honestly, assorted other vicious beasts, ate away the very beginning—but I've set down here all the rest, in deep reverence for all things ancient.

Chapter Two // Antidotal Jokes, Found in an Ancient Tomb*

[Comes] the great Tamer of the Celtic Cimbri,
[So afraid] of dew that he flies through the air.
[Against] his coming they've stuffed the troughs
[With] fresh butter, falling like a shower.
[And when] grandma was well watered with the stuff
She yelled out loud, "O God, please!
Fish it on up. His beard's all mucky.
At least, lower him down a ladder."

Some people say that licking his slipper
Is worth more than winning his pardons.
But then a slimy fool appeared,
Popping from the bottom where roach fish swim,
And he said, "Gentlemen, for God's sake, no.
The eel's down there, hidden in his cage.
You'll find him there (if you look good and hard),
With a great big spot at the bottom of his neckcloth."

He was just about to read the chapter
When all he could find there was a pair of calf's horns.
"The bottom of my bishop's staff (he said)
Is so freezing cold that my brain's gone icy."
They warmed him up with turnip fragrance
And he was happy to stay near the fire,
On condition that a harness was clapped on someone
Else, from the crowd of crazies all around.

They analyzed Saint Patrick's gaping hole,
And Gibraltar, and a thousand other assholes,
Wondering how to get them down
To a scar so small that it might be invisible,
For they all agreed it just wasn't right

* "We've understood almost nothing of this," observes M. A. Screech.

To see them hanging open when the wind blew.
Perhaps if they got them tightly closed
They could even be pledges for commercial loans.

They'd gotten that far when the crow got skinned
By Hercules, freshly arrived from Libya.
"Hey!" said Minos. "Why not call me?
You've brought in everyone else in the world,
And it's all too much, much too much:
They want me to dish them up oysters, and frogs.
Well, if they keep from cutting my throat
I'll get them one hell of a trade in bedposts."

Up limped Q.B., to argue them flat
(His pass was signed by some cheerful starlings).
Cyclops' cousin, that cinder sifter,
Beat them to death. So they blew their noses!
This well-plowed field didn't yield much asshole
Buggery (the tanner's mill took care of 'em).
Hey! Run and sound the alarm:
The crop's way up from the one last year.

A little later, Jupiter's bird
Made up his mind to bet on the worst of them,
But seeing how exceedingly angry they got
Was worried they'd huff and puff down the empire,
So he thought it better to steal the Empyrean
Fire from the stump where herrings are sold.
Otherwise he'd have to filter tranquil
Air through a haze of Masoretic texts.

And in spite of Até, with her heron's thighs,
They got it all down to the point of a pin.
Até just sat there, watching Penthesilea,
So old she looked like a watercress pond.
And everyone cried, "You stinking peddler!
Why must we find you blocking the road?
You took it, you did, that Roman banner
They turned into parchment texts and tomes!"

Juno was high under heaven, with her royal
Horned owl, busily snaring birds.
They played a dirty trick on her,
Which looked like really doing her in.
They let her have two of Proserpina's eggs—
That was the final agreement—provided

They never catch her there again,
Or they'd tie her up on a mountain of hawthorns.

Seven months later (subtracting twenty-
Two) that man who'd ruined Carthage
(The soul of courtesy) appeared among them,
Demanding his heritage. Or better yet,
That it should all be divided up,
Share and share alike, as the law
Provided. He offered a bit of soup
To the friends and scumbags who drew up the deed.

But that year will come, marked by a Turkish
Bow (and five spindles, and three
Old pots), when the back of a barbarous king
Will be pockmarked, despite his hermit's cloak.
For shame, for shame! So many acres
Lost to a mealymouthed licker of asses.
Stop it, stop it! The game's a bad one.
Give up, go home to the snake's older brother.

When that year's gone, he who is
Will be king, and peaceful, together with his friends.
And there'll be no rudeness, no insults, in that reign:
All good wishes will be brought to pass.
And the joy, promised so long ago
To the hosts of heaven, will ring out in bells.
And then all the stud horses, struck dumb for years,
Shall march in triumph as royal steeds.

And this time of magic and tricks will last
Until Mars is finally put in chains.
And a time will come surpassing all time
Cheerful, delightful, lovely beyond
Compare. Raise your hearts toward that banquet,
My faithful friends, for he has gone
Beyond us, and nothing could tempt him back,
Which is how it will be when we mourn for time.

And finally, he who was fashioned of wax
Will live at the door hammer's door. And the jumping
Jack who tends the potbellied kettle
Will never be called "My Lord, My Lord."
Ah, if you got your broadsword out
You could put an end to this swarming mess,
And then a spool of good thick thread
Could bind up all this rotten stuff.

Chapter Three ⁄⁄ How Gargantua Was Carried in His Mother's Belly for Eleven Months

In his time, Grandgousier was a fine tippler and a good friend, as fond of draining his glass as any man walking the earth, cheerfully tossing down salted tidbits to keep up his thirst. Which is why he usually kept a good supply of Mainz and Bayonne hams, plenty of smoked beef tongues, lots of whatever chitterlings were in season and beef pickled in mustard, reinforced by a special caviar from Provence, a good stock of sausages, not the ones from Bologna (because he was afraid of the poisons Italians often use for seasoning), but those from Bigorre and Longaulnay (near Saint-Malo), from Brenne and Rouergue.

When he became a man, he married Gargamelle, daughter of the King of the Butterflies, a fine, serviceable female—with a good-looking face, too. And they whacked away at making the beast with two backs, happily whipping their lard together, so successfully that she conceived a handsome boy and carried him for eleven months.

Because even that's not as long as women can carry a child, above all when the baby's a masterpiece, someone who's bound to do great deeds in his time, as Homer said of the child that Neptune conceived in the nymph Tyro, who was born only after an entire year: that was twelve months. And as Aulus Gellius says, in book three of his *Attic Nights,* such a long time was completely appropriate for Neptune's majesty, because it took that long to form the child perfectly. For the same reason, Jupiter made the night he spent with Alcmena last forty-eight hours, because in anything less than that he couldn't possibly have forged the infant Hercules, who would go on to cleanse the earth of monsters and tyrants.

All the ancient Pantagruelists are agreed that what I say is not only possible, but they have declared that the child born to a woman eleven months after the death of her husband is that husband's legitimate son:

Hippocrates, *Concerning Nourishment,*
Pliny the Elder, *Natural History,* book 7, chapter 5,
Plautus, *The Jewel-Box,*
Marcus Varro, in his satire called *The Testament,* alleging the authority of Aristotle on this matter,
Censorinus, *Concerning the Days of Birth,* book 6,
Aristotle, *Concerning the Nature of Animals,* book 7, chapters 3 and 4,
Aulus Gellius, *Attic Nights,* book 3, chapter 16,
Servius, *On the Eclogues,* explaining a line in Virgil,

—and a thousand other fools, the number of which has been vastly swollen because of the increase in lawyers: see Justinian's *Digest,* law 3, paragraph 13, and *Concerning Legal Restitution and the Female Who Bears a Child in the Eleventh Month after the Decease of Her Husband.* They've even scribbled it into their bacon-gnawing Gallic law, *Concerning Posthumous Children and Heirs Unprovided for by Will or Disinherited,* and so on, including other laws that, right now, I'd better not refer to. And thanks to laws like these, widows can play squeeze-your-ass to their hearts' content (and not just their hearts), and bet the whole bank, for two whole months after their husbands have kicked the bucket.

So I beg you by all that's holy, you upstanding young fellows, if you find any juicy widows worth opening your fly front for, hop up—and ride them over here. Because if they get pregnant by the third month, whatever pops out will inherit from the dead man—and once she's visibly pregnant, they can bang on as hard as they like and what the hell! the stomach's already stuffed full—the way Julia, Emperor Octavian's daughter, would never abandon herself to those who played drumroll on her belly until she knew she was pregnant, just like a cargo ship that won't take on a pilot until she's all freshly caulked up and loaded. And if anyone criticizes them for letting the game go on when they're pregnant, since even animals won't stand for males being male-ish, not while they're carrying their young, well, they'll answer that those are animals, but they're human beings, women who understand perfectly well the beautiful, joyous (if minor) privilege of double impregnation, as Populia put it, once upon a time, according to what Macrobius tells us in book two of his *Saturnalia.*

Anyway, if the devil didn't want them to get pregnant, he'd have to turn off the faucet and shut the hole.

Chapter Four ⁄⁄ How Gargamelle, When She Was Pregnant with Gargantua, Proceeded to Stuff Herself with Tripe

Here's how and when Gargamelle went into labor—and if you don't believe it, may your ass fall off!

Her ass fell out, one afternoon, on the third day of February, from having eaten too much fatty beef tripe—tripe from oxen fattened both in the stall and also by grazing in meadows where the grass is so rich that it has to be mown twice a year. And in fact they had killed three hundred and sixty-four thousand and fourteen of these fat oxen, to be salted on Shrove Tuesday, so that in the springtime they'd have plenty of good pressed beef and, before they really sat themselves down and started to eat, they could have a little ritual in celebration of meat salting—which would also make it easier to enjoy their wine.

There was no shortage of tripe, believe me, and so delectable that they were all licking their fingers. But that was the trouble, damn it! and a big trouble, too: they just couldn't keep all that delicious tripe: it was bound to go rotten. This struck them as downright indecent. So they decided it was their duty to wolf it all down, as fast as they were able. And to accomplish this most expeditiously they invited all the citizens of Cinais, and Seuilly, and La Roche-Clermault, and Vaugaudry and, not far behind them, the folks from Coudray Monspensier, and Gué de Vède, and a slew of their other neighbors—good guzzlers, all of them, good friends, and fellows who knew what to do when a bottom was up.

That good man Grandgousier, relishing the occasion, ordered double portions for everyone. But he was careful to warn his wife not to eat too much, since she was nearing her time and, anyway, tripe was not the best meat going:

"You've really got to love chewing on shit," he said, "to swallow all these bowel pipes."

But in spite of these cautionary words she ate sixteen barrels, two casks, and six pots besides. Oh, the lovely load of shit that must have swollen up inside her!

After dinner they ran, all helter-skelter, down to the willow grove and there, on the thick, tough grass, they danced to the happy sound of flutes and the gay piping of bagpipes, and it was absolutely celestial to see them having such a grand time.

Chapter Five ⁄ The Chatter of Well-Oiled Drunks

And then they thought of going back and having another meal. And flasks started to pass from hand to hand, and hams picked themselves up and trotted about, and goblets flew, and bottles chinked and clinked:

"Pour it, pour it!"

"Over here!"

"My turn!"

"Mix it, mix it!"

"Give me mine straight. . . . Ah, like that, my friend."

"Drink that down in one gulp—quick!"

"Bring me a glass of nice light wine, full to the top!"

"Down with thirst!"

"O you false fever, won't you go away?"

"Oops, my dear (burped a woman): I can't get it down."

"My love, are you too cold?"

"It looks like it."

"By Saint Quenet's belly, let's talk about drinking."

"I only drink when church bells ring—or a papal bull bellows."

"Me, I only drink when my prayer book says so—just like a good and proper abbot."

"Which came first—thirst or drinking?"

"Thirst. How could you drink if you weren't thirsty, back in the days when we were all innocent?"

"No, drinking. Because *privatio presupponit habitum*: 'if there's something missing, then there's got to be something that used to be there.' Me, I'm a scholar. *Faecundi calices quem non fecere disertum?* 'Is there anyone who hasn't been turned into an orator by having his glass continually refilled?'—as Horace puts it."

"The rest of us innocents drink quite enough, even without being thirsty."

"No. I may be just a sinner, but I can't guzzle without having a thirst. Maybe not a thirst right now, but at least one in the future—so I can take care of it, if you know what I mean. I drink for the future to come. I drink eternally. For me, eternity is drinking and drinking is eternity."

"Sing—drink—let's have a song!"

"Where's my funnel? Wine going into a barrel: that's the only song I want to hear!"

"What? Am I drinking only by proxy? Let's have another one over here!"

"Query: Do you wet your whistle so you can get dry again, or do you get dry so you can pour in some more?"

"I don't know a thing about theory. Practice helps a little, now and then."

"Hurry up, you over there!"

"A drop here, a drop there: I drink, and all because I'm afraid of death."

"Just drink all the time and you'll never die."

"If I don't drink, I'll be dry: to me, that would be death. My soul is always running off to some swamp. A dry soul is a dead soul. *Anima certe, quia spiritus est, in sicco habitare non potest,* as Saint Augustine tells us. 'Surely the soul, because it is spirit, cannot dwell in dryness.' "

"O wine stewards, you workers of miracles, creators of new life-forms, you who turn ordinary men into drinkers, transform me from a non-drinker to a drinker!"

"An eternal flood along these dry, these tough and palpitating guts of mine!"

"He who drinks and feels nothing drinks for nothing."

"It gets right into your veins: you don't piss away a drop of it."

"How gladly I bathe the tripe of this calf—this calf that I sliced up just this morning."

"My stomach has just the right ballast!"

"Ah, if the paper on which I wrote my promissory notes would soak up ink as I'm soaking up wine, there wouldn't be a thing for my creditors to show the judge."

"That hand lifting your glass is ruining your nose."

"Oh how many others will go in, before that one comes out!"

"If you keep diving down to the bottom of your glass, you'll get to be like a horse straining to reach a shallow stream."

"They could call this bird catching: what are all those bottle birds doing, just standing there like bait?"

"What's the difference between a bottle and a flask?"

"Tremendous: you close a bottle with a plug, but a flask you stopper by screwing."

"Hey ho!"

"Our fathers knew how to drink" (singing)—"They emptied their mugs."

"Now that's a shit bitch of a song. Drink!"

"This one's going down there to wash those tripes. Got anything you want to send to the riverbank?"

"I don't drink any more than a sponge does."

"Me, I drink like a trooper."

"I drink *tanquam sponsus,* like the bridegroom in the Song of Solomon."

"And me, *sicut terra sine aqua,* like parched ground where there's no water."

"Who's got another word for ham?"

"That's a barkeeper's writ; it's a barrel ramp. The ramp lets you run wine barrels down into the cellar. Ham lets you run the wine into your belly."

"Now that—I'll drink to that! But the indictment isn't complete. *Respice personam; pone pro duos; bus non est in usu*—Pay attention to whom you're serving and pour enough for two—and pay no attention to my bad grammar—or to how much we've already drunk."

"If I could climb up as well as I can put it down, I'd be long gone, flying through the air."

"How did Jacques Cuer get rich? Like this."

"This is how you make money out of uncut timberland."

"And how do you think old Bacchus conquered India?"

"Or the Portuguese took Zanzibar—smart buggers, they used wine instead of gunpowder."

"Light rain smothers a high wind. And good hard drinking smashes thunder."

"If my balls could piss out a urine like that, how'd you like to suck on it?"

"I can hold my liquor."

"Hey, boy, it's my turn! Do you want me to get a ticket for passing illegally?"

"Suck it up, Gilly! There's at least one more bottle."

"I'm obliged to appeal this condemnation to thirst—it's sheer abuse. Boy, you've got to do these things according to form."

"Is that all that's left?"

"Once upon a time I drank everything in sight. Now it's different: I leave nothing."

"There's no hurry. Let's just keeping pouring it down."

"Ah, this is tripe worth spinning the dice for, and again, and again— from that striped black ox, remember him? Oh, God, let's honor this household, let's do it right!

"Drink, or I'll—"

"No, no!"

"But drink, please."

"Sparrows only drink when you whack them on the tail. Me, I only drink when you coax me."

"Hey there—booze! There isn't a rabbit hole anywhere in my body where this wine won't go hunting after thirst."

"This stuff really whips me."

"This is really going to drive it out of me."

"Let's make a proclamation, to the sound of bottles and flasks: who-ever's lost his thirst had better not look for it here. All these hefty injec-tions of drinking and we've shat it away, out back."

"Our Lord in heaven made the moon and the stars besides, but what we've done is clean off some sideboards."

"Jesus's final words are on my lips: *Sitio,* 'I thirst.' "

"And when He spoke of that which is so eternally hard that it will never burn, His words were no more quenchable than my priestly thirst."

"Eating gives you an appetite, said the bishop of Mans. But drinking chases away thirst."

"Is thirst curable?"

"It's exactly the opposite of how you treat dog bites: if you're always chasing a dog, he never bites you; if you always drink before you get thirsty, it will never happen to you."

"I've got you with your eyes shut: now I'll shake you awake. O eternal wine steward, keep us from snoozing! Argus could see with a hundred eyes: a wine steward needs a hundred hands—like Briareus, that giant with fifty heads—so he can pour and pour without interruption."

"Let's soak it up. Thirst is a noble thing!"

"White wine, that's what I want! Pour it all, pour it right out, in the devil's own name! Pour it over here, right to the top: my tongue is split-ting."

"Oh, ja. Mein friends, trink it up!"

"To you, my friend! From the heart—straight from the heart!"

"Ho, ho, ho! This is real guzzling, that's what this is."

"O lachrima Christi, Christ's holy tears!"

"That one's from La Devinière, it's a good black Burgundy."

"O noble white wine!"

"And, by my soul, it's just like velvet to the stomach."

"Hey, hey, it's one of a kind, it's choice, it's velvet well cut, spun out of the best stuff going."

"Be brave, my friend!"

"This won't be a game where we go flying off, because I've already done too much lifting."

"*Ex hoc in hoc:* And the Lord pours it from one to the other. But there's no magic about it: you've all of you seen it. I'm just a past master, that's all. No, wait a minute! I'm just Master Paster."

"To you, all drinkers! Oh, let us all be thirsty!"

"Boy, boy—my friend—fill this, please—let the good wine pour forth. Who cares if it runs right over?"

"Like a cardinal's crown!"

"*Natura abhorret vacuum,* Nature abhors a vacuum."

"Wouldn't you say a fly was drinking here, not a man? Only a fly could find anything to drink in this glass!"

"Drink—as if you came from Brittany!"

"All of it, all of it—drink!"

"Drink—oh, it's good—and it's good for you!"

Chapter Six How Gargantua Was Born in an Extremely Odd Way

While they were chattering away on the subject of drinking, Garga-melle began to feel sick in her lower parts. So Grandgousier rose from his seat on the grass and courteously tried to cheer her up, expecting that her labor had begun. He told her that she was lying on good grass under willow trees and that, before very long, there'd be someone new lying next to her. She ought to be encouraged by the imminent arrival of her little baby. It was certainly true that the pain would make her feel bad, but it would all be over very soon, and the happiness that always fol-lowed a birth would completely wipe away all the discomfort. Nothing would be left but a memory.

"I'll prove it to you," he said. "God—our Savior Himself—declares in the Gospel according to Saint John, chapter sixteen, 'A woman in labor is sad, yes, but once she has her child she remembers nothing of all her pain.' "

"Ha!" she said. "It's easy enough for you to talk—you and all other men. By God, I'll do everything I can, since it's what you want. But I wish to God you'd cut it off!"

"What?" said Grandgousier.

"Oh," she said, "you're a fine one, you are! You know exactly what I mean."

"My tool?" said he. "Holy cow! If that's what you want, tell them to bring me a knife."

"Ha!" she said. "God forbid. May He forgive me! I didn't really mean it, so don't do it just for me. But I'll have plenty on my hands, today, without God's good help, and it's all because of that tool of yours, which makes you feel so good."

"Be brave, be brave!" said he. "Don't worry about anything. I'll just get myself something to drink. Remember: when you've got all your oxen harnessed to the plow, and they're hauling away at it, just let the lead ox do the job. If you start to feel really bad, I won't be far off. Just cup your hands around your mouth and let out a good yell. I'll come right back."

Not long after, she began to moan and cry and wail. And then mid-wives came from everywhere, to help her. Groping around underneath, they found some fleshy excrescences, which stank, and they were sure this was the baby. But in fact it was her asshole, which was falling off, because the right intestine (which people call the ass gut) had gone slack, from too much guzzling of tripe, as we have already explained.

Then one of them, a dirty old hag who was said to be a great doctor (she'd come from Buzançais, near Saint-Genou, sixty years earlier), made her a good stiff astringent—so ghastly that every sphincter in her body was locked up tight, snapped so fiercely shut that you couldn't have pulled them open with your teeth, which is pretty awful to think about. You couldn't have done it any better than the devil, listening to Saint Martin's mass and trying to get down on paper all the stupid chattering of a couple of stylish women: the parchment he was using was too short, so he tried to stretch it with his teeth (knocking himself silly in the process, his head banging up against a stone pillar).

This was not useful. It made her womb stretch loose at the top, instead of the bottom, which squeezed out the child, right into a hollow vein, by means of which he ascended through the diaphragm up to her shoulders, where that vein is divided in two. Taking the left-hand route, he finally came out the ear on that same side.

As soon as he was born, instead of crying, like other children, "Wa! Wa! Wa!," he shouted in a loud voice, "Drink! Drink!"—as if inviting the whole world to join him—and he spoke so loud, and so clearly, that they heard him all over Toper and Tipple (where his words were naturally very well understood).

I'm not sure you're going to believe this strange birth. If you don't, I don't give a hoot—but any decent man, any sensible man, always believes what he's told and what he finds written down. Doesn't Solomon say, in Proverbs, 14, *Innocens credit omni verbo,* "An innocent man believes every word"? And doesn't Saint Paul say, in I Corinthians, 13, *Charitas omnia credit,* "Charity believes everything"? Why shouldn't you believe me? Because, you say, there's no evidence. And I say to you that, for just this very reason, you must believe with perfect faith. Don't all our Orthodox argue that faith is precisely that: an argument for things which no one can prove?

And is there anything in this against the law? or our faith? or in defiance of reason—or Holy Scripture? Me, I find nothing written in the Holy Bible that says a word against it. And if God had wanted this to happen, can you possibly say it wouldn't have happened? Ha! But don't trouble your spirit with any such useless thoughts, because I tell you that for God nothing is impossible and, if He chose, from now on women would all have their babies coming out of their ears.

Wasn't Bacchus spawned by Jupiter's thigh?

And the giant Rocquetaillade, wasn't he born from his mother's heel?

And Croquemouche, wasn't he born out of his nurse's slippers?

And what about Minerva: wasn't she born out of Jupiter's head—and through his ear?

And Adonis, didn't he appear through the bark of a myrrh tree?

And Castor and Pollux, out from the shell of an egg laid and then hatched by Leda?

But you'd be even more flabbergasted and struck dumb if I took the trouble to lay out for you that whole chapter in Pliny, in which he speaks of strange, unnatural births. Anyway, I'm hardly the kind of established liar that he was. Read the seventh book of his *Natural History,* chapter three, and stop bothering me about this whole business.

Chapter Seven ⁄⁄ How Gargantua Got His Name, and How He Tossed Down Wine

That good man Grandgousier, drinking and laughing with the others, heard the horrible cry uttered by his son, as he first saw the light of this world, bellowing out, "Drink, drink, drink!" At which Grandgousier said (speaking of the child's throat), "What a grand gargler you've got!" And everyone said, hearing this, that the child simply had to have the name Gargantua, since that had been his father's first word as he was being born—according to the old Hebrew tradition. Grandgousier graciously agreed, which pleased the mother, too. And to pacify the child they gave him enough to drink to fill up that splendid throat, and then they carried him to the font and baptized him, as good Christians usually do.

And for his daily nourishment they allocated seventeen thousand nine hundred and thirteen of the best cows from Pontille and Bréhémont, near Chinon—because it would have been impossible to find him an adequate wet nurse, even if they'd scoured the entire country: he needed such a tremendous quantity of milk. Still, certain disciples of Duns Scotus have insisted that his mother fed him herself, and that she could pump out of her breasts fourteen hundred and two casks, plus nine small pots, of milk at a time. This is simply unrealistic—a scholastic proposition solemnly declared (by other scholastics) to be mammarily scandalous, offensive to pious ears, and even smelling a bit of heresy.

And so a year and ten months went by, at which time, on the doctors' advice, they began to take him out of doors, and Jean Denyau invented a lovely little oxcart specially for this purpose. Riding around in this cart, he went happily here and there. He was a fine sight, with a great fat face and very nearly eighteen chins, and he almost never cried. But he did shit himself all the time, because his bowels were wonderfully phlegmatic—as much by natural character as by accidentally acquired predisposition (since he'd been guzzling far too much new wine). Not that he ever drank a drop without good reason, because whenever he was out of sorts, or angry, or sad and upset—whether he was jumping up and down in a rage, or bawling his eyes out, or screaming, they'd bring him wine to set him right again, and just like that he'd be peaceful and happy.

One of those who took care of him, swearing by all that's holy, once told me he was so used to this way of being handled that, just at the first clink of a bottle or a glass, he'd go into ecstasies, as if he were already tasting the joys of paradise. And so, carefully keeping in mind this divine temperament, to start off his day in a good mood they'd arrange to have glasses banged with a knife, or they'd tap stoppers against their flasks, or they'd clink the lids on their beer mugs—and at these cheerful sounds he'd brighten up, quivering with joy—he'd even rock himself, keeping time with his head, strumming on an invisible keyboard and farting.

Chapter Eight ✍ How Gargantua Was Dressed

And when he'd reached this age of one year and ten months, his father ordered him dressed in the colors that by right belonged to him, which were white and blue. They got to work at once, and worked with a will, and his clothes were soon ready, cut and sewn in the prevailing fashion. According to ancient documents in the Accounts and Records Department at Montsoreau, I find that these clothes were made as follows:

For his shirt they had to use nine hundred yards of Châtellerault linen, plus two hundred more for the armpit gussets (cut almost in squares) which they put in to make the garment more comfortable. And they didn't pucker the collar, because puckered shirts hadn't been invented yet—an event that didn't take place until seamstresses broke the points of their needles and had to turn around and use the blunt ends (with the holes in the middle).

For his jacket they used eight hundred and thirteen yards of white satin, and for the shoulder ties fifteen hundred and nine and a half dog hides. That was when people were beginning to tie their jackets to their long breeches, instead of the jacket to the breeches—which is of course distinctly unnatural, as William of Ockham, that great philosopher, has more than sufficiently proven in his commentaries on the *Commentaries* of Master Highpockets.

For his breeches they used eleven hundred and six yards of light white linen, slashed in columns, ribbed and grooved in back, in order not to overheat his kidneys. And they were puffed out, from inside the columns, by as much blue damask as the effect required. Note, please, that he had singularly handsome legs, remarkably well proportioned to the rest of his body.

For his codpiece they used sixteen and a quarter yards of this same fine light linen. And they made it in the shape of a flying buttress, carefully and merrily fastened by two beautiful gold buckles with enameled clasps, each of which gleamed with a large emerald, fat as an orange. Because (as Orpheus says in his *Book of Gems,* and Pliny, too, in the last book of his *Natural History*) this stone has an erective as well as a soothing effect on the natural member.

The opening of the codpiece was about two yards long, striped like his breeches, and once again with flaring blue damask. But if you could have seen the beautifully wound thread, all gold and silver, and the handsomely bejeweled interlacing, garnished with sparkling diamonds, the gorgeous rubies and turquoise stones, and the emeralds and all the Persian pearls, you would have compared it to a lovely horn of plenty, the sort you see in famous antiquities, like the one Rhea, the mother of all the gods, gave to the nymphs Adrastea and Ida, Jupiter's nurses—oh, a horn eternally fresh and strong, juicy and nutritious, overflowing, forever green and flowering and fruitful, full of good humor, full of fruit and flowers and all manner of delicacies. Let me never see the face of God if it wasn't a magnificent sight! But I'll tell you more about this entire subject in a book I've written, *On the High Importance of Codpieces.* However, do let me tell you one thing: it was good and long, and it was large, but it was also loaded to the brim, as nourishing as it could be, not a bit like the hypocritical codpieces of all those fops and dandies, stuffed with nothing but wind—to the great regret of the feminine sex.

For his shoes they used four hundred and six yards of bright purple velvet, slashed in delicate parallel lines, dotted across with cylinder shapes, all the same size. The soles took eleven hundred brown cowhides, cut swallow-tail style.

For his overcoat—a kind of cape with huge, open sleeves—they used eighteen hundred yards of blue velvet, tinted with bright scarlet, embroidered all around with lovely vines, with rows of drinking mugs down the middle, worked in silver thread, and everything bordered with gold and clusters of pearls. The scene depicted was of course intended to show that, in his time, he would be a high and mighty drinker.

His belt was made of just over three hundred yards of silk serge, half white and half blue (unless I've been misinformed).

His sword hadn't been made in Spain, nor his dagger, because his father hated all those drunken hidalgos, Moors, and Marranos and God only knows what else—he hated them like the devil himself. No, it was a good wooden sword, and his dagger was boiled leather, gilt and painted as prettily as anyone could want.

His purse was made of an elephant's testicle, given him by Herr Pracontal, the Libyan proconsul.

For his gown they used nine thousand six hundred yards (less two-thirds) of the same blue velvet mentioned already, all laced with diagonal gold figures: if you looked at it correctly, you'd catch a glimpse of an absolutely unnameable color, something like what you see on the necks of turtledoves, and the flickering, shifting hues were marvelously satisfying to the eye.

For his hat they used three hundred and two and a quarter yards of white velvet. Large and round, it perfectly fit the shape of his head: his father swore that all those Moorish and Marrano hats, shaped like a pastry crust, would surely bring down bad luck on the cropped heads that wore them.

His plume was a beautiful big feather, bright blue, plucked from a Persian pelican; it hung prettily from his right ear.

A slab of gold weighing over thirty-nine pounds was fixed to his hat. It bore, appropriately enameled, a design showing a two-headed human body, the heads turned to face each other, and four arms, four feet, and two pairs of buttocks—portraying exactly what Plato describes in the *Symposium* about human nature in its mystical beginnings. And around this design was written, in capital Ionic letters:

CHARITY DOES NOT SEEK ITS OWN REWARD

He had a gold chain around his neck, weighing over twelve thousand pounds (Troy measure, of course), shaped into huge berries, and between each of them a great green gem of jasper, cut and engraved in dragon shapes, surrounded on every side with beams of light and flashing sparks— exactly like Pharaoh Nechepso, that great old astrologer. It hung all the way down to his belly button—and all his life that jasper was highly beneficial to his digestion (as Greek doctors understand perfectly well).

His gloves were fashioned from sixteen goblin skins, trimmed with the pelts of three werewolves: and this was done at the express command of the monkish cabalists at Saint-Sheepshead.

His rings—and his father insisted that he wear them, to carry on this ancient insignia of nobility—were:

on the index finger of his left hand, a bright red garnet as big around as an ostrich egg, delicately set in pure gold;

on the ring finger of that same hand, a ring fashioned of the alchemic four metals, worked as if into just one metal, in the most marvelous fashion ever seen, the steel never splitting away from the gold, the silver never twisting against the copper—the whole thing managed by my good friend Captain Chappuis and by Alcofribas, his good assistant;

on the ring finger of his right hand, a spiral ring, set with an utterly perfect ruby, a half-cut crystal diamond, pointed, and an emerald from one of the four rivers of the Garden of Eden (worth more than one can possibly say, because Hans Carvel, royal jeweler to the king of Zanzibar, estimated its worth at sixty-nine million eight hundred and ninety-four thousand and eighteen gold pieces—and the Fuggers of Augsburg agreed).

Chapter Nine ⁄⁄ Gargantua's Personal Colors

Gargantua's colors were white and blue, as you may have read just a little bit ago, and by such colors his father wished it to be understood that, to him, his son was a positively celestial joy. To him, white meant joy, pleasure, delight, and rejoicing, and blue meant heavenly things.

I understand perfectly well that, reading these words, you'll scoff at the old guzzler, and consider his exposition of coloristic matters distinctly coarse and primitive, not to say absurd. You'll say that white means faith and blue means steadfastness and determination. But without getting you all upset, or angry, without getting your blood pressure up or indeed changing it in any way (because in this weather that might be dangerous), just answer me, please, if it seems to you worthwhile. I won't use any other pressure on you—or on anyone else, either, no matter who they may be—but let me say this:

Just who's upsetting you, eh? Who's pointing your nose into the wind? Who tells you that white means faith and blue means determination? Well (you answer), a beaten-up old book, sold by door-to-door peddlers: its title (first appearing around a century ago), *All about Colors*. And who wrote it? Whoever, he was certainly smart enough not to put his name on the thing. But, for the rest, I'm not sure whether to give him more credit for his arrogance or for his stupidity:

—arrogance, because without reason or cause or any likelihood of sense or accuracy, he has laid down prescriptions (founded only on his own personal authority) for what the various colors mean—and this is the method always used by tyrants who want what they say to take the place of good sound reason; it is emphatically not the method of truly wise men and scholars, who satisfy their readers strictly by reasonable argument;

—stupidity, because he fancied that, without any evidence and without the slightest show of rational discourse, the world would adjust its approach to these important heraldic matters according to his idle rules and regulations.

Now, in fact (as the proverb says, "A dirty asshole always has a good supply of shit"), what he found was that a few doddering old idiots, left over from the last century, have trusted his book and shaped their aphoristic observations and high pronouncements according to his views. They have actually harnessed their mules, dressed their pages, designed their breeches, embroidered their gloves, fringed their bed curtains, painted their banners and flags, composed their songs, and (this is the worst of it) created deception and all manner of deviltry (but secretly) among sedate and otherwise respectable married women—for who knows what evil messages can be sent by wearing the wrong colors?

And this same darkness descends on those high and mighty court followers, those courtly word weighers, who symbolize "hope" in their heraldic drawings by using a "hoop," who depict "feathers" by "fetters," "flowers" by "bowers," "the man in the moon" by "the pan and the spoon," a "broken bench" by a "token wench," a "fool" and a "horse" by "force," a bed with no "curtains" by an absolute "certainty"—all of which is simply inept, insipid, heavy-footed and barbarous homonymerie without the slightest sense. Such exceedingly ghastly stuff, now that in this day and age we in France have finally rediscovered real literacy, ought to require anyone who even thinks about using it to have a fox tail tied to his collar and his face smeared with cow shit.

Using the same kind of reasoning (if we have to call this "reason streaming" rather than "seasonal dreaming"), I could "pamper" a "hamper," indicating that those opposed had better "scamper"; and my "heart's desire" could be my "fart's hot fire"; and a "priestly judge" could be a "beastly drudge"; and the "seat of my pants" could be the "heat of my aunts"; and my "glorious codpiece" could be my "uproarious oddities"; and even "dog shit" could become "a frog's tit," so I'd be well provided for if I happened to fall in love with a frog.

But the wise men of Egypt, in the old days, proceeded completely differently, when they wrote the magical letters that we call hieroglyphics—which no one understood who had no understanding, and which everyone understood who had any understanding of the powers, the nature and the special qualities of that writing. All of which has been fully and usefully discussed by Horapollo, who wrote two treatises in Greek (one of them called *On Hieroglyphics*), and by Polyphilus in his *Dream of Love*. Here in France we have some inkling of all this, too, in the heraldic device adopted by our lord admiral, showing a dolphin as a symbol of speed and an anchor as a symbol for caution. Octavian Augustus used this same motto: "Make haste slowly."

Enough: this little boat of mine sails no farther, out among all these whirlpools and evil-smelling swamps: I propose to come back and dock exactly where I started from. But some day I hope to write of these things more fully, showing—by philosophical reasoning as well as by accepted authority, in full accord with what the ancients have said—just which colors exist in nature and what each one can be understood to mean. I will, at least, if God gives me the chance, because as my old grandmother used to say, your hat's the best wine mug you'll ever find.

Chapter Ten ⁄⁄ What the Colors White and Blue Mean

Thus: white means happiness, comfort, and gaiety. And this is the truth, not some piece of concocted idiocy. No, this is established and testified to by good authority—as you'll be able to prove for yourself if, putting aside all your prior notions, you just listen to what I'm going to tell you.

As Aristotle says, if we postulate two things of the same sort, but of opposite natures—like good and bad, virtue and vice, cold and hot, white and black, delight and sadness, happiness and sorrow, and many others— and if we then match the opposite of one pair with the opposite of another, inevitably the other extremes also match. For example: virtue and vice are opposites, and so are good and bad. Now, if one of these opposites matches the other, like virtue and good (because clearly virtue is good), then the other halves of the pairs will match, too, as bad and vice plainly do, since vice is unquestionably bad.

Having grasped this logical rule, consider these opposites, happiness and sadness. Then take this pair, white and black (because they're physically opposite). So if black plainly matches sorrow, good sense indicates that white matches happiness.

Nor is this a meaning imposed by merely human contrivance, but understood and agreed to by the whole wide world—what the philosophers call *jus gentium,* "the customs of all nations," universally valid in every country on earth.

Now you know perfectly well that all peoples, all nations (I leave out the ancient dwellers in Syracuse, as well as other ancient Greeks who had eccentric souls), speaking whatever language, when they wanted to give some clear sign of sadness would put on black clothing, and pain and sorrow always wear black. This universal agreement would only exist provided nature herself offered solid, rational argument in its favor, argument that anyone and everyone can easily understand for himself, without outside help or instruction—and this we call natural law.

By the same natural inference, the entire world understands that white means happiness, gaiety, comfort, pleasure, and delight.

In ancient times the Thracians and Cretans marked their lucky days with white stones, but their sad and unlucky days with black ones.

Isn't night a hostile time, sad and melancholy? Deprivation and loss make it black and dim. Doesn't everything in nature take pleasure in clarity? And it's whiter than anything else that exists. To prove which, I might refer you to Lorenzo Valla's *Book in Opposition to Bartolus*—but the testimony of the Gospels ought to be sufficient. In the Gospel according to Saint Matthew, 17, it is written that at the Transfiguration of Our Lord, *vestimenta ejus facta sunt alba sicut lux,* "his raiment was white as light," that is, his clothing was made as white as light, by which gleaming whiteness His three Apostles were shown both the idea and the face of eternal happiness. Because light and clarity are a delight to all human beings—in proof of which you have the words of an old hag who didn't have a tooth in her skull but still declared, *Bona lux,* "The light is good." And Tobit, chapter 5, when he'd gone blind and the angel Raphael greeted him, answered, "What happiness can I possibly have, I who can't even see the light of heaven?" The angels bear witness to their happiness, and that of the entire universe, in exactly this color, at the Resurrection of our Savior: see the Gospel according to Saint John, 20. And at His Ascension: see Acts, 5. And Saint John the Baptist (see Revelation, 4 and 7) had a vision of the faithful in the heavenly and blessed city of Jerusalem, wearing clothing of just this color.

Read the ancient histories, the Greek as well as the Roman. There you'll find that the city of Alba, the first model for Rome, was founded and built and even named because of a white sow.

You will find that any man, after having defeated one of the city's enemies, was by law permitted to enter Rome in triumph, on a chariot drawn by white horses; so too those who had had lesser victories. In short, no sign and no color could more emphatically express the happiness of these heroic entrances than white.

You will find that Pericles, duke of Athens, divided his soldiers into eight equal groups, and those who drew the white beans would spend their entire day in happiness, comfort, and rest, while those in the other seven groups would be fighting. I could tell you a thousand other examples along these same exact lines, but this is not the place.

But knowing these things should help you to solve a puzzle, which Alexander of Aphrodisias (though he wrote a whole book about problems and puzzles) did not think could possibly be solved: "Why the lion, whose very roar strikes terror into all other animals, fears and reveres the white rooster?" Because (according to Proclus, in his *Sacrifice and Magic*) the sun's powers—and the fact that the sun holds and dispenses all the light of earth and of the heavens—more fittingly belong to the white rooster than to the lion, both on account of his color and his exact nature. Devils are often seen in the shape of lions, he also says, and the very presence of a white rooster makes them suddenly disappear.

And this is why the Gauls (that is, the French, a people who are by nature white as milk, which in Greek is *gala*) like to wear white feathers on their hats. For by their very nature the French are happy, open, gracious, and loved by everyone, and their sign and symbol is the whitest of all flowers: the lily.

If you ask me how nature leads us to see happiness and gaiety in the color white, I answer that those are in fact the true comparisons and resemblances. Consider: the outward nature of white separates and reflects that which is seen, visibly dissolving all visual spirits (according to Aristotle, in book 31 of his *Problems,* and also other students of perspectival matters)—as you can see for yourself when you cross a snow-covered mountain and grumble that you can't see more clearly (which is what Xenophon says happened to his men, and is fully explained by Galen in *On the Use of the Various Parts of the Human Body,* book 10). Thus transcendent happiness seems to split the heart, which experiences a kind of physical dissolution of its vital spirits, and this can reach such an intensity that the heart is no longer properly nourished and such an excess of happiness can result in death, as also noted by Galen in his *Method of Healing,* book 12, in his *Where Sickness Is Found,* book 5, and in his *Causes of Certain Symptoms,* book 2. And in previous times this same effect was observed and reported by Cicero, in his *Tuscan Questions,* book 1, as well as by Marcus Verrius and Aristotle and Livy (when he describes what took place after the battle of Cannae), by Pliny in his *Natural History,* book 7, chapters 32 and 53, by Aulus Gellius in *Attic Nights,* book 3, chapter 15, and others, including such well-attested examples of people dying of excess happiness as Diagoras of Rhodes, Chilo, Sophocles, Dionysius, tyrant of Sicily, Philippides, Philemon, Polycrita, Philistion (who laughed himself to death), Marcus Juventia, and more. Avicenna's *The Heart's Strength,* book 2, asserts that saffron, though it quickens the heart, can also kill it, by a general weakening and an overdilation, if an excessive dose is administered. For more on this matter see Alexander of Aphrodisias, in his book on problems, book 1, chapter 19—and that's that.

But, good God, that's more than enough! When I set out, I had no intentions of wandering this far. So let me lower my sails right here, leaving all the rest—and there's an immense amount still to be said—to the book devoted entirely to the subject of colors. Let me just say, in a word, that blue definitely means heaven and heavenly things, according to the same exact processes by which we know that white means happiness and pleasure.

Chapter Eleven ⁄ Gargantua's Adolescence

From age three to age five, Gargantua grew and was taught all the proper discipline, by his father's orders, and those years went by just as they do for ordinary children. He drank, ate, and slept; he ate, slept, and drank; and he slept, drank, and ate.

He was always wallowing in mud and muck, making his nose smutty, his face dirty, wearing out his shoes, his mouth open as he chased flies, running wildly after butterflies (of which, by marriage, his father had become king). He pissed all over his shoes, shat on his shirt, blew his nose on his sleeves and in his soup, and splashed and paddled and drabbled everywhere. He drank from his slipper and rubbed his belly on any wicker basket he could find. He sharpened his teeth on wooden shoes, washed his hands with soup, combed his hair with a wineglass, flopped down on a pair of stools with his ass dragging on the ground, wore a wet gunnysack, guzzled and slopped up his soup, ate his butter-and-egg sandwich without bread, chewed as he laughed and laughed as he chewed, often spat in the collection plate, emitted good fat farts, pissed at the sun, hid under water to avoid the rain, tried to play blacksmith with cold iron, walked around in a daze, daydreaming, played at billing and cooing, threw up all over, made his teeth clack like a monkey reciting a prayer, said the first thing that came into his head (and then forgot it), did the wrong thing at the right time, kicked a slave so the master would learn a lesson, put the cart in front of the horse, scratched when he didn't itch, wormed out other people's secrets, grabbed at everything and picked up nothing, ate his cake before he ate his meal, tilted at windmills, tickled himself so he could laugh, ate like a horse, made fun of the gods, sang the Magnificat in the morning instead of at night (and thought it sounded better his way), ate cabbage and shat beans, knew which end was up, made a fool of himself (and tried to make a fool of Mother Nature), ruined reams of expensive paper, ran like hell, drank like a fish, reckoned without his host, beat around the bush (without catching any birds), believed that clouds were curtains and the moon was made of green cheese, ground his grain twice, made an ass of himself if he got paid for it, used his fist for a hammer, never waited for Peter before he paid Paul, believed that Rome was certainly built in a day, always looked a gift horse in the mouth, couldn't tell cock from bull, dropped a pinch of sugar in a vat of vinegar, collected water in a sieve, made fish talk, waited to catch skylarks when the clouds fell, made a virtue of necessity, never put his elbows in his ears, split all the hairs he liked, and vomited every morning, like a drunken fox. His father's little dogs ate from his plate, and he ate with them. He bit their ears and they scratched his nose; he blew down their assholes and they licked his lips.

And do you know what, fellows? May your guts rot! This little lecher was always feeling up his nurses, groping up and down and all around—whoopsy daisy!—and he was already beginning to make use of his codpiece. Every day his nurses decorated it with lovely bouquets, blooming flowers, beautiful flowers, gorgeous garlands; they spent hours working it back and forth between their hands like doctors shaping a suppository. And then they burst out laughing when it lifted its head, as if the game were really an amusing one.

One of them called it my little spigot, another my pinhead, another my coral branch, another my barrel plug, my bung stopper, my drill bit, my little cannon, my wood borer, my baby prick, my hard little toy—so stiff and so low, my ladder, my glove stretcher, my little red sausage, my little empty-balled treasure.

"It's mine," said one.

"Mine!" said another.

"Mine," said a third. "Are you trying to cut me out? By God, I'll chop it off!"

"Oh ho," said another. "That wouldn't do him any good, madame. How can you cut it off a little child? You'd turn him into a docked puppy."

And so he could play just like any ordinary child, they made him a hoop out of the vanes of a fine windmill from Mirebalais.

Chapter Twelve ⁄⁄ Gargantua's Hobbyhorses

Then, so he'd be a good horseman all his life, they made him a great wooden horse, which he taught how to buck, leap, dance on a rope, kick and prance at the same time, pace, trot, step high, gallop, amble, canter, jog, camel-walk, and wild-donkey trot. And he also got it to change its hide (like Dalmatian monks, who dress differently on different holidays), from bay brown to chestnut to spotted gray to dun to fawn to roan to brindle to mottled to striped to piebald to snow white.

Gargantua himself made a hunting horse, out of a huge beam on two wheels (which had been used for carrying tree trunks), and another everyday steed out of the great beam of a winepress, and from a towering oak tree he made himself a mule, using furniture covers from his bedroom for its saddlecloth. And he had ten or twelve other horses, too, which he used for riding relays, and still another seven for playing mailman. And all of them got to sleep beside him.

One day Lord Squeeze-a-Penny came to visit Gargantua's father, arriving with many followers and a great deal of fuss—and on the very same day, in exactly the same style, there also arrived the duke of Sponge-a-Meal and the count of Wetwind. I tell you, the house wasn't quite big enough for so many people, and especially the stables. So Duke Sponge-a-Meal's chief steward, and the master of his horses, to make sure there weren't any vacant stables elsewhere in the house, went calling on Gargantua, who was still a small boy, asking him on the sly where the stables for the war horses were located. Their notion was that all you had to do was ask a child and he'd tell you whatever you wanted to know.

So he led them up the great castle staircase, past the second floor, and into a large gallery, from which they went into a high tower. And then, as he took them up yet another staircase, the master of horses turned to the steward and said:

"This child is playing games with us. Stables are never this high in a house."

"Ah-ha," said the steward, "you don't know very much, do you? I know of places—in Lyons, at La Baumette, at Chinon, and other places too—where the stables are in fact the very highest part of the house. Maybe there's a back entrance, facing into the mountain. But I'll ask him more specifically."

Then he asked Gargantua:

"My sweet little boy, just where are you taking us?"

"To the stable," he said, "where my war-horses are kept. We're almost there—it's right up this ladder."

Then they went through yet another huge room, and he led them into his bedroom and, pulling open the door:

"Here," he said, "here are the stables you wanted. Here's my Spanish racehorse, and there's my mare—she's a walking horse, and that one's my racehorse, and that's one of my trotting horses."

And then, loading them up with a huge beam:

"You can have this Frisian horse," he said. "I got him from Frankfort, but he'll be yours. He's really a nice little clothes horse and he works hard. With a male hawk, half a dozen spaniels, and a pair of greyhounds, why, you'll be king of partridges and rabbits all winter long."

"By Saint John!" they said. "We've been taken! We've been hoaxed up to the eyes: oh, we've really gotten the monk this time."

"Oh no," he said. "You're wrong. He was here just three days ago."

You can guess whether they should have hidden their heads in shame or just laughed at the joke.

As they were starting down, totally embarrassed, he asked:

"Would you like an obbler?"

"An obbler?" they said. "What's that?"

"Right here," he said. "Five turds: they make a great muzzle."

"From this day on," said the steward, "if they ever try to roast us, we won't burn, because as far as I'm concerned we've now been thoroughly cooked. Oh, you sweet little boy, you've put the horns on our heads and hung the warning straw between them. I expect some day they'll have to make you pope."

"I expect so," he said. "But when *you* get to be pope, this nice parrot of mine will be spouting approved doctrine."

"Quite so, quite so," said the master of horses.

"Now," said Gargantua, "guess how much needlepoint there is in my mother's shirt."

"Sixteen," said the master of horses.

"Ha!" said Gargantua. "That's wrong, you're not talking by the Book. Because there's *some* in front and *some* in back, and you haven't done the *sum* right, not at all."

"When?" asked the master of horses.

"When they made your nose into a spigot," said Gargantua, "and drew out of it a thousand quarts of shit—and your throat got used for a funnel, so they could pour it into another barrel, because the bottom of that one was all stunk up."

"By God!" said the steward, "we've gotten ourselves a chatterbox. Master Tongue-wagger, God keep you safe from all harm, because your mouth knows what it's up to."

As they were hurriedly going down, they dropped the great beam he'd given them, just below the arc of the staircase. And at that Gargantua said:

"Oh boy, you're not good riders, you two! That hack of yours let you down, just when you really needed him. Suppose you had to ride from here to Cahuzac, would you rather saddle up a goose or just lead a pig on a leash?"

"I'd rather get myself a drink," said the master of horses.

And as he spoke they reached the lower room and joined the rest of the company. And when they told their little story, everyone laughed like a swarm of buzzing flies.

Chapter Thirteen ⁄⁄ How Grandgousier Became Aware of Gargantua's Wonderful Capacities, When His Son Invented an Ass Wiper

At the end of his fifth year, Gargantua was visited by his father, Grandgousier, who had just returned from defeating the Canarrians. Grandgousier was as happy as such a father could possibly be, seeing such a son, and, kissing and hugging him, asked him about a number of suitably childish matters. And Grandgousier drank a good bit, both with the boy and with his governesses, asking the latter most earnestly, among other things, if they had kept him fresh and clean. To which Gargantua replied that he had made sure that, nowhere in all the land, was there a boy cleaner than he was.

"And how do you manage that?" said Grandgousier.

"By long and careful experience," said Gargantua, "I have invented a method for wiping my ass which is the most noble, the best, and also the simplest ever seen."

"What is it?" asked Grandgousier.

"I'll tell you," said Gargantua, "right now.

"Once I wiped myself with a lady's velvet veil, and I liked that very much, because it was so soft that it made my ass feel really good;

—and then with a lady's hood, made of the same stuff, and it was just as good;

—and then with a man's scarf;

—and then with an embroidered red satin veil, but the gilt came off and rolled up into all sorts of shitty balls, and they scraped half the skin off my ass—may Saint Anthony's fire roast the ass of the goldsmith who made the thing—and the lady who wore it!

—I got over that by wiping myself with a page's hat, handsomely plumed in Swiss style.

"Then, once when I was shitting behind some bushes, I found a March cat and wiped myself with him, but his claws scratched my whole rear end.

"I cured myself of that, next day, by wiping myself with my mother's gloves—nicely scented with cunt flavor.

"Then I wiped myself with sage, with fennel, with dill and anise, with sweet marjoram, with roses, pumpkins, with squash leaves, and cabbage, and beets, with vine leaves, and mallow, and *Verbascum thapsus* (that's mullein, and it's as red as my asshole), and lettuce and spinach leaves— and a lot of good it all did me!—and mercury weed, and purslane, and nettle leaves, and larkspur and comfrey. But then I got Lombardy dysentery, which I cured by wiping myself with my codpiece.

"Then I wiped myself with the bedclothes, the blankets, the bed curtains, with a cushion, a tablecloth (and then another, a green one), a dishcloth, a napkin, a handkerchief, and with a dressing gown. And I relished it all like mangy dogs when you rub them down."

"To be sure," said Grandgousier, "but which ass wipe did you find the best?"

"I'm getting there," said Gargantua. "In just a minute you'll hear the *tu autem,* the real heart of it. I wiped myself with hay, with straw, with all sorts of fluffy junk, with tag wool, with real wool, with paper. But:

> Wipe your dirty ass with paper
> And you'll need to clean your ass with a scraper."

"What?" said Grandgousier. "My little fat-head, have you drunk the magic potion and started rhyming?"

"By God, yes, my king," Gargantua answered. "I rhyme so much

that, sometimes, it makes me sick. Here's what our shit house says to the
assholes who sit in it:

> Plop
> A whopper,
> Blast it,
> You pig shit
> Asshole,
> Drop her
> A big shit
> Past all
> Blast holes—
> Oh, dripping,
> Slipping
> Slop!
> But Saint Anthony's fire come cracking
> If you plop
> And drop
> Without stopping
> To wipe your ass after cacking.

"Would you like to hear more?"

"Most certainly," said Grandgousier.

"Well, then," said Gargantua, "here's a nice rondeau:

> Shitting, the other day, I knew
> Exactly how much I owed my ass;
> The stink was so strong, so compelling, so nasty,
> That my nose curled up and my ears turned blue.
> Oh! If only someone would bring me
> Her for whom I long, and I sing me,
>   While shitting!
> I could have closed her water spout,
> Although she'd try to keep me out,
> Turning her fingers to a wall of glass,
> And only shit could protect my ass
>   While shitting.

"Now try to tell me I don't know anything! By the smother of God, I
didn't actually make that up, but I heard that noble lady—the one over
there—recite it, and I plunked it right into my memory pouch."

"But now," said Grandgousier, "let's get back to the subject."

"Which is," said Gargantua, "shitting?"

"No," said Grandgousier. "It's ass-wiping."

"Well," said Gargantua, "will you give me a big barrel of Breton wine if I put you to shame on that subject?"

"Certainly," said Grandgousier.

"There's no need," said Gargantua, "to wipe your ass, if you haven't unloaded any shit. There can't be any shit if you haven't shat. So you've got to shit before you can wipe your ass."

"O my little rascal," said Grandgousier, "how clever you are! Pretty soon I'll have you made a doctor of poetic science—by God I will! Because you're smarter than your years. Now stay with this matter of ass-wipery, please. And by my beard! instead of giving you a barrel, I'll give you sixty casks—and not just any Breton wine, about which I know a thing or two: it doesn't grow in Brittany at all, but in Veron."

"Later on," said Gargantua, "I wiped myself with a headband, with a pillow, with a nice cloth slipper, with a game bag, with a basket—but that was an awful way to wipe your ass!—and then with a hat. Let me emphasize that there are hats and hats: some are smooth and plain, some are furred, some have velvet, some have taffeta, and there are others with satin. Best of all are the furry ones, because they do the best job of cleaning off shit.

"Then I wiped myself with a hen, a rooster, a baby chick, with a calf's skin, with a hare, a pigeon, a hawk, a lawyer's leather briefcase, a big hooded cape, a cap, and a falconer's wristband.

"But, to make a long story shorter, it's my solemn opinion that there is no ass wiper like a fluffy goose, if you keep its head between your legs. On my honor, this is the truth. Because you feel a miraculous voluptuousness in your asshole, as much from the soft smoothness of that goose down as from the good warm bird, and this is readily communicated right into your asshole and up to the upper intestines, all the way through to the heart and the brain. Don't think that the bliss of all the heroes and demigods, out there on the Elysian Fields, comes just from their asphodel or their ambrosia or their nectar, as the old hags around here say it does. As I see it, their heavenly bliss comes from the fact that they wiped their asses with a soft goose—and that's the opinion of Master John Duns Scotus, too."

Chapter Fourteen ⁄⁄ How Gargantua Was Taught Latin by a Terribly Learned Philosopher

This subject disposed of, that good man Grandgousier was ravished with admiration, thinking about the good sense and marvelous comprehension of his son Gargantua. And so he said to his governesses:

"Philip, king of Macedonia, understood the good sense of his son

Alexander by his skill in handling a certain horse, which was so terrible, ,
so completely wild, that no one could even get up on its back. He bucked
and threw everyone who tried to ride him, breaking the neck of one, the
legs of another, cracking one man's skull and shattering another's jaw-
bone. When Alexander went down into the Hippodrome (which was
where they trained and exercised their horses) and analyzed the problem,
he saw that the horse's desperate fury came, simply enough, from being
afraid of his own shadow. Having come to this understanding, he jumped
up on the horse's back and forced him to run straight toward the sun, so
that his shadow fell behind him, and by this procedure turned the horse
gentle and obedient. And that showed his father what divine understanding his son possessed, and he arranged that the boy be thoroughly trained
by Aristotle, who was at that time considered the best philosopher in
Greece.

"But I tell you that from this one discussion, which my son and I have
just had, right here in front of you, I too understand that his understanding has something divine about it—so acute, subtle, profound, and yet
serene—and will attain to a singularly lofty degree of wisdom, provided
he is well taught. Accordingly, I wish to put him in the hands of some
scholarly man who will teach him everything he is capable of learning.
And to this end I propose to open my purse as freely as need be."

So they sent for a great philosopher, Maître Tubalcain Holofernes,
who taught him the alphabet so well that he could say it backward, by
heart, at which point he was five years and three months old. Then he
read with the boy a Latin grammar by Donatus, plus a dull and well-
meaning treatise on courtesy, and a long book by Bishop Theodulus, in
which he proves that ancient mythology is all a heap of nonsense, and
finally an exceedingly long poem in dreadfully moral quatrains. All this
took thirteen years, six months, and two weeks to accomplish.

Of course, it's also true that he learned to write in Gothic letters, and
wrote out all his own books that way, since this was before the art of
printing had been invented.

Most of the time he carried a large writing desk, weighing more than
thirty tons, with a pencil box as big and heavy as the four great pillars of
Saint-Martin d'Ainay, the old church in Lyons. And the inkpot hung
down on huge iron chains, capable of supporting barrels and barrels of
merchandise.

And then they read *De modis significandi,* "The Methods of Reasoned
Analysis," with the commentaries of Broken Biscuithead, Bouncing Rock,
Talktoomuch, Galahad, John the Fatted Calf, Balogny, Cuntprober, and
a pile of others. And this took more than eighteen years and six months.
And by then Gargantua knew it all so well that, if you asked him, he
could recite every single line, backward, proving to his mother that he
had the whole thing at his fingertips and, most important of all, that *de*

modis significandi non erat scientia, the methods of reasoned analysis were neither reasonable nor a science.

Then they read that great book *Calculation,* surely the longest almanac ever compiled: this took another sixteen years and two months. And then, suddenly, his teacher died, being four hundred and twenty years old: it was the pox that carried him off.

So they brought in another old cougher, Maître Blowhard Birdbrain, with whom he read Bishop Huguito of Ferrara, Eberhard de Bethune's *Greekishnessisms,* Alexander de Villedieu's barbarous Latin grammar, Remigius' *Petty Doctrines* and also his *What's What,* a charming discourse set in question-and-answer form, the *Supplement to All Supplements,* a fat glossary of saints' lives and the like, Sulpicius' long, long poem on the psalms and death, Seneca's *De quatuor virtutibus cardinalibus,* The Four Cardinal Virtues (which wasn't by Seneca at all), Passavantus' *Mirror of True Penitence,* and the same author's *Sleep in Peace,* a collection of sermons chosen to make happy days still happier—and he also read other tough birds of the same feather. And in reading all this he became quite as wise as any blackbird ever baked in a pie.

Chapter Fifteen ⁄⁄ How Gargantua Got to Study with Other Teachers

By that point his father could see that although he was studying as hard as he could, and spending all his time at it, he didn't seem to be learning much and, what's worse, he was becoming distinctly stupid, a real simpleton, all wishy-washy and driveling.

When he complained of this to Don Philippe des Marais, viceroy of Papeligosse, he was told that it would be better for Gargantua to learn nothing at all than to study such books with such teachers, whose learning was nothing but stupidity and whose wisdom was nothing but gloves with no hands in them—empty. They were specialists in ruining good and noble spirits and nipping the flowering of youth in the bud.

"To show you what I mean," he said, "take some modern youngster, who has only been studying for two years. If he doesn't show better judgment, better use of words, better ability to analyze and discuss than your son, as well as greater ease and courtesy in dealing with the world, then call me a fat-head from Brenne."

Grandgousier was delighted and told him to do exactly that.

That night, at supper, des Marais introduced one of his young pages, a young fellow named Rightway (in Greek, Eudemon), who was from Villegongis, near Saint-Genou. And he was so well-groomed, so beautifully dressed, so clean and neat in every respect, so courteous in his bearing, that he more nearly resembled a little angel than a human being. And des Marais said to Grandgousier:

"See this child? He's only twelve years old. Shall we see, if you care to, what a difference there is between the learning of your bird-chirping old philosophers and modern youngsters like this?"

Grandgousier liked the idea, and told the page to give them a demonstration of what he knew. Then Rightway, after asking his master's permission to proceed, stood on his feet, his hat in his hands, his face open, his lips red, his eyes confident, his glance fixed on Gargantua with a modesty appropriate to his age, and began both to praise and to glorify Grandgousier's son, first for his virtue and his good manners, second for his knowledge, third for his nobility, fourth for his physical beauty, and then, fifth, sweetly urged him always to honor his father, who had taken such pains to have him well brought up, finally begging Gargantua to consider Master Rightway the most insignificant of his servants, for the boy asked no other gift from the heavens but the grace of pleasing Gargantua by some cheerfully rendered service. And all of this was spoken with such extraordinarily tactful gestures, with a pronunciation so clear, a voice so eloquent, and in language so elegant and such good Latin, that he more nearly resembled a kind of ancient Gracchus, or Cicero, or Ennius than a young person of his own time.

But all Gargantua could do was weep like a cow. He hid his face behind his hat, and it was no more possible to draw a word from him than to get a fart from a dead donkey.

All of which made his father so furious that he wanted to kill Maître Blowhard Birdbrain. But des Marais checked him with a well-turned word of warning, so neatly administered that it cooled his anger. But he ordered that Blowhard Birdbrain be paid what he was owed and allowed to guzzle like a philosopher. And when he'd drunk to his heart's content, he was to be told to go to the devil.

"It won't cost me a thing," he said, "not today at least, if he gets so drunk that he dies of it, like an Englishman."

Maître Blowhard Birdbrain left the house. Grandgousier sought des Marais' advice about who might be available to be Gargantua's new teacher, and the two of them decided that Powerbrain (in Greek, Ponocrates), Rightway's teacher, would be the best man for the job. The three of them would then travel to Paris, the better to understand how the young men of France were pursuing their studies.

Chapter Sixteen // How Gargantua Was Sent to Paris, Riding an Enormous Brood Mare, Which Waged War against the Cow Flies of Beauce

Now, at this same time Fayoles, fourth king of Numidia, happened to send Grandgousier, all the way from Africa, the biggest, tallest brood mare anyone had ever seen. And the most monstrous, too (it being well known that Africa always brings forth new things), for it was the size of six elephants and it had toes, like Julius Caesar's horse; its ears hung down like a Languedoc goat, and it had a horn sticking out of its ass. For the rest, it had a kind of burned chestnut hide, mottled with gray. Most impressive of all was its ghastly tail, because—give a pound, take a pound— it was as big as the old ruin of Saint-Mars, near Langeais (which is forty feet high), and every bit as wide, with hair as closely woven as the tassels on an ear of corn.

And if that strikes you as astonishing, what do you think of those amazing Scythian rams, weighing in at more than thirty pounds apiece, and those Syrian sheep, which (if Jean Thenaud is telling the truth) have an ass so heavy, so long and massive, that they have to tie a supporting cart to its rear end so it can get about at all. You haven't got anything like it, you lowland ass bangers!

It came by sea, in three Genoan schooners and a man-of-war, to the port of Les Sables-d'Olonne, in Talmont.

When Grandgousier saw it:

"This is exactly the right thing," he said, "to carry my son to Paris. Now, God be thanked, everything will turn out all right. Someday he'll surely be a great scholar. If it weren't for our friends the animals, we'd all have to live like philosophers."

The next day, but of course only after having drunk their fill, Gargantua, his new teacher Powerbrain, and all his attendants, together with the young page Rightway, took to the road. And because the weather was calm and moderate, his father had them make soft laced boots for Gargantua. (That great bootmaker Babin tells me they go by the name of buskins.)

So they went merrily down the highway, laughing and singing, until they had almost reached Orléans. There they entered a large forest, ninety miles long and forty miles wide. The place swarmed with horrible cow flies, millions of them, and wasps and hornets, too, the sort that were true highway robbers for all poor mares and mules and horses. But Gargantua's mare took an appropriate revenge for all the outrages her species had suffered, playing a trick that those insects had never expected. Suddenly, as they entered the wood and the flies and wasps began their assault, she whipped out her tail and swatted them so vigorously that in fact she knocked down the entire forest. Left, right, here, there, length and width, over and under, she smashed those trees like a mower cutting grass, until finally there were neither any trees nor any insects, but just a nice flat stretch of land, which is all you can see to this day.

Gargantua watched this performance with immense delight. But he didn't want to sound vainglorious, so all he said to his companions was, "This is fine, but I don't want to boast." And ever since that part of the country has been known as Beauce. But all they got to put in their open mouths was their own yawns—in memory of which the gentlemen of Beauce (and everyone knows how poor they've always been) still dine by yawning and opening and closing their empty mouths, which they've grown to like, especially since it helps them spit.

When at last they reached Paris, Gargantua spent two or three days resting and recovering from their journey, drinking and chatting with the townsfolk and asking what scholars happened to be in the city at that time and what wine Parisians liked to drink.

Chapter Seventeen ⁄⁄ How Gargantua Gave the Parisians as Good as He Got and Took the Great Bells of Notre Dame Cathedral

Some days later, when he was feeling more like himself, Gargantua went to visit the city and was stared at by the city folk with great admiration, because Parisians are such idiots, such gapers, such natural fools, that any juggler, any common comedian, any seller of holy relics, any mule with cymbals tied to his back, any hurdy-gurdy man standing in the middle of a crossroads, gathers a bigger crowd than a good, sound evangelical preacher.

And they pushed and shoved around him so annoyingly that he was obliged to take refuge on the towers of Notre Dame Cathedral. From which vantage point, seeing so many people all around him, he said in a loud, clear voice:

"I think these good-for-nothings want me to pay them a welcoming fee and make them a whacking good present. That's all right. I'll give them some good fresh wine—but just in jest."

Whereupon, smiling broadly, he unbuttoned his handsome codpiece and, sticking his tool right out into the air, bepissed them so violently that he drowned two hundred sixty thousand, four hundred and eighteen people, not counting women and small children.

Some of them were able to escape this flood of urine, being light on their feet. And once they were safely up on the heights of Sainte-Geneviève, coughing and spitting and out of breath, they began to curse and swear, some of them furious, others laughing:

"God's plagues on him!"

"There can't be a God!"

"Francine! Do you see that?"

"Mother of God!"

"By Chriyst's hooly heayd!"

"Ze bassion of Gott gonfound him!"

"God-a-mighty!"

"By the belly of Saint Quenet!"

"God's heavy hand!"

"O Saint Fiacre of Brie!"

"Saint Trinian help us!"

"By Christ's last supper!"

"By God's bright day!"

"May the devil take me!"

"Upon my honor as a gentleman!"

"O holy Saint Andrew!"

"By Saint Godegrin, stoned to death with apples!"

"By Saint Foutin the apostle!"

"O Saint Vitus!"

"O Saint Mamica, you virgin martyr!"

"By all pigs in all pokes! We've been soaked for a joke!"

And from then on the city was called Pa-ris (*par ris,* "for a joke"), although it had always been known as Lutetia, as Strabo explains in his third book—that is, in Greek, "Snow White," because of the lovely white thighs of the ladies of the city. Moreover, since this new christening was accompanied by suitable oaths from all of those present, each according to his or her particular parish and its ways, and since Parisians are none of them natives anyway, the city being composed of people of all sorts and from everywhere on earth, they became by inevitable nature both good oath makers and good oath takers, especially in the legal line, in which they became swaggering and fearfully cocksure. John of Barranco, in his *De copiositate reverentiarum,* "On all the oaths we can swear," gives it as his opinion that "Parisians" is indeed a Greek-derived term, meaning "people with brass tongues."

And then, he looked very carefully at the great bells hanging in Notre Dame's towers, and made them ring most pleasantly. Hearing this, it occurred to him what fine cowbells they'd make, hanging around his mare's neck, for he'd already decided to load her up with Brie cheese and fresh herrings and send her back to his father. And so he took them down and brought them to his rooms.

In the meantime, along came a mouth-stuffing officer of the legions of Saint Anthony, pig lovers all of them, hunting the daily pork ration of his order. And he tried to sneak away with the bells, which would have let him be heard for miles around—so loud and clear, indeed, that he could make bacon tremble in the frying pan. But he chivalrously left them where they were, not because they were too hot but because, weighing about twenty thousand pounds each, they were a trifle too heavy for him to carry. But this particular pig stuffer wasn't Antoine du Saix, Saint Anthony commander at Bourg-en-Bresse, because he's too good a poet for such things. Besides, he's a friend of mine.

The whole city was in a violent uproar—because, remember, Parisians riot in the streets so regularly, and so often, that foreigners are amazed at the patience—or, truthfully, the stupidity—of the kings of France, who are not otherwise known for their reluctance to enforce the laws. I wish to God I knew the den where these plots and counterplots are hatched! I'd spill the beans, I would, and every monastery and nunnery in *my* parish would know everything!

Now, the place where all these tumbling, rioting people were gathered was that hotbed of right-wing radicalism, the famous School of Theology, where—at that time—they could consult the oracle of Lutetia (which isn't there any more). The whole episode was set before these priestly judges and, in particular, they pleaded the difficulties caused by Gargantua's having taken away the bells. After long and thorough splitting of every hair, both *pro* and *contra,* it was concluded (in the best scholastic style) that they ought to send the oldest and most deeply learned member of the Faculty to Gargantua, to prove to him what a dreadful loss they had suffered in losing these bells. And over the objections of some of the distinguished theologians, who felt that this mission should be assigned to an orator rather than to a philosopher, they chose as their emissary that notable scholar Maître Janus Twosides.

Chapter Eighteen ⁄⁄ How Janus Twosides Was Sent to Gargantua, to Get Back the Huge Bells

Maître Twosides, his hair cropped like Julius Caesar's, wearing his most classical doctoral robes, his stomach fortified with the finest oven-baked bread and the most wickedly delightful of wines (from deep in the Faculty's special cellars), journeyed to Gargantua's lodgings, preceded by three red-snouted academic flunkies and followed by five or six artless masters of arts, all mud-smeared and wormlike.

They were met at the door by Powerbrain, Gargantua's new teacher. Seeing how weird and fantastic they looked, and thinking they were a band of insane actors or street musicians, he asked some of those artless masters of arts what the masquerade was all about. And they told him they had come to ask for the return of the bells.

Hearing this, Powerbrain ran to tell Gargantua, to give him time to meditate on his reply and on how it would be best to deal with these people. Duly warned, Gargantua at once took counsel with Powerbrain, and with Down-the-hatch, his steward, Gymnast, his squire, and also with Rightway, and quickly, in as few words as possible, discussed with them what the best course of action might be. They all agreed that the best plan was to take them down to the pantry and get them to drink like peasants (or, more accurately, like theologians and philosophers). And to keep that old flathead Maître Twosides from swelling out like a turkey-cock, when the bells were handed back, while he was swilling away they sent for the provost marshal, the vice-chancellor of the School of Theology, and the parish priest, to whom—after the learned doctor had made a full statement of his mission—they would in fact deliver up the bells. And so, when everyone was gathered, they would be ready to hear his fine-toned harangue. And when in fact everyone had arrived, the meeting was officially convened, the learned philosopher was duly introduced, and he rose, coughing and trying to clear his wheezy throat, and began his speech:

Chapter Nineteen // Maître Janus Twosides' Speech to Gargantua, Seeking the Restoration of the Bells

"Hrrumph, humph, humph! Collar-eagues—Sir—Collar-eagues and also you non-collar-eagues, all of you. It wouldn't be nice if you don't return our bells to us, because we really need them. Hrrumph, hrrumph! Those people in Londres (near Cahuzec), and Cahors, not to mention Bordeaux and Brie as well, have many times offered us good money for those bells, and we've refused. They wanted to buy them for the substantive quality of the elementary metallic temperament created in the terrestriality of their quidditive essence by means of an effective separation between rain and whirlwinds in our vineyards—well, not really ours, but those around ours—because if we were to lose the wine we would lose everything, both sensually and in the accepted meaning of the law.

"If you will return them to us, at my request, it will be worth six foot of sausage to me, as well as a very handsome pair of breeches which will distinctly flatter my legs, unless they fail to keep to what they promised me. Hah! By God, my lord, a pair of breeches is a very good thing, *et vir sapiens non abhorrebit eam*—no wise man will take a dislike to them. Ha, ha! Everyone who may want a pair of breeches does not necessarily get one: I know that very well from my own experience! Now listen, my lord: it's already eighteen hours since I've preparatrated this lovely speechifying. *Reddite que sunt Cesaris Cesari, et que sunt Dei Deo:* Render unto Caesar that which is Caesar's, and unto God that which is God's. *Ibi jacet lepus,* that's the point, that's the heart of it.

"By my faith, my lord, if you wish to dine with me—privately, of course—by the body of Christ! *charitatis nos faciemus bonum cherubin,* we'll make good cherubim—I mean, good cheer—in the banquet hall. *Ego occidi unum porcum, et ego habet bon vino,* I've had a pig killed and I has—have? has?—anyway, there's plenty of good wine. But you can't make bad Latin out of good wine, eh?

"Well then, now, *de parte Dei,* for the sake of God, *date nobis clochas nostras,* give us back our bells. Now, in the name of the Faculty I'll give you a *Sermones de Utino,* a truly divine sermon if, *utinam,* in the name of heaven, you will return to us our bells. *Vultis etiam pardonos?* Would you like to buy some official pardons? *Per diem, vos habetitis et nihil poyabitis,* by God, you'll have them, and you won't have to pay anything, either.

"O Mister Lord, sir, *clochidonna minor nobis!* Give us back our insignificant bells! *Dea, est bonum urbis,* really, they belong to the city. Everybody benefits from them. If they're just right for your mare, they're just right for our Faculty, too, *que comparata est jumentis insipientibus et similis facta est eis, psalmo nescio quo,* which Faculty can be compared to the dumb beasts—which saying comes from a psalm, though I don't know which one. But the proper quotation is in my notebook, *et est unum bonum Achilles,* and it's a good one, as invincible as Achilles himself. Humph, humph, hrrumph—arggh, arggh.

"There! You see? I prove to you that you have to give them back to me. *Ego sic argumentor,* and this is what I argue:

"*Omnis clocha clochabilis, in clocherio clochando, clochans clochativo clochare facit clochabiliter clochantes,* All the bells are bell-like, and they all bell in the bell tower, because bells make bellness which makes bell sounds bell out. *Parisus habet clochas,* Therefore Paris has bells. *Ergo gluc,* and that's the end of it.

"Ha, ha, ha! That's real speechmaking, that is! It's *in tertio prime,* the third mood of the first syllogistic question, in *Darii,* I think, or somewhere else. By my soul, there have been times when I was the very devil at argument, but right now all my mind does is wander this way and that, so all I really need is good wine, a good bed, my back to the fire, my belly at the table, and a good full plate in front of me.

"Hey, my lord, I beg you, *in nomine Patris et Filii et Spiritus Sancti,* in the name of the Father and the Son and the Holy Spirit—amen—give us back our bells, and may God keep you from all harm, and Mary Our Lord's Mother keep you in good health, *qui vivit et regnat per omnia secula seculorum,* who lives and rules for all eternity, world without end, amen, amen! Hrrump, hump, arggh, rrrrragharggh!

"*Verum enim vero, quando quidem, dubio procul, edepol, quoniam, ita certe, meus Deus fidius,* But yes truly, seeing that, without a doubt, by God, because, accordingly, certainly, my God in heavens. A city without bells is like a blind man without his stick, a donkey without a harness strap, or a cow without cowbells. Until you give them back to us we will go on crying after you, like a blind man who has lost his stick. We will go on braying after you like a donkey that has lost its harness strap. And we will go on mooing after you like a cow without cowbells.

"Some fellow who liked to jabber in Latin—he lived near the hospital—well, once he said, citing the authority of a certain Fontana—no, no, I'm wrong, it was Pontana, that Italian, the secular poet—anyway, he said he wished that bells were made out of feathers and that the clapper was made out of a fox tail, because the bells ringing gave him a severe pain in the guts of his brain while he was writing his poems. But bing, bang, bash and smash, snicker snacker, we got him labeled a heretic: we can do that just as fast as melting a wax seal and sticking it onto the paper. Anyway, your deponent sayeth nothing more. *Valete et plaudite,* farewell—feel free to applaud. *Calepinus recensui,* It was Calepinus who did this, and now he's done."

Chapter Twenty ⁄⁄ How Maître Twosides Went Off with His Gift, and How He Sued the Other Professors

Maître Twosides had barely finished when Powerbrain and Rightway burst into such wild laughter that they thought they'd die of it—just like Crassus, when he saw a donkey eating thistles, or Philemon, when he saw a donkey eating figs that had been readied for his dinner. And then Maître Twosides began to laugh with them, which made them laugh still harder, until all the heaving and shaking they were giving their brains brought tears to their eyes—or, in short, their brains expressed these lachrymal humidities and, via the optic nerves, made them come rolling forth (in which action they well represented Democritus heraclyzing and Heraclitus democratizing).

When all the laughter had subsided, Gargantua consulted with his people about what to do. Powerbrain was of the opinion that the grand orator should be set to drinking again—and since he'd given them such pleasure, making them laugh harder even than that great actor Songecreux, he ought to be given the six feet of sausage mentioned in his happy harangue, plus a pair of breeches, three hundred cords of good firewood, twenty-five hogsheads of wine, a triple-sized bed stuffed with goose feathers, and a really deep dish which could hold all he'd ever want—that is, all the things he'd said his old age required.

So everything was done, exactly as they'd agreed, except that Gargantua, not at all sure it would be readily possible to find a pair of breeches big enough to go around his lovely legs, and unsure, too, how best they could fit breeches on this noble speechmaker—whether to cut them deep around the ass, so he'd have no trouble shitting; or to make them as ample as sailors' breeches, to lighten the pressure on his old kidneys; or to trick him out like a Swiss, to keep his belly warm; or to put him into a swallowtail coat so his kidneys wouldn't get too warm—decided to give him seven yards of black cloth, plus three yards of white wool for the lining. His porters took the wood; the masters of arts carried the sausages and the deep dish; Maître Twosides decided to carry the cloth himself.

One of the aforesaid masters of arts, named Maître George Pirate, argued with the old professor, pointing out that it wasn't proper and respectable for someone of his standing to parade through the streets bearing sausages. He therefore proposed to hand his burden over to one of the others.

"Ha!" said Janus Twosides. "You donkey, you ass, you don't have any idea how to think *in modo et figura,* according to the principles of formal logic. There! That shows you what the *Suppositions* and the *Beginner's Logic* are worth! *Pannus pro quo supponit,* eh? To what object is this cloth related?"

"*Confuse,*" said Maître Pirate, "*et distributive,* it relates to a lot of things and to no one in particular."

"Jackass!" said Maître Janus, "I didn't ask you that. *Quo modo supponit,* in what way is it related, which means *pro quo,* for whom? Donkey! And the answer to that is *pro tibiis meis,* for my legs. And for that reason I'm going to carry it—me, because *egomet, sicut suppositum portat adpositum:* the substantive carries the attributive!"

And so he stole off with it, just like that rascal Patelin in the farce.

But the best part of the joke came when the old wheezer rose up—oh how gloriously!—at a full meeting of the Faculty of Theology and demanded his sausages and his breeches. They were denied him on the spot, because according to all the information available he'd already gotten his reward from Gargantua. He replied that this had been *de gratis,* just a gift, and had proceeded simply from Gargantua's great generosity, so it did not release them from their promises. Nonetheless, they told him that in all good reason he should be content, and in any case he wouldn't get another scrap.

"Reason?" said Maître Twosides. "We don't use that around here. You miserable traitors, you're all worthless! You won't find more vicious, spiteful rascals anywhere on earth: I see that perfectly clearly. Don't try this stuff about being lame when you can see you're dealing with a cripple: you and I have done too much flimflamming together. By God's sacred spleen! I'll go to the king, I will, and I'll tell him all the incredible abuses you've been concocting here, all with your own hands. And you just see—may I be cursed with leprosy if I don't!—if I don't have all of

you burned alive as pederasts and traitors and heretics and seducers, enemies of God and of virtue!"

At these words, they had an indictment brought against him, and he
for his part filed a summons against them. The long and short of it was
that jurisdiction of the dispute was accepted by the courts—who still have
jurisdiction, though nothing has been decided. His opponents took a vow
not to bathe until the issue was settled. Maître Twosides, and his sup-
porters, swore that they would not blow their noses until a definitive
judgment had been handed down.

The result of these oaths has been that all of them are walking around
either filthy or snotty, to this very moment, because the court still hasn't
reviewed all the documents. The judgment is supposed to be handed down
on the first of the month, according to the Greek calendar—which of
course means never, because when it comes to courts nothing in all nature
can outdo them: they're easily able to ignore even their own rules and
regulations, in the interests of keeping a case going. The Articles of Paris
assure us that only God can accomplish things of an infinite nature. Nothing on this earth is immortal, because all things are fashioned with a time
to live and a time to die: *Omnia orta cadunt,* etc., Everything that's born
will die. But once these monsters of pretense get hold of a case, they
make it last forever—both infinite and immortal. They make you
remember—and believe—the words of Chilon of Sparta, consecrated at
Delphos:

"Misery walks hand in hand with Law. All litigants are miserable,
because most of them will be dead long before they'll ever have what
they went to Law to get."

Chapter Twenty-one // Gargantua's Studies, and His Way of Life, according to His Philosophical Teachers

Some days after the bells had been put back, and in recognition of
Gargantua's courtesy in thus restoring them, the citizens of Paris offered
to feed and maintain his mare for as long as he might like, an offer which
Gargantua found most acceptable. So the mare was put to pasture in Fontainebleau Forest. I don't think she is still there.

Gargantua was absolutely determined to study under Powerbrain. To
begin with, however, Powerbrain directed his new pupil to proceed exactly
as he always had, the better to understand how, over such a long period
of time, his former teachers had turned him into such a fop, such a fool
and ignoramus.

Accordingly, Gargantua lived just as he usually did, waking up between eight and nine (whether it was daylight or not), exactly as his old teachers had prescribed. And they cited the words of King David: *Vanum est vobis ante lucem surgere,* It does you no good to wake before day begins.

So he fooled about, swaggering, wallowing away the time in his bed (the better to enliven his animal spirits), and then dressed himself as the season dictated. But what he really liked to put on was a great long gown of heavy wool, lined with fox fur. And then he combed his hair as that great Ockhamist philosopher Jacob Almain always did—that is, with four fingers and a thumb, because his teachers used to say that, in this world of ours, to pay any more attention than that to your hair—or to washing and keeping yourself clean—was simply a waste of time.

Then he shat, pissed, vomited, belched, farted, yawned, spat, coughed, sighed, sneezed, and blew his nose abundantly. Then he put away a good breakfast, the better to protect himself against the dew and the bad morning air: good fried tripe, some nice broiled steak, several cheerful hams, some good grilled beef, and several platters of bread soaked in bouillon.

Powerbrain objected, observing that, fresh out of bed and before he'd been exercising, he hardly needed to take in so much refreshment. Gargantua replied:

"What! Haven't I already done enough exercise? I turned over in bed six or seven times before I got up. Isn't that enough? That's exactly what Pope Alexander used to do, and he was following the advice of his great Jewish doctor and astrologer, Bonnet de Lates. And he lived until he died, too, in spite of those who did not wish him well. This is what my prior teachers got me used to doing, saying that breakfast helped you develop your memory: that was why they started drinking at breakfast, too. I think it's marvelous—and it starts me off so well that I eat an even better supper. And Maître Tubalcain Holofernes (who was right at the head of his class, here in Paris) used to say there was no point at all just to running well: the idea was to leave early enough. So true good health for all of us doesn't require, does it, that we gulp it down, cup after cup after cup, like ducks, but certainly that we start to drink in the morning—*unde versus,* as the little poem says:

> To wake up early in the morning isn't the point:
> You've got to wet your whistle and bend that joint."

And so, after a hearty breakfast, he went to church, where they brought him, in a huge basket, a great fat prayer book, all wrapped in velvet, so heavily oiled, with such heavy clasps, and on such luxurious parchment that it must have weighed at least twenty-five hundred pounds. And then they heard twenty-six or maybe thirty masses. And then his private chaplain would come, dressed like a society swell, and with his breath nicely fortified by wine. He and Gargantua would mumble through the litany, thumbing the rosary so carefully that not a single bead ever fell to the ground.

As he walked out of church, they brought in a heavy-wheeled log carrier and delivered for his personal use an entire cask of carved-wood rosaries, each of them as round around as the rim of a man's hat. And as he and his chaplain strolled through the cloister of the church, and its galleries and gardens, they worked at their beads, saying more prayers than sixteen hermits.

Then he put in a scant half-hour of studying, keeping his eyes on his book. But, like the character in Terence's play, his soul was in the kitchen.

Then he pissed his urinal full, sat down to table, and—being naturally of a calm and imperturbable disposition—began his meal with several dozen hams, smoked beef tongues, caviar, fried tripe, and assorted other appetizers.

Meanwhile, four of his servants began to toss into his mouth, one after the other—but never stopping—shovelfuls of mustard, after which he drank an incredibly long draft of white wine, to make things easier for his kidneys. And then, eating whatever happened to be in season and he happened to like, he stopped only when his belly began to hang down.

His drinking was totally unregulated, without any limits or decorum. As he said, the time to restrict your drinking was only when the cork soles of your slippers absorb enough so they swell half a foot thick.

Chapter Twenty-two ⁄⁄ Gargantua's Games

Then, heavily mumbling a few fragments of prayer, he washed his hands in cool, fresh wine, picked at his teeth with a pig's foot, and chatted happily with his servants. After which, spreading out a green cloth, they laid out piles of cards and dice and game boards. And what they played was:

> four-card flush
> piquet
> Italian bridge
> grand slam
> gotcha
> trumps
> spades
> hunt 'em
> old maid
> cheating
> thirty-one
> one after the other

triple piquet
Italian poker
call your card
face down
poor Jack
cuckoo the devil
slapjack
cross your cards
marriage
I got 'em
who thinks so?
see what happens
this one, that one
follow the leader
tarot
winners, losers
gulls
torture
sneeze
German happiness
honors
how many fingers?
chess
fox and geese
squares
checkers
white lady
roll 'em
triple dice
backgammon
nick-nack
lurch
queens
Italian backgammon
trick-track
ladies' backgammon
ladies' nick-nack
down with God
jump
draughts
boo
tiddlywinks
hit the knife
around the millstone
knives

hit the stone
guess
heads or tails
jacks
knuckle-bone
croquet
tag
owl
baby
helter-skelter
hare and hounds
magpie hopping
horns
musical chairs
screech owl
keep a straight face
you're next
donkey shoes
giddy up
hurry up
going to Jerusalem
gold beard
high shoes
shit in your face
school beard
lend me your bag
ram ball
where's the ball?
up yours
arrow in the hole
blind man's buff
tripping
sow your wild oats
blow the coal
hide and seek
live judge, dead judge
oven and iron
fake thief
dibs
hunchback
horseshoes
pinch my ear
pear tree
kick my ass
hop and skip

jump rope
crooked stick
head to foot
stack the blocks
whipping sticks
quoits
I'm it
blow out the light
ninepins
skittles
bowls
bows and arrows
fly to Rome
redbeard
cherubs
English bowls
badminton
leapfrog
catch the pot
yes I can
twirl and whirl
jackstraws
whack 'em
tug-of-war
blindfold
marbles
off to school
bang the nut
taws
chuckhole
tops
whirling tops
monks
thunder
amazement
bang the bladder
shuttler
doctor
dung beetle
where's your green?
Lent just went
upside down
piggyback
single file
double roll

hand me my spear
bump on a log
treasure hunt
ox foot
secrets
question and answer
blind man's buff
London bridges
shuttlecock
hopscotch
run and hide
hit the stick
I spy
frogs
cross
wooden leg
cup and ball
kings and queens
master and servant
heads-up
flicks and flips
stuff your finger
soak your head
nose banger
pig
hand springs
gobble the bread
circle round
whip your ass
climb the ladder
head banger
dead man
cover your thumb
fat pig
bang your ass
flying pigeon
thirds
burning bush
soldiers
crosses
cross tag
stitch in time
buzzard
gangway
a fig to you

fart 'em away
bang the mustard
shake a leg
backslides
darts
jump your back
how high
nose bone
slap your ass
flick your finger.

And then, having played to his heart's content, and sifted and sieved and generally fooled away his time, they'd drink a bit more—roughly three gallons apiece—and then he'd eat and curl up on a nice bench or a good soft bed and take a nap for two or three hours, neither thinking nor speaking an evil word.

When he woke up, he'd shake his ears a little. And then more wine would be brought, and he drank better than ever.

Powerbrain scolded him: drinking just before sleeping, he objected, was not healthy.

"But this," said Gargantua, "this is the true way of life of the Holy Fathers. For me, sleep is like salted food—it works just as well as ham, and I wake up wonderfully ready to drink."

Then he'd go back to studying, though not for long. And he'd recite his Our Father and say his rosary—and to say it more efficiently he'd climb up on an old mule that had carried nine kings on its back. Mumbling and nodding his head as he rode, in fulfillment of his sacred obligation, he'd trot off to watch a rabbit hunt.

When he got back he'd visit the kitchen, just to be sure what kind of roast was on the spit.

He dined well, by God! And he'd gladly break bread with some of his neighbors, good drinkers all, and as they boozed away they told stories, old ones, new ones, on and on. Among these noble friends and neighbors were the squires du Fou, Gourville, Grignaux, and—a very ancient family—Marigny.

And after dinner they turned to the Bible—game boards shaped like Bibles, anyway—and all you could hear was "Banco!" or "Straight flush!" or "One, two, three!" Sometimes they'd hunt up the willing girls in the neighborhood, and wine and dine them liberally. And then Gargantua would sleep for eight good hours at a stretch and not wake up till the next day.

Chapter Twenty-three // How Gargantua Was So Well Taught by Powerbrain That He Never Wasted a Single Hour of the Day

Once Powerbrain understood Gargantua's vicious way of life, he began to reflect on other—and better—ways of instructing him in humanistic matters. But for the first few days he did not make any changes, realizing that nature would not allow abrupt shifts without cataclysmic violence.

Accordingly, to begin his work in the best way possible, he sought the advice of a wise physician, Holygift, with whom he discussed how to set Gargantua on a better path. The learned doctor, proceeding according to his profession's canonical rules, first purged the young man with a sovereign remedy for madness, Anticyrian hellebore, which powerful herb quickly cleaned away all the deterioration and perverse habits to which his brain had succumbed. This procedure had the advantage, also, of making Gargantua forget everything he had learned from his early teachers, just as in ancient times Timotheus did with disciples who'd studied under other musicians.

To help in the good work, Powerbrain introduced Gargantua to some of Paris's truly learned scholars. In trying to be like them, he came to understand their spirit, wanting to acquire knowledge and to make something of himself.

And then he got him into such a way of studying that no hour in the day was wasted: all his time was spent in pursuit of humanistic learning and honest knowledge.

Accordingly, Gargantua now woke up at four in the morning. He would be given a massage, while a portion of the holy Scriptures was read aloud to him, in a high, clear voice, with precise and accurate pronunciation. A young page named Reader, a native of Basché, was given this task. The subject, and also the argument, of this lesson often led Gargantua into reverence and adoration of God, the majesty and marvelous wisdom of whom had thus been exhibited to him, and into prayer and supplication.

Then he would go off and, in some private place, permit the natural result of his digestive process to be excreted. While he was thus occupied, his teacher would repeat what had been read to him, clarifying and explaining the more obscure and difficult points.

Coming back, they would examine and reflect on the state of the heavens: was everything as it had been when they'd seen the sky the night before? into what constellations had the sun newly entered, and likewise the moon?

And then he was dressed and combed, his hair was properly done, and he was equipped and perfumed, while all the time the lessons he'd been given the day before were repeated for him. He recited them by heart, showing by some practical and compassionate illustrations that he understood their meaning. This often lasted two or three hours, though ordinarily they stopped when he was fully dressed.

Then he was read to for three solid hours.

After which they went outdoors, always discussing the meaning of what had been read, and went to the park or somewhere near it, where they played various games, especially three-handed palm ball, giving their bodies the same elegant exercise they had earlier given their souls.

Their games were entirely free: they stopped whenever they felt like stopping—usually when they'd worked up a sweat or when they grew tired. Then they had a vigorous massage, and were wiped clean; they'd change their shirts and, walking quietly, would go to see if dinner was ready. And as they waited they'd recite, clearly and eloquently, remembered portions of the lesson.

However, Sir Appetite arrived, and when they could they seated themselves at the table.

Some entertaining story of ancient heroism was read to them, at the start of the meal, until wine was poured in Gargantua's cup.

Then, if they liked the idea, the reading was resumed, or else they'd begin to chat happily. At the beginning of this new regime, they talked about virtue, proper behavior, the nature and effect of everything placed on their table that day: bread, wine, water, salt, meat, fish, fruit, herbs, roots, and about the preparation of these things. In so doing, Gargantua soon learned all the appropriate passages from Pliny, Athenaeus, Dioscorides, Julius Pollux, Galen, Porphyry, Oppian, Polybius, Heliodorus, Aristotle, Claudius Aelian, and others. In order to be sure they had their authorities right, they'd often have the books brought right to the table. And what was said became so clearly and entirely fixed in Gargantua's memory that no doctor alive understood anything like as much as he did.

Then, talking about the lessons read that morning, and finishing their meal with some quinced sweet, Gargantua would clean his teeth with a bit of fresh green mastic twig. He'd wash his hands and his eyes with good fresh water, and give thanks to God with sweet hymns of praise for His munificence and divine kindness. And cards were brought, not for playing games of chance, but to learn a thousand gracious things and new inventions, all founded in arithmetic.

And in this way Gargantua developed a genuine liking for the numerical science. Every day, after both dinner and supper, he passed his time in arithmetical games just as pleasantly as when he'd been in the habit of playing at dice or cards. Indeed, he came to understand both the theory and the practice of arithmetic so well that Cuthbert Tunstall, the Englishman who had written so much on the subject, was obliged to admit that, truly, in comparison to Gargantua, all he understood was a pack of non-sense.

But arithmetic wasn't the end of it, for they went on to other mathematical sciences, like geometry, astronomy, and music. While waiting for their meal to be digested and properly absorbed, they worked out a thousand pleasant geometrical figures, and shaped appropriate instruments, and practiced astronomical laws in the same way.

Later, they had a wonderful good time, singing four- and five-part rounds, and sometimes singing variations on some melody that was a delight to their throats.

As for musical instruments, Gargantua learned to play the lute, the clavier, the harp, the transverse flute as well as the recorder, the viol, and also the trombone.

As this hour passed, digestion was indeed accomplished, and so he proceeded to purge himself of his natural excrement. Then he at once returned to his main studies for three hours or even more, in order to repeat the morning's lesson and also to continue with whatever book had been set for him. And he practiced writing in the Italian and the Gothic alphabets, and also drawing.

And then they'd go back to their rooms, and along with them went a young gentleman from Touraine, Squire Gymnast by name, who was teaching Gargantua the arts of knighthood.

After changing his clothes, Gargantua would mount a battle horse, a traveling steed, a Spanish stallion, an Arabian racehorse, and a light, quick horse, and ride a hundred laps, making his mount fairly fly through the air, jump ditches, leap over fences, make quick circular turns, both to the right and to the left.

Nor did he break his lance, for it is sheer nonsense to say, "I broke ten lances in battle." Any carpenter could do as much. Real glory comes from breaking ten of your enemies' with one of your own. So, with his steel-tipped, solid, firm lance he learned to break down a door, crack open a suit of armor, uproot a tree, strike right through the center of a hoop, knock a knight's saddle right off his horse, and carry away a coat of mail or a pair of armored gloves. And all the time he was himself in armor, from his head right down to his toes.

When it came to marching his horse in rhythm, or making the animal obey his commands, there was simply no one better. Even Cesare Fieschi, the famous equestrian acrobat, seemed no better than a monkey on horseback, in comparison. He was especially good at leaping from one horse to another, without ever setting foot on the ground—the horses were known as leapers—and he could do this from either side, lance erect, without stirrups. Without any reins or bridle he could make a horse do anything he wanted it to do. In short, he was accomplished at everything useful in military matters.

Some days he exercised with the battle-ax, which he could wield like a razor, swinging it so powerfully, slicing it around in a circle so deftly, that he was ranked a knight at arms, passing every sort of trial and declared fit for any battle.

And then he'd practice with the pickax, or at wielding the two-handed sword, or with the short sword (so perfect for thrusting and parrying), and the dagger—sometimes wearing armor, sometimes not, or using a shield, or wearing a cape, or carrying a small wrist shield, known as a *rondelle*.

He hunted deer—stag and doe and fallow buck—bears, wild boar, hares, partridge, pheasant, buzzards. He played with the big kickball, making it bound high in the air, sometimes with his foot, sometimes with his fist. He fought and ran and leaped and jumped—but not a mere three-foot hop and leap, or a high jump in the German style—because, as Gymnast said, jumps of that sort were useless and of no good whatever, when it came to real war—but he'd jump great wide ditches, go flying over a hedgerow, climb six paces up a wall, and thus get in through a window as high off the ground as a lance.

He swam in deep water, breaststroke, backstroke, sidestroke, using his entire body or only his legs, or with one hand high in the air and holding a book, crossing the Seine River without getting a page wet. He swam with his cloak in his teeth, as Julius Caesar did (says Plutarch). Then, pulling himself right into a boat with just one hand, he'd throw himself back into the water, head first, going all the way down to the bottom, sinking among the rocks and swimming to great depths, plunging down to all sorts of chasms and deep abysses. Then he'd turn the boat, and steer it, sometimes quickly, sometimes slowly, now downstream, now upstream, sometimes bringing it to a halt by pressing it against a milldam, guiding it with one hand, his other wielding a great oar or raising the sail. He'd climb up the guide ropes, right to the top of the mast, and run out along the spars. He'd adjust the compass, brace the bowlines, tighten the helm.

Leaving the water, he'd go directly up a mountain and then come right down again. He'd climb trees like a cat, jumping from one to the other like a squirrel, tearing down thick branches as if he were another Milo of Croton. With a pair of sharp-pointed daggers and a couple of good marlinespikes, he'd climb to the top of a house exactly like a rat, then leap down so expertly that the drop wouldn't cause him so much as a twinge.

He threw the javelin, and the iron bar, the millstone, the boar spear, the hunting spear, the spiked halberd. He drew the longbow like an archer, pulled crossbows taut (though this was usually done with a winch), sighted a rifle right against his eye (though usually it had to be rested against the shoulder), set up and mounted cannon, centering them right in on target, aimed them so they could knock a stuffed parrot off a pole, pointing them straight up a mountain or right down into a valley, directing their fire up ahead or to the side or, like the ancient Parthians, back behind him.

They would attach a rope cable to some high tower, hanging down to the ground, and he would climb this, hand over hand, then come down so strongly and with such confidence that he might just as well have been strolling along some nice, flat meadow.

They would rig up a long pole, supported on each side by a tree, and he'd hang from it by his hands, going this way and that without his feet ever touching the ground—and at such a speed that, even running on flat ground, it would have been impossible to catch him.

And in order to exercise his chest and lungs, he would shout like all the devils in hell. Once, I heard him call to Rightway, from the Saint Victor Gate all the way across Paris to Montmartre. Even bull-throated Stentor, at the battle of Troy, could not shout so loud.

To toughen his nerves, they made him two huge molded lead weights, cast in the shape of salmon, each just over eighty thousand pounds: he called them his dumbbells. He'd lift one in each hand, starting from the ground, and hold them both high up over his head—and then he'd keep them there, not moving a muscle, for three-quarters of an hour or even more. This was literally unmatchable strength!

No one was stronger, not in barriers or tug-of-war or any of the games. When it was his turn, he stood his ground so firmly that he could afford to let the most adventurous try to move him a single inch from his place, exactly as Milo of Croton used to do—and in imitation of whom he would clasp a pomegranate in his hand and offer it to anyone who could take it from him. Nor would he permit the fruit to be damaged in the attempt.

Having thus spent his time, he'd have another massage, then clean himself and change his clothes, returning with a smile and, strolling through meadows and other grassy spots, he'd turn his attention to trees and plants, examining them in the light of what the ancients wrote—Theophrastus, Dioscorides, Marinus, Pliny, Nicander, Aemilius Macer, and Galen. He and his companions would fill their hands with herbs and roots and flowers, then bring it all back to their lodgings, where a young page, Rootgatherer, was in charge of all such matters, including care of the hoes, picks, rakes, spades, shovels, and everything else needed for the proper care of growing things.

And once they were back at their lodgings, and while waiting for their supper, they would repeat selected passages from what they had read, earlier, and also what they had discussed at table.

Note, please, that although dinner was a sober and even frugal meal, at which Gargantua would eat only just enough to control the growling in his stomach, supper was a great abundant affair. He would consume everything he needed to sustain and properly nourish himself, which is exactly the sort of diet prescribed by any good, knowing doctor, though there are plenty of medical hacks (in constant dispute, of course, with learned academic philosophers) who advise exactly the opposite.

Gargantua continued his lessons all during supper, or for as long as he felt in the mood. And then he would turn to good solid discussion, literate, informed, useful.

After a final grace had been said, they would turn to music, singing, the harmonious playing of various instruments, or to pleasant card and dice games. And there they would stay, having a fine time, often amusing themselves until it was time to go to bed. And sometimes they would go visiting the houses of learned people, or perhaps those newly returned from foreign countries.

When night had truly arrived, but before they climbed into bed, they would stand in their lodgings, in the spot from which the sky could be most closely observed, and compare notes about any comets they might see, and the configuration of the stars, their location and aspect, their oppositions and conjunctions.

And then Gargantua and Powerbrain would briefly recapitulate, according to the Pythagorean fashion, everything Gargantua had read and seen and understood, everything he had done and heard, all day long.

They would both pray to God their Creator, worshiping, reaffirming their faith, glorifying Him for His immense goodness and thanking Him for all they had been given, and forever placing themselves in His hands.

And then they would go to sleep.

Chapter Twenty-four ⁄ What Gargantua Did When It Was Rainy

When the weather turned rainy and bad, the time before dinner went exactly as usual, except that Gargantua had a good bright fire lit, to help moderate the intemperate air. But after dinner, in place of exercise, they would stay indoors and, according to the best therapeutic approach, amuse themselves by baling hay, sawing and splitting wood, and threshing the grain stored in the barn. Then they would study the art of painting and sculpture, or else (following ancient custom) play knucklebones, an entertainment about which Leonicus Thomaeus has written so well—and a game which Andreas Lascaris, teacher and friend of Erasmus, and my good friend too, has played with such pleasure. And while they played they turned over in their mind all the passages from classical authors in which the game is either mentioned or used as a metaphor.

In the same way, they would either go to watch the work at metal foundries, or the casting of cannon, or go to observe jewelers, goldsmiths, and those who cut precious stones, or else alchemists and coin makers, or tapestry weavers, silk weavers, velvet makers, watchmakers, mirror makers, printers, organ manufacturers, dyers, and other crafts- men of that sort. And treating all of them to wine, they learned from the mouths of these masters what their various trades and inventions were all about.

They would go to hear public lectures, solemn convocations, and the careful orations, declamations, and pleadings of wellborn lawyers, or the sermons of evangelical preachers.

He went to all the places where swordsmanship was practiced and taught, and tested himself against those who taught it, in every aspect of fencing and with all the sorts of swords and foils known. And he demonstrated to them that he knew as much as they did, and more.

Instead of going off to collect herbs and examine plants and flowers, they would go to drugstores, herb sellers, and other apothecaries, and contemplate with great care the fruits, roots, leaves, gums, seeds, and all the exotic unguents, and then how they were prepared and diluted for more effective use.

He went to see the jugglers and clowns, the magicians and those who peddled wonderful, half-magical remedies, and contemplated their games and tricks, their somersaults and smooth patter, especially those famous mountebanks from Chauny, in Picardy—born with a silver tongue, every one of them, able to sell water to people swimming in a lake or firewood to those who live inside a volcano.

They would return for supper, and eat more sparingly than on other days—in particular, meats that tend to dry and tame the body. This was made necessary by the excessive humidity in the air, which under the circumstances there was no way to avoid. These simple dietary measures corrected that natural imbalance and saved them from being bothered by the loss of their usual exercise.

And this was how Gargantua's life was regulated. He kept to these rules every day, and he benefited—to be sure!—as a young man of his years can, a youth with good sense. All regular exercise, no matter how hard it may at first seem, becomes pleasant and easy and finally great good fun, more like a royal pastime than a scholar's plodding.

In spite of which, and in order to allow him some relief from such a whirlwind way of life, Powerbrain made sure that Gargantua took off at least one day a month, some day of great clarity and calm brightness. They would leave Paris early in the morning and go to one of the pleasant villages beloved of all Parisian students—Gentilly, perhaps, or Boulogne on the Seine, or Montrouge, or Pont-Charenton, or Vanves, or Saint- Cloud. And they would spent the entire day there, just as happily as they could manage, laughing, telling jokes, drinking gaily, playing, singing, dancing, lying on their backs in beautiful meadows, hunting for spar- rows' nests, catching quail, and fishing for frogs and crayfish.

But even on this day spent without books and reading, they didn't completely neglect higher matters, because even lying there in the lovely meadows they would recite from memory cheerful verses from Virgil's *Georgics,* from Hesiod, from Politian's *Rusticus* (Farming), or some pleasant Latin epigrams, which they'd then turn into equally pleasant poems in their own language.

And when they feasted they would not simply mix their wine and water. Instead, as Cato advises in his *Country Matters,* and Pliny too, they would use a cup of ivy wood and wash the wine in a full basin of water, then pour it back out with a funnel. And they would pour the water from one glass to another and construct tiny automatic engines that seemed to work of their own accord, like automatons.

Chapter Twenty-five ⁄⁄ How the Bakers of Lerné and the Bakers of Gargantua's Country Got into a Great Argument, and the Great War Which Resulted

At the beginning of autumn, which was the season for harvesting their vineyards, all the shepherds in the country were out guarding the vines, trying to keep cows from eating up their grapes.

And at just that time the bakers of Lerné came down the highroad from Lerné to Chinon, bringing ten or twelve loads of flatcakes to that city.

So the shepherds asked, very politely, if they could buy some of their cakes. I should explain that these flatcakes make an utterly delicious breakfast, eaten with fresh grapes—especially pinot grapes, Anjou grapes (with a lovely fig flavor), and muscatel, and grapes from Poitou, and a kind of grapes that are a sovereign cure for constipation, because they turn out turds as long as a pickax, and people who think they're only going to fart suddenly find their breeches full of shit, which makes this variety go by the name "hopeful harvesters."

The bakers were not particularly receptive to the shepherds' request. Worse still, they proceeded to give them, instead, a stream of gross insults, calling them toothless beggars, redheaded clowns, drunken bums, bed shitters, thieves, pickpockets, cowards, sweet little morsels, big bellies, fat mouths, slobs, clodhoppers, patsies, bloodsuckers, saber rattlers, prettyboys, practical jokers, shovel watchers, boors with big mouths, fat-heads, jerks, fools, sharp-tongued bastards, fops, motor tongues, turd herders, shit shepherds, and assorted other unpleasant names. And they added that good flatcakes of the kind they were selling weren't for the likes of them: they ought to be happy with half-baked crumble cakes and peasant's bread.

To which outrageous performance one of the shepherds, Jacques Frogier by name—a respectable young man of good family—responded pleasantly:

"Since when have calves like you grown horns and turned into ferocious bulls? What big mouths you've got! By God, you used to sell to us cheerfully enough—and now you turn us down. This isn't how good neighbors are supposed to act, and it's not how we treat you when you come here to buy our fine wheat, which you need for making your bread and your flatcakes. And we would have given you some of our grapes, into the bargain. But now! By the holy mother of God, you'll live to regret this. The day will come when you'll want something from us. And we'll treat you, then, the way you're treating us now, and you'll remember my words."

Then Marquet, leader of the bakers' guild, answered:

"Hah! You're feeling your oats this morning, aren't you? You must have eaten some pretty cocky stuff, yesterday. Well, come on over here, come on, and I'll let you have some flatcake!"

At which Frogier innocently went over to him, pulling a coin out of his purse, expecting Marquet to open his sack and take out some flatcakes. But Marquet drew back his whip and gave the young fellow such a cut across the legs that great welts appeared. And then Marquet thought he'd better leave there pretty quickly. But Frogier yelled as loud as he could and, at the same time, pulled his great shepherd's staff from under his arm and threw it at the baker, hitting him directly on the forehead, on the right side where the temporal artery is located, and Marquet tumbled off his mule, looking more like a dead man than a live one.

Now all the farmers, who were out there shelling walnuts, came running over and, drawing their thick staffs, began to pound on the bakers as though they were green grain. And the shepherds and shepherdesses, hearing Frogier's cry, also came running, with their slingshots and their staffs, and hurled such a flurry of stones that it seemed to be hailing. And then they caught up to the fleeing bakers and grabbed four or five dozen of their flatcakes—for which, however, they paid them the usual price. And they also gave them a hundred walnuts and three baskets of white grapes. After which the bakers helped Marquet, who was badly hurt, to get back up on his mule, and then they went back to Lerné, not trying to follow the road all the way to Chinon, lined as it was with threatening hordes of farmers and shepherds and cowherds.

And then the shepherds and shepherdesses had a fine feast of flatcakes and grapes, dancing and singing to the lovely sound of the bagpipe, and making fun of the puffed-up bakers, who had surely risen that morning and made the sign of the cross with the wrong hand—which would explain the bad luck they'd fallen into. And they carefully bathed Frogier's aching legs with soothing grapes, which virtually cured him at once.

Chapter Twenty-six // How the People of Lerné, at the Command of Picrochole, Their King (Whose Very Name Signifies Bitter Bile), Launched a Surprise Attack on Gargantua's Shepherds

After they got back to Lerné, and even before they ate or drank, the bakers went to the royal household and there, in front of their king, Picrochole (the third of that name to wear that crown), they uttered their complaint, showing their broken bread baskets, their crumpled hats, their torn coats, their crushed flatcakes, and especially the badly wounded Marquet, and saying that all this had been done by Grandgousier's shepherds and farmers, on the highroad to Chinon.

And Picrochole immediately flew into a wild rage and, without trying to find out anything more, neither why nor how nor anything else, called up all the warriors in his kingdom. Under penalty of death by hanging, they were all to assemble in the courtyard outside his house, fully armed and equipped, by noon that same day.

And the better to ensure his success, he sent the town crier all around his city, to beat the drum and notify the townsfolk. He himself, while his dinner was being cooked, went to see to it that the royal cannon were mounted and ready, the royal flags and banners unfurled, and the necessary supplies of gunpowder and food all loaded up.

Then, as he dined, he signed the commissions for his officers, ordering (although custom required that he himself or perhaps his son take the responsibility) that Lord Tatter-rags be in charge of the avant-garde, which would be constituted of sixteen thousand and fourteen archers, plus thirty-five thousand and eleven volunteers.

His master of the horse, Loudmouth, was put in charge of the artillery, which had nine hundred and fourteen large brass cannon, double cannon, siege pieces, rifle cannon, snake cannon, mortars, shrapnel cannon, cannon on wheels, small snake cannon, and other pieces as well. The rearguard was given to the duke of Pennyrake, while the main army was led by the king and the princes of the realm.

Thus promptly readied, before setting out they still dispatched three hundred light cavalrymen, commanded by Captain Goatsucker, to spy out the land and see if any ambushes had been set. These gallant soldiers, having made a diligent search, found the entire countryside calm and peaceful, without any sign of military activity whatever.

Hearing this, Picrochole commanded them to march forth at once, banners high.

Accordingly, they rushed into the field pell-mell, without any discipline or order, pillaging and burning everywhere they went, sparing neither poor nor rich, and no place either secular or holy. They carried off oxen and cows and bulls and heifers, ewes and sheep and she-goats and billy goats, hens and capons and chickens and goslings and ganders and geese, and pigs and sows and piglets. They knocked the walnuts out of the trees, stripped vines bare, stole the seedling vine plants, and in general pulled all the fruit they could find out of the branches. They created an ungodly mess, and never met with the least resistance—except one man, who threw himself on their mercy, begging to be treated more humanely, just as they had always, before this, been good neighbors, never under any circumstances being guilty of any excess or outrage, and certainly nothing to justify being so badly treated, for which God Himself would swiftly and surely punish them. To all of which they replied not a word, except that they would teach them to eat flatcakes!

Chapter Twenty-seven ⁄⁄ How a Monk of Seuilly Saved the Abbey from Being Sacked by Its Enemies

So they went wildly on, pillaging and stealing, until they came to Seuilly, where they robbed men and women alike, taking everything they could: nothing was too hot or too heavy. Although there was plague in the town, and virtually every house was afflicted, they broke in everywhere, plundering anything they found—and they were never in any sort of danger, which is absolutely miraculous, because all the priests and vicars and preachers, the doctors, surgeons, and druggists who went to visit the sick, and dealt with their illnesses, and tried to cure them, or at least preached and tended to them, all of them died, while these devils stole and murdered and nothing ever happened to them. How can that be, I ask you? Please: think about it.

Having pillaged the city, they proceeded to the abbey, more like a riot than an army. But they found the inner enclosure all shut up and bolted. So the main part of their army marched off toward Gué de Vède, leaving seven companies of foot soldiers and two hundred knights at arms to stay there and break down the walls and destroy the vineyards.

The monks, poor devils, didn't know which of their saints to pray to. Having nothing better to try, they rang the bells *ad capitulum capitulantes,* summoning everyone to the main building. And there they decided to mount a handsome procession, reinforced by solemn psalms and other holy songs and by prayers *contra hostium insidias,* against the enemy's snares, and also by responses *pro pace,* in favor of peace.

Now, at that time there resided in the abbey a cloistered monk, Brother John Mincemeat—young, strong, lively, always in a fine humor, good with his hands, bold, adventurous, thoughtful, tall, lean, noisy, with a handsome nose, who knew the breviary inside out and could read it like a flash (and could say a mass, too, without wasting any time), who got through vigils in the twinkling of an eye—in short, a true monk if ever there monked one since the days when monks first practiced monking through this unmonkish world of ours, and in all breviary matters a priest right up to the teeth.

And hearing the noise their enemies were making, down in the vineyard, Brother John went to see what was happening. Finding that they were stealing the grapes on which next year's entire supply of wine depended, he quickly went back into the heart of the church. And there he found the other monks, all as dazed as people who have just been testing the clappers on giant bells: they were chanting *Impetum inimicorum ne timueritis,* Fear not the enemy's attack—except what they were saying was more like *Ini nim, pe, pe, ne, ne, ne, ne, ne, ne, ne, tum, ne, num, num, ini, i, mi, i, mi, co, o, ne, no, o, o, ne, no, ne, no, no, no, rum, ne, num, num.*

"Oh, you sang the shit out of that!" he said. "But why don't you sing:

Good-bye, wine baskets—the grape harvest's gone?

"May I go straight to the devil if they're not right here in the enclosure of this abbey, stripping the vines and cutting them right down to the roots so there won't be anything left—by the blood and bones of Christ! All we'll have for the next four years will be scraps. By Saint James' belly! What will we drink, eh, we other poor devils? O dear Lord God, *da mihi potum,* let me have something to drink!"

And the monastery priest said:

"What is this drunkard doing here? Someone take him and lock him away. To break in on divine service in this riotous way!"

"But the *wine* service," said Brother John. "Let's make sure that's not broken—because you yourself, My Lord Prior, you love your wine better than anyone. All good men feel that way: no man of true nobility dislikes wine. Now that's a true monastic rule! But by all that's holy! these responses you're chanting don't answer the real question.

"Why do we keep short hours, when it's time to bring in the harvest and pick the grapes? And why are our hours long before Christmas and all through the whole winter? Well, Brother Macé Pelosse, may he rest in peace, he had the true Christian spirit—may I be damned if he didn't— he once told me, and I've never forgotten it, that the reason was so we could bring in the grapes and make good wine in this autumn season, so in the winter we could drink it.

"So listen to me, all of you, if you love wine: by the body of Christ, follow me! May Saint Anthony's fire strike me if those who haven't tended the vine will get to drink the wine! By God's belly, it belongs to Holy Mother Church! Ha—no, no, you devil! Saint Thomas à Becket was willing to die for this—and if I die, won't I be a saint, too? But listen: it's not going to be me that ends up dead. It's going to be them!"

And so saying he tucked up his long monk's robe and grabbed the heavy staff of the cross, good solid apple wood, that the monks carried aloft in processions. It was as long as a lance, as thick around as a man's fist; it was decorated with well-rubbed, half-invisible fleurs-de-lis. And so, wearing his handsome monk's uniform, he rushed out, his cowl flung back like a sash, and began banging away at his enemies with the cross, hitting as hard as he could. And scattered all over the vineyard as they were, gathering grapes with both hands—in no military deployment, without their banners and their trumpets and their drums—because the standard-bearers and the banner-bearers had leaned their poles against the wall, and the drummers had bashed in the sides of their drums, the better to fill them with grapes, and the long brass trumpets had been stuffed full of vine stems, leaves and grapes and all, and couldn't have sounded an alarm if they'd tried—Brother John came down on them so hard, striking out left and right and center, in the best old-fashioned style, that they went flying topsy-turvy like a herd of frightened pigs.

He crushed the skulls of some of them, smashed others' arms and legs, broke necks, stove in kidneys, beat in noses, blackened eyes, cracked jaws, bashed in teeth, broke shoulder blades, turned flesh and skin all black and blue, dislocated hips, shattered forearms.

Any who tried to hide among the thick vines, he clubbed all down the spine, breaking their backs like dogs.

Any who tried to run, he sent their heads flying in pieces instead, splitting them down the occipito-parietal lobe.

Any who tried to climb a tree, hoping they'd be safe up there, he took his stick and impaled them right up the asshole.

Any who knew him and cried out:

"Hey, Brother John, my old friend, O Brother John, I surrender!"

"You've got a lot of choice," he answered. "Surrender your soul, too, to all the devils in hell."

And without another word he would proceed to bashing and banging.

Any who got so carried away that they tried to stand up to him, face to face, then he really showed how strong he was, because he would stab them through the chest, down into the thorax and right through to the heart.

Others he would club on the ribs, smashing them and turning their stomachs inside out, making them drop dead like flies. Others he would club so savagely in the belly that their guts fell out. And others he smashed so hard on the balls that he broke their asses.

It was easily the most horrible sight ever seen on earth.

Some cried, "O Saint Barbara, protect your faithful!"

Others cried, "O Saint George!"

And others, "O Saint Touch-me-not! O Our Lady of Cunault! Our

Lady of Lorette! Our Lady of Good Tidings! Our Lady of Lenou! Our Lady of Rivière!"

Some prayed to Saint James of Compostéla.

Some prayed to the Holy Shroud at Chambery, though that relic burned three months later and they couldn't save a single thread.

Some prayed to the holy shrine at Cadouin.

Some prayed to Saint John of Angery.

Some prayed to Saint Eutropius of Saintes, or Saint Maximus of Chinon, or Saint Martin of Candes, or Saint Cloud of Cinais, or to the relics at Javarsay, and to a thousand other nice little saints.

Some died without talking, others talked without dying. Some died as they were talking, others talked as they were dying.

Some cried out, "Confession! Confession! *Confiteor! Miserere! In manus!* I confess! Have mercy on me! I am in Your hands!"

The wounded made so much noise that the monastery priest and all his monks came out and, seeing these poor men lying strewn on the ground all over the vineyard, mortally wounded, gave some of them holy confession. But while the priests waited to hear confessions, the younger monks ran to Brother John and asked him what they could do to be helpful.

To which he answered that they could cut the throats of those who were lying around on the ground and were still alive.

So, hanging their long capes on the nearest vineyard trellis, they began to cut the throats and finish off those who were mortally wounded. Can you imagine what tools they used? Small pruning knives—the kind little children use, where I come from, to shell walnuts.

Which is how, wielding his cross, Brother John finally got to the hole their enemies had smashed in the abbey walls. Some of the younger monks carried off the fallen flags and banners, to cut them up into garters. But when the enemy soldiers who had made their confessions tried to sneak out through this same breach in the wall, Brother John began to club away at them, crying:

"These men have confessed! They've made their repentance, they've been pardoned for their sins! They're ready to go right to heaven, their road's as straight as a sickle knife—or that winding mountain road up to Faye-la-Vineuse!"

So his bravery had beaten the entire army, everyone who had broken into the abbey—and there had been thirteen thousand six hundred and thirty-two of them, not counting the women and little children, to be sure.

Even that legendary fighting hermit Maugist d'Aigremont never wielded his pilgrim's staff so valiantly, in all his battles against the Saracens (described so glowingly in the old stories about the four Aymon brothers), as Brother John had swung his cross against a marauding enemy.

Chapter Twenty-eight // How King Picrochole Stormed the Castle of La Roche-Clermault, and Grandgousier's Sadness and Reluctance at Having to Go to War

❧

While the monk was skirmishing against those who'd broken into the abbey, as we have said, Picrochole and the main part of his army went quickly past the Gué de Vède and attacked the town of La Roche-Clermault, which made no resistance whatever. And because it was already dark, Picrochole decided to put up for the night there, he and his people, to let his stinging anger cool down a bit.

In the morning he attacked the outer fortifications and then the castle itself, and captured them, then set them to rights again, stocking them with the necessary supplies in case he in his turn was attacked and had to retreat there. It was a strong place, both because of what men and what nature had done: the location was superb, and the walls and other fortifications had been well constructed.

So: we will leave him there, for the moment, and return to our good Gargantua. He was in Paris, studying hard both at humane letters and athletically. And our good old friend Grandgousier, his father, warming his balls after supper in front of a good, clear big fire, watching the chestnuts roast, sat drawing on the hearth with a broken stick—it had been used for stirring up the fire, and so was nicely charred at one end—and telling stories of the old days to his wife and family.

Just then, one of the shepherds who watched over Grandgousier's vineyards, named Pillot, came and told him about all the outrages and the violence perpetrated in his domain by Picrochole, king of Lerné, telling how Picrochole had ravaged and ruined and plundered all through the kingdom, except the abbey in Seuilly, where Brother John Mincemeat had saved his king's honor. And Pillot said that Picrochole was now at the castle of La Roche-Clermault, which with great care he and his men had repaired and readied for defense.

"Alas! alas!" said Grandgousier. "What's going on, my good people? Am I dreaming, or is it true, all this you've just been telling me? Picrochole, my dear old friend, so very long my good friend—my kinsman—my ally—has attacked me? Who has been stirring him up? Who has been making him angry? Who has been leading him on? Who has urged such a course on him? Oh! Oh! Oh! Oh! Oh! My God, my Savior, help me, breathe Your spirit into me, help me decide, with Your counsel, what I should do! Lord: I swear before You—and may You be gracious to me, knowing that this is true!—that I have never displeased him, this Picrochole, nor hurt any of his people, nor stolen anything from his lands. On the contrary, I have always helped him, whenever I knew I could—with people, with money, with goodwill, with advice. The devil himself must have prompted him, for Picrochole to perpetrate such an outrage. O God, You know my heart: nothing is hidden from You. If something has driven him out of his mind, and I am meant to be here, as Your emissary, to help bring him to himself again, give me the power and the knowledge to teach him, once more, to live under the yoke of Your holy will.

"Oh! oh! oh! my good people, my friends, my faithful servants, must I trouble you to help me? Alas! Until now all my old age needed has been calm and repose, and all my life I have sought nothing but peace. But I see it clearly: now I have to put armor and weapons on my poor weak shoulders, and in my trembling hand I must take up my lance and all the weight of battle, in order to help and protect my poor subjects. Reason and justice demand it, for it is my people's labor which sustains me, and their sweat which feeds me—me, my children, and all my family.

"Nevertheless, I will not engage in war until I have tried all the ways and arts of peace. On this subject, I am determined."

And so he convened his advisers and told them everything that had happened, and they counseled him to send some sensible man to Picrochole, to find out why he had suddenly left the pathways of peace and invaded lands to which he had absolutely no claim or right. Moreover, they should also send someone to bring back Gargantua and his people, in order to preserve and defend the country in its hour of need. And all of this pleased Grandgousier, who ordered that it be done exactly as they had said.

And he promptly sent his personal servant, a loyal Basque, to hurry to Paris and bring Gargantua home. And he wrote the following letter to his son:

Chapter Twenty-nine ⁄⁄ A Copy of the Letter Which Grandgousier Wrote to Gargantua

"The intensity of your studies has made it essential that, for a long period of time, your philosophical repose not be disturbed. But the friends and ancient allies in whom I have always had such trust have now sadly disappointed me and threatened the security of my old age. Since it is my fatal destiny to be made anxious on account of those in whom I had always had such confidence, I have no choice but to call you back, to save and preserve people and property which, by right and justice, have been entrusted to your care.

"For just as soldiers sent abroad are useless, if there is no wisdom at home, so too both study and wisdom are as nothing if, when the time comes, they are not carried into effect by courage.

"On due reflection, I have decided not to provoke but to pacify—not to attack but to defend—not to conquer but simply to protect my loyal subjects and rightful territory, which King Picrochole, without cause or reason, has angrily invaded: and day by day he has pursued this insane undertaking, with a fury and immoderation which no free man can tolerate.

"It is my plain duty to cool his tyrannical rage, offering him whatever I am able, in order to bring him back to peaceful paths. I have accordingly several times sent him messages, to try to determine why, and by whom, he felt he had been so injured, but all I have succeeded in doing is to make him angrier still. I have had no answer whatever from him, except defiance and the assertion that he holds my lands only at his good pleasure. And so I have come to understand that our eternal Lord has consigned Picrochole to the commands of his own free will, his own sense of what is right and just, and that he can only continue in his wicked ways because he is not continually guided by God's good grace. And I have come to understand that, in order to check and restrain him, to remind him of his duty and return him to a proper understanding, He has given me the duty of teaching Picrochole unpleasant lessons.

"Furthermore, my beloved son, once you have seen this letter, return as soon as you are able, in order to assist not me alone (though natural piety of course obliges you to do that), but to save and preserve those whom by right and justice you must help and relieve. Our warfare will be conducted with the least possible shedding of blood: indeed, if we possibly can, we shall use all the ways and devices we know, all the precautions and tricks of war, to save every life we can, and to return everyone happily and safely to their homes.

"My dearly beloved son, may the peace of Christ our Redeemer be with you. Give my greetings to Powerbrain, Gymnast, and Rightway.

"Signed and sealed on this twentieth day of September,

Your father,
GRANDGOUSIER."

Chapter Thirty ⁄⁄ How Ulrich Gallet Was Sent to Picrochole

Having dictated and dispatched this letter, Grandgousier ordered that Ulrich Gallet—his lawyer, a wise and discreet man who had proven his soundness and his ability in a variety of quarrels and disputes—go to Picrochole and let him know what had been decided.

So good Gallet left at once. Crossing the Gué de Vède, he inquired of the miller on Picrochole's estate, who answered him that Picrochole's soldiers had stripped his cupboards bare, leaving him neither a cock nor a hen. And he said that the king was now shut away at La Roche-Clermault, and advised Gallet to go no farther, because there were patrols all over and they were exceedingly dangerous. Gallet did not need much convincing, so that night he lodged with the miller.

The next day, in the morning, he went to the castle gate with a trumpeter, and asked the guards to allow him to speak to the king, for the king's own good.

When his words were repeated to the king, Picrochole refused to allow them to open the gates. Going to the top of the castle wall, he called down to the ambassador:

"Have you any news? Have you anything worth saying?"

At which Gallet spoke as follows:

Chapter Thirty-one ⁄⁄ Gallet's Speech to Picrochole

"No man ever has more reason for sorrow than when, instead of receiving the goodness and kindness which in justice he expects, he finds himself experiencing torment and pain. Nor is it unjustified or unreasonable that many who have suffered such a calamity have thought it worse than losing their lives, and when neither force nor any other method was available to them, to cure the evil, they have voluntarily ended their existences.

"Nor is it remarkable that King Grandgousier, my master, is extremely unhappy and troubled by your wild and hostile foray into his territory. It would indeed be remarkable if he were unaffected by the unparalleled excesses perpetrated by you and your people, from which no species of inhumanity has been omitted. Because of the warm regard he has always had for his subjects, all of this has caused him more pain than any human being has ever known. And yet it is incomparably more painful still to him that these injuries and wrongs have been at your hands, you and your people, since from the beginning of time you and your forefathers have always lived alongside him, and all his ancestors, in a state of perfect friendship, always regarded on both sides as a sacred and inviolable state, carefully maintained and preserved from that day to this—and always so regarded not only by his people and by yours but by all other peoples, whether Poitevins or Bretons or the folk of Mans or those who dwell beyond even the Canary Islands or the lands discovered by Christopher Columbus—all of them have thought it as easy to tear down the skies and raise the abyss higher than the clouds as to break your alliance, and they have behaved so warily in everything they have done because they feared to provoke or irritate or endanger either one of you, out of fear of the other.

"And more. This sacred friendship has enjoyed such a reputation that there are precious few peoples, among those inhabiting all the continents, and all the islands in the world's great oceans, who have not longed to also become your friends, on terms you yourselves would dictate—valuing your mutual association as highly as they value their own lands and territories. In consequence, no one can even recall either a king or any league of states so wild and savage, or so arrogant, that they would dare attack—not just your territories, but even those of your allies. And those who, acting rashly and without sufficient forethought, may have begun to encroach on lands so nobly protected have withdrawn, at once, as soon as they realized against whom they would be proceeding.

"And in the light of all this, what madness has possessed you to break all alliances, to trample on all friendship, to violate right and justice alike, rampaging into my master's lands without having been in any way injured either by Grandgousier or by any of his people, without having suffered the slightest irritation or provocation? What has happened to faith? What has happened to law? What has happened to reason? What has happened to humane understanding? What has happened to fear of God? Can you imagine that such outrages will be hidden from heavenly eyes and from that almighty God from whom we may all expect our just reward? If you believe anything of the sort, you are deceived, because He is the judge of all things. Are there astrological juxtapositions and effects which signal the end of your time of ease and peace? There is indeed a time and a season for all things, and when they have reached their apogee they are cast down in ruin, no longer able to sustain themselves. This marks the end of those who cannot employ reason and balance to moderate and thus preserve their fortunes and their prosperity.

"But if it has been thus decreed, and your happiness and peace must now come to an end, must it be accomplished by doing wrong to my king, he by whom you yourself were set in power? If your dynasty was bound to collapse, was it necessary that in its ruin it should fall on the hearths of those who had helped create it? The idea is so completely outside the bounds of reason, so alien to common sense, that mere human comprehension can scarcely take it in. And those not party to such a thing will also find it impossible to believe, until they come to understand, watching what follows, that nothing is sacred or holy to those who have cast off their allegiance to God and to reason, those who are determined to heed only their perverse whims and desires.

"If we had committed any wrong against your people and your lands, if we had accepted favors from your enemies, if we had failed to support you in the things which concern you, if we had in some way injured either your name or your honor—or, to put it better, if the lying, evil-thinking spirit, wanting to tempt you into evil, had conjured up false appearances and fantastic illusions, making you imagine that we had done something unworthy of our ancient friendship, your first obligation was to find out if this was indeed the truth, and then you should have warned us about it, and we should have given you all the assurances you could possibly have wanted. But, O eternal God! What did you do instead? Did you plan, like some traitorous tyrant, to ravage and ruin my master's kingdom? Do you think him such a coward, so stupid a king, that he would not resist your unjust assault? Could you think him so destitute of men and money and sound advice and opinions, so unaware of the arts of war?

"You must leave here at once, and no later than tomorrow be gone from his lands, creating no disorder and committing no violence as you go. You must pay a million pieces of gold for the damage you have caused to his people and his kingdom. Half of that must be paid tomorrow; the other half must be paid by the fifteenth of next May, on the ides of May. And you must leave as hostages the dukes of Whirling Millstone, Droopy Ass, and Scumbag, as well as the prince Scratching His Ass and the count Louse Itch."

Chapter Thirty-two ⁄⁄ How Grandgousier, Hoping to Buy Peace, Sent Back Flatcakes

And then good Gallet held his peace. But all Picrochole would say was:

"Come and get 'em, come and get 'em! We'll bake you some flat-cakes!"

So Gallet went back to Grandgousier and found him in a small corner of his chambers, on his knees, his bare head bowed, praying to God that He would soften Picrochole's anger and bring him to reason, without the necessity of force. When he saw that the good man had come back, he asked him:

"Ah, my friend, my friend, what news are you bringing me?"

"Nothing has been arranged," said Gallet. "This man is completely out of his mind: he has been abandoned by God."

"Yes, yes," said Grandgousier. "But tell me, my friend: did he give you any explanation for this explosion?"

"Nothing," said Gallet. "He said nothing about anything, except a few furious angry words about flatcakes. Perhaps something outrageous happened to his flatcake bakers."

"Ah," said Grandgousier. "I wish to be fully informed on that subject before we decide on our next move."

So he investigated the matter and discovered that, in truth, some flatcakes had in fact been forcibly taken from Picrochole's flatcake bakers, and also that Marquet had been struck on the head by a shepherd's staff. On the other hand, whatever had been taken had certainly been paid for and, as for the aforesaid Marquet, before he'd been struck he had wounded Frogier by a whip stroke on the legs. And it seemed to all Grandgousier's counselors that, under the circumstances, Frogier had no choice but to defend himself. Notwithstanding, Grandgousier said:

"If it's only a question of a few flatcakes, let me try to satisfy him, for war is not something I care to engage in."

Accordingly, he inquired how many flatcakes had been taken and, hearing that it had been four or five dozen, ordered that they should immediately prepare five wagonloads of flatcakes, one of which—baked with the best butter, golden with good eggs and saffron, and seasoned with fine spices—was to go to Marquet, and further, in damages and interest, the injured man should be given seven hundred thousand and three gold coins, so he could pay the surgeon-barbers who had tended him—and in addition Grandgousier gave him the little farm at Pomardière, for him and his heirs to have and to hold forever.

He sent Gallet to make these arrangements, and along the road to Roche-Clermault he had huge heaps of reeds collected—a traditional symbol of peace—and hung them all around the wagons, and had the carters wear them, too. And Gallet himself took a branch in his hand, thus signifying that all he was interested in was peace and that he had come to secure it.

When they reached the castle gate, they asked in the name of Grandgousier for Picrochole to come and speak to them. But Picrochole would neither allow them to enter nor exchange a word with them. He ordered that they be stopped where they were, unless they informed Captain Loudmouth, who was busy mounting a cannon up on the outer walls, what they wanted.

So the good man spoke to him:

"My lord, to put an end to this dispute and leave no reason for you not to adhere to our long-standing alliance, we hereby return to you the flatcakes which are the gist of this entire controversy. Our people took five dozen, which they paid for most handsomely. But we care so much more for peace that we bring you five wagonloads, of which this one is for Marquet, who has suffered the most. In addition, to be sure that the injured man is completely satisfied, I present you with seven hundred thousand and three gold pieces, and as interest I also give Marquet and his heirs, in perpetuity and in fee simple, the little farm at Pomardière. Here are the documents so certifying. Let us now, in the name of God, live in peace forever after. You will go happily back from whence you came, giving up this castle to which you have no lawful claim whatever, as you will surely agree. And we can once again be friends."

Captain Loudmouth told all this to Picrochole and, to inflame his heart still further, said:

"These hicks are really afraid. By God! Grandgousier is shitting in his pants, that poor old guzzler! He's not made for war: all he's good at is emptying wineglasses. I think we should keep the flatcakes, and the money, and then dig ourselves in right here and see what good fortune brings us. What kind of fools do they think they're dealing with, to try to fob us off with flatcakes? Let me tell you something. You've been too good to them, you've been too friendly, and now they think you're not worth taking into account. Try to be nice to one of these dirty rascals, and they bite you. But treat them rough and they eat out of your hand."

"Oh yes, yes, yes!" said Picrochole. "By Saint James, we'll let them have it! We'll do it exactly as you said."

"Let me explain one more thing," said Loudmouth. "We're pretty badly supplied. We don't have nearly enough food. If Grandgousier were to lay siege to us right now, I'd go and have all my teeth pulled out, except maybe three, and the same for all of your men. With just three teeth we wouldn't go through our food so quickly."

"We've got more than enough food," said Picrochole. "Are we here to eat or to fight?"

"To fight, of course," said Loudmouth. "But you can't dance on an empty stomach—and where hunger is in charge, strength leaves."

"That's enough babbling!" said Picrochole. "Confiscate what they brought."

And so they took the money and the flatcakes and the oxen and the wagons and sent Gallet and his people away without a word, except a warning not to come this close again, for a reason which would be explained to them on the following day. And they went back to Grandgousier, having accomplished nothing, and told him everything, adding that there was no hope whatever of making peace, except by vigorously making war.

Chapter Thirty-three ⁄⁄ How Some of Picrochole's Officers, by Giving Him Rash Advice, Put Their Master in Great Danger

The flatcakes in hand, the duke of Slobdom, together with Count Boastwell and Captain Shitface, came to Picrochole and said to him:

"Sire, today we make you the happiest, the noblest prince to have walked the earth since Alexander the Great."

"You may put your hats on," said Picrochole. "You have my permission."

"A thousand thanks," they said. "Sire: we are at your service. Here is what we have in mind:

"You will leave this castle in charge of one of your captains, with a small company—enough to hold the fort, which seems to us more than sufficiently strong, as much by its natural position as on account of the fortifications you have commanded us to build. Your army will leave in two segments, as of course you perfectly well understand how to do. One company will attack Grandgousier and his people. And they will easily defeat them, by which means you will lay hold of vast amounts of money, for that rascal certainly has a lot of it. And we call him a rascal, Your Highness, because a truly noble prince never has a penny to his name. Hoarding up money is a sure sign of a rascal.

"But the other portion of the army will move toward Aunis, Saintonge, Angoumois, and Gascony, as well as Périgord, Médoc, and Landes. They will capture cities and castles and fortresses, and meet no resistance. At Bayonne, Saint-Jean-de-Luz, and Fontarabia you will seize all the ships, after which, following the coastline toward Galicia and Portugal, you will capture the entire maritime region as far as Lisbon, and there you will be able to recruit all the reinforcements you might need: men flock to the banners of a conqueror. By the three-headed body of God, all Spain will surrender to you, because they're just a bunch of hicks! And then you'll cross the Straits of Gibraltar, where you will put up a pair of columns more magnificent than Hercules himself ever erected, and they will stand in perpetual memory of your name, and the Mediterranean will be rechristened the Picrocholean Sea. And then, beyond the Picrocholean Sea you'll come to Redbeard, king of Algeria, who will become your slave . . ."

"But I'll be merciful," said Picrochole.

"Yes," they said, "provided that he becomes a Christian. And then you'll attack other kingdoms: Tunis, Hippo, Algeria, Bizerte, Cyrenaica—you'll smash the whole Barbary Coast, the whole of Arab North Africa. And then you'll sweep past there and snatch up Majorca, Minorca, Sardinia, Corsica, and all the other islands in the Gulf of Genoa and the Balearic Sea. Turning left, down the coast, you'll command all of Transalpine Gaul, Provence, and the fierce Allobrogians, Genoa, Florence, Lucca, and then good-bye to the power of Rome! Our poor Mister Pope will die of fright."

"By God," said Picrochole, "I won't kiss his slipper."

"Once Italy's been captured, there'll be Naples, Calabria, Apulia, and Sicily ready to be sacked, and Malta too. I'd like to see the jolly knights of Rhodes fight back: it would be nice to see what their piss is made of!"

"I'd like to see Notre-Dame de Lorette," said Picrochole.

"Ridiculous, ridiculous," they said. "Save that for when you're coming back. From there we'll take Crete, Cyprus, Rhodes, and the Cyclades, and that will give us Peloponnesus. We'll take it. By Saint Ninian! The Lord had better protect Jerusalem, because the sultan of Egypt is simply no match for you!"

"Will I rebuild Solomon's Temple?" he asked.

"Not yet," they said. "Wait a bit. Don't ever be so hasty about things. Do you remember what the emperor Augustus said? *Festina lente,* Make haste slowly. Before you get around to that you'll need to have Asia Minor, Anatolia, Lycia, Pamphylia, Cilicia, Lydia, Phrygia, Ilium, Bithynia, Sardis, Samaria, Kastamonu, Luga, Cappadocia, all the way to the Euphrates."

"Will we see Babylon and Mount Sinai?" said Picrochole.

"There's still no need for that," they said. "Not yet. Won't it be enough to ride and conquer all the way to the Caspian Sea, trampling Greater and Lesser Armenia and the three realms of Arabia?"

"By God!" he said. "We're really out of our minds, now! Oh, we're going to be in such trouble!"

"Why?" they said.

"What will we drink in those deserts? They say that Julian the Apostate and all his armies died of thirst, out there."

"We've arranged for everything," they said. "At the Red Sea there'll be nine thousand and fourteen great boats, loaded with the best wines in the world. They'll dock at Jaffa. And there we'll find twenty-two hundred thousand camels and sixteen hundred elephants, which you'll have captured while hunting near the African oasis of Sidijilmassa, when you marched into Libya, just after you seized the caravan headed for Mecca. Won't that be enough wine?"

"Lord, yes!" he said. "But we won't drink it fresh."

"By all that's holy," they said, "that's pretty piddling stuff. A hero, a conqueror, a claimant to the universal throne, can't always have everything he wants. May God just grant it that you come to the shores of the Tigris River, you and your men, safe and sound!"

"But," he said, "now tell me what the other part of my army will be doing—the part that defeated old guzzling Grandgousier?"

"They won't be standing around," they said. "We'll meet up with them pretty soon. They'll have captured Brittany for you, and Normandy, Flanders, Hainaut, Brabant, Artois, Holland, Zeeland. They'll have crossed the Rhine, walking on the bellies of Swiss soldiers and their mercenaries, too, and one company will have subdued Luxemburg, Lorraine, the Champagne, Savoy—all the way to Lyons, at which point they'll have found your armies coming back from their naval victories on the Mediterranean, and they'll all have gathered in Bohemia, after having sacked Swabia, Württemberg, Bavaria, Austria, and Moravia. And then they'll have descended en masse, and furiously, onto Lübeck, Norway, Sweden, Denmark, Gotland, Greenland, and all the cities of the Hanseatic League, up to the Arctic Sea. And then, after conquering the Orkney Islands, they'll subjugate Scotland, England, and Ireland. Then they'll cross the Baltic Sea into Russia and conquer Prussia, Poland, Lithuania, Russia,

Romania, Hungary and Transylvania, Bulgaria, Turkey—and then on to Constantinople."

"Should we perhaps meet up with them sooner?" said Picrochole. "Because I'd also like to be the emperor of Trebizond. Shouldn't we kill all those Turkish and Muslim dogs?"

"Why the devil should we do anything else?" they said. "You'll give their lands and all their possessions to those who have served you so graciously."

"Reason requires it," he said. "It's simple justice. You—I'll give you a good slice of Turkey, and Syria, and all of Palestine."

"Ha!" they said. "Lord, how good of you. Many thanks! May God grant you unending prosperity!"

There was an old gentleman with them, who had proven his mettle in all sorts of dangerous situations—a true old warrior. His name was Commonsense and, hearing these declarations, he said:

"I'm very much afraid that this whole affair will turn into nothing more than the old story about the shoemaker and his pail of milk. He dreamed that it was going to make him rich—but when the pail tipped over he didn't even have anything to eat for dinner. What do you think these lovely conquests of yours really mean? Where do you think you're going to get, with all that work and running here and there?"

"What it will mean," said Picrochole, "is that, when we get back, we'll rest in comfort."

Commonsense replied:

"And suppose you don't ever come back, since the journey is long and dangerous? Wouldn't it be better to rest right now, without putting ourselves in such danger?"

"Oh," said Boastwell. "By God, here's a real lunatic! Let's all go hide in the corner, near the fire, so we can spend the rest of our lives with the ladies, stringing beads—or maybe spinning, like old Sardanapalus. He who never takes any chances, he ends up without a horse or a mule. That's what Solomon says."

"Yes," said Commonsense, "and do you remember what Malcon answers, in the same poem? He who takes too many chances loses both his horse and his mule."

"Enough!" said Picrochole. "On to other things. What worries me are all those damned soldiers who fight for Grandgousier. Suppose we get to Mesopotamia; what do we do if they set on us from behind?"

"Very good," said Captain Shitface. "A handy little mobilization, which you'll send to the Muscovites, and in the twinkling of an eye you'll have four hundred and fifty thousand elite troops, all equipped and ready for battle. Oh! My lord, if you make me your lieutenant, there's nothing I won't do! I chomp at the bit, I kick up my heels, I hit out, I get them, I kill them, I stop at nothing!"

"Forward, forward!" cried Picrochole. "Hurry, everyone hurry—and whoever loves me, follow me now!"

Chapter Thirty-four ⁄⁄ How Gargantua Left the City of Paris, in Order to Save His Country, and How Gymnast Met the Enemy

At exactly this time Gargantua, riding his great mare, had crossed the Nonnain Bridge, well along on the highroad to Chinon. He had left Paris immediately after reading his father's letter; Powerbrain, Gymnast, and Rightway rented post-horses in order to accompany him. The others in their household were coming right after them, traveling at a regular but more moderate pace, and carrying all their books and their scientific instruments.

When they reached Parilly, very near Chinon, a farmer named Gouget warned them that Picrochole had captured and fortified La Roche-Clermault and sent Captain Drinkup Gutsout and a large army to attack the woods of Vède and Vaugaudry, and that he had already rounded up all the chickens and hens as far away as Pressoir-Billard. It was a strange thing, he said; he found it hard to believe the outrages they were committing right here in his own country. This news made Gargantua so much afraid that he knew neither what to say nor what to do. But Powerbrain urged him to go directly to the lord of La Vauguyon, who had always been their friend and ally. He would be better able to give them sound advice about everything that was happening. Which was what they did, as quickly as possible. And they found him already pondering how best to help them. It was his considered opinion that they ought to send someone to scout out the land and see what the enemy was up to, so that anything they finally decided to do would be based on an informed judgment of the actual situation. Gymnast volunteered, but they thought it better for him to take along someone who knew the paths and back roads and the creeks and rivers in that neighborhood.

So Readiwell, Vauguyon's squire, was sent along with him, and they went fearlessly spying about on all sides. Meanwhile Gargantua rested and ate a bit, and had a peck of oats fed to his mare: that is, to be exact, seventy-four bushels. Gymnast and his companion rode until they found the enemy—scattered all about, completely disorderly, burning and looting everything they could. And as soon as they saw him in the distance they all came running toward him, to rob him, too. And he cried to them:

"Gentlemen, I'm just a poor devil. I beg you for mercy. I still have a few pennies and you shall drink it all up, because this is *aurum potabile,* drinkable money, and we'll sell this horse here to pay for my welcome. And after that, why, let me join you, because there's never been a better man than me for catching, roasting, frying, or by God! cutting up and seasoning a chicken. And for my *proficiat,* my official welcome, I hereby drink to all good drinkers."

At which he pulled out his portable flask and, tipping his head back, poured a good dose down his gullet. The scoundrels stared, their mouths gaping, sticking out their tongues like panting dogs, waiting their turns. But just then Captain Drinkup Gutsout came over to see what was going on. And Gymnast offered the flask to him, saying:

"Here, Captain, have yourself a good pull. I've already tested it, and the stuff couldn't be better. It's vintage La Foye Monjault, by God."

"What!" exclaimed Drinkup Gutsout. "This joker is pulling our legs! Who are you?"

"Just a poor devil," said Gymnast.

"Ha!" said Drinkup Gutsout. "Since you're just a poor devil, it's only reasonable that we let you go your way, because poor devils can go anywhere without paying tolls or taxes. But devils don't usually ride up on such damned good horses. So, Mister Devil, down you come: this pony is mine, now—and if *he* doesn't trot along the way I like, Mister Devil, *you* get to carry me yourself. And let me tell you, I like the idea of being carried off by a devil like you."

Chapter Thirty-five // How Gymnast Gracefully Killed Captain Drinkup Gutsout and Others in Picrochole's Army

As soon as they heard these words, many of the soldiers were frightened and started making the sign of the cross as fast as they could, thinking this was a devil in disguise. One of them, Good Jack by name, a captain in a rural brigade, pulled his prayer book out of his codpiece and shouted:

"*Agios ho Theos!* God is holy! If you come from God, say so. And if you come from the Other One, get away from us!"

Gymnast did not move, but some of the listening soldiers turned and left, which Gymnast carefully noted.

He pretended to dismount but, as soon as he was on the horse's left side—the mounting side—stepped into the stirrups, his single-bladed sword at his side, then swung himself straight through, completely under the animal, after which, without his feet ever touching the ground, he leaped high in the air, landing in an upright position on the saddle, facing backward. Then he said:

"Ah! I'm not doing things right."

Accordingly, standing just where he was, he leaped up on one leg, pirouetted quickly to the left, and dropped into the saddle as if he had never left it. And Drinkup Gutsout said:

"Ha! I won't try that, right now—and for good reason."

"Shit!" cried Gymnast. "I got it all wrong. Let me try that jump again: this time I'll lick it."

So with great strength and agility he repeated the pirouette, but in reverse, this time turning swiftly to the right. Then he put his right thumb on the saddlebow and lifted himself straight up in the air, holding himself simply by the strength of that one thumb. And then three times he spun himself around in a circle. But the fourth time he completely reversed himself, though touching nothing, so that he hung between the horse's ears, just above the animal's head, except now he was supported not by the right thumb but by the left, and on that pivot he swung himself in yet another full circle. And then, slapping his right hand smack down in the center of the saddle, he performed a flying leap that left him seated on the horse's rump, like a woman riding sidesaddle.

Then he swung his right leg lightly over the saddle and sat ready to ride from the hindquarters.

"But still," he said, "it would be a better jump if I got right into the saddle."

So he put both thumbs in front of him, on the horse's rump, and did a back somersault in the air, then landed smack in the middle of the saddle, ready to ride. Another somersault lifted him back into the air, his feet together, and then he turned around and around, more than a hundred times, his arms extended in the shape of a cross, crying in a loud voice:

"I'm ready to kill, devils—kill, kill! Look out, devils, look out, look out!"

While he was flying this way and that, the soldiers were dumbfounded and said to one another:

"Oh, holy shit! He's a god damned goblin or maybe a devil in disguise. *Ab hoste maligno libera nos, Domine,* Save us from the Evil Ones, Lord."

And they went running down the road, looking behind them like a dog trying to steal a goose wing.

At which point Gymnast, seeing his advantage, leaped off his horse, drew his sword, and swinging furiously charged at the cocky ones who hadn't run off. He knocked them into heaps, stabbed, mortally wounded, and dying, and none of them tried to fight back, thinking they had been attacked by a ravening devil—and what had convinced them was both the incredible flying performance he had staged and also the way their captain had greeted him, addressing him as "poor devil." Drinkup Gutsout sneaked up behind him, swinging his short, heavy sword at Gymnast's head, trying to split it open. But Gymnast's armor was so solid that all he felt was the weight of the blow. And then he swung swiftly around and took a mighty swing at Drinkup Gutsout, who managed to get his shield in front of his face. But the sword struck him in the belly and the guts and half the liver, too, so he fell to the ground, and as he fell threw up more than four pots of soup and, mixed in with the soup, his mortal soul.

After which Gymnast retreated, understanding that luck cannot be pushed too far. Knights ought to treat good fortune with immense care, never embarrassing it or making it uncomfortable in any way. So he climbed back up on his horse and, giving him the spur, rode straight down the road toward La Vauguyon, and Readiwell rode with him.

Chapter Thirty-six ⁄ How Gargantua Demolished the Castle of Gué de Vède and He and His Men Crossed the Ford There

As soon as they got back, Gymnast reported on the enemy's condition and the stratagem he had employed against a whole troop of them, single-handed, swearing that they were nothing more than thieves and robbers, completely ignorant of military discipline, and that Gargantua and his men could quickly rout them: it would be simplicity itself to club them down like oxen.

So Gargantua got up on his great mare, accompanied as we have previously described. Finding on his way a thick, tall tree (which people thereabouts called Saint Martin's Tree, believing it had been a pilgrim's staff planted there by that saint), he said:

"This is exactly what I needed. This tree will be both my staff and my spear."

He pulled it out of the ground with no trouble, then stripped off its branches and made it ready for use.

Now the mare began to piss, to relieve the pressure in her belly, but she pissed so copiously that there was a flood for fifteen miles around, and that piss flood flowed toward the ford at Vède, making the current swell so high that an entire company of Picrochole's men, watching in horror, were swept away and drowned, except a few who ran up the road toward the hills.

When he got to the Vède wood, Gargantua was informed by Rightway that those among their enemies who had survived the flood were in the castle there. So Gargantua called out, as loudly as he could:

"Are you in there or aren't you? If you're there, you'd better not be. If you're not, I have nothing to say."

But a drunken cannonier, stationed near the gateway, fired his cannon at Gargantua and hit him a tremendous shot right on the right temple. But it did no more damage than if the man had thrown a fat plum.

"What's that?" said Gargantua. "Are you throwing grape seeds? That's going to be an expensive harvest!"—for he really thought the cannonball was a grape seed.

Those fellows in the castle, having fun and stealing everything in sight, heard the noise and ran up to the fortified towers and walls and from there fired more than nine thousand and twenty-five rounds of small artillery at him, and also crossbows, all of it aimed at his head. Such a hail of bullets and balls rained down on him that he called out:

"Powerbrain, my friend: there are so many flies around here that I can't see through all these pesky clouds! Give me a willow branch, so I can chase them away"—for he thought the bullets and cannonballs were cow flies.

Powerbrain explained to him that those were not flies at all but artillery being fired at him from the castle. So Gargantua banged at the castle with his big tree staff, and with tremendous blows knocked down all its towers and fortresses, and leveled the castle right down to the ground. Those inside, too, were similarly broken into small pieces.

Leaving there, they came to the mill bridge and found the whole ford so covered with dead bodies that they had choked the mill stream. These were the men who had been drowned in the flood of mare's piss. They stood there in silence, wondering how they were going to get past all that jumble of corpses. But Gymnast said:

"If devils can get over, by God, I can too."

"Devils," said Rightway, "crossed over so they could carry off damned souls."

"By Saint Ninian!" Powerbrain said. "In all good logic, he ought to be able to get over, too."

"Oh yes, yes," said Gymnast. "Or else I'll find myself planted right in the road."

And spurring his horse, he leaped right over, his horse totally unafraid of the dead bodies, having been trained, according to the methods set out by Aelian in *De natura animalium,* On the Nature of Animals, not to be afraid of either dead men's souls or their bodies. Aelian's method doesn't involve killing their grooms, as Diomedes did the Thracians, nor does it work by throwing the bodies of your enemies at your horse's feet, the way Ulysses did (as Homer tells us), but makes use of a human-sized dummy, placed in the animal's fodder: the horse then has to step on the dummy every time he takes his oats.

The other three leaped over after him, but not Rightway, whose horse jammed his right foot up to the knee in the belly of a huge fat scoundrel, lying flat on his back, drowned. The horse's leg wouldn't come out until Gargantua, using the end of his great staff, pushed the rest of the fellow's intestines out into the water. And then the horse was able to lift out his leg. What's more, the animal was cured of a bone tumor in his foot—what a miracle of veterinary science!—simply by having touched this fat oaf's guts.

Chapter Thirty-seven ⁄⁄ How Gargantua, Combing His Hair, Made the Cannonballs Fall Out

Leaving the Vède river behind them, they soon came to Grandgousier's castle. The king had been eagerly awaiting them: Gargantua was received joyously and with open arms. Happier people were never seen, as the *Supplementum supplementi chronicorum,* The Supplement to the Chronicles' Supplement, declared, noting that Gargamelle, Gargantua's mother, absolutely died of joy. I don't know a thing about it, and I frankly don't give a damn about her or any other woman.

The truth was that Gargantua, changing his clothes and combing his hair (his comb was almost two hundred yards long, fashioned of huge elephant teeth), with each sweep of his comb shook out more than seven bales of cannonballs, stuck in his hair after the battle in the woods at Vède. Seeing this, his father, Grandgousier, thought his son had lice, and said to him:

"Good lord, my son, I hope you haven't brought us any flying creatures from the School of Theology? I didn't want you to be living *there.*"

To which Powerbrain replied:

"My lord, please don't think I'd put him in such a louse house. He'd be better off begging outside the cemetery, from what I know of the cruel savagery in such colleges. Why, the Moors and the Tartars treat their galley slaves better—murderers in prison are treated better—certainly, the dogs right here in your house are treated better—than anyone unlucky enough to be resident at that college. Were I the king of Paris, may the devil carry me off if I wouldn't light a fire and burn the place down—and I'd make sure the headmaster was in it, and the whole board of governors, too, for permitting such inhumanity to flourish right under their eyes!"

Then, picking up one of the cannonballs, he said:

"These are from the cannon shot at your son Gargantua not long ago by your treacherous enemies, as he was going by the wood at Vède. But they got what they deserved, every one of them: they all died in the ruins of the castle, like the Philistines when Samson pulled the roof down on their heads, or those who died when the tower of Siloam fell on them, as our Lord tells in the Gospel according to Saint Luke, 13. And I suggest that we continue to fall on them, while luck is with us. Opportunity knocks only once, and then she passes you by, and once she's gone you can't call her back. She's stone deaf, if you haven't listened to her when she comes to you."

"Not quite yet," said Grandgousier, "not quite yet. Tonight I intend to give you a banquet and show you a proper welcome."

And so supper was prepared, and what they piled on was: sixteen oxen, three heifers, thirty-two veal calves, sixty-three suckling kids, ninety-five sheep, three hundred young pigs in wine sauce, two hundred and twenty partridges, seven hundred woodcocks, four hundred full-grown Loudunoys and Cornish capons, six thousand young hens and just as many pigeons, six hundred grouse, one thousand four hundred rabbits, three hundred and three plovers, and one thousand seven hundred young capons. There was no time to round up any game, except for eleven wild boar sent by the abbot of Turpenay, and eighteen fallow deer sent by the lord of Grandmont (near Chinon), and a hundred and forty pheasants from the lord of Les Essarts (closer to Langeais but not too far from Chinon), plus a few dozen wood pigeons, river birds, freshwater ducks, herons, curlews, golden plovers, wildfowl, wild geese, sandpipers, lapwings, flat-tailed ducks, spoonbills, speckled herons, fledgling herons, waterfowl, white herons, storks, moorhens, orange flamingos (*phoenicoptera,* in Latin), cranes, and turkeys, garnished with heaps of chopped, boiled grain, the whole thing reinforced with platter after platter of potatoes.

They had plenty to eat, no doubt about it, and Grandgousier's cooks served them gladly—Saucesucker, Beefpot, and Sweetandsour.

Their wine—and there was plenty of it—was served by Janot, Michael, and Emptyglass.

Chapter Thirty-eight ⁄ How Gargantua Ate Six Pilgrims in a Salad

In the interests of truth and accuracy we now have to tell what happened to six pilgrims from Saint Sebastian, near Nantes. Taking shelter, that night, for fear of all the marauding armies, they hid themselves in the garden, under heaps of discarded pea vines, between the cabbages and the lettuce.

Finding himself a little unwell, Gargantua asked that some lettuce be picked to make him a salad. And having been told that they had some of the biggest and most beautiful lettuce plants anywhere in the country—as big as plum or fat walnut trees—he decided to go and pick the ones he liked for himself. He plucked the six pilgrims along with the lettuce, and they were so terrified that they didn't dare speak or even cough.

And then he went to wash the lettuce in the fountain, and the pilgrims began to whisper to each other:

"What can we do? We'll be drowned, here in this lettuce. Should we say something? But if we do, he'll kill us as spies."

And while they were deliberating, Gargantua put the lettuce, and the six pilgrims, onto a huge platter, as broad around as three hundred hogsheads. And then, after dousing them with oil and vinegar and salt, he ate them, in order to refresh before supper. He swallowed five of the pilgrims: the sixth was still on the platter, hidden under a leaf of lettuce—except for his staff, which was sticking out. And seeing it, Grandgousier said to Gargantua:

"That looks like a snail shell, there. Don't eat it."

"Why not?" said Gargantua. "The snails are fine all this month."

And lifting up the staff, and the pilgrim along with it, he swallowed it right down. Then he washed it down with a long gulp of strong red wine, and waited for supper to be ready.

The pilgrims he had swallowed, terrified of his huge grinding teeth, tried to keep out of their way. They thought they had been thrown into the deepest, darkest of prison dungeons. And when Gargantua took that great gulp of wine, they feared they would be drowned right there in his mouth. Indeed, the torrent almost swept them down into the pit of his stomach. But they managed to save themselves, using their staffs like the pilgrims who climb Mont Saint-Michel, leaping to shelter behind his teeth. Unfortunately, however, one of them, tapping as hard as he could with his staff to see if they were on safe, solid ground, happened to strike right through the hole in a hollow tooth and smashed down on the mandibular nerve. This caused Gargantua an excruciating pain, and he cried out wildly. And then, to ease the pain, he took out his toothpick and, as he strolled in the garden, near the young walnut tree, he dug you out, my fine pilgrim friends. He caught one of them by the legs, another by the shoulders, another by his knapsack, another by his traveler's purse, another by his shoulder sash—and the poor sinner who had struck him with his staff, him he caught by the codpiece, except that turned out to be a great stroke of luck, because the toothpick went right through a swollen ulcer that had been tormenting him ever since they passed Ancenis (near Nantes), and drained it clean out.

So the pilgrims, all rooted out, ran off through the vineyard at a good hard trot, and Gargantua's mouth stopped hurting.

At which point Rightway called him to come for supper, which was ready.

"In that case," said he, "I'll go and piss away my bad luck."

And he pissed so copiously that the urine cut the pilgrims' road, making it necessary for them to cross the great canal. Skirting around the edge of a wood they all—except for Fornillier—fell into a trap that had been set for wolves, and the thick ropes caught all of them except Fornillier, who by singular cleverness got the others free by breaking all the ropes and knots. Once out of there, they spent the night in a hut near Coudray.

And one of them, Wearyway, made them forget their misfortune by his well-chosen words, reminding them that this very adventure had long since been predicted in the psalms of King David:

"*Cum exurgerent homines in nos, forte vivos deglutissent nos,* Then they would have swallowed us up, when their wrath was kindled, that is, when we were eaten in a salad, with a pinch of salt; *cum irasceretur furor eorum in nos, forsitan aqua absorbuisset nos,* then the waters overwhelmed us, the stream went over our soul, that is, when he took that great gulp of wine; *torrentem pertransivit anima nostra,* our soul went over the torrent, that is, when we crossed the great canal; *forsitan pertransisset anima nostra aquam intolerabilem,* then the proud waters went over our soul, that is, the flood of his urine, which cut off our path; *benedictus Dominus, qui non dedit nos in captionem dentibus eorum,* blessed be the Lord, who did not let us become a victim of their teeth; *anima nostra, sicut passer erepta est de laqueo venantium,* our soul was caught, as a bird is caught in a snare, that is, when we fell into the trap; *laqueus contritus est,* the snare is broken, that is, by Fournillier; *et nos liberati sumus,* and we are freed; *adjutorium nostrum,* our help is in the Lord's name, etc."

Chapter Thirty-nine // How Gargantua Gave the Monk a Banquet, and How Well the Monk Talked As He Ate

After Gargantua had come to the table, and the first course had been tucked away, Grandgousier began to discuss how the war between himself and Picrochole had started. He told how Brother John Mincemeat had so triumphantly defended the inner walls of the abbey, and praised him even higher than Marcus Furius Camillus, savior of Rome and conqueror of the Gauls, or than Scipio, Pompey, Julius Caesar, and Themistocles. So Gargantua asked that this monk be sent for at once, so that his advice could be sought on what they ought to do next. The chief steward was asked to go and fetch him, which he did, returning with him, happily, his heavy cross in hand, on Grandgousier's mule.

He was greeted by a thousand hugs, a thousand handshakes and pats on the back, a thousand hello's and how-are-you's.

"Hey, Brother John, my friend!"

"Brother John, my old buddy, Brother John, by all that's holy!"

"Welcome, welcome, old friend!"

"Let me get my arms around you!"

"Oh, you old fart, I'll hug you so hard you'll burst!"

And what a fine time Brother John was having! There was never anyone so courteous, so gracious.

"Well, well," said Gargantua, "come on over here, have a stool next to me, right down here."

"That's fine with me," said the monk, "since you want me over there. Waiter: water! Pour it, my son, pour it: it's good for my liver. Give me something to gargle."

"Deposita cappa, Take off your cowl," said Gymnast. "Off with that monkish stuff."

"Ha, by God," said the monk, "my dear sir, there's a whole chapter *in statutis ordinis,* the regulations of my order, which wouldn't like that."

"Shit," said Gymnast, "shit on your chapter! Those robes are just a weight on your shoulders. Take them off."

"My friend," said the monk, "leave them where they are—because, when I wear these robes, they make me drink better: they make my whole body feel good. And suppose I take my habit off. Your pages will just cut everything up into garters, as they did to me, once, when I was at the castle of Coulaines. And besides, I wouldn't have any appetite left. But if I sit down at the table, wearing these robes, by God, I'll drink! I'll drink to you, I'll drink to your horse—and gladly. May the Lord keep you all safe! I've already eaten—but that just means I'll eat a little less now, because I have a brick-lined stomach, as empty as the great wine cask in Bologne, in the convent there—my guts gape open like a lawyer's purse. I eat any fish going, if they're soft enough, and I nibble on a partridge wing now and then, or a young nun's thighs. Wouldn't it be crazy to die with a stiff prick? The prior at our abbey is crazy about white meat."

"But he's not," said Gymnast, "crazy like a fox. They snatch up any chicken they can get, but they never eat the white meat."

"Why not?" said the monk.

"Because," said Gymnast, "they haven't got any cooks to cook it, and if it's not cooked right it stays red, and never gets white. When meat is red, that shows it's undercooked, except for lobsters and crayfish, because they turn red when they're boiled."

"By all that's holy!" said the monk. "Then we've got a man at our abbey who hasn't had his head properly boiled yet, because his eyes are as red as a redwood bowl! These rabbits' legs are good for the gout, you know. And while we're on the subject of trowels: why are a girl's thighs always so nice and cool?"

"Now, that question," said Gargantua, "is not discussed by Aristotle, nor by Alexander of Aphrodisias, and not even by Plutarch."

"It stems," said the monk, "from three causes, which tend to make a place naturally cool: *primo,* because the water runs all the way down; *secundo,* because it's a shaded place, dark and hidden, where the sun never shines; and third, because it's continually ventilated by breezes from the asshole, from the lady's chemise, and—most frequently and especially— from the codpiece. And joyously! Boy: something to drink! (gulp, gulp, gulp) How good God is, letting us have this fine wine! I swear, right here in the sight of God: if I'd been alive in the time of Jesus Christ, the Jews would have had a damned hard time getting him up on that Mount of Olives. And damn the devil if I wouldn't have sliced their hamstrings, those Gentleman Apostles, when they turned out to be such cowards, after they'd eaten their fine supper—abandoning their master when he needed them! A man who runs away, when he needs to make good use of his knife: Lord, I hate that sort worse than poison! Hey, if only I were king of France for eighty or a hundred years! By God, that battle of Pavia, when they all ran and France lost! I'd have clipped them like so many little dogs—and I don't mean just their ears and their tails. May they rot with fever! Why didn't they stand and die for their king when he needed them? Isn't it better, isn't it more honorable, to die fighting in a virtuous battle than to live by running like a cowardly dog? Well, we'll hardly eat any goslings, not this year. So, my friend, let me have a piece of that pig over there. Satan! There's no more of that green wine: *Germinavit radix Jesse,* a stem flowered from Jesse's roots, and I swear by my life a thirst is flowering out of mine. This isn't the worst wine I've ever drunk. What kind do you get in Paris? The devil take me if I wasn't there, once, for more than six months, and I let anyone in who wanted to come in. Did you happen to meet Brother Claude of Saint-Denis? Oh, how he could put it away! But some fly or other bit him, damn it: he's been doing nothing but study since I don't know when! Me, I don't study, never. In our abbey, you know, we never study, because we're worried about the mumps. Our late abbot always said that a scholarly monk was a monstrous thing to behold. By God, sir, my dear good friend, *magis magnos clericos non sunt magis magnos sapientes,* the greatest priests are not the greatest scholars. You've never seen so many rabbits as we've had this year. But I haven't been able to find a goshawk anywhere, neither a female nor a male. My Lord Bellonnière promised me a falcon, but he writes that the bird's gone short of breath. The partridges will gobble up our corn, this year. There's not much fun hunting birds with a net: you freeze your ass off. I'm never happy unless I'm running this way and that. It's true, though: when I'm jumping over hedges and bushes, these robes of mine lose a little of their fur. But I've got me a really fine greyhound. I'll be damned if any rabbits get away from him! One of his lackeys was taking him to Lord Maulevrier, and I nabbed him. Was that the wrong thing to do?"

"By God, no, Brother John," said Gymnast, "no, no, by all the devils, no!"

"All right," said the monk, "let's drink to all those devils: may they live forever! By all that's holy! What could that cripple-legged nobleman do with such an animal? God's holy heart! What he really likes is when they bring him a couple of good fat oxen!"

"What?" said Powerbrain. "What? Were you swearing, Brother John?"

"Hardly," said the monk. "That was just verbal decoration—just Ciceronian rhetoric, you know."

Chapter Forty ⁄ Why Monks Are Shunned by the World, and Why Some of Them Have Longer Noses than Others

"By the Christian faith!" said Rightway. "It's a wonderful thing, this monk's incredible honesty, his good humor, his courtesy. He's a delight to everyone here. Tell me why monks are chased out of good company, why they're called spoilsports? It's like bees chasing wasps away from their roses:

"*Ignavum fucos pecus, a presepibus arcent,* 'They chase away the lazy wasps,' as Virgil puts it."

To which Gargantua answered:

"Here's the simple truth: it's the way monks dress, their robes, their cowls, that make men look down on them—that make men curse at them, even strike out at them. It's exactly the same thing as the north wind attracting clouds. But the real reason is that they eat the world's shit, men's sins, and shit eaters get pushed off into their shit houses, their convents and their abbeys, just as separate from polite society as a shit house is from a house. But if you understand why a family that keeps a monkey is always mocking and teasing it, then you'll also understand why monks are rejected by everybody, old and young alike. A monkey isn't a watchdog; it doesn't pull a plow, the way an ox does; it doesn't produce milk or wool, like a sheep; you can't use it to carry things, like a horse. All he does is shit all over himself and break things, which is why all he gets in return is insults and blows. It's just the same with monks— I mean the lazy ones, of course. They don't work the way peasants do, they don't watch over the land like warriors, they don't cure sickness like doctors, they don't preach and teach the way a good evangelical doctor and teacher does, they don't carry the things that people in a republic need, as a merchant does. And this is why everyone mocks at them and despises them."

"Indeed," said Grandgousier, "but they pray to God for us."

"Not a bit of it," answered Gargantua. "The truth is that they bother everyone for miles around with the noise of their bells."

"Yes, yes," said the monk. "A mass that's really well rung is half sung."

"They mumble their way through yards of saints' lives and psalms, without understanding a word they're saying. They're more than happy with a lot of 'Our Father Which Art in Heaven' mixed with some good long 'Hail Mary, Mother of Grace,' without stopping to think or even listen—and I call that making fun of God, not praying to Him. But if they really do pray for us, and not because they're afraid of losing their thick loaves of bread and their nice fat soups, then may God reward them. All true Christians pray to God, no matter what their rank or where they are or when, and the Holy Spirit prays for them, and pleads for them, and God gives them His grace. And this is how it is with our Brother John, which is why everyone likes to be with him. He's no bigot; he doesn't walk around all dressed in rags; he's honest, happy, thoughtful, he's a good friend; he works, he works hard; he defends the oppressed; he comforts the sick; he comes to the aid of those in need; he's a true guardian of the abbey's inner walls."

"I do a lot more than that," said the monk, "because, while we're hurrying through all our prayers, which we've long since memorized, I knot up strings for our crossbows and I polish the bows, the big ones and the smaller ones, too, and I make nets and sacks for catching rabbits. I'm never just sitting around, let me tell you. But hey! It's time to drink! Bring on the wine! And some fruit, too: these chestnuts come from the trees in Saint-Hermine, the best you'll ever find. Some of these, and some good green wine, and you'll blow out some fine farts. You haven't got the fun really going, not yet. By God, I drink wherever the water's running, like a church inspector's horse."

Then Gymnast said to him:

"Brother John, would you mind wiping up the snot hanging off your nose?"

"Oh ho!" said the monk. "Would I be in danger of drowning, since I'm in water right up to my nose? No, no. *Quare?* Why not? *Quia*—Because it'll drop off all right, but nothing is going to get in, since wine is a sovereign preventative. Ah, my friend, if you owned a pair of winter boots of solid leather like this, you could go preaching to the oysters as much as you liked: they'd never let in a drop."

"Now why," said Gargantua, "does Brother John have such a fine nose?"

"Because," Grandgousier answered, "God wanted him to have one, and He shapes all things as He wishes, according to His divine will, just as a potter makes his pots."

"Because," said Powerbrain, "Brother John was the first to get to the Nose Fair. So he got the handsomest—and the biggest."

"Ridiculous!" said the monk. "According to true monastic wisdom, it's because my wet nurse had such soft breasts. When I was sucking away, my nose sank in as if she'd been made of butter. And then when it was lying in there, my nose swelled up and grew, just like yeast dough in a bowl. Wet nurses with tough tits make for snub-nosed kids. But hey ho! *Ad formam nasi cognoscitur ad te levavi,* They shall be known by the shape of their noses; unto thee I lift my . . . I never eat jam. Boy! Over here: wine! And meat, if you please!"

Chapter Forty-one ⁄ How the Monk Put Gargantua to Sleep, and All about His Prayers

Supper done, they turned to the issue at hand and concluded that at about midnight they would stage a skirmish, to see how careful a lookout their enemies were keeping. And then, while waiting, they lay down a bit, to make themselves all the fresher. But no matter in what position he put himself, Gargantua couldn't sleep. So the monk said to him:

"I can never really sleep, unless I'm listening to a sermon or saying my prayers. So let's recite the seven penitential psalms, you and I, and we'll see if that doesn't get you to doze right off."

Gargantua thought that was an excellent idea. So they began with the first psalm, and by the time they got to the first words of the second, *Beati quorum,* Blessed are they whose transgressions are forgiven, they both fell asleep, one after the other. Still, the monk managed to wake himself up just before midnight, because that was the hour at which he was accustomed to saying prayers. And once he was awake, he woke up all the others, singing as loud as he could:

"Hey Rainier, my shepherd, wake up, wake up,
O Rainier, Rainier, wake up!"

And when all of them were awake, he said:

"Gentlemen, we say that morning prayers begin with coughing and supper with drinking. Let's turn that on its head: we'll start our morning with drinking, and tonight, just before supper, we'll all cough as hard as we can."

To which Gargantua replied:

"Drinking so soon after sleeping goes against all the rules of medicine. First you have to empty everything you don't need out of your stomach, and you have to shit, too."

"Hah!" said the monk. "That's marvelous medicine, all right! But may a hundred devils jump all over my body if you don't see a lot more old drunks than old doctors! My appetite and I, we've made an agreement. It always lies down and goes to sleep when I do, and all day long I make sure to take care of it. And then, when I wake up, it wakes up with me. Take all the purges and laxatives you like: me, I'll tickle myself with a pile of feathers."

"Feathers?" said Gargantua. "What are you talking about?"

"My prayer book," said the monk. "You know what falconers do, when they're going to feed their hawks. They stick a chicken foot down their throats, which gets rid of all the phlegm in their heads and makes them hungry. Me, I have this little flask right here, shaped exactly like a prayer book, and I dip into it every morning and it clears my lungs right up and gets me ready for really serious drinking."

"Is that the Greek Orthodox way," said Gargantua, "of saying such pleasant prayers?"

"It's the good Catholic style of the abbey at Fécamp," said the monk. "Those good Benedictine monks say three psalms and three short prayers—and those who don't want to join in say nothing at all. I've never tied myself down to any kind of regular schedule for prayers. Men weren't created for hours: hours were created for men. So I make mine the way you make stirrup straps: I shorten them or stretch them as I please. *Brevis oratio penetrat celos, longa potatio evacuat cyphos,* A short prayer reaches heaven, but a long one drains your cup. Now: where might that be written?"

"By my faith," said Powerbrain, "I don't know. But you, you've really got balls, and you're worth more than any of them!"

"And you," said the monk, "you've got them, too. But *venite apotemus,* let's get down to drinking."

So a heap of grilled meat was prepared for them, and some good rich soup, and the monk drank his fill. Some of them drank with him; some abstained. And then they got themselves into their armor, and took up their fighting gear, and against his will put armor on the monk, too, although all the armor he wanted was his robe hanging in front of his stomach and the thick staff of the cross in his hand. All the same, they got him armored from head to toe, and then they mounted him on a royally good horse, a handsome sword at his side, just like Gargantua, Powerbrain, Gymnast, Rightway, and twenty-five of the boldest of Grandgousier's men, all armed to the teeth, spears in their hands, riding into battle like Saint George chasing dragons, and a soldier with a crossbow riding behind every one of them.

Chapter Forty-two // How the Monk Filled His Friends with Courage, and How He Hung from a Tree

So these noble warriors rode off on their adventure, determined to understand just how they ought to meet their enemies and what they needed to guard against, when the awesome day of battle arrived. And the monk filled them with courage, saying:

"My children, have no fear and no doubt: I will lead you with a sure hand. May God and Saint Benedict be with us! Oh, if I had as much strength as I have courage, by God's holy grave! I'd pluck them for you like a duck! I'm not afraid of anything except cannons. Besides, I know a prayer, which the assistant sexton at our abbey gave me, which protects you against all kinds of bullets. But it won't do me a bit of good, because I don't believe in stuff like that. Anyway, this staff from a cross performs all the miracles I need. By God, maybe one of you will feel like cutting and running, but the devil take me if I don't wind my robe around his neck and turn him right into a monk: these robes are a sovereign remedy for cowardice. Have you heard about Lord de Meurles' greyhound, which was worthless once they let him off the leash? Well, they tied a monk's habit around his neck. By the body and blood of Christ! There wasn't a rabbit or a fox that could get away from him after that, and what's more, he screwed every bitch in the county, though he'd never been able to get it up before: he'd always been *frigidis et maleficiatis,* impotent and incompetent."

Saying these angry words, the monk rode under a walnut tree, heading toward Saullaye (near Lerné), and jammed the visor of his helmet right into a notch in one of its thick branches. In spite of this, he jabbed his spurs into his horse, which was a damned ticklish animal. Whereupon the horse leaped forward and the monk, trying to yank his visor out of the notch, let go of the bridle and took hold of the branch. But his horse rode right out from underneath him. So the monk was left hanging from the tree and yelling for help, shouting out, "Murder! Treason!"

Rightway was the first to see him, and called to Gargantua:

"My lord, come and see Absalom hanging from a tree!"

Gargantua rode up and, examining the monk's face and the way he was suspended from the branch, said to Rightway:

"You've got it all wrong. How can you compare Brother John to Absalom? Absalom was hanging by his hair and this close-cropped monk of ours is hanging by his ears."

"Get me down," said the monk, "for the devil's sake! Is this the time to stand around jabbering? You're like a pack of formalist preachers, who see one of their neighbors in danger of death but, before they help them, think they have to worry about being excommunicated if they don't first hear the man's confession and put his soul in a proper state of grace. So next time I see someone fall into the river, as he's going down for the third time I won't run over and give him my hand—oh no, I'll preach him a fine long sermon *de contemptu mundi et fuga seculi,* of contempt for worldly things and the slipperiness of everything secular. And when he's stiff and dead, I'll go and fish him out."

"Stay where you are," said Gymnast, "my fine fellow. I'm going to come and help you—because you're such a sweet little monk:

> *Monachus in claustro*
> *Non valet ova duo;*
> *Sed quando est extra*
> *Bene valet triginta.*

> A monk in his cell
> Isn't worth an eggshell,
> But once let him out
> He's worth thirty, no doubt.

"I've seen more than a hundred men hang from trees, but I've never yet seen anyone who hung with such grace, such charm. If I could be hanged like that, I think I'd like to spend my whole life hung from a tree."

"Have you done enough preaching?" said the monk. "For the love of God, help me, unless for the love of the devil you don't want to. I swear by the holy robes I wear, you'll live to regret it, *tempore et loco prelibatis,* in good time and in some good place."

So Gymnast got down from his horse and, climbing up into the walnut tree, put one hand under the monk's armpit and with the other tugged his visor out of the notch in the branch, and so let him fall to the ground, and then followed after himself.

As soon as he was safely on solid ground, the monk pulled off every bit of his armor and threw it, one piece after the other, all over the field. And then, taking up the staff of the cross, he got back on his horse, which Rightway had been holding for him.

And then they went happily on their way, still on the road to Saullaye.

Chapter Forty-three ⁄⁄ How Gargantua Met Picrochole's Scouting Party and the Monk Killed Captain Tiravant and Then Was Captured by the Enemy

Hearing the story of those who escaped, when Drinkup Gutsout was disemboweled, Picrochole fell into a fury, thinking that demons had been running rampant among his men. So he and his counselors sat up all night, debating what to do next. It was the opinion of Hastyman and Loudmouth that they were strong enough to stand up to all the devils out of hell, if they showed up for a fight, an opinion which Picrochole didn't believe for a minute, though he also didn't disbelieve it.

However, he sent out a scouting party of sixteen hundred cavalrymen, riding in strict combat formation on light, fast horses, under the command of Count Dasharound. Each of them had been thoroughly sprinkled with holy water and so they would be prepared for whatever might happen they also wore, as their battle insignia, a shoulder sash which the sainted Gregorian water had so impregnated that it had the power to make devils absolutely evaporate and disappear. So they rode near La Vauguyon and Saint-Lazare, but saw no one they could question. Then they came back along the heights and, in a shepherd's hut near Coudray Montpensier, they found the five pilgrims, whom they tied up, hand and foot, and blindfolded. Then they led them off like spies, though the pilgrims protested and swore to their innocence and begged to be released. Coming down toward Seuilly they were spotted by Gargantua, who said to his companions:

"My friends, here we see the enemy, and they are more than ten times our number. Should we engage them?"

"What the devil are we doing out here?" said the monk. "Do you weigh men by number and not by their courage and their strength?" Then he cried out, "Lay on, you devils: let's get them!"

Hearing this, Picrochole's troops thought these were certainly real devils and began to run as fast as they could, except Dasharound, who positioned his lance and charged at the monk, hitting him right in the middle of his chest. But when the steel tip smashed into those awesome robes it buckled and went blunt, as if you'd clubbed an anvil with a little wax taper. Then the monk gave him such a blow on the side of his neck, just over the shoulder blade, that he was stunned and fell senseless on the ground at his horse's feet. And seeing the sash on the man's shoulder, Brother John said to Gargantua:

"These men are only preachers, which is barely the first step toward becoming a monk. But by Saint John! I'm a real monk, and I'll kill them for you like flies."

Then he galloped after them and caught up with the stragglers, and clubbed them like a farmer reaping grain, whipping them up and down.

At which point Gymnast asked Gargantua if they ought to pursue the rest of them. To which Gargantua answered:

"Definitely not, because true military wisdom advises you never to drive your enemy into utter desperation, because that kind of necessity only makes him stronger and more courageous, even if he's already been defeated and humbled. The best way to revive soldiers who are weary and stumbling about is to leave them absolutely without any hope. How many victories have been snatched out of the hands of conquerors by those they were vanquishing, when they overreached themselves and would not listen to reason, but tried to kill every last man and utterly destroy their enemy, wanting not to leave even a single man left alive to carry the news back home! Always leave your enemy some doors to go through and some roads to run on—indeed, build them a silver bridge so they can cross over and get away."

"True," said Gymnast. "But they've got the monk."

"They've got the monk?" said Gargantua. "Oh my honor, they're going to regret that! Well, since we don't know exactly what will happen, we won't retreat just yet. Let's wait here, quietly: I think I've gotten to understand our enemy's mind. They don't think and plan: they simply dash whichever way looks best at the moment."

So they waited, there under the walnut trees, watching the monk chase after Picrochole's men, clubbing everyone he met without any mercy, until he came to a cavalryman riding along with one of the pilgrims sitting behind him. Brother John was just about to add them to his list when the pilgrim cried out:

"Oh, my Lord Prior, my friend, Lord Prior, save me, I beg you!"

And Picrochole's men, hearing these words, turned to face their pursuers and, seeing that it was only the monk who was after them, turned on him and began to rain blows on him the way you load wood onto a donkey. The monk didn't feel a thing, especially when they hit his robes, because he had a tough hide. So they left two archers to guard him and, turning around, saw that there was no one else there, which made them think that Gargantua and his troop had fled. Accordingly, they rode down toward the walnut trees as fast as they could, trying to find them, leaving the monk alone with his two guards.

Hearing the sound of their horses, their hooves and their whinnying, Gargantua said to his men:

"Friends, I hear our enemies coming, and I can already see some of them rushing at us. Stand together and we'll hold this road like soldiers. That way we'll welcome them honorably, and make them pay for coming."

Chapter Forty-four ⁄⁄ How the Monk Killed His Guards and Picrochole's Scouting Party Was Defeated

Seeing them leave in such a hurry, the monk suspected that they were charging down on Gargantua and his men, and was mightily upset that he could not help them. Then, noticing the faces of the two archers guarding him, he saw how sorry they were, too, not to be dashing along with their friends and picking up what loot they could; indeed, they kept looking down toward the valley where the others had ridden. Thinking logically, he said to himself:

"These fellows have been badly trained for their profession: they haven't asked me to agree not to run off, and they certainly haven't taken away my short sword."

So he quickly drew out that same sword and swung it at the archer to his right, slicing clean through the jugular veins and the arteries in his neck, as well as the base of the throat all the way to the thyroid glands. Then, pulling back the blade, he cut through the top of the spinal cord, between the second and third vertebrae—and the archer fell like a stone, dead. After which the monk turned his horse to the left and charged at the other man, who saw that his companion was dead and that the monk had the draw on him, and began crying in a loud voice:

"Ah, My Lord Prior, I surrender! O Lord Prior, my good friend, My Lord Prior!"

And the monk shouted right back:

"My Lord Backside, my friend, O My Lord Backside, I'm going to knock you on your ass."

"Oh," said the archer, "My Lord Prior, my dear, dear Lord Prior, may God make you an abbot!"

"By these robes I'm wearing," said the monk, "I'm going to make you a cardinal. Are you trying to bribe a man of the cloth? I'm going to make sure you get to have a red head, and right now."

And still the archer cried out:

"My Lord Prior, My lord, O Prior, My Lord Future Abbott, My Lord Cardinal, My Lord Everything! Oh, oh—no, no, My Lord Prior, my good little, my noble little Prior, I surrender, I surrender!"

"And I," said the monk, "I surrender you to all the devils in hell."

And with a blow he split his head, cutting right through the temporal bone, chopping through the two parietal bones and the junctures of all the bones that hold the skull together, which also involved slicing across the membranes which hold the brain in place and opened a huge hole in the two rear ventricles of the brain itself. The man's head hung down from his shoulders by no more than the skin on the back of his skull, rather like the academic hat worn by doctors, which is black on the outside and red within. And then he too fell dead to the ground.

And so the monk spurred his horse and rode down in the direction the enemy had taken. The enemy, meanwhile, had gone down the highroad and met up with Gargantua and his companions, who had significantly reduced them in number because of the incredible slaughter accomplished by Gargantua with his huge tree—but he was helped by Gymnast, Powerbrain, Rightway, and the others. So Picrochole's forces began a brisk retreat, frightened and deeply upset, incapable of understanding, as if they had seen death's own shape and form right in front of their eyes.

And then—have you ever seen a donkey with a huge horsefly on his asshole or any kind of fly stinging his ass, running this way and that, never knowing where he's going, knocking his load to the ground, breaking his bridle, snapping his reins, neither breathing nor stopping to rest, and no one knows what he's going to do next, because no one can see what's bothering him? Well, that's how Picrochole's soldiers acted, utterly out of their minds, without any notion of what they were running from— because in sober fact the only thing that was chasing them was the sheer panic, the terror, which they had conceived in their souls.

And when the monk saw that the only thought in their heads was to run away as fast as they could, he dismounted and then climbed up on a huge rock that stood in the middle of the road. And then, with his long sword, he took mighty swings at those who were madly fleeing, showing them no mercy and never holding back a bit. He killed so many, dropping them to the ground all around him, that his sword finally broke in two. Which made him think that this ought to be enough massacring and killing, and the rest ought to be left to escape and bring the news to their master.

So he climbed down, picked up a battle-ax that had belonged to one of those lying there on the ground, then climbed back up on the rock, passing the time of day by watching their enemies run wildly through the heaps of corpses. But he did make them leave their weapons—all their axes and swords and lances and crossbows. And he also obliged those who were escorting the pilgrims, who were still tied up, to dismount and let the pilgrims have their horses. And he had the pilgrims stay with him at the edge of the wood—along with Captain Loudmouth, whom he had taken prisoner.

Chapter Forty-five ⁄⁄ How the Monk Brought Back the Pilgrims, and the Wise Words Spoken to Them by Grandgousier

This skirmish over, Gargantua and his men withdrew (except for the monk, who for all they knew was still a prisoner), just at daybreak, and returned to Grandgousier. He was still in bed, praying that they come back safely and victoriously. Seeing them all safe and sound, he embraced them warmly and asked about the monk. But Gargantua told him that the enemy had certainly captured Brother John. "It will be a bad day for them," said Grandgousier, which was in fact all too true. Nevertheless, this is still how we say that a man has something to worry about: *he's been given the monk.*

Then they gave orders for a handsome breakfast, because they needed the refreshment. When it was ready they called Gargantua, but he was so worried about the monk's nonappearance that he had no interest in either food or drink.

And then, suddenly, the monk arrived and, standing at the lower gate, called out:

"Fresh wine, fresh wine, Gymnast, my old friend!"

Gymnast leaped up and saw that it was indeed Brother John, and that he was leading five pilgrims and a prisoner, Captain Loudmouth. Gargantua went out, too, and gave the monk the warmest welcome in the world, and brought him to Grandgousier, who asked for every detail of his adventure. The monk told him everything—how he had been taken prisoner, and how he had killed the two archers guarding him, and the butchery he'd accomplished out on the highroad, and how he'd recovered the pilgrims and led off his prisoner, Captain Loudmouth. So they all sat down and feasted merrily.

And then Grandgousier asked the pilgrims where their home was, and where they had come from and where they were going.

Wearyway spoke for all of them:

"My lord, I come from the Benedictine abbey at Saint-Genou. My friend here is from Palluau, and he's from Onzay, and he's from Argy, and this last fellow is from Villebernin. We came here from holy Saint Sebastian, near Nantes, and we've been returning home by slow stages, as pilgrims do."

"Indeed," said Grandgousier. "But what were you doing at Saint Sebastian?"

"We went," said Wearyway, "to offer up our prayers for protection against the plague."

"Oh," said Grandgousier, "you poor people. Do you believe that the plague comes from Saint Sebastian?"

"Most certainly," answered Wearyway. "Our preachers say so."

"Really?" said Grandgousier. "Those false prophets proclaim such falsehoods? But they're blaspheming against God's true and holy saints, comparing them to devils who can only do us harm—just as Homer writes that the Greeks were given the plague by Apollo, or the way poets in general concoct a mad jumble of Joves and wicked gods! There was a hypocrite preaching at Cinais, not long ago, claiming that good Saint Anthony shot fire into men's legs, or that Saint Eutropius swelled them up with dropsy, or that Saint Gildas was responsible for madmen, or Saint Genou brought us the gout. But I punished that liar, though he called me a heretic, and ever since no religious hypocrite has dared to approach these lands of mine. Indeed, it astonishes me that your king allows such scandalous creatures to preach in his kingdom, because they are more deserving of punishment than magicians or other hoaxers—who probably did bring the plague with them. Plague only kills the body, but these fakers infect the soul."

As he spoke to them, the monk marched in and asked the pilgrims:

"Where are you from, the rest of you miserable wretches?"

"From Saint-Genou," they said.

"And how's Abbott Tranchelion," he said, "my good drinking friend? And the monks, how are they doing? By God's sacred heart! They must be having a fine time with your wives while you're off on Rome's business!"

"Hey, ho," said Wearyway, "I'm not worried about mine. Anyone who's seen her by daylight isn't going to be breaking his neck to visit her at night."

"What a house of cards *you're* living in!" said the monk. "She can be as ugly as Proserpina, the queen of hell, and, by God, she'll be humped if there's a monk anywhere around, because a good workman makes use of everything that finds its way into his hands. The pox on me, but you'll find them growing monks' seed by the time you get home: a woman can get knocked up just by the shadow of a monastery bell tower."

"Yes," said Gargantua, "like the waters of the Nile, if you believe Strabo. And Pliny, book 7, chapter 3, warns it can be done by monks' robes, even by the food they eat, as well as by their bodies."

At which point Grandgousier said:

"Go then, you poor folk, in the name of God the Creator: may He keep you forever in His hands. And hereafter don't be so quick to venture out on these difficult and unprofitable journeys. Stay with your families, work at your occupations and trades, teach your children, and live as the good Apostle Saint Paul has taught you. If you do, you'll live in God's grace, and all the angels and the saints will be with you, and no plague nor any other misfortune will bother you."

So Gargantua brought them into the dining hall, to take their meal. But all the pilgrims did was sigh, and they said to him:

"Oh what a blessed country, to have such a man as its ruler! We've been more enlightened and instructed by what he just said to us than by all the sermons ever preached in our hometown."

"It's exactly what Plato said," explained Gargantua, "in book five of his *Republic:* republics will be happy places only if kings philosophize and philosophers rule."

After which he made them fill their knapsacks with food, their traveling flasks with wine, and gave each of them a horse to make the rest of their journey easier, as well as enough gold to help them on their way.

Chapter Forty-six // Grandgousier's Humane Treatment of His Prisoner, Captain Loudmouth

Captain Loudmouth was formally presented to Grandgousier, who questioned him about what Picrochole was up to and, in particular, about what that king saw as the goal of this wild uproar. Loudmouth answered that Picrochole's goal, and his destiny, was to conquer the entire country (if he could), because his flatcake bakers had been so flagrantly wronged.

"That," said Grandgousier, "is terribly overambitious: if you try to take too much, you're likely to get precious little. These are no longer the times when you can go around conquering Christian kingdoms and inflicting injuries on your brothers in Christ. To imitate the ancients in that way—Hercules, Alexander, Hannibal, Scipio, and the Caesars and all the others—is directly contrary to what the Bible teaches us. We are each of us ordered to protect and save and rule and administer our lands, not angrily to invade. The Saracens and all the other barbarians were once considered heroes, but now we call them pirates and evildoers. How much better to be content with that which is rightly your own, and govern it properly, like a good king, rather than to commit such wrongs against these lands of mine, savagely robbing and destroying. If he had been content to govern well, his worldly kingdom would have been increased. But since he has chosen to ravage my kingdom, by that very act he will be destroyed.

"You are free to leave as you will, in the name of God. Try to do good. Tell your king his errors, which now you understand, and never advise him to think of what may be good only for you yourself, for when the state perishes so too does the individual. Whatever your ransom may be, I hereby waive it. I also direct that you be given your armor and weapons, and your horse.

"So should it be, between neighbors and old friends, since our dispute is truly not a war, as Plato says in his *Republic,* book five: don't call it war but sedition, when Greeks take arms, one against the other—and if by some bad luck that does happen, Plato's advice is to use all the restraint of which you are capable. And if you do call it war, it's barely that, for it can never proceed from the true depths of our hearts. There's been no great insult to our honor: all that's truly needed is to repair a minor wrong committed by our people—and I mean both yours and ours, for surely you must understand that you should have let this silly business simply blow over. Those who began the quarrel should have been scolded rather than praised, above all because I offered them fair compensation, fully equal to any injuries they suffered. Whatever dispute we have, may God weigh it in His balance. And I pray that death may sooner take me from this life, and tear everything I own from me, in front of my very eyes, than for me or mine to be guilty of anything sinful."

Having thus spoken, he called the monk and asked him:

"Brother John, my good friend, are you the one who captured Captain Loudmouth, who stands here before us?"

"My lord," said the monk, "he does indeed stand before us, and he is a grown man and has a grown man's judgment. I would rather have you hear these things from him than from me."

Whereupon Loudmouth said:

"My lord, it is indeed true that he captured me, and I surrendered myself to him of my own free will."

"And," said Grandgousier to the monk, "did you set a ransom for him?"

"No," said the monk. "I don't care about such things."

"What would you like his ransom to be?" said Grandgousier.

"Nothing, nothing," said the monk. "That doesn't mean anything to me."

So Grandgousier directed that, in Loudmouth's presence, sixty thousand and two gold pieces be counted out as ransom, and this was done while they offered Captain Loudmouth food and drink. And Grandgousier asked him if he wished to stay or would prefer to return to his king.

Loudmouth answered that he would do whatever Grandgousier advised.

"In which case," said Grandgousier, "return to your king, and may God be with you."

Then he gave Loudmouth a fine sword, forged in Dauphiné, with a scabbard of worked gold, all traced around with vine leaves, and a golden necklace weighing three hundred and one thousand pounds, garnished with splendid gemstones worth a hundred and sixty thousand gold ducats, and an additional ten thousand gold crowns as a reward of honor. And then Loudmouth got up on his horse. To ensure his safety, Gargantua provided thirty men at arms and a hundred and twenty archers, under Gymnast's command, who would conduct him, if need be, as far as the gates of La Roche-Clermault.

After he had gone, the monk gave back to Grandgousier the sixty-two thousand gold pieces he had received, saying:

"My lord, this is not the time for giving such gifts. Wait until this war is over, because no man can predict exactly what will happen and a war fought without a good stock of money is only a wispy shadow of what a war should be. The true sinews of battle are silver."

"All right," said Grandgousier. "When this is over I will reward you handsomely, as I will all those who have served me well."

Chapter Forty-seven // How Grandgousier Marshaled His Forces, and How Loudmouth Killed Hastyman and Then Was Executed by Picrochole's Order

At this same time the people of Bessé (near Chinon), Marché Vieux, the faubourg de Saint-Jacques, Trainneau, Parilly, Rivière, Roche Saint-Paul, Vaubreton, Pautille, Bréhémont, Pont-de-Clan, Cravant, Grandmont, Bourdes, Ville-au-Maire, Huismes, Segré, Hussé, Saint-Louant,

Panzoust, Couldreaux, Verron, Coulaines, Chosé, Varennes-sur-Loire, Bourgueil, L'Ile-Bouchard, Croulay, Narsy, Candes, Montsoreau, and other nearby places all sent ambassadors to Grandgousier, saying that they had heard of the wrongs done him by Picrochole, and, on account of their ancient league of alliance, they all offered him anything they could supply that might be of assistance, whether soldiers or money and other necessary war supplies.

The sums raised, according to the treaties to which they all were party, came to a hundred and thirty-four million, two and a half gold pieces. The soldiers raised came to fifteen thousand men at arms, thirty-two thousand light cavalrymen, eighty-nine thousand archers, a hundred and fourteen thousand volunteers, eleven thousand two hundred cannon, double cannon, mortars, and spiral mortars, plus forty-seven thousand scouts. And every man of them had been fully paid and provisioned for six months and four days. Gargantua neither refused nor accepted everything thus offered, but extended them his most gracious thanks, explaining that he intended to end this war in such a way that there would be no need to impose upon so many good men. All he asked was that they send him such troops as, in the ordinary course of affairs, they kept stationed at such places as La Devinière, Chavigny, Gravot, and Quinquenays, in all perhaps two thousand five hundred men at arms, sixty-six thousand foot soldiers, twenty-six thousand archers, two hundred large pieces of artilery, twenty-two thousand scouts, and six thousand light cavalrymen, organized into proper companies and sufficiently supplied with the necessary paymasters, quartermasters, marshals, armorers, and whatever other auxiliary forces might be required, all of these men, to be sure, so well trained in all the military arts, so well armed and equipped, so ready to decipher and carry out any orders transmitted to them by military signs, and so quick to listen to and obey their captains, moving so rapidly, so ready to attack, so careful in their skirmishing, that they might better be thought of as a blending of musical instruments or a simultaneous chiming of clocks than a mere army or police force.

Now, when Captain Loudmouth arrived at La Roche-Clermault, he presented himself to King Picrochole and told him in detail everything he had seen and done. And when he was finished he advised, in the strongest of language, that Picrochole seek some sort of accommodation with Grandgousier, who had proven himself to be a man of the very greatest goodwill to be found anywhere on earth. And he added that, in his own mind, it did not seem either useful or right to harass their neighbors as they had done, since their neighbors had never been anything but neighborly to them. So far as the main argument was concerned, he did not think there would be any way out of what they had gotten themselves into except immense shame and ill fortune, for Picrochole was simply not powerful enough to easily defeat Grandgousier. He had barely finished speaking when Hastyman said, in a loud voice:

"What an unlucky prince, to be served by such men as this, so easily corrupted, as I see Loudmouth has been. His heart has been so entirely changed that he would gladly have taken our enemy's side, ready to fight against us, to betray us, had they been willing to enlist him. But just as everyone—friends and enemies alike—praises and values virtue, so too does everyone readily recognize, and mistrust, wickedness. I submit that even if our enemies are glad to make use of wickedness, they still think wicked men and traitors are nothing but abominations."

Hearing this, Loudmouth impulsively drew his sword and ran Hastyman through, the blade transfixing him just a little above the left nipple, killing him at once. Then, pulling out his sword, he said boldly:

"May they all perish, those who falsely slander a faithful servant!"

But Picrochole flew into a fury, seeing the handsome new sword all smeared with blood, and cried:

"Is this why they gave you that fine new sword, eh? So—in my very presence—you could wickedly kill my good friend Hastyman?"

And he commanded his archers to cut him to bits, which they immediately did, and so savagely that the room was covered with blood. Then they gave Hastyman an honorable burial and threw Loudmouth's body from the castle walls, down into the valley below.

News of this violent barbarity spread all through the army, and there were words muttered against Picrochole, and Winegrabber said to the king:

"My lord, I don't know what will come of all this. Your men seem to me deeply unsettled. They think we don't have enough provisions, and they also see that the two or three skirmishes we've experienced have significantly depleted our ranks. Moreover, your enemy has been receiving vast numbers of reinforcements. If they lay siege to us, I don't see how we can expect anything but total disaster."

"Shit, shit!" said Picrochole. "You're all a bunch of Melun eels: you squeal even before they put you in the pot! Let them just attack us."

Chapter Forty-eight // How Gargantua Attacked and Defeated Picrochole's Army in the Castle at La Roche-Clermault

The army was completely in Gargantua's charge. His father stayed in his fortress at La Devinière and, inspiring them with wise words, promised great rewards to those who did heroic deeds. When they came to the ford at Vède they constructed small boats, and also bridges which they quickly hammered together, and crossed directly over. Then that night, as they planned their assault on the town and castle, which stood commandingly on high ground, they discussed what it might be best to do. But Gymnast said to Gargantua:

"My lord, the French temperament is such that they're only good at the start of a battle. At that point they're fiercer than the very devils—but if things go on too long they're worth less than women. So it seems to me that right now, after your men have had time for a quick rest and a chance to catch their breath and eat a little, is the time for you to attack."

The advice was taken. Accordingly, Gargantua deployed his army, setting his reserves alongside the mountain. Taking six companies of foot soldiers and two hundred men-at-arms, the monk quick-marched them across the marsh and reached the peak, just at the point where the highway from Chinon to Loudun crosses it.

The assault continued all this time, and Picrochole's men couldn't decide whether it was better to charge out and engage them or to stay where they were and hold on to their fortified position. But one band of house guards, led by Picrochole himself, burst out from behind the walls in a furious sally. They were greeted and suitably entertained by a tremendous burst of artillery fire, which fell like hail all across the slopes, from which Gargantua's men had withdrawn, the better to position their cannon in the valleys just below.

The defenders fought as best they could, firing back with their own artillery, but their range was too long and the shells dropped uselessly out beyond the Gargantuan lines, hitting nothing. Those among the band of house guards who had not been killed by our artillery made a fierce attack, but accomplished very little, for Gargantua's troops split to the side to let them rush in, and then dashed them to the ground. Seeing which, they tried to retreat, but the monk had cut off the way, which threw them into a disordered and panicked flight. Though some of his troops wanted to chase after them, the monk held them back, concerned that if they ran after the fleeing men they would themselves fall into disorder, leaving themselves open to a counterattack from the other troops in the town. Accordingly, after waiting a bit and finding no one else coming out to meet them, he sent Duke Thoughtful to urge Gargantua to bring up his men and take control of the slope to their left, thus further cutting off the possibility of retreat for Picrochole and his house guards. Gargantua promptly put this plan into effect, sending four legions of Lord Sobriety's men. But before they could get to the top they came face-to-face with Picrochole and those of his men who had fallen back alongside him. So Lord Sobriety's men threw themselves at the enemy, although—since they were by this time close to the defenders' walls—they suffered seriously from gunfire and artillery poured down on them from above. And seeing this, Gargantua and a huge force of his soldiers ran to help them, and also ordered their own cannon to begin firing directly at that section of the walls, thus drawing all the defenders to this position.

The monk, seeing that the sector he'd been attacking was now stripped of soldiers and guards alike, made a noble dash toward the fortress. He and some of his men succeeded in climbing over the walls and right in, his theory being that more fear and terror are created by those who suddenly burst into a battle than by those who have been fighting all along. So none of them made a sound until every man jack of them had climbed the wall (except for two hundred men-at-arms that they left outside, just in case). And then they yelled as horribly as they could, all of them together, and promptly killed all the guards at that gate, without meeting any effective resistance. Then they opened the gate from the inside, so the two hundred men-at-arms could join them, and the entire troop ran proudly straight to the left, where the fighting was centered, and striking at them from the rear totally overwhelmed Picrochole's forces. Seeing that they were surrounded on all sides by attackers, and that Gargantua's men had already conquered the town, the enemy troops surrendered to the monk, who made them hand over their banners and their weapons, then shut them up in the town's churches. But he made sure that all the crosses mounted on staffs were removed, and he placed guards at all the doors, to keep the prisoners safely inside. And then, opening the gates, he went to assist Gargantua.

But Picrochole, thinking it was he who was being helped by soldiers sallying forth from the town, threw himself ever more recklessly into the battle, fighting with no caution at all, until the moment Gargantua cried out:

"Brother John, my friend, Brother John: how welcome you are!"

And Picrochole suddenly understood, and all his men with him, that there was no hope left for them, and they turned and ran. Gargantua chased them as far as Vaugaudry, killing and butchering, then ordered retreat to be sounded.

Chapter Forty-nine ⁄⁄ How the Fleeing Picrochole Suffered Misfortune, and What Gargantua Did after the Battle

Desperate, Picrochole fled toward L'Ile-Bouchard, not far from Chinon. On the Rivière road his horse stumbled and fell to the ground, which made him so wildly angry that he drew his sword and killed the animal on the spot. Then, finding no one who might provide him with another steed, he tried to steal a donkey belonging to a nearby mill. But the millers beat him black and blue, destroying his clothing in the process, so to cover his nakedness they gave him a torn and dirty peasant shirt.

So on he went, the miserable, ill-tempered wretch. Crossing the river to Port-Huault, and telling everyone what bad luck he had had, he was assured by an old witch that his kingdom would be restored to him when the Cockamamies came flying overhead. But no one knows what happened to him after that. On the other hand, I have heard rumors about his being a poor day laborer, these days, off in Lyons, just as bad-tempered as ever, and afflicting any stranger he can collar with tales of the Cockamamies coming, absolutely confident—as the old witch had prophesied—that when they finally arrived he would be put back on his throne.

The first thing Gargantua did, when he and his men got back, was to call the rolls, and he learned that remarkably few had been killed in battle, other than a few foot soldiers from Captain Boldyboy's command; Powerbrain, too, had been wounded by a bullet which had pierced his coat. So he ordered food brought for them, company by company, and gave orders to all the paymasters that they could expect repayment from him. He also commanded that no rioting or any outrages were to be perpetrated on the town or its people, because it belonged to him. And then, after they had eaten, they were ordered to appear in the square in front of the castle, where he would reward them with six months' pay; and this was done. And afterward, all those who had been on Picrochole's side were commanded to appear in that same place, all of them together, and in the presence of his princes and captains he spoke to them as follows:

Chapter Fifty ⁄ Gargantua's Speech to the Conquered

"Our fathers, our grandfathers, and our ancestors from the beginning of time have all felt that, once battles were over and done with, the best memorial of their triumphs and victories should be trophies and monuments created in the hearts of those who had been conquered, brought into being by acts of kindness—and these, they were convinced, were better by far than any architectural symbols erected in those conquered lands. It seemed to them that the living memories of human beings won by liberality were worth infinitely more than cold, silent inscriptions chiseled onto arches, columns, and pyramids, open to all the injuries to which stone and marble are subject, and forever liable to evoke jealousy and anger.

"Just remember the kindness they showed to the Bretons, when they were defeated at Saint-Aubin-du-Cormier, and how Parthenay was utterly destroyed but its defeated defenders were permitted to leave with both their freedom and their weapons. You have heard and admired the generosity they exhibited to the barbarians of Haiti, who had ravaged and devastated all the maritime territories of Les Sables-d'Olonne and Talmont.

"Heaven itself was flooded to the brim by the thankful prayers offered

by you and your fathers when Alpharbal, king of Canarre, not satisfied
with what fortune had already brought him, stormed into the land of
Aunis and, like the pirate he was, did immense damage in the Armoric
Islands and all the lands nearby. My royal father, may God keep and
protect him, defeated Alpharbal in a fierce battle at sea, and made that
king his prisoner. And what then? Had he been captured by other kings
and emperors, and certainly by those who like to call themselves Catho-
lics, he would have been miserably treated, thrown into prison for long
periods, and ransomed only at immense cost. But Alpharbal was treated
with all due courtesy. He lived in my father's own castle, as a friend, and
by incredible gentility and graciousness was given safe-conduct home,
loaded with gifts and favors and blessed by every sign of friendship. And
what happened after that? Once again on his throne, Alpharbal called
together all his princes and officials, told them of the great humanity with
which he had been treated, and begged them all to think how the world
could be made to see that, having encountered such graciousness and
integrity in us, they too were capable of such heights of uprightness and
courtesy. It was thereupon decided, by unanimous consent, that their
entire kingdom should be ours, completely subject to our will. Alpharbal
himself immediately returned to my father, bringing with him nine thousand and thirty-eight huge freight-bearing ships, laden not only with all
the treasures of his household and of his royal dynasty but with virtually
all the wealth in his kingdom—for as he set sail, the wind blowing west-
northeast behind him, the entire populace rushed down and threw on
board their gold, silver, rings, jewels, and all their precious spices and
medicines and perfumes, their parrots and pelicans and monkeys, their
rare civet cats, their hedgehogs and porcupines. Not a man was worthy
to be his mother's true son who didn't throw in whatever he owned that
was rare and costly. And when he landed, Alpharbal tried to kiss my
father's feet, but this was deemed unworthy and he was greeted like all
other men. Then he offered his gifts, but my father would not accept
them; they were far too extravagant. So Alpharbal tried to consign himself and all his descendants to perpetual slavery, but my father would not
accept this either, saying it was unjust. So Alpharbal tried to hand over
all rights to his kingdom, signed and sealed in a document ratified by
everyone whose signature might be required for such a deed, but this too
was absolutely refused, and the documents were tossed into the fire. And
finally my father broke out into tears of pity and compassion, seeing the
open goodwill and the true simplicity of the Canarrians. With exquisitely
chosen words and measured wisdom he made light of any kindness he
had shown them, saying that whatever he might have done wasn't worth
more than a button, adding too that if he had done some insignificant
nothing of merit it was in any case only what he had been obliged to do—
nothing more. But Alpharbal only pressed him harder. And what was
the result? Instead of a ransom, wrung out of him, a tyranny which might

have gotten us two million gold pieces and his oldest children as hostages for its payment—instead, they placed themselves in a posture of perpetual tribute to us, obligating themselves to pay us, each and every year, two million pieces of the purest gold, twenty-four carats pure. The first payment was made on the spot. The second year, freely and gladly, they paid us two million three hundred thousand gold pieces, then in the third year two million four hundred thousand, and in the fourth year a flat three million—and their goodwill goes on growing so steadily that, soon, we will be obliged to forbid them to send us anything at all. And this is the true nature of gratitude. Time gnaws and diminishes all things, but it increases and adds to our good deeds: anytime we have extended a generous hand to a rational human being, that goodness keeps growing and glowing in the man's heart, forever remembered, constantly contemplated.

"And so, not wishing either to retreat or to detract from the hereditary kindness of my forefathers, I hereby discharge and release you, making you once again the free men you were before. In addition, as you leave here through those gates you will each receive three months' pay, so you will be able to return to your homes and your families, and to help you return in safety you will have an escort of six hundred men-at-arms and eight thousand foot soldiers, under the command of my squire, Alexander, so that no harm will be done to you by the peasants. May God be with you!

"With my whole heart I regret that Picrochole is not here, because I would have liked to make him understand that for me this war has been a completely involuntary affair, entered into without the slightest thought of enlarging either my possessions or my reputation. But since he is completely gone from our sight, and no one knows where or how he has vanished, I wish his son to have his entire kingdom, and since the child is far too young (being still no more than five years old), he will have to be governed and instructed by the oldest princes and the most learned men in the realm. But since a kingdom without a king is easily ruined, unless the greed and avarice of its officials are held in check, it is my decree, as it is my wish, that Powerbrain should take charge of all those who govern here, with full and complete authority, and that he be regularly in attendance upon the child until he thinks him able to govern and rule by himself.

"It is my judgment, however, that to weakly and idly pardon evildoers is simply to encourage them to again do evil, imparting to them a dangerous belief that they will be pardoned a second time, too, as they were the first.

"It is my judgment that Moses, though he was in his time the most good-natured man who walked the earth, severely punished those among the people of Israel who were guilty of mutiny or treason.

"It is my judgment that Julius Caesar, though he was so kind a ruler that Cicero said of him that nothing seemed to him worth more than the power to save and pardon as he chose, even Julius Caesar would rigorously punish those who rose in rebellion.

"And so, according to these examples, I wish you to hand over to me, before you leave here: first of all, that fine fellow Marquet, whose gross, senseless arrogance was the source and the primary cause of this war; and second, his fellow flatcake bakers, who were negligent about instantly correcting his headstrong folly; and, finally, all of Picrochole's advisers, captains, officers, and domestics who in any way incited or encouraged or counseled him to so far overreach himself and thus seriously inconvenience us."

Chapter Fifty-one // How Those Who Fought for Gargantua Were Rewarded after the Battle

After he finished his speech, they brought him the troublemakers he had asked for, except Count Boastwell, Captain Shitface, and the duke of Slobdom, who had fled six hours before the battle, one dashing right through the pass at Laignel, in the Maritime Alps, another running all the way to the Vire Valley, and the third to Logroño, in Spain, none of them stopping either to look back or to take a breath along the road, plus two flatcake bakers who had died during the day's fighting. But Gargantua did nothing more to any of them than to order that they run the treadles for the new printing presses he had just had installed.

Then he had those who had been killed honorably buried in Walnut Valley, and in the fields at Scorchville. He had the wounded dressed and treated in his great hospital. Then he looked into the damage done to the town and its dwellings, and had all the losses reimbursed, on the basis of sworn statements. And he had a strong castle built, and had it manned and supplied, so that in the future they might be better protected against sudden uprisings.

When he left, he gave gracious thanks to all the soldiers of his legions, and sent them to the winter quarters of their several stations and garrisons, except for some from the Tenth Legion, for he had seen them performing brave deeds during the battle, and except, too, the captains of the bands, for he intended to take them directly to Grandgousier.

When that good man saw them coming, his happiness was so great that it would be impossible to describe. He made a feast for them—so magnificent, so overflowing with such delicious things that nothing like it had been seen since the times of King Ahasuerus. As they rose from the table, he gave each of them the utensils they had dined from, which were of gold and weighed eight hundred thousand and fourteen troy ounces, and included great antique vessels, large jugs, huge bowls, tall drinking glasses, cups, smaller-sized pots, candlesticks, bowls of all sorts, containers shaped like ships, vases for flowers, small dishes for candies and other sweets, and a host of others like them, all hammered in massive gold, decorated with precious stones, or enameled, and so elaborately worked that, by universal opinion, the workmanship was worth still more than the materials. And more: for each of them he had counted out, from his treasury, twelve hundred thousand gold pieces, and in addition he gave each of them, in perpetuity (except those who might die without heirs), those castles and the lands around them as seemed to them most fitting. So Powerbrain received La Roche-Clermault, Gymnast got Le Coudray, Rightway was given Montpensier; Le Rivau went to Tolmère, Montsoreau to Scrupulosity, Candes to Indefatigable, Varennes to Handworker, Gravot to Upright, Quinquenays to Alexander, Ligré to Wiseman, and so on.

Chapter Fifty-two ⁄ How Gargantua Built the Abbey of Desire (Thélème) for Brother John

The only one still left to be provided for was the monk. Gargantua wanted to make him abbot of Seuilly, but the monk refused. Gargantua also offered him the abbey of Bourgueil or that of Saint-Florent, whichever best pleased him—and said he could have both those rich, old Benedictine cloisters, if he preferred that. But the monk answered him in no uncertain terms: he wanted neither to govern nor to be in charge of other monks:

"And how," he asked, "should I govern others, when I don't know how to govern myself? If you really think I've done something for you, and I might in the future do something to please you, grant me this: establish an abbey according to my plan."

The request pleased Gargantua, so he offered him the whole land of Thélème, alongside the river Loire, two leagues from the great forest of Port-Huault. And the monk then asked Gargantua to establish this abbey's rules and regulations completely differently from all the others.

"Obviously," said Gargantua, "it won't be necessary to build walls all around it, because all the other abbeys are brutally closed in."

"Indeed," said the monk, "and for good reason. Whenever you've got a whole load of stones in front and a whole load of stones in back, you've got a whole lot of grumbling and complaining, and jealousy, and all kinds of conspiracies."

Moreover, since some of the cloisters already built in this world are in the habit, whenever any woman enters them (I speak only of modest, virtuous women), of washing the ground where she walked, it was decreed that if either a monk or a nun happened to enter the abbey of Thélème, they would scrub the blazes out of the places where they'd been. And since everything is completely regulated, in all the other cloistered houses, tied in and bound down, hour by hour, according to a fierce schedule, it was decreed that in Thélème there would not be a single clock, or even a sundial, and that work would be distributed strictly according to what was needed and who was available to do it—because (said Gargantua) the worst waste of time he knew of was counting the hours—what good could possibly come of it?—and the biggest, fattest nonsense in the whole world was to be ruled by the tolling of a bell rather than by the dictates of common sense and understanding.

Item: because in these times of ours women don't go into convents unless they're blind in one eye, lame, humpbacked, ugly, misshapen, crazy, stupid, deformed, or pox-ridden, and men only if they're tubercular, low born, blessed with an ugly nose, simpletons, or a burden on their parents . . .

("Oh yes," said the monk, "speaking of which: if a woman isn't pretty and she isn't good, what sort of path can she cut for herself?"

"Straight into a convent," said Gargantua.

"To be sure," said the monk, "especially with a scissors and a needle.")

. . . it was decreed that, in Thélème, women would be allowed only if they were beautiful, well formed, and cheerful, and men only if they were handsome, well formed, and cheerful.

Item: since men were not allowed in convents, unless they sneaked in under cover of darkness, it was decreed that in Thélème there would never be any women unless there were men, nor any men unless there were women.

Item: because both men and women, after they'd entered a cloister and served their probationary year, were obliged to spend the entire rest of their lives there, it was decided that men and women who came to Thélème could leave whenever they wanted to, freely and without restriction.

Item: because monks and nuns usually took three vows—chastity, poverty, and obedience—it was decided that in Thélème one could perfectly honorably be married, that anyone could be rich, and that they could all live wherever they wanted to.

As an age limitation, women should be allowed in at any time from ten to fifteen, and men from twelve to eighteen.

Chapter Fifty-three ⁄ How the Abbey of Desire (Thélème) Was Built and Endowed

In order to build and equip the abbey, Gargantua gave two million seven hundred thousand eight hundred and thirty-one gold pieces. Further, until everything had been completed, he assigned the yearly sum of one million six hundred and sixty thousand gold pieces, from the tolls on the river Dive, payable in funds of an unimaginable astrological purity. To endow and perpetually maintain the abbey he gave two million three hundred thousand and sixty-nine English pounds in property rentals, tax-free, fully secured, and payable yearly at the abbey gate, to which effect he had written out all the appropriate deeds and grants.

The building was hexagonal, constructed so that at each angle there was a great round tower sixty feet in diameter, and each of the towers was exactly like all the others. The river Loire was on the north side. One of the towers, called Artice (meaning "Arctic," or "Northern"), ran down almost to the riverbank; another, called Calaer (meaning "Lovely Air"), was just to the east. Then came Anatole (meaning "Oriental," or "Eastern"), and Mesembriné (meaning "Southern"), and then Hesperia (meaning "Occidental," or "Western"), and finally Cryere (meaning "Glacial"). The distance between each of the towers was three hundred and twelve feet. The building had six floors, counting the subterranean cellars as the first. The second or ground floor had a high vault, shaped like a basket handle. The other floors were stuccoed in a circular pattern, the way they do such things in Flanders; the roof was of fine slate, the coping being lead-decorated with small figurines and animals, handsomely colored and gilded; and there were rainspouts jutting out from the walls, between the casement windows, painted all the way to the ground with blue and gold stripes and ending in great pipes which led down to the river, below the building.

This was all a hundred times more magnificent than the grand chateau at Bonnivet, or that at Chambord, or that at Chantilly, because it had nine thousand three hundred and thirty-two suites, each furnished with an antechamber, a private reading room, a dressing room, and a small personal chapel, and also because each and every room adjoined its own huge hall. Between each tower, in the middle of the main building, was a spiral staircase, its stairs made of crystal porphyry and red Numidian marble and green marble struck through with red and white, all exactly twenty-two feet wide and three fingers thick, there being twelve stairs between each landing. Further: each landing had a beautiful double arch, in Greek style, thus allowing light to flood through and also framing an entryway into overhanging private rooms, each of them just as broad as the stairway itself. The stair wound all the way to the roof, ending there in a pavilion. Off the stair, on each side, one could come to a great hall; the stair also led the way to the private suites and rooms.

Between the tower called Artice and that called Cryere were great beautiful reading rooms, well stocked with books in Greek, Latin, Hebrew, French, Italian, and Spanish, carefully divided according to the languages in which they had been written.

In the center of the main building, entered through an arch thirty-six yards across, stood a marvelous circular ramp. It was fashioned so harmoniously, and built so large, that six men-at-arms, their lances at the ready, could ride clear up to the top of the building, side by side.

Between the tower called Anatole and that called Mesembriné were beautiful galleries, large and open, painted with scenes of ancient heroism, episodes drawn from history, and strange and fascinating plants and animals. Here, too, just as on the side facing the river, were a ramp and a gate. And on this gate was written, in large antique letters, the poem which follows:

Chapter Fifty-four ⁄⁄ The Inscription on the Great Gate of Thélème

Hypocrites, bigots, stay away!
Old humbugs, puffed-up liars, playful
Religious frauds, worse than Goths
Or Ostrogoths (or other sloths):
No hairshirts, here, no sexy monks,
No healthy beggars, no preaching skunks,
No cynics, bombasts ripe with abuse:
Go peddle them elsewhere, your filthy views.

   Your wicked talk
   Would clutter our walks
   Like clustering flies:
   But flies or lies,
   We've no room for your cries,
   Your wicked talk.

Hungry lawyers, stay away!
People eaters, who grab while praying,
Scribes and assessors, and gouty judges
Who beat good men with the law's thick cudgels
And tie old pots to their tails, like dogs,
We'll hop you up and down like frogs,

We'll hang you high from the nearest tree:
We're decent men, not legal fleas.

> Summons and complaints
> Don't strike us as quaint,
> And we haven't got time
> For your legal whine
> As you hang from the line
> Of your summons and complaints.

Money suckers, stay away!
Greedy gougers, spending your days
Gobbling up men, stuffing your guts
With gold, you black-faced crows, busting
Your butts for another load of change,
Though your cellar's bursting with rotten exchange.
O lazy scum, you'll pile up more,
Till smiling death knocks at your door.

> Inhuman faces
> With ghastly spaces
> That no heart can see,
> Find other places:
> Here you can't be,
> You inhuman faces.

Slobbering old dogs, stay away!
Old bitter faces, old sour ways,
We want you elsewhere—the jealous, the traitors,
The slime who live as danger creators,
Wherever you come from, you're worse than wolves:
Shove it, you mangy, scabby oafs!
None of your stinking, ugly sores:
We've seen enough, we want no more.

> Honor and praise
> Fill all our days:
> We sing delight
> All day, all night:
> These are our ways:
> Honor and praise.

But you, you, you can always come,
Noble knights and gentlemen,
For this is where you belong: there's money
Enough, and pleasure enough: honey
And milk for all, and all as one:
Come be my friends, come join our fun,

O gallants, sportsmen, lovers, friends,
Or better still: come, gentlemen.

Gentle, noble,
Serene and subtle,
Eternally calm;
Civility's balm
To live without trouble,
Gentle, noble.

And welcome, you who know the Word
And preach it wherever the Word should be heard:
Make this place your holy castle
Against the false religious rascals
Who poison the world with filthy lies:
Welcome, you with your eyes on the skies
And faith in your hearts: we can fight to the death
For truth, fight with our every breath.

For the holy Word
Can still be heard,
That Word is not dead:
It rings in our heads,
And we rise from our beds
For that holy Word.

And welcome, ladies of noble birth,
Live freely here, like nowhere on earth!
Flowers of loveliness, with heaven in your faces,
Who walk like angels, the wisdom of ages
In your hearts: welcome, live here in honor,
As the lord who made this refuge wanted:
He built it for you, he gave it gold
To keep it free: Enter, be bold!

Money's a gift
To give, to lift
The souls of others:
It makes men brothers
In eternal bliss:
For money's a gift.

Chapter Fifty-five // How They Lived at Thélème

In the middle of the inner court was a magnificent fountain of beautiful
alabaster. Above it stood the three Graces, holding the symbolic horns of

abundance: water gushed from their breasts, mouths, ears, eyes, and every other body opening.

The building which rose above this fountain stood on giant pillars of translucent quartz and porphyry, joined by archways of sweeping classical proportions. And inside there were handsome galleries, long and large, decorated with paintings and hung with antlers and the horns of the unicorn, rhinoceros, hippopotamus, as well as elephant teeth and tusks and other spectacular objects.

The women's quarters ran from the tower called Artice all the way to the gates of the tower called Mesembriné. The rest was for men. Right in front of the women's quarters was a kind of playing field, an arena-like space set just between the two first towers, on the outer side. Here too were the horse-riding circle, a theater, and the swimming pools, with attached baths at three different levels, all provided with everything one could need, as well as with an endless supply of myrtle water.

Next to the river was a beautiful pleasure garden, and in the middle of it stood a handsome labyrinth. Between the other two towers were fields for playing palm ball and tennis. Alongside the tower called Cryere were the orchards, full of fruit trees of every description, carefully arranged in groups of five, staggered by rows of three. At the end was a great stretch of pastures and forest, well stocked with all kinds of wild animals.

Between the third pair of towers were the target ranges for muskets, bows, and crossbows. The offices were in a separate building, only one story high, which stood just beside the tower called Hesperia, and the stables were just beyond there. The falcon house was situated in front of the offices, staffed with thoroughly expert falconers and hawk trainers: every year supplies of every sort of bird imaginable, all perfect specimens of their breed, were sent by the Cretans, the Venetians, and the Sarmatian-Poles: eagles, great falcons, goshawks, herons and cranes and wild geese, partridge, gyrfalcons, sparrow hawks, tiny but fierce merlins, and others, so well trained and domesticated that, when they left the chateau to fly about in the fields, they would catch everything they found and bring everything to their handlers. The kennels were a bit farther away, in the direction of the woods and pastures.

All the rooms in all the suites, as well as all the smaller private rooms, were hung with a wide variety of tapestries, which were regularly changed to suit the changing seasons. The floors were covered with green cloth, the beds with embroidery. Every dressing room had a mirror of Venetian crystal, framed in fine gold, decorated around with pearls, and so exceedingly large that one could in truth see oneself in it, complete and entire. Just outside the doorways, in the ladies' quarters, were perfumers and hairdressers, who also attended to the men who visited. Every morning, too, they brought rosewater to each of the ladies' rooms, and also orange and myrtle water—and brought each lady a stick of precious incense, saturated with all manner of aromatic balms.

Chapter Fifty-six ⁄⁄ How the Men and Women Who Dwelled at Thélème Were Dressed

In the beginning, the ladies dressed themselves as they pleased. Later, of their own free will, they changed and styled themselves all as one, in the following way:

They wore scarlet or yellow stockings, bordered with pretty embroidery and fretwork, which reached exactly three fingers above the knee. Their garters were colored like their bracelets (gold, enameled with black, green, red, and white), fastened both above and below the knee. Their shoes, dancing pumps, and slippers were red or purple velvet, with edges jagged like lobsters' claws.

Over the chemise they wore a handsome corset, woven of rich silk shot through with goat hair. Over this they wore taffeta petticoats, in white, red, tan, gray, and so on, and on top of this petticoat a tunic of silver taffeta embroidered with gold thread, sewn in tight spirals—or if they were in the mood and the weather was right, their tunics might be of satin, or damask, or orange-colored velvet, or perhaps tan, green, mustard gray, blue, clear yellow, red, scarlet, white, gold, or silvered linen, with bordered spirals, or embroidery, according to what holiday was being celebrated.

Their dresses, again according to the season, were of golden linen waved with silver, or red satin decorated with gold thread, or taffeta in white, blue, black, or tan, or silk serge, or that same rich silk shot through with goat hair, or velvet slashed with silver, or silvered linen, or golden, or else velvet or satin laced with gold in a variety of patterns.

Sometimes, in the summer, they wore shorter gowns, more like cloaks, ornamented in the ways I have described, or else full-length capes in the Moorish style, of purple velvet waved with gold and embroidered with thin spirals of silver, or else with heavier gold thread, decorated at the seams with small pearls from India. They were never without beautiful feathers in their hair, colored to match the sleeves of their gowns and always spangled in gold. In the winter they wore taffeta dresses, colored as I have described, lined with lynx fur, or black skunk, or Calabrian marten, or sable, or some other precious pelt.

Their prayer beads, rings, neck chains, and collar pieces were made of fine gems—red garnets, rubies, orange-red spinels, diamonds, sapphires, emeralds, turquoises, garnets, agates, green beryls, pearls, and fat onion pearls of a rare excellence.

They covered their heads, once again, as the season demanded: in winter, in the French style, with a velvet hood hanging down in the back like a pigtail; in spring, in the Spanish style, with a lace veil; in summer, in the Italian mode, with bare ringed hair studded with jewels, except on Sundays and holidays, when they used the French fashion, which seemed to them both more appropriate and more modest.

And the men wore their fashions, too: their stockings were of light linen or serge, colored scarlet, yellow, white, or black; their breeches were velvet, in the same colors (or very nearly), embroidered and patterned however they pleased. Their jackets were of gold or silver cloth, in velvet, satin, damask, taffeta, once again in the same colors, impeccably patterned and decorated and worn. Their shoes were laced to the breeches with silken thread, colored as before, each lace closed with an enameled gold tip. Their undervests and cloaks were of golden cloth or linen, or silver cloth, or velvet embroidered however they liked. Their gowns were as costly and beautiful as the women's, with silk belts, colored to match their breeches. Each of them wore a handsome sword, with a decorated hilt, the scabbard of velvet (the color matching their stockings), its endpiece of gold and heavily worked jewelry—and their daggers were exactly the same. Their hats were of black velvet, thickly garnished with golden berries and buttons, and the feathered plumes were white, delicately spangled in gold rows and fringed with rubies, emeralds, and the like.

But there was such a close fellowship between the men and the women that they were dressed almost exactly alike, day after day. And to make sure that this happened, certain gentlemen were delegated to inform the others, each and every morning, what sort of clothing the women had chosen to wear that day—because of course the real decisions, in this matter, were made by the women.

Although they wore such well-chosen and rich clothing, don't think these women wasted a great deal of time on their gowns and cloaks and jewelry. There were wardrobe men who, each day, had everything prepared in advance, and their ladies' maids were so perfectly trained that everyone could be dressed from head to toe, and beautifully, in the twinkling of an eye. And to make sure that all of this was perpetually in good order, the wood of Thélème was surrounded by a vast block of houses, perhaps half a league long, good bright buildings well stocked and supplied, and here lived goldsmiths, jewelers, embroiderers, tailors, specialists in hammering and filamenting gold and silver, velvet makers, tapestry weavers, and upholsterers, and they all worked at their trades right there alongside Thélème, and only for the men and women who dwelled in that abbey. All their supplies, metals and minerals and cloths, came to them courtesy My Lord Shipmaster (Nausiclète, in Greek), who each year brought in seven boats from the Little Antilles, the Pearl and Cannibal islands, loaded down with gold ingots, raw silk, pearls, and all sorts of gemstones. And any of the fat pearls which began to lose their sparkle and their natural whiteness were restored by feeding them to handsome roosters (as Avicenna recommends), just as we give laxatives to hawks and falcons.

Chapter Fifty-seven ⁄⁄ How the Men and Women of Thélème Governed Their Lives

Their lives were not ordered and governed by laws and statutes and rules, but according to their own free will. They rose from their beds when it seemed to them the right time, drank, ate, worked, and slept when they felt like it. No one woke them or obliged them to drink, or to eat, or to do anything whatever. This was exactly how Gargantua had ordained it. The constitution of this abbey had only a single clause:

DO WHAT YOU WILL

—because free men and women, wellborn, well taught, finding themselves joined with other respectable people, are instinctively impelled to do virtuous things and avoid vice. They draw this instinct from nature itself, and they name it "honor." Such people, if they are subjected to vile constraints, brought down to a lower moral level, oppressed and enslaved and turned away from that noble passion toward which virtue pulls them, find themselves led by that same passion to throw off and break any such bondage, just as we always seek out forbidden things and long for whatever is denied us.

And their complete freedom set them nobly in competition, all of them seeking to do whatever they saw pleased any one among them. If he or she said, "Let's drink," everyone drank. If he or she said, "Let's play," they all played. If he or she said, "Let's go and have fun in the meadows," there they all went. If they were engaged in falconry or hunting, the women joined in, mounted on their good tame horses, light but proud, delicately sporting heavy leather gloves, a sparrow hawk perched on their wrists, or a small falcon, or a tiny but fierce merlin. (The other birds were carried by men.)

All of them had been so well educated that there wasn't one among them who could not read, write, sing, play on harmonious instruments, speak five or six languages, and write easy poetry and clear prose in any and all of them. There were never knights so courageous, so gallant, so light on their feet, and so easy on their horses, knights more vigorous, agile, or better able to handle any kind of weapon. There were never ladies so well bred, so delicate, less irritable, or better trained with their hands, sewing and doing anything that any free and worthy woman might be asked to do.

And for this reason, when the time came for anyone to leave the abbey, whether because his parents had summoned him or on any other account, he took one of the ladies with him, she having accepted him, and then they were married. And whatever devotion and friendship they had shown one another, when they lived at Thélème, they continued and even exceeded in their marriage, loving each other to the end of their days just as much as they did on the first day after their wedding.

But I must not forget to set out for you an enigmatic poem which turned up, set into the abbey's foundations on a great bronze plaque. It went as follows:

Chapter Fifty-eight   Prophetic Riddle Found on the Foundations of the Abbey at Thélème*

All you poor people, hoping for fortune to bless you,
Feel better, come here, and listen while I address you.

If we are allowed to believe, and with conviction,
That the spirit of man, resting in solid human
Bodies, can somehow teach itself to tell
The future, the things to be that have not come,
Or else if God Himself would lend us the power
To see how fate intends the future to unfold,
To see and speak it clearly and understand
How distant times unroll, and what they bring,
Then let me inform you, all who are willing to learn,
That as soon as winter comes, not a bit later
And maybe sooner, we'll find walking this earth
A certain kind and style of men, weary
Of anything restful and bored to tears with leisure,
And never bothering to hide a thing they'll go
To work provoking people high and low,
Creating bitter divisions and contrary views.
And any who want to hear them—or worse, believe them,
Indifferent to what they can do, what they can cost us—
They'll quickly find themselves in open debate

*Except for the first two lines, and a snippet at the end, this poem is not by Rabelais but by his friend Mellin de Saint-Gelais, 1487–1558, a poet known for polished verse of high fluency and no great weight. The original is in rhymed couplets: except for the first couplet, I have translated into iambic pentameter blank verse. [Translator's note]

With their closest friends, and cousins will fight with cousins,
And sons will see no harm, and nothing wrong,
In joining with those who oppose their very fathers.
And even the greatest of great, our noblest men,
Will find themselves attacked by those they rule.
Those bound by law and custom to show respect
Will lose all knowledge of order, all sense of distinctions,
For the word of the hour, spoken for all to hear,
Will be that any man can lead, and any
Follow, and this will turn the whole world quarrelsome,
Fighting and bickering, yammering this and that,
That nowhere in history, despite its incredible tales,
Will there be such stories of riots and public displays.
Then brave men will be seen on every side,
Spurred by courage and youth and passion, but far
Too trusting of their own desire: they'll die
In their prime, cut down before they ever grow old.
And no one will think of leaving what he's started,
Once his courage pushes him on, until
He quarrels and argues and finally fills the sky
With empty noise, the earth with marching feet.
Then faithless men will share authority
With men of virtue, and men all over the earth
Will follow foolish leaders and foolish ideas,
Bred by ignorance and believed by mobs of ignorant
Fools, the worst of whom will become our judges.
Oh, an arduous flood, a damning deluge!
A flood, yes, and I speak the word with reason,
For this will be a piece of work to last
Forever, and our world will never be free again
Until those waves come gushing forth, swift
And sudden, and all those locked in combat will drown
Before they know it, and rightly, for their hearts
Care only for combat and spare no one, not even
Herds of innocent oxen and sheep, offering
Their smoking bowels and bleeding flesh not
To the gods, not even in pagan sacrifice,
But simply to feed the mouths of mortal men.
Think it out for yourself: I leave it to you:
How will the world and all of us go along,
How can our spinning globe, this round machine
We ride on, find peace in the midst of so much quarrelsome
Noise! Happiest of all will be those most devoted
To this world, least willing to lose or harm it,
Trying as hard as they can to find a way

To help our earth, to hold her ruined frame
Together and hope for God's good grace for us all:
For the worst of all this sorry, sickening business
Will be that the sun, once so clear as it set
In the west, now will only shed darkness, covering
Earth more blackly than eclipses or darkest night,
Which loss will come like a blow, ending our world's
Freedom, depriving the earth of heaven's light,
Or at least leaving it empty, deserted by life.
But even before this ruinous loss the earth
Will have known, millions of years ago but still
To be seen, a violent, an incredible trembling which even
Etna could never have matched, thrown as she was
From the heights of heaven down on hundred-headed
Typhon, rebelling against Zeus—a shaking of the earth
Hardly more sudden than the tremor that shook all Ischia
When that Titan's son, mountains pressing down
Around him, in defeat and fury threw mountains in the sea.
How long will it take to reduce our earth to rubble?
Not long—and then she'll be so sadly changed
That even those who held her reins and ruled her
Will release their hold and leave her for those to follow.
And finally, then, the good, the smiling times
Will be near, and all the agony will almost be over:
For the giant floods of which I have written will split
And pull back and begin to disappear—although
Before they withdraw, before they leave, the air
Will burn with a singular flame, immense, too bright,
Too hot, for even giant waves to withstand.

All that remains, once we've survived these horrors,
Is to bring the elect, blessed of heaven, all
The joys and rewards that heaven can put in their hands:
Eternal riches. And those on whom heaven frowns
Will have nothing. Reason and justice require it: the struggle
Over, each and all receive what each
And all deserve. That was the bargain. How noble
Those who struggle and stand and stay to the end!

After reading what was inscribed on the bronze plaque, Gargantua gave a profound sigh and said to those who were watching:

"It isn't just our own times that have persecuted those who truly believe in the Gospel. The happiest men are those who can never be led astray, who always hold in their hearts the shining goal that God sets before us, in the person of His beloved Son—those who cannot be turned aside, or in any way diverted from that holy path, by merely worldly concerns."

The monk said:

"And what do you think this enigmatic poem is trying to say? What do you think it means?"

"What?" said Gargantua. "The nature of divine truth, and how to preserve it."

"By Saint Goderan!" said the monk. "That's not how I take it. It reads as though Arthur's old wizard, Merlin the Prophet, wrote every word of the thing. Stick in all the allegories and all the terribly serious intellectual stuff you like, and let all that carry you away, you and the rest of the world. Go ahead. As far as I'm concerned, all we've been reading is a description of a game of tennis, written in obscure language. Those who were supposed to be provoking people, they're the ones who choose up sides before a game, and they're usually friends. They get to serve twice, and the one who was playing leaves and the one who wasn't playing takes his place. The cord hangs right across the court, and whoever speaks up and says it went under or over, everybody takes his word for it. The waters: that's the sweat they work up. And all that about the guts of sheep and goats, why, that's the strings on the racquet. And the round machine is just the tennis ball. After you play, you take a rest, you sit in front of a good fire and you change your shirt, and you eat with a will, but just the same, the happiest are still the ones who won the game. So here's to your good health!"

Pantagruel
King of the Dipsodes
Restored to
His True Character
with All His Terrible
Deeds and Acts
of Heroism,

◈

Written by the Late

Maître Alcofribas, Extractor of the

Fifth, or Celestial, Essence

Poem Written for the Author of This Book by Maître Hugues Salel

Sometimes, for blending sweetness with use,
An author wins himself applause:
You win that praise, and deserve it, in truth.
  Understanding how well you saw
With a smile, in this little book, wise
And important matters, and made them clear
Enough for all to read, my eyes
Seem to see another seer
Laughing as he shows the facts of our lives.
Continue! And if no one praises you here,
Know that you're known in heaven, where you'll rise.

LONG LIVE ALL GOOD PANTAGRUELISTS!

THE AUTHOR'S PROLOGUE

OH WONDERFULLY FAMOUS, magnificently heroic heroes, noble gentlemen, and the rest of you, who willingly lend yourselves to all sorts of graciousness, and every kind of courtesy, you have recently read, fed, and taken to bed a book I did not write, *The Great and Absolutely Priceless Chronicles of the Great Giant Gargantua*. Like true believers, you have swallowed literally every word written there, as if it were the text of the Holy Bible, spending hours with it, in the company of worthy ladies and virtuous maidens, telling them lovely long tales drawn from its pages (when you had nothing better to tell them), for all of which you are worthy of infinite praise and to be remembered eternally in all of our prayers.

If it were up to me, I'd have everyone leave off whatever he was supposed to be doing, forgetting about his trade, his profession, letting everything else go, so he could concentrate on this book so completely that nothing could possibly distract him or keep him away, until he came to know the whole thing by heart, so that just in case by any bad luck we forgot the art of printing, or all the books in the world were destroyed, every man would be able to teach it to his children, and his heirs, and all his assigns and successors forever and forever, passing it down from hand to hand, just as if it were a secret religious cult—because there's far more to be found in these pages than a bunch of lazy braggarts, lousy with lice and scabs, could possibly imagine, since they understand even less of these bright little pleasures than Professor Raimbert Raclet knows about his legal ABC's.

I have known many powerful huntsmen, out in the field after great wild beasts, or hawking after ducks, who would be pretty unhappy if they couldn't track the animal or if their hawk began to care more about reaching the clouds than catching birds. And that's only natural. Ah, but their comfort and their refuge (it also protected them against the cold wind) was to remember the priceless, noble deeds of Gargantua.

There are others (and these aren't just fairy tales) who, racked with a horrible toothache that the doctors couldn't cure (no matter how much they were paid), have found no more sovereign remedy than to wrap this same *Chronicles of the Great Giant Gargantua* in a couple of good linen tablecloths, properly heated, and apply it to the painful spot, along with a plaster of magic-dog powder.

But what should I say about the poor pox-ridden or the gout sufferers? Oh, how many times have we seen them, just when they were nicely oiled up, shining with grease, their faces gleaming like a well-rubbed pantry lock, their teeth clattering like the keys on a church organ, or maybe a small harpsichord, when a musician is rattling along, and their throats are foaming up like a wild boar when the bloodhounds have driven him right into the trap! And what were they doing? Their only hope of happiness was to have a page or two of this same book read to them—and they'd say they would have rolled themselves into a hundred barrels, chock full of ripe old devils, if they hadn't felt real relief, hearing those pages read as they took their baths, just the way women in labor feel better when they hear *The Life of Holy Saint Margaret*.

Isn't that worth something? Just show me a book—in any language and on any subject you can think of—which can do such things, have such powers, display such virtues, and I'll fork over a good half-pint of tripes. No, my friends, no. This book we've been talking about simply has no equal, it is incomparable, utterly original. And I'll go on saying this—at least, until the heretic hunters come after me, to burn me in the fire. And those who say differently—well, clearly they're nothing but impostors, Calvinists, liars, and vile seducers.

Now, it's true that there are some high-quality books that do have certain mystical properties, like *Guzzlepot, Robert the Devil, The Giant Fierabras, Fearless William, Huon of Bordeaux, Monteville,* and *Matabrun.* But you can't really compare them to the book we've been talking about. The whole world has learned, and knows perfectly well, the wonders, the high utility of the *Chronicles of the Great Giant Gargantua*—because the booksellers sold more copies of this book in two months than the Bibles they sold in nine years.

Accordingly, I, your humble servant, wishing to do something still more pleasant and diverting for you, hereby present another book cast in the same golden mold, except that it's a little bit more rational and easier to believe. I don't want you thinking (because it would be a deliberate error) that I speak immodestly, like Jews boasting about their law. I wasn't born under the influence of any such planet, and I never tell lies or say things which aren't plain fact. I'm a real pelican, let me tell you, with my beak stuffed full of holy martyrs and martyrs for love: *Quod vidimus testamur,* We testify to what we ourselves have seen. And what I have seen are the awesome deeds, the heroic deeds, of Pantagruel, in whose employ I have been ever since I was old enough to work, and in whose service I still labor. With his permission I am right now visiting my homeland, to see if any of my relatives are still alive.

But before I end this prologue, let me hereby swear that I consign myself—body and soul, guts and bowels—to a thousand basketfuls of good devils if in this entire tale I put down a single untruthful word. And so too may Saint Anthony's fire burn you, may you twitch and roll on the ground with epileptic fits, may lightning strike you, may your legs turn lame and rotten with running sores, may your insides fairly boil with dysentery,

> May your skin shiver and crawl
> And creep like a sick cow's hide,
> May pain like liquid mercury
> Come running up your asshole,

and may you be burned in a living fire of sulfur, like Sodom and Gomorrah, dropped deep in the bottomless pit, if you don't devoutly believe everything I tell you in *this* chronicle!

Chapter One ⁄ The Origin and Antiquity of the Great Pantagruel

It won't be a waste of time, since we're in no particular hurry, if I begin by reminding you of the primal roots from which our good Pantagruel flowered. Besides, all good historians begin their chronicles that way, and not just the Arabs, the Barbarians, and the Romans, but also the noble Greeks, who really knew how to hold their liquor and drank it religiously.

It's appropriate to point out how, at the beginning of the world (I speak here of distant things, more than forty forties of nights gone by—if we count the way the old Druids used to), not long after Abel was killed by his brother, Cain, the earth soaked with that righteous blood became so prodigiously fertile in all the fruits the soil offers us (and especially the medlar apple) that everyone ever after has always called it the year of the giant medlar apples, because it took just three of them to make a bushel.

And that year they set the first day of the month according to the Greek calendar, as it was printed in all the prayer books. Lent didn't come in March, and the middle of August was in May. It was in October, I think, or maybe in September (because I don't want to make a mistake, and I'm trying very hard not to), that we had the famous week, written about in all the history books, known as the Week of Three Thursdays. There were three of them, you see, because in our irregular leap years the sun slips a little to the left (as if it were limping), and the moon wanders more than six thousand miles off course, and it's easy enough to see how all the Ptolemaic spheres get to shaking and trembling, so the star in the center of the Pleiades slides away from the other stars in that constellation and dips toward the equinox, and the star called Spica, in the Virgin's constellation, slipped down toward Libra. All of this is immensely frightening, so convoluted and difficult that even the astrologers simply couldn't deal with it: they'd have had pretty good-sized teeth, to have bitten *that* off!

You'd better believe that everyone gladly ate those apples, because they were lovely to look at and they tasted delicious. But just as Noah, that saintly man (to whom we owe so much, and are so bound, since it was he who planted for us that glorious vine from which we get that nectarous, fragrant, precious, heavenly, joyous, godlike drink we call wine), was misled when he drank, because he forgot just how powerful wine is, and what it can do, so too the men and women of that time ate that beautiful huge fruit with great pleasure.

And then all sorts of disasters began to occur. Every single one of them suffered horrible swellings all over their bodies, but in different places. Some puffed out at the belly, and their stomachs rounded out like a great cask, because of which it is written, *Ventrum omnipotentum,* O Almighty Belly—and these were all wags and punsters, from which race sprang Saint Fatbelly and Fat Tuesday, or Mardi Gras.

Others swelled along the shoulders, and got to be so humpbacked that they were called Manmountains, or Mountain Carriers, and you still see them, all over the world, male and female, noble folk and commoners. Their race gave us Aesóp, whose wonderful words and good deeds we have in writing.

Still others swelled along that part we call nature's digging tool, so that it got to be magnificently long, and large, hard, and thick all around, and proud as a peacock, the way it used to be in the old days, so men used it as a belt, tying it around their waists five or even six times. And if it was really feeling its oats and the wind was in its sails, well, you'd have to say, seeing such men, that they were carrying their spears at the ready, all of them on their way to target practice. And this race is extinct, according to the ladies, because they're always complaining that

> Those great great big ones are gone, gone, gone—

you know how the song goes.

Still others swelled up in the balls—so enormously that three filled a large barrel. From them we have the race who live in Lorraine, whose balls never stay in their codpieces but are always hanging down to the bottom of their breeches.

And others got huge in the legs and feet, so that if you saw them you'd say they were cranes or flamingos, or even men walking on stilts. And little schoolboys, studying grammar and versification, called them Metermen.

Still others grew such immense noses that they looked like the long beak of a flask, but speckled, as sprinkled with pimples as the sky is filled with stars, swelling up everywhere, purple and blotched, flecked all over with eruptions, decorated with red—and you've seen them, if you've ever seen Canon Fatgut or Doctor Woodfoot of Angiers. Not many of this race were crazy about barley water or tea: they were all of them lovers and guzzlers of wine. Publius Ovidius Naso, better known these days as Ovid, came from this race—of whom we write, *Ne reminiscaris,* Don't remember my sins, though what we really mean is, Forget about my no's.

Others grew big ears, so big you could make a jacket out of just one of them, plus a pair of breeches and even a scarf to tie around your head, and a Spanish cape from the other one. It's said that this race still exists, in Bourbonnais somewhere, which is why we talk about Bourbon ears.

Others grew immense bodies. From them, finally, came the race of giants, from whom, ultimately, Pantagruel was born:

And the first of the giants was Chalbroth,
Who begat Sarabroth,
Who begat Faribroth,
Who begat Hurtaly, who loved bread soaked in soup: he reigned at
    the time of the Flood,
Who begat Nimrod,
Who begat Atlas, whose shoulders kept the world from falling,
Who begat Goliath,
Who begat Eryx, the Sicilian giant who invented the shill game:
    which shell has a nut in it?
Who begat Titus,
Who begat Eryon,
Who begat Polyphemus,
Who begat Caccus,
Who begat Etion, the first man to catch the pox because he didn't
    drink enough cool, fresh wine in the summertime (which is
    attested by Bartachim, the great Italian jurist),
Who begat Enceladus,
Who begat Ceus,
Who begat Typhus,
Who begat Alus,
Who begat Otho,
Who begat Aegeon,
Who begat Briarus, who had a hundred hands,
Who begat Porphyrion,
Who begat Adamastor,
Who begat Antaeus,
Who begat Agatho,
Who begat Porus, against whom Alexander the Great did battle,
Who begat Aranthas,

Who begat Gabbara, who was the first ever to drink a toast,

Who begat Goliath of Secundille,

Who begat Offot, who had a magnificent nose for drinking straight out of the barrel,

Who begat Artacheus,

Who begat Oromedon,

Who begat Gemmagog, who invented those horrible pointed shoes they still wear in Poland,

Who begat Sisyphus,

Who begat the Titans, who fathered Hercules,

Who begat Enac, who was a true professional at digging mites and other small insects out of the meat of your hands,

Who begat Firebras, who was defeated by Olivier, peer of France and Roland's faithful companion,

Who begat Morgan, the first in the world ever to play dice while wearing spectacles,

Who begat Fracassus, who was written about by Merlin Coccaius (who was really Teofilo Folengo),

Who begat Ferragus, the Saracen giant,

Who begat Happemouche, who was the first to smoke beef tongues in the fireplace, since before his time everyone just salted them, the way they do hams,

Who begat Bolivorax,

Who begat Longass,

Who begat Gayoff, whose balls were poplar wood and whose prick was carved from a rowan tree,

Who begat Machefain,

Who begat Bruslefer,

Who begat Engolevent,

Who begat Galahad, who invented bottle stoppers,

Who begat Mirelangault,

Who begat Galaffre,

Who begat Falourdin,

Who begat Roboaster,

Who begat Sortibrant of Coimbra,

Who begat Brushant de Mommiere,

Who begat Bruyer, who was defeated by Ogier the Dane, a peer of France,

Who begat Mabrun,

Who begat Foutasnon,

Who begat Hackleback,

Who begat Vitdegrain,

Who begat Grandgousier,

Who begat Gargantua,

Who begat the noble Pantagruel, my lord and master.

Now, I perfectly understand that, reading this passage, you begin to experience completely reasonable doubts and ask how this could all be, since back in the days of the Flood everyone on earth perished, except Noah and the seven people who were with him in the ark—which number does not include the aforesaid Hurtaly.

It's a very fair question, to be sure, and pretty obvious, too. But my answer will make you happy, unless my brains are leaking out. And because I wasn't there myself, and I can't tell you all about it as I'd like to, I'll have to rely on the ancient Hebraic commentators, good old cocks and handsome Jewish bagpipers, who affirm that in fact our friend Hurtaly was definitely not in Noah's ark; also that he couldn't have gotten in, because he was too big; but he did ride up on the roof, one leg on this side, one leg on the other, the way little children ride on wooden horses, or the way the great bull bugler of Berne, who was killed at the battle of Marignan, rode along on a fat mortar cannon—surely a steed that keeps up a smart, jolly pace, and doesn't get tired, either. And that was how Hurtaly, thank God, saved old Noah's ark from going right to the bottom, because he kicked it along with his legs, turning it whichever way he wanted with his feet, which he used exactly as you might use a boat's rudder. The people inside sent up all the food he needed, passing it through a smokestack: they could see what a splendid job he was doing. And sometimes they'd exchange a word or two with him, as the philosopher Ikaromenippus chatted with Jupiter, as he looked up through the trapdoors that conduct men's prayers to the gods.

Have you understood everything, and clearly? Then take a good swig, and don't put any water in it. On the other hand, if you don't believe me—well I don't, she said, she said.

Chapter Two ⁄⁄ The Birth of the Very Formidable Pantagruel

When he was four hundred and ninety-four, plus four more, Gargantua begat his son Pantagruel on his wife, the daughter of the king of the Amaurotes, in Utopia. Her name was Bigmouth, or Babedec, as we say in the provinces, and she died giving birth to the baby: he was so immensely big, and weighed so incredibly much, that it was impossible for him to see the light without snuffing out his mother.

Now, to truly understand how he got his name, which was bestowed on him at the baptismal font, you must be aware that in the year of his birth there had been such a fearful drought, all across the continent of Africa, that it had not rained for more than thirty-six months, three weeks, four days, thirteen hours, and a little bit over, and the sun had been so hot, and so fierce, that the whole earth had dried up. It wasn't any hotter even in the days of the prophet Elijah than in that year, for not a tree on earth had a leaf or a bud. Grass never turned green, rivers dried up, fountains went dry; the poor fish, deprived of their proper element, flopped about on the ground, crying horribly; since there was no dew to make the air dense enough, the birds could not fly; dead animals lay all over the fields and meadows, their mouths gaping wide—wolves, foxes, stags, wild boars, fallow does, hares, rabbits, weasels, martens, badgers, and many, many others. And it was no better for human beings, whose lives became pitiful things. You could see them with their tongues hanging out, like hares that have been running for six solid hours. Some of them threw themselves down into wells; others crawled into a cow's belly, to stay in the shade (Homer calls them *Alibantes,* desiccated people). Everything everywhere stood still, like a ship at anchor. It was painful to see how hard men worked to protect themselves from this ghastly change in nature: it wasn't easy to keep even the holy water in churches from being used up, though the pope and the College of Cardinals expressly ordered that no one should dare to dip from these blessed basins more than once. All the same, when a priest entered his church you'd see dozens and dozens of these poor parched people come crowding around behind him, and if he blessed anyone the mouths would all gape open to snatch up every single drop, letting nothing fall wasted to the ground—just like the tormented rich man in Luke, who begged for the relief of cool water. Oh, the fortunate ones, in that burning year, whose vaults were cool and well stocked!

The Philosopher tells us, asking why seawater is salty, that once, when Phoebus Apollo let his son Phaeton drive his gleaming chariot, the boy had no idea how to manage it, nor any notion how to follow the sun's proper orbit from tropic to tropic, and drove off the right road and came so close to the earth that he dried up all the countries over which he passed, and burned a great swath through heaven, called by the philosophers *Via Lactea,* the Milky Way, but known to drunkards and lazy louts as Saint John's Road. But the fancy-pants poets say it's really where Juno's milk fell, when she suckled Hercules. Then the earth got so hot that it developed an enormous sweat, which proceeded to sweat away the entire ocean, which thus became salty, because sweat is always salty. And you can see for yourself that this is perfectly true, because all you have to do is taste it—or the sweat of pox-ridden people when they're put in steam baths and work up a great sweat. Try whichever you like: it doesn't matter to me.

It was almost exactly like that, in this year of which I write. One Friday, when everyone was saying prayers and making a beautiful procession, and litanies were being said, and psalms chanted, and they were begging omnipotent God to look mercifully down on them in their desolation, they could suddenly see great drops of water coming out of the earth, exactly as if someone were sweating profusely. And the poor people began to rejoice, as if this were something truly useful, some of them saying that since there wasn't a drop of liquid in the air from which one could have expected rain, the very ground itself was making up for what they lacked. Others, more scholarly, said that this was rain from the opposite side of the earth, as Seneca explains in the fourth book of *Questionum naturalium*, in which he speaks of the source and origin of the river Nile. But they were deceived: once the procession was over, and they went back to collect this precious dew and drink down a full glass, they found that it was just pickle brine, even worse to drink, and even saltier, than seawater.

And it was precisely because Pantagruel was born that very day that his father named him as he did: *Panta* in Greek means "all," and *Gruel* in Arabic means "thirsty," thus indicating that at the hour of his birth the whole world was thirsty—and he saw, prophetically, that someday his son would be lord of the thirsty, for this was shown to him at that same time and by a sign even more obvious. For when the child's mother was in labor, and all the midwives were waiting to receive him, the first thing that came out of her womb was sixty-eight mule drivers, each one leading a pack mule loaded with salt by its halter, after which came nine one-humped camels loaded with hams and smoked beef tongue, and then seven two-humped camels loaded with pickled eels, followed by twenty-five carts all loaded with onions, garlic, leeks, and spring onions. The midwives were frightened out of their wits. But some of them said to the others:

"Here's God's plenty. It signifies that we shouldn't either hold back, when we drink, or, on the other hand, pour it down the way the Swiss do. It's a good sign: these are truly wining signs."

And while they were gabbling and cackling about such trivialities, out popped Pantagruel, as hairy as a bear, at which one of them pronounced prophetically:

"He's been born all covered with fur, so he'll do wonderful things, and if he lives he'll live to an immense age."

Chapter Three // Gargantua's Sorrow at the Death of His Wife

And when Pantagruel was born, who was flabbergasted and utterly perplexed? Gargantua, his father, that's who. On the one hand, seeing that his wife was dead, and on the other that his son Pantagruel was born, so exceedingly handsome and so large and strong, he knew neither what to say nor what to do. What particularly troubled him was to understand whether he ought to weep with sorrow for his wife or laugh for joy because of his son. He rehearsed logical arguments from one side and then from the other, but all they did was stifle him, for he argued as the academics do, by rule and rote. And that could not resolve anything. So he remained confused and entangled, like a trapped mouse or a bird caught in a noose.

"Shall I weep?" he said. "Yes, but why? My lovely wife is dead, who was the best this, and the best that, in all the world. I'll never see her again, nor will I ever find another like her: what a boundless, endless loss! O my God, what have I done to be thus punished? Why didn't you send death to me rather than to her? To live without her will be nothing but pining away. Ah, Badebec, my darling, my love, my sweet little cunt (though it was a good three acres and more across), my tender sweetheart, my codpiece, my comfortable old shoe, my slipper—I'll never see you again! Oh, poor Pantagruel, you've lost your lovely mother, your sweet suckler, your well-beloved lady! Ah, you traitorous death, how maliciously you treat me, how you've attacked and injured me, to deprive me of her for whom immortality was her just due!"

And saying all this, he cried like a cow. And then all of a sudden he laughed like a calf, thinking of Pantagruel.

"Oh ho, my little son," he said, "oh, bully balls, my tootsy-wootsy, how pretty you are, and how grateful to God I am for having given me such a handsome son, so laughing and happy and pretty! Oh—oh—oh, how good it makes me feel! Drink up, drink up! Away with all sadness! Pages: bring in the best wine, rinse out the glasses, set out the tablecloth, get rid of the dogs, start the fire burning good and hot, light candles, close that door over there, slice up bread and soak it in soup, send for the poor and let them have anything they want! Take away this cloak, so I can get down to my underjacket and really entertain my friends."

But as he said this, he heard the litanies and the prayers of the priests who were bearing his wife to her grave, at which he abandoned everything he had started and was swept away in the exact opposite direction:

"O my Lord: must I be forever sad? That makes me unhappy. I'm no longer young, and I'll grow older. It's a dangerous season: I could catch a fever: I stand here, stricken. By my faith as a gentleman, it would be better to weep less and drink more. My wife is dead—but by God!—*Da jurandi,* forgive me for swearing: my tears won't bring her back to life. She's not suffering, she's in paradise—at least—if there isn't someplace better. She's praying for us, she's very happy, she isn't worried any more about all our miseries and our disasters. We all face the same fate: may God keep those who still remain! I have to start thinking about finding myself another woman.

"But what on earth are you doing?" he said to the midwives—wise women all (where? where? my friends, *I* can't see any!). "Go see her buried, all of you, and I'll stay here and cradle my son. I feel as if I've been turned inside out; I think I'm in serious danger of falling ill. But have a good stiff drink first, it will make you feel better, believe me, on my honor."

They did as he asked, and went to the burial and the funeral, and poor Gargantua stayed at home. The inscription he had carved on his wife's tombstone went as follows:

> She died, my lofty wife,
> In childbirth: I like the child.
> Her face was like a fiddle;
> She was thin, but fat in the middle.
> Pray that God is gracious
> And forgives anything halacious
> She did, for she was good.
> Here is her body, in a wooden
> Box. She lies inside,
> And lived till the day she died.

Chapter Four ⁄ Pantagruel's Childhood

According to the ancient historians and poets, lots of people have come into this world in exceedingly strange ways—too many of them, and tales much too long-winded, to repeat here. Go and read chapter seven of Pliny's *Natural History, De prodigiosis partubus,* "All about Prodigious Births," if you happen to have the time. But nothing you read will tell you about anyone as marvelous as Pantagruel, because it's hard to believe how quickly he grew and became strong. What Hercules did was nothing, killing two serpents in his cradle, because in fact those were really pretty small serpents, and not very powerful. But when he was still in his cradle, Pantagruel performed truly incredible feats.

I won't bother to tell you how at each of his meals he drank the milk of four thousand six hundred cows, and how, to make him a saucepan for boiling that milk, they called up all the pot makers of Saumer, in Anjou, and Villedieu, in Normandy, and Bramont, in Lorraine, and how they poured that boiled milk into a huge wooden trough (which still exists, in Bourges, near the palace)—and his teeth were already so big and so strong that he broke a big chunk right out of that trough, as you can see for yourself if you go take a look.

One day, toward morning, when they wanted him to suckle from one of those cows (because they were the only wet nurses he had, the histories tell us), he got one of his arms out of the straps that kept him in his cradle, and got a good grip on the cow, just under the knees, and ate both her udders and half her stomach, and her liver and kidneys, and would have eaten all the rest of her if she hadn't bellowed and roared, and they thought wolves had gotten at her, and they all came rushing up and pulled her away from Pantagruel. But they didn't manage it very well and the knee joint was still in his grip, and he chewed on it nicely, as you might bite on a fresh sausage. And when they wanted him to let go of the bone, he bolted it right down, like a seagull with a little fish, after which he began to cry out, "Good! good! good!"—because he still couldn't talk well and wanted them to understand that he'd thoroughly enjoyed his snack and they should certainly let him have more. Seeing this, his servants tied him with the biggest ropes they could find, like those made at the port of Tain for the voyage to Lyons, with cargoes of salt, or as they certainly used for that huge ship the *Grande-Française,* tied up at the port of Havre-de-Grâce, in Normandy.

His father kept a great bear, and once it escaped and approached the baby to lick his face (because his lazy nursemaids had barely wiped his lips). Pantagruel pulled off those ropes as easily as Samson got out of the Philistines', and picked up My Lord Bear and popped him in in one bite, crunching him up like a chicken, and making a fine hot mouthful of him.

Gargantua was worried that the child might really hurt himself, so he had them make four huge chains to bind him with and had flying buttresses built for his cradle, solidly mounted and braced. One of those chains can be seen at La Rochelle, where at night they stretch it between the two great harbor towers; there's another at Lyons, another at Angiers— and the fourth was carried off by devils, to tie up Lucifer himself, who had gotten loose just then because he was horribly tormented by colic, because he'd eaten a bailiff's soul, fricasseed, for breakfast. Trust what Nicholas of Lyra says about that passage in Psalms which reads, *Et Og regem Bashan,* "And Og, king of Basan." Og, still a small child, was so strong and lusty that they had to tie him up in his cradle with chains. And this kept Pantagruel peaceful and quiet, because he couldn't easily break those chains, especially because there wasn't room enough in his cradle for him to really get his arms into action.

But here's what happened, one day, when his father, Gargantua, gave a handsome banquet for the princes of his court. All the officers of that court, naturally, were too much occupied with preparations for the feast to worry about poor Pantagruel, who was therefore left *à l'écart, reculorum,* to fend for himself. What did he do?

What did he *do,* my good friends? Listen.

First he tried to break his cradle chains, but could not, because they were too strong. So he kicked and kicked until he beat in the side of his cradle, though it had been fashioned of a great square beam ten yards thick, and once he could get his feet out he climbed down as best he could, so that his feet touched the ground. And then, using his immense strength, he pushed himself up, carrying the cradle tied to his back, like a tortoise climbing a wall and looking for all the world like a five-hundred-ton Genoan barque sailing head-on to the wind. Which was how he made his entrance into the banquet room, so boldly that the guests were terrified. Since his arms were still chained, he couldn't take any food, but with great difficulty he managed to bend enough so he could lap up a few mouthfuls. Seeing all of which, his father immediately realized that he'd been left without anything to eat and ordered the chains taken off, as he was advised to do by the assembled council of princes and lords, not to mention the fact that Gargantua's doctors informed him that keeping the child tied up in his cradle would leave him, for the rest of his life, vulnerable to serious disorders of the bladder.

When the chains were off, they sat him down and he dined exceedingly well. And with one angry blow of his fist he smashed that cradle into five hundred thousand pieces, or maybe more, vowing never ever to be put back into it.

Chapter Five // What the Noble Pantagruel Did as a Young Boy

So Pantagruel grew from day to day: it was easy enough to see how much he was learning, and natural affection made his father take great delight in the boy's progress. Since he was still only a child, Gargantua had a crossbow made for him, so he could shoot at baby birds, which bow is today known as the great siege engine of Chantelle. And then the boy was sent to school, to acquire knowledge as he went through his formative years.

Accordingly, he was sent to the university at Poitiers, where he indeed learned a great deal. Seeing that some of the students, when they had free time, had no idea what to do with it, he took pity on them and, one day, pulled a rock out of a huge crag called Passelourdin—a rock measuring roughly twenty-four yards around and just under four yards thick—and without any difficulty set it up on four columns, in the middle of a field. And then those students, when they had nothing else to do, could climb up and indulge themselves in as much wine and ham and pâté as they wanted, and cut their names in the rock with knives. And today they call it the Raised Stone. In memory of Pantagruel, no one is allowed to matriculate at the University of Poitiers unless he has drunk from the Caballine Fountain, at Croutelle, and then traveled to Passelourdin and climbed the Raised Stone.

Later, when he read the fine histories of his ancestors, he learned that Geoffrey of Lusignan, called Geoffrey Longtooth, his stepmother's daughter-in-law's uncle's son-in-law's aunt's older sister's cousin-in-law's grandfather, was buried at the Benedictine abbey of Maillezais. So he took a day of academic leave to pay his respects, as a good man ought to. Leaving Poitiers, he and some of his friends went through Legugé, visiting the noble abbot Ardillon, and Lusignan, Sanxay, Celles-sur-Belle, Coulonges-sur-l'Autize, Fontenay-le-Comte, there greeting the learned Doctor Tiraqueau, and finally arriving at Maillezais, where they visited the tomb of Geoffrey Longtooth. It was a bit frightening, because the tomb portrait showed him angrily drawing his saber. So he asked why his ancestor was depicted in this fashion, and the religious custodians of the place told him it was simply as Horace said, *Pictoribus atque poetis,* etc., Painters, like poets, can do as they like. But he didn't much like their answer, and said:

"He wouldn't have been painted like this for no reason, and I suspect that his death was brought about by foul play, which he wants his kinsmen to avenge. I will have to look into this more deeply and do whatever seems right."

Instead of returning to Poitiers, he decided to make a tour of other French universities. So going on to Rochelle, he took a boat to Bordeaux, where he found nothing much going on, except that the stevedores were playing Spanish rummy on the beach.

Then he came to Toulouse, where he learned how to dance beautifully, and how to fence with a two-handed sword, as all the students at that university do. But he didn't stay there long when he saw them burning their professors alive, like smoked red herring. And he said:

"May it please God never to let me die like that, because I was born more than dry enough: I don't need to be heated up any more!"

Then he went to Montpellier, where he found magnificent Mirevaux wine and good fellowship. He thought of studying medicine, but decided it was simply too boring, and saddening, and doctors reeked of enemas, like old devils.

So he decided to study law. But seeing that the only law teachers they had were three rogues and a nobody, he left. The highroad to the Roman bridge at Gard and the amphitheater at Nîmes (which seems as if it had been built by gods rather than by humans) took him less less than three hours, and brought him to Avignon, and before he'd been there three days he was in love—because it's papal territory and the women screw around with great gusto.

And seeing all this, his tutor, whose name was Epistemon (meaning "learned," in Greek), took him away to the University of Valence, in Dauphiné, but not much was going on there, and the town toughs beat up the students, which made him angry. One lovely Sunday, when there was a public dance, those toughs wouldn't let one of the students join in, so Pantagruel drove them all right down to the banks of the Rhône and felt like drowning the lot of them. But they burrowed into the ground like moles, hiding a good mile and a half under the river. You can still see the holes they dug.

Then they left, and with three steps and a hop they got to Angiers, which they liked very much, and they would have stayed a while, but the plague drove them off.

So they went to Bourges, where he studied long and profitably in the faculty of law. And sometimes he said that lawbooks seemed to him like a gorgeous golden gown, triumphant, precious, wonderful, but trimmed with shit:

"Because," he said, "no books in the world are so lovely, so beautifully decorated, and so elegant as the texts of the Roman *Pandects*. But their embroidery, and specifically the commentary of François Accurse, is so filthy, so vile and stinking, that it's simply worthless muck."

Leaving Bourges, they came to Orléans, which was full of student bumpkins who were exceedingly happy to see him, and quickly taught him to become an expert at tennis, because these were students who believed in physical activity. And sometimes, too, they took him to the islands in the middle of the Loire, for a game of bowling—or balling. But as for cracking his head with studying—well, he didn't, out of concern for his eyesight. Besides, one of his teachers used to say, in his lectures, that nothing was as bad for the eyes as eye disease. One day, when one of the students he knew was taking his law degree, a fellow who didn't know any more than the others but, to compensate for his ignorance, was a magnificent dancer and played a splendid game of tennis, Pantagruel composed a little poem, a kind of motto for the graduates of that university, which went as follows:

> Tennis balls in your codpiece,
> Racket in your hand,
> Diploma as a mouthpiece:
> You dance so grandly
> You'll win the land.

Chapter Six // How Pantagruel Met a Man from Limousin Who Spoke Fractured French

One day, I'm not exactly sure just when, Pantagruel and his companions went for a walk after supper, taking the gate through which you pass on the way to Paris. There he met a well-dressed student coming along that road, and after they'd exchanged greetings Pantagruel asked him:

"My friend, where are you coming from, at this hour?"

The student answered him:

"From the spirit-evocative, grandiosely illustrious, manifoldly celebrated academy which one vociferates as Lutetia."

"What did he just say?" Pantagruel asked one of his companions.

"From Paris," he answered.

"Ah, so you come from Paris," Pantagruel continued. "And what do you do all day, you and all the other gentlemanly students in Paris?"

The student answered:

"We transmigrate the Seineian flow, both matutinally and nocturnally. We perambulate the transecting metropolitan arteries and assorted urban intersectional quadrant points. We converse continuously in Latinate verbalizations, and like veritable connoisseurs of aspects amatory we endeavor to captivatingly incur the benevolence of the universally magistrate, multiplicitously engendered, and ultimately endogenous feminine sex. At suitably appropriate intervals we ensure that we incarnate ourselves in certain well-defined habitations and, in an utterly ecstatic venereal transport, we inculcate our virile members into the most interiorly located recesses of the pudenda of these meretricious but supremely amiable personages. Then we engage in gustatorial ingestion at the meritorious quaffing establishments of the Pine Cone, the Castle, the Magdalen, and the Mule, imbibing inter alia appropriately elongated comestibles, liberally perforated with quantities of aromatic herbal concoction. On occasion, the hazards of aleatoric existence being what they are, and our pecuniary chambers being entirely evacuated of their contents, inclusive of all assorted metallic substances of recognized potency in such affairs, we obligatorily terminate our parsimony through the vendation of our printed textual sources, and equally of the habilitating furnishings of our persons, pending to be sure the anticipated arrival of alleviating remunerations from the trusted ancient source of original domestic succor."

To which Pantagruel said:

"What the devil kind of language is all this? By God, you must be some kind of heretic."

"Your Lordliness, no," said the student, "for most willingly, from the instant that nocturnal crepuscularity commences to be withdrawn, I ambulate to one or another of those beautifully architecturated ecclesiastical structures, where I proceed to aspergate myself with blessed lustration, and briefly articulate fragments of some worshipful sacrificial evocation, and I murmurate my personal precations exactly as the astronomically determined divisions dictate: I lave and obviate my personal spiritual essence from all nocturnal contaminations. Those who habituate those astronomical regions are the sources of my intense adoration. The omnipotent regent of those astral realms, in particular, is the object of my interminable veneration. I practice reciprocal amicability with those in my proximity, I adhere to the proscriptions incorporated in the decalogue, and insofar as my minuscule capabilities permit I do not deviate therefrom even a single ungulate width. Veritably, however, since it is circumstantially accurate to observe that Mammon does not overgenerously endow me, I am but infrequently constituted and enabled to in my turn endow those who implore donations at the portals."

"Oh, shit, shit!" said Pantagruel. "What is this idiot talking about? I suspect he's weaving some diabolical language, trying to enchant us with an evil spell."

To which one of his companions said:

"My lord, it seems clear that this gallant gentleman wants to imitate the language of Paris, but all he's doing is butchering Latin. He thinks that, like Pindar, he expresses himself in the loftiest of sentiments. He seems to see himself as a splendid orator, making eloquent use of French, since he's so contemptuous of ordinary ways of speech."

To which Pantagruel said:

"Is this true?"

The student replied:

"My noble lord, my native genius is scarcely apt to the expressions employed by this shameless nebulosity, who asserts that I excoriate the epidermis of our vulgar Gallic tongue. I operate viceversusly: all my attentiveness, all my sail matter and oarings work for the enricherment of that vulgar speech by a splendid redundancy of Latinate word wrappings."

"By God," said Pantagruel, "I'll teach you how to speak! But first tell me: where do you come from?"

To which the student answered:

"The primal origin of my domestic hearth and fire may be locatable in the Limousinish region, where requiescats in noble pace the sainted corpse of venerable Saint Martial."

"Ha: I understand perfectly," said Pantagruel. "You're a Limousin through and through, and here you are pretending to be a Parisian. Come here and I'll whip that out of you!"

And he grabbed him by the neck, saying:

"You rip up Latin. By Saint John, I'll rip it all right out of your throat— I'll rip you right apart."

Then the poor Limousin began to cry:

"Hey, boss, hey there! O Saint Martial save me! Hey, let me go, in the name of God, and stay away from me, you hear?"

To which Pantagruel said:

"Now he talks like a human being."

And he let him go, since the poor Limousin had shat in his pants, which were cut swallowtail style rather than full across. Panagruel observed:

"By Saint Alipentin! what a stinking skunk! The devil with this turnip-eater. Lord, how he smells!"

So he released him. But the student was so conscience smitten that the whole rest of his life was changed around, as he often said, when Pantagruel grabbed him by the neck. Some years later, he died the death of

Roland, that is, of thirst, which was clearly an act of divine vengeance, thus proving to us what Aulus Gellius makes his philosopher say, in *Attic Nights:* rare and unusual words should be carefully shunned, exactly as navigators steer their ships away from rocks in the sea.

Chapter Seven ⁄⁄ How Pantagruel Came to Paris, and the Lovely Library of Saint Victor

When Pantagruel had completed a vigorous course of study at Orléans, he decided to visit the great University of Paris. But before leaving he heard that at Saint-Aignan, just to the southeast of the town, there was an immense bell that had fallen to the ground more than two hundred and fourteen years earlier. It was so huge that no device known could so much as budge it, although they had tried all the methods set out by Vitruvius, in *De architectura,* Albertus' *De re edificatoria* (or The Art of Building), Euclid, Theon, Archimedes, and Hero of Alexandria's *De ingeniis* (On Machinery), all of which were worthless. Gladly heeding the citizens and other inhabitants of the town, who humbly requested that he repair the situation, Pantagruel decided to put the bell where it was meant to go.

So he went to where it was lying on the ground and, with just his little finger, lifted it as easily as if it had been a sleigh bell or one of those little bells you tie to a hawk's leg. But before putting it back in its tower, Pantagruel felt like serenading the city, carrying the bell through the streets in his hand and ringing it everywhere, which made everyone exceedingly happy—until they became aware of a serious inconvenience, namely, that carrying it everywhere and ringing it as he had, Pantagruel had made all the fine wine in Orléans turn to vinegar. They had no idea until the next night, when they felt so incredibly thirsty after drinking such spoiled wine that all they could do was spit as white as Maltese cotton, saying, "We've been Pantagruelized: our throats have been well salted."

And when this was done, he and his people went to Paris. As he entered the city, they all poured out of their houses to see him—since, as you surely know, Parisians are natural fools, inside out and outside in. They stared at him in great astonishment, and not a little fear, concerned that he might just pick up the municipal courthouse and carry it *a remotis,* to some far-off country, just as his father, Gargantua, had taken the bells of Notre Dame, in order to tie them around his mule's neck.

After he'd been there for some time, studying long and hard at the seven liberal arts, he said that Paris was a good city to live in but a bad place to die, because the beggars and bums who hung around the cemetery at Saint Innocent warmed their asses by burning dead men's bones. But he thought the library at Saint Victor's abbey was magnificent, especially for certain books he found there, a catalogue of which follows: *et primo,* to begin with:

Bigua salutis, Riding High on Salvation
Bragueta juris, The Law's Codpiece
Pantofla decretorum, Soft Slippers and Hard Decrees
Malogranatum vitiorum, How to Blow Up Vice
Theology's Tennis Ball
The Preacher's Featherduster, written by a bum
Heroes' Elephant Balls
Bishops' Antidotes for Aphrodisiacs
Marmotretus, De Baboinis et cingis, cum commento Dorbellis, Apehead, On Baboons and Monkeys, with commentary by our Franciscan friend Des Orbeaux
Decretum universitatis Parisiensis super gorgiasitate muliercularum ad placitum, University of Paris Rule about Well-Dressed Whores
How a Vision of Saint Gertrude Appeared to a Nun, at Poissy, When She Went into Labor
Ars honeste petandi in societate, per M. Ortuinum, The Proper Method for Farting in Company, by Maître Hardouin de Graetz
The Musty Mustard-Pot of Penitence
Garters, or Patience's Knee-Boots
Formicarium artium, Art's Anthill (translated from the German)
De brodiorum usu et honestate chopinandi, per Silvestrem Prieratem, Jacospinum, How to Use Soups, and The Respectability of Boozing, by Silvester of Priero, Jacobin friar
Cheated Husbands in Court
The Notary's Basket
Marriage Tied Around with a String
The Crucible of Contemplation
Fairy Tales of the Law
How Wine Spurs You On
And Cheese, Too
Decrotatorium scholarium, On Scholarly Filth
Tartaretus, De modo cacandi, Pierre Tartaret (professor of theology), *How to Shit*
Roman Fanfares
Guillaume Bricot, another professor of theology, *De differentiis soupparum,* The Differences between and among Soups
How to Get to the Bottom, in Discipline
Humility's Worn-out Shoe
The Tripe-Pod of Noble Thought
Magnanimity's Stewpot
What Bothers Priests about Holy Confession
How Priests Say No

Reverendi Patris Fratris Lubini, Provincialis Bavardie, De croquendis lar-donibus, libri tres, Father Brother Bother Lubin of Tonguetown, *How to Bolt Down Bacon* (in three volumes)

Pasquilli, Doctoris marmorei, De capreolis cum chardoneta comedendis, tempore Papali ab Ecclesia interdicto, Pasquin, Broken-Statue Doctor of Lampoonery, *How to Eat Goats with Artichokes, Even When the Church Forbids It*

Faking the Holy Cross, for six characters, acted by assorted subtle priests

Blinders for the Road to Rome

Majoris, *De modo faciendi boudinos,* How to Make Blood Puddings and Sausages

The Bishops' Bagpipes

Beda, *De optimitate triparum,* Aristocrats of the Belly

Lawyers' Complaints about the Abolition of Bribes

Magistrates in Cat Fur

Peas in Lard, *cum commento,* with commentary

Making Money on Indulgences

Praeclarissimi juris utriusque Doctoris Maistre Pilloti Raquedenari, De bob-elinandis glosse Accursiane baguenaudis repetitio enucidiluculidissima, The famous doctor of this law and the other law, Maître Pillot Penny-Squeezer, *On the Stupidity of Trying to Patch Up Accursius' Windy Commentaries*

Stratagemata Francharchieri de Bagnolet, Wheeling and Dealing according to the Militiaman de Bagnolet

Franctopinus, De re militari, cum figuris Tevoti, Military Maneuvers, with drawings by Tevot

De usu et utilitate escorchandi equos et equas, authore M. nostro de Quebecu, How to Skin Horses and Mules Profitably, written by Our Maître Quebecu

On the Clownishness of Country Priests

M. n. Rostocostojambedanesse, *De moustarda post prandium servienda lib. quatuordecim, apostilati per M. Vaurillonis,* Serving Mustard after a Meal, the 14th book, marginal (and other foot-) notes by the theologian Maître Vaurillon

Ball-biting Promoters

Quaestio subtilissima, utrum Chimera in vacuo bombinans possit comedere secundus intentiones, et fuit debatuta per decem hebdomadas in concilio Constantiensi, The infinitely subtle problem of the Imaginary Object vibrating out in empty space: can it or can it not feed off secondary intentions?—a subject closely debated for ten weeks at the Council of Constance

The Hungry Jaws of Lawyers

Barbouilamenta Scoti, Duns Scotus' Scribblings

Batwing Hats for Cardinals

De calcaribus removendis decades undecim, per M. Albericum de Rosata, The Use, Misuse, and Nonuse of Spurs: Eleven Poems by Maître Aubry de Rosata, legal commentator

Ejusdem, De castrametandis crinibus lib. tres, from the same author, How to Ornament Your Hair, three volumes

Antonio de Leva's Landing in Brazil

Marforii bacalarii cubantis Rome, De pelendis mascarendisque cardinalium mulis, The statue of Marforius, a fading old Roman bachelor, *How to Beat the Shit out of a Cardinal's Mules*

An apology, written to protest against those who claim that the pope's mule eats only when he feels like it

Prognostication *que incipit Silvia Triquebille balata per M. n. Songecruyson,* Prediction and prophecy, beginning "By Silvus Trickballs": staged by our Maître Songecruyson, better known as Master of Useless Dreams

Boudarini episcopi, De emulgentiarum profectibus enneades novem, cum privilegio papeli ad triennium, et posteanon, Bishop Boudarin, Nine Novenas on how much you can make from milking everyone in sight, with a special papal printing authorization for three years but not a day longer

How Virgins Shit

Widows' Bald Asses

Monks' Cowls

Stupid Noises by Celestine Monks

The Cost of Letting Monks Beg

Thieves' Dens

Theologians' Rat Traps

Advanced Asslicking, for Graduate Students

Ockham's Close-Shaven Clerks

Magistri n. Fripesaulcetis, De grabellationibus horarum canonicarum lib. quadraginta, Our learned Maître Lickitup, *Scientific Analysis of the Canonical Hours,* in forty volumes

Cullebutatorium confratiarum, incerto authore, Religious Brotherhoods and How They Stand on Their Heads, author unknown

The Guzzlers' Den

The Sweat Stink of Spaniards, all cock-and-bulled-up by Brother Inigo de Loyola

Worm Powder for the Poor

Poiltronismus rerum Italicarum, authore magistro Brulefer, The Laziness of Italians, by Maître Etienne Brulefer

R. Lullius, better known as Ramon Lull, *De batisfolagiis principium,* How Princes Waste Time

Callibistratorium caffardie, actore M. Jacobo Hostratem hereticometra, The Humbug's Sexuality, as measured by Maître Jacob Hochstraten, grand inquisitor and calculator of heretics

Chaultcouillon, or Hotballs, *De magistro nostrandorum magistro nostra-*
   torumque beuvetis lib. octo galantissimi, Favorite Drinking Places of
   Our Would-be Theologians and Those Already Enrolled in the
   Professional Ranks, in eight jolly volumes
Regis, compiler, The Incessant Fartings of Ecclesiastical Scrive-
   ners—scribes, copyists, abbreviators, court clerks, and calendar
   fixers
Perpetual Almanac for Those Afflicted with Gout or the Pox
Maneries ramonandi fournellos, per M. Eccium, How to Clean Stoves, by
   Maître Jean Eck
Commercial Rope Tricks
Pleasures of the Monastic Life
Bigots' Stew
The History of Elves, Brownies, and Hobgoblins
Old Soldiers and Other Bums
Official Swindlers
Misers' Mountains
Badinatorium Sophistarum, Philosophers' Bad Jokes
Antipericatamentanaparbeugedamphibricationes, or Discussions on
   All Manner of Subjects, by Shit Monks
Poetasters' Bellybuttons
Alchemists' Windpipes
How Grabby Beggars Grab, a collection made by Brother Cutyour-
   wallet
The Chains of Religion
Bell Ringers' Ballgames
How to Keep It Up Till You're Ninety
How to Make a Nobleman Shut Up
Why Monkeys Smack Their Lips When They Pray
Piety's Handcuffs
A Pot for All Seasons
Political Glue
Why Hermits Have Pendulous Beards
How Priests Cover Themselves
How Fast Friars Fool Around
Lourdadus, *De vita et honestate braguardorum,* Dumbbell, *On the Lives*
   and Integrity of Fops
Lyripipi Sorbonici Moralisationes, per M. Lupoldum, Sermons on Schol-
   ars' Hats, by Maître Lupoldus
Travelers' Trinkets
Dribbling Tipplings by Useless Bishops
Tarraballationes Doctorum Coloniensium adversus Reuchlin, Noises
   Nosed at the Great Reuchlin by the Scholarly Nitwits of Cologne
Ladies' Finger Bells
Rear-Flapping Trousers for Shitheads

Virevoustatorium nacquettorum, per F. Pedebilletis, Ballboys' Games, by
   Brother Pinhead
Boots for the Stouthearted
Tricks by Trixies and Elves
Gerson, *De auferibilitate pape ab ecclesia,* How the Church Might
   Depose a Pope
Catalogue of Academic Candidates
Jo. Dytebrodii, *De terribiliditate excommunicationum libellus acephalos,*
   Jean Ditebrodius, Brainless Book on the Utter Awfulness of
   Excommunication
Ingeniositas invocandi diabolos et diabolas, per M. Guingolfum, How to
   Call Up Male Devils, and Also Female Devils, by Maître Guingol-
   fus
Begging Monks' Stew
Folk Dances for Heretics
Cardinal Cajetan's Whinnyings
*Moillegroin doctoris cherubici, De origine patepelutarum et torticollorum riti-
   bus lib. septem,* Wetnose, cherubic doctor, *On the Origin of Liars and
   Hypocrites,* in seven volumes
Sixty-nine handsome, heavy, greasy, and well-thumbed prayer books
The five mendicant orders' "Hail Mush-Belly"
Heretics' Hides, pulled out of that musky container which is incorn-
   fistibulated in Thomas Aquinas' massive writings
Forcible Removal in Matters Requiring a Conscience
Judges' Bulging Bellies
Abbots' Donkey-Size Pricks
*Sutoris, adversus quemdam qui vocaverat eum fripponatorem, et quod frip-
   ponatores non sunt damnati ab Ecclesia,* The monk and theologian
   Pierre Couturier, Against Someone Who Called Him a Rascal, and
   Also Proving That the Church Does Not Condemn Rascals
Cacatorium medicorum, Medical Dung Drops
Astrology's Chimney Sweep
Campi clysteriorum, per S.C., Symphorien Champier, physician,
   Proper Use of Suppositories
The Pharmacist's Fart Sucker
Surgery's Kiss-My-Ass
Justinianus, *De cagotis tollendis,* Wiping Out Sanctimonious Hypo-
   crites
Antidotarium animae, Soul-Healing Medicinals: A Catalogue Merlinus
   Coccaius (Th. Folengo), *De patria diabolorum,* The Devils' Home-
   land

Some of these volumes have already been printed. The rest are currently being printed in the noble city of Tübingen, which is full of good
books.

Chapter Eight // How Pantagruel, at Paris, Received a Letter from His Father, Gargantua, with a Copy of That Letter

Pantagruel studied hard, of course, and learned a great deal, because his brain was twice normal size and his memory was as capacious as a dozen kegs of olive oil. While he was thus occupied in Paris, one day he received a letter from his father, which read as follows:

"My very dear son,

"Among the gifts, the graces and the prerogatives with which from the very beginning our sovereign Creator and God has blessed and endowed human nature, that which seems to me uniquely wonderful is the power to acquire a kind of immortality while still in this our mortal state—that is, while passing through this transitory life a man may perpetuate both his name and his race, and this we accomplish through the legitimate issue of holy wedlock. And by that means we partially reestablish that which we lost through the sin of our first parents, Adam and Eve, to whom it was declared that, because they had not obeyed the commands of God their Creator, they would know death and in dying would utterly destroy the magnificent form in which mankind had been shaped.

"But this seminal propagation permits what the parents lose to live on in their children, and what dies in the children to live on in the grandchildren, and so it will continue until the hour of the Last Judgment, when Jesus Christ will return to the hands of God the Father His purified and peaceful kingdom, now utterly beyond any possibility or danger of being soiled by sin. And then all the generations and all the corruptions will come to an end, and all the elements will be taken from their endless cycle of transformations, for the peace so devoutly desired will be achieved, and will be perfect, and all things will be brought to their fit and proper ending.

"So I have very fair and just cause to be thankful to God, my preserver, for having permitted me to see my hoary old age blossoming once again in your youth. Whenever, at His pleasure, He who rules and governs all things, my soul leaves this human dwelling place, I will not consider myself entirely dead, but simply transported from one place to another, for in you, and by you, my visible image lives on in this world, wholly alive, able to see and speak to all honorable men, and all my friends, just as I myself was able to do. I confess that my life on this earth, though I have had divine help and divine grace to show me the way, has not been sinless (for indeed we are all sinners and continually beg God to wash away our sins), and yet it has been beyond reproach.

"Just as the image of my flesh lives on in you, so too shine on the ways of my soul, or else no one would think you the true keeper and treasure of our immortal name, and I would take little pleasure in seeing that, because in that case the least part of me, my body, would live on, and the best part, my soul, in which our name lives and is blessed among men, would be decayed and debased. Nor do I say this because I have any doubt about your virtue, which I have long since tested and approved, but simply to encourage you to proceed from good to still better. And the reason I write to you now is not so much to ensure that you follow the pathways of virtue, but rather that you rejoice in thus living and having lived, and find new joys and fresh courage for the future.

"To consummate and perfect that task, it should be enough for you to remember that I have held back nothing, but have given help and assistance as if I had no other treasure in the world but to someday see you, while I still lived, accomplished and established in virtue, integrity, and wisdom, perfected in all noble and honorable learning, and to be able to thus leave you, after my death, as a mirror representing me, your father—perhaps in actual practice not so perfect an image as I might have wished, but certainly exactly that in both intention and desire.

"But though my late father of worthy memory, Grandgousier, devoted all his energy to those things of which I might take the fullest advantage, and from which I might acquire the most sensible knowledge, and though my own effort matched his—or even surpassed it—still, as you know very well, it was neither so fit nor so right a time for learning as exists today, nor was there an abundance of such teachers as you have had. It was still a murky, dark time, oppressed by the misery, unhappiness, and disasters of the Goths, who destroyed all worthwhile literature of every sort. But divine goodness has let me live to see light and dignity returned to humanistic studies, and to see such an improvement, indeed, that it would be hard for me to qualify for the very first class of little schoolboys—I who, in my prime, had the reputation (and not in error) of the most learned man of my day. Nor do I say this as an empty boast, though indeed I could honorably do so in writing to you—for which you have the authority of Cicero in his book *On Old Age,* and also the judgment of Plutarch, in his book *How a Man May Praise Himself without Fear of Reproach.* No, I say these things to make you wish to surpass me.

"For now all courses of study have been restored, and the acquisition of languages has become supremely honorable: Greek, without which it is shameful for any man to be called a scholar; Hebrew; Chaldean; Latin. And in my time we have learned how to produce wonderfully elegant and accurate printed books, just as, on the other hand, we have also learned (by diabolic suggestion) how to make cannon and other such fearful weapons. The world is full of scholars, of learned teachers, of well-stocked libraries, so that in my opinion study has never been easier, not in Plato's time, or Cicero's, or Papinian's. From this day forward no one will dare to appear anywhere, or in any company, who has not been well and properly taught in the wisdom of Minerva. Thieves and highwaymen, hangmen and executioners, common foot soldiers, grooms and stableboys, are now more learned than the scholars and preachers of my day. What should I say? Even women and girls have come to aspire to this marvelous, this heavenly manna of solid learning. Old as I am, I have felt obliged to learn Greek, though I had not despised it, as Cato did: I simply had no leisure for it, when I was young. And how exceedingly glad I am, as I await the hour when it may please God, my Creator, to call me to leave this earth, to read Plutarch's *Morals,* Plato's beautiful *Dialogues,* Pausanias' *Monuments,* and Athenaeus' *Antiquities.*

"Which is why, my son, I strongly advise you not to waste your youth, but to make full use of it for the acquisition of knowledge and virtue. You are in Paris, you have your tutor, Epistemon: you can learn from them, by listening and speaking, by all the noble examples held up in front of your eyes.

"It is my clear desire that you learn languages perfectly, first Greek, as Quintilian decreed, and then Latin. And after that Hebrew, for the Holy Bible, and similarly Chaldean and Arabic. I wish you to form your literary style both on the Greek, following Plato, and on the Latin, following Cicero. Let there be nothing in all of history that is not clear and vivid in your mind, a task in which geographical texts will be of much assistance.

"I gave you some awareness of the liberal arts—geometry, arithmetic, and music—when you were still a child of five and six. Follow them further, and learn all the rules of astronomy. Ignore astrology and its prophecies, and all the hunt for the philosopher's stone which occupied Ramon Lull—leave all those errors and vanities alone.

"As for the civil law, I wish you to know by heart all the worthy texts: deal with them and philosophy side by side.

"I wish you to carefully devote yourself to the natural world. Let there be no sea, river, or brook whose fish you do not know. Nothing should be unknown to you—all the birds of the air, each and every tree and bush and shrub in the forests, every plant that grows from the earth, all the metals hidden deep in the abyss, all the gems of the Orient and the Middle East—nothing.

"Then carefully reread all the books of the Greek physicians, and the Arabs and Romans, without turning your back on the talmudic scholars or those who have written on the Cabala. Make free use of anatomical dissection and acquire a perfect knowledge of that other world which is man himself. Spend several hours each day considering the holy Gospels, first the New Testament and the Apostles' letters, in Greek, and then the Old Testament, in Hebrew.

"In short, plumb all knowledge to the very depths, because when you are a grown man you will be obliged to leave the peace and tranquillity of learning, and acquire the arts of chivalry and warfare, in order to defend my house and lands and come to the aid of our friends if in any way they are attacked by evildoers.

"And soon I shall ask you to demonstrate just how much you have learned, which you can do in no better way than by publicly defending, in front of the entire world and against all who may come to question you, a thesis of your own devising. And continue, as you have been doing, to frequent the company of those leaned men who are so numerous in Paris.

"But since, as the wise Solomon says, wisdom can find no way into a malicious heart, and knowledge without self-awareness is nothing but the soul's ruin, you should serve, and love, and fear God. Put all your thought in Him, and all your hopes, and by faith which has been shaped by love unite yourself with Him so firmly that sin will never separate you away. Be ever watchful of the world's wicked ways. Never put your heart in vanity, for ours is a transitory existence and the Word of God lives forever. Help your neighbors and love them as you love yourself. Honor your teachers. Avoid the company of those you do not desire to imitate; do not take in vain the blessings God has given you. And when, finally, you know that you have learned all that Paris can teach you, return to me, so that I may look on you and, before I die, give you my blessing.

"My son, may the peace and grace of our Lord be with you. *Amen.*

"Written from Utopia, this seventeenth day of the month of March.

Your father,
GARGANTUA"

After receiving and reading this letter, Pantagruel was filled with new zeal, positively on fire to learn more than ever before—so much so that, had you seen him at his studies, and observed how much he learned, you would have declared that he was to his books like a fire in dry grass, burning with such an intense and consuming flame.

Chapter Nine // How Pantagruel Found Panurge ("He Who Is Good at Everything") and Loved Him All the Rest of His Life

One day, as Pantagruel was walking outside the city, headed for the Cistercian abbey of Saint-Anthony, chatting and debating with the members of his household and a number of other students, he met a tall, elegantly handsome man, but pitifully wounded all over his body, and in such a state of disarray that he seemed to have just escaped from a pack of furious dogs—or, better still, he looked like the proverbial raggle-taggle apple picker from Perche.

Seeing him in the distance, Pantagruel said to his companions:

"See that man coming along the Charenton Bridge road? By my faith, it's only fortune that's made him poor, because I swear that nature made him in some rich and noble mold, and the bad luck that often befalls people with curious minds has reduced him to such beggary."

And as soon as he'd come right up to them, Pantagruel asked him:

"My friend, let me ask you, please, to stop a moment and answer a few questions. You won't regret it, I assure you, for I feel a great urge to help you in any way I can, seeing the disaster you have plainly experienced. I feel an immense pity for you. So tell me, my friend: Who are you? Where do you come from? Where are you going? What are you hunting? And what is your name?"

The man answered him in German:

"Junker, Gott geb euch Glück unnd Hail. Zuvor, lieber Junker, ick las euch wissen, das da ihr mich von fragt, ist ein arm unnd erbarmglich Ding, unnd wer vil darvon zu sagen, welches euch verdruslich zu hoeren, unnd mir zu erzelen wer, wie vol die Poeten unnd Orators vorzeiten haben gesagt in iren Sprüchen und Sententzen, das die Gedechtnus des Ellends unnd Armuot vorlangst erlitten ist ain grosser Lust."

("My lord, may God grant you happiness and prosperity. My dear sir, I must tell you that what you ask of me is a sad and pitiful thing, and that what must be said, on that subject, would be full of matters it would tire you to hear, and weary me to relate. On the other hand, as the ancient poets and rhetoricians have declared in their maxims and other words of wisdom, the memory of pain and poverty is a great joy.")

To which Pantagruel answered:

"My friend, I don't understand a word of that gibberish. If you want to be understood, please speak in some other tongue."

So the man answered him:

"Al barildim gotfano dech min brin alabo dordin falbroth ringuam albaras. Nin porth zadikim almucathin milko prim al elmin enthoth dal heben ensouim: kuth

im al dim alkatim nim broth dechoth porth min michas im endoth, pruch dal
marsouim hol moth dansrikim lupaldas im voldemoth. Nin hur diavolth mnar-
bothim dal gousch pal frapin duch im scoth pruch galeth dal chinon, min foulthrich
*al conin butbathen doth dal prim."**

"Do you understand any of that?" Pantagruel asked his companions.

To which Epistemon answered:

"It might be the language of Upside-down Land. The devil himself
would break his teeth on it."

So Pantagruel said:

"Friend, I don't know if the walls understand you, but we don't, not
a word."

And so the man said:

"Signor mio, voi vedete per exemplo che la cornamusa non suona mai s'ela
non a il ventre pieno. Cosi io parimente non vi saprei contare le mie fortune, se
prima il tribulato ventre non a la solita refectione. Al quale è adviso che le mani
et li denti abbui perso il loro ordine naturale et del tutto annichillati."

(In Italian: "My lord, you know from experience that a bagpipe can't
make a sound unless its belly is full. And so too with me: I wouldn't
know how to tell you what has happened to me unless my unhappy belly
first got what it's used to. My stomach feels as if my hands and my teeth
have lost their natural abilities—been quite annihilated.")

To which Epistemon answered:

"It's six of one and half a dozen of the other."

And Panurge said:

"Lard, ghest tholb be sua virtiuss be intelligence ass yi body schall biss be
naturall relvtht, tholb suld of me pety have, for nature hass ulss egually maide:
bot fortune sum exaltit hess, an oyis deprevit. Non ye less viois mon virtius
deprevit and virtiuss men discrivis, for, anen ye lad end, iss non gud."

(In Scots: "My lord, if you are as noteworthy for intelligence as you
are, in your own person, elevated in form, you ought to have pity on
me, because nature has indeed made us equal, but chance raises some and
lowers others. Nonetheless, virtue is often looked down on and virtuous
men despised, since after all it's true that, before the final end, no one is
truly good.")

"Still less," answered Pantagruel.

So Panurge said:

"Jona andie, guaussa goussyetan behar da er remedio beharde versela ysser lan
da. Anbates oyto y es nausu eyn essassu gour ray proposian ordine den. Nonys-
sena bayta fascheria egabe, genherassy badia sadassu noura assia. Aran hondovan
gualde cydassu nay dassuna. Estou oussyc eguinan soury hin, er darstura eguy
harm, Genicoa plasar vadu."

(In Basque: "Great lord, there is a remedy for every evil. What's really
hard is to do the right thing. I've already asked you, over and over! Let

---

*Spoken in an imaginary language, meaning nothing.

us have things settled. We'll get to that, and in pleasant style, if you'll let me satisfy my hunger. After that, ask me whatever you like. And it wouldn't be a bad idea to fork up enough for two, may God be willing.")

"Are you there?" answered Epistemon. "Hey, Genicoa!"

And Carpalim (meaning in Greek, "Quickman") said:

"By Saint Trinian, you're Scots, or I haven't understood a word!"

And Panurge answered:

"Prug frest strinst sorgdmand strochdt drhds pag brledand Gravot Chavigny Pomardière rusth pkallhdracg Devinière pres Nays. Bcuille Kalmuch monach drupp delmeupplistrincq dlrnd dodelb up drent loch minc stzrinquald de vins ders Cordelis hur jocststzampenards."*

To which Epistemon said:

"Are you speaking some Christian tongue, my friend, or jabbering the way they do in Maître Patelin's farce? Ah, no: it must be the language of Lanternland."

And Panurge said:

"Heere, ie en spreke anders gheen taele, dan kersten taele; my dunct nochtans, al en seg ie u niet een woordt mynen nood verklaart ghenonch wat ie beglere; gheest my uyt bermherticheyt yet waer ie ghevoed magh zung."

(In Dutch: "I speak none but Christian tongues. However, it seems to me that, without my saying a single word, the rags I'm wearing would show you well enough what I wish. Be sufficiently charitable, please, to give me that which will nourish and restore me.")

To which Pantagruel answered:

"And that's more of the same."

And Panurge said:

"Seignor, de tanto hablar yo soy cansado. Por que suplico a Vuestra Reverencia que mire a los preceptos evangelicos, para que ellos movent Vuestra Reverencia a lo que es de consciencia; y si ellos non bastarent para mover Vuestra Revenerencia a piedad, yo supplico que mire a la pieded natural, la qual yo creo que le movra como es de razon, y con esto non digo mas."

(In Spanish: "My lord, I grow tired of too much talking. Which is why I beg Your Reverence to consider the Bible's precepts, so they may move Your Reverence to act according to the dictates of conscience; and if those precepts are not enough to move Your Reverence to pity, I beg you to consider natural piety, which I believe will move you, as it is right it should. And having said that, I have nothing else to say.")

To which Pantagruel answered:

"Certainly, my friend, I haven't the slightest doubt that you can talk all sorts of languages. But tell us, please, in some language we can understand, what it is you want."

And Panurge said:

"Myn Herre, endog, jeg med inghen tunge ta lede, lygeson boeen, ocq uskuulig

---

*Another imaginary language, sprinkled with occasional French words and place-names.

creatner! Myne Kleebon och my ne legoms magerhed udviser alligue klalig huuad tyng meg meest behoff girered somder sandeligh mad och drycke: hvuarpor forbarme teg omsyder offuermeg; oc befarlat gyffuc meg noguethi: aff hvylket ieg kand styre myne groeendes magher lygeruff son man Cerbero en soppe forsetthr. Soa shal tuloeffue lenge och lycksaligth."

(In Danish: "Sir, even were this a situation where, like children or animals, I spoke no language at all, my clothes and the bony, half-starved nature of my body should clearly show you what I need: that is, to eat and drink: so have pity on me and give me that which will subdue my howling stomach, just as one puts a sop in front of Cerberus. And may you live long and happily.")

"I believe," said Eusthenes (meaning in Greek, "Strongman"), "that the Goths talked like this. And if God wanted us to talk through our assholes, we'd talk that way, too."

So Panurge said:

"Adoni, scholom lecha: im ischar harob hal habdeca, bemeherah thithen li kikar lehem, chancatbub: Laab al Adonia chonenral."

(In Hebrew: "Lord, greetings to you: if you care to help your servant, give me, right away, a bit of bread: as it is written, he who has pity on a poor man says a prayer to God.")

To which Epistemon answered:

"Now I've understood him, because this time he spoke in Hebrew, most eloquently pronounced."

And Panurge said:

"Despota tinyn panagathe, diati sy mi uc artodotis? horas gar limo analiscomenon eme athlios. Ce en to metaxy eme uc eleis udamos, zetis de par emu ha u chre, ce homos philologi pantes homologusi tote logus te kerhemata peritta hyparchin, opote pragma afto pasi delon esti. Entha gar anankei monon logi isin, hina pragmata (hon peri amphisbetumen) me phosphorus epiphenete."

(In classical Greek: "Dear master, why, why don't you give me some bread? You see me virtually dying of hunger, and you have no pity for me, none at all, and you ask me improper questions. Yet all those who love learning agree that words are superfluous when the facts are obvious to everyone. Words are necessary only when the things we discuss don't clearly reveal themselves.")

"What!" said Carpalim, Pantagruel's servant. "That's Greek, I understood that. How come? Have you lived in Greece?"

And Panurge said:

"Agonou dont oussys vou denaguez algarou, nou den farou zamist vou mariston ulbrou, fousquez vou brol tam bredaguez-moupreton den goul houst, daguez daguez nou croupys fost bardou noflist nou grou. Agou paston tol nalprissys hourtou los echatonousm prou dhouquys brol panygou den bascrou no dous cagnous goukfren goul oust troppasou."*

---

* Yet another imaginary language, with a few real words to season the mixture.

"I understand that," said Pantagruel. "Or at least I seem to, because it's the language we speak in Utopia—or at least it sounds a lot like it."

And then, as Pantagruel was about to go on, Panurge said:

"Jam toties vos, per scara, perque deos deasque omnis obtestatus sum, ut, si qua vos pietas permovet, egestatem meam solaremini, nec hilum proficio clamans et ejulans. Sinite, queso, sinite, viri impii, Quo me fata vocant *abire, nec ultra vanis vestris interpellationibus obtundatis, memores veteris illius adagii, quo venter famelicus auriculis carere dicitur."*

(In Latin: "I have already conjured you, and several times, by the holiest of objects, by the gods and by the goddesses themselves, that if any pity stirs in you, you might relieve my poverty, but my cries and lamentations have been useless. Give it up, I beg you—give it up, O hard-hearted men, and let me go wherever my destiny calls me. Nor weary me any more with your empty interpolations, but remind yourselves of the old adage that a famished belly has no ears.")

"Truly, my friend," said Pantagruel, "don't you know how to speak French?"

"Very well indeed, my lord," answered Panurge, "and God be thanked for it. French is my native tongue, and my mother tongue, for I was born and nourished in the very garden of France: that is, in Touraine."

"And so," said Pantagruel, "tell me your name and where you're going, because—by my faith!—I've taken such a liking to you that, if you're willing, I'll never let you leave my company, and you and I will make a new pair of friends to rival Aeneas and Achates."

"My lord," was the answer, "my true and proper baptismal name is Panurge, and I have just come from Turkey, where I was taken prisoner when, in an evil hour for us, we tried to take Mytilene. And I'll gladly tell you everything that's happened to me, which is more marvelous than the adventures of Ulysses. But since it pleases you to keep me with you (and I cheerfully accept your offer, and declare I will never leave you but follow you, if you like, straight to the devil), there will be more convenient times, and more leisure, to tell you everything, because right now I have a singularly urgent need to eat. My teeth are sharp, my belly is empty, my throat is dry, my appetite is eating me alive: everything's ready. If you'd like to see me get to work, it will please you to watch me put it away. By God, just give the order."

Then Pantagruel commanded that Panurge be led to his lodgings and that food be brought to him at once. This was done, and that night Panurge ate very well indeed, and then fell asleep like a chicken, and slept until it was dinner time the next day, so that all it took him to get from his bed to the table was three steps and a jump.

Chapter Ten ⁄ How Pantagruel Makes an Equitable Judgment in a Matter Quite Incredibly Obscure and Difficult, and Does It So Well That Everyone Admires His Conclusions

Remembering well the words of his father's letter, Pantagruel one day decided it was time to test his knowledge. So he had his arguments posted on every street corner all over the city, in the number of nine thousand seven hundred and sixty-four, arguments dealing with all manner of subjects and raising the very strongest uncertainties that could be formulated about all the various branches of knowledge.

And first, on Straw Street (right in front of the Faculty of Arts), he attacked all the professors, and the students, and the rhetoricians, and upended every one of them. Then he proceeded to the Faculty of Theology and over the course of six weeks attacked all the theologians, starting at four o'clock in the morning and going until six at night, except that he took two hours to dine and to refresh himself.

Most of the city's men of law were present: the high judges, presidents of councils, counselors, treasury officers, secretaries, lawyers, and others, as well as the municipal counselors, and also the physicians and the masters of canon law. And mind you, most of them threw themselves into the discussion as vigorously as they knew how, but for all their quibbling and lying little tricks Pantagruel checkmated them, showing them up like a pack of puppies in petticoats.

His incredible learning became a sensation: everyone was talking about him, even old ladies and laundrywomen, brokers and roast-beef merchants, pocketknife peddlers, and others, who would cry out as he passed through the streets, "It's him!" All of which pleased him, as it did Demosthenes, prince of Greek orators, when an old hag, pointing at him, cried, "That's the man."

Now, just at that time there was a lawsuit pending between two great lords, the plaintiff being Sir Kissmyass, the defendant Sir Fartsniffer. Their dispute involved a point of law so abstract and difficult that the high court of appeals understood it about as well as it understood Old High German. Accordingly, by royal command, four of the largest and most learned bodies in France were convened, being the Great Council and all the senior professors from the best universities—and not just from France but from England and Italy, too, including Mainus Jason, of Padua, Philippe Dece of Pisa, Peter Pickleater, and a whole host of other gray-headed men of ancient wisdom. For forty-six weeks they sat in council without being able to get their teeth into it or even clearly formulate the problem so that the law could begin to dispose of it, which made them so wildly angry that they beshat themselves for sheer embarrassment.

But one day, when they were all wracking their brains, the humanist scholar Briand Vallée, lord of du Douhet, who was the most learned, skillful, and sensible of them all, rose and said:

"Gentlemen—how long have we been here, now, without having accomplished anything but wasting time? Not only have we been unable to get to the bottom of this matter, we have been unable even to find its banks, and the more we contemplate it the less we understand. We are put sadly to shame; this has become a great burden on our consciences. It seems to me we can only rise from these deliberations in dishonor, because all our debate is pure drivel. So here is what I suggest. You have heard much talk of that great and noble person Maître Pantagruel, who has acquired the highest of scholarly reputations, disputing publicly against the entire world. I believe we should call him in and confer about this matter, for if he can't get to the bottom of this, then no one can."

To which the entire learned assemblage cheerfully agreed.

So they promptly sent for him and begged him to consider the matter in the most careful detail, and provide them with a report that made legal sense of it. They gave him all the bundles and bags of documents they had in their hands, which it took four fat donkeys to carry. But Pantagruel said to them:

"Gentlemen, are the two litigants to this dispute still alive?"

To which they answered that, yes, they were.

"Then why the devil," said he, "bother ourselves with this rubbish heap of papers and copies of papers? Isn't it better to hear from their own living voices what they're quarreling about, rather than to read about it in all this monkey business, which is simply tricks and legalistic devices designed to evade and subvert, not to carry out the rules and principles of law? I am convinced that you, and all those who have had a hand in judging this case, have supplied every scrap you could for this side or that. Even if this had been an obvious matter, simple to judge, by now you've got it totally obscured with stupid irrationalities, and ridiculous opinions, from Accurse, Peter Baldus, Bartolus of Bologna, Paul de Castro from Naples, Alexander de Imola (also of Bologna: I think bologna is a speciality in such matters as these), Hippolytus of Ferrara (also known as Riminaldus), Panormitanus (whose real name, as you know, was Nicolas Tedesco), Bertachin de Fermo, Alexander Tartagno, Curtius (who was so well employed in Montferrat), and all those other old bulldogs who never understood a word of what Justinian wrote—fat dumb calves, all of them, ignorant of everything needed to truly understand the law.

"It's completely clear that none of these men knew any more Greek than they did Latin, but only Gothic and Barbarian. Yet our law begins in Greece, as Ulpian tells us in his *Liber de origine juris,* On the Origin of Law, and all our laws are full of words and phrases in Greek, and furthermore have been drafted in the most elegant and elaborate Latin to be found anywhere, exceeding even that of Sallust, Varro, Cicero, Seneca, Livy, or Quintilian. How then can these old fuzzy-brains understand the very text of the laws, since they've never so much as seen a good Latin book, as their own style shows perfectly well, for they write like chimney sweeps or cooks and scullions, not like legal thinkers?

"And more: since laws have their origin and context in moral and natural philosophy, how can these idiots possibly understand—for, by God, they have studied less philosophy than the mule I ride on. And as for knowledge of humane letters, and of history and all other ancient matters, they know about as much as a frog with feathers. And yet all such learning is essential for understanding law, and without it there can be no understanding at all, as I propose to demonstrate in a book, someday, at considerably greater length.

"And thus, if you wish me to take charge of this lawsuit, the first thing to do is burn all these papers, and then have the two parties brought before me. And once I have heard them, I will give you my opinion, without any more legal fictions or pretenses."

There were those who objected to this solution, for as you know in every assemblage there are more fools than wise men, and the loudest voices always overrule the best ones, as Livy says, speaking of the Carthaginians. But the lord of du Douhet fought them tooth and nail, insisting that Pantagruel had spoken well, and that all their records and receipts, their depositions, rejoinders, disclaimers, motions and countermotions, and all their other deviltries, were nothing but subversions of law which prolonged the lawsuit. The devil himself would carry off those who refused to proceed down a better path, one that made use of biblical and philosophical justice.

In the end, all the papers were burned, and the two gentlemen brought forward in person. And then Pantagruel said to them:

"Are you the two men who have this huge quarrel?"

"Yes, sir," they said.

"Which of you is the plaintiff?"

"Me," said the lord Kissmyass.

"Now, my friend, give me a true, point-by-point account of the whole affair. And by the body of God, if you tell me one single lie, I'll cut the head off your shoulders and show you that in legal matters the truth, and nothing but the truth, must be told. So be careful neither to add to nor detract from the facts of your case. Speak."

Chapter Eleven ⁄⁄ How My Lords Kissmyass and Fartsniffer Testified, without Their Lawyers

Then Kissmyass began as follows:

"Sir, it's true that an old lady from my house went to market with some eggs . . ."

"I'm not the king. Put your hat back on, Kissmyass," said Pantagruel.

"Many thanks, sir," said My Lord Kissmyass. "But, back to the subject: there came between the two tropics, six pennies toward the zenith but diametrically opposite to the Great Cave Dwellers, since of course in that particular year the Riphée Mountains had experienced a great sterility of practical jokers, caused by a mutiny of Blabbermouths breaking out between the Babblers and the Windmill Spinners, on account of the Swiss rebellion, who had assembled, just as numerous as bumblebees, in order to go to the celebration of the year's first hole, when they bring soup to the oxen and the key to the coal cellar goes to the girls so they can give the dogs their oats.

"Well, all they did the whole night long was keep their hands on the pot, getting the bulls to hurry off, on foot and on horseback, to keep the boats from sailing, because there were some stolen goods and the tailors wanted to make them into a blowpipe that would cover the whole ocean, which right then was pregnant with a stewpot of cabbage (according to the hay balers). But the doctors said there was no obvious sign in her urine of hawk's tracks, eating double-bladed axes with mustard, unless to be sure the gentlemen of this honorable court issue a B-flat command to the pox, ordering it not to scrounge around after silkworm cocoons, since the bums had already begun to dance around the tuning fork, one foot in the fire and their heads right in the middle, as that great old bum Ragot used to say.

"Oh ho, gentlemen! God arranges everything as He wants it, and a carter flicked his whip against changeable Fortune, and broke it. This was coming back from the battle of Bicoque, which we lost, and Maître Antitus Watercress was granted his graduate degree—in the highest mistakenness, as the canonical lawyers say: *Beati lourdes, quoniam ipsi trebuchaverunt,* Blessed be the stupid, who work hard at it.

"But the reason Lent is so expensive, by Saint Fiacre of Brie, is simply because

We celebrate Pentecost
And it costs and costs,

But hey ho and a big fat grin:
A little rain beats the strongest wind.

I suppose the sergeant put the blank so high up on the target for me only
so the clerk of the court wouldn't go licking all around his fingers (which
have feathers exactly like a gander's), and we can see perfectly clearly that
everyone goes pulling their own nose, unless they've managed to see
themselves in a duly ocular perspective, in the direction of the chimney,
right where the sign's hanging that shows a wine barrel with forty hoops,
which are all necessary for twenty bottoms with a five-year waiting period.
At least, who wouldn't let birds come before cheesecakes in order to
uncover them, since things so often get forgotten when stockings are put
on inside out? Ah, ah, may God protect Thibault Mitaine!"
     At which Pantagruel said:
     "Easy, my friend, easy, speak slowly and don't get angry. I understand
the case: go on, please."
     "Now, sir," said Kissmyass, "that old woman I mentioned, saying her
Gaudes, Rejoice, Rejoice, and her *Audi nos,* Oh, Hear Us, was unable to
protect herself against a swordsman's feint by invoking the privileges of
the university, except by a thorough bath in holy water, covering it with
a seven of diamonds and then giving him a good swift thrust right near
the place where they sell the old rags that the Dutch painters use when
they really want to take a bite out of the moon, and I am truly astonished
that no one lays eggs when we're all so good at hatching them."
     At this point My Lord Fartsniffer wished to interrupt and say some-
thing, but Pantagruel said to him:
     "Hey, by Saint Anthony's belly, are you supposed to speak before I
tell you to? Here I am, struggling as hard as I can to understand just what
your quarrel is, and you're going to bother me? Be quiet, in the devil's
name, be quiet! You'll get to put in your penny's worth when this fellow
here is done. Now go on," he said to Kissmyass, "and don't rush yourself."
     "And in view of the fact," said Kissmyass, "that when our royal lord,
Charles the Second, issued the Pragmatic Sanction of Bourges, limiting
the pope's authority, no mention was made of these matters, and furthermore that the pope himself has given each of us the liberty to fart as we
please, provided we don't mess our pants, no matter how poor the world
might be (provided that no one crosses himself in any sort of ribald way),
accordingly the rainbow, which had been newly sharpened in Milan so it
could hatch out skylarks, agreed that the old woman should serve those
who suffer from sciatica in a soup bowl, according to the protest of the
little fat-balled fish who were by that point indispensable in figuring out
how to make old boots.
     "However, John the Calf, her first cousin, knocked around by a burn-

ing log, advised her under no circumstances to take the risk of continuing on with the bubbling lye unless she first mixed some good astringent alum in with the paper, two, four, shut the door, because

> *Non de ponte vadit,*
> *qui cum sapientia cadit.*
>
> From bridges no one can fall
> Who thinks even a little at all.

—especially since the gentlemen of the treasury couldn't agree on the number of German flutes, otherwise known as recorders, from which they created *Royal Eyeglasses,* Jean Meschinot's new book, just printed in Antwerp.

"Now there, gentlemen, is what makes for a badly drawn document, and I think the other party gets what credence it has from this: after all, *in sacer verbo dotis,* we have a priest's word for it. Because wishing to comply with the king's express wish, I armored myself from head to toe in good solid boot-sole leather, right over my belly, so I could go see how my grape pickers had trimmed down their towering hairdos, in order to play better on *their* flutes, since it wasn't the right season for the fair and might even be a bit dangerous, seeing that some of the king's militia-men had been denied the right to put on a show of their own, even though the chimneys were certainly tall enough, according to the proportions of the horse chancres and other leg sores on our friend Baudichon, whose song we all know so well.

"And so it was a fine year for snail shells all over Artois, so the basket makers all did very well, eating crabs and lobster shells and all, until they were stuffed to the gills. And I wish everyone could sing as well as they did: it helped them play a much finer game of tennis, and all those little tricks we use to etymologize ladies' slippers would flow far more easily into the Seine and could always be used like the Meuniers Bridge, the way it used to be, by the king of Canarre's royal decree, and that order is still right on file with the clerk of the court.

"Thus, sir, I ask you in your wisdom to decide this case in my favor, in all solemnity, on the facts and according to the strictest rules of reason, with costs, damages, and interest."

And Pantagruel said:

"My friend, is there nothing else you wish to add?"

And Kissmyass answered:

"No, sir, because I have already said everything, *tu autem,* right to the end, and I haven't changed a bit of it, on my honor."

"Now then," said Pantagruel, "My Lord Fartsniffer, you say whatever you wish to have me hear. Try please to be brief, without however leaving out anything necessary to your argument."

Chapter Twelve ⁄⁄ How Lord Fartsniffer Testified

And My Lord Fartsniffer began as follows:

"My dear sir, and gentlemen all: if the evil that men do were as readily visible, and could be as conveniently and categorically catalogued, as the flies one sees in milk, the entire world—by the four great oxen that stand at each of its corners!—would not be eaten up by rats as, demonstrably, it now is, and there would be many, many ears here on this earth that would not be so disastrously and cowardly gnawed as now they most certainly are. Because, although every word that my opponent has said may be goose-featherly true, according to the letter and the precise history of the *factum,* the facts in the case before you, nevertheless, gentlemen, the subtleties, the lies, all the little snags and difficulties are hidden under the pot of roses.

"Should I be obliged to endure it that, just as I sit down at my table and begin to eat my soup, which is as good as anyone's, thinking evil of no one, speaking evil of no one, they start to scrabble around and trouble my brain, singing and dancing at me?

> Whoever spoils his food by drinking as he eats
> Will die and never see another treat.

"Now, by the Holy Mother, how many great captains have we seen, right out on the battlefield, slammed about with monkish holy wafers, so they could be more graciously and forthrightly cuddled, go playing their lutes, farting, and performing pretty little dance steps right out in public!

"And now the world is completely unhinged, and all because of these bales of English linen: one goes to the dogs, here, and over there five, or four, or ten, and if this court does not insist on order it will be just as bad, this year, when it comes to bringing in the grain, as it has been all along, or else it will all turn to weeds. If some poor person goes to the bathhouse to light up his snout with a bit of cow shit or maybe buy a pair of winter boots, and the court officers going by, or maybe the constables out on patrol happen to get drenched by a successful enema, or maybe by a chamber pot dumping shit all over them, is that any reason to clip gold and silver off the edges of coins and positively burn up wooden money?

"Sometimes we think about things going this way, but God goes the other way instead, and once the sun has gone down all the animals lie in the shade. Don't take my word for it: I want to be believed only if I've given you living proof, right here in broad daylight.

"In 1536 I bought a short-tailed German horse, and his ears were docked,

too, and he was tall and he was short, with good wool and as red as a
cardinal's hat, guaranteed by all the goldsmiths, though the notary stuck
in an *et cetera*. I'm no learned man, who can get the moon between his
teeth, but in the tub of butter where they put the volcanic instruments,
well, it was said that salt beef made you go look for wine even without a
candle, no matter that they might have hidden it down at the bottom of
a coal miner's sack, covered all over with armor for your arms and your
shoulders and also all the leg pieces you need for country cooking, namely,
a sheep's head. As the proverb nicely says, it's good to see black cows
properly roasted when making love is really right. I made sure to talk all
this over with those gentlemen, the court clerks, and using the *frisesomo-*
rum, the fifth figure in the syllogism, they decreed that in the summer
there's nothing quite like messing around in some cool cellar, with a good
supply of paper and ink, and pens, and a good penknife from Lyons on
the Rhône, hey nonny-nonny. Because as soon as your armor gets a garlic
smell, mildew and rust eat up his liver, and then all you can do for yourself is get a stiff neck, scented with an after-dinner nap. And that, believe
me, is why salt is so expensive.

"Gentlemen, please don't think for a moment that when that old woman,
of whom you have heard so much, trapped that passenger pigeon with
bird lime, hoping to improve the sergeant's memory, and the lungs and
heart and kidneys they plucked out of that pigeon went wriggling around
in the usurers' moneybags, there was nothing better to protect us against
cannibals than to take a string of onions, tied together with three hundred
turnips, and just a bit of lamb's wool (the best alloy the druggists can give
you), and smear his slippers with mud and rust, all muffle-duffle, with a
good hayseed sauce, and then get down in a tiny molehill, being careful,
of course, to save the sliced bacon.

"And if the dice keep giving you bad numbers, maybe a pair of threes
at the butt end, keep your eye on the ace and get that dame on the corner
of the bed, jump around with her, tourra-lourra-ley, and drink right down
to the bottom, *depiscando grenoillibus,* never mind the frogs down there,
in your best boots and buskins. This will be for the little geese, penned
up in the fattening cage and hopping around on their hot little feet, waiting to hammer out the metal and heat up the wax for the beer drinkers.

"Now, it is certainly true that those four oxen we spoke of don't have
long memories. Nevertheless, to follow the tune, they weren't afraid of
any hawks or Savoy ducks, and the good people who live on my land
expected fine things of them, saying, 'These children are going to master
arithmetic, and for us this will become a basic point of law.' We can't
help catching the wolf, as long as we keep our hedges higher than the
windmill, which my learned opponent has already referred to. But the
devil in hell was jealous of that and shoved the Germans back, because
they were devils for drinking: '*Herr, tringue, tringue!*' Beer over here, drink,
drink!—and the dice roll a pair of identical twins, right when you want

them, because there's no truth in the old saying that at the Little Bridge in Paris there are fresh chickens for sale, just out of the straw, with crests like swamp gulls, unless in fact you cut the tassles with freshly sharpened ink (in either capital or cursive letters), which is all the same to me, provided that kind of binding doesn't invite in the worms.

"Now, let's just suppose that, when the dogs started copulating as they ran, the sweet little ladies had stuck out their tongues, or anything else, before the notary gave his report (by cabalistic art), it would not necessarily follow—unless of course this court so decides—that six acres of grassland, measured generously, will yield three barrels of the best ink without a lot of huffing and puffing, considering that at King Charles' funeral you could buy a good lamb's fleece for a good roll of the dice, really, by my woolly oath.

"And I see that in all good bagpipes, ordinarily, when you go bird hunting, you dance around the chimney three times and hand in your commission, and all you have to do is tighten up your kidneys and blow it out your ass, and if by any chance it's too hot, then, well, just roll 'em,

> As soon as they saw the letter
> The cows went back to their betters.

"And just that kind of decree was issued on Saint Martin's Day, in 1517, on account of the misgovernment of Louzefougerouse—I mean, La Loge-Fougueuse, near Fontenay—and may the court take note of that.

"It is not my position that one cannot equitably cancel title when it comes to drinking holy water, as indeed is done with a weaver's loom, from which one frames suppositories for those who refuse to resign, unless they get as good as they give.

"*Tunc,* gentlemen, *quid juris pro minoribus?* Then what law applies to minors? As we know, the ordinary usage, under Salic law, is that the first firebrand who breaks a cow's horns, and who blows his nose while the music is playing, without hitting the shoemakers' notes, is obliged, when it's festival season, to minimize the insufficiency of his member with moss collected during midnight mass, in order to beat down those Anjou white wines that trip you up, neck for neck, just the way they do in Brittany.

"So I conclude as above indicated, and request costs, damages, and interest."

And when My Lord Fartsniffer was finished, Pantagruel turned to My Lord Kissmyass:

"My friend, do you have any reply to make?"

To which Kissmyass replied:

"No, sir, because I have spoken the plain truth—and, by God, let's be done with this whole case, because it's cost both of us a lot just to come here."

Chapter Thirteen ⁄⁄ How Pantagruel Ruled on the Quarrel between the Two Lords

Then Pantagruel rose and assembled around him all the presidents of councils, and the counselors, and the doctors of law and theology who were there, and said to them:

"Now, there it is, gentlemen! You have heard, *vive vocis oraculo,* in their own voices, the dispute in question. What do you think?"

To which they answered:

"We have heard indeed, but—in the name of the devil!—we certainly haven't understood. And so we implore you *una voce,* unanimously, as if with one voice, we beg you to graciously give judgment as you see fit. *Ex nunc prout et tunc,* From this day forth and for all days past, we approve that judgment and hereby fully ratify it."

"Very well, gentlemen," said Pantagruel, "since you wish it, that's what I'll do. But I don't really find this case so extraordinarily difficult. The paragraph you use in *Cato,* the law on brotherhood, the Gallic law, the laws *Quinque pedum, Vinum, Si dominus, Mater, Mulier bona, Si quis, Pomponius, Fundi, Emptor, Pretor, Venditor*—these and a host of others seem to me a great deal more difficult."

Having said which, he walked around the room a bit, and it was easy to see how deep in thought he was, because he was wheezing like a donkey whose load has been strapped on too tight, trying to see how he could do justice to both sides, without being inconsistent or favoring either of them. Then he came back, sat down, and began to deliver the following judgment:

"*Whereas,* having heard, understood, and thoroughly analyzed the dispute between the lords Kissmyass and Fartsniffer, the court hereby decrees:

"*That,* considering how the bat's recoil can be observed to wane after the summer solstice, in order to woo the crackbrained notions which have checkmated the pawn, making use of the wicked, vexatious measures of those who flee from the light, who are in the region of Rome like some false-faced idiot stretching a crossbow across a horse in full gallop, *therefore,* the plaintiff was well within his rights to caulk up the treasure ship which the old lady had bloated, one foot in his shoes, the other bare, paying him back at the lowest valuation and without the slightest hesitation, conscientiously aware that there was as much stupidity involved as there are hairs in eighteen full-sized cows, with as many more for the embroidery maker.

"*Furthermore,* plaintiff is also innocent, on grounds of privilege, of the charge of filthiness which has been brought against him, because he could not shit freely, according to the ruling of a pair of gloves nicely perfumed with fart sniffings, by a walnut-wax candle of the sort regularly employed in his Mirabeau homeland, letting out the bowline with bronze pellets from which, most questionably, the stableboys baked his interlined Loire vegetables, along with all the delicate hawk bells tuned in Hungary, which his brother-in-law had made a point of bringing, in a nearby basket decorated with three faded red stripes, in hemp and in a herringbone pattern, for the angular shooting shed from which one fires at the gaudy parakeet with long plumes.

"But since the defendant is also charged with being a hack, a cheese eater, and the sort of person who covers mummies with tar, all of which after careful examination has been found not to be true, exactly as the aforesaid defendant has so well argued himself, the court hereby directs the said plaintiff to furnish the said defendant with three glassfuls of seasoned buttermilk, ready for drinking and spiced in the usual fashion, payable in the middle of August, in the month of May.

"But the said defendant will be obliged to furnish the hay and stubble necessary for the swallowing of thorn apples, all of which materials shall be well smothered in monks' cowls, properly sieved for the presence of other slices.

"And be it decreed that henceforth they shall be friends, exactly as they used to be, with no costs awarded, and this entire judgment given for good cause."

When that judgment had been pronounced, the two parties immediately left, both of them well satisfied with the decision, which was an almost incredible feat. No such thing had occurred since the heavy rains had fallen; nor will it happen again for thirteen Holy Years (each fifty years long) that any two parties, contending in directly opposed arguments, will walk away from a final judgment, each of them equally pleased.

And as for the counselors and other legal experts who were there, they swooned away in ecstasy and did not come to themselves for three full hours, overwhelmed with admiration for Pantagruel's superhuman wisdom, which they could clearly see in the decision he had reached in this difficult, this thorny matter. And they might have remained in their swoons, had not vinegar and rosewater been used to bring them back to their senses, for which in particular may God be praised.

Chapter Fourteen ⁄⁄ Panurge's Tale of How He Escaped from the Turks

Pantagruel's decision was immediately made known to all the world, and many copies were printed; and it was duly recorded in the official archives, and everyone said:

"Not even Solomon, who figured out how to restore the child to its mother, could have produced such a masterpiece of wisdom as our good Pantagruel has done. We are happy to have him living among us."

Indeed, they invited him to become chief judge and president of the high court, but he refused all their offers, thanking them graciously:

"All of these offices," he said, "are too limiting; they require too much, and only with the greatest difficulty can those who hold them be saved, so great is human corruption. I believe that if the vacant seats among the angels are not filled by very different people, the Last Judgment won't come for thirty-seven Holy Years, and Cardinal Cusa's predictions will be wrong. Take careful notice of this: I have given you fair warning. On the other hand, if you have some barrels of good wine, I'd be pleased to have them as a gift."

Which suggestion was cheerfully accepted, and they sent him the best the city had to offer, from which he drank well. But poor Panurge truly lapped it up, for he was as thin as a dried herring; he even walked like a hungry cat. And they warned him, as he was gulping from a great tankard of red wine, saying, "Hey, easy there! You're drinking like a lunatic."

"Go to hell," Panurge said. "I'm not one of your delicate little Paris drinkers, who spend a whole night over one jug of wine and only get their beaks full when you slap them on the tail, like sparrows. Oh, my friend, if I could fly up high as well as I can put it down, I'd be long gone over the moon, with Empedocles! But I don't know what the devil's going on: this is damned good wine, but the more I drink, the thirstier I get. I guess Mr. Pantagruel's shadow makes you thirsty, the way moonlight gives you a cold."

At which they all began to laugh. And seeing this, Pantagruel said:

"Panurge, what's there to laugh about?"

"My lord," said he, "I've been telling them how those Turkish devils are incredibly unlucky: they never get to drink a drop of wine. If Muhammad's Koran did me no other bad turn, I'd still never put myself under its laws."

"Now tell me," said Pantagruel, "how you got away from them."

"By God, my lord," said Panurge, "I'll tell it to you just the way it happened.

"Those sinful Turks had put me on a spit, all greased up like a rabbit, wrapped in good frying bacon, because I was so skinny that otherwise I would have made damned awful meat, and their idea was to roast me alive. And as they started to roast me, I prayed for divine grace, remembering how our good Saint Lawrence, too, was roasted on a grill, but I was always hoping God would deliver me from my torment, which He did, very queerly—for as I consigned myself to His great mercy, crying, 'Lord God, help me! Lord God, save me! Lord God, free me from this torment, in which these traitorous dogs have thrust me because I kept Your law!' the Turk who was turning the spit suddenly fell asleep, as God willed—or else it was some good god Mercury, tricking Argus with the hundred eyes into falling asleep.

"And when I noticed that the spit wasn't turning me any more, I saw that he'd gone to sleep. So I grabbed a half-burned stick with my teeth, using the end that hadn't caught on fire, and threw it into my roaster's lap, and then I threw another one, as best I could, right under a camp bed, near the chimney, where Sir Roaster had his straw mattress laid out.

"The fire blazed up in the straw, and from the straw to the bed, and from the bed to the ceiling, which was lined with pine posts. The best part of it was that the fire I'd started in my roaster's lap, tossing the burning stick in there, burned off his penis and was working away at his balls, but he was so caked with dirt that he wouldn't have felt it till the next day. Jumping up like a billy goat, he ran to the window, yelling as loud as he could, 'Dal baroth, dal baroth!'—which means 'Fire, fire!'—and then came straight over to me, meaning to take me off the spit and throw me smack into the flames. He'd cut the ropes on my hands and was working on my feet.

"But then the lord of the house, hearing the cry of 'Fire!' and smelling the smoke from the street (where he was out walking with some other pashas and learned Muslims), came running in as fast as he could, to help and also to try to save his household goods.

"As soon as he got there, he pulled out the spit I'd been roasting on and killed my roaster right on the spot, maybe because he'd made such a mess of things—but who knows? In any case, he rammed the spit right through the fellow, a little below the belly button, just to the right a bit, and pierced the third lobe of the liver, after which the spit swung upward through the diaphragm and, cutting through the pericardium, which surrounds the heart, emerged at the top of the shoulders, between the dorsal vertebrae and the left shoulder blade.

"Now, of course, when that spit was pulled out, I fell to the ground, near the andirons, and the fall made me feel rather sick, but it wasn't too bad, because the thick grease and the bacon wrapping absorbed the blow.

"And then the pasha, seeing how desperate the situation was, and that his house was going to burn straight to the ground, and everything he owned was going to be lost, surrendered himself to the devils in hell, calling out, nine times, to Grilgoth, Astaroth, Rappalo, and Gribollis.

"Seeing this, I was pretty seriously worried, fearing that all those devils would immediately come and carry off this crazy fellow. And they'd certainly be the sort to take me along with him! I was already half roasted. And what really worried me was the bacon, because devils have an itch for bacon, a fact supported by the authority of the Neoplatonist Iamblichus, and also by Johannes Murmel, in his tract *De bossutis et contrefactis, pro Magistros nostros,* On Hunchbacks and Fakers, A Scholar's Guide. But I made the sign of the cross, crying, '*Agyos athanatos, ho Theos!* God is Holy, God is Eternal!' And none of them came.

"And realizing this, that rascal of a pasha tried to kill himself with my spit, stabbing himself through the heart. He shoved it at his chest, but it couldn't get through, because it just wasn't sharp or pointed enough. No matter how he banged away, it simply wouldn't work.

"So I went over to him, saying:

" 'Hey, you pig, you! You're wasting your time: you're never going to get yourself killed like that. The best you're going to do is break something, and they you'll spend the rest of your life in the surgeons' hands. But if you want me to, I'll really kill you, and you won't feel a thing. Believe me, because I've killed lots of other people, and they felt all the better for it.'

" 'Ha, my friend,' he said, 'please, I beg you! Do it, and I'll give you my purse. Here, take it, take it. There are six hundred gold pieces in there, and some absolutely perfect diamonds and rubies.' "

"And where are they now?" said Epistemon.

"By Saint John!" said Panurge. "They've gone pretty far, if they're still moving:

But where are the snows of yesteryear?

That was what worried Villon, the Parisian poet."

"Go on," said Pantagruel, "please. Tell us how you took care of your pasha."

"On my honor," said Panurge, "I'll tell it exactly as it happened. I trussed him up with some of their big baggy trousers that were lying there, half burned. I got him tied up like a pig, hands and feet both— using the same ropes I'd been bound with—and he was so snug he couldn't have kicked if he'd wanted to. Then I stuck my spit through his throat and strung him up, running the spit across two big spikes where they hung their spear axes. Then I stoked up a good fire just below him and, by God, I cooked My Lord Pasha just like a dried herring smoked over the fireplace. After which I snatched up his purse and a good short spear that had been hanging on those hooks, and God knows I stank like a dead pig myself!

"When I got down to the street, I found everyone gathered around, trying as hard as they could to put out the fire with water, and seeing me, half roasted as I was, they naturally took pity on me and turned all their water on me, which made me feel very good indeed, and strengthened me enormously. Then they gave me something to eat, but I could hardly get a bite down, because all they gave me to drink was water, which is how they always do it.

"They didn't do anything else to me, except one small Turkish rascal with a hump on his chest, who tried to sneak a few bites of my bacon, but I rapped him on the knuckles so sharply with my short spear that he didn't try that again. And there was one girl who brought me a bowl of their best aphrodisiac plums, candied just the way Turks like them: she kept looking at my poor flea-bitten penis, which really looked as if it had been held in a fire—and it only hung down to my knees. On the other hand, this bit of roasting and basting did completely cure me of a sciatica I'd had for more than seven years—at least, on the side that my roaster let cook, while he snoozed.

"And while they had fun with me, the fire ran wild—please: don't bother me for details—and burned down more than two thousand houses, and one of them finally saw that and started to scream: 'By the belly of Muhammad! The whole city's burning down and we're sitting here playing games!' So they all ran off to their assigned places.

"Me, I took the highroad straight to the city gates. When I got to a little hill nearby, I turned around and looked back, like Lot's wife, and saw the whole city burning, which made me so happy that I felt like shitting for joy. But God punished me right enough."

"How?" asked Pantagruel.

"Like this," said Panurge. "While I was watching that fire, and grinning with delight, making fun of them: 'Oh, you poor fleas—you poor mice—you're going to have a bad winter: the fire's burning up your beds!'—suddenly more than six dogs—no, really, more than a thousand three hundred and eleven, big ones and little ones—came rushing out of the city, running from the fire. And they all ran straight to me, because they could smell the fragrance of my half-roasted flesh. I'd have been eaten up in an instant if my ever-watchful good angel hadn't intervened and given me a fine cure for toothache."

"And why," said Pantagruel, "do you call it toothache? Wasn't it sciatica you got cured of?"

"Blessed God!" answered Panurge. "Is there any worse toothache than when dogs sink theirs into your legs? But I suddenly thought of all that bacon I'd been wrapped in and I threw it down in the middle of the howling pack. And the dogs began to run in circles and fight each other for the bacon. Which allowed me to get away, and I left them to fight it out for themselves. So I escaped, happy and healthy—and long live roasting!"

Chapter Fifteen // Panurge's Fine New Method for Building the Walls of Paris

One day, to refresh himself after long studying, Pantagruel went for a walk to the Saint-Marcel area, wanting to have a look at the Gobelins' country house. Panurge was with him, as usual with a flask under his gown and carrying a chunk of ham: he never went anywhere without them, saying these were his bodyguards. He carried no other weapon. When Pantagruel wanted to give him one, he replied that wearing a sword would overheat his spleen.

"Indeed," said Epistemon. "And if someone attacks you, how will you defend yourself?"

"I'd make good use of my legs," Panurge answered, "since swordplay would be out of the question."

On the way back, Panurge contemplated the walls of Paris and said to Pantagruel, mockingly:

"Just look at those handsome walls. Oh, how strong they are—and how wonderfully useful for keeping little geese in a pen! By my beard, they're just awful enough for a city like this: a cow could knock six yards of them over with a single fart."

"Oh, my friend," said Pantagruel, "don't you remember what Agesilaus said, when they asked him why the Spartans' capital city had no walls? Because, he said, pointing to the citizens of Sparta, all of them trained to the hilt in military matters, and strong, and well armed, these are the city's walls—meaning that the only walls that matter are made of bone, and that no town, no city ever has a more secure wall, or a stronger one, than the virtues of its citizens. And this city is powerful because of all the warlike people who live in it, so they don't give a hoot about other walls. Besides, if you wanted to wall it around like Strasbourg, or Orléans, or Ferrara, it simply wouldn't be possible. It would cost more than anyone could muster."

"Oh, really?" answered Panurge. "It's still good to have some sort of stone face when your enemies invade, and not only because you can look down and ask, 'Who's that down there?' But as for all that enormous expense, which according to you would be necessary if it was decided to put up walls, if the gentlemen of the city would furnish me with a good barrel of wine, I'd teach them a fine new method, and they could build at bargain rates."

"How?" said Pantagruel.

"If you'll keep quiet about it," answered Panurge, "I'll teach it to you.

"In this part of the world, women's cunts are cheaper than stones. So build your walls with *them,* nicely arranged, with proper balance and due attention to architectural detail, with the biggest cunts in the front row, and then, sloping gradually down like a donkey's back, the middle-sized cunts, and finally the littlest ones. Then make a nice little row—diamond pointed, like the tower at Bourges—of all those stiff pricks that have to stay inside monkish trousers.

"What devil could attack walls like that? There is no metal more resistant. And then, if the really heavy cannonballs, or any balls at all, came and rubbed up against that wall, by God! you'd see a sudden shower of the blessed fruit of the great pox, as fine as rain, and dry and hard, in Satan's name! Besides, lightning wouldn't ever hit a wall like that, either, and do you know why? It would be blessed and consecrated.

"In fact, I see only one disadvantage."

"Ho, ho, ha, ha, ha!" said Pantagruel, "And what's that?"

"It's the flies: they have a fantastic taste for cunts, and they'd all flock over and make a stink—and there you'd be, the whole construction ruined. But there's a way to take care of that, too. You've got to whack them away with handsome foxtails, or the big fat donkey pricks they grow in Provence. And, on that subject, let me tell you (now that we're sitting down to supper) a nice example from *Frater Lubinus,* Friar Lubin, in his *libro,* his book, *De compotationibus mendicantium,* How the Begging Friars Drink.

"Back in the days when animals could talk (which wasn't just three days ago), a poor lion walking through the woods at Fontainebleau, saying his prayers after hearing mass, went past a tree where a rascally charcoal maker had climbed up, the better to cut the tree down. And seeing the lion, the man hurled his ax down at him and cut an enormous gash in his thigh. So the lion limped out of the forest as fast as he could, trying to find help. And he met a carpenter, who was glad to inspect the wound and clean it as well as he knew how, putting in moss and explaining to the lion that he had to keep the flies away so they wouldn't shit in it. Meanwhile, the carpenter said, he'd go hunt for some healing yarrow weed.

"Well, the lion was cured, and he went walking through the forest. And just then he saw an old hag who was older than old, gathering sticks and bits of wood in that forest, and she, seeing the lion approaching, fell head over heels in fear. The wind blew her dress, and her petticoat, and her chemise up around her shoulders. And seeing this the lion came running over, hoping she hadn't been hurt, and seeing her *comment a nom,* thing which he had no name for, he said:

" 'O poor woman, who could have hurt you like that?'

"And then, as he spoke, he saw a fox, and called to him, saying:

" 'Brother Fox, hey, hey, over here, hurry up!'

"And when the fox came over, he said to him:

" 'Brother, my friend, someone has given this old woman a dreadful wound, right between the legs, and there's a genuine cleft; you can easily see it. See how huge a wound it is? From her ass to her belly button it measures, four—no, maybe five or five and a half spans. It has to be an ax blow; I suspect it's an old wound. Now, to keep the flies out of it, swat it good and hard, please, inside and out. You have a good long tail: swat at it, my friend, swat, I beg you, and meanwhile I'll go hunt for some moss to put in that dreadful wound, because we are all obliged to help and succor each other. Swat hard. That's it, my friend, swat it well, because this is a wound that needs a lot of swatting, or the woman can't possibly be comfortable. Now swat away, little brother, swat, swat! How good of God to bless you with such a tail, so good and long, and just as thick as it is long. Just keep swatting and don't give up. A swatter who swats away without ever stopping is a first-class swatter, and flies won't ever get on him. So swat, little fellow, oh swat, my tiny soldier! I won't be gone for more than a moment.'

"Then he hurried off, hunting for moss. And when he'd gone a little way, he called back to the fox:

" 'Just keep on swatting, brother. Swat, and don't hold back, O little brother. By God, I'll get you made swatter in waiting to Queen Mary, or Dom Pietro de Castillo's personal swatter. Just keep on swatting— swat, and don't do anything else.'

"The poor fox swatted as hard as he could, this way and that way, inside and out. But the old woman farted and farted, and she stank like a hundred devils. The poor fox started to get good and sick, because he couldn't figure out which way to turn in order to avoid those farts and their wicked stench. And as he faced first this way, and then that, he saw that down back the old woman had another hole, not quite as big as the one he was swatting, but certainly the place from which those stinking, ugly winds were blowing out at him.

"The lion finally came back, carrying enough moss to make eighteen bales, and began to shove it into the wound with a stick he'd found. And pretty soon he'd shoved in sixteen and a half bales, and was astonished:

" 'What the devil! This wound is incredibly deep: I've already put in more than two wagonloads of moss!'

"But the fox warned him:

" 'Oh, brother lion, my friend, please, don't put all the moss in there. Save a little, because there's still another little hole that stinks like five hundred devils. It smells so awful that it's poisoning me.'

"And that's how we have to keep the flies off these walls and pay good wages to our swatters."

And Pantagruel said:

"How can you say honest women's cunts are so cheap? This city has a lot of decent women, chaste women and virgins, too."

To which Panurge answered:

"*Et ubiprenus?* And where shall we find them? What I tell you is not opinion, not at all, but true certainty and most assuredly so. I'm not going to boast just because I've screwed four hundred and seventeen of them since I've been here (and that's exactly nine days). But just this morning I met an old man who was carrying two tiny girls, two or three years old, maybe a bit more. He had them in a kind of double-pouched sack, one in front, one in back, exactly like old Aesop's (you put your own shortcomings in back, out of sight, and other people's right out front). He asked me for money, but I told him I had more balls than gold pieces. And then I asked him, 'Old man, are these little girls virgins?' 'Brother,' he said, 'I've been carrying them like this for two years, and I never take my eyes off the one in front, so I'd say, yes, she is. Still, I wouldn't put my hand in the fire to vouch for her. But as for the one in back—well, I can't vouch for a thing.' "

"Really," said Pantagruel, "you're a pleasant fellow to have around. I'd like to have you dressed in the same uniform all my people wear."

And so they had him dressed gallantly, in the current fashion, except that Panurge insisted on having his codpiece almost a yard long, and cut square rather than round, which was how it was done. And it was a fine sight to see. He often remarked on how little the world understood about the advantages of wearing a good-sized codpiece, remarking philosophically that someday they would learn, as the wheel of time eventually reveals all good things.

"May God preserve," he would say, "your friend whose very life was saved by a long codpiece! May God preserve the man whose long codpiece has brought him a hundred and sixty-nine thousand gold pieces, in just a single day! May God preserve the man whose long codpiece keeps a whole city from dying of starvation! By God, I'm going to write a book on the advantages of long codpieces, just as soon as I have the time."

And indeed he did write a handsome, fat book on the subject, beautifully illustrated. But it hasn't been printed yet, as far as I know.

Chapter Sixteen ⁄⁄ Panurge's Character, and How He Lived

Panurge was of middle height, neither particularly tall nor especially short, and he had a rather aquiline nose—in fact, very like a razor handle. He was thirty-five years old, more or less (to put a little gilding on a lead dagger), dashing looking, except that he was something of a skirt chaser, and also that he was naturally ill with a disease called, in those days,

Short of money, what a sorrow, what a pain

(as students used to sing)—but all the same, he had at least sixty-three ways of finding what he needed, the most honorable (and usual) of which was sly thievery. He was mischievous, a cheat, a drinker, a hobo, a scrounger (as long as he was in Paris), and for the rest, the best son of a bitch in the world, always cooking up something to make trouble for the constables and watchmen.

Once he got together three or four good country fellows and set them to drinking like Templars the whole night long. Then he brought them down in front of the church of Saint Geneviève, or out in front of Navarre College, and just when the watchmen of the guard were coming by— which he made sure of by resting his sword on the pavement, and his ear against his sword, and when he heard the sword shake he knew it was an infallible sign that the guard was coming—he and his friends would take a dung cart and give it a good shove, making it run rapidly down the slope of those streets and knocking the poor guardsmen down like so many pigs ready to be trussed for roasting. And then they'd run off in the other direction, because in less than two days he'd made it his business to know every street and alley and byway in Paris as well as he knew his grace after meals, *Deus det nobis,* May God grant us. . . .

Another time, knowing exactly where the night guardsmen would be passing, he laid down a train of gunpowder and, just as they came march- ing by, threw a match into it and proceeded to thoroughly enjoy himself, watching how gracefully they ran, thinking Saint Anthony's fire had grabbed at their legs.

But it was the poor masters of arts, in theology above all, that he truly enjoyed persecuting. Anytime he met one of them in the street, he did them some mischief or other, either sticking a fresh turd in their big broad-brimmed hats, or tying foxtails to the backs of their coats, or maybe rabbit ears, or something unpleasant, it didn't matter what.

One day, when all the theologians had been told to assemble on the Rue de Feurre, so their faith and belief could be properly tested, he cooked up a proper treat, starting with a ton of garlic, and adding *galbanum, assa fetida,* and *castoreum,* three noxious, toxic, vomit-producing flavors, some nice fresh shit (still warm), all of which he soaked in hot pus from good canker sores, and then that morning he did a fine job pouring it all over, anointing the pavement in every direction, so the devil himself couldn't have stood it. All those good folk proceeded to throw up, right in front of everyone, as if they'd been skinning fox hides; ten or twelve of them died of the plague, fourteen got leprosy, eighteen came down with sca- bies, and more than twenty-seven got the pox, but he didn't give a damn. And he always carried a whip under his gown, so he could whip the devil out of any servants he ran across, fetching wine for their masters, so he could make them go faster.

His overcoat had more than twenty-six little pockets and pouches, which were always filled:

one, with a pair of little dice, well loaded with hidden lead, and a small knife as sharp as a furrier's needle, which he used to cut open purses;

another, with sour wine or vinegar he could throw in people's eyes;

another, with burrs and prickles to which he'd tied little goose or chicken feathers, so he could throw them on the gowns and hats of respectable folk, and often he managed to create first-class horns, which they would then parade all over the city—sometimes for the whole rest of their lives;

another, especially for women, specially fashioned little penises he'd sometimes stick on their hats, or on the back of their gowns;

another, a bunch of horns stuffed with fleas and lice, borrowed from the beggars at Saint Innocent's cemetery, which he threw, with little reeds or writing pens, down the backs of the sweetest-looking ladies he could find, even in church, for he'd never sit high up in the organ loft or where the choir was. He always stayed down in the nave with the women, whether at mass or vespers or when the sermon was being preached;

another, a good supply of fishhooks and knitting needles, so whenever there was a crowd he could stick men and women together, and especially when they were wearing thin taffeta dresses, so when they started to walk away they'd rip their gowns to shreds;

another, a good flint stone, and a sufficiency of fuses, matchsticks, and everything else required;

another, two or three magnifying glasses, which he could use to drive both men and women out of their minds and get them to lose all control, even in church; as he used to say, there wasn't anything to choose from, as between a woman who was crazy for religion and a woman whose ass moved like crazy;

and in another, a supply of needles and thread, with which he played a thousand wicked little jokes. Once, at the door to the Justice Building, in the Grand Ballroom, when a Franciscan monk was to say mass for the magistrates, Panurge helped him to dress himself for the occasion. But in getting him properly attired, he stitched the long robe of white linen, which priests wear for mass, both to his monk's robe and to his undershirt, then quietly disappeared when the magistrates came and took their seats. Now, when the poor friar got to the *Ite missa est,* Go forth, the mass has now been said, and tried to take off his white robe, he also took off his monk's robe and his undershirt, all tightly sewn together, and got everything he was wearing rolled up as far as his shoulders, exhibiting his genitals to the whole world—and without any question he was a very well-hung friar. And the more the poor man pulled and tugged, the more he uncovered himself, until one of the magistrates finally said, "What the devil is this? Is the good father offering us his ass to kiss? May it get kissed by Saint Anthony's fire!" And it was decreed that henceforth the poor good monks were not to dress themselves in public, but only in their robing room, especially when there happened to be women present, who might be driven to the sin of desire. And everyone wondered just why these monks were so exceedingly well hung, a problem that Panurge neatly solved, saying:

"What makes donkey's ears so big is that their mothers never get them to wear hoods on their heads, as that noted theological scholar Pierre d'Ailly writes in his book *Conjectures and Assumptions.* By the same logic, what's responsible for the size of these poor blessed monks' equipment is that their breeches never have bottoms, and so it's all free to drop down as far as it feels like going, swinging down to their knees like the big strings of rosary beads women wear at their belt. But the thickness, which is just as notable—that's caused by the bodily essences swinging right down into their genitals, since as we all know shaking and continual motion create attractive impulses."

Item: Panurge's overcoat had another pocket full of powdered alum, a fierce astringent and itching agent which he liked to toss down the backs of haughty women, making them strip down right in public, or else dance like a chicken on a bed of hot coals, or like a stick beating on a drum, or else run wild through the streets, in which case he would go running after them, while for those who stripped off their clothes he'd most graciously offer his cape and drape it over them like the most courteous, kindest gentleman in the world.

Item: in another pocket he had a flask full of used oil, and when he saw a woman, or a man, who was especially handsomely dressed, he'd grease them up and completely ruin all the best parts, under the pretext of touching and admiring them, saying, "What a fine piece of goods this is, ah, what beautiful satin, what lovely taffeta, madame: may God grant you whatever your noble heart desires! You have a new gown and a new friend: may God permit you much joy of them both!" And as he spoke he'd run his hand down over the collar, and the back, and the deep spots he'd make would stay forever—carved so deep into the soul, as the saying goes, stamped so indelibly onto the body, that the devil himself couldn't remove them. And then he'd say, "Madame, do be careful not to fall: there's a great dirty hole right over there."

And another pocket was full of a pungent, bitter drug that sadly disturbs the stomach and the intestines, which he kept finely powdered, and he'd put a fine lace handkerchief in there, one that he'd stolen from a pretty washerwoman at the Justice Building while pulling a louse out of her bodice (which louse he had of course put there himself). When he found himself surrounded with gentlewomen, he'd turn the talk to lacework and put his hand on their breasts, asking, "Now this, was it made in Flanders or in Hainaut?" And then he'd pull out his handkerchief, saying, "See? See? Just look at how *this* was worked! It's from Frontignan— or from Fontarabie," and he'd give it a good shake under their nose, and they'd sneeze for four hours without being able to stop. And then he'd fart like a horse, and the women would laugh and say to him, "What? Is that you farting, Panurge?" "Hardly, madame," he'd say. "That was just a good harmonious counterpoint to the music you're making with your nose."

In another pocket he had a burglar's wrench, a locksmith's jimmy, a hook, and other iron tools: there wasn't a door or a store box he couldn't pry open.

And yet another pocket he kept full of tiny glasses with which he could play all sorts of cunning tricks, because his fingers were as supple as Minerva's or Arachne's. Indeed, he had once been a traveling showman. And when Panurge gave change, you'd have had to be sharper sighted than Master Flim-Flam-Fly himself if, every single time, five or six small coins didn't somehow disappear, right out in the open, under your very nose, but without any sign of wrongdoing, so that all you were aware of was a slight puff of air as they vanished.

Chapter Seventeen ⁄⁄ How Panurge Won a Pile of Indulgences and Married Off a Crowd of Old Maids, and the Lawsuits He Fought in Paris

One day I found Panurge down in the dumps and silent, and I was pretty sure he didn't have a cent. So I said to him:

"Panurge, you're sick. I can see it written all over you, and I understand the sickness: you've had a sudden outflow of cash. But don't let it worry you. I've still got five or six francs that never saw their father or their mother, and they won't let you down when you need them, any more than the pox ever does."

To which he answered:

"Shit to your money! Someday I'll have too much of it—because I have a philosopher's stone, which pulls money out of people's purses the way a magnet sucks in iron. But," said he, "would you like to come and pick up a few indulgences?"

"By my faith," I answered him, "I'm not much for pardons and indulgences, not in this world, anyway. I don't know how I'll feel when I get to the other one. But all right, let's go: I'm in for one franc, by God, neither more nor less."

"But," said he, "lend me a franc. I'll pay you interest."

"You'll never pay me any interest, never," I said. "I'll give it to you freely."

"*Grates vobis, Dominos,* My sincere thanks," he said.

So off we went, beginning at the church of Saint Gervais, and I got some indulgences just from the first box, and no others, because I'm happy with nothing very much in these matters. And then I said a few quick prayers, and especially to Saint Bridget. But Panurge stopped at every box and bought indulgences at each of them, and paid cash every time.

From there we went to Notre Dame, to Saint Jean's, to Saint Anthony's, and so on to all the other churches where they did business in indulgences. Me, I didn't buy any more, but Panurge, he knelt and kissed the relics at every box, and always bought more, and paid cash each time. To make a long story short, when we were coming home again he took me to the Chateau Restaurant and showed me ten or twelve purses stuffed with money. At which I made the sign of the cross and said:

"How did you get your hands on so much in so short a time?"

To which he answered that he'd taken it from the collection plates.

"You see," he said, "when I gave them the first coin, I put it down so grandly that they thought it was a big fat gold piece. So with one hand I took twelve coins, or maybe twelve triple coins, or doubles anyway, and with the other I took three or four dozens. And I did the same thing in every church we went to."

"By God," I said, "then you've damned yourself for a snake—you're a thief and you've committed sacrilege!"

"Oh yes," he said, "that's how it may seem to you. But not to me, let me tell you. Because the indulgence sellers gave me that money, when they showed me which relics to kiss. *Centuplum accipies,* they said, You will receive a hundredfold—so for each coin I took a hundred, and *accipies,* you understand, was spoken according to the Hebrew mode. They used the future where we would use the imperative, as in the Bible: *Diliges Dominum,* You will love the Lord, instead of *dilige.* So when the indulgence seller said to me, *Centuplum accipies,* what he meant was *Centuplum accipe,* Take a hundredfold. Rabbi Kimy and Rabbi Eben Ezra explain it exactly that way, and do so all the Masoretic commentators, and Bartolus, too. Besides, Pope Sixtus gave me an income of fifteen hundred gold pieces, payable on his lands and his treasury, because I cured him of a cankerous sore that tormented him so terribly he thought he'd be lame the rest of his life. So all I'm doing is paying myself with my own hands, out of that same ecclesiastical treasure, because in fact he isn't lame.

"Ho, my friend," he said, "if you knew how I'd feathered my nest with the Crusades, you'd be astonished. They've been worth more than six thousand florins."

"Then they've all flown off," I said, "because you haven't got a cent."

"They went where they came from," he said. "All they did was change owners.

"But I've put three thousand to good use, arranging marriages—but not for young girls, because they find only too many husbands, but old, old hags who have lived forever and don't have a tooth in their heads. I thought, 'These old women worked hard when they were young, lifting their asses so all comers could screw them, until finally no one wanted to bother any more—and by God I'll let them get back to work one more time before they kick off!' So I gave one of them a hundred florins, a hundred and twenty to another, three hundred to a third, depending on how disgusting they were, how ugly, how loathsome—and besides, there were some even more horrible and ghastly, and they had to have even more dowry to give or the devil himself wouldn't have screwed them. Then right away I'd go to some big fat woodchopper and arrange the marriage myself—but before I showed him the old hags, I'd show him the money, and I'd say, 'Brother, here's what's in it for you if you screw them right.' And that would make the poor fellows stiffen up like jack-asses. So then I'd prepare a good banquet, the best wine around, and lots of spice in it, to get the old bags heated up and ready for it. And in the end, they did their jobs like all good fellows, except that when the hags were just too awful even to look at, I'd cover their faces with a sack.

"And besides, I lost a lot of money in lawsuits."

"And how did you get involved in lawsuits?" I said. "You don't own any land, or a house."

"My friend," he said, "the women in this city, inspired by the devil in hell, have figured out a style of wearing their collars and their neck scarves—a high fashion—which conceals their breasts so well that you can't get your hand in there, because the opening is down their backs and the front is closed up tight, so the poor sad lovers are miserable even thinking about it. One bright Tuesday I filed a suit in court, constituting myself an interested party plaintiff against those ladies, showing the great interest I took in the whole matter, and complaining that by the same logic I could put my codpiece on the back of my breeches, unless the court ordered the problem cured. The result was that all the women joined together, thus demonstrating how alike they were in fundamental matters, and retained lawyers to defend their cause. But I went after them so vigor-ously that the court issued an order banning those high collars and tight neck scarves, unless there was at least some kind of opening in front. But all that cost me a bundle.

"I had another lawsuit against Maître Toilet Cleaner and his associates that was so filthy, so disgusting, arguing that they should no longer be permitted to read *Barrels of Shit* in the darkness, at night, or *Small Stink Mugs,* but should read them right out in the broad daylight, and in front of the School of Theology, with all the theologians and the other hypo-crites watching, but I lost on some purely formal ground, because my lawyer made a mistake in drafting the pleadings, and I even had to pay court costs and all the other expenses.

"Another time I sued because of the judges' and counselors' mules, alleging that when they were given their straw to eat, down in the court-yard of the Justice Building, they ought to have nice little bibs hung around their necks, so when they slobbered and driveled they didn't mess up the pavement, and then when the judges' and counselors' servants wanted to play a pleasant, relaxing game of dice, or any other cheerful sport, they wouldn't have to get their breeches filthy all the way to the knees. I won that case, too, but it cost me plenty.

"Now, just add in, also, how much it costs me, giving those regular little banquets to the judges' servants."

"And why do you do that?" I said.

"My friend," he said, "you don't enjoy yourself. But I have more fun than the king. And if you like you can join me: we'd be very devils!"

"No, no," I said, "by Saint Upintheair! Because you're going to end up at the end of rope."

"And you," he said, "you'll end up in the ground. Which is better, the air or the earth? Hey, you fat pig! While those servants are stuffing their faces, I watch their mules and I snip the stirrup leather on the mounting side, so it just hangs by a thread. When their great windbag counselors, or anybody else, jumps up, they fall on the ground like a side of meat, right in front of everyone, and that laughter's worth a lot more than a hundred francs. But I get still more laughs out of it, because when they get home, they beat the shit out of their servants. So I don't complain about what it costs me to feast them."

So the long and the short of it was, as he told me, that he had sixty-three ways of getting money, but he had two hundred and fourteen ways of spending it, not counting what he owed that yawning gap just under his nose.

Chapter Eighteen ⁄⁄ How a Great English Scholar Wanted to Dispute with Pantagruel, But Was Beaten by Panurge

At about the same time, a scholar named Thaumaste (in Greek, "Wonderful"), hearing all the fuss over Pantagruel's incomparable learning, and seeing how famous he'd become, came from England with the sole intention of meeting Pantagruel and finding out if his knowledge matched his reputation. Arriving in Paris, he immediately went to Pantagruel's lodgings, which were at the abbey of Saint Denis. At that moment, Pantagruel was in the garden with Panurge, walking up and down and philosophizing after the fashion of the ancient Peripatetics. Thaumaste quivered with fear, seeing how huge Pantagruel was, but then he greeted him in customary style and said, with great courtesy:

"How true it is, as Plato, prince of philosophers, says, that if the image of wisdom and learning is a physical matter, visible to human eyes, it excites the whole world with admiration. The very word of such accomplishments, spread through the air and received by the ears of those who study and love philosophy, prevents them from taking any further rest, stirring them, urging them to hurry to where they may find and see the person in whom knowledge has erected its temple and given forth its oracles. Which was clearly demonstrated for us by the queen of Sheba, who traveled from the farthest reaches of the Orient and the Persian Sea to visit the house of the wise Solomon and hear his sage words;

"and by Anacharsis, who came from Scythia only to see Solon;

"and by Pythagoras, who journeyed to the prophets of Memphis;

"and by Plato, who visited the Egyptian magi, and also Archytas of Tarentum;

"and by Apollonius of Tyana, who went to the Caucasian mountains, who journeyed among the Scythians, the Massagetae, and the Indians, who sailed down the great river Physon, all the way to the land of the Brahmans, to see Hiarchos, and who traveled in Babylonia, Chaldea, the land of the Medes, Assyria, Parthia, Syria, Phoenicia, Arabia, Palestine, and Alexandria, and in Ethiopia, too, to see the Gymnosophists.

"We have another example in Livy, to see and hear whom certain studious folk came to Rome from the farthest boundaries of France and Spain.

"I am not so presumptuous as to include myself among the ranks of such illustrious men. But I deeply desire to be thought of as a student and lover not only of humanistic learning but also of men of such learning.

"And, in fact, hearing of your priceless learning, I have left my country, my parents, and my home and come here, indifferent to the weariness of the journey, the anxiety of a voyage by sea, the strangeness of different lands, solely for the purpose of seeing and conferring with you about certain passages of philosophy, and geometrical divination, and also of cabalistic knowledge, passages of which I am myself unsure and about which I cannot rest content. If you can resolve these difficulties for me, I will be your servant from this day forth, and not only me but all my posterity, for I command no other gifts sufficient to repay you.

"I will put all of this in writing, and tomorrow I shall notify all the learned men of this city, so that we can discuss these matters publicly and in their presence.

"But I intend that our discussions, and any disputes in which we may engage, shall be conducted as follows. I do not wish to argue any bare-bones *for* and *against,* as do the besotted sophistical minds of this and other cities. Nor do I wish to dispute after the fashion of academics, by declamation, or by the use of numbers, as Pythagoras did and as Picodella Mirandola, at Rome, wished to do. I wish to dispute simply by signs, without a word being spoken, for these are matters so intricate and difficult that, as far as I am concerned, mere human speech will not be adequate to deal with them.

"May it please Your Magnificence to accept my invitation and join me, at seven in the morning, in the great hall of the College of Navarre."

When he had finished, Pantagruel said to him, courteously:

"My dear sir, how could I deny anyone the right to share in whatever blessings God has given me? All good things come from Him, and surely He wishes us to spread the celestial manna we have from Him among men both worthy and capable of receiving true learning—among whose number in our time, as I know very well, you belong in the very first rank. Let me say to you, therefore, that you will find me ready at any time to accede to any of your requests, to the extent that my poor powers may enable me, and well aware as I am that it is I who should be learning from you. And so, as you have declared, we will discuss these doubts of yours together, and hunt as hard as we can for their resolution, diving even as far as the bottom of that bottomless well in which, according to Heraclitus, the truth is said to be hidden.

"And I highly commend the style of argument you have proposed, that is to say, by using signs, without any words, for thus you and I will truly understand one another, free from the sort of hand clapping and applause produced during their discussions by these puerile sophists, whenever one party has the better of the argument.

"So, then, tomorrow I shall appear without fail at the time and place you have requested. I ask of you only that, as between us, there may be no contentiousness and fuss, and that we seek neither honor nor men's applause, but only the truth."

To which Thaumaste replied:

"Sir, may God keep you in His grace. I thank Your High Magnificence for being so willing to condescend to my humble talents. Until tomorrow, I leave you in His hands."

"Farewell," said Pantagruel.

Gentlemen, you who may read this book, please don't imagine that anyone was ever more exalted, more transported, that whole night long, than Thaumaste and Pantagruel. Thaumaste told the concierge at his lodgings, in the abbey of Cluny, that in his entire life he had never been so incredibly thirsty:

"It feels to me," he said, "as if Pantagruel has me by the throat. Order me wine, if you please, and make sure that there's enough fresh water so I can lubricate the roof of my mouth."

And for his part, Pantagruel felt himself carried away, so that all that night he did nothing but tear through:

The Venerable Bede's *De numeris et signis,* Numbers and Signs;
Plotinus' *De inenarrabilibus,* Inexpressible Things;
Proclus' *De sacrificio et magia,* Sacrifices and Magic;
Artemidorus' *Per onirocriticon,* On the Interpretation of Dreams;
Anaxagoras' *Peri semion,* On Signs;
Dinarius' *Peri aphaton,* Unknowable Things;
Philistion's books;
Hipponax's *Peri anecphoneton,* Things Better Left Undiscussed;

And many, many others, so that finally Panurge said to him:

"My lord, stop all this intellectual groping and go to bed, for I can see you're far too agitated—indeed, such an extravagance of thinking and straining may well make you feverish. But first, have twenty-five or thirty good drinks, then go to bed and sleep comfortably—for tomorrow I will answer our English friend, I will argue with him, and if I don't get him *ad metam non loqui,* to the point where he can't say a word, well, then you can say anything you like about me."

"All right," said Pantagruel, "but Panurge, my good friend, he's a deeply learned man. How will you deal with him?"

"Very easily," said Panurge. "Please: don't even speak about it. Just leave the whole thing to me. Do you know any man as learned as the devils in hell?"

"Not really," said Pantagruel, "unless blessed by some special divine grace."

"You see?" said Panurge. "I've had many arguments with devils, and I've made them look like idiots, I've knocked them on their asses. So tomorrow you can be sure I'll make this glorious Englishman shit vinegar, right out in public."

Then Panurge spent the night boozing with the servants and playing games, at which he lost all the roses and ribbons from his breeches. And then, when the agreed-upon hour came, he conducted his master Pantagruel to the assigned meeting place, where as you can easily understand everyone in Paris, from the most important to the least, had assembled, all of them thinking:

"This devil of a Pantagruel, he's beaten all our clever fellows, and all those naive theologians and philosophers. But now he'll get what's coming to him, because this Englishman is a regular devil. We'll see who beats whom today."

Everyone was assembled; Thaumaste was waiting for them. And when Pantagruel and Panurge arrived in the hall, all the students—elementary, high school, and college—began to applaud, in their usual ridiculous way. But Pantagruel shouted at them, his voice as loud as the sound of a double cannon:

"Quiet! In the name of the devil, quiet! By God, you rascals, bother me and I'll cut the heads off every last one of you!"

Which announcement struck them as dumb as ducks: they were afraid even to cough, no matter if they'd swallowed fifteen pounds of feathers. And the very sound of his voice left them so parched and dry that their tongues hung half a foot out of their mouths, as if Pantagruel had roasted their throats.

Then Panurge began to speak, saying to the Englishman:

"Sir, have you come here seeking a debate, a contest, about these propositions which you have posted, or are you here to learn, to honestly understand the truth?"

To which Thaumaste answered:

"Sir, the only thing which has brought me here is my deep desire to understand that which I have struggled all my life to understand, and which neither books nor men have ever been able to resolve for me. As far as disputing and arguing is concerned, I have no interest whatever in that. That is a vulgar affair, and I leave it to villainous sophists, who never truly seek for truth when they argue, but only contradict each other and emptily debate."

"And so," said Panurge, "if I, who am no more than a minor disciple of my master Pantagruel, am able to satisfy you in all these matters, it would be an indignity and an imposition to trouble my master. Accordingly, it would be better if for now he simply presided over this discussion, judging what we say—and I need hardly say that he will himself satisfy you, should I be unable to fully quench your scholarly thirst."

"Indeed," said Thaumaste, "that's perfectly true."

"Then let us begin."

But note, please, that Panurge had hung a handsome tassel of red, white, green, and blue silk at the end of his long codpiece, and inside it he had stuffed a fat, juicy orange.

Chapter Nineteen ⁄⁄ How Panurge Made the Englishman Who Argued by Signs Look Like an Idiot

Then, with everyone watching and listening in absolute silence, the Englishman raised his hands high in the air, first one and then the other, holding his fingertips in the shape called, in Chinon, the hen's asshole. He struck the nails of one hand against the nails of the other four times in a row, then opened his hands and slapped his palms together with a sharp crack. Joining his hands once again, as he had done at the start, he clapped them twice, then opened them out and clapped them four times more. Then he clasped them and extended one right over the other, as if praying devoutly to God.

Suddenly Panurge raised his right hand and stuck his thumb into his nose, keeping the other four fingers extended in a row straight out from the tip of his nose. He closed his left eye and winked the right one, making a deep hollow between eyebrow and eyelid. Then he lifted his left hand, the four fingers held rigidly extended, the thumb raised, and lined it up precisely with his right hand, keeping it perhaps half again the width of his nose distant. Then he lowered both hands, keeping them just as they were, and ended by raising them halfway and holding them there, as if aiming at the Englishman's nose.

"And yet if Mercury—" the Englishman began.

But Panurge interrupted him:

"You have spoken. Be silent."

Then the Englishman made the following sign: With palm open, he raised his left hand high in the air, then closed its four fingers in a tight fist, with the thumb lying across the bridge of his nose. And then, suddenly, he raised his right hand, palm out, and lowered it again, placing the thumb against the little finger of his left hand, the four fingers of which he moved slowly up and down. Then, in reverse, he repeated with his right hand what he had just done with his left and with his left hand what he had done with his right.

Not a bit surprised, Panurge lifted his immense codpiece with his left hand, and with his right pulled from it a piece of white ox rib and two bits of wood in the same shape, one of black ebony, the other of rose-colored brazilwood. Arranging these objects symmetrically, in the fingers of his right hand, he clapped them together, making a sound exactly like that produced by the lepers in Brittany, to warn people off—but a sound infinitely more resonant and harmonious. And then, pulling his tongue slowly back into his mouth, he stood there, humming happily, staring at the Englishman.

The theologians, physicians, and surgeons thought this sign meant that the Englishman was a leper.

The counselors, jurists, and canon lawyers, however, thought his meaning was that being a leper brought with it a certain sort of happiness, as once our Lord had declared.

Not at all frightened, the Englishman raised both hands, holding them with the three largest fingers balled into a fist, then placed both thumbs between the index and middle fingers, with the little fingers sticking straight out. He presented his hands to Panurge, then rearranged them so that the right thumb touched the left one, and his little fingers, too, were pressed against each other.

At this, without a word, Panurge raised his hands and made the following sign: he put the nail of his right index finger against the thumb-nail, shaping a loop. He bent all the fingers of his right hand into a fist, except for the index finger, which he jabbed in and out of the space framed by his other hand. Then he extended both the index and the middle fingers of his right hand, separating them as widely as he possibly could and pointing them at Thaumaste. Then placing his left thumb in the corner of his left eye, he extended his entire hand like a bird's wing or a fish's backbone, and waved it very delicately up and down. Then he did the same thing with his right hand and his right eye.

Thaumaste began to turn pale and tremble, then made the following sign: he struck the middle finger of his right hand against the muscle of his palm, just below the thumb, then inserted the index finger of his right hand into a loop shaped exactly like that Panurge had made, except that Thaumaste inserted it from below, not from above.

Accordingly, Panurge clapped his hands together and breathed into his palms. Then, once again, he shaped a loop with his left hand and, over and over, inserted into it the index finger of his right hand. Then he thrust his chin forward and stood staring at Thaumaste.

And though no one there understood what these signs meant, they understood perfectly well that he was asking Thaumaste, without a word being spoken:

"Hey, what do you make of that, eh?"

And indeed Thaumaste began to sweat heavily, looking like a man swept away by high contemplation. Then he stared back at Panurge and put the nails of his left hand against those of his right, opening all the fingers into semicircles, then raised his hands as high as he could, exhibiting this sign.

At which Panurge suddenly put his right thumb under his jaw, and stuck the little finger into the loop fashioned by his left hand, and proceeded to vigorously snap his jaw, making his teeth crash harmoniously together.

In great anguish, Thaumaste stood up, but as he rose let fly a fat baker's fart, with the dung right after it. He pissed a good dose of vinegar, and stank like the devils in hell. All those in the hall began to hold their noses, because, clearly, it was anxiety that was obliging him to beshit himself. Then he raised his right hand, the ends of all the fingers clutched together, and spread out his left hand, flat against his chest.

At which Panurge pulled out his long codpiece with its waving tassel, stretching it a good foot and a half or more, holding it in the air with his left hand and with his right, taking the ripe orange, he threw it in the air seven times, the eighth time catching it in his right fist and then holding it quietly, calmly high in the air. Then he began to shake his handsome codpiece, as if displaying it to Thaumaste.

After this, Thaumaste began to puff out his cheeks like a bagpipe musician, blowing as hard as if he were inflating a pig's bladder.

At which Panurge stuck one finger of his left hand right up his ass, sucking in air with his mouth, as if eating oysters in the shell or inhaling soup. Then he opened his mouth a bit and slapped himself with the palm of his right hand, making an immensely loud sound which seemed to work its way up from the very depths of his diaphragm all along the trachial artery. And he did this sixteen times.

But all Thaumaste could do was snuffle like a goose.

So Panurge next stuck his right index finger into his mouth, clamping down hard on it. Then he pulled it out and, as he did so, made a loud noise, like little boys firing turnips from an elderwood cannon. And he did this nine times.

And Thaumaste cried:

"Ah ha, gentlemen! The great secret! He's got his hand in there up to the elbow."

And he pulled out a dagger, holding it with the point facing down.

At which Panurge grabbed his great codpiece and shook it against his breeches as hard as he could. Then he joined his hands like a comb and put them on top of his head, sticking out his tongue as far as he could and rolling his eyes like a dying goat.

"Ah ha, I understand," said Thaumaste. "But what?" And he set the handle of his dagger against his chest, and put his palm over the point, letting his fingertips turn lightly against it.

At which Panurge bent his head to the left and put his middle finger in his left ear, raising his thumb. Then he crossed his arms on his chest, coughed five times, and the fifth time banged his right foot on the ground. Then he raised his left arm and, tightening his fingers into a fist, held the thumb against his forehead, and with his right hand clapped himself six times on the chest.

But Thaumaste, as though still unsatisfied, put his left thumb to the end of his nose and closed the rest of that hand.

So Panurge put his forefingers on each side of his mouth, pulling back as hard as he could and showing all his teeth. His thumbs drew his lower eyelids as far down as they would go, making an exceedingly ugly face, or so it seemed to everyone watching.

Chapter Twenty // What Thaumaste Said about Panurge's Virtues and His Learning

Then Thaumaste stood up and, removing his hat, thanked Panurge graciously, then turned to the audience and said in a loud voice:

"Gentlemen, now I can truly speak the biblical words: *Et ecce plus quam Solomon hic,* And here is one who is greater than Solomon. You see in front of you an incomparable treasure: and that is Monsieur Pantagruel, whose fame drew me from the farthest reaches of England in order to discuss with him certain insoluble problems, involving not only magic, alchemy, cabalistic learning, geometrical divination, and astrology but philosophy as well, which had long been troubling me. But now his fame bothers me, because it seems to be afflicted with jealousy—certainly, it hasn't granted him a thousandth part of what he deserves.

"You have seen for yourselves how his only disciple has satisfied my questions—has even told me more than I'd asked. Moreover, he has first shown and then solved for me other problems of inexpressible difficulty and importance, and in so doing he has opened for me, I can assure you, the deepest, purest well of encyclopedic learning, and in a fashion, indeed, that I had never thought any man could accomplish—not even begin to accomplish. I refer to our disputation by signs alone, without a word being spoken. But in due time I will record everything he has said and shown me, so no one will think that this has been mere tomfoolery in which we have been engaged, and I will have that record put into print so others can learn from it as I have. Then you will be able to judge how little the master is truly esteemed, when the mere disciple can demonstrate such ability, for as it is written, *Non est discipulus super magistrum,* The disciple is not superior to his master.

"And now let praise be given to God, and let me humbly thank you all for the honor you have shown us. May the good Lord repay you through all eternity."

Pantagruel said similarly courteous things to all who were gathered there, and as he left took Thaumaste with him, to dine—and you will believe they drank until they had to open their breeches to let their bellies breathe. (In those days men buttoned up their bellies, the way they button up their collars today.) They drank, indeed, until all they could say was, "Where do *you* come from?"

Holy Mother of God, how they guzzled, and how many bottles of wine they put away:

"Over here!"

"More, more!"

"Waiter, wine!"

"Pour it, in the name of the devil, pour it!"

No one drank fewer than twenty-five or thirty jugs, and do you know how? *Sicut terra sine aqua,* Like a dry land with no water—for it was warm weather and, besides, they were good and thirsty.

But as for Thaumaste's explanation of the signs they used, in their disputation, well, I'd be glad to explain them all myself, but I'm told that Thaumaste in fact wrote a huge book, printed in London, in which he sets out everything, omitting not a single item. In consideration of which, for now at least I'll just leave the subject.

Chapter Twenty-one ⁄⁄ How Panurge Fell in Love with a Noble Parisian Lady

Because of his success in this disputation against the Englishman, Panurge began to develop a certain reputation in Paris. This made his codpiece an even more valuable instrument, and he festooned it with bits of embroidery (in the Roman style). They sang his praises everywhere, even making up a song about him, which was sung by the little boys going to fetch mustard. And he became so welcome wherever women and girls were gathered, such a glamorous figure, that he began to think about tumbling one of the city's greatest ladies.

Indeed, not bothering with the long prologues and protestations poured forth by the usual whining, moody Lent lovers, who have no affection for flesh and blood, he said to her:

"Madame, the whole country would find it useful, and it would be a delight to you, an honor to your descendants and, for me, a necessity, for you to be bred to my blood: believe me, experience will show you how truthfully I speak."

At these words the lady pushed him more than a hundred yards away, saying:

"You wicked idiot, what makes you think you have the right to talk to me like that? To whom do you think you're speaking? Go! Don't let me ever see you again—indeed, I'm tempted to have your arms and legs chopped off."

"Now," he said, "it would be perfectly agreeable to lose my arms and legs, provided you and I could shake a mattress together, playing the beast with two backs, because"—and here he showed her his long cod-piece—"here's Master John Thomas, who's ready to sing you a merry tune, one you'll relish right through the marrow of your bones. He knows the game very well indeed: he knows just how to find all the little hidden places, all the bumps and itchy spots. When he's been sweeping up, you never need a feather duster."

To which the lady answered:

"Go, you wicked man, go! If you say one more word to me, I'll call for help and have you beaten to a pulp."

"Ho!" he said. "You're not as nasty as you say you are—no, or I've been totally taken in by appearances. The earth will float up into the clouds, and the high heavens drop down into the abyss, and all of nature be turned upside down and inside out, before someone of such beauty, such elegance, possesses so much as a drop of bile or malice. It's truly said that you don't often find

> A woman who's truly beautiful
> Inclined to make herself dutiful

—but then, they say that about vulgar beauties. Yours is a beauty so excellent, so rare and unusual, so celestial, that I believe nature intended you as a model, letting us know what she could do when she wished to use all her power and all her knowledge. Everything about you is honey, is sugar, is heavenly manna.

"It's you to whom Paris should have given the golden apple, not Venus, no, or Juno, or Minerva, for Juno was never so magnificent, Minerva never so wise, or Venus so elegant, as you.

"O celestial gods and goddesses, how happy he will be, whoever you grant the grace of coupling with this woman, of kissing her, of rubbing his bacon against her. By God, it's got to be me, I see it perfectly well, because she already loves me. I see it, I know it, I was destined for this by all the fairies and elves. No more wasting time, push it, pull it, let's get to it!"

And he tried to take her in his arms, but she started toward the window, as if to call in her neighbors. So Panurge left at once, and as he went said to her:

"Wait right here, madame. Don't trouble yourself: I'll fetch them for you."

And so he went off, not terribly concerned about the rebuff he'd experienced, and not particularly unhappy.

The next day he appeared at church right when she came to hear mass. As she entered the church, he sprinkled holy water on her and made her a profound bow, and then, as they were kneeling in prayer, he approached her familiarly and said:

"Madame, understand: I love you so much I can't piss or shit. I don't know what you think—but suppose I fall sick, whose fault will it be?"

"Go away," she said, "go away, I don't care! Leave me alone, let me say my prayers to God."

"Ah," he said, "but think about *To Beaumont le Vicomte.*"

"I don't know it," she said.

"Here's what it means," he said. "*A beau con le vit monte,* A prick climbs on a beautiful cunt. And pray to God that He grants me what your noble heart longs for. Here, let me have those prayer beads."

"Take them," she said, "and leave me alone."

And she tried to take off her rosary, which was fashioned of scented wood; the large beads were solid gold. But Panurge quickly pulled out one of his knives and neatly cut it for her, and started off to the pawnshop, saying:

"Madame, may I offer you my knife?"

"No, no!" she said.

"But remember," he said, "it's always at your service, body and baggage, guts and bowels."

But losing her rosary beads didn't make the lady very happy, for they were an important part of her appearance in church, and she thought to herself, "This babbler is out of his mind; he must be a foreigner. I'll never get those beads back. What will I say to my husband? He'll be angry at me. But I'll tell him a thief cut them off while I was in church, and he'll surely believe me, seeing the end of the ribbon still tied to my belt."

After dinner, Panurge went to see her, carrying hidden in his sleeve a fat purse, stuffed with tokens used in high-court business. And he began by saying:

"Who's more in love, me with you, or you with me?"

To which she answered:

"I certainly don't hate you, because as God commands I love the whole world."

"But more specifically," he said, "don't you love me?"

"I've already told you," she said, "and over and over, that you're not to say such things to me! If you insist on speaking to me like this, I will show you, sir, that dishonorable words may be directed at some women, but not me. Leave—and give me back my rosary beads, in case my husband asks for them."

"What?" he said. "Your rosary beads, madame? Ah no, I can't do that, on my honor I can't. But I'd be delighted to give you others. Which would you prefer? Enameled gold, with large beads, or handsome love knots, or something truly enormous, with beads as fat as ingots? Or perhaps you'd prefer ebony wood, or big blue jacinth stones, or well-cut red garnets, and every tenth stone a gorgeous turquoise, or else maybe a fine topaz, or a shining sapphire, or maybe all in rubies with a fat diamond every tenth stone, something cut with twenty or thirty gleaming faces?

"No—no—that's not good enough. I know a beautiful necklace of fine emeralds, and every tenth stone marked with great round ambergris, and the clasp set with an oriental pearl as fat as an orange! It costs only twenty-five thousand gold pieces. I'd love to give you that; I can afford it without any trouble."

And as he spoke he jiggled the court counters in his sleeve so they rang like gold pieces.

"Would you like a bolt of bright crimson velvet, striped with green, or some embroidered satin, or maybe crimson? What would you like—necklaces, gold things, things for your hair, rings? All you have to do is say yes. Even fifty thousand gold pieces doesn't bother me."

He was making her fairly salivate, but she answered:

"No. Thank you, but I want nothing from you."

"By God," said he, "I damned well want something from you, and it's something that won't cost you a cent, and once you've given it you'll still have it, every bit of it. Here"—and he showed her his long codpiece—"here's my John Thomas, who wants a place to jump into."

And then he tried to take her in his arms, but she began to scream, although not too loud. So Panurge dropped all pretense and said to her:

"You won't let me have even a little of it, eh? Shit to you! You don't deserve such a blessing, or such an honor. By God, I'll get the dogs to screw you."

And then he got out of there as fast as he could, afraid of being beaten—for he was a terrible coward.

Chapter Twenty-two ⁄⁄ How Panurge Played a Nasty Joke on the Parisian Lady

The next day was the great feast of Corpus Christi, for which all the women wore their very best gowns. And that day this particular Parisian lady wore a beautiful dress of red satin and a very expensive white velvet petticoat.

The day before the feast, Panurge hunted everywhere till he found a bitch in heat, then tied her to his belt and brought her to his rooms, where he fed her extremely well all day long, and that night, too. And then in the morning he killed her and cut out that portion so well known to the ancient Greek magicians and diviners. He cut it into the smallest possible pieces and, taking it with him, well hidden, he went where the lady would be sure to come, as (by custom and tradition) she followed the holy procession. And when she came by, Panurge sprinkled her with holy water, greeted her most courteously, and a little later, after she had said her prayers, went and sat by her on a bench and gave her a poem carefully written out as follows:

> O lovely lady, just this once
> I told my love: you called me dunce
> And drove me off, said "Don't return!"
> Though what I could have done to earn
> Your hate, by word or deed, I'll never
> Know. What trusting lover was ever
> So shamed? Why not just gently sever
> The knot and tell me my passion must burn
> Uselessly, just this once?
>
> Look in my heart: what your heart hunts
> Is there—not venom, but only chunks
> Of flaming desire, longing that burns
> Like the sun, and all my desire turns
> On my need to stuff your lovely cunt,
> But just this once.

And as she unfolded the sheet to read this poem, Panurge quickly sprinkled the hidden substance all over her, here, there, and everywhere, even into the folds of her sleeves and her dress. Then he said:

"Madame, unhappy lovers are rarely at peace. As for me, I hope that the hard nights, the pains, and all the anxiety my love for you has given me will be taken into account, when the fires of purgatory are lit for me.

At least, pray to God on my behalf, that He may grant me patience in my suffering."

He had barely finished when all the dogs hanging around the church came running at the lady, drawn by the smell of that which he had sprinkled on her. Little ones and big ones, fat ones and thin ones, they all came, penises at the ready, sniffing and snuffing and pissing all over her. It was one of the nastiest scenes you'll ever hope to see.

Panurge chased away a few of them, but the lady fled, and he went into a small chapel, from which he could watch the show. Those wretched dogs completely pissed up her clothes, a huge wolfhound pissing on her head, others on her sleeves, some on her backside, while the littlest ones pissed on her shoes, with the result that the women who gathered around had a hard time saving her.

And Panurge laughed, saying to a Parisian gentleman:

"By God, that lady must be in heat, or else some wolfhound screwed her not too long ago."

And when he saw that the dogs were snarling and growling all around her, exactly as if she'd been a bitch in heat, he ran off in search of Pantagruel.

And on every street where he found dogs, he kicked them, saying, "Why aren't you at the wedding with all the others? Hurry up, hurry up, by the devil! Hurry!" And when he got to their lodgings, he said to Pantagruel:

"Master, I beg you, come see how all the dogs in the whole country are after a woman, the prettiest in the whole city, and trying to screw her."

And Pantagruel was quite happy to come see this sight, this intensely dramatic spectacle, which struck him as most interesting, as well as brand-new.

But the best of it all was the procession, in which you could see more than six hundred thousand and fourteen dogs all around her, making her life miserable in a thousand ways. Everywhere she went, the dogs came running along behind her, pissing on the road wherever her dress had touched it.

Everyone stopped to watch the show, watching the dogs' fabulous tricks, some of them leaping as high as her shoulders. They completely ruined her beautiful clothes, and finally there was no help for it but to run back to her home, dogs running after her. And when she got home she hid herself, while the chambermaids giggled. Still, even when she'd closed the door behind her, all the dogs from half a mile around came running and bepissed the front door so thoroughly that their urine made a stream in which ducks could have swum. And indeed it is this same stream which, today, flows past Saint Victor, and in which the Gobelins dye their red wools, precisely because of the endowment these pissing dogs gave that water, as our beloved Maître Oribus has publicly declared in a sermon.

And so—God help you! A mill could have ground corn alongside that torrent, but Bazacle's mills, in Toulouse, do it still better.

Chapter Twenty-three // How Pantagruel Left Paris, Hearing That the Dipsodes ("Bloodthirsty," in Greek) Had Invaded the Land of the Amaurotes ("Hard to See," in Greek); Also, Why the French Mile Is a Short One

Not long after, Pantagruel heard that Morgan le Fay had translated his father, Gargantua, to the land of the fairies, like Ogier and Artus before him. And at the same time, word of this event having spread, the Dipsodes had poured across their borders and destroyed a large part of Utopia; they were at that very moment besieging the great city of the Amaurotes. So he left Paris without bidding farewell to anyone, the situation calling for the utmost speed, and went directly to Rouen.

Now, as he traveled, Pantagruel saw that the French mile was far too small, compared with that of other countries, and asked Panurge why this was so. And Panurge told him the tale told by Marotus du Lac, a monk, in *Stories of the Kings of Canarre*: "Once upon a time, the country was not divided up into miles, Roman paces, Greek furlongs, or Persian parasangs. And then King Pharamond put them into effect, in the following way. He went to Paris and picked out a hundred young, handsome gallants, good fellows and tough, and a hundred pretty wenches from Picardy, and he took them home and treated them well and courteously for a week. Then he called them in and gave each fellow a girl, with more than enough money to spend, ordering them to go wherever they liked, this way, that way, but wherever they flipped the girls on their backs they were to deposit a stone, and that distance would be called a mile.

"So they all left, happy, and because they were fresh and well rested they made love at the end of every field, which was why the miles in France were so short. But after they'd been on the road a while, and were getting worn down with it, and had less oil in their lamps, they didn't make love as often, being perfectly satisfied (and here I speak only of the men) with one weary, scrabbly time a day. And that's why the miles in Brittany, and in Gascony, and in Germany and other countries still farther away are all so long. Now, there are others who give different reasons, but this seems to me the best."

And Pantagruel was glad to agree.

Leaving Rouen, they came to the port of Honfleur, from which Pantagruel, Panurge, Epistemon, Carpalim, and Eusthenes booked passage by sea. While waiting for a favorable wind, and having their boat caulked,

Pantagruel received from a lady in Paris (who had been his mistress for quite some time) a letter inscribed as follows:

To the best loved of the handsome
and the least faithful of the brave,
P. N. T. G. R. L.

Chapter Twenty-four // The Letter Which a Messenger Brought Pantagruel from a Lady in Paris, and the Explanation of What Was Carved on a Gold Ring

When Pantagruel read this inscription, he was astonished, and asked the messenger who it was that had sent him the letter. Then he opened the letter and found nothing written inside, but only a gold ring, set with a single diamond, cut flat across rather than in facets. So he called Panurge and explained the situation to him.

Panurge informed him that the sheet of paper had indeed been written on, but in some secret way, so that no one could see the writing.

Accordingly, he said, in order to find out, they would have to hold the paper near the fire: perhaps the letter had been written in sal ammoniac dissolved in water.

Then he tried putting it in water, to see if the letter might have been written in the milky sap of a euphorbia plant.

Then he held it near a candle, to see if it had been written in white onion juice.

Then he rubbed one part of it with walnut juice, to see if it had been written in ink made from fig-wood ash.

Then he rubbed another part with milk from a mother nursing her first child, to see if it had been written in toad's blood.

Then he rubbed one corner with ashes from a swallow's nest, to see if it was written in winter-cherry dew.

Then he rubbed another end with earwax, to see if it was written in crow bile.

Then he soaked it in vinegar, to see if it had been written in the sap of the spurge plant.

Then he rubbed it with bat grease, to see if it had been written in that whale sperm we call ambergris.

Then he put it very gently in a basin of cool water and suddenly pulled it out, to see if it had been written with alum crystals.

And finally, seeing that he had learned absolutely nothing, he called the messenger over and asked him, "Brother, did the lady who sent you here give you any kind of stick to bring with it?"—thinking it might be the ancient Greek trick of making a message unclear until it was rolled out on a stick of some special dimensions.

But the messenger answered, "No, sir."

Then Panurge wanted to shave his head, to see if the lady might have written her message, in some strong ink, on his bare skull, but seeing how long the man's hair was, he desisted, since in so short a time his hair could not possibly have grown so long.

So he said to Pantagruel:

"Master, by the holy virtues of God Himself, I don't know what to do or to say! To learn if anything has been written here I've drawn on the secret wisdom of Signor Francesco of Nothingness, the famous Tuscan scholar, and I've also used Zoroaster's great book, *Peri grammaton acriton,* Writing Which Is Hard to Decipher, and Calphurnius Bassus', too, *De literis illegibilibus,* On Invisible Writing. But I see nothing. So it seems to me that this ring says nothing except that it's a ring. But let's look at it."

And then, looking at it, they found it was inscribed, in Hebrew, with the last words of Christ upon the cross:

LAMAH HAZABTHANI

So they called Epistemon and asked him what this was supposed to mean. To which he answered that these were Hebrew words, meaning "Why have you forsaken me?"

To which Panurge immediately replied:

"I see it all. Do you see this diamond? It's a *false* diamond. So what the lady means is as follows:

"Tell me, false lover, why you have forsaken me?"

Pantagruel understood at once, and recalled that he hadn't taken the time to say farewell to the lady, for which he was extremely sorry. He wished to return to Paris to make his peace with her. But Epistemon reminded him of how Aeneas left Dido, and Heraclitus of Tarentum's saying that when the ship is at anchor, and it must sail at once, it is better to cut the rope than to take the time to wind it back up. He had to forget memory itself, in order to defend his native city, which was in such danger.

And indeed, just an hour later, the north-northwest wind began to blow and it was time to open their sails and take to the high seas. In just a few days they passed Porto Santo and Madeira, on their way to the Canary Islands.

From there they sailed past Cape Blanco, Senegal, Cape Verde, Gambia, Sagres, and Melli, in Liberia, then past the Cape of Good Hope, and then they had reached the kingdom of Melinda, near Zanzibar. From there, blown by the north wind, they passed Meden, Uti, Uden, Gelasim, the Fairy Islands, and then along the coast of the kingdom of Achorie, at last landing in Utopia, some three miles and a little more from the city of the Amaurotes.

When they'd gotten their land legs back, Pantagruel said:

"My boys, we're not far from the city. Before we go any farther, we need to think about what's to be done, so we won't be like the Athenians, who never planned anything except after the fact. Are you prepared either to live or to die at my side?"

"My lord, yes," they all said. "You can be as certain of us as you are of the fingers on your own hands."

"Then," he said, "there's only one thing that bothers me, and that is: I don't know how many besiegers there are, or how they're deployed in front of the city. Once I know these matters, I can proceed against them with great assurance. Accordingly, let us consider how best to find out these things."

To which they all answered, as one:

"We'll go and see, and you wait for us here. Before the day is over, we'll bring you definite word."

"My plan," said Panurge, "will be to sneak into their camp, right in the middle of the guards and sentries. I'll eat and drink with them, and I'll screw around at their expense. But no one will know who I am, so I'll stroll over and have a look at their artillery, and which tents their officers are in, and generally strut around in all their regiments, without their ever knowing a thing. I can match wits with the devil himself, because I'm a direct descendant of Zopirus, who cut off his own nose and ears so he could disguise himself from the enemy."

"And I," said Epistemon, "since I understand all the stratagems and heroic deeds of all the great heroes and champions of history, and all the tricks and subtleties of the military art, I will go there and even if they sniff me out and unmask me, I'll make them believe whatever I like, and I'll escape, because I'm a direct descendant of Sinon the Greek, who got the Trojan horse into Troy."

"And I," said Eusthenes, "I'll go in right across their trenches, in spite of the sentries and all their guards, because I'll walk on their bellies and break their arms and legs, even if they're as strong as the devil himself, because I'm a direct descendant of Hercules."

"And I," said Carpalim, "will go in as the birds do, because my body's so flexible, so light on its feet, that I can jump their trenches and go right into their camp before they even know I'm there, and I don't have to worry about bullets or arrows, or horses. I'm as light as a feather, so even if they had Perseus' magic horse, Pegasus, or the horse the dwarf Pacolet made out of wood, I'd run away from them, laughing as I went, and unhurt. By God, I can walk on the blades of wheat, or the grass in the meadow, without their bending under me, because I'm a direct descendant of Camilla, the Amazon princess who fought Aeneas."

Chapter Twenty-five ⁄⁄ How Pantagruel's Companions, Panurge, Carpalim, Eusthenes, and Epistemon, Cleverly Defeated Six Hundred and Sixty Enemy Knights

As Carpalim was speaking, they became aware of six hundred and sixty knights, well armored and riding fast horses, who were coming to see what ship it was that had newly docked in that port, galloping at full speed so they could capture the newcomers, if there weren't too many of them.

So Pantagruel said:

"Boys, get back in the boat. These are our enemies, galloping down, but I'll kill them all for you like dogs, even if there were six times as many. But you go back and enjoy the fun."

But Panurge answered:

"No, my lord, it wouldn't be right to do it that way. No, exactly the opposite: *you* go back in the boat, you and all the others, and I alone will take care of them. But go quickly—quickly!"

And the others said:

"My lord, he's right. You go back in the boat and let us help Panurge. Just wait: we know what we're doing."

So Pantagruel said:

"All right, I agree. But in case you're getting the worst of it, you can count on me."

Then Panurge took two thick ropes from the ship and tied one end to the capstan, on the main deck. Then he laid them out on the ground in two circles, one longer than the other, and said to Epistemon:

"Go back in the boat, and when I give you the signal, turn the capstan as hard and fast as you can, and wind in these ropes."

Then he said to Eusthenes and Carpalim:

"Boys, wait right here, and surrender to the enemy, do whatever they want. Let them think you're captives. But don't get in the circle between these two ropes: make sure you stay outside."

So they quickly went back into the boat. And Panurge took a bale of straw and a barrel of gunpowder, and spread it in the circle between the two ropes. With a lit torch in hand, he stood close by.

The troop of knights came galloping up. But the ones in front, forty-four in all, reined in just short of the boat, and since the banks were wet they slipped and, horses and all, fell into the water. And those behind them, seeing their comrades go down, thought they had met with resistance. But Panurge said to them:

"Gentlemen, I believe your friends have had an accident. Excuse us, please, because it's not our fault but just the slipperiness of seawater, which indeed is always inclined to be slippery. We surrender ourselves to you, freely and willingly."

The others said the same thing, including Epistemon, who was up on deck.

But Panurge drew back and—seeing that the knights were all in the rope circle, and that his two companions had stayed outside it, giving way to all the knights who were pushing and shoving in close, to see the ship and whoever might be in it—suddenly called out to Epistemon:

"Pull, pull!"

And when Epistemon began to wind the capstan, the ropes got all tangled up in the horses' legs, which quite naturally resulted in beasts and riders both being thrown to the ground. Seeing which, the knights drew their swords and got ready to kill Panurge and his friends. But Panurge lit the train of gunpowder and burned them up like damned souls. Horses and men, not one of them escaped, except one, who was riding a Turkish steed, and managed to gallop off. But when Carpalim saw this, he ran after him so quickly, so easily, that he caught him in less than a hundred paces and, leaping onto the horse's back, grabbed the man from behind and brought him back to the boat.

Pantagruel was delighted at the destruction they'd wrought. He gave endless praise to his companions' cleverness and skill, and made them a fine banquet right there on the bank, with much good food and drink. He had them drinking right where they lay, belly on the ground, and their prisoner with them, as pleasantly as you please, except that the poor devil wasn't entirely sure that the giant Pantagruel wouldn't eat him in one bite, as he could easily have done, for his throat was so huge that he could have swallowed the man like a bit of sugared almond and no more known he was even in his mouth than a donkey would have known he'd swallowed a grain of millet.

Chapter Twenty-six ⁄ How Pantagruel and His Companions Were Unhappy about Eating Salt Meat, and Carpalim Went Hunting for Venison

As they were feasting, Carpalim said:

"But by Saint Quenet's belly, don't we ever get to eat venison? This salt meat makes me incredibly thirsty. Let me go fetch a leg from one of those horses we burned up. It should be well roasted."

As he got up, he saw a fine big stag come out at the edge of the wood, probably because he'd seen Panurge's fire. Carpalim immediately set out after the animal, moving so fast that he might have been fired from a crossbow. He caught the stag in an instant—and as he ran, he reached up and plucked out of the air:

> four fat plovers,
> seven cranes,
> twenty-six gray partridges,
> thirty-two brown ones,
> sixteen pheasants,
> nine woodcocks,
> nineteen herons, and
> thirty-two wood pigeons.

While with his feet, he killed ten or twelve good-sized hares and rabbits,

> eighteen swamp hens, running two by two,
> fifteen young wood pigs,
> two badgers, and
> three large foxes.

Striking the stag across the head with his scimitar, Carpalim killed him, and as he was bringing him back also collected the hares and rabbits, the swamp hens and the young wood pigs, and as soon as he got within earshot called out:

"Panurge, my friend, vinegar! vinegar!"

Which made Pantagruel think he was faint, and he ordered that vinegar be brought to him. But Panurge understood perfectly well that he had rabbits in his stewpot and, indeed, pointed out to his noble master how Carpalim carried the buck over his shoulders and had stuck hares and rabbits into his belt, all around.

In the name of the nine Muses, Epistemon quickly fashioned nine Greek-style spits, carving them out of fresh wood; Eusthenes helped with the skinning; and Panurge laid out two of the dead knights' saddles, so they did very well as andirons. Their prisoner was put in charge of roasting, and with the same fire in which they had consumed the knights, they roasted their venison. And then they had a grand time, and used the vinegar liberally—and the devil take the hindmost! It was marvelous to see them wolfing it down.

Then Pantagruel said:

"If only God would put a pair of hawk bells on your chins, and on

mine the great clocks at Rennes, and Poitiers, and Tours, and Cambray—
oh, what a song we'd sing as our chops went up and down."

"Yes," said Panurge, "but we'd do better to think about what we're
doing here, and how we can topple our enemies."

"That's very well considered," said Pantagruel.

So he asked their prisoner:

"My friend, tell us the truth, and not a lying word, if you don't want
to be skinned alive—because I eat little children. Tell us exactly how many
men there are in your army, and how they're deployed, and what fortifications have been built."

To which the prisoner answered:

"My lord, the truth is that there are three hundred giants in the army,
all of them armed with big blocks of quarried stone, and they're incredibly big, though not as big as you, except their leader, whose name is
Werewolf, whose armor is made of gigantic anvils. There are also a hundred
and seventy-three thousand foot soldiers, all wearing goblin skins that are
just as hard to pierce as werewolf hide; and these are all courageous men,
and strong. And there are eleven thousand and fourteen hundred men-at-
arms, plus three thousand six hundred double cannon, and more siege
guns than a man can count. And there are ninety-four thousand scouts,
and a hundred and fifty thousand whores, as beautiful as goddesses—"

"That's for me," said Panurge.

"—And some of them are Amazons, and some come from Lyons, and
from Paris, from Touraine, and Anjou, and Poitou, and Normandy, and
Germany—from everywhere in the world, and speaking every language
known to men."

"Very good," said Pantagruel. "But where's the king? Is he there?"

"Yes, sire," said the prisoner, "he's there in person, and his name is
Anarch, king of the Dipsodes. Dipsodes means 'thirsty people,' because
you'll never see people anywhere who can match us for thirst, or who
are happier to drink. The giants guard the king's tent."

"Enough," said Pantagruel. "How about it, boys? Are you sure you
want to come with me?"

To which Panurge answered:

"God blast anyone who stays behind! I've been trying to figure out
how I could deliver them to you, like a row of dead pigs who couldn't
get away even if they sold their legs to the devil. But there's just one
thing that still bothers me."

"Which is?" said Pantagruel.

"Which is," said Panurge, "how I can manage to screw all those whores
in just one afternoon, so not a single one escapes and I get to have every
damned one of them."

"Ha, ha, ha!" laughed Pantagruel.

And Carpalim said:

"I'll be damned! By God, I'll stuff some of them myself!"

"And me," said Eusthenes. "What! I haven't even had it straight up since we left Rouen—at least, only so my needle pointed at ten or eleven o'clock. So now I'm hard and strong like a hundred devils."

"Indeed," said Panurge. "You can have the plumpest ones, the ones in best condition."

"What's all this?" said Epistemon. "Everyone else goes screwing and I get to hold the donkey's reins? May the devil carry off whoever just sits around and watches! This is war, and we claim its privileges: *Qui potest capere capiat,* Anyone who can take it, take it."

"No, no," said Panurge. "Tie up your donkey and go screwing like everyone else."

And Pantagruel laughed at them all, and then said:

"You're forgetting all about your host. I'm worried that, before night-fall, I might see you in such a state that you won't be much interested in standing up at all, and instead they'll be screwing you with a quick thrust of a spear or a lance."

"That will do!" said Epistemon. "I'll deliver them to you, and you decide if you'd prefer them roasted or boiled, fricasseed or in a batter. And are there more of them than Xerxes had, who commanded three million warriors—if you believe Herodotus and Pompeius Trogus. But Themistocles had only a handful of men, and he defeated them. Don't feel the slightest concern, please!"

"Oh, shit, shit!" said Panurge. "My codpiece by itself ought to be enough to sweep up all the men. And Saint Ballandcunt, who lives here inside, will clean up the women."

"Then off we go, boys!" said Pantagruel. "Let's start walking."

Chapter Twenty-seven // How Pantagruel Built a Monument to Their Bravery, and Panurge Built One to the Hares and Rabbits They'd Eaten; Also, How Some of Pantagruel's Farts Created Tiny Men, and Some Created Tiny Women; And How Panurge Broke a Thick Stick over Two Glasses

"Before we leave," said Pantagruel, "in memory of the brave deeds done here, I wish to put up a nice monument."

Gaily, and singing little country songs, they decorated a large tree, on which they hung: a warrior's saddle, a horse's leg armor, harness pom-

poms, stirrup leathers, spurs, a mail shirt, a complete set of horse armor, an ax, a heavy short sword, a chain-link glove, a mace, shoulder armor, leg armor, the throat piece of a helmet, and so on, until they had everything needed for a triumphal arch or battle trophy.

Then, in eternal memory, Pantagruel wrote the following victory song:

> Here we saw heroic skills
> Displayed by valiant champions, four
> In all, who snuffed out hundreds more,
> Fighting not with armor but wills
> Of iron, and honest wits: like hills
> Of straw they burned the proudest knights.
> Wit is the fiercest engine of war:
> Let chessmen learn before they fight
>> That what all history
>> Teaches of victory
>> Blows like the wind.
>> The only story
>> Of eternal glory
>> Is what God brings
> To whoever pleases Him: you win
> With God at your side, not strength, not power.
> We built this trophy here in our hour
> Of triumph, our hearts free of sin.

While Pantagruel was writing this poem, Panurge raised up a big pole and from it hung the buck's horns, as well as his hide and both his right feet; then the ears of three hares, a rabbit's back, a hare's jaws, two plover's wings, the feet of four wood pigeons, a flask of vinegar, one salt-shaker, a wooden spit, a lard stick, a banged-up pot all full of holes, a saucepan, a clay saltcellar, and one cut-glass goblet from Beauvais. And then, in imitation of Pantagruel's monument, and of his poem, he wrote the following:

> Four happy drunks sat squatting here,
> Honoring Bacchus in a joyous feast,
> Down on their asses, guzzling beer
> And wine till they nearly dropped. Beasts
> Of the forest hung overhead, their ears
> Cropped, their paws cut off, but honoring
> Bacchus in their deaths, while vinegar and salt
> Followed them, led them, down our guts.
>> The best defense
>> Of common sense
>> In weather this hot

Is to drink a bot-
tle, and then another,
And all of the best.
How sad to think of rabbits and hares
Eaten unsauced, vinegarless:
Vinegar makes them taste their best,
Vinegar's their sauce beyond compare.

Then Pantagruel said:

"Let's go, boys. We've spent too much time feasting here: it's hard for great banqueters to do great things in battle. There's no shade like that cast by unfurled banners; there's no steam like a war-horse's breath, and no jingling like armor in action."

At which Epistemon began to smile, and said:

"There's no shade like that in a kitchen, no steam like a pie baking, and no jingling like that of glasses and mugs."

To which Panurge answered:

"There's no shade like the curtains on a bed, there's no steam like a pair of sweaty breasts, and no jingling like a pair of merry balls."

And getting up, he farted, and jumped, and whistled, and cried out happily, as loud as he could:

"Long live Pantagruel!"

But when Pantagruel tried, this time, to copy Panurge, his fart made the earth shake for twenty-nine miles around, and the foul air he blew out created more than fifty-three thousand tiny men, dwarves and creatures of weird shapes, and then he emitted a fat wet fart that turned into just as many tiny stooping women, of the kind you see all over the place, and who never get bigger, except that like cows' tails they grow down toward the ground—or else, like Limousin radishes, they just get fatter and fatter.

"Hey!" said Panurge. "Are your farts as productive as all that? By God, here are some good worn-out men and some nice fart-headed women. They ought to get married: their children will turn out to be horseflies."

And Pantagruel did indeed marry them, and called them Pigmies, and he sent them to live on an island not far off, where ever since they have flourished and multiplied. But the cranes are always making war on them, though they defend themselves courageously, because these little human stumps (the Scots call them comb handles) are pretty short-tempered. There's a physical reason, too: their hearts are very close to their shit.

At the same time, Panurge picked up two glasses, both very good-sized, and filled them to the brim. Then he put each of them on a wooden stool, perhaps five feet apart. Then he took a spear shaft, five and a half feet long, and put it on top of the glasses, so that the ends of the shaft were exactly even with the rims of the glasses. Then he took a big stick and said to Pantagruel and the others:

"Gentlemen: just think how easily we're going to defeat our enemies. Exactly as, now, I will proceed to break this spear shaft without break-ing—no, without even cracking—these two glasses, and what's more, without spilling a single drop from either of them, so we'll break these Dipsodes' heads, without any of us being wounded and without losing anything we own. But in case you think this is just magic—here," he said to Eusthenes, "you take this stick and swing it down as close to the center as you can."

And Eusthenes did, and the spear shaft broke cleanly in half, and not a drop of water fell from either of the glasses. And Panurge said:

"I know a lot of these tricks. All right: let's go, knowing we can't lose."

Chapter Twenty-eight // How Pantagruel Won an Exceedingly Strange Victory over the Dipsodes and the Giants

After this discussion, Pantagruel called over their prisoner and set him free, saying:

"Go back to your king, in his camp, and tell him what you've seen. Tell him he'd better make a feast for me, tomorrow at about noon. For as soon as my other ships arrive, which will be tomorrow morning at the very latest, I will prove to him, by means of one million eight hundred thousand soldiers and seven thousand giants, each of them bigger than me, how absolutely idiotic and irrational it is for him to attack my coun-try."

And thus Pantagruel pretended that he had an army arriving by sea.

But the prisoner replied that he surrendered himself to Pantagruel as his slave, and was perfectly happy never to return to his own people, and indeed would rather fight with Pantagruel against them, if, in the name of God, he would permit it.

Pantagruel did not like the idea, and ordered him simply to go and do as he had been told. He gave the man a jar of euphorbium, which makes castor oil seem mild and gentle, sweetened with brandy and seasoned with Cnide-berry water, which matches castor oil in spirit and power, the whole thing molded into candies, and told him to bring it to his king. If that royal monarch could eat a single ounce without having to drink, then he could think himself able to resist Pantagruel without fear.

The prisoner knelt down and begged with folded hands that, when the time for battle came, Pantagruel would have mercy on him. And Panta-gruel answered:

"Once you have given your king my messages, put all your hope in

God, who will not abandon you. I won't tell you, as those professional hypocrites do, 'Help yourself and God will help you,' because what that really means is, 'Help yourself, because the devil's going to break your neck.' Look at me: powerful as I am, as you can see for yourself, and possessed as I am of an infinite number of fully armed soldiers, nevertheless I place no trust either in my strength or in my cleverness. All my faith is in God, my protector, who never abandons those who have turned their thoughts and place their hope in Him."

And then the prisoner begged that, as far as ransom was concerned, Pantagruel would prove himself a reasonable man. To which Pantagruel replied that it was not his intention to rob or ransom men, but to enrich them and raise them to complete freedom.

"Go then," he said, "and may the peace of God go with you, and stay away from evil men, so bad luck never comes to you."

Once the prisoner had gone, Pantagruel said to his men:

"Boys, I've let our prisoner think that we have an army coming by sea, and I've also let him think we won't attack them before tomorrow at about noon. I want them to worry about all those armed men so they spend the whole night getting themselves and their fortifications ready. But my real intention is that we attack just about when they'll be closing their eyes for the first time."

Let us now leave Pantagruel and his apostles, and turn to King Anarch and his army.

As soon as the prisoner returned, he was brought to the king, to whom he told how a great giant had come, named Pantagruel, who had beaten and indeed cruelly roasted a troop of six hundred and fifty-nine knights, and that only he had been saved to bring the news. Moreover, the giant had commanded him to tell the king to prepare dinner for him, tomorrow at noon, because that was when he had decided to attack.

Then he gave the king the box containing the candied herbs. But as soon as the king had swallowed a spoonful, his throat burned so fiercely that it instantly developed deep sores, and the skin was peeled off his tongue. Whatever he did to try to relieve the pain did not work, except to drink without stopping, because as soon as he took the bottle out of his mouth his tongue began to flame up again. So all they could do was pour wine down his throat, using a funnel.

Seeing this, his captains and pashas and guardsmen tasted the concoction themselves, to find out if they were able to manage it without drinking and so could fight without fear, but it worked on them exactly as it had on their king. As a result, they all drank so wildly that word spread all through the camp that the prisoner had returned and they were to expect an attack tomorrow, for which the king and his officers were already preparing, along with the guardsmen, by drinking like mad. So everyone in the army set to work tippling, lifting up their glasses and putting them down again just as their king was doing. Pretty soon, they had put away so much wine that they were snoring like hogs, sleeping wherever they happened to fall down, all over the entire camp.

Now let's return to our good Pantagruel and tell how he behaved in this business.

Leaving the spot where they'd erected their monuments and hung their trophies, he pulled out the mast of their boat, as if it had been a pilgrim's staff, and put in two hundred and thirty-seven barrels of good Anjou white (all that remained of what he'd brought from Rouen). Then, after filling the ship itself with salt, he hung it from his belt, carrying it as easily as soldiers' wives carry their little baskets. And then he and his companions set out down the road.

As they drew close to the enemy camp, Panurge said to him:

"My lord, would you like to do things right? Then take down that good Anjou wine and let's bend our elbows a little."

Which Pantagruel cheerfully agreed to, and they put it away so efficiently that not a drop of the two hundred and thirty-seven barrels was left, except a leather bottle flask made in Tours, which Panurge carefully filled for himself, calling it his *vade mecum,* his guide and companion, and some miserable leavings fit only for making vinegar.

After they'd drunk their fill, Panurge fed his master a fiendish purgative of his own manufacture, made of lithontriptic (so strong it can dissolve gallstones while they sit in your bladder), nephrocatarticon (which can empty your kidneys faster than the devil's tail), and quince marmalade laced with Spanish fly, plus a few other suitable diuretics. After which, Pantagruel said to Carpalim:

"Go down to that poor besieged city of ours: climb over the walls like a rat, as you know how to do so well. Tell them that right now they must sortie out and fall on the enemy as hard as they can. And then you climb down again and, with a flaming torch, set fire to all the tents in the camp. Then shout as loud as you can, in your most booming voice. And then get out of the camp."

"To be sure," said Carpalim. "But wouldn't it be a good idea if I spiked their cannon?"

"No, no," said Pantagruel. "But do set fire to their gunpowder."

Prompt to obey him, Carpalim left at once, and did exactly as Pantagruel had ordered. Then all the soldiers left in the city came sallying forth.

And when Carpalim had set fire to all the tents, he left the camp, moving so lightly that they never knew he was there, so deeply asleep and snoring so loudly as they were. He went where they kept their cannon and set fire to the gunpowder, which was exceedingly dangerous, because the flames flared up so quickly that they almost set fire to poor Carpalim. If it had not been for his incredible quickness, he would have been roasted like a chicken. But he left so swiftly that an arrow shot from a crossbow could not have fled any faster.

When he'd gone beyond their trenches, he shouted so horribly that it seemed as if the devils in hell had been unchained. And that sound woke their enemies, but do you know how? Just as heavily as the first tolling of the bells in the morning, which in the Vendée they call *scratch-your-balls*.

But by now Pantagruel had begun to spread around the salt in the boat, and because they slept with their mouths gaping open, he filled their gullets and the miserable wretches coughed like foxes, crying, "Ha, Pantagruel, you're making the fire inside us burn like crazy!" And then Pantagruel had a sudden, urgent need to piss, and he pissed all over their camp, so thoroughly and in such quantities, that his private and personal flood drowned everyone for ten miles around. And history records that, if his father's great mare had been there, and pissed as freely, there would have been a flood greater than that caused by Prometheus' son Deucalion, because that mare could never piss at all without creating a river greater than anything except the Rhine and the Danube.

And those who came out of the besieged city, seeing this, said: "They're all most savagely killed: just see the blood run."

But they were wrong, thinking that Pantagruel's piss was the enemy's blood, because they saw only by the faint light from the tents, with a little help from the moon.

And their enemies, after having been thus awakened, saw both the fire in their camp and the tremendous flood of urine, and didn't know what to think. Some said it was the end of the world, the Final Judgment, when the world would perish in fire. Others said that the sea gods Neptune, Proteus, Triton, and others were attacking them because, clearly, this was seawater, all salty.

Now who could properly tell how Pantagruel fought against the three hundred giants? O my muse, my Calliope, my Thalia, come and inspire me! Raise and restore my spirits, because now I have come to Logic's insupportable bridge of donkeys: here is where one finally pays, here is the true difficulty of ever putting into proper words a ghastly battle as it was truly fought.

I wish that it were in my power to give a bottle of the best wine to those about to read on, in this tale of things told exactly as they happened!

Chapter Twenty-nine // How Pantagruel Defeated the Three Hundred Giants Armed with Great Blocks of Stone, and Also Defeated Werewolf, Their Leader

The giants, seeing how their camp was flooded, carried King Anarch to safety on their backs, and brought him outside the fortifications, just as Aeneas had carried his father Anchises, during the fire that destroyed Troy. When Panurge saw this, he said to Pantagruel:

"My lord, see: the giants have come out. Now swing your staff as hard as you can, in the old French style, because this is the time when true men must prove themselves. None of us will let you down. Let's do it boldly: I'll kill a bunch of them for you myself. Why not? David easily killed Goliath. And this great rake, Eusthenes, who's as strong as four oxen, won't show them any mercy. Take courage; give it to them this way and that."

And Pantagruel said:

"I've got plenty of courage. But man! Even Hercules never dared to fight against two at once."

"Ha!" said Panurge. "You're shitting up my nose. You compare yourself to Hercules? By God, you've got more strength in your teeth and more brains in your ass than Hercules ever had in his whole body and soul. A man is worth as much as he thinks he is."

As they were speaking, Werewolf and his giants reached them, and seeing Pantagruel alone, their captain felt a surge of arrogant boldness, thinking he could surely kill the poor fellow. So he said to the other giants:

"By Muhammad's beard, if any of you siege-gun poppers fight with these fellows, you'll die a savage death at my hands! I want to kill them myself. But you can enjoy yourselves, watching."

So the other giants, together with King Anarch, fell back and picked up their wine bottles. And Panurge and his companions, who were pretending to be poxy beggars, went with them. Panurge twisted his throat and bent his fingers every which way, and making his voice hoarse, he said to them:

"In the name of God, brothers, we're not fighting anyone. Let us eat with you, while our masters fight."

Which was perfectly agreeable to the king and the giants, so they all sat together, feasting. And while they ate and drank, Panurge told them stories from Turpin's lying *Chronicles,* and tales about Saint Nicholas, and all kinds of Mother Goose stuff.

Werewolf then turned toward Pantagruel, carrying a great steel staff that weighed nine thousand seven hundred and a quarter tons, and was fashioned of Syrian steel. At the tip it had thirteen diamond points, the smallest of which was as big as the biggest bell hanging in the cathedral of Notre Dame, in Paris. Well, it might have been just a nail's width thinner, or maybe, to be completely accurate, just a touch thicker, say about the width of a dozen of the knives we call ear cutters—used to nip off convicts' ears—but only that much, just a little, not too much either way. And that staff was enchanted, rendered unbreakable by the fairies: exactly the opposite happened to anyone and anything it touched, for they would suddenly be smashed into little pieces.

And as Werewolf came arrogantly toward him, Pantagruel threw his glance toward heaven and consigned himself to God with a pure heart, praying as follows:

"Lord God, who has always protected and preserved me, You see the distress in which I now find myself. The only thing that has brought me here is that natural concern to protect themselves, with which You have endowed all humankind, and to protect their wives and children, their lands and their families, though never against Your decrees, which all must learn to accept with patience and faith. For Your only wish in such cases is for humans to make a good Catholic confession and obey Your words, forbidding us all weapons and defenses, since when You so desire, and in matters You have reserved to Yourself, You are all-powerful. You can defend Yourself far better than we can even imagine; You who have thousands of millions of billions of trillions of angels of whom the very least could kill every man alive and turn the heavens and the earth upside down, exactly as You wish, as long ago was made clear to the army of Sennacherib, when in one night an angel slaughtered almost two hundred thousand of those unbelieving soldiers. And if it should be Your pleasure to help me now, You in whom rests my complete faith and trust, I promise You that everywhere in this world, in my country of Utopia and everywhere where I have power and authority, I will preach Your Holy Word purely, simply, and in its entirety, so that the abuses of no matter how many pretended believers and false prophets, those who have by merely human words and corrupt inventions poisoned this whole earth, shall be exterminated as far as my hand can reach."

And then he heard a voice from heaven, saying, *"Hoc fac et vinces,"* which means, "Do this, and you shall prevail."

Then, seeing Werewolf coming at him, his mouth gaping open, Pantagruel charged bravely at him, shouting as loud as he could, to make him afraid: "Death to you, rascal! Death!" This was how the Spartans taught their men to fight, using their voices as well as their weapons. And then, dipping into the ship which hung from his belt, he threw eighteen herring barrels at him, and a great box of salt, which he got well up his throat and his windpipe, not to mention his nose and his eyes.

Angry at this, Werewolf swung his staff, trying to crush his opponent's skull. But Pantagruel was quick, always light on his feet and watchful, so he simply stepped back a bit with his left foot. Still, he couldn't keep the blow from landing on the ship, which broke into four thousand and eighty-six pieces, and made the rest of the salt fall to the ground.

And seeing this, with a vigorous stroke of his arms, and following the art of ax fencing, in which he had been trained, Pantagruel gave him a solid blow with his own staff, hitting him with the point just below the nipple. And then, swinging the staff back again, this time from left to right, he struck him right on the neck. After which, stepping forward with his right foot, he whacked him in the balls with the upper part of his staff, a blow which broke off the tip of the staff and spilled out three or four barrels of wine that were still stored there. And Werewolf thought his bladder had been cut open, and the wine pouring out was his urine.

Not satisfied with this, Pantagruel shifted his ax and prepared to attack again, but Werewolf, raising his huge staff high in the air, rushed forward, trying with all his might to drive the staff right through him. And indeed, he struck so swiftly that, if God had not helped our good Pantagruel, he would have been split open from the top of his head all the way down to his spleen. But because Pantagruel leaped quickly to his left, the blow fell just to his right, and the staff went more than seventy-three feet straight into the ground, smashing through a great rock as it went and flaring up with more sparks and fire than nine thousand and six burning barrels.

When Pantagruel saw his enemy giving all his attention to his staff, trying to pull it back out of the ground (it was stuck in that huge rock), he rushed at him, intending to smash him right on the head, but by bad luck his own staff glanced against Werewolf's—which as we have said was enchanted—and was immediately shattered, three fingers from the end of the handle. Which struck him dumber than a man in a foundry, casting bells, when he breaks away the mold and suddenly sees that the bell is cracked.

"Ha, Panurge, where are you?"

Hearing this, Panurge said to the king and the giants:

"By God, they're really going to hurt each other, if we don't separate them."

But the giants were as relaxed and happy as guests at a wedding. So Carpalim started to get up, to help his master, but a giant said to him:

"By Guffrin, Muhammad's nephew, if you move a muscle I'll shove you down my breeches like a suppository! And I'm so constipated these days, I can hardly shit at all, except by really grinding my teeth."

So Pantagruel, deprived of his staff, picked up the leftover stub of the handle and tried to whip it against the giant, but with that sort of weapon he couldn't do any more damage than flicking your finger against an anvil. And then Werewolf got his own staff out of the ground and swung it at Pantagruel, but Pantagruel backed up swiftly and ducked each blow, until Werewolf came very close and Pantagruel cried out, "Now, you villain, I'll chop you into mincemeat, and you'll never again raise a thirst in any poor devil!" And as he spoke, he kicked Werewolf so savagely in the belly that he fell over backward, with his legs in the air, at which Pantagruel immediately grabbed him and dragged him along the ground for the length of a good bow shot. And Werewolf screamed, blood spurting out of his mouth:

"Muhammad! Muhammad! Muhammad!"

And hearing this, all the giants jumped up, in order to help him. But Panurge said to them:

"Gentlemen, I think you'd better not go over there, because our master is a wild man, and he'll hit out right and left, without any regard for what he strikes. He might make you distinctly unhappy."

But the giants paid him no attention, since they saw that Pantagruel had no staff.

Seeing them approaching, Pantagruel lifted Werewolf (still wearing his armor of anvils) like a spear and, still holding him by the feet, smashed him into the giants and their blocks of stone like a mason making stone chips, swinging him this way and that until every one of them was beaten to the ground. And the sound of their stone armor cracking and splitting made such an incredible racket that it reminded me of the time when the great tower at Saint Etienne de Bourges, built all of butter, melted down in the sun. With the help of Carpalim and Eusthenes, Panurge quickly slit the throats of the giants, as they hit the ground.

Please realize that not one of them got away and, indeed, Pantagruel looked for all the world like a mower whose scythe (which was Werewolf) was cutting grass in a meadow (which was the giants), but in that fencing game Werewolf lost his head. And that happened when Pantagruel smashed him against one of the giants, Riflandouille by name, whose armor, made of soft sandstone, covered the giant from head to toe. (Most of the others wore less elaborate armor, usually of soft stone, but a few fashioned of harder stuff.) But when Werewolf slammed into the soft stone, it splintered and one fragment sliced right through Epistemon's throat.

Finally, seeing that they were all dead, Pantagruel threw the body of Werewolf as far as he could, off into the distant city, where it fell into the central square, flopping on its belly like a dead frog, and in falling killed a spotted tomcat, a wet kitten, a little field duck, and a bridled goose.

Chapter Thirty // How Epistemon, Whose Head Had Been Cut Off, Was Cleverly Restored to Life by Panurge, with Some News about Devils and the Damned in Hell

Having finished this gigantic routing of his enemies, Pantagruel went back to where they'd left their wine flasks and called Panurge and the others, who ran over to him, all safe and sound, except Eusthenes, whose face had been a bit scratched by one of the giants as he bent over to slit his throat, and Epistemon, who could not come at all. Which made Pantagruel so sad that he felt like killing himself. But Panurge said to him:

"Indeed, my lord, just wait a little, and we'll hunt for him, among all those corpses, and then we'll see what's what."

And when they went hunting for him, they found him, all stiff and dead, and his bloody head in his arms. And Eusthenes cried out:

"Ha! O you unlucky corpse, you've deprived us of the most perfect of men!"

And hearing this, Pantagruel rose, seized by the fiercest sorrow ever known on this earth, and said to Panurge:

"Ha! My friend, the prophecy of your two glasses and your spear shaft has been thoroughly mistaken!"

But Panurge said:

"Boys, don't shed a single tear. He's still good and warm: I'll fix him up for you, just as good as new."

So saying, he took the head and held it against his codpiece, both to keep it warm and to keep the air off it. Eusthenes and Carpalim carried the body back to where they'd done their feasting, not because they had any expectation of bringing him back to life, but just so Pantagruel could see him. But suddenly Panurge rallied their spirits, saying:

"If I don't cure him, let me lose *my* head—and where will you find a more idiotic pledge than that, eh? Now stop all that crying and come help me."

Then they carefully bathed his neck and afterward his head in good white wine, and sprinkled them well with diamond dung powder (which he always carried in one of his pockets). Then he rubbed on some ointment, I don't know what, and carefully fitted the head to the body, vein to vein, muscle to muscle, nerve to nerve, bone to bone, to make sure Epistemon wouldn't become one of those hunched-over people (hypocrites that he hated worse than death). And then he sewed him around, taking fifteen or sixteen stitches, so his head wouldn't fall off again, and finally he rubbed the wound all around with a bit of some ointment that he called a resuscitative.

Suddenly Epistemon began to breathe, then opened his eyes, then yawned, then sneezed, then blew out a fat domestic fart. At which Panurge said:

"Now I know he's cured!"

So he gave him a big glass of coarse white wine to drink, with a sugared sop of bread.

And so Epistemon was cleverly cured, except that he was hoarse for more than three weeks and suffered from a dry cough, which he couldn't get rid of unless he drank wine.

And then he began to speak to them, explaining that he'd seen the devils themselves, had had a nice intimate chat with Lucifer, and had a fine time both in hell and on the Elysian Fields. He swore to them that devils were damned good drinking friends. As far as the souls of the damned were concerned, he said he was really sorry Panurge had called him back to life so soon.

"Because," he said, "I took great pleasure in seeing them."

"How's that?" said Pantagruel.

"They're not as badly treated as you might think," said Epistemon. "But their condition is strangely changed. For example, I saw Alexander the Great, who eked out a poor living by patching up old breeches,

Xerxes was a mustard seller,
Romulus peddled salt, when he wasn't repairing shoes,
Numa sold nails,
Tarquin was a miserly money-lender,
Piso, a peasant,
Sulla, a ferryman,
Cyrus, a cowherd,
Themistocles was a glassblower,
Epaminondas, a mirror maker,
Brutus and Cassius were both surveyors,
Demosthenes tended a vineyard,
Cicero stoked a blacksmith's forge,
Fabius wove rosary beads,
Artaxerxes was a rope maker, when he wasn't skimming the scum
    off soup pots
Aeneas was a miller,
Achilles, who had scabies, was a hay baler,
Agamemnon went around licking out pots and pans,
Ulysses was a mower,
Nestor, a pickpocket,
Darius, a cesspool cleaner,
Ancus Martius caulked boats,
Camillus was a bootmaker,
Marcellus shelled beans,
Drusus cracked nuts for a living,
Scipio Africanus went up and down the streets, peddling wine dregs,
Hasdrubal was a lantern maker,
Hannibal, an egg seller,
Priam peddled old clothes,
Lancelot of the Lake skinned dead horses, and all the other Knights of
    the Round Table were poor starving wretches who made a living
    as galley slaves on the rivers of Cocytus, Phlegethon, Styx, Ach-
    eron, and Lethe, whenever my lords the devils felt like taking to
    the water, like the boatmen of Lyons and the gondoliers of Venice,
    except that all they got for each passage was a flick of the finger
    and, at night, a chunk of moldy bread,

Trajan fished for frogs,
Antoninus was a servant who scurried when his master called,
Commodus carved tourist toys of onyx,
Pertinax shelled walnuts,
Lucullus grilled roast meat,
Justinian sold secondhand games,
Hector whipped up sauces,
Paris went around in rags,
Cambyses drove a mule,
Nero was a street fiddler, and Fierabras was his servant, but he played
   his master a thousand bad turns and made him eat dry crusts and
   drink sour wine, while he himself ate and drank the best stuff
   going,
Julius Caesar and Pompey tarred boat bottoms,
Valentin and Orson, those heroes of popular romance, were bath-
   house servants in hell,
Gawain and Giglan were poor pig keepers,
Geoffrey Longtooth, of Lusignan, made matches and then peddled
   them,
Godefroy de Bouillon made dominoes,
Jason was a bell ringer,
Don Peter the Cruel, king of Castile, sold pardons and indulgences,
Morgan, another romantic hero, brewed beer,
Huon of Bordeaux put hoops on barrels,
Pyrrhus was a kitchen scullion,
Antiochus, a chimney sweep,
Octavian picked up paper scraps,
Nerva was a stableboy,
Pope Julius peddled little pastries and pies, but they trimmed off his
   huge, ugly beard,
John of Paris, another romantic hero, was a shoeshine boy,
King Arthur of England cleaned hats,
Bethis, yet another legendary English king, lugged around baskets
   with bits of firewood,
Pope Boniface the Eighth, like Artaxerxes, skimmed the scum off
   soup pots,
Pope Nicholas the Third was a bookseller,
Pope Alexander was a rat catcher,
Pope Sixtus rubbed ointment into pox sores."

"What?" said Pantagruel. "People have the pox down there?"

"Certainly," said Epistemon. "I've never seen so many: there are more
than a hundred million of them. Believe me, anyone who doesn't have
the pox in this world will have it in the next."

"By God's heart!" said Panurge. "In that case, I'm all right, because

I've had it since I dipped down into the Hole of Gibraltar, and stuffed Hercules' great columns, and I've knocked over some of the poxiest you'll ever see!"

"Ogier the Dane," Epistemon went on, "was an armorer,
King Tigranes, a roofer,
Galien, the great restorer of chivalry, was a mole catcher,
Aymon's four sons became tooth pullers (and liars, to boot),
That half-snake, half-woman Melusine was a kitchen wench,
Matabrune, our lovely heroine of romance, was a washerwoman,
Cleopatra sold onions,
Helen ran an employment service for chambermaids,
Semiramis pulled lice off loafers and bums,
Dido peddled mushrooms,
Penthesilea sold watercress,
Lucretia emptied bedpans,
Hortensia spun yarn,
Livia scraped off rust and grime.

—"So the great and mighty in this world earn their livings as poor, suffering creatures down there. Now it's just the opposite for philosophers and those who've been poor in this world, because now it's their turn to be rich and mighty.

"I saw Diogenes strutting in all his magnificence, wearing a long purple robe and carrying a scepter in his right hand, and when he got angry at Alexander the Great, who hadn't properly patched his pants, he gave him some pretty smart whacks.

"And I saw Epictetus all dressed up in the latest French style, walking in a beautiful tree-lined garden with a whole crowd of pretty girls, laughing and joking, drinking, dancing, and in general having a fine time, and he had a huge heap of gold coins right there next to him. And he'd put up an inscription—verses he wrote himself:

Jump, dance, whirl,
Drink red, drink white with the girls,
Do nothing but lie in the sun
And play at counting your money!

"And when he saw me, he most courteously invited me to drink with him, which I was only too glad to do, and we certainly put it away. But then Cyrus came over, begging for pennies in the name of Mercury, so he could buy some onions for his supper. 'Nothing, nothing,' said Epictetus. 'I'm not giving you any pennies. No, wait, you rascal: here's a gold piece instead. See if you can be an honest man.' Cyrus was thrilled to get booty like that, but those other royal rogues, Alexander, and Darius, and the others, stole it from him that night.

"I saw Pathelin, Rhadamanthus' treasurer, haggling over the little pies Pope Julius was peddling, and asking him, 'How much for a whole dozen?' 'Three cents,' said the pope. 'Ah no,' said Pathelin, 'three whacks with a stick! Hand them over, you good for nothing, hand them over and go find yourself more!' The poor pope went off, crying. And when he got to the pastry maker, and told him that his pies had been stolen, his boss beat him silly—you couldn't have made a bagpipe out of his hide, after the pastry maker got finished with him.

"I saw that great poet Jean Lemaire imitating the pope, so all these poor worldly kings and popes had to kiss his feet—and how he swaggered as he gave them his blessing, saying, 'Buy your pardons, you rascals, buy them. They're a good bargain. I hereby absolve you of bread and soup, and I grant you a special dispensation, allowing you to remain worthless.' And then he called over two professional clowns, Caillette and Triboulet, and said to them, 'My Lord Cardinals, dispatch your bulls: they each get a rap of the stick on their kidneys.' And they got them, quick as a wink.

"I saw Maître François Villon, who asked Xerxes, 'How much mustard for a gold piece?' 'A gold piece worth,' said Xerxes. To which Villon replied, 'May you rot with fever, you thief! It isn't worth a tenth of that—you're trying to gouge us down here!' So he pissed in Xerxes' mustard tub, just the way mustard sellers do in Paris.

"I saw the militiaman of Bagnolet, that mercenary whore, who was an inquisitor of heretics. He found that old romantic hero King Bethis of England, pissing against a wall, and there was a painting of Saint Anthony's fire on the wall, so he declared the king a heretic and would have had him burned alive, if he hadn't been bought off by Morgan, who gave him nine barrels of beer (which was enough to buy off a bishop)."

Now Pantagruel said:

"Let's save some of these fine stories for another time. But just tell me how usurers are treated, down there."

"I saw them," said Epistemon, "down on their hands and knees in the street, scrabbling around in the gutters for rusty pins and bent old nails, just like beggars in this world. But a hundredweight of all that junk is worth barely a chunk of bread, and since they haven't got much of it, down there, the poor skinflints sometimes have to go three weeks without a bite to eat—not even a single crumb—even though they're working day and night, waiting for something to fall in their laps. But they're so busy bustling around, and so utterly damned, that they don't pay much attention to all their work and their suffering, just as long as the end of the year shows them some miserable sum ahead of the game."

"Well then, boys," said Pantagruel, "it's time we had a good round of merrymaking. Let's drink up: please. This is supposed to be a fine month for drinking."

So they pulled out a heap of flasks and, drawing on their enemy's supplies, had a fine feast. But poor King Anarch couldn't join in their merrymaking. So Panurge said:

"What kind of job should we find for Sir King over here, so he'll be an expert in something when he goes down there with all the devils?"

"Indeed," said Pantagruel, "that's a splendid idea. Do whatever you like: he's yours, I give him to you."

"My sincere thanks," said Panurge. "I won't turn down a present like that, especially not from you."

Chapter Thirty-one ⁄⁄ How Pantagruel Entered the City of the Amaurotes, and How Panurge Married Off King Anarch and Turned Him Into a Sauce Peddler

After this wondrous victory, Pantagruel sent Carpalim to the city of the Amaurotes, to announce that King Anarch had been captured and all their enemies defeated. And once that news had been received, everyone in the city came out, rank upon rank in good order, making a great triumphant parade and celebrating solemnly. And they brought Pantagruel to the city, and built big bright bonfires all over town, and out in the streets they set handsome tables, loaded down with all sorts of good food. This was truly a renewal of the ancient Golden Age, so happily did they rejoice.

And with the whole senate assembled, Pantagruel said to them:

"Gentlemen, we must strike while the iron is hot. Accordingly, before we allow ourselves to relax any further, I wish to attack and conquer the entire Dipsode kingdom. Those who wish to accompany me should be ready tomorrow after breakfast, because that is when I shall set out—not that I need more men to help me in this conquest, because we've virtually accomplished it already. But I see that this city is so full of people that they can barely turn around in the streets. Therefore, I propose to take them to the Dipsode realm as colonists and hand the entire country over to them, for it is the loveliest, most bountiful, healthiest, and most agreeable country in the world, as those of you have been there know. Anyone who wishes to come with me, be ready at the appointed hour."

This decision was announced throughout the city, and the next day the square in front of the palace was crowded with a million eight hundred fifty-six thousand and eleven people, not counting women and little children. So they began their march straight into Dipsodia, in such good order that they looked like the children of Israel, when they went out of Egypt and crossed the Red Sea.

But before I follow them any further, I want to tell you how Panurge treated his prisoner, King Anarch. He kept firmly in mind what Epistemon had told them about how the kings and rich men of this world were treated, down in the Elysian Fields, and especially how they earned their livings in hard and dirty occupations.

Accordingly, he had the king dressed in a nice little linen jacket, striped like a royal guardsman's, and a pair of baggy sailor's breeches, but without any shoes (because shoes would spoil his eyesight, he said). And he covered his head with a cute little blue hat with a big feather stuck in it—no, that's wrong: I've been told there were two feathers—and gave him a handsome blue-and-green sash, explaining that this was a proper outfit for him, since he'd made so many other people blue.

And then he brought him to Pantagruel, asking:

"Do you know this peasant?"

"Not at all," said Pantagruel.

"This is our polished and perfect king; I propose to turn him into a useful man. These devilish kings are nothing more than calves, who know nothing and are worth exactly that much—except they do know how to make trouble for their poor subjects and, by making war, for the rest of the world as well—which they do because their brains are warped and to them it's a lot of fun—disgusting fun. I intend to teach him how to make green sauce, and then to peddle it though the streets. You: let me hear you call out, 'Who'd like some green sauce?' "

And the poor devil did as he was told.

"That's not loud enough," said Panurge, and he grabbed him by the ear, saying, "Sing it louder, in do, re, mi, fa, sol. Go on, you devil! You've got a healthy throat. The best thing that ever happened to you was when you stopped being a king."

And Pantagruel liked the idea, because I dare say the king had become the nicest little peasant you'll ever see—at the end of a stick. So Anarch was turned into a first-rate peddler of green sauce.

Two days later, Panurge married him to an old whore and gave the wedding feast himself, including juicy sheep heads, good roast pork with mustard, and fine tripe stew with garlic—five loads of which were sent to Pantagruel, which he thoroughly enjoyed and ate up every bite—plus some local wine and cider to drink. And so they could dance, Panurge hired a blind fiddler.

After dinner he brought them to the palace and exhibited them to Pantagruel. Gesturing to the new wife, he said:

"She doesn't have to worry about farting."

"Why?" said Pantagruel.

"Because," said Panurge, "she's already been well opened."

"Which means?"

"Don't you get it?" said Panurge. "When you roast chestnuts, the whole ones fart and pop like mad, so to keep them from farting you cut them open. Well, this new wedded wife's been thoroughly opened underneath, so she won't ever fart."

Pantagruel gave them a little shop, in the workingmen's quarter, and a stone mortar for grinding the sauce. And so they set up their little household, and Anarch became the best peddler of green sauce Utopia had ever seen. But I've been told that, since then, his wife has taken to beating him up, and the poor fool is such an idiot that he doesn't dare defend himself.

Chapter Thirty-two ⁄⁄ How Pantagruel Shielded an Entire Army with His Tongue, and What the Author Saw in His Mouth

As Pantagruel and all his people entered the land of the Dipsodes, the inhabitants were delighted and immediately surrendered to him, bringing him of their own free will the keys to every city to which he journeyed— all except the Almyrods, who intended to resist him and told his heralds that they refused to surrender, except on good terms.

"What!" said Pantagruel. "They want more than their hand in the pot and a cup in their fist? Let's go, so you can knock down their walls for me."

So they got themselves ready, as if about to launch their attack.

But as they marched past a huge field, they were struck by a huge downpour, which began to knock their lines about and break up their formation. Seeing this, Pantagruel ordered the captains to assure them that this was nothing and he could see, past the clouds, that it was only a bit of dew. Whatever happened, however, they should maintain military discipline and he would provide them with cover. And when they had restored good marching order, Pantagruel stuck out his tongue, but just barely halfway, and shielded them as a mother hen protects her chicks.

Now I, who report these totally true tales to you, had hidden myself under the leaf of a burdock weed, which was at least as big as the Mantrible Bridge. But when I saw how well they had been shielded, I went to take cover alongside them, but I couldn't, since there were so many of them and (as they say) "all things come to an end." So I climbed up as best I could and walked along his tongue for a good six miles, until I got into his mouth.

But, O you gods and goddesses, what did I see there? May Jupiter blow me away with his three-pointed lightning if I tell you a lie. I walked along in there, as you might promenade around Saint Sophia's Cathedral in Constantinople, and I saw immense boulders, just like the mountains of Denmark (I think they were his teeth), and great meadows, and huge forests, with castles and large cities, no smaller than Lyons or Poitiers.

The first person I met was an old man planting cabbage. And quite astonished I asked him:

"My friend, what are you doing here?"

"I," he said, "am planting cabbage."

"But why, and how?" I said.

"Oh ho, sir," said he, "we can't all walk around with our balls hanging down like mortars, and we can't all be rich. This is how I earn my living. They take this to the city you see over there, and sell them."

"Jesus!" I said. "Is this a whole new world in here?"

"Not at all," he said, "it isn't completely new, no. But I've heard that there is a new world outside of here, and that there's a sun and a moon out there, and all kinds of things going on. But this world is older."

"Well, my friend," I said, "what's the name of that city where they sell your cabbage?"

"It's called Throattown," he said, "and the people are good Christians, and will be pleased to see you."

So, in a word, I decided to go there.

Now, as I walked I found a fellow setting pigeon snares, and I asked him:

"My friend, where do these pigeons of yours come from?"

"Sir," he said, "they come from the other world."

And then I realized that, when Pantagruel yawned, pigeons with fully extended wings flew right down his throat, thinking it was a great bird house.

Then I came to the city, which seemed extremely pleasant, well fortified, and nicely located, with a good climate. But at the gates the porters asked for my passport and my certificate of good health, which truly astonished me, so I said to them:

"Gentlemen, is there any danger of plague here?"

"Oh, sir," they said, "they're dying of it so rapidly, not very far from here, that the body wagon is always rattling through the streets."

"Good God!" I said. "And just where is this?"

So they informed me that it was in Larynx and Pharynx, which were two cities as big as Rouen and Nantes, rich and doing a fine business, and that the plague was due to a stinking, infectious odor recently flowing up to them from the abysses below. More than twenty-two hundred and seventy-six people had died of it in the last week. So I thought about this, and added up the days, and realized that this was a foul breath from Pantagruel's stomach, which had begun after he'd eaten so much garlic (at Anarch's wedding feast), as I've already explained.

Leaving there, I walked between the great boulders that were his teeth, and climbed up on one, and found it one of the loveliest places in the whole world, with fine tennis courts, handsome galleries, beautiful meadows, and many vineyards. And these delightful fields were dotted with more Italian-style summerhouses than I could count, so I stayed on there for four months and have never been happier.

Then I climbed down the back teeth, in order to get to his lips, but as I journeyed I was robbed by a band of highwaymen in the middle of a huge forest, somewhere in the neighborhood of his ears.

Then I found a little village on the slope (I forget its name), where I was happier than ever, and worked happily for my supper. Can you guess what I did? I slept: they hire day laborers to sleep, down there, and you can make five or six dollars a day. But those who snore really loud can make seven or even seven and a half. And I told the senators how I'd been robbed in the valley, and they told me that, truthfully, the people in that neighborhood were naturally bad, and thieves to boot, which made me realize that, just as we have the Right Side of the Alps and the Wrong Side of the Alps, so they have the Right Side of the Teeth and the Wrong Side of the Teeth, but it was better on the Right Side, and the air was better, too.

And I began to think how true it was that half the world has no idea how the other half lives, seeing that no one has ever written a thing about that world down there, although it's inhabited by more than twenty-five kingdoms, not to mention the deserts and a great bay. Indeed, I have written a fat book entitled *History of an Elegant Throat Land,* which is what I called that country, since they lived in the throat of my master Pantagruel.

Finally, I decided to go back, and going past his beard I dropped onto his shoulders, and from there I got down to the ground and fell right in front of him.

And seeing me, he asked:

"Where are you coming from, Alcofribas?"

And I answered him:

"From your throat, sir."

"And how long have you been down there?" he said.

"Since you marched against the Almyrods," I said.

"But that," he said, "is more than six months. How did you live? What did you drink?"

I answered:

"My lord, just as you did, and I took a tax of the freshest morsels that came down your throat."

"Indeed," he said. "But where did you shit?"

"In your throat, sir," I said.

"Ha, ha, but you're a fine fellow!" he said. "Now, with God's help, we've conquered the entire land of the Dipsodes. And you shall have the castle of Salmagundi."

"Many thanks, sir," I said. "You're far more generous than I deserve."

Chapter Thirty-three ⁄⁄ How Pantagruel Got Sick, and How He Was Cured

Not long after, my good Pantagruel fell sick and had so much difficulty with his stomach that he could neither drink nor eat. And since sicknesses never come singly, he was tormented by a burning piss that tortured him almost beyond belief. But his doctors were able to help him, and they did a fine job, with the assistance of lots of sedatives and diuretics, so that soon he was able to piss away his illness.

But his urine was so burning hot that from that day to this it has never cooled down, and we have a number of such places right here in France, depending on how the urine happened to flow away. And these are the hot baths of Cauterets, Limoux, Dax, Balaruc-les-Bains, near Montpellier, Néris, Bourbon-Lancy, and others. And in Italy there are: Monte Grotto, Abano, San Pietro Montagone, Santa Elena Battalia, Casa Nova, and San Bartolomeo. And in Bologna: at Porretta—and a thousand other places.

And that crowd of stupid doctors (and would-be philosophers) absolutely astonish me, wasting time debating where each of these hot baths might come from, whether perhaps borax might have caused them, or sulfur, or alum, or saltpeter from a mine. Because all they're doing is playing games: they'd do better rubbing their asses on a spike thistle than making so much empty noise about something they don't understand at all. Because the answer is simple, and there's no need to look any farther for it. These hot baths are hot because they began as our friend Pantagruel's hot piss.

Now, to tell you how he was cured of his principal ailment, let me just note that he took a diuretic sedative, in a dosage of four hundredweights of colophonic resin, a hundred and thirty-eight wagonloads of cassia, eleven thousand nine hundred pounds of rhubarb, not to mention other items.

You must realize that, according to the doctors' best opinions, it was decided that they had to get rid of whatever was upsetting his stomach. To accomplish this, they made seventeen great copper balls, bigger than those you see at Rome, on Virgil's Needle. Each of these balls opened in the middle and could be closed by a spring. One of his men climbed into the first great ball, carrying a lantern and a burning torch, and was lowered down into Pantagruel as if he'd been a tiny pill. Five good-sized fellows, each carrying a pick, got into five other balls, and three peasants got into three more, each of them with a shovel on his back. Seven strong porters got into seven other balls, each of them with a big basket on his back, and they, too, were lowered down like pills.

When they got into his stomach, they unhooked the springs and left their cabins, headed by the man with a lantern, and thus they groped their way for more than a mile, across a ghastly chasm, fouler and more stinking than the fumes of Mephitis, or the Swamp of Camerina, or the fetid Lake of Serbonis that Strabo wrote about. If they had not been protected by the heart, the stomach, and that wine pot we call the head, they would surely have been suffocated to death by those horrible vapors. Oh what a perfume, oh what a scent, to foul the delicate masks of whores and sluts!

And then, feeling their way and sniffing as they went, they located and drew near the fecal matter and corrupt essences, until finally they reached a small mountain of shit. The pick carriers smashed at it, to break it into smaller chunks, and then the men with shovels loaded it into their baskets, and when everything was thoroughly cleaned up, they all got back into their balls. And then Pantagruel obligingly threw up, and they were back out again in a moment, and it made no more difference to his throat than a belch would to yours. They jumped out of their balls happily—it made me think of the Greeks jumping out of the wooden horse, in Troy— and thus Pantagruel was cured and put back on the road to good health.

And one of these bronze balls can be seen, to this day, in Orléans, on the bell tower of the church of the Holy Cross.

Chapter Thirty-four // Conclusion of This Book, and the Author's Apology

Now, gentlemen, you have heard the beginning of the awesome history of my master and lord, Pantagruel. And here I must end this first book: I have a bit of a headache and I have the clear sense that the organ stops of my brain have been somewhat disordered by this unsettled fresh September wine.

The rest of this history will be ready for sale at the next Frankfurt Fair, and you will see how Panurge got married, and was cuckolded from the very beginning; and how he found the philosopher's stone, and just how he located and then used it; and how he climbed the Caspian Mountains; how he sailed across the Atlantic Ocean, and routed the cannibals, and conquered the Antilles Islands; how he married the king of India's daughter (Prester John was that king's name); how he fought the devils and burned up five rooms in hell, and utterly destroyed the great black room, and threw Proserpina into the flames, and broke four of Lucifer's teeth, not to mention one of the horns on his ass; and how he traveled to the moon in order to find out if, in fact, the moon was not all there (since women have at least three-quarters of it in their heads); and a thousand other little gay tales, each and all of them absolutely true. These are jolly matters.

Farewell, gentlemen. *Pardonnate my:* Excuse me, as they say in Italy, and don't think as much about my faults as you do about your own.

If you say to me, "Maître, it doesn't look as though you have to be particularly wise, to write us all this nonsense and these pleasant little jokes," I'll answer that you don't seem much wiser yourself, since you read them and had a good time doing it.

Anyway, if you read them to have a good time, as I wrote them to have a good time, you and I both deserve a pardon more than a whole crowd of lecherous monks, sanctimonious hypocrites, lazy good-for-nothings, liars, imitation believers, fakers, humbugs, and all the others of that sort, who walk around disguised in masks, to deceive the rest of us.

You see, letting it be generally understood that their only concern is contemplation and true devotion, fasting and mortification of the flesh, in order truly to nourish and sustain the slender fragility of their poor human natures, in reality they do exactly the opposite—God alone knows all they do. As Juvenal says:

Et Curios simulant, sed bacchanalia vivunt,
They pretend to be as austere as Curius, but they lead riotous lives.

And you can read the facts, in capital letters, illustrated, right on their bright red noses and their soft round bellies—except when they perfume themselves with the scent of sulfur.

And as for their studying, they spend all their time reading pantagruelistic books—but not for pleasure. No, they read in order to injure others, wickedly—by articulating, monarticulating, lyingly articulating, sitting on, shitting on, and diabolically spitting on—which means viciously. They're just like those country clods who poke around in little children's shit, during the cherry season, so they can dig out the pits and sell them to druggists, who use them for oils and perfumes.

Run from such men, avoid them at all costs, hate them as much as I do, and by my faith it will improve you. And if you want to be good Pantagruelists (which means to live peacefully, happily, healthily, always having a good time), never trust anyone who looks out at you from under a cowl.

The end of the chronicles of Pantagruel, king of the Dipsodes,
restored to his true character, with all his terrible
deeds and acts of heroism, written by
the late Maître ALCOFRIBAS,
extractor of the fifth,
or celestial, essence

The Third Book
of the Heroic Words
and Deeds of
Our Good Pantagruel

Written by M. Fran. Rabelais,

Doctor of Medicine

Revised and Corrected

by the Author in the

Light of Earlier Criticism

The aforesaid author

implores his benevolent readers

to save their laughter for

the seventy-eighth book.

From François Rabelais
to the Noble Mind of the Queen of Navarre

O rapt spirit, entranced, ecstatic,
Your soul lives in heaven, its home,
Deserting your servant body, domestic
And amiable host, letting it roam
This fleshly world like mobile stone,
Aware of nothing, lost, alone.
Why not step down from heaven, make
A journey away from forever, try
This earth—where Pantagruel and I
Still travel together, for laughter's sake?

THE AUTHOR'S PROLOGUE, BY MAÎTRE FRANÇOIS RABELAIS

for the Third Book of the Heroic Words and Deeds of Our Good Pantagruel

GOOD PEOPLE, most illustrious guzzlers, and you exceedingly precious gout stricken, have you ever seen Diogenes, the heroic Cynic philosopher? If you have, either you haven't lost your vision, or I've lost all logic and logical sense. It's a wonderful thing to see the clear golden sparkle of wine—the bright clarity of gold and the sun. Just think of that man, blind from birth, celebrated in the most holy Bible: when He who is All Powerful, whose words are in an instant transformed into deeds, asked the man to say what he wanted, all the man wanted was to see.

And you too are no longer young, which qualifies you to judge wine—and not only not uselessly but actually more than merely physically, which is to say, metaphysically, and also enrolls you in the Council of Bacchus, since simply by drinking you can decide such matters as the substance, color, fragrance, excellence, eminence, individuality, power, capacities, effects, and dignity of that blessed and universally beloved beverage.

If you've never seen him (which isn't hard for me to believe), at least you've heard him spoken of. His praise has been heard everywhere on earth and in heaven, and to this very day his name remains both memorable and more than celebrated. And then too, all Frenchmen are descended from the ancient Phrygians (unless I'm very much mistaken), and even if you don't have as many gold pieces as Midas, you inherit something else from him—his huge ears, perhaps, which the Persians valued so highly in their spies and the emperor Antoninus longed for (at least, in *his* spies), and which later on were immortalized in the duke of Rohan's chateau, known as Handsome Ears.

And if his name is totally unfamiliar to you, I'll tell you a story about him, to get us started on our wine (drink up, drink up) and on our conversation (hey, listen). Let me make it clear right away, so your brains won't be as blank and unseeing as barbarians', that in his day Diogenes was a rare philosopher, and a truly happy man. If he had a few faults, well, you have a couple yourself, as all the rest of us do. Nothing's per-

241

fect, except God. But even though Aristotle was both tutor and servant to Alexander the Great, that great emperor thought so well of this noble philosopher of whom we speak that, if he could not be himself, he would have chosen to be Diogenes.

When Philip, king of Macedonia, planned to lay siege to Corinth, and destroy that city, the Corinthians' spies warned them that he was marching against them with a huge army, which gave them good reason to be afraid. So they were extremely careful: every man among them did everything he ought to do, to try to resist the attackers and to defend their city.

Some of them brought animals, grain, wine, fruit, supplies, and necessary equipment—everything and anything they could carry—inside the city.

Others repaired walls, set up fortifications, straightened and reinforced the earthworks out in front of their fort, dug ditches, cleaned out tunnels, loaded baskets with rocks and stones, tightened and braced shooting platforms, emptied latrines, put new bars on outside passageways, set up earthen platforms, piled up outside slopes, re-cemented the walls between fortifications, built sentry boxes, made parapet ramps, set stones around small spy windows, lined with steel the vertical openings through which stones and other objects were dropped on their enemies' heads, repaired the sliding grills in fortified gates (both those in the Arab and those in the Greek style), stationed sentries, and sent out patrols.

They were all of them watchful, all of them working. Some polished armor, varnished light shields, cleaned horse armor and head plumes, and coat of mail, armored cloaks, helmets, neck armor, hoods, hooked pikes (the sort foot soldiers carry), helmets with beaked nose plates, archers' helmets (with tall crests), mail shirts and coats, shoulder armor, thigh armor, underarm armor, throat armor, arm and leg harnesses, breastplates, light-armored breastplates, short mail coats, shields, huge light shields for protection against arrows, Roman leg armor, mail gloves, foot armor, and spurs.

Others worked on bows, slingshots, crossbows, heavy balls for slingshots, catapults, fire-setting arrows, bombs, fireballs, spears and rings of fire, machines for hurling stones of various sizes, as well as other machines for repelling and destroying mobile siege towers.

They sharpened lances, axes, hooked claws, spikes and ax blades mounted on long shafts, iron lances with bent tips, long-handled billhooks, spears, cavalrymen's axes, long-handled pitchforks, spiked spears, heavy clubs with spiked tips, hatchets, javelins and half-axes, long and short, and heavy-tipped spears. They filed the edges of Turkish swords, short swords, scimitars, short spears, rapiers, heavy foot-soldier swords, daggers both small and large, spiral daggers, dirks, Roman rapiers, knives, and every blade, missile, and arrow they found.

They all practiced cutting and thrusting with their daggers; they all worked at their swordsmanship. No woman was too proud or too old to get herself thoroughly ready—for, as you know, the ancient Corinthians were courageous in all manner of combat.

Now, Diogenes, seeing the whole city in such a whirl of activity, and himself not having been assigned to any task at all, for a few days simply watched and said nothing. Then, as if impelled by the warlike spirit, he pulled back his cloak and, belting it tight, rolled his sleeves up to the elbows, tucked up his clothes like an apple picker, handed his beggar's sack, his books, and his writing tablets to an old friend, then went outside the city toward the Cranium (a ridge of high land, with a hill, near Corinth), which was a fine parade ground. And he rolled out there the clay barrel in which he lived—his only shelter against the elements—and with singularly violent motions began to turn it this way and that, moving it wildly every which way, without apparent rhyme or reason—twisting, turning, spinning, beating on it, turning it over, turning it back again, caressing it, whipping it around, flogging it, bashing it, bumping it, shaking it, tumbling it, trampling it, banging it, sticking in the plug, pulling it out again, speeding it up, prancing it, dancing it, thumping it, dumping it, rolling it, tolling it, rocking it, socking it, lifting it, shifting it, veering it, steering it, whirling it, hurling it, clamping it, damping it, setting it, getting it, tying it, trying it, sticking it, pricking it, spreading it, heading it, squeezing it, wheezing it, clapping it, tapping it, cranking it, yanking it, whacking it, cracking it, clacking it, hacking it, tacking it, backing it, sacking it, racking it, packing it, crashing it, bashing it, rapping it, zapping it, running it down from the hill into the valley, then tossing it off the Cranium, then lugging it back up to the hilltop once more, like Sisyphus with his endlessly rolling stone, and all with such passion and violence that he very nearly smashed it to pieces.

And seeing this, one of his friend asked what earthly reason he had, in mind or body, to so punish and torment his barrel. To which the philosopher answered that, since the republic had given him no other job to do, he raged about with his barrel because, with everyone else rushing around, totally occupied, dedicated, he could not be the only one standing empty-handed and still.

And I, too, though I have no reason for personal concern, how can I keep from being excited, finding myself with nothing worthy to occupy my hands when this whole noble realm of France, on both sides of the mountains, shows me everyone working as hard as possible, some to fortify and defend their country, others to push back its enemies, and attack them in their turn, everything in such perfect order, so beautifully regulated, and so clearly aimed at future advantages (because France's borders will be superbly extended, and every Frenchman will be guaranteed peace and security), that it wouldn't take much for me to agree with Heraclitus that war is the father of all good things, and to believe that the Latin word for war, *bellum,* and the French word for beautiful, *belle,* are hardly opposites at all, though there have been mumblers of rusty Latin who have believed them deeply opposed, there being in their eyes no beauty in war. I could believe in the linking of these two words plainly and simply, because only in war can we see every variety of goodness and beauty, just as we are shown every variety of evil and ugliness. And so the wise and peaceful King Solomon understood there was no better way to show us the unutterable perfection of divine wisdom than to compare it, in the Song of Songs, to the ordered arrangements of an army in camp.

And so, since I have not been enlisted, to serve with other Frenchmen in our military ranks (being thought too feeble, too helpless), nor been drafted to help with our defense, either—not even digging dirt, shoveling shit, cracking sticks, or stuffing turf: I'd have done anything asked of me—it would seem to me more than mildly shameful to be seen as a mere spectator, in the presence of so many brave, eloquent, and chivalric men, who with the eyes of all Europe on them have played out their roles in this worthy fable, this tragicomedy. So I, too, must exert myself to the utmost, giving this nothing, which to me is everything I still possess. For it seems to me that in these matters there is small glory in simply watching, conserving your strength, hiding your gold and your silver, scratching your head with one finger, like a weary sluggard, yawning at flies like a clumsy calf, occasionally pricking up your ears like an Arcadian ass who hears musicians singing and then indicates in simpering silence that he approves the performance.

Having chosen this path, I thought it would not be entirely useless or tiresome to roll my own barrel of Diogenes—indeed, all I have left since I went aground, trying to sail past the lighthouse of bad luck. And what do you think I ought to do, as I whirl my barrel? By that holy virgin who tucked up her skirts, I still don't know. Hold on: wait just a minute, while I take a pull at this bottle: this—this is my true, my only fountain of inspiration, my spring of Helicon, my bubbling Hippocrene, my unique rapture. As I drink I think, I consider, I resolve, I come to conclusions. Only after that epilogue can I laugh, and write (even write poems), and then drink some more. Old Ennius drank as he wrote, and wrote as he drank. If Plutarch's telling the truth in his *Symposiaca,* Aeschylus drank as he wrote, and wrote as he drank. Homer never wrote on an empty stomach. Cato would never write except after drinking. I cite these eminent predecessors so you won't tell me my way of life is unique: I'm simply following famous models with high reputations. And this is good, fresh wine—you might say it's just reaching its second degree of perfection. May God, the good God Sabaoth (which means, you know, the Lord of hosts) be eternally praised! So if the rest of you take a swig or two (maybe with a flask hidden in your cloaks), it won't bother me a bit, as long as you take the time to thank the Lord.

And so, since this is my lot, my fate (because we can't all be so lucky as to live in Corinth), I have decided to serve both sides in this conflict. At least, that's better than just standing helplessly on the sidelines and doing nothing at all. The diggers and builders and fixers will have from me exactly what Neptune and Apollo gave King Laomedon, when they built Troy for him at Zeus' command, and exactly what Renaud de Montalban gave, when as an old man he worked with the stone masons, erecting the cathedral at Cologne. I will work right alongside the masons, I'll boil a kettle for them, and, when they've finished eating, they'll have their fun fooling around to the music I make for them. Which was exactly how Amphion founded and built and peopled the great and justly famous city of Thebes, all to the sound of his lyre. So here I am, ready to stick another spigot in my barrel, all for the benefit of those now at war: and what I pour out of that barrel (which you would already know pretty well, from the two volumes which preceded this one, if humbugging printers hadn't done their best to spoil and scramble my books) will come from our after-dinner entertainment: it will be a bold third—and later, a happy fourth—effusion of Pantagruelian wisdom. You have my permission to call them worthy of Diogenes. And those now at war, who cannot have me truly at their side, as their comrade in arms, will at least have me as the loyal organizer of their festivities, refreshing them when they come back from battle, to the extent my poor powers will allow. And I will sing—sing indefatigably—their praise for all their bravery and their glorious feats of arms. Nor will I ever let them down, by the passionate patience of Christ, unless Lent doesn't come in March—but the old sinner won't ever do that.

But I remember reading, anyway, how one day Ptolemy, Lagus' son, in the middle of a crowded open-air auditorium, all full of the spoils and plunder of his conquests, presented the Egyptians with a pitch-black Bactrian camel, and a slave partly white, partly black—not striped across the middle, one color above his diaphragm, one color below it (like the Indian woman, a worshiper of Venus, seen by Apollonius of Tyana as that philosopher journeyed between the Hydaspes River and the Caucasus mountains), but perpendicularly. This was something never before seen in Egypt, and by offering them such a novelty Ptolemy hoped to swell the people's affection for him. But what happened? Seeing the camel, the people were either frightened or indignant; seeing the striped man, some of them began to mock him, while others bemoaned him as an infamous monster, created by nature's error. And so his hope of pleasing the Egyptians, thus extending and enlarging the affection they naturally felt toward him, slipped right through his fingers. And he came to understand that they took their pleasure and delight in beautiful things, rather than in ridiculous and monstrous ones. After which both the slave and the camel seemed contemptible, and not long afterward, through neglect and lack of attention, they exchanged life for death.

This illustration leaves me hanging between hope and fear, not sure if, expecting pleasure, I still may have to deal with dislike, my treasure all turned to dust, my desire to turn up the lovely Venus card turned into the horrible sight of the card bearing the Unholy Dogs—not certain if, intending to be useful, I'll make people angry; wishing to cheer them up, I'll offend them; trying to please them, I'll only displease—and it will all work out, for me, the way it did for Euclion's famous rooster, celebrated by Plautus in his *Pot of Gold,* and by Ausonius in his poem *Gryphon,* and by others, too—the rooster whose scratching uncovered the treasure was then rewarded by having his throat cut. And in that case, wouldn't it be annoying? Such things have indeed happened: they could happen again. But no, it won't happen, by Hercules! For in each and all of these warriors for whom I write I see a certain specific form (as the old scholars used to say), a definite, unique character trait which our ancestors called Pantagruelism, proving that they will never take offense at things which, as they know perfectly well, spring from a good, loyal, open heart. I've often seen them take goodwill for their only payment, and take it gladly, when their debtor clearly couldn't pay them with anything else.

Now, with that out of the way, I can go back to my barrel. Drink up, my friends! Boys, drink hearty! And if you don't like it, leave it. I'm not one of those insistent Germans, who use force and outrage and violence on their friends and countrymen, to get them to guzzle—even to get them drunk, which is worse still. Every honest drinker, every gouty guzzler, every truly thirsty man who approaches this barrel of mine and doesn't feel like drinking, needn't drink. But if they feel like it, and their Lordly Lordships like the wine, let them drink as much as they like, swill it right down: it won't cost them a cent, and they don't have to hold back. That's an order. And there's no need to worry about the wine running out, the way it did at the wedding feast at Cana, in Galilee. Whatever you pull out through the spigot, I'll put right back in through the bung hole. And the barrel will be forever inexhaustible. It has a living source; it will flow eternally—like the liquid in Tantalus' cup, as portrayed by Brahman wise men, or that Spanish mountain of salt celebrated by Cato, or that golden branch sacred to the goddess of the underworld, made famous by Virgil. It's a true cornucopia of happiness and good cheer. Sometimes you'll think it's drained right down to the bottom, but it will never go dry. It's hope that lies at the bottom, as in Pandora's bottle, not the kind of despair the wretched Danaides find in their bottomless tub.

Listen to me carefully; notice the kinds of people I invite to my banquet. Like Lucilius, I wish to deceive no one. He protested that he wrote only for the Tarentines and Calabrians (who spoke both Latin and Greek and therefore were critics of neither). Me, I've opened this barrel of mine only for you, men of goodwill, drinkers of the best stuff going, men who have earned their cases of gout. Our great bribe-guzzling judges, men who suck up mists and fog, they already have hot asses, they can stuff pounds of flesh into handy briefcases: they won't find what they're looking for here. This isn't big enough game for hunters like them.

And as for the doctors in their padded hats, those nit-picking scavengers, don't talk to me about them, please: in the name of—for the honor of—the four bouncing buttocks who brought you into being, and also the stout, life-spouting peg that tied those bouncing bottoms together. The so-called philosophers, those whining hypocrites? Don't even mention them, even though they're incredible, outrageous drinkers, crusty with pox, endowed with inextinguishable thirsts and insatiable jaws. Why not? Because they're men who come from evil, not good—and exactly that evil which, every day of our lives, we pray to God to deliver us from. And how they pretend to be nothing more than poor beggars! You'll never see an old monkey making a pretty face.

Get back, you mutts! Out of the way—stop blocking my sunshine, you hooded devils! Did you come here, wagging your tails behind you, to sniff around my wine and piss all over my barrel? See this stick? Diogenes put it in his will that this was to be laid next to his body, after he was dead, so he could whip off and drive away these graveyard ghouls and hounds of hell. Get back, hypocrites! Sic 'em, dogs! Get away, humbugs, off to hell with you! What? You're still here? If I can just get my hands on you, I'll give up all my rights in the pope's kingdom. Gzz. Gzzz. Gzzzzzz. At them, at them! Are they running away? May you never be able to shit without being whipped—may you never piss without being flogged—may you never get hot except under the blows of a good solid stick!

Chapter One ⁄⁄ How Pantagruel Brought a Colony of Utopians to the Land of the Dipsodes

Having completely conquered the land of the Dipsodes, Pantagruel brought there a colony of Utopians, numbering 9876543210 men (not counting women and children), craftsmen in all trades known to man and students of every liberal science, his purpose being to revive, improve, and more densely people the country, since for the most part it consisted of unpopulated desert. Nor did he bring them there because of the immense overpopulation in Utopia, where men and women were multiplying like locusts—for as you very well know, and there is absolutely no need to explain, Utopian men have enormously productive genitalia, and Utopian women have wombs so large, so appetent, so tough and retentive, and biologically so extraordinarily well structured, that every marriage produces, in each nine-month period, at least seven children, males and females occurring in equal proportions, just as the Jewish people did when they were in exile in Egypt (unless Friar Nicholas of Lyra is mistaken). Nor was Pantagruel's primary motivation the fertilizing effects of the sun, the healthfulness of the climate, and the great comfort of life in the land of the Dipsodes, but rather that the Dipsodians be helped to fulfill their civic duties and to maintain their obedience to their ruler by this new importation of Pantagruel's faithful old subjects, who could not remember ever having had any other ruler—had neither known nor wanted nor served any other. And these faithful Utopians, from the moment they were born into the world, had sucked in, along with their mothers' milk, the sweetness and good humor of his reign, in which they were continuously steeped and sustained. Pantagruel was sure that they would sooner give up their lives than this primary and unique subjugation, naturally owed their prince, no matter where they might be scattered and sent—and not only would this be true of them and all the descendants who might thereafter be born to them, but further, they would introduce this loyalty and obedience to all the nations newly added to his empire.

And this was exactly what happened: his decision did not disappoint him in any way. Because if the Utopians had been thus loyal and faithful before he brought them to the land of the Dipsodes, the Dipsodes themselves, after just a few days of acquaintance with their new neighbors, displayed these traits even more prominently. And this was because of who knows what natural fervor, the sort of gushing enthusiasm that comes to all human beings when they start some new enterprise that pleases them. Their only complaint, calling on the heavens above and all the powers that spun the eternal spheres, was that Pantagruel's fame had not been brought to their attention sooner.

And you mark well, my drinking friends, that the way to maintain and stay in possession of a newly conquered country (in spite of the erroneous opinions of certain tyrannical writers, much to their shame and dishonor) is not to rob, abuse, conscript, ruin, and angrily mistreat the people, ruling them with iron whips—in short, gobbling them up, devouring them, as Homer calls an evil king *Demovore,* "Devourer," he who consumes his own people. Nor will I cite you all the examples from ancient history, but just remind you of what your fathers have seen for themselves, and you too have seen, unless you're too young. Like a child, conquered people must be allowed a new freedom to suckle at the breast, to be rocked and soothed in their cradles, to play and enjoy themselves. Like newly planted trees, they need to be supported, made secure, defended against all storms, and injuries, and disasters. Like someone rescued from a long, threatening illness, and just entering convalescence, they must be fussed over, treated with infinite kindness, restored. This is how to make them realize that nowhere in the world will they find a king or prince less anxious to be their enemy, more concerned to be their friend. Thus the great Egyptian king Osiris conquered the entire world, not so much by force of arms as by holding back on reparations and seizures of conquered property, by teaching people how to live healthily and well, by appropriate and well-made laws, and gracious acts, and all manner of good deeds. Which is why Jupiter himself, speaking through an Egyptian woman at Thebes, Pamyle, had announced that he would be called the great king *Evergètes,* or Benefactor—and why the world so spoke of him.

Indeed, in his *Hierarchies* Hesiod speaks of good demons (which we might think of as angels, or genies) as the gods' intermediaries in their dealings with men, creatures higher than mere mortals, but lower than the deities. And just as kings are always opening their hands and showering down on us heaven's riches, and all manner of good things, so too function these intermediaries, forever helping us, preserving us from evil, doing good and never doing evil—which are surely the actions of kings. Alexander of Macedonia, the emperor of the universe, ruled in that way. So too Hercules came to rule over an entire continent, freeing human beings from oppressive monsters, and from all other oppressions, exactions, and tyrannies, treating well those he governed, preserving equity and justice, giving them a gentle administration and laws well suited to stability in each of the countries where he decreed them, compensating for whatever was lacking, adding to what was already abundant, and forgiving all prior offense, and wiping out whatever had been, with an unending ability to turn away from the past—like the amnesty extended by the Athenians, when the heroism and ceaseless efforts of Thrasybulus wiped tyrants from the face of the earth, a graciousness referred to by Cicero and then rekindled in Rome under Emperor Aurelius.

These are the magic love potions, the charms and lures that enable you to stay in peaceful possession of that which, with infinite difficulty, you have conquered. Nor can any conqueror—king, prince, or philosopher—reign more truly than by letting Courage lead the way for Justice. We see his courage in his victory, in his conquest; we see his justice when, wanting only good for the people, and cherishing them, he gives them laws, publishes decrees, establishes religions, treats everyone with an even, honest hand—as Virgil says of Octavius Augustus:

> He who wishes true victory, gives
> The conquered laws by which to live.

And this is why Homer, in his *Iliad,* calls good princes and great kings Adorners of the People. Numa Pompilius, the Romans' second king and an honest politician, as well as a philosopher, had exactly such considerations in mind when he ordered that on the feast day of the god Terminus (the feast called Terminalia) no dead animal should be consecrated to the god, thereby demonstrating to all of us that boundaries, frontiers, and appendages of the realm should be guarded and ruled in peace, friendship, and gentleness, not by the governors soiling their hands with blood and theft. Those who follow a different path not only lose what they have gained but also endure the scandal and shame of being judged evil, and wrongful conquerors, since what they conquered has slipped through their hands. What we wrongfully acquire withers away as we try to hold it. And he who keeps peaceful title in his lifetime, but whose heirs lose it, finds that even death is no protection, for exactly the same scandal descends on him, on his now accursed memory, as fell on the evil conqueror. As our proverb says, "Things wrongfully acquired never reach the heir's heir."

And you, who inherit your gout, pay attention to this—note how Pantagruel turned a single angel into two, which is exactly the opposite of Charlemagne's decision, when he turned one devil into two by moving the Saxons into Flanders and the Flemish into Saxony. He was unable to hold down the Saxons, whose territories he had added to his empire: every time his attention was occupied elsewhere—perhaps in far-off Spain, or some other distant part of his kingdom—they rebelled against him. So he brought them into his own country, where obedience was a tradition, namely, into Flanders. And his natural subjects, the Flemish, he sent to Saxony, convinced they would be loyal even if living in foreign lands. But as it happened the Saxons persisted in their original obstinacy and rebelliousness, and the Flemish who were living in Saxony learned the ways and manners, and especially the obstinacy, of the Saxons.

Chapter Two ⁄⁄ How Panurge Was Made Lord of Salmagundi, in Dipsodia, and Spent All His Money before He Got It

As he set about governing Dipsodia, Pantagruel gave Panurge the lordship of Salmagundi, worth 6789106789 gold pieces, not counting fluctuating revenues from the sales of may-bugs and snails, and adding up, year after year, to a grand total of anywhere from 2435768 to 2435769 gold pieces. In a good year for snails, with may-bugs in demand, revenues could reach as high as 1234554321 gold pieces. But, of course, this did not happen each and every year. The new lord governed so well, and so prudently, that in less than two weeks he had squandered all of the revenue, fixed and fluctuating alike, for a good three years. Not strictly speaking squandered, you might say, by setting up monasteries, building temples, founding schools and hospitals, or tying up his dog with a rope made of sausages, but spent it on a thousand small banquets and happy feasts, open to everyone who cared to come, but especially all good drinkers, pretty young girls, and other sweet, elegant little things—and also cutting down timber, burning up huge stumps to sell the ashes, taking money in advance, buying dear, selling cheap, and—in general—spending all his money before he got it.

Notified of what was happening, Pantagruel was neither indignant, angry, nor sad. I've already told you, and will tell you again, that he was the best fellow, small or large, who ever buckled on a sword. He took everything just as it came, putting everything in the best possible light. He never tortured himself with anxiety, and never permitted himself to be scandalized by anything. And he would have turned himself out of the divine palace of Reason had he done otherwise, allowing himself to grieve or to change, for all the possessions the sky can cover or the earth can hold, in all its dimensions—height, depth, longitude, and latitude—are not worth stirring up our emotions or troubling our good sense and our spirits.

He simply took Panurge aside and gently warned him that, if he really wanted to live this way, and not run his household differently, it would be quite impossible—or at least exceedingly difficult—for him ever to be rich.

"Rich?" answered Panurge. "Is that what you've been thinking of? You're worrying about making me rich in this world? Think about being happy, in God's good name, and man's! No other concern—none—should be allowed into the holy sanctuary of your celestial brain. Your serenity should never be troubled by intellectual clouds draped in disappointment or annoyance. You stay happy, and healthy, and be jolly—and I'll be rich enough. Everyone shouts at me, 'Don't spend so much! Be careful!' But those who talk that way don't know what they're saying. They should be asking me for advice. And what they're warning me about, what they call a vice when they find it in me, I have learned from the University of Paris, and from the court of law in that same great city, both of them true sources and living embodiments of universal theology. And of justice, also. It would be sheer heresy to doubt it—even to believe it less than fervently. They eat up their bishops in one day—or the bishop's revenues for an entire year: they're one and the same thing—and sometimes they eat up two years' worth. Think of the banquets, on the day a bishop enters the city. And the bishop can't hide or get away, unless he'd like to be stoned to death, right then and there.

"And furthermore, what they call my vices have all been strictly regulated by the four cardinal virtues:

"Prudence, first of all, in taking money in advance, because how can you tell who's going to die or refuse to pay up? Who knows if the world will last another three years? And besides, even if it lasts longer, can a man be so foolish as to promise himself another three years?

The gods have never been that easy to know:
We might be here, tomorrow; we might be below.

"And Justice: the justice of exchange, which lies in buying dear (that is, on credit) and selling cheap (that is, in hard money). What does Cato tell us about this, in his *The Art of Management?* He says, simply enough, that the father of a family must be a perpetual seller. And so it is impossible for him not to become rich, if, that is, his provisions hold out. As for the justice of distribution: well, that lies in feasting your good (note the emphasis on *good*) and noble friends and drinkers, who have been shipwrecked on the rocks of good appetite, without food or wine, just as Ulysses was stranded—and also, in feasting gallant young women (note the emphasis on *young:* as Hippocrates says, young people have very little patience with hunger, especially when they're bright, lively, vigorous, changeable, quick moving), for these young women are only too glad to bring pleasure to good men: they're such devoted followers of Plato and Cicero that they can't imagine having been placed in the world solely for themselves: they dedicate their lovely bodies half to their country and half to their good male friends.

"And as for Strength: well, knocking down great trees, like that Greek lumberjack Milo, blasting away dark forests—the home of wolf dens, wild boars, foxes, the repository of thieves and murderers, riddled with assassins, counterfeiters, not to mention heretics—and thus creating nice cleared land and beautiful meadows—the trees sell well and their stumps make pleasant seats where people can wait for the Last Judgment.

"And now for Temperance: you see me, in effect, eating my crops before they're even out of the ground: why, I might be a hermit living on leaves and roots, thus liberating myself from all sensual appetites and saving real food for the sick and infirm. Just think how much I save on gardeners, who need to be paid with good, hard money; and reapers, who get to drink as much as they like (and never add water to their wine); and gleaners, who eat so much flatcake; and threshers, who pull up all the garlic and onions and lettuce in the garden, because they say Virgil's Thestylis did exactly that; and millers, who are usually thieves anyway; and bakers, who aren't much better. Is this such a negligible savings?— not to mention the disasters that mice make, and what you always lose in the granaries, where the mites and weevils eat you out of house and home.

"You can make a fine green sauce out of green wheat, light and easy to digest, which quickens your brain, delights your animal spirits, revivifies sight, starts up the appetite, pleases the palate, comforts the heart, tickles the tongue, clears up the complexion, strengthens the muscles, moderates the blood, quickens the diaphragm, purifies your liver, relieves the spleen, calms the gall gladder, soothes the kidneys, loosens up your spine, cleans and empties your bladder, dilates your sperm glands, tightens up your balls, puffs up your genitals, gives the foreskin a bit of exercise, straightens and stiffens your prick, so your stomach's in good order, and you belch well, and fart, and shit, and piss, and sneeze, and weep, and cough, and spit, and vomit, and yawn, and blow your nose, and your breath is sweet, and you breathe easily, both in and out, you snore, you sweat, you have good erections—and thousands of other singular advantages."

"Oh, I understand very well," said Pantagruel. "What you mean is that you have to be pretty lively to spend so much money is so short a time. But you're not the first to think up such a heretical notion. It was Nero's idea, too, and he admired above all other men his uncle Caligula, who by miraculous ingenuity managed to spend, in just a few days, the entire patrimony that Tiberius had left him. Yet, instead of faithfully following all the Roman laws about eating and drinking—those statutes referred to as Orchia, Fannia, Didia, Licinia, Cornelia, Lepidiana, and Anti—and the laws of the Corinthians, too, all of which rigorously forbid anyone to spend more on his belly than he receives by way of income, you've consumed enough for your travels as well, and for the Romans that would be a sacrifice like the Jews slaughtering their Passover lamb: when they conducted that ritual, the Romans would eat everything they could, then burn the rest, leaving nothing whatever for the next day. I can truly say of you, as Cato said of Albidus, when his extravagance had led him to eat everything he owned and he was left all alone in his house, and set it on fire, so he could pronounce, *Consummatum est,* It is finished—just as Saint Thomas Acquinas declared after he'd eaten up the king's eel—but *he* was thinking of Christ on the cross. Well, never mind, it doesn't matter."

Chapter Three // Panurge's Eulogy of Debtors and Borrowers

"But," said Pantagruel, "when will you be out of debt?"

"When we count by the Greek calendar," answered Panurge, "and when everyone in the world is happy, and you're your own heir. May God keep me from being out of debt! Because no one would ever lend me a thing. If you don't have any baking powder when you go to bed at night, you'll never be able to bake a pastry in the morning. You've got to always owe something to *some*one. That way, there'll always be someone praying to God that He'll grant you a good, long, happy life—because he's terrified that he'll lose what you owe him. And wherever he goes, he'll always say good things about you, so you'll always be able to acquire new creditors, so you can borrow from them to pay him off and he can fill up his ditch with somebody else's dirt. Which was how it used to be in Gaul, under the Druids' regime: serfs and slaves and others who belonged to a man were always burned alive at their masters' funerals—and wouldn't they have lived in perpetual fear of their masters' deaths? When the masters died, the slaves knew they had to die with them. So wouldn't they be praying just as hard as they could to their great god Mercury, and to the god of their underworld, the father of all riches, to preserve those masters of theirs in good health and for as long as long might be? And wouldn't they be as careful as they knew how to treat them well and serve them faithfully, because together they could at least live until they died? Believe me: your creditors will pray to God on your behalf even more fervently—because they'd rather lose their arm than the sleeve it's wearing—rather lose their lives than a couple of gold pieces. Just think of the moneylenders in Landerousse, who hanged themselves when they saw wheat and wine going back up in price and good times returning."

When Pantagruel said nothing, Panurge went on:

"In the name of God! Come to think of it, you're trying to get me to trump my own ace, criticizing me for my debts and my creditors. Good Lord! This is the one characteristic in which I have an absolutely august reputation—the one thing for which I'm revered and considered truly formidable—because in spite of the fact that, according to all the philosophers, nothing can be created out of nothing, I had nothing, not even the beginnings of anything, but something originated with me, I was the creator of something.

"And what do I think I created? A crowd of good, lovely creditors. And creditors—as I will argue until just before they throw me into the fire—are good and lovely creatures. The man who refuses to lend money is an ugly, wicked creature, a deformed monster spawned straight out of hell by the devil himself.

"And what else did I create? Debts. O rare and venerable things! More debts, let me tell you, than all the combinations of syllables you can make with all the consonants and all the vowels in the language, according to Xenocrates' calculations. If you judge a debtor's perfection in terms of the number of his creditors, you'll never make a mistake in practical arithmetic.

"Can you imagine how comforting it is, waking up every morning and seeing all around me this flock of creditors—so humble, so useful, so numerous, so reverential—and when I observe that if I smile more openly at one of them than at the others, the idiot thinks he'll surely get his money sooner, probably the very first of all, thinking my smile as good as having the cash counted into his hands? I feel as if I'm playing God in a passion play, with my angels and cherubim gathered around me. And what are they? They're my suitors, my followers, who always greet me, who always wish me good day, the people who always have a word for me. And it has seemed to me that to be truly in debt is the equivalent of Hesiod's summit of heroic virtues, an exalted state some parts of which I have already achieved and toward which all human beings try to draw near, and for which they long (though not many succeed in climbing, for the road is a hard one). And looking around me, today, I see the entire world madly rushing, hungrily hurrying to acquire new debts, and new creditors.

"But not just anyone can be a debtor; creating creditors isn't work for just anyone. And you want me to give up such exquisite happiness? You actually ask me when I'll be out of debt?

"Worse and worse! May Saint Babolin take my soul if, all my life, I haven't seen debts as a tie, a chain running between heaven and earth, a unique link in human heredity—a connecting pin, it seems to me, without which the whole human race would soon perish from the earth—even perhaps that great universal Oversoul which, according to Plato and his followers, breathes life into all things.

"And to see that this is indeed the truth, just imagine—calmly—the notion of a world, its shape, its form—perhaps, if you like, the thirtieth of the worlds conjured out of the mind of Metrodorus, or the seventy-eighth conceived by the fancy of Petron of Hymera—but a world in which there will be neither debtors nor creditors. A completely debt-free world! None of the heavenly bodies, there, will have a predictable orbit. Everything will be in disarray. Jupiter, not thinking himself in debt to Saturn, his royal father, will push him out of his orbit and hang high—from that mighty chain described by Homer—all gods and heavens and demons and genies and heroes and devils, all intelligence, the earth, the sea, everything that exists. Saturn will link up with Mars and throw the entire world into eccentric motion. Mercury would no longer care to be of service to the others—no longer be their Camillus, as the Etruscans called him, because he would owe them nothing. No one will venerate Venus, because she will have lent nothing to anyone. The moon will remain red and dark: what reason will the sun have to give her his light? He won't be bound to anything of the sort. The sun won't shine on the earth, in that world; the stars will exert no useful influence—for the earth will have stopped lending them nourishment in the form of vapors and other gaseous exhalations, from which, as Heraclitus said, and the Stoics proved, and Cicero too argued, the stars are fed and sustained. The very elements would no longer change, or combine, or be transformed, since none will think itself obligated to any other: no element will have lent any other a thing. Then earth won't be turned into water; water won't be turned into air; air won't be turned into water; and fire won't warm the earth. All the earth will produce is monsters—titans, giants, and then still more giants. Rain won't fall, light won't shine, wind won't blow, there'll be neither summer nor autumn. Lucifer will be unchained and, rising up out of the depths of hell with the furies, fiends, and horned devils, will set about driving from the heavens all the gods of all the nations, big and little alike.

"This world where nothing is borrowed would be nothing but a gross indecency, a conspiracy more monstrous even than the election of the rector of Paris, a more jumbled piece of devilishness than the ancient mysteries they perform in Doué. No human being will help another. You'll hear them shouting, "Help! Fire! Water! Murder!"—but no one will come to their aid. And why not? He won't have lent anything, no one will owe him anything. Why worry about his fire, or shipwreck, his ruin or his death? He not only lent nothing, but after a disaster like that he wouldn't go on to lend anything.

"In short, Faith, Hope, and Charity will be driven out of this world, because men are born to help and take care of other men. And when Faith, Hope, and Charity are gone, what we'll get instead are Suspicion, Contempt, Spite, with all the evils that come with them, all the curses and all the miseries. You'll think, and justly, that Pandora turned her bottle of fortune upside down. Men will behave like wolves toward other men, like werewolves, like imps and hobgoblins: just like Lycaon, transformed into a wolf, and Bellerophon, and Nebuchadnezzar—thieves, assassins, poisoners, evildoers of all sorts, men who think nothing but evil, malicious, malevolent, all of them hating every other man alive, like Ishmael, Metabus—forever cast out from decent men—like Timon of Athens, who was justly renamed *Misanthropos,* the Misanthrope. Would it be simpler for nature to have fish swim through the air, or deer live at the bottom of the ocean, or to tolerate this beggarly world where nothing is ever borrowed, nothing ever lent? By God, I hate the whole lot of them!

"And if, with this never-lending world as your model, you turn your attention to that other little world, namely, man himself, you'll uncover a ghastly mess. The head won't lend its eyesight to the feet and the hands, so they can know what they're doing. The feet won't condescend to carry the body. The hands will refuse to work for the head. The heart will be furious, having to work so hard to keep up the pulse, and won't pump any more. The lungs will keep all their breathing to themselves. The liver won't send out blood for the rest of the body. The bladder will refuse to be in debt to the kidneys, and so urine will be abolished. The brain, reflecting on this whole unnatural sequence, will go quietly mad and stop supplying emotion to the nerves or motion to the muscles. In short, in such a lunatic world, nothing owed, nothing lent, nothing borrowed, you'll see a conspiracy far more vicious than anything Aesop dreamed of, when he wrote his dialogue between the stomach and the rest of the body. Such a man, and such a world, will surely die—and not just die, but die quickly, even if the man had been Aesculapius himself. And the dead body will rot right off, for the soul will be off to hell, chasing after the money I sent there, consigning it to the devils when I did something so sinful as paying off my debts."

Chapter Four // Panurge's Eulogy of Debtors and Borrowers: Continued

"Now imagine a completely different world, in which everyone lends, everyone owes, we're all debtors, we're all lenders.

"Oh, what harmony there would be in all the regular movements of the heavens! I think I could hear the music of the spheres as well as Plato ever did. What mutual sympathy among all the elements of the universe! Oh, what delight nature will take in all its works, in everything it produces! Ceres will be bent with wheat, Bacchus with ripe grapes, Flora with flowers and blossoms, Pomona with fruit. And Juno, high in her ethereal realm, will turn the air serene, healthy, delightful. The very thought of it carries me away. For human beings I see peace, love, delight, loyalty, repose, banquets, festivals, joy, gaiety, gold, silver, and small change, too, and chains and rings and all manner of goods passing back and forth. No lawsuits, no war, no arguments; there'll be no usurers, no gluttonous thieves, no misers, no one who holds back and refuses a loan. By God, won't this be the Age of Gold, the fabled reign of Saturn, the glorious ancient model of Olympus, where all the lesser virtues will become functionless, for there Charity alone will rule, queen, empress, triumphant? Everyone will be good, everyone will be beautiful, everyone will be just. O happy world! O lucky dwellers in that happy world, blessed three and four times over! I can imagine myself right there. I swear to you, by the name of all that's holy, that if this blessed, blessed world, in which everyone lends and no one ever says no, were ever endowed with a pope and all the army of cardinals of the sacred college, in just a few years you'd see saints so thick on the ground, and performing more miracles, than in all the saints' lives you've ever heard recited, with more prayers and processionals and burning candles than in the nine fanatical bishoprics of Brittany put together (except Saint Yves, patron saint of lawyers, who believe in paying back their divine helpers).

"Just think, please, how the noble Patelin, in the famous play we all know so well, when he wanted to absolutely deify William Jousseaume's father, praising him to the third sphere of heaven, all he'd say was:

> And he lent anything he had
> To anyone who asked for it.

"Oh, how beautifully said! Imagine our microcosm, our little world, man himself, according to *this* model—every part of him lending, borrowing, owing—in a word, in his natural state. Because nature created man precisely for this: to lend and to borrow. Even the harmony of the spheres can be no nobler, no matter what plan it follows. He who created this microcosm meant to plant in it the soul, and also life itself, like a guest residing with a host. Life is made of blood. Blood is what preserves the soul. Which is why the world is afflicted with just that one task: to go on making blood. And in this task all the parts of the body have their jobs, and the arrangement is such that each is forever borrowing from the other, lending to the other; one part is always in debt to another. Nature supplies the raw materials which are meant to be transformed into blood: bread and wine. This includes all the nourishment we take in—what in the Gothic language is called *compagne,* meaning everything we put on the table, in addition to bread and wine. In order to find these things, to prepare them and cook them, the feet must walk and carry the body here and there; the eyes must guide all the rest; down in the stomach, the appetite must produce a bit of the acid bile sent it by the spleen, thus giving the order to bring in food. The tongue tries it; the teeth chew it up; the stomach receives and digests and starts it on its way. The abdominal veins suck out of it whatever is good and can be used; they reject all the excrement, which an expulsive force evacuates from the body, via special passageways; and then the good and useful materials are brought to the liver, which once again transforms them, this time into blood.

"And how happy all the body is, each and every part rejoicing to see this golden stream, which is their unique restorative. The alchemists were no happier when, after long, hard labor and immense trouble and expense, they saw the base metal in their furnaces being transmuted into gold.

"Then every part of the body gets ready and works as hard as it can to purify and refine this treasure. The veins in the kidneys draw the water out of it, which you call urine, and pass that down through the urethral channels, all the way to its special receptacle, that is, the bladder, which when it has the opportunity voids it out of the body. The spleen draws out all the dirt and dregs, which you call melancholy. The gallbladder removes any excess of yellow bile. Then it's brought to yet another mechanism, to be still more perfectly refined: the heart, which warms and volatilizes it by diastolic and systolic movement, so the right ventricle can make it absolutely perfect and the veins can then send it forth to all the parts of the body. Each part draws it to itself and takes what it's supposed to take: feet, hands, eyes—everything. And then they're debtors, though earlier they were lenders. The heart's left ventricle so refines this golden treasure that we call it spiritual, and then sends this, too, via its arteries, to all the parts of the body, so it can warm and aerate the rest of the blood in the veins. The lungs never stop renewing and refreshing it, using their lobes and their bellows. And the heart, recognizing this extremely useful service, sends the lungs the best portions, via the pulmonary artery. And then, at last, it's so utterly refined, in a marvelous network, that it can be turned into animal spirits, which enable us to imagine, speak, judge, resolve, discuss, think, and remember.

"By God's holy greatness, how I swoon, and faint away, and utterly lose myself, when I sink into the profound, unfathomable depths of this world so beautifully balanced on taking and owing. What a divine thing it is to lend! Debt is a truly heroic virtue! But this still isn't all. This taking, owing, borrowing world is so extraordinarily fine that, once this feeding is finished, it starts to think about lending to those as yet unborn and by such loans to perpetuate itself, if it can, and multiply itself in images of its own likeness: which are, of course, children. And to this end, each part of the body chooses and trims off a portion of its own nourishment, and sends it back down to where nature has prepared the proper vessels and receptacles. That carefully selected nourishment is led from these receptacles, down through long and winding passageways, to the genitals, where it takes appropriate and wholly functional form in both men and women, so it can conserve and perpetuate the human race. And all of this is done by taking and owing, back and forth: and so we speak of the debt that is marriage.

"And to refuse to acknowledge and pay this debt is to be punished by nature with a bitter irritation of one's private parts, and a wild rage in one's senses. But whoever acknowledges the debt, and pays it, is rewarded with pleasure, happiness, and sensual delight."

Chapter Five // Pantagruel's Hatred of All Debtors and Borrowers

"I hear you," said Pantagruel. "You seem to me a first-rate debater who truly believes in his cause. But you could preach and plead from here to Pentecost and you wouldn't persuade me of any of it, nor would I go into debt for all your fine words. Owe nothing to anyone, said Saint Paul, except love and mutual delight.

"You've shown me some lovely images and descriptions, and they're very nice indeed. But I say to you that if you try to imagine a shameless, disgraceful pest of a borrower coming back to a city that already knows what he is and how he operates, you'll find the citizens more frightened and worried than if the plague had come to visit them, dressed like a human being—which is how, Apollonius of Tyana tells us, the philosopher saw it in Ephesus. And I agree with the Persians, who thought the second-greatest vice was lying, but being in debt was the first, for debts and lies usually go hand in hand.

"I don't mean to suggest that you should never ever be in debt, or that you should never lend. No one is so rich that, now and then, he can keep from having to owe money. Nor is there any man so poor that, sometimes, he might not need to lend. But it ought to be the way Plato puts it in his *Laws:* you shouldn't let your neighbors draw water from your well, he says, unless they've first dug so deep on their own land that they've hit rock and potter's clay and never found a spring or any water source at all. At that depth the earth holds water; it's thick and soft and smooth and dense, and it isn't easy to make anything come gushing out.

"It's always an immense shame—everywhere on earth—to go around borrowing rather than working and earning your own living. You ought to lend (as far as I'm concerned) only when the man's been working as hard as he can but hasn't been able to make anything, or when he's suffered some sudden disaster and lost everything.

"But let's leave this subject. And in the future don't tie yourself up with creditors: I will free you from your past."

"And the very least I can do," said Panurge, "is thank you—and if thanks are to be measured by the benefactor's affection, then here my thanks should be infinite, eternal. For the love which you so graciously extend to me is far beyond any calculation: it utterly transcends weight, number, measure—it is indeed infinite and eternal. Truly, to measure it even by the benefactor's own nature, or the beneficiary's satisfaction, is simply to grossly underestimate. You do so many good things for me, far, far more than I have any right to, and surely more than anything I've done for you could possibly deserve, and without question more than I am worthy of—that, I have no choice but to admit. But here, my lord, you do less than you think.

"But that isn't what bothers me, that isn't what gnaws and bites at me. Consider: from now on I'm out of debt—but how will I manage? The first months are bound to be awkward, for I wasn't brought up this way, nor has it been my way of life. That fills me with fear.

"And consider, too, that every fart blowing into the air, anywhere here in Salmagundi, will be aimed directly at my nose, since all the farters in the world always say, as they fart, 'Now we're even!' It's going to shorten my life, I can see that very well. I'll let you write my epitaph: I'm going to die pickled in farts. Someday, when old hags afflicted with windy colic need to be able to fart, and can't, well, if ordinary medicines aren't good enough for the doctors, all they'll need is a little mummy oil squeezed out of my worn-out befarted body, and everything will be made right. They'll need to take only a little—less than prescribed—and they'll fart more freely than they could have dreamed.

"And that's why I beg you, please, to leave me a few debts, a hundred or so—as Miles d'Illiers, bishop of Chartres, when he was thrown out of court, begged King Louis the Eleventh to leave him just a few lawsuits, to keep his mind busy. I'll be happy to let them have all the money I get from selling snails, plus the income from the sale of may-bugs—though of course none of this will reduce the actual debts."

"Let's put this subject aside," said Pantagruel. "I've already told you that."

Chapter Six ⁄ Why Newly Married Men Were Excused from Fighting Wars

"Now," asked Panurge, "by what law has it been decided and decreed that those who have just planted new vines, those who have just built new houses, and those who have just gotten married have a one-year exemption from going off to fight wars?"

"By the law of Moses," answered Pantagruel.

"But why," asked Panurge, "include the newly married? Vine planters: well, I'm too old to worry about *them*. I'm willing to let vine trimmers take care of themselves. As for the good folk who pile up dead stones and make houses out of them, they're not written in my book of life, either. I build only with living stones: I mean, with men."

"As far as I know," answered Pantagruel, "so that they got the first year to make love as much as they liked, and took the time to produce descendants and provide themselves with heirs. That way, at least, if they were killed in war during the second year, their names and their coats of arms lived on in their children. It's also so they could know for sure if their wives were fertile or sterile (a year's trial seemed sufficient, considering how old they were, in those days, when they got married), so after the first husband was dead the widows would be able to decide about a second marriage: the fertile ones could marry those who wanted a lot of children, the sterile could marry those who had no interest in propagation and were interested in a woman for her abilities, her knowledge of the finer things in life—men who were concerned only with domestic pleasures and living well.

"The preachers in Varennes," said Panurge, "can't stand second marriages: they call them idiotic and disgraceful."

"They burn," answered Pantagruel, "like men with fevers."

"Indeed," said Panurge, "and Brother Hotpants agrees with them. At Parilly, he preached a blunt sermon against second marriages, swearing that he'd let the fastest devil in hell run off with him if he didn't think it would be better to screw a hundred virgins than to jump in bed with just one widow.

"I think you're right, and your argument's well founded. But what if their exemption were granted because, all during this first year, they'd banged away so hard at these new love objects (as they certainly ought to do), and so thoroughly drained their sperm ducts, that they'd worn themselves out, gone all limp and weak and wilted? When the time came for fighting, they'd be more likely to dive into the baggage like ducks than to stand up among the warriors and brave champions, there where Bellona, goddess of war, whips up the struggle, and fierce blows are

given and taken. Could they rear themselves up, under Mars' bold banner—Mars, Venus' brave husband—and strike a single worthwhile blow?
All their whacking would have been banged away, long since, behind the
curtains on Venus' bed.

"And the proof that that's really how it was can still be seen, among
sensible people. One of the customs we've inherited from ancient times
is that, after a certain number of days, these newly married men are sent
off to visit their uncles, to get them away from their wives and have a
little rest and be fattened up and restored so they're better fitted for a
return to combat—whether or not they in fact have either an uncle or an
aunt. I remember how King Clodhopper, after the battle of Blowhard,
didn't really discharge us, strictly speaking—that is, me and Birdbrain—
but told us to take a rest at home. Birdbrain's still hunting for his. My
grandfather's godmother once told me, when I was still a child, that

> Hail Marys and all the rest of your prayers
> Are good for those who hold back.
> A piper ready to push his wares
> Does better than two who are whacked.

"And what really persuades me is that people who plant vines hardly
eat a grape or drink a glass of wine that whole first year. And people who
put up houses never live in them that first year: they're afraid of dying of
suffocation (caused by an insufficiency of air), as Galen has observed, in
book two of his *Difficulties in Breathing*.

"You see, my lord, I didn't ask this question without having a good
reason, founded in proper reasoning and resonating most resoundingly.
Don't be annoyed."

Chapter Seven ⁄⁄ How Panurge Got a Flea in His Ear and Stopped Wearing His Magnificent Codpiece

The next day, Panurge had his right ear pierced, Old Testament style,
and started to wear a little gold ring, ornamented with hammered silver
and set with a jeweled flea. It was an ebony flea—and just so you have no
doubt of its costliness (it being a good thing, in any case, to be well
informed), carefully posted and double-checked by his Salmagundian
accountants, please understand that it came to scarcely twenty-five per-
cent per three-month period more than the marriage dowry of a Hyrcan-
ian tigress: roughly speaking, about six hundred thousand very fat gold
pieces. That sort of excessive expenditure annoyed him, now that he was
out of debt, so that, afterward, he proceeded thereafter to pay it off as

tyrants and lawyers always do: namely, with the blood and sweat of his subjects.

He took four yards of heavy brown wool and wore it like a long robe, tied around. He also stopped wearing the upper part of his breeches and hung his spectacles from his hat.

And looking like this, he presented himself to Pantagruel, who thought his outfit exceedingly odd—noticing especially that he was no longer wearing his handsome, his magnificent codpiece, which had always been Panurge's sacred anchor, his ultimate refuge against the shipwrecks of adversity.

Not understanding what this mystery was all about, the good Pantagruel asked what this new appearance was supposed to mean.

"I," answered Panurge, "have a flea in my ear. I want to get married."

"May it be so," said Pantagruel. "You make me very happy. But I wouldn't want to hold a hot coal in my hand, to prove it was true. This is hardly the way lovers dress, their codpiece fallen off, their shirts hanging down over their knees, and the tops of their breeches missing, all wrapped in a long robe of coarse wool—and a most unusual color, too, for the full-length clothing of good, virtuous folk.

"When certain heretics, and followers of strange sects, used to dress like this, they were considered fakers—imposters—a tyrannical imposition on the plain people of this world, though on that account alone I don't want to accuse them of anything and make something ominous out of their getup. Everyone is full of his own ideas, especially when it comes to things we don't know a lot about—things foreign and not important to us, and which we don't know as either good or bad, because they don't come from our own hearts and thoughts—and the heart, of course, is the center of all that's good about us and also all that's bad: good, if it really is good, if it's ruled by good feeling; bad, if it's unfair and impelled by evil, depraved feeling. What bothers me is simply the novelty of this outfit of yours—its contempt for ordinary manners."

"The color," answered Panurge, "fits the man who's wearing it. I swear it, this stuff is the right stuff, right enough. But from now on I mean to keep a close watch on my accounts. Now that I'm out of debt, you'll never hope to see a nastier fellow, if God doesn't help me.

"See my spectacles? Watching me coming, from a long way off, you'd say I was that famous Franciscan preacher Brother Jean Bourgeois. I think next year I'll give a good sermon on the Crusades. May God keep my balls safe and sound!

"And this good brown wool? There's something magical about it—something damned few people know about. I just put it on this morning, but I'm already wild, mad with excitement; I'm burning to get married and work my good coarse cloth back and forth over my wife like the devil himself—without worrying about anyone beating me for it. Oh, what a fantastic housekeeper I'll be! When I'm dead, they'll burn me on a noble pyre, just so they can preserve the ashes of such a splendid, such a perfect, unforgettable housekeeper. Jee-sus! They use brown wool like this to cover counting tables—and those accountants of mine had better not fool around with *my* accounts, or my fist will play little brown horse's hooves all up and down their faces!

"Study me front view, back view: this is exactly how a toga must look, that ancient garment worn by the Romans in times of peace. I've copied Trajan's column in Rome—and also the triumphal arch of Septimius Severus. I'm tired of war—of wise men—of bulky padded clothes. My shoulders are all worn out from being in harness. Down with weapons, up with togas! At least this next year, anyway, if I get married—as you suggested, yesterday, talking about Moses and his Old Testament laws.

"And about the tops of my breeches: my great-aunt Laurence explained to me, a long time ago, that breeches were made for codpieces. I agree with the argument of that good rascal Galen, who says in the ninth book of his *On the Use of Our Arms and Legs* that our heads were made for our eyes. You don't see nature putting our heads on our knees, or on our elbows. No: making sure that our eyes will see into the distance, she set them on our head—as if on a stick jutting up over the body. It's the same thing as lighthouses and tall towers in harbors, built so their lanterns can be seen from far off.

"And since I wish to leave the military arts for a while, at least a year, so I can get married, I'm not wearing my codpiece any more, and because I'm not wearing my codpiece I'm not wearing the upper part of my breeches. The codpiece is a man of war's most important piece of armor. And I would argue—until they've got me tied to the stake and they're ready to light the fire—that the Turks are all improperly armored, because their law forbids them to wear a codpiece."

Chapter Eight ⁄⁄ Why the Codpiece Is a Man of War's Most Important Piece of Armor

"Do you seriously argue," said Pantagruel, "that the codpiece is a man of war's most important piece of armor? That's an exceedingly paradoxical and novel notion: we always say that it's when you've put on your spurs that you're beginning to get yourself armored."

"I do argue it," answered Panurge, "and I'm not wrong, either.

"Consider how nature—wishing the plants and trees and shrubs, the grasses and corals and sponges she created, to live on and perpetuate themselves over and over, so that no species would ever die out even though the individual died—has so strangely and carefully armored their seeds, which are their guarantees of eternal life. She has fitted them, covered them with her wonderful ingenuity, giving them pods, sheaths, shells, pits, calyxes, husks, spikes, tufts, bark, thorns, which for them are like strong, handsome natural codpieces. You see the same thing in peas, beans, nuts, peaches, apricots, cotton, crab apples, wheat, poppy seed, lemons, chestnuts, and indeed generally speaking in all plants in which the seed germs plainly need to be better covered, fitted, and armored than any other part. But nature couldn't do the same thing for human beings, in assuring the perpetuation of our race, having in that Golden Age at the beginning of time created man in a state of innocence, naked, weak, vulnerable, without armor or weapons, without scales or a shell, like an animal rather than a plant, and like an animal—as I see it—born for peace and not for war, an animal born to seek its nourishment by enjoying the marvels of all plants and fruits, an animal intended to take peaceful domination over all other animals.

"But when that Golden Age gave way to the Age of Iron, and the reign of Jupiter, evil and bad feeling began to spread among men, and the earth began to produce nettles, spikes, thorns, and all manner of vegetable rebellion against mankind. And almost all the animals displayed a deadly disposition to assert their independence of us and even began to conspire among themselves, resolved to serve us no longer, and to refuse to obey us, and to resist us in every way they could, and as their abilities and strength permitted, to injure us.

"So man, wishing to preserve and continue his original dominance, and being unable easily to abandon the services of at least some of the animals, found it necessary to start arming himself."

"By Saint Quenet's belly!" cried Pantagruel. "Since the last rains fell you've turned into quite a tippler—or should I say philosopher?"

"Just consider," said Panurge, "how nature gave man the idea of armor, and what part of the body she first armed. And, by God, it was the balls:

> And when Master Priapus was shod
> The job was well and snugly done, by God!

"And just think of that great captain, and Hebrew philosopher, Moses, who tells us in Genesis that Adam put on a gallant, dashing codpiece, fashioned—by a fine bit of ingenuity—out of fig leaves, a natural commodity and perfectly appropriate: tough, properly shaped, neatly curved, smooth, large enough, nicely colored, sweet smelling—in short, with all the qualities necessary for covering and protecting a pair of swinging balls.

"Now, I'm not talking about the stupendous balls you find in Lorraine, which, since those fellows don't like high-flown codpieces and won't wear anything else, dangle straight down to the bottom of their breeches. Just think about that noble jester Viardière, whom I met one fine May day: he had his balls all spread out on a table, like a Spanish cape, and was scrubbing away at them, to make them even more elegant.

"So, if we want to speak properly when we're sending the rural militia off to war, we shouldn't always say, 'Hey, Etienne, take care of your wine pot,' (which means his head). No: from now on we ought to say, 'Hey, Etienne, take care of your cream pot,' which by all the devils in hell means your balls! If you lose your head, it's just the particular individual who dies. But when you lose your balls, you kill human nature itself.

"And this is what our gallant old friend Galen boldly concluded, in book one of his *On Sperm:* it's better—that is, it's less bad—to be without a heart than to try to do without your genitals. Because what you have in there, as in some sacred repository, are the seeds of the human heritage. Nor would it take even a hundred francs to persuade me that these were in fact the very stones from which Deucalion and Pyrrha once reconstituted the whole human species, after that Great Flood of which the poets tell us.

"And it was this, too, which moved the valiant Justinian to assert, in book four of his *De cagotis tollendis,* Wiping Out Sanctimonious Hypocrites, that *summum bonum in braguibus et braguetis,* the highest virtue of all resides in codpieces and breeches.

"For these as well as for other causes, the lord of Merville, intending to follow his king into war, one day tried on new battle gear (because his was old and half rusted through, and it couldn't be used any more, because it had been a good many years since the skin on his belly was anywhere near his kidneys), and his wife stood and thoughtfully watched him, noting that he couldn't be much worried about that bundle and staff which were the shared property of their marriage, since the only armor he put over it was iron mail. It seemed to her that he'd much better provide for and protect it by buckling on a great helmet that she could see in the cupboard, just lying there useless.

"The third book of *How Virgins Shit* contains the following verses about this same lady:

> Seeing her husband wearing his armor
> But not his codpiece, and ready for war,
> She said, 'My love, it might be harmed:
> Protect it: I love it the best by far.'
> Hey? You think she was wrong to say it?
> No! Why not be afraid of losing
> The heart and soul of her marriage, and choosing
> To cherish that candy stick she played with.

"So, my lord, don't be astonished at my new clothing."

Chapter Nine // How Panurge Consulted Pantagruel, to See If He Really Ought to Get Married

Since Pantagruel did not answer, Panurge sighed deeply and went on:

"My lord, you've heard my thoughts: you know I mean to marry, unless all the cunts in the world are closed up, locked, and buckled. I beg you, for the sake of the love you've so long shown me, to give me your advice."

"Well," answered Pantagruel, "since you've already rolled the dice, and firmly made up your mind, there's no need for talk. All you need to do is do it."

"Yes, of course," said Panurge, "but I don't want to do it without your counsel and your good advice."

"I counsel you to proceed," said Pantagruel. "That's my advice."

"But," said Panurge, "suppose you knew that it would be better for me to remain as I am, and not try anything new: in that case I'd rather not get married at all."

"Then don't get married," answered Pantagruel.

"To be sure," said Panurge. "But do you want me to stay all alone the rest of my life, with no wife to keep me company? You know what the Bible says: *Voe soli,* Woe to the man who lives alone! A man by himself has no pleasures like those of married people."

"Then get married, by God!" answered Pantagruel.

"But," said Panurge, "suppose my wife deceived me—and you know what a good year this has been for cuckolds. That would drive me wild! I'm very fond of diddled husbands, and they strike me as good fellows, and good company. But I'd rather be dead than wear a pair of horns. This is something that really bothers me."

"Then just don't get married," answered Pantagruel, "because what Seneca said is universally true: whatever you've done to others will certainly be done to you."

"Really?" said Panurge. "Without any exceptions?"

"He says with no exceptions at all," answered Pantagruel.

"Ho ho!" said Panurge. "The little devil! But I suppose he means either in this world or maybe in the next one.

"Well, yes. But since I can't manage without a woman, any more than a blind man can do without a stick (because I've got to keep this tool of mine active, or I don't know how I'd go on living), wouldn't it be better to tie myself to some respectable, chaste woman, instead of always changing from this one to that one, and always worried about getting beaten—or worse still, getting the pox? No good woman has ever had an affair with me—not that I mean to upset their husbands."

"Then get married, by God!" answered Pantagruel.

"But if by God's will," said Panurge, "I happened to marry a good woman, and she beat me, I'd have to be a miniature Job to stop myself from going wild. And they say these terribly virtuous women usually have ugly tempers: there's a lot of good vinegar in those kitchens! But I'd do better than that: I'd slaughter her goose for her! I mean, I'd beat her arms, and her legs, her head, her chest, her liver and spleen, and I'd tear up her clothes so fast that the devil himself would be standing outside the door, waiting to collect her damned soul. I'd just as soon not go through all that—not this year—not ever, in point of fact."

"Then don't get married," answered Pantagruel.

"Of course, yes," said Panurge. "But now that I'm out of debt and still not married—but notice, out of debt and into bad luck! Because when I was up to my ears in debt, my creditors couldn't have been more careful about my paternity. But now, free of debt, and unmarried, I have no one to take care of me, no one to love me—I mean, as a married woman is supposed to love her husband. And suppose I fell sick, I'd probably be treated really badly. The Bible says: Where there's no woman—I mean, the mother of a family, properly married—sickness is a real problem. I've seen exactly that happen to popes, and papal ambassadors, and cardinals, bishops, abbots, priors, priests, and monks. I don't want it happening to me."

"Then get married, by God!" answered Pantagruel.

"But suppose," said Panurge, "I get so sick that I can't perform my marital duties; my wife might get impatient and give herself to someone else. And then she wouldn't just abandon me in my hour of need—no, she'd be poking fun at my misfortune, and (this is even worse) she'd be robbing me, as I've often seen it happen, and that would be the last straw. You'd see me running through the fields in my shirt."

"Then don't get married," said Pantagruel.

"Yes," said Panurge. "But then I wouldn't have any legitimate sons or daughters, through whom I could hope to carry on my name and my coat of arms—to whom I could leave everything I myself have inherited and acquired (I'm going to do well, one of these days: don't you doubt it: and I'll even pay off the estates I've mortgaged to the hilt)—with whom I can have fun, and without whom I'd be sad—the way I see your kind, gentle father always is with you, as all good men are, in the shelter of their own homes. But being out of debt, unmarried, and maybe angry, too—But instead of cheering me up, all you're doing is laughing at my misfortune!"

"Then get married, by God!" answered Pantagruel.

Chapter Ten ∕∕ Pantagruel Explains to Panurge How Difficult It Is to Give Advice about Marriage, Plus Some Comments about Telling Fortunes Using Homer and Virgil

"Your advice," said Panurge, "unless I'm very much mistaken, is like that song about Ricochet, which keeps repeating itself and never comes to an end. All you've offered me are ironies, jokes, and contradictory repetitions. They all negate each other. Which am I supposed to pay attention to?"

"Just as in your arguments," said Pantagruel, "there's so much 'maybe yes' and 'maybe no' that I can't find any solid ground: there's nothing I can try to make clear. Don't you know what you want? That's the main point: everything else is just happenstance and depends on what heaven decides—not you.

"We find so many men so very happy in marriage that, watching them, we seem to glimpse the joys of paradise. And others are so miserable that the devils who tempt hermits, out in the deserts of Thebes or Montserrat, aren't any worse off. You've got to go into the thing with your eyes shut, lowering your head, kissing the ground, and—for the rest—putting your trust in God, as long as you've decided to do it. Can I give you any greater comfort than that, or make you any stronger promises?

"Now, here's what you can do, if you want to. Bring me Virgil's works, and open the book three times, and wherever your finger rests we'll see if we can find an answer for you, some prediction about the future of your marriage. It's been done many times, using Homer's words:

"Socrates, for example, when he was in prison, heard Achilles' speech from book nine of the *Iliad:*

> It won't take long: in three days more
> I'll land in Phthia, my lovely home.

"And so he predicted that he himself would die three days later, and told his disciple Aeschinus, as Plato explains in his *Crito,* and also Cicero in the first book of his *De divinatione,* On Divination, and also Diogenes Laërtius.

"And Opilius Macrinus, too, wanting to know if he would become the Roman emperor, came upon this passage, from book eight of the *Iliad:*

> Oh, old man, younger and stronger
> Soldiers will be weary of you, no longer

The man you were: harsh, impatient
Age will snarl and snap in your face.

"And indeed he was already an old man, and he'd been on the throne barely a year and two months when the young, powerful Heliogabalus overthrew and killed him.

"And Brutus, when he wanted to know how the battle of Pharsalia would turn out—it turned out that he was killed—came across this verse, spoken by the dying Patroclus in book sixteen of the *Iliad:*

I was killed by spiteful Fate
And Leto's son, who hated
Me.

"He meant Apollo, and they made that angry god's name the password for the battle.

"The ancients also used Virgil for making predictions, and seeking information about large and important matters—including accession to the throne. Witness Alexander Severus, who used this technique of divination and found, in the *Aeneid,* book six, the following verse:

Son of Rome, when you take the throne
Make ruling your business, and ruling alone.

"And not many years later, he in fact did become emperor of Rome.

"And Hadrian, before he came to the throne, wondered how Emperor Trajan felt about him and whether or not he truly loved him. So he used Virgil as a source of magical information, and found this verse from book six of the *Aeneid:*

And who is this, coming from a distant place,
Who bears an olive branch with imperial grace?
His graying head and sacred robe show me
An ancient Roman king, who clearly knows me.

"And later he was adopted by Trajan, and succeeded him to the throne.

"And Claudius, Rome's much-praised second emperor, found this prediction in book six of the *Aeneid:*

Think of the third year
Of your reign as emperor,

"And in fact he ruled for only two years.

"And he also sought magical advice about his brother, Quintilian, when he thought about making him his imperial equal—and found the following, again in book six of the *Aeneid:*

> Fate only gives the world a glimpse of him.

"And after he became co-ruler of Rome, it happened exactly as the prophecy had indicated, for he died just six or seven days later.

"The same fate befell Emperor Gordian the younger.

"And Clodius Albinus, anxious to hear how well the future would treat him, came upon this passage, once more from book six of the *Aeneid:*

> This knight, finding Rome swept
> By storms, made sure the empire was kept
> Alive, with victories in Carthage
> And Gaul, where rebels wanted war.

"And Marcus Aurelius' predecessor as emperor, Divus Claudius, anxious to see how his descendants would fare, found the following prediction in book one of the *Aeneid:*

> I say they'll last for many years
> And live well: have no fear.

"And in fact his descendants had long, successful histories.

"And that learned friar Maître Pierre Amy, when he wanted to learn if he'd ever escape the traps set for him by hobgoblins—that is, by ignorant, jealous monks—found this verse from book three of the *Aeneid:*

> Leave these barbarous people!
> Leave these miserable shores!

"And then he did flee from them, and escaped safe and sound.

"And there are thousands more, though it would take far too long to tell what prediction each of them encountered and exactly what happened.

"Of course, I don't mean to suggest that this sort of prediction is invariably accurate, for that would be to mislead you."

Chapter Eleven ⁄⁄ How Pantagruel Explained to Panurge That Using Dice to Predict the Future Is Improper

"All of this," said Panurge, "could be quicker and more readily accomplished with just three pretty dice."

"No," answered Pantagruel. "That kind of prediction is deceptive, improper, and indeed distinctly scandalous. Don't ever trust it. That accursed book *Fun with Dice* was spawned a long time ago by our great enemy, the devil himself. It comes from Greece, near Bura—and right there, in front of the statue of Hercules, he used to catch simple souls and pull them into his grip and make them fall—there and in many other places. He's still doing it. Surely you know that my father, Gargantua, has banned this book in every kingdom he rules. Indeed, he's had it burned, along with the type used to print it, and all its illustrations: he's completely stamped it out, suppressed it, eliminated it, as if it were a dangerous plague.

"And everything I've said to you about dice I repeat about knucklebones: it's exactly the same sort of fraud. And don't say to me, Oh no, just think about Tiberius' wonderfully revealing rolling of knucklebones, right in front of Aponnus' fountain, at the oracle of Gerion. That's just another of the hooks with which the devil pulls simple souls down into eternal damnation.

"But just to please you, go ahead: throw your three dice right here on this table. Whatever number you throw will be the page you'll open to. Did you bring any dice with you?"

"A whole bagful," answered Panurge. "It's the devil's gambling cloth, as Merlin Coccaius shows, in the second book of his *De patria diabolorum,* The Devils' Homeland. The devil would grab me and not bother about the cloth, if he ever found me without my dice."

He took out the dice and threw them, and they showed a five, a six, and a five.

"That," said Panurge, "makes sixteen. We'll take the sixteenth line on the page. I like that number: I think we're going to come up with some jolly things. I'll throw myself into all the devils' arms, like a bowling ball crashing into a set of ninepins or a cannonball right down a line of foot soldiers. Watch out for yourselves, devils, if I don't screw that hypothetical wife of mine sixteen times, the very first night of our marriage!"

"I don't doubt it a bit," answered Pantagruel. "But there was no need to swear such a ghastly oath. The first point in tennis is worth fifteen, so we'll call your first stroke a fault; then, when you climb down out of the saddle, you'll do better; and that way you'll easily get to sixteen."

"And is that," said Panurge, "how you understand me? Well, that valiant who stands guard for me, right here under my belly, has never committed a fault in his life. Have you ever found me in the brotherhood of
defaulters? Never—never—right down to the end, never! I'm faultless—
as a father or a church father, no matter which, I appeal to my fellow
players!"

And when they were done with their verbal jousting, they had Virgil's
works brought to them. Before opening the book, Panurge said:

"How my heart's pounding! Just have a look at the pulse in this artery,
here in my left arm. The way it's going you'd say I was trying to defend
a thesis at the Sorbonne, and not doing too well. Maybe, before we go
any farther, we ought to say a prayer to Hercules and the goddesses who
rule the inner sanctum of Fortune?"

"Neither one," said Pantagruel, "nor the other. Just open the book."

Chapter Twelve   How Pantagruel Uses Virgilian Fortune-telling to Find Out about Panurge's Marriage

So Panurge opened the book, and on line sixteen found this verse:

> God's holy table needs no great display,
> And no one needs a goddess' bed to play.

"That," said Pantagruel, "won't do you much good. It means your
wife will fool about and you'll surely be cuckolded.

"The goddess who'll refuse to smile at you is Minerva, a deadly virgin
and extremely powerful, indeed a fire breather, and the enemy of all
cuckolds and seducers and adulterers, the enemy of all loose women and
especially those who break their marriage vows and give themselves to
other men. The god is Jupiter, cracking thunder and hurling lightning up
in the skies. And note that, according to the ancient Etruscans, thunderbolts (they thought the rumbling of volcanoes was like thunder) were
exclusively the province (they cited the fire that destroyed Ajax Oileus'
navy) of Minerva and her royal progenitor, Jupiter. The other gods up
on Mount Olympus weren't allowed to hurl fire, which is why men weren't
as afraid of them.

"Let me explain a bit more: you can take this as a page out of the
highest old mythologies. When the giants declared war on the gods, at
the beginning the gods just made fun of them, saying they'd let their
servants fight with attackers of that sort. But when they saw that the
giants had succeeded in putting Mount Pelion on top of Mount Ossas,

and felt how Mount Olympus itself was beginning to shake, as the giants
got ready to lift it onto the other two, they got frightened. So Jupiter
called a meeting, and all the gods agreed that they had to start really
defending themselves. And since they'd seen that battles were often lost
because women, who in those days accompanied armies, got in the soldiers' way, they decreed that, for the time being, they would drive all the
whorish goddesses out of the skies and into Egypt and the borders of the
Nile. So they changed them into weasels, skunks, bats, shrewmice, and
assorted disguises of that sort. Only Minerva was left, to stand at Jupiter's
side, hurling thunder and lightning, because she was the goddess of poetry
and war, of counsel and action, a goddess born with weapons already in
her hands, a goddess feared in heaven—in the air, on the seas, and on the
ground."

"By God's belly!" said Panurge. "Am I supposed to be like Vulcan, a
figure of fun for poets to write about? No. I'm not lame, like him; I'm
not a counterfeiter, or a forger, as he was. Maybe my wife will be as
beautiful and seductive as Venus—but not as wild as Venus, and certainly
she won't cuckold me, the way Venus did him. That bent-leg rascal got
himself openly declared a cuckold—right in the presence of all the other
gods. But this—this has to be understood differently.

"This prophecy means that my wife will be chaste, modest, loyal, not
at all belligerent or rebellious, or brainless (or born out of anybody else's
brain) like Minerva—and that randy ram Jupiter won't be after her, trying
to dip his bread in my soup while we're sitting and eating together.

"Just think of the stories about Jupiter, and what he did. He was the
most infamous scoundrel, the worst whoring monk—I mean, skunk that
ever was, always rutting around like a pig—he was even suckled by a
sow, in the caves of Mount Dicté, on Crete, unless Agathocles the Baby-
lonian is a liar. He's like a sex-starved goat: some people say he was even
suckled by that she-goat Amalthea. Damn! One day he screwed a third
of the whole world, animals and people both, and rivers and mountains,
too—I'm talking about Europa. That memorable bit of rutting made the
Ammonians picture him like a goat caught in action—and a goat with
horns.

"But I know how to stop the bastard. He's not going to find some
stupid Amphitryon, some idiot Argus with his hundred eyeglasses, or
that coward Acrisius, that head-in-the-clouds Lycus of Thebes, that dreamy
Agenor, that lazy Asopus, that daddy wolf Lycaon, that lumpy-brained
Corytus of Tuscany, or Atlas with his strong back (and no brain at all).

"He'll have to turn himself into a hundred swans, or bulls, or satyrs,
or showers of gold, or cuckoos—as he did when he deflowered his sister
Juno, or eagles, or billy goats, or pigeons—as he did when he was lusting
after young Phthia, who lived in Aegia, or fires, or snakes, or, yes, into
fleas or Epicurean atoms or theomagisterially into thoughts of other
thoughts—but I'll grab him, no matter what. And do you know what I'll

do? Jee-sus! I'll do what Saturn did to his father (Seneca said it would happen, and Lactantius confirmed it)—what Rhea did to Athys: I'll cut off his balls, so he's flat smooth all the way to his ass—I won't leave him a hair. Which is why he'll never become pope, because *testiculos non habet,* he won't have any balls."

"Easy, easy there, boy," said Pantagruel. "Easy! Just open the book a second time."

And then they came on this verse:

> His back was broken, his limbs were cracked,
> By the fear that turned his blood to glass.

"Which means," said Pantagruel, "that she'll beat you black and blue."

"On the contrary," answered Panurge. "This is talking about me, and it prophesies that I'll beat her like a tiger if she ever makes me angry. Saint Martin's staff will do the job. And if there's no stick handy, may the devil swallow me up if I don't eat her alive, the way Cambles, king of the Lydians, ate his wife."

"You're very brave," said Pantagruel. "Hercules wouldn't dare fight with you, when you're this worked up. It's like backgammon, when John's worth two points: Hercules all by himself wouldn't dare fight against two of you."

"And I'm John?" said Panurge.

"Never mind, never mind," answered Pantagruel. "I was just thinking about backgammon."

And on the third try they found this verse:

> He burned and flamed with a woman's desire,
> The passion to steal glowing like fire.

"That means," said Pantagruel, "that she'll rob you blind. And from these three prophecies, I can see exactly how it's going to be. You'll be cuckolded, you'll be beaten, you'll be robbed."

"On the contrary," answered Panurge, "what this last verse means is that she'll love me with a perfect, true love. Juvenal doesn't lie about this, telling us how a woman burning with supreme love sometimes likes to steal things from her beloved. And what will she steal, eh? A glove, a comb, just so you have to go hunting for it—some little thing—nothing of any importance.

"It's the same with these little quarrels, these niggling disagreements that sometimes spring up between lovers: they actually freshen love up, they spur it on. It's the way you see knife sharpeners bang on their grind-stones, so they'll do a better job on steel blades.

"And that's why I think all three of these prophecies predict good things for me. Otherwise I'd appeal them."

"Go ahead and appeal," said Pantagruel, "but you always lose, when the case is decided by fortune-telling and fate, as the old legal authorities all say, and also Baldus, in the last book of his *De legibus,* On the Laws. And that's because Fortune doesn't think anyone or anything is her better or that anything she decides can be changed. And in this case, too, you can't argue that the disciple can be treated as if he had full and separate rights, as Baldus also says, and accurately, in his *Ait praetor,* Legal Digest, title IV, paragraph 7."

Chapter Thirteen // How Pantagruel Advises Panurge to Forecast the Success or Failure of His Marriage by the Use of Dreams

"Now, since we don't agree about what these Virgilian fortune-tellings tell us, let's try another kind of divination."

"Which?" asked Panurge.

"A good one," answered Pantagruel, "an old one, and reliable: dreams. Because the soul often sees things yet to come, when we dream in the way Hippocrates writes about, in his book *On Dreams*—and so too Plato, and Plotinus, Iamblichus, Synesius of Cyrenaica, Aristotle, Xenophon, Galen, Plutarch, Artemidorus, Herophilus, Quintus Calaber, Theocritus, Pliny, Athenaeus, and many others.

"I don't need to say much more to prove this, do I? A common example should be enough to make the point. When little children have been all cleaned up, and fed well, and they've sucked as much as they want, they fall into a deep sleep—and then their nurses go off and have fun. They feel as if they've been turned loose to do whatever they want to: hanging around the crib wouldn't accomplish a thing. And just so our soul, when the body's asleep, and digestion's all done with, and nothing more is needed until later, when it wakes up, it flies happily off and revisits its original home, which is heaven.

"And there it's reminded of its divine origins, and—while contemplating this infinite and intellectual sphere, the center of which lies everywhere in the universe, with a circumference that is nowhere to be found (which, according to Hermes Trismegistus, is God), where nothing happens, there is no time, nothing fades away, all time is continuously present—our soul observes not only the lesser movement of all things past and done with, but also the future. Then, reporting these things back to its body, and through that body's senses and its various organs making them known also to its friends, the soul is called a prophet and a seer. Of course, it cannot be absolutely candid or truly tell all it has seen, because it is hampered by the imperfections and weaknesses of the body's senses—

just as the moon receives its light from the sun but cannot transmit that light to us as clear and pure and lively or even as hot as it was originally received. So these dream predictions need an interpreter—someone skilled, wise, ingenious, experienced, rational: *onirocritical,* the Greeks called them, meaning able to read dreams, and also *oniropolic,* accustomed to dealing with dream matters.

"Which is why Heraclitus said that dreams never explain anything to us, or ever conceal anything, but just give us hints and tokens of things to come, whether happy or sad, either for us or for anyone else. The Bible, too, bears this same witness, and secular history adds still further support, offering us a thousand instances where dreams came true, either for the dreamer himself or for others about whom he had dreamed.

"But those who lived in Atlantis and on the island of Thasos (one of the Cyclades) were deprived of that capacity: in those lands, no one ever dreamed. Cleon of Daulia was like that, too, and Thrasymedes—and in our own time, the learned Simon de Neuville, who never dreamed a dream in his life.

"So tomorrow, when the glorious dawn parts the shadows of night with her rosy fingers, allow yourself to dream as deeply as you can. But free yourself of of all human concerns: love, hate, hope, and fear.

"That great seer Proteus, whenever he disguised himself, transformed himself into fire and water, into a tiger or a dragon, or wore a thousand other strange masks, and being so disguised could no longer see into the future, had to be restored to his own proper form before he could see what was to come. So too man cannot take into himself that divinity which is the seer's high art unless that part of himself which is the closest to the divine—that part we call *Nous* and *Mens,* Spirit and Mind—is calm, peaceful, untroubled, not worried or distracted by external passions and emotions."

"I'll do that," said Panurge. "Should I eat lightly or heavily, tonight? I don't ask casually, because if I don't eat well, then I don't sleep well, all night long I'm just woolgathering, and when I do dream I only dream about my stomach."

"No supper," answered Pantagruel, "would be better, since you're in good condition. Amphiaraus, Apollo's son, who was a famous prophet, required those who wanted the oracle to speak to them in their dreams not to eat at all for an entire day—and to drink no wine for three whole days. We won't have to resort to a diet quite so rigorous.

"I find it hard to believe that a man stuffed with food and rolling in debauchery could possibly absorb anything spiritual. All the same, I don't agree with those who feel that long, hard fasting makes it easier to understand heavenly things. Just think how often my father, Gargantua (honor to his name!), has told us that the writings of these self-flagellating hermits are as flabby, grim, and sour spittled as their bodies were when they wrote them. It isn't easy to feel peaceful and calm in your soul when your body is starving: all the philosophers, and certainly all the doctors, agree that the animal spirits come flowing up, created and first set in motion by the arterial blood, then purified and refined to perfection in that marvelous network the *plexus retiformis,* which (though no one has yet seen it) we know lies spread out just under the ventricles of the brain. Consider the example of a philosopher who, the better to analyze and discuss and set down his thoughts, thinks he has made himself completely solitary, placed himself far from the noisy rabble, and yet all around there are dogs constantly barking, wolves howling, lions roaring, horses whinnying, elephants trumpeting, snakes hissing, donkeys braying, crickets chirping, turtledoves cooing—in short, there's more noise and confusion than if he'd been at the Fontenay Fair, or the even more raucous fair at Niort, and all because his body is hungry. And hunger makes your stomach bark, your eyes grow dim; your veins start to suck the life out of all the body's parts and pull down that wandering, careless spirit which is indifferent not only to what it needs but also to what its natural host—the body—simply has to have. It's just as if a falcon, perched on your fist, wants to soar off into the air but suddenly gets yanked back by its leash. And we have the authority of the father of all philosophy for this: Homer tells us that the Greeks did not end their sad mourning for Patroclus, Achilles' great friend, until hunger reared up its head and their bellies told them there would be no more tears. A body depleted by long fasting has nothing left for tears or weeping.

"We always praise moderation: preserve it, here. At supper you'll eat neither beans, nor rabbit or any other meat, nor squid or octopus either (they call it devilfish), nor cabbage or anything else that might disturb or confuse your animal spirits. Just as a mirror can't show us what we hold up in front of it, if mist or changeable weather obscures its shiny surface, so too the spirit can't take in the prophecies extended to it by dreams if the body is troubled and upset by the smoke and fumes of what the body has been eating: the bonds between body and spirit are indissoluble.

"So you'll eat good pears from Crustumemia and Bergamot, a single fragrant apple, some plums from Tours, and a few cherries from my own orchard. And that way you won't have to worry that your dreams will be uncertain, or untrue, or suspicious—although some of the old Peripatetic philosophers used to argue that dreams were always of dubious reliability in this autumn season, since that is when people eat more fruit than at any other time of the year. Those old poets and mystic seers used to claim that futile, foolish dreams lay hidden and waiting for us under the piles of dead leaves fallen from the trees. Well, at least they could see that it was autumn when the leaves fell. But the natural power that new fruit contains in abundance, and which can be quickly absorbed and spread through the whole body (exactly as it is by new wine), has in reality long since been used up and dissolved. And what you'll drink is good clear water from my spring."

"I find these terms," said Panurge, "a bit difficult. But I consent to them, all the same, for better or worse. But I insist on having my breakfast good and early, tomorrow morning, right after my dream sessions! Also, I commend myself to Homer's dream gates of horn and ivory, to Morpheus the god of sleep, to Icelon and Phobetor, twin gods of fear, and to Phantasus, the god of appearances. Let them help me, if I need help, and I'll make them a joyous altar of fine goose down. And if I were in Laconia, at the temple of Ino, between Oetylus and Thalames, that goddess (who once saved Odysseus) would have solved my problem as I slept and dreamed all sorts of beautiful, happy dreams."

Then he asked Pantagruel:

"Wouldn't it be a good idea if I put some laurel branches under my pillow?"

"It's not necessary," answered Pantagruel, "not now. That's just superstition, a bad mistake made by Serapion of Ascalon, and also by Antiphon, Philochorus, Artemon of Miletus, and Fulgentius Planciades, bishop of Carthage, who all wrote on the interpretation of dreams. And I could say just about the same thing about a crocodile's left shoulder, or a chameleon's, except that I think too well of old Democritus. And also that Bactrian stone they call Eumetrides, or Ammon's horn (which old Scaliger thought was so good for dreaming)—and the Ethiopians have a precious stone, which looks like gold and has the shape of a ram's horn, like Jupiter Ammon: they swear it brings you infallible dreams, as true as any divine oracles.

"Maybe these are just the two dream gates Homer and Virgil wrote about, which you just invoked. The ivory one admits all the confused dreams, mistaken, hesitant—exactly the way you can't possibly see through ivory, no matter how thin you make it. It's so dense and opaque that it keeps physical spirits from getting through, just as it blocks reception of visible spirits. But the other gate is of horn, and clear, distinct dreams come through there, true and certain, exactly as all immaterial images can flow right through horn because it's so diaphanous, so shining, and you can see them perfectly."

"Ah," said Brother John, "do you think the dreams of horned cuckolds, which is what Panurge will be (with God's help and, of course, his wife's), are always true, not to say accurate?"

Chapter Fourteen // Panurge's Dream and Its Interpretation

At seven o'clock the next morning, Pantagruel was in his rooms, along with Epistemon, Brother John Mincemeat, Powerbrain, Rightway, Car-

palim, and others, when Panurge presented himself. And Pantagruel said
to them:

"Here's our dreamer."

"Those exact words," said Epistemon, "proved costly, once, when
they were spoken by the sons of Jacob, as young Joseph approached."

And Panurge said:

"I've been dreaming like some enchanted hero. I've had lots of dreams,
but I don't understand any of them. Except that in my dreams I had a
young wife, dashing, beautiful to perfection, who behaved charmingly
and took care of me like a living doll. No man has ever been more comfortable, or happier. She was always caressing me, touching me, feeling
me, stroking my head, kissing me, hugging me, and—just for a joke—
put two pretty little horns on my forehead. I laughed and told her they
really ought to be below my eyes, so I could see what I was supposed to
stick with them, because that persnickety god Momus was very particular about just where you had your horns and I didn't want him criticizing
me. But she kept fooling around, in spite of me, and pushed the horns
even farther in. And it didn't hurt me at all, which is pretty remarkable.

"A little later—I don't know how—it seemed to me I was changed into
a drum and she into a screech owl. And right there my dream was broken
and I jumped up, wide awake and annoyed, and puzzled, and indignant.
So there's my nice little bowl of dreams for you: I hope they make you
happy and you can say what they mean. Now let's have breakfast, Carpalim."

"If I know anything at all about interpreting dreams," said Pantagruel,
"it's clear that your wife won't stick real horns on your forehead—the
kind satyrs wear—but she won't be a faithful, loyal wife, and she'll give
herself to other men, and—in a word—you'll be cuckolded. This is all
settled by what Artemidorus says: that much is clear.

"Nor will you be turned into a drum, but she'll beat you as if you were
a tom-tom being played at a wedding. And she won't turn into a screech
owl, but she'll rob you blind, the way an owl naturally does. Now, just
see how your dreams match our Virgilian predictions: you're going to be
cuckolded; you're going to be beaten; you're going to be robbed."

Then Brother John howled, saying:

"By God, he's telling the truth. You're going to be a cuckold, my
good man, I promise you that, and you'll wear a really fine pair of horns.
Ho, ho, ho: our horny Pierre Cornu—except that fat Franciscan just has
the name and you'll have the real thing—God keep and protect you! Give
us a little Franciscan preaching, will you, and I'll go around begging for
alms!"

"On the contrary," said Panurge, "my dream predicts that I'll be granted
everything I want, poured straight out of the horn of plenty.

"You say I'm going to have satyr's horns. *Amen, amen, fiat! ad differ-
entiam papae!* Let it be done, let it be done, except not the way the pope

does it. So: I'll always have a stiff, strong prick, exactly as satyrs do, which is something lots of people want, though heaven doesn't grant it very often. And so how could I be cuckolded? Because there's exactly where the problem always lies—the only reason men are ever cuckolded!

"Why are there rogues out there begging? Because they haven't got anything at home they can fill their sacks with. What makes the wolf leave the forest? Because he hasn't got enough to eat. What makes women wild and loose? You know exactly what I'm talking about. Let me just refer you to our learned friends the priests, and our learned judges and lawyers and counselors-at-law and procurers—prosecutors, I mean—and everyone who's ever written a commentary on that ancient subject *de frigidis et maleficatis,* laws about frigid and impotent people.

"I'm sorry if I misunderstand you, but you're obviously wrong when you think that horns always mean cuckolding. Didn't the goddess Diana wear them on her head, in the form of a handsome crescent moon? But was she cuckolded? How the devil could she be cuckolded, when she wasn't even married? Try to talk sensibly, please, and remember: she might make you a pair of horns like the ones she planted on Acteon.

"Our good Bacchus wore horns, and so did Pan and so did Jupiter Ammon, and lots of others. Were they cuckolds? Was Juno a whore? If you follow out your argument, in good logic, that's what you'd have to conclude, just the way you'd be saying a child's father was a cuckold and his mother a loose woman if you said, right there to his father and mother's face, that he was a bastard.

"Choose your words more carefully. The horns my wife put on me were horns of abundance, filled with all sorts of good things. I swear it. As for the rest of it, I'll be as happy as a drum at a wedding, always singing, always booming, always noisy and thundering. Believe me, this is when everything goes right for me. My wife's going to be as trim and pretty as a beautiful little owl. And if you don't believe it,

> Go hang yourself in hell:
> Noel, Noel, Noel."

"Let's take your last point," said Pantagruel, "and compare it with your first one. When you started your dream, you were in absolute raptures. But at the end you woke up, suddenly angry, bewildered, and indignant . . ."

"Of course," Panurge said, "because I didn't have any dinner!"

". . . It will go badly, I can see it. That's the absolute truth: every dream that ends by making the dreamer angry and indignant either means something bad or predicts something bad.

"To mean something bad signifies a serious illness, something malign, pestilential, hidden deep in the center of the body—and medical theory tells us that sleep, which always works hand in hand with digestion, starts these things moving toward the surface, where they then manifest themselves. Which unfortunate movement would break into the dreamer's repose, and the heart, our first organ of consciousness, would be warned to offer sympathy and support. It's just the way the proverb says: stay out of a hornet's nest, don't stir up a muddy lake, let sleeping dogs lie.

"To predict something bad, that's when the sleeping soul comes to understand that some disaster is already coming our way and will soon reach us.

"For example: Hecuba's frightful dream and awakening; and Eurydice's dream—Orpheus' wife—which according to Ennius ended in her sudden and horrible awakening. After Hecuba woke up, she saw her husband, Priam, and her children, and her entire country butchered and destroyed. And not long after she awoke, Eurydice died a miserable death.

"When Aeneas dreamed he was talking to the dead Hector, he woke up with a start. And that same night Troy was sacked and burned. Another time he dreamed that he saw all his household gods and again he woke up in a terrible fright, and the very next day his fleet sailed into a horrible storm.

"And Turnus, when the Fury's phantasmic vision drove him to declare war on Aeneas, woke up suddenly, flooded with indignation. And after many long and unfortunate events, that same Aeneas killed him. And thousands more.

"And when I remind you of Aeneas, remember that Fabius Pictor tells that he never did a thing, launched no enterprise, that nothing in fact ever happened to him, unless he'd first been informed and counseled by dream predictions.

"Nor is there any doubt about why these things turned out as they did. If sleep and rest come to us as a special grace and gift of God, as philosophers claim and poets declare, saying:

> Then sleep, heaven's great gift, came
> To tired humans, and care was tamed—

"—then how could such a marvelous gift be snatched away and not leave the sleeper angry and indignant, and without signifying some imminent misfortune? Otherwise repose would not be repose, and a gift would not be a gift, nor would sleep descend from our helpful friends the gods, but rather rise up from the devils our enemies. As the proverb says: An enemy's present is no present at all.

"If the father of the family sits down to a well-set table, and has a good appetite when he starts to eat, you'd be surprised to see him suddenly getting up. Without knowing the cause, you'd be absolutely astonished. But hey! He heard his servants crying 'Fire!' or 'Thief!' or his children crying 'Murder!' He had no choice but to leave the table and run to take care of things, set them back in order.

"And let me tell you: the Cabalists and other interpreters of the Holy Word, wondering whether we can really know whether angelic apparitions are true or false (since Satan's fallen angels often turn themselves into angels of light), explain that the difference between the two is that when the good, consoling angel appears to man, at first he's stunned, but at the end he feels better, having been made to feel satisfied and happy. But the evil, seductive angel makes man happy at first, but finally leaves him upset, angry, and bewildered."

Chapter Fifteen ⁄⁄ Panurge's Excuse, and the Mysterious Monastic Doctrine of Pickled Beef

"Lord!" said Panurge. "God protect those who see but can't hear! I see you perfectly well, but I can't hear a thing you're saying. I haven't any idea what you're talking about: a raging stomach has no ears. By God, I'm absolutely burning with hunger. I've been working on an extraordinary assignment. It's going to take more than some master magician to get me to give up my supper again, all this year, just so I can go dreaming.

"Not eat my supper, in the devil's own name? A pox on me if I ever do it again! Come on, Brother John, let's have breakfast. When I've eaten well, and my stomach's stuffed with straw and fodder, in an emergency I might be able to pass up dinner. But to eat nothing at all? Pox on it! That's just plain wrong. That's scandalous—that's unnatural.

"Nature made daytime for exercise and work and so people could go about their business. And to make things easier, nature gave us a marvelous candle, which is the clear, joyous light of the sun. But by nightfall she's ready to take that away and tell us, without needing to say a word, 'Children, you're good people. You've worked hard enough. Night's coming: now you need to stop working and refresh yourself with good bread, good wine, good meat—and then you need to have a little fun, and then lie down and rest, so tomorrow you can be bright and fresh and ready to work again.'

"That's how falconers do it. When they've just fed their birds, they don't send them out flying: they let them sit on their perches, digesting. The first of our holy popes understood that, too, when he decreed fasting. He ordered that you shouldn't fast any later than about three in the afternoon; the whole rest of the day you were free to banquet as much as you liked. In the old days not many people ate at midday, except monks and canons—because of course they don't have anything else to do: every day's a feast day for them, and they have a monkish rule which they followed faithfully: *de missa ad mensam,* right from mass to the dining room. And they don't sit there waiting for the abbot, so they can get started: once they're stuffing it down, they wait for the abbot if they happen to feel like it, and for no other reason and under no other circumstances. Well, the rest of the world may not eat at noon, but everyone has always eaten at night, except some dreamy-eyed dreamers, which is why that meal is the one that everyone eats together.

"You know all that, Brother John. Come on, my friend—by all the devils, come on! My stomach's so sick with hunger that it's barking like a dog. Let's toss down some chunks of bread soaked in soup to keep it quiet, the way the Sibyl did with Cerberus. You love those light soups monks get, early in the morning. Me, I like a good heavy soup and a chunk of plowman, salted with nine lessons."

"Oh, I know what you're talking about," answered Brother John. "That's a good monastic metaphor, right out of a monastery soup pot. The plowman, that's the ox doing the plowing—and nine lessons means cooked to a turn.

"Because the good fathers of our religion, according to an old cabalistic principle, didn't write out all their rules, but passed them down from hand to hand. In my time they'd get up in the morning and do certain special things before they went to church: they'd shit in the shitteries, piss in the pisseries, spit in the spitteries, cough in the cougheries—but harmoniously, snooze in the snoozeries—all so they wouldn't bring anything inappropriate with them, when they got to holy service. When they'd done these preliminary things, they'd go into the sacred chapel with devoted steps (the sacred chapel was what they called the kitchen) and with incredible devotion they'd make sure that the beef was on the fire and getting ready for these religious brothers of our Lord to have their breakfasts. They'd even light the fire under the soup pot with their own hands.

"Now, since they started their days with nine holy lessons, they'd be careful to get up even before dawn, because they got even hungrier and thirstier, chanting holy songs—so they had to cut morning prayers short—maybe one holy lesson or three at most. According to that ancient unwritten tradition I mentioned, the earlier they got up, the sooner they got to eat their breakfasts; the longer the beef was boiled, the better cooked it got; the better cooked it was, the tenderer it was; the less they had to bother chewing, the better it all tasted; the less work their stomachs had to do, the better nourished were these good religious folk. Which was the founders' precise intention—in consideration of which they didn't eat so they could live; they lived so they could eat, having nothing in this world except their lives. Let's go, Panurge!"

"Now," said Panurge, "now you're talking, old velvet balls, old convent balls, old cabalistic balls! Forget my share of the capital: I'll do without predictions and usury and interest payments. Expenses are enough for me, now that you've so eloquently informed us on this interesting subject, told us all about monastic mysteries and culinary cabals. Let's go, Carpalim! Let's go, Brother John, my great good friend! Good day to you, gentlemen! I've done enough dreaming: now it's time to drink. Let's go!"

Panurge had barely finished speaking when Epistemon cried out, in a loud voice:

"How easy it is for us to understand other people's misfortunes: we can foresee them, predict them, understand them right down to the ground. But, oh, what a rare thing it is to foresee, and understand, and predict, and understand your own misfortune! As Aesop so wisely illustrated in his *Fables,* explaining how we're all born with a bag around our necks. The front part hangs heavy with other people's faults and misfortunes, which we can see and understand perfectly. But the back part hangs heavy with our own faults and misfortunes, and we never see or understand them at all, without benevolent heaven's good grace."

Chapter Sixteen ⁄ How Pantagruel Advises Panurge to Consult the Sibyl of Panzoult

Not long after, Pantagruel sent for Panurge and said to him:

"Because of my deep-rooted love for you, which has grown stronger over time, I try to think what's best for you. Now listen: I'm told that at Panzoult, near Croulay, there's a remarkable Sibyl, who's been able to predict everything that happens. Take Epistemon as your traveling companion and go to see her, and find out what she has to tell you."

"Perhaps," said Epistemon, "she'll turn out to be like Horace's Canidia and Sagana—a snake in human form, a witch. I wonder about that because there are nasty stories about Panzoult. It's supposed to have even more witches and sorcerers than there ever were in Thessaly. I wouldn't be glad to go. It's an unlawful business—forbidden by Mosaic law."

"But," said Pantagruel, "we're not Jews, and there's no proof whatever that she's a witch. When you come back, we'll consider all the evidence.

"Suppose she's an eleventh Sibyl, a second Cassandra? And even if she's not a Sibyl, and doesn't deserve to be called one, what harm can it do to discuss your problem with her? Especially since she has the reputation of being more knowing, more perceptive, than most people in this country—of either sex. When did it ever hurt a man to keep acquiring knowledge, whether from a sot, a pot, a bottle, a feather, or shoe leather?

"Remember how Alexander the Great, after defeating King Darius at Arbela, and sitting with all his subordinates around him, wouldn't listen to a fellow, and afterward regretted it a thousand thousand times over? He'd won a great victory in Persia, but was so far from his own kingdom of Macedonia that it made him exceedingly sad, having no way of getting news. He was separated from his home by enormous tracts of land and immense rivers, kept from communication by huge deserts and blocked by tall mountains. This was a painful difficulty, and not a trivial one, since perhaps his kingdom could have been invaded and conquered, and a new king set on his throne, and a whole colony of foreigners set in the midst of his country, long before he would have any warning and any chance to do anything about it. And then a traveling merchant from Sidonia came to him, a sensible man but poor and dressed shabbily, who informed him that he'd discovered a way to let Macedonia know about his Indian triumphs, and let him know about Macedonia and Egypt, and all in less than five days. But Alexander thought the idea was so ridiculous, so impossible, that he wouldn't even listen, and had the fellow taken away.

"What would it have cost him to listen to what the man had in mind? What harm, what damage could have been done by finding out what the fellow had devised, what the technique was that he wanted to show the emperor?

"I don't believe nature didn't know what she was up to when she provided us with wide open ears, ears that can't be closed or shut in any way, though our eyes, and our tongues, and all the other openings in our body can be. And I think the reason was so that we'd always—day and night—be able to hear, and by hearing always be able to learn, for of all our senses that is the most appropriate for learning. And maybe Alexander's visitor, that day, was in fact an angel, that is, a messenger of God, sent to him as Raphael was sent to Tobias. Alexander was too quick to turn him away, and for a long time thereafter he regretted it."

"Those are eloquent words," said Epistemon. "But you'll never make me believe that anything worth knowing can be learned from a woman—and such a woman—living in such a place."

"And I," said Panurge, "I've done very well with women's advice, and especially old hags. Thanks to them, I always shit once or twice more than usual. My friend, they're true hound dogs, they have real noses for the law. And especially midwives, who are knowing women indeed—but me, I'd rather call them foreseeing women, because in fact they can peer into the future and tell you how it's going to be. Sometimes I call them handy baby takers, rather than randy baby makers: Juno was the goddess of midwives, and the Romans called on her all the time, and she always gave them plenty of warning. Just ask Pythagoras about her, and Socrates, Empedocles, and our own Maître Ortuinus.

"And I praise to the skies the old Germanic custom: taking old women's words as if they were worth their weight in gold—because for them, indeed, they truly were, and they did very well, listening to what the old women advised. Just think of old Aurina and our good mother Velleda, back in Vespasian's time.

"Believe me: old women are always richly sublime—I mean to say, sibylline. Let's go, then, with God's help—let's go! Good-bye, Brother John. I'll leave you my codpiece to take care of."

"Fine," said Epistemon, "I'm coming with you—but if I find out there's any witchcraft involved, I'm leaving you right at the door and you'll go on all by yourself."

Chapter Seventeen ⁄⁄ How Panurge Spoke to the Sibyl of Panzoult

It took them three days to get there. On the third day they found the prophetess' house, high on a mountain ridge, under a huge, spreading chestnut tree. It was easy enough to walk into that thatch-covered cottage, poorly built, poorly furnished, all thick with smoke-filled air.

"Enough!" said Epistemon. "That great Duns Scotus of vague philosophers, Heraclitus, wasn't surprised when he walked into a house like this: he just told his followers and disciples that the gods dwelled even in such places, just as much as in palaces stuffed with delicacies and delights. And unless I'm much mistaken, this was the kind of house the celebrated Hecaté enjoyed, when she entertained the young Theseus. And the same for Orion's father, which Jupiter, Neptune, and Mercury weren't too proud to enter, and where they ate and slept and then, to pay for their night's lodgings, they gave their poor, wifeless host a fine son, by pissing on a bull hide."

They found the old woman sitting near the chimney.

"She's really a Sibyl!" cried Epistemon. "She looks exactly like Homer's old woman crouching near her oven."

The old woman was in sorry shape—badly dressed, half starved, toothless, bleary-eyed, bent over, limp, her nose running. She was cooking a pot of green cabbage soup, with a bit of pigskin and an ox bone that had been cooked before in this same pot.

"Mother of all the gods!" said Epistemon. "We've made a mistake. We won't get anything out of her. We haven't got a gold coin for the gatekeeper at the door of hell."

"Ah," answered Panurge, "I've got it. Here in my purse: a gold ring—and some good King Charles coins."

So saying, Panurge made her a deep bow and gave her six smoked beef tongues, a big butter pot full of couscous, a tall flask filled to the brim, and a small purse made of an ox's balls, all filled with newly minted coins. And then he finished by placing on her middle finger, with deep reverence, a gorgeous gold ring, set with a magnificently worked toadstone from Beuxes. With a few brief words, he told her why he'd come, asking her most courteously for her advice and how she thought his marriage would go.

For a time the old woman sat in silence, thoughtfully grinding her teeth. Then she sat at the edge of a great, floppy sack and, picking up three spindles, turned and spun them between her fingers, this way and that. She tested their points and kept only the sharpest, tossing the others under a great stone mortar. And then she took the pulley wheels for the three spindles and spun them nine times; on the ninth revolution she peered intently at the revolving wheels, not touching them, and waiting until they had completely stopped. Then she pulled off one of her wooden shoes (we call them "sabots"), turned her apron up over her head, the way a priest flaps up the white linen behind his neck when he's saying mass, and tied it in place with a strip of worn, multicolored striped cloth. She took a long swig from the flask Panurge had given her, then took the three gold coins out of the ox-ball purse, put each of them in a walnut shell, and stuck them under a vase filled with chicken feathers. Then she swept around the chimney three times, and threw half a bundle of heather and a dried laurel stick into the fire. She stood there, silently watching them burn, duly noting that they neither crackled nor made any sound at all. Then she gave a horrible shriek, and spoke (from between clenched teeth) a few barbarous words, in a wildly unfamiliar accent, which made Panurge turn to Epistemon and say:

"By God, I'm shaking all over! I feel as if I've been enchanted: this woman's not talking in any Christian tongue. She looks ten feet taller than before she turned up her apron and stuck it over her head. The way she's moving her lips: what does it mean? And all that shoulder shrugging: what's she *doing*? There! Why is she wiggling her lips like a monkey cleaning shrimp? My ears are burning: I feel as if I can hear Proserpina, Lucifer's wife: in just a minute all the devils will be coming up out of hell. Oh, those ugly beasts! Let's get out of here! You serpent: I'm dying of fear! I don't like devils. They irritate me, they're not at all pleasant. Let's get out of here! Good-bye, madame, thank you for everything! I'm not going to get married after all, no! From this moment on I give it all up: I'll stay a bachelor."

He started out of the room, but the old woman got there first, holding the sharp spindle in her hand, and led him out into a small garden adjoining the house. There was an old sycamore tree out there: she shook it three times and, using the spindle, quickly wrote some brief verses on the eight leaves that fell. Then she threw them into the wind and said to Panurge and Epistemon:

"Go look for them if you like; find them if you can: the deadly future of your marriage is written on those leaves."

And having said this, she went back into her dark hut. But right on the doorstep she suddenly pulled her dress and petticoat and chemise up to her armpits and stuck out her ass at them. Panurge stared, then said to Epistemon:

"By all that's holy, look! There's the Sibyl's cunt."

And then she slammed and bolted the door; they never saw her again. They ran after the leaves and caught them, though it wasn't easy, for the wind had blown them down in the bushes below. Arranging them properly, they found this poetic sentence:

> She'll rob you blind
> Of whatever you're due.
> She'll be bred in kind
> But not by you.
> She'll suck and suck
> At the end of your diddle.
> She'll beat you up
> But leave just a little.

Chapter Eighteen // Pantagruel and Panurge's Different Readings of the Sibyl of Panzoult's Poem

When they'd gotten all the leaves, Epistemon and Panurge went back to Pantagruel's court, in part pleased, in part annoyed. They were happy to be going back; they were irritated by the trip, for the road seemed to them singularly rough, rocky, and badly made. They gave Pantagruel a full report of their journey and of how they had found the Sibyl. And finally they gave him the sycamore leaves and showed him the brief verses written thereon.

Pantagruel read them all and, sighing, said to Panurge:

"You've done well: the Sibyl's prophecy directly confirms everything we've already been told, both by our Virgilian prophecies and by your own dreams—which is that you'll be dishonored by your wife; that she'll cuckold you, giving herself to other men, and indeed that she'll be pregnant by another man; that she'll steal freely from you; and that she'll beat you, seriously injuring some part of your body."

"You understand about as much of these prophecies we've just had," said Panurge, "as a sow knows about cooking. Don't be angry if I tell you this, but I'm a little annoyed. It's the exact opposite that's the truth. Listen carefully. The old hag says: Just the way a bean can't possibly be seen unless and until it's shelled, so too my abilities, my high competencies, will never be known if I don't get married. How many times have I heard you saying that taking on high office, and that office itself, truly reveal the man, and show what he's really worth? Which means that when it's known for sure what a man is, and what he's worth, then he's called to the management of important matters. Which is to say that when a man remains unknown, private, no one knows for certain what he is—any more than you can tell anything about an unshelled bean. So much for the first verse. Or do you want to argue that a good man's honor and reputation hang from a whore's ass?

"Now, the second verse says: My wife will be pregnant (and isn't this marriage's primary happiness?), but not with me. Well, of course that's true! She'll be pregnant with a fine bouncing baby boy! I already love him—I'm crazy about him: he'll be my first little calf. Nothing that makes me angry at the whole world, no matter how big and irritating, will ever be able to endure, just as soon as I catch sight of him and hear him prattling away in his own lovely little language. My blessings on that old hag! Really, I'd like to set her up in some nice property here in Salmagundi—not some mere life estate, but a vested title, like some important legal eagle. According to you, my wife ought to carry *me* in her belly, as if she'd somehow conceived me, brought me to life—and people would say, 'This Panurge is a second Bacchus—born twice over. He's reborn the way Hippolytus was; and Proteus, who was first born of Thetis and then delivered a second time by the philosopher Apollonius' mother; and the way the two Palici were, alongside the Simethus River, in Sicily. His wife was pretty big with him! This Panurge embodies and brings to life the Megarians' ancient doctrine of palintocius, and Democritus' palingenesis.' Good lord, what nonsense! No one's ever going to say such things about *me*.

"Now, the third verse says: My wife's going to suck my diddle. That's fine with me. You know perfectly well that what hangs between my legs is a staff that has just one end. Let me tell you, by God, that I propose to always keep it succulent and juicy. If she sucks on me, she won't suck in vain. There'll always be oats in that feed bag, or maybe something better. You insist on interpreting the poem allegorically, on this head, and taking it to mean something stolen. I admire the argument; I like the allegory—but not the way you understand it. Perhaps the sincere affection you feel for me pulls you into a contradictory and negative mood: scholars always say that love is a wonderfully fearful thing, and there's no real love without an abundance of fear. But (as I see it, at least) you really must understand, deep in your hearts, that this theft the old hag refers to must mean—here as in so many Latin and other ancient authors—the sweet fruits we steal in love, which Venus likes to pluck secretly, furtively. And why? Because grabbing a little on the sly, hiding between doorways or on a flight of stairs, or behind a hanging tapestry, sneaking around, or lying on an opened bundle of firewood, somehow makes the Cyprian goddess happier (though I admit there are other authorities who hold contrary views) than when you do it right out in broad daylight—even in public, if you listen to Diogenes the Cynic—or lying between a pair of gorgeous bed curtains, maybe all embroidered in gold, but do it only at long intervals, and when you're in exactly the right mood, but first chasing off the flies with a silk flyswatter and a brush of Indian feathers, while the bitch lies there waiting, picking her teeth with a bit of straw she pulled out of the mattress.

"You can't mean to say she'd actually be robbing me by sucking on me, like eating oysters on the half shell, or the way the women in Cilicia (according to Dioscorides) suck the seeds out of acorns? Impossible. Robbers don't suck, they pinch and poach; they don't stop to eat, they stuff things into their pockets, grab them up and off they go!

"Now, the fourth verse says: My wife will beat me, but not completely. Oh, what a wonderful phrase! You think this means assault and injury. It certainly sounds like that, God help us all! But please: think loftier thoughts—rise above the merely worldly perspective and consider nature's higher marvels—and thereby realize what mistakes you've made, perversely twisting the divine Sibyl's prophetic words.

"Just think: let's say, arguendo—not conceding the point, but just postulating that the devil in hell might try to inspire my wife to do me wrong, slander me, cuckold me up to the eyes, rob me, attack me—that still doesn't mean she gets to do it. And I say this, based on the following argument, which Brother Ass-shaker once explained to me—it was a Monday morning—we were working our way through a bushel of chitterlings—and, if I remember rightly, it was raining—may God give him happiness!

"But the point is this: when the world began, or not long after, women got together and decided to skin men alive, because all over the world they wanted to be in the driver's seat. So they all swore this great holy oath—but how silly women are! Oh, the endless fragility of the entire female sex! They did indeed begin to skin men alive (peel them, as Catullus puts it), and they began with the part they liked best, namely, our nerveless, swerveless stick—and here we are, more than six thousand years later, and in all that time they haven't gotten past the head of it. And so, with a wonderful flair for revenge, the Jews actually circumcise themselves, cutting all around the head: they'd rather be called snipped pricks or chopped-off Marranos than be skinned by women the way other people are. My wife, too, will be part of this communal enterprise: she'll skin me, if nobody beats her to it. That's fine with me—but not the whole thing, I assure you—not the whole thing!"

"But what about the laurel wood," said Epistemon, "which we both saw burn without a single sound—and the ghastly, terrifying shriek she uttered! You know perfectly well what a dismal omen that is—and a powerful one, too, as Propertius says, and Tibullus, Porphyry (that shrewd philosopher), Eustathius (in his book on the *Iliad*), and many others."

"Indeed!" answered Panurge. "You cite some fine fat calves! Those fellows were all idiots as poets, and dreamers as philosophers—all of them stuffed just as full of high-sounding nonsense as their books were."

Chapter Nineteen // Pantagruel's Praise of Dumb People's Advice

After hearing this, Pantagruel was silent for a long time, and seemed exceedingly thoughtful. Then he said to Panurge:

"You've been seduced by the evil spirit—but listen. I've read that in the old days the truest and most reliable oracles weren't those that got written down or those that were spoken. People who relied on such predictions, even people who were considered shrewd and knowing, were often misled, either because the oracles were deeply ambiguous, evasive, and obscure or simply because they were so terribly brief. Blame that on Apollo, god of prophecies, called by the Greeks the Devious One. The most valuable prophecies, the truest and most accurate, were those that came via signs and omens. That was Heraclitus' opinion. And that was how Jupiter prophesied in Ammon; also Apollo among the Assyrians— which is why the Assyrians depicted him as a calm old man with a long beard, never naked and young and beardless, the way the Greeks saw him. Let's rely on these same tokens—signs and gestures, but no words: let's take counsel with a dumb mute."

"I agree," answered Panurge.

"But," said Pantagruel, "it's important that he be born deaf and that he be dumb for that reason. Because the most innocent dumb mutes are those who've never been able to hear."

"How so?" answered Panurge. "If it's true that no one speaks unless he's been spoken to, I should think that, in logic, you'd be led to an impossible and paradoxical conclusion. But never mind. Still, you won't believe what Herodotus says about two little children, kept locked away in absolute and perpetual silence by Psammetichus, king of Egypt. After a time they spoke the word *becus,* which in Phrygian means 'bread.' "

"I don't believe a word of it," answered Pantagruel. "It's ridiculous to claim that we have a natural language. Languages are social institutions, conveniences which we create for ourselves arbitrarily and by general agreement. The analytical philosophers assure us that words have no intrinsic meanings, until and unless we assign meanings to them. I don't say this casually. In *The Purpose of Language,* book one, Bartolus tells us that in Italy, in his day, there was a man named Nello de Gabriele, who'd been accidentally rendered deaf. However, he understood those who spoke to him in Italian, no matter how softly they spoke: he was a lip-reader, and he knew what people's gestures meant. And I've also read a learned and sophisticated author who claims that Tyridates, king of Armenia, visited Rome in Nero's days and was received with great dignity and high pomp, for the Romans wished to keep him forever friendly to their people. There was nothing worth seeing in the whole city that they didn't show him. When he finally left, the emperor heaped him high with gifts of all kinds, and also told him that he could pick out whatever he'd seen in Rome that he liked best, promising that he could have anything he wanted, no matter what it was. All he asked for was a comedian he'd seen at the theater: the Armenian hadn't understood the actor's words, but he'd understood him perfectly because of the gestures and signs he used. And he explained that, in his kingdom, there were many people, speaking all sorts of different languages: he had to use translators in order to communicate with them. But this one comic actor would serve for all of them, indicating his meaning so well by signs and gestures that he seemed to be speaking with his fingers.

"Accordingly, you have to pick a mute who's been deaf since birth, so his signs and gestures will be simply, naturally prophetic, not unclear, or all tricked out, or false. But you still have to decide whether a man or a woman would be better."

"I'd prefer a woman," answered Panurge, "but there are two things that bother me:

"First, what women see, they immediately re-create in their own minds, and then think about exclusively in terms of the sacred Priapus, carried in, all stiff and erect, to honor the great god Bacchus. Whatever signs and gestures and behavior you show them, they interpret it all in terms of how that sacred instrument moves. And we'd be deceived, since any sign we made would be understood sexually. Remember what happened two hundred and fifty years after the founding of Rome. A young gentleman happened to meet a young lady up on Mount Caelian; her name was Verona and, though he didn't know it, she'd been deaf and dumb since birth. Well, he asked her, gesturing as freely as Italians still do today, which senators she'd met, up there. Not understanding his words, she thought he was thinking about the same thing she was, which was what a young man quite naturally asks of a young woman. So, using signs (which in all matters of love are worth far more, and work far more effectively, than mere words), she led him home to her own house, letting him know—again by signs—that the idea pleased her. And in the end, without a word being said, they made love like mad.

"The second thing I'm worried about is this: what if she just lies down, as if agreeing to what she thinks we're asking of her? Or else, if she answers us with signs of her own, they're likely to be so foolish, so silly, that we'd simply have to understand that she thought we were thinking sexually. Remember how, at Croquinoles, when the young nun Sister Fatass got pregnant by the young friar Brother Stiffprick, and the abbess found out and called her up in front of the whole nunnery and accused her of

dishonoring their order, the nun defended herself by insisting that she
hadn't ever done it willingly and Stiffprick had used force and violence.
But the abbess answered, 'You wicked girl, it was right there in the dor-
mitory: why didn't you scream as loud as you could? We'd all have run
to help you!' The nun answered that she didn't dare scream in the dor-
mitory, because everyone slept there in an eternal silence. 'But,' said the
abbess, 'wicked as you are, why didn't you signal to those who were
sleeping near you?' 'But I did,' answered Fatass, 'I wiggled my ass as hard
as I could, but no one helped me.' 'Ah,' barked the abbess, 'you wicked
girl, why didn't you come to me at once and make a formal accusation
against him? That's what I would most certainly have done, if anything
like this had ever happened to me, so I could prove my innocence.'
'Because,' answered Fatass, 'I was so afraid of living in a state of sin and
damnation, and he was a priest, and I was terrified that I might die suddenly and never be able to make my confession, so I confessed to him
before he left the room, but the penance he gave me was that I should
never say a word or reveal a thing to anyone. And it's a tremendous sin
to tell anyone what was said in confession: God and all the angels hate
anyone who does such an evil thing. It might even have made God burn
down the entire abbey, and every one of us would have been hurled into
hell, along with Dathan and Abiram, who rebelled against Moses.' "

"You're never going to make me laugh at that," said Pantagruel. "I
know perfectly well that monks are a lot less worried about God's commandments than they are about the rules of their order. All right: let's
not use a woman. I think Goatnose would do fine. He was born both
deaf and dumb."

Chapter Twenty ⁄⁄ How Goatnose Answers Panurge with Gestures and Signs

Goatnose was sent for, and came the next day. When he arrived, Panurge gave him a fat calf, half a pig, two barrels of wine, a wagonload of
wheat, and thirty francs in small change. Then he brought him to Pantagruel and, in the presence of all the gentlemen of Pantagruel's court, did
the following: first he yawned extravagantly, then as he yawned held his
right hand in front of his mouth and over and over, with his thumb,
shaped the Greek letter tau, or T. Then he lifted his eyes to heaven and
rolled them like a she-goat in labor, coughing and sighing deeply. Then,
pointing to where his codpiece should have been, but wasn't, he grabbed
his penis and rattled it melodically around between his thighs. Then he
bent his left knee and bowed, holding that posture, his arms folded across
his chest.

Goatnose watched him attentively, then raised his left hand and clenched it, except for the thumb and index finger, which he joined, nail to nail.

"I understand," said Pantagruel. "I know just what he means by this sign. It means marriage; according to the Pythagoreans, it also means thirty. So you'll be married."

"A thousand thanks," said Panurge, turning toward Goatnose, "my little banquet maker, my slave driver, my jailhouse keeper, my own policeman, my chief of policemen."

At which Goatnose raised his left hand still higher, fanning out his five fingers as far as he was able.

"Here," said Pantagruel, "he again informs us, but this time even more fully, by the use of what mathematicians would call a quinary number, that you're definitely going to be married. And not just engaged, and betrothed, and married, but also that you'll live together even before the wedding. According to Pythagoras, five, the quinary number, was the marriage number, and indicated consummation of the marriage and also that a wedding would take place: three, after all, forms a triad, which is the first of the odd-number groups, and two is the first number which combines male and female in one. In Rome, indeed, on the day of a wedding, they used to light five wax candles and it was forbidden to light more, even when the richest people were getting married. Nor could they light fewer than five, no matter how poor the bride and groom might be. The old pagans also used to pray to five gods, or make five prayers to one god, for blessings on the newlyweds: to Jupiter, for the wedding itself; Juno, who presided over the celebration; Venus, for beauty; Pitho, the goddess of persuasion and elegant speech; and Diana, for help in childbirth."

"Oh," cried Panurge, "my sweet, sweet Goatnose! I'm going to give you a farm near Cinais and a windmill in Mirebalais."

And then the mute sneezed so violently that his whole body shook, turning him to the left.

"What in God's name is that!" said Pantagruel. "It can't be good for you. It must mean your marriage will be unlucky. According to Terpsionian doctrine, sneezing always represents the Socratic daemon. When you sneeze to the right, it means you can go ahead with your plans boldly and in perfect confidence: you'll start and finish in happiness and success. But when you sneeze to the left, it means exactly the opposite."

"And you," said Panurge, "always look at things in the worst possible light: you're always as worried as a Roman slave. I don't believe a word of it. Nor have I ever known anyone to tell lies like that wretched Terpsion."

"Just the same," said Pantagruel, "Cicero talks about it, too, in the second book of his *Prophecies and Signs.*"

Then Panurge turned toward Goatnose and made the following sign: he rolled back his eyelids, swung his jaw from right to left, and stuck his tongue partway out of his mouth. Then he held out his left hand, open except for the middle finger, which he kept perpendicular to his palm, setting it (again) where his codpiece would ordinarily have been. He kept his right hand clenched in a fist, except for the thumb, and thrusting it directly behind him, pressed it against his back, just over his rump, in the spot the Arabs call *al katim* and we call the sacrum. Then he quickly reversed his hands, putting the right one where the left had been, as if it were now his codpiece, and the left one on his sacrum. He proceeded to do this back and forth, nine times over. The ninth time, he lowered his eyelids to their normal position, stopped wagging his jaw, let his tongue go where it belonged, then squinted at Goatnose, making his lips quiver like a thoughtful monkey or a rabbit nibbling oats.

Then Goatnose opened his right hand and lifted it high in the air, placing the thumb (up to the first joint) between the middle and ring fingers, tightening those fingers tightly around the thumb and making a fist, but with the index and little fingers sticking straight out. Then he stuck this hand into Panurge's navel and twisted it from side to side, almost as if it were walking on the two extended fingers. Then he moved his hand up, first to Panurge's belly, then to his stomach, his chest, and his neck, and finally to his chin, after which he shoved the rotating thumb right into Panurge's mouth. Then he rubbed it on Panurge's nose and, climbing over his eyes, pretended to gouge out his eyes with the thumb.

By then Panurge was angry, and tried to disentangle himself and move away from the mute. But Goatnose went on, pressing that moving thumb into him, now on the eyes, now on the forehead, all the way out to the edge of his hat. Finally Panurge shouted:

"By God, you idiot, I'm going to beat you if you don't leave me alone! If you make me any angrier you're going to find my hand pressing into your ugly face like a mask!"

"He's deaf," said Brother John. "He doesn't know what you're saying, fat-head. Show him with your fist that you're going to whack him on the muzzle."

"For God's sake," said Panurge, "who the devil does this high and mighty fool think he is? He's almost poached my eyes in black butter. By God, *da jurandi,* just this once let me swear as much as I want. Idiot! I'll let you swallow a whole meal of raps on the nose, with a few good stiff jabs in between."

Then Panurge jumped away, lip-farting at the deaf mute—who, seeing Panurge moving off, stepped in front of him, stopped him by brute force, and made the following sign: he dropped his right arm toward his knee, extended downward as far as it would go, clenching his hand into a fist, with the thumb between the middle and index fingers. Then with his left hand he rubbed his right arm, just below the elbow, and as he rubbed gradually lifted the right hand until first it was horizontal and then almost vertical. And then, abruptly, he let that right hand fall again, then kept lifting it and dropping it, and all the while showing it to Panurge.

Annoyed at all this, Panurge raised his fist as if to strike the mute, but remembered that he was in Pantagruel's presence and refrained. And Pantagruel said:

"But if the signs and gestures make you angry, how much angrier will you be when the things they predict actually happen! It all fits together. What the mute is predicting is that you'll be married, cuckolded, beaten, and robbed."

"Married, yes," said Panurge. "I concede that much. I deny the rest. Please: do me the favor of believing that, both in women and in horses, no man has ever had such luck as I am absolutely predestined to experience."

Chapter Twenty-one « How Panurge Seeks the Advice of an Old French Poet, Raminagrobis

"I never thought," said Pantagruel, "I'd ever meet a man so set in his predetermined opinions as, clearly, you are. All the same, to clear up your doubts, let's try to turn over every stone we can. Here's my idea. Swans—birds sacred to Apollo—never sing except when they feel death coming, especially on the river Meander in Phrygia. (I say this because Aelian and Alexander Myndius claim they saw several dying elsewhere, but heard none of them sing.) Now, when the swan sings it knows for sure it's going to die, and it never dies unless it's sung this preparatory song. So too poets, guided and protected by Apollo, when they feel themselves coming to their deaths usually rise to prophetic heights, inspired by Apollo, and become seers of things yet to come.

"I've often heard it said, too, that all old men, decrepit and near their ends, find it easy to see into the future. I remember that Aristophanes, in one of his comedies, calls old men Sibyls. We stand on a pier and look far out at sailors and all those who set out across the high seas in their ships, and we watch them in silence, praying they'll come to land again in safety, and when they come into harbor we greet them with words and gestures, congratulating those who have safely arrived among us. But angels and heroes and all the good daemons (according to Platonic doctrine) think of humans who are close to death as people arriving at a very sure and welcome port, a harbor of repose and tranquillity far from all earthly troubles and concerns, and greet them, comfort them, and speak with them, too, and even before their actual deaths begin to teach them the art of seeing into the future.

"I hardly need to mention the many, many ancient examples: Isaac and Jacob, Patroclus and Hector, Hector and Achilles, Polynestor and both Agamemnon and Hecuba, that Rhodian made famous by Posidonius, Calanus the Indian and Alexander the Great, Orodes and Mezentius, and many more. I'll just remind you of the learned and brave knight Guillaume du Bellay, who was lord of Langey and died on Mount Tarar on the tenth of January, in the climacteric year of his life, the year 1543 by our standard Roman calculation. Three or four hours before his death, tranquil and serene and in full possession of his senses, he spoke in clear, strong words, predicting both what we have already seen come true and what we still await. All the same, when he told us of these things we thought his prophecies strange and unpleasant, because whatever *he* had seen, we had glimpsed no warning signs of what he so confidently predicted.

"And here, near Ville-au-Maire, we have a man doubly poetic, old and in truth a poet: this is Raminagrobis, whose second wife was the magnificent Pock-face, who gave birth to the beautiful Bazoche. I've heard that he's at the very point of death: go to him and hear what he has to sing. Perhaps you can get what you need from him; through him, perhaps Apollo can resolve your doubts."

"Gladly," answered Panurge. "Let's go, Epistemon—and quickly, so death can't get in our way. Would you like to come too, Brother John?"

"Gladly, gladly," answered Brother John. "Cheerfully—for love of you, you charming fat-head. My liver grows warm whenever I think of you."

So they left at once and, arriving at the poetic home, found the good old man in his death throes, but happy, his face open, his glance luminous.

Greeting him, Panurge put on the ring finger of his left hand, strictly as a gift, a gold ring with a large and beautiful oriental sapphire. Then, imitating Socrates, he offered him a handsome white rooster that, as soon as it was set on his bed, raised its head and happily flapped its wings, crowing vigorously. Then Panurge politely asked the old poet's opinion about whether he should or should not get married.

The old man ordered them to bring him ink and pen and paper, which was done at once. Then he wrote the following:

> Maybe you'll take her, maybe you won't.
> Take her: you'll do quite well.
> But if you don't
> That, too, will ring the bell.
> Hurry, but not too fast;
> Step back, just let it last;
>   Maybe you'll take her, maybe you won't.
>
> Don't eat, but eat for two when you do.
> Undo whatever's redone.

Redo whatever's undone:
Wish her long life, wish her few.
Maybe you'll take her, maybe you won't.

Then he handed them the sheet of paper, saying:
"Go, my children, and may God in His heaven watch over you. Don't bother me any more about this or about anything else. Today is the last of May, and the last of my days, and I've just with great weariness and difficulty chased out of my house a whole horde of villainous creatures, foul and filthy beasts, a disgusting, motley, monkish crowd, in black and brown and white and gray, speckled vultures, who wouldn't let me die in peace—no, with their crafty, lying insinuations, their rapacious claws, their stinging insistence, nurtured and nourished in who knows what factory of greed, they dragged me back out of a sweet dreamy rest into which I'd sunk, and in which I seemed to be considering and seeing and already touching and tasting that happiness and delight which our good God has prepared for His faithful, His chosen ones, in that other life, that other condition, which is immortality. Shun them—don't ever be like them—and don't bother me any more; leave me here in silence, I beg you!"

Chapter Twenty-two // Panurge's Defense of Begging Monks

As they left Raminagrobis' room, Panurge exclaimed with great fear:
"By all the holinesses of God, either the man's a heretic or you can hand me over to the devil! He slanders our good begging monks, Franciscans and Dominicans, who are in fact Christianity's two hemispheres. They're the gyroscopic calendricals from which, like a pair of celestial balance weights, the whole antonomastic empty-headed colossality of the true Roman church—whether hyperagitated by articulate error or by outright heresy—homocentrically spins and revolves. But by all the devils! What have those poor Capuchin monks, those poor begging friars, ever done to him? Aren't they quite sufficiently afflicted already, the poor devils? Haven't they been abundantly smoked and scented with misery and disaster—oh, the poor calumniated products of too much fish eating! Brother John: do you think this Raminagrobis is ready for heaven? By God, he's on a direct serpent pathway to thirty thousand baskets full of devils! Slandering these good, courageous pillars of the church! Is that what they call poetic passion? I don't like it a bit: it's vulgar sinning, that's what it is—it's antireligious blasphemy. I'm deeply shocked."
"And I," said Brother John, "don't give a hoot. Those monks slander

everybody else: if everybody decides to slander them, I don't care. Let's see what he wrote."

Panurge carefully read out what the good old man had written, then said:

"He's dreaming, the old drunk. But I forgive him: he's obviously very near the end. Let's get his epitaph ready! According to the answer he's given us, I'm as wise as anyone who's ever lived. Just listen to that, Epistemon, old boy. Don't you think his answers are perfectly clear? By God, he's terrifically ingenious; he's a real philosopher, as honest and hair-splitting as they come. I'll bet he's a Marrano—one of those secret Jews. By all that's holy, how carefully he protects himself against being misread! Every time he says yes, he also says no: he can't help speaking the truth, because half of what he says is bound to be right. Oh, what a smooth-tongued liar! By Saint Iago of Bressuire, you can still find some of that sort, can't you?"

"Remember Tiresias," answered Epistemon. "That's exactly how that great seer spoke to those who came to him for advice, every time he prophesied: what I tell you will either come true or it won't. That's how all sensible prophets speak."

"All the same," said Panurge, "Juno put out his eyes."

"Indeed," answered Epistemon, "because she was angry that he'd answered Jupiter's question better than she had."

"But," said Panurge, "what devil could have possessed Maître Raminagrobis, to make him rail so irrationally, so thoughtlessly, and without the slightest cause, against the poor Dominicans and Franciscans and the other begging monks? I'm really shocked, let me tell you, and I can't keep quiet about it. That's a terrible sin. His blessed soul (and his poor ass, too!) will get nipped by thirty thousand baskets full of devils."

"Not at all," answered Epistemon. "And you yourself shock me, twisting what the good poet said about black and brown and other beasts as if he'd actually said begging monks. As I understand it, he meant no such fantastic, sophistical allegory. All he was talking about, and quite rightly, were fleas, bedbugs, biting spiders, flies, mosquitoes, and such other pests, some of which are black, some brown, some ash colored, some tan and bronze, and all of them a nuisance, an affliction, and a bother, not just to sick people but also to those who are strong and healthy. Perhaps he himself has intestinal worms, or pin worms, or maybe even tapeworms. Maybe—the way everybody does in Egypt or all along the Red Sea—he's suffering from hair-worm bites on his arms or his legs—that ugly insect the Arabs call the Medina worm. It's wrong of you to take his words differently: you not only slander a good poet, but you slander all those monks, too, by such an angry accusation. Especially when you're dealing with people you know, you should always try to interpret for good rather than bad."

"You'll teach me," said Panurge, "how to recognize flies when I see them floating in milk! By all that's holy, the man's a heretic. And I mean a fully developed heretic, a mangy heretic, a heretic who ought to be burned! His soul's going to be fried by thirty thousand cartloads of devils. And do you know where? By God, my friend, he's going to roast right under Queen Proserpina's shitting stool, right in that infernal pot where she succumbs to the fecal workings of her suppositories, on the left-hand side of that great caldron, just three feet from Lucifer's claws, dragging him down into Demigorgon's black cave! Hah! the scoundrel!"

Chapter Twenty-three ⁄⁄ Panurge's Argument for Going Back to Raminagrobis

"Let's go back," Panurge continued, "and—in the name and for the sake of God—make him understand what dangerous words he's spoken. It will be an act of charity: though he may die and lose his body, at least he won't abandon his soul to eternal damnation! We'll lead him to repent his sin, and to ask pardon of the good monks—those absent as well, Brother John, as those present. And we'll get it all in writing, solemnly sealed, so after he dies he won't be declared a heretic and damned for his errors, like those Franciscans because of the provost's wife, in Orléans. He'll have to compensate them for the injury, of course: all the monasteries and convents throughout this province will have to have money for lots of alms, and lots of masses, including anniversary masses for the day of people's death, and forever after, on the day of his death, they'll have to have quintupled rations—and great flasks of wine, full of the best stuff, will have to go from table to table, for the monks and the lay brothers and those who go begging for the nuns, not to mention the canons and the priests, or to omit the novices or those who have already made their first vows. That's how he can make sure God will pardon him.

"Ho, ho, I'm kidding myself, I'm making one mistake after another! The devil carry me off if I go back in there! By God, the room's already full of devils! I can hear them quarreling and scrapping over Raminagrobis' soul, trying to be the first to snatch that soul up in their mouths and bring it to their master, Lucifer. Let's get away from there! I won't go—no, the devil take me if I'll go. Who knows if they'll use their *qui pro quo*, one soul for another, and instead of snatching up Raminagrobis', maybe they'll take poor Panurge's soul, now that he's out of debt? They tried and failed, many times, when I was mortgaged up to the ears and wearing a bankrupt's colors. Let's get out of here! I won't go. By God, I'm dying of fear and fury! O lord, to be found among famished devils! devils on sentry duty! swapping and trading devils! Let's get away! I'll bet they'll all be afraid to help with his burial—the Dominicans, the Fran-

ciscans, the Carmelites, the Capuchins, the Theatines, the monks of Saint
Francis de Paul. And they'll be smart! Anyway, he won't leave them
anything in his will. Devil take me if I'll go back in there! If he's damned,
too bad for him! Why did he have to slander the good begging monks?
Why did he throw them out of his room, just when he needed them
most—their devoted prayers, their holy warnings? Why didn't he at least
provide in his will for a few extra rations for them, something to eat,
something to keep their bellies warm—something for those poor people
whose worldly possessions begin and end with their own lives? Anyone
who wants to can go in there and help him! Devil take me if I'll go! And
if I went, the devil *would* take me. A pox on him! Let's get out of here!

"Brother John, would you like to have thirty thousand cartloads of
devils carrying you right off? Do these three things: first, let me have
your purse, because the sign of the cross, stamped on all that money in
there, flies right in the face of the magic, and what happened to Jean
Dodin, not long ago, would happen to you. He's the bailiff at Coudray
and he wanted to cross the ford at Vède, but the soldiers had broken
down the bridge. Well, the old cock, meeting Brother Adam Heavyballs,
one of those really observant Franciscans from Mirabeau, offered to buy
him a new habit if he'd piggyback him across, because the friar was a
powerful son of a gun. It was agreed. Brother Heavyballs tucked up his
gown all the way to his balls, and put the imploring Dodin up on his
back, just as if he were some fine little Saint Christopher carrying the
infant Jesus. And he lugged him easily, the way Aeneas carried his father,
Anchises, out of the burning city of Troy, singing merrily, '*Ave maris
stella,*' Hail the Virgin Mother, Who Stands Waiting. When they got to
the deepest part of the ford, above the mill wheel, the monk asked if he
had any money on him. Dodin replied that he was loaded and he certainly
would not go back on his promise about buying a new habit. 'What!' said
Brother Heavyballs. 'You know perfectly well that we Franciscans are
strictly forbidden, by an absolutely clear interdiction in our rules, ever to
carry money on us. You've done a very bad piece of business, making
me sin against so plain a commandment. Why didn't you leave your purse
with the miller? You'll be punished for this, and soon. And if I ever get
you in our cloister at Mirabeau, you'll be listening to the Miserere all the
way to the very last word.' And then he suddenly dumped Dodin right
into the water, head first.

"And so, Brother John, my sweet friend, give me your purse, so the
devils can carry you off more comfortably: don't carry any gold-coin
crosses on you. You can see how dangerous it is. If you have those crosses,
they'll toss you down on rocks, the way eagles drop tortoises, to break
their shells. Remember how they dropped a tortoise down on Aeschylus'
bald head—it won't be good for you, my friend, and I'd be really sorry.
Or maybe they'll let you fall into the ocean, I don't know where, but way

far out, the way Icarus fell, and forever after they'd call it the Mincemeat Ocean.

"Second, stay out of debt, because the devils really love people without debts. I know this from close personal experience. The rascals haven't stopped soft-soaping me, courting me, and I can tell you I wasn't used to such treatment, not when I was over my ears in debt. When a man's deep in debt, his soul is all weak and anemic. That's not devil's meat.

"Third, go back to Raminagrobis, in your habit and that great hood of yours. And if thirty thousand boatloads of devils don't carry you off, dressed so appropriately for the job, I'll drink your health—and pay for it, too. And if, to make sure all's well, you want someone to go with you, don't come looking for me—no, no! I'm warning you. Get away from there—I'm not going. Devil take me if I go!"

"It doesn't worry me that much," answered Brother John, "though they say it ought to—not while I have my good short sword in my fist."

"That's it exactly," said Panurge, "and spoken like a subtle doctor of fat-headedness. When I was a student in Toledo, where magic is king, our reverend father in the devil, Picatrix, rector of that diabolical faculty, told us that shining swords naturally frighten devils as much as bright sunlight. In fact, Hercules, when he went down into hell after all the devils, didn't really frighten them at all, because all he had was the lion skin he wore and that great stick in his hands—but Aeneas was wearing shining armor and a razor-sharp sword, all polished and rubbed till it gleamed, because that was what the Sibyl of Cumae had told him to do. Maybe that was why Lord Jean Jacques Trivulzi, as he lay dying at Castres, called for his sword and died with the bare blade in his fist, swinging it all around his bed like the brave, chivalric knight he was—that final swordplay routing all the devils who were lying in wait for him on his road to death. When you ask the cabalistic doctors why no devils could get into the earthly paradise, the only reason they give is that there's an angel at the gate, holding a flaming sword in his hand. And, you know, to speak like the real Toledo devil-worshipers, I have to admit that sword strokes can't kill devils. Still, I would argue that, according to proper devil lore, they can suffer a kind of disruption of continuity, just as when you slice your sword through the flames of a hot fire or a thick, dense smoke. They certainly howl like devils, when they feel this disruption, so it must be devilishly painful for them.

"And when you see two armies clash, my old fat-head friend, do you think that that immense, frightening noise you hear comes from human voices? from armor clashing? from steel-clad horses smashing into each other? from the collision of great masses of men? from axes banging? from spears cracking? from the cries of the wounded? from the sound of drums and trumpets? from the whinnying of horses? from the thunder of blunderbuss and cannons? That's all part of it, no question. But the immense uproar, the incredible noise, comes from the devils' pain and shrieking as, falling pell-mell on the poor souls of the wounded, they stumble into swift sword strokes and suffer disruptions in the continuity of their aerial and invisible substance. It's like a kitchen boy sneaking a munch on bits of broiled bacon and Maître Dirtyhands raps him on the knuckles with his stick. So the devils cry and shriek like Mars, when Diomedes wounded him at Troy; Homer says he screamed so loud and so horribly that it was worse than if ten thousand men had all shrieked at the same time.

"But so what? We were talking about polished armor and shining swords. That doesn't apply to your sword, Brother John. Because disuse and lack of opportunity have left it, by God, rustier than the lock on an old storeroom. So you can do one of two things: you can either scrape it clean and shine it up, or you can leave it as it is and be careful not to go back to Raminagrobis' house. Me, I'm not going. Devil take me if I'll go!"

Chapter Twenty-four ⁄⁄ How Panurge Sought Epistemon's Advice

Leaving Ville-au-Maire and setting off on the road back to Pantagruel, Panurge turned to Epistemon and said:

"My good old friend, my buddy, you see what difficulties I'm having. And you know so many good remedies! Can't you help me?"

Epistemon rose to the occasion, scolding Panurge because everyone was making fun of his strange disguise, and suggesting that he take a bit of hellebore, purge himself of his odd and unacceptable behavior, and start wearing his normal clothing once again.

"Epistemon, old buddy," said Panurge, "I have a fantasy about getting married. But I'm afraid of being cuckolded, and I'm afraid of being unlucky in my marriage. So I've made a vow to Saint Francis the Younger (who gets talked about, at Plessis-les-Tours, by all the terribly devout ladies, because he founded the order of *good men,* which naturally appeals to them) that I'd wear spectacles on my hat, and never wear a codpiece on my breeches, until I've managed to resolve this perplexity of spirit."

"Truly," said Epistemon, "it's a fine and happy vow. But I'm astonished that you don't just come back to your senses, get rid of all this craziness, and once again be your natural tranquil self. Listening to you talk, I'm reminded of the vow made by the long-haired Argive Greeks, after they'd lost a battle against the Spartans, when they were fighting over Thyrea, and they swore they'd walk around bald until they'd won back both their honor and their lands. And you also make me think of that pleasant Spaniard Michael Doris, who refused to take off a piece of broken leg armor until some English knight fought with him.

"Nor do I know which of the two better deserves a green-and-yellow cap with rabbit ears: that glorious Spanish champion, or Enguerrant de Monstrelet, who wrote such long, detailed, boring historical accounts—completely forgetting Lucian's prescriptions for the writing of history. Reading his immense narration about Michael Doris, you feel sure that it must signal the beginning of a major war, or a tremendous national development. But by the time you finish his story, all you feel is contempt for the poor innocent Spaniard, and for the Englishman who finally challenged him—and also for Enguerrant, their scribe, who drivels worse than a pot of mustard. It's as ridiculous as that mountain in Horace, weeping and wailing like a woman in labor. People come running from miles around, on account of all the racket, expecting to see some phenomenal, monstrous birth, but in the end all that pops out of the mountain is a tiny mouse."

"But," said Panurge, "it isn't funny. That's just the pot calling the kettle black. I must do as I have sworn myself to do. We've been together a long time, you and I, sworn to friendship by Jupiter, god of friends. By God, tell me what you think: should I get married or not?"

"I concede," said Epistemon, "that it's chancy. I don't think I know enough to honestly advise you. If what Hippocrates of Lango said about medicine was ever true, it's true here: It's hard to judge. Certainly, I can think of things that would solve your problem. But none of them really satisfies me. There are Platonists, you know, who say that if you can see your own *daemon,* you can understand your destiny. I'm not truly that much of a Platonist, so I don't think you ought to listen to them. It's a doctrine shot full of errors. I've had some experience of that, seeing what happened to a scholarly, intellectual gentleman, in Estrangore. That's the first point.

"There's another. If we could still appeal to the ancient oracles—Jupiter's, in Egypt; Apollo's, on Mount Helicon, and in Delphos and Delos and Cyrrha, and Patara and Boetia, and Latium and Lycia and Colophon, or in the Castalian Fountain, near Antioch, in Syria, between the Branchides, or in Dodona; or Mercury's, in Pharae, near Patras; or the oracle of Apis, again in Egypt; or that of Serapis, in Canopus; or that of Faunus, in Maenalia or at the Albunian Fountain near Tivoli; or that of Tiresias, in Orchomenus; or that of Mopsus, in Cilicia; or that of Orpheus, on Lesbos; or that of Trophonius, on Leucadia in the Ionian Sea—then I could tell you (though maybe I wouldn't) to go there and hear what the oracles had to say about your plan. But you know they've all gone dumb as fish since the coming of our King and Savior, who brought to an end all oracles and prophecies—just the way, when the clear sunlight shines, it chases away all goblins, vampires, wicked spirits, werewolves, sprites, and ghosts. And even if those oracles were still able to speak, I wouldn't put too much trust in their responses: an awful lot of people have been fooled.

"Besides, I remember that Agrippina scolded the beautiful Lollia Paulina for having asked the oracle of Apollo at Clarus if she and the emperor Claudius would ever be married. And that was why she was first banished and afterward miserably put to death."

"Well," said Panurge, "let's do better than that. The Ogygian Islands aren't far from the port of Saint Malo: let's speak to the king and go sail there. They say that on one of those four islands, the one that most squarely faces the setting sun—and I've read about this myself, in good classical authors—there are a number of fortune-tellers and soothsayers and prophets. Saturn is supposed to be there, bound on a golden rock with golden chains, fed by ambrosia and divine nectar, carried to him every day, direct from the heavens, by I don't know what species of bird (maybe the same crows that fed Saint Paul, the first hermit, in the desert), and he clearly foretells the future for anyone who wants to hear about it—his whole destiny, everything that's going to happen to him. Because there's nothing the Fates weave, nothing that Jupiter intends to do, nothing they even talk about doing, that Jupiter's old father doesn't know about. It would save us a lot of work, hearing a bit of what he'd say about my problem."

"And that," answered Epistemon, "is simply too ridiculous—a wildly fantastic fable. I'm not going."

Chapter Twenty-five // How Panurge Consults with Herr Trippa

"But," said Epistemon, continuing, "I think there's still something you can do, before we go back to our king. Right near here, at L'Ile Bouchard, near Chinon, lives Herr Trippa. You know how, using astrology, geomancy, chiromancy, physiognomy, and other such stuff, he predicts everything that's going to happen. Let's discuss your business with him."

"I don't know anything about all that," answered Panurge. "I do know that one day, while he was speaking with the king of all France about assorted celestial and transcendent matters, the court attendants were busy on the stairs and in the hallways, screwing his wife one after the other, and having a ball, because she was really pretty. And there he was, needing no spectacles to see all things on earth and in the skies, lecturing learnedly about everything past and present, predicting everything that was to come, except that he couldn't see his wife wagging her tail and indeed never knew a thing about it. Lord! Well, let's go see him, since you want to. You can never know too much."

The next day they got to Herr Trippa's house. Panurge gave him a wolf-skin robe, a magnificent short sword with a handsomely gilded velvet hilt, and fifty shiny gold pieces. And then they openly discussed his problem.

The moment he saw Panurge, Herr Trippa, studying his face, said:

"You have the head and face of a cuckold—a gross and shocking cuckold."

And then, carefully examining Panurge's right hand, he said:

"This broken line, the one I see just above the *Mons Jovis,* the Jupiterean Bump, occurs only on the hands of cuckolds."

Then he took up a pen and quickly plotted out a series of unrelated points, matching them up by means of geomancy, and said:

"There's not a doubt in the world: it's quite certain that, right after you're married, you'll be cuckolded."

And then he asked Panurge for his birth horoscope, which he was given, and at once he drew up a complete astrological chart, with all the heavenly bodies suitably arranged. Then, studying the zodiacal arithmetic spread out before him, he sighed heavily, saying:

"I've already said bluntly that you'll be cuckolded: it can't fail. And here I see it even more clearly. And I say again: you'll be cuckolded. Moreover, your wife will beat you, and rob you, for I see the seventh house in a fearfully bad aspect, plus a whole host of signs with horns, like Ares, Taurus, Capricorn, and others. And in the fourth house I find Jupiter declining, together with Saturn in his tetragonal aspect, associated also with Mercury. You're going to be well and thoroughly poxed, too, my good man."

"Oh will I?" answered Panurge, "you old fool, you disgusting idiot! When the cuckolds have a parade, you'll be carrying the banner. But how did this little bug get between these two fingers?"

And as he spoke, he stuck out his first two fingers at Herr Trippa, making them into a pair of horns and closing the other fingers into a fist. Then he turned to Epistemon and said:

"Here's the real Ollus that Martial made fun of, who made it his sole business to watch and study and understand other people's accidents and misfortunes. Meantime, his wife ran a gambling den and whorehouse. For his part, though he was poorer than that beggar Irus, he lived gloriously—no, vaingloriously, more cocksure and impossible than seventeen devils—in a word, a boastful beggar, as the ancients used to call such worthless scum. Let's go: this idiot foaming at the mouth, this dog-faced fool, can go raving out his belly to his private devils. But would devils be willing to serve a rascal like him? He doesn't even know the first rule of philosophy—which is: Know yourself—and he puffs himself up so stupidly about seeing a mote in someone else's eye, he can't see the great

fat logs poking out both of his. He's exactly that eternal busybody Poly-
pragmon, described by Plutarch. He's another Lamia, who saw more
keenly than a lynx—in other people's houses, in public, among ordinary
people. But in her own house she was blinder than a mole. Once she was
back in her own house, she saw nothing because, in private, she yanked
the eyes out of her head, the way other people take off their spectacles,
and hid them in a wooden shoe she had hanging behind the front door."

Hearing all this, Herr Trippa picked up a twig of heather.

"A good choice," said Epistemon. "Old Nicander called it a fortune-
telling twig."

"Would you like to know the truth in greater detail," said Herr Trippa,
"as told to us by fire reading, or by reading the air and the clouds and the
wind, so celebrated by Aristophanes in his *Clouds,* or by water reading,
or by the forms of reflections, once so famous among the Assyrians and
employed by Hermolaus Barbarus? In a basin full of water I'll show you
your future wife screwing with a pair of peasants."

"But when you stick your nose up my ass," said Panurge, "remember
to take off your spectacles."

"Or would you prefer me to use mirrors," said Herr Trippa, going on,
"by which method Didus Julianus, emperor of Rome, was able to see
everything that was going to happen to him? You don't need spectacles,
either: you'll see your future wife screwing just as clearly in a mirror as if
I showed her to you in the fountain of Minerva's temple, near Patras. Or
would you prefer sieve reading, once employed so religiously in Roman
ceremonies? We've got a sieve and some tongs: you'll see devils. Or would
you prefer barley-meal reading, which Theocritus discusses in his *Phar-
maceutria*—or perhaps flour reading, wheat mixed with corn? Or perhaps
chickpea reading? I have the apparatus right at hand. Or perhaps cheese-
hole reading? I have a fine Bréhémont cheese we can use. Or perhaps
divination by walking in circles? You'll turn yourself around and around
and around—and you, you'll fall to the left, I can tell you that right now.
Or perhaps we can read your chest: by God, yours is certainly out of
proportion! Or perhaps you'd prefer to read incense fumes? For that, all
we need is just a bit of incense. Or perhaps belly reading? Lady Jacoba
Rhodogina, the famous ventriloquist of Ferrara, has used that for a long
time. Or perhaps we can try reading a donkey's skull? The Germans used
that, roasting a donkey's head in red-hot charcoal. Or falling wax, perhaps? That way you can see your future wife and those who are thumping
her, right in the wax at the bottom of the water. And then there's cap-
nomancy: we put poppy seeds and sesame seeds on hot charcoal . . . oh,
what a marvelous thing, reading those smells, those colors, those crac-
kling sounds! And then there's ax-onomancy, which requires only an ax
and a chunk of onyx: we can burn some of the gemstone or else tune into
the subtle, lingering vibrations of the ax. Oh, what splendid use Homer
makes of axes, in dealing with Penelope's lovers! And there's oil-ono-

mancy: all we need is oil and wax. Or ash-onomancy? You'll see how the ash floating away through the air will portray your wife all dressed to kill. Or botono-nomancy? I have some sage leaves right here. Or reading fig leaves? Ah, such a divine art! All fig leaved! Or fish reading—so famous, once, as practiced by Tiresias and Polydamas, and certainly employed in her deep pit of divination by Diana, there in Apollo's sacred wood, in the land of the Lycians? Or pig predicting? If there are enough hogs, by my faith, you'll get to have the bladder all for yourself. Or might you prefer cleromancy—the way you hunt for the bean hidden in the cake, on Epiphany Eve? Or we could strangle some babies and study their entrails, like Heliogabalus, emperor of Rome? It's not the nicest thing, but you'll manage well enough, since you're a foredoomed cuckold. Or would you like to try reading sibylline verses? Or using names—people names, place names, whatever? What's your name?"

"Eatshit," answered Panurge.

". . . Or perhaps cock-omancy? I'll draw a perfect circle right here and, while you're watching, I'll divide it into twenty-four equal portions. Under each one I'll put a letter of the alphabet; under each letter I'll put a grain of wheat; and then I'll let a good virgin cock go across: you'll see, I swear it, how he'll eat the grains under the letters C U C K O L D—just as prophetically as the divine cockamamie rooster, when Emperor Valens couldn't figure out who his successor would be. T H E O D was what he pecked, and the next emperor's name was Theodosius.

"Or we can work from the flesh of sacrificed animals. Does that interest you? Or their entrails, perhaps? Or we can study the flight of birds, or the songs of omen birds. Or the sun-dancing grains dropped by sacred hens."

"How about turd reading!" answered Panurge.

"Or perhaps corpse reading? I'll reawaken someone who's just died for you, as Apollonius of Tyre did for Achilles, or the witch did for Saul, and the corpse will tell us everything—the way Erichtho had a dead man predict for Pompey what would happen at the battle of Pharsalia. But if you're afraid of the dead, as all cuckolds naturally are, I can simply study ghosts and shadows."

"Get out of here," answered Panurge, "you crazy fool—the hell with you. Go get yourself screwed by an Albanian: that way you can wear a pointed hat, the way they do. Damn! Why don't you tell me to hold an emerald under my tongue—or maybe a hyena's eyeball? Or how about hoopoe tongues? Or the hearts of green frogs? Or maybe I should eat a dragon's heart and liver, so I can figure out my destiny from the songs of swans and other birds, the way the Arabs used to do in Mesopotamia? May thirty devils take you, you double-horned monster, you cuckold, you secret Jew, you devil's own magician, you Antichrist witch!

"Let's go back to our king, Epistemon. I know he won't be happy with us, if he ever hears that we came to this long-skirted devil's den. I regret coming: I'd cheerfully donate a hundred noble gold coins, and then fourteen plebeian ones, if the spirit that used to blow on the bottom of my breeches would pop up right now and smear this fellow's mustache with his spit. In the name of God! How he's stunk me up with his devilish irritating stupidities—all those charms and that dumb witchcraft! The devil can have him whenever he wants him! Say *amen* and let's go get a drink. I won't be smiling for another two days—no, make that four days, by God."

Chapter Twenty-six // How Panurge Sought the Advice of Brother John Mincemeat

Panurge was still angry about Herr Trippa. So, after they passed the village of Huismes, he turned to Brother John and, stammering and scratching at his left ear, he said:

"Cheer me up a little, my fat old friend. My soul's positively flattened by what that devil-driven idiot said. Just listen to this, you old fat-head, you ball bag:

stumpy balls,	lumpy balls,
famous balls,	squamous balls,
lead balls,	bread-and-milk balls,
soft balls,	caulked balls,
spotted balls,	potted balls,
dotted balls,	grotto balls,
graceful balls,	faithful balls,
trussed-up balls,	mussed-up balls,
rolled-up balls,	holed-up balls,
speckled balls,	freckled balls,
banged-up balls,	ganged-up balls,
sworn balls,	worn balls,
humped-up balls,	pumped-up balls,
tooted balls,	fluted balls,
wrapped-up balls,	slapped-up balls,
cape balls,	ape balls,
glossy balls,	flossy balls,
redwood balls,	deadwood balls,
organic balls,	Latin balls,
harbor balls,	barber balls,
antic balls,	frantic balls,
crazy balls,	lazy balls,
huddled balls,	puddled balls,

stuffed balls,
witty balls,
seasoned balls,
actual balls,
possessive balls,
immensual balls,
dinosaur balls,
monken balls,
manly balls,
respectful balls,
waiting balls,
huge balls,
handy balls,
emphatic balls,
power balls,
double balls,
spice-giving balls,
glistening balls,
bouncing balls,
needy balls,
crossing balls,
humping balls,
successful balls,
coral balls,
glossy balls,
important balls,
dangling balls,
leopardy balls,
bear-y balls,
noble balls,
paternal balls,
telescope balls,
higher-math balls,
lusty balls,
unflagging balls,
cooperative balls,
rocking balls,
gracious balls,
distinguished balls,
solid balls,
additional balls,
tragedy balls,
bridge-like balls,
soothing balls,
spirit balls,

puffed balls,
pretty balls,
unreasoned balls,
factual balls,
excessive balls,
good sensual balls,
minotaur balls,
sunken balls,
canny balls,
dejectful balls,
impatient balls,
lewd balls,
dandy balls,
dramatic balls,
by-the-hour balls,
no-trouble balls,
life-giving balls,
whistling balls,
flouncing balls,
seedy balls,
assaulting balls,
jumping balls,
messed-up balls,
moral balls,
flossy balls,
im-potent balls,
jangling balls,
in-jeopardy balls,
hairy balls,
sober balls,
eternal balls,
tell-a-joke balls,
mercury-bath balls,
busty balls,
unstaggering balls,
nicely operative balls,
shocking balls,
advantacious balls,
lingering balls,
stolid balls,
requisitional balls,
badgering balls,
rigid balls,
confusing balls,
you-can-hear-it balls,

manning balls,
rushing balls,
explosive balls,
thunder balls,
bang-up balls,
shrill balls,
tolling balls,
spruced-up balls,
hooting balls,
bouncing balls,
knitting balls,
dropped balls,
woven balls,
balling balls,

stamping balls,
gushing balls,
proposive balls,
wonder balls,
sang-up balls,
well-filled balls,
rolling balls,
goosed-up balls,
looting balls,
flouncing balls,
hitting balls,
plopped balls,
roaming balls,
falling balls,

"Oh, you battling balls, you rattling balls—oh, Brother John, my old friend, how much I admire and respect you, so I've saved you for the last and best: tell me, I beg you, give me your advice. Should I get married or not?"

Brother John answered him gaily, saying:

"By the devil himself, get married, get married, and peal out a double bell on your balls. Do it as soon as you can, that's what I say, and that's what I mean. Get the banns said today and get her to bed tonight. In the name of God, what are you waiting for? Don't you know that the end of the world is right around the corner? Today we're two rods and half a fathom closer to it than we were yesterday. They tell me the Antichrist's already been born. True, he's still just working on his nurse and his governesses, and the devils haven't shown him all the treasures they're saving for him, because he's still so little. *Crescite,* Believe this. *Nos qui vivimus, multiplicamini,* Those of us who are alive, increase, multiply—that's what's written: it's right there in the prayer book—just so a bag of wheat doesn't cost more than three pence and a barrel of wine more than six pieces of gold. When the Day of Judgment comes, do you want to get caught with your balls full, *dum venerit judicare,* when it comes time to be judged?"

"Your soul, Brother John," said Panurge, "is perfectly clear and wonderfully serene: you've got a bishop's balls, by God, or a cardinal's, and you speak right to the point. That's how Leander prayed to Neptune and all the other sea gods, back in Abydos, in Asia, when he was swimming across the Hellespont to visit his beloved Hero, at Sestos, which was in Europe:

> If in coming I come to you,
> Who cares if I die coming back?

"He didn't want to die with his balls full. And it's my opinion that hereafter, all through this Salmagundi which I rule, before a criminal is to be executed he ought to have a day or two to screw like a pelican, so there won't be enough spermatic fluid left in him to write the Greek letter Y. Something so exceedingly precious must not be foolishly wasted! Perhaps he'll have created another man, and then he can die without regret, knowing he's left a life for his life."

Chapter Twenty-seven // Brother John's Happy Advice for Panurge

"By Saint Rigomer," said Brother John, "Panurge, my sweet friend, I won't advise you to do anything I wouldn't do, if I were in your place. Just be watchful and careful to keep at it, and never give up. If you take an intermission, you're lost, my poor friend, and what happens to wet nurses will happen to you. If they ever stop feeding babies, they lose all their milk. If you don't keep using the weapon God's given you, it will lose its milk, too, and all it'll be good for is pissing, just as all your balls will be is hanging bags. Listen to me, my friend. I've seen it happen— men who didn't have enough when they wanted it, because they didn't use it when they could have. And as the scholars say, if you don't use it, you lose it. So, my son, keep these little, low-slung, common cave dwellers working away. Make sure they don't try loafing like gentlemen, living off their income and doing nothing."

"Not a chance, Brother John, my good left ball," answered Panurge. "Believe me. You're not wasting any time, and you're saying what needs to be said. You're not beating around the bush: everything you've said just blows away the things I've worried about, the fears that have been holding me back. May heaven grant you the power always to work so straight to the point. Now that I've heard what you have to say, I'm going to get married. Nothing will go wrong. There'll always be pretty chambermaids, when you come to see me, and you'll be the protector of their sisterhood. And that's the first part of my sermon."

"Listen," said Brother John. "There are the bells at Varennes. What are they saying?"

"I hear them," answered Panurge. "By my thirst! They're clanging more prophetically than the great caldrons hung all around Jupiter's sanctuary at Dodona. Listen: *Get married, get married, married, married. If you get married, married, married, you'll like it fine, you'll see, you'll see. Married, married.* So I'll definitely get married: the whole universe is urging me on. Let these words stand in your mind like a great bronze wall.

"Now, as for the second point, you strike me as somewhat doubtful—

indeed, it seems to me you're challenging my powers of paternity—you think the stiff-limbed god Priapus doesn't truly smile at me. I beg you, please, to believe me when I say that he does what I want him to—he's obedient, benevolent, attentive, always doing exactly what I want whenever and wherever I want it. All I have to do is untie his leash—I mean, his belt buckle—show him the prey and say, 'At 'em, boy!' And even if my future wife is as greedy for sexual pleasure as Messalina or the marquise of Winchester, in England, believe me, please: there'll always be more to keep her happy.

"And I'm not forgetting what Solomon said, speaking as both a priest and a scholar. Nor that Aristotle declared, long after him, that a woman's cunt is insatiable. I just want it known that I have an iron tool quite as indefatigable. Don't talk to me about such fantastic fornicators as Hercules, Proclus, Caesar, or Muhammad, who boasted in his Koran that his genitals had as much power as any sixty strong men. He lied, the rascal. And don't talk to me about that Indian, the one Theophrastus prates about, and also Pliny and Athenaeus—the one who, with the help of a certain herb, in one day screwed seventy times, and more. I don't believe a word of it: that's an imaginary number. Don't believe it, please. But do believe (it's nothing that isn't literally true) that my unaided, natural penis, when it stands to attention, is *the* penis—first and best in the whole wide world.

"So listen, my small-bored friend. Did you ever see the monk of Castres' robes? All you had to do was put his clothing in a house, no matter whether anyone knew it was there or whether it was hidden away, and all of a sudden, because of its incredible supernatural power, everyone who lived there went into heat—animals and people alike, men and women, even the cats and the rats. And I can tell you, on my honor, that at times I've felt an even more awesome power right in my codpiece.

"I won't tell you about houses and huts, or sermons and marketplaces. But once, when they were acting out the Passion play at Saint-Maixent, I'd just walked into the audience and I saw, so help me, that the power, the occult force, of what was inside my codpiece suddenly overwhelmed everyone there, actors and spectators alike, and there wasn't an Angel, a Man, a Devil, or a She-devil who didn't feel an immense and incredible urge to screw. The director threw away his script; the man who was playing Saint Michael climbed down from his angelic machine; the devils climbed up out of hell and dragged all the poor girls down with them; even Lucifer threw off his chains. And seeing what I'd done, and what a mess I'd made, I immediately left, like Cato the Censor, who when he saw that his presence had created havoc at the Festival of Flora, turned and walked away."

Chapter Twenty-eight // How Brother John Fortified Panurge against His Fear of Being Cuckolded

"I understand you," said Brother John, "but time conquers all things: neither marble nor granite ever escapes age and decay. It may not be a problem now, but not too many years from now I'll hear you admitting that, for lots of men, their balls hang down because there's nothing to hold them up. I can already see gray hairs on your head. And the shades of gray and white and brown and black in your beard remind me of a map of the world. Look right here: that's Asia, and over here's the Tigris and the Euphrates. There's Africa; here are the mountains of the moon. Don't you see the marshes of the Nile? Europe's over there. Can you see Thélème? This tuft over here, the one that's all white, is the Hyperborean mountains, far in the north. By my thirst, my friend, when there's snow on the mountains—I mean, the head and the chin—there can't be that much heat down in the valleys of the codpiece!"

"May your feet freeze!" answered Panurge. "You don't know a thing about logic. When the snow's on the mountains, that's exactly when, down in the valleys, thunder rumbles and lightning crackles and flashes, and the wind whips around and it storms, and all the devils are loose down there. Would you like to see for yourself? Go to Switzerland and watch the lake at Wunderberlich, four leagues from Bern, toward Sion. You scold me for my graying head without stopping to consider that that's just how onions are—white up on top but with green tails, erect and lusty.

"It's true, I see some signs of aging in myself—but it's green aging. And don't you tell anyone: this is a secret, just between the two of us. What I find is that wine tastes better—it's more savory—than it ever used to be. And I worry more about bad wine than I used to. I suppose that points to a touch of sunset; it means that noon's gone by. But so what? I'm still as good company as I ever was—and maybe more. In the devil's name, I'm not worried about that! That's not what bothers me. What I'm worried about is that I'll have to go somewhere with our king Pantagruel, because I have to go with him, even if he goes to all the devils, and I'll be away a long time, and that's when my wife will cuckold me. That's what it comes down to: because everyone I've talked to has warned me, swearing that heaven has fixed that as my fate."

"You don't get to be a cuckold," answered Brother John, "just by wanting to be. If you're cuckolded, *ergo,* therefore, your wife will have to be beautiful; *ergo,* she'll have to treat you well; *ergo,* you'll have lots of friends; *ergo,* you'll be saved. Now *that's* logic, monk style. It'll be all the better for you, you old sinner. You'll never have had it easier. There won't be any the less for you. You'll grow wealthier and wealthier. And if that's your destiny, why would you want to fight it? Tell me, my shrunken-balled friend, old mildew balls,

water-logged balls,
water-bogged balls,
icicled balls,
slice-ickled balls,
chilled balls,
spilled balls,
dropped balls,
plopped balls,
faded balls,
jaded balls,
dying balls,
sighing balls,
scruffy balls,
stuffy balls,
splitty balls,
shitty balls,
hung-up balls,
bunged-up balls,
teased balls,
squeezed balls,
runty balls,
stunted balls,
mule's balls,
presumed balls,
aching balls,
breaking balls,
blocked-up balls,
knocked-up balls,
dead balls,
lead balls,
diseased balls,
displeased balls,
corked balls,
untorqued balls,
splashed balls,
trashed balls,
drained balls,
strained balls,
dreaded balls,
shredded balls,
scattered balls,
battered balls,
locked-up balls,
boxed-up balls,
churning balls,
burning balls,
troubled balls,
bubbled balls,
smeary balls,
bleary balls,
used-up balls,
abused-up balls,
sad balls,
bad balls,
unscrewed balls,
blue balls,
wormy balls,
squirmy balls,
flagging balls,
sagging balls,
wrinkled balls,
shrinking balls,
chopped-off balls,
lopped-off balls,
ripped-off balls,
slipped-off balls,
split-off balls,
bitten-off balls,
cooking balls,
ill-looking balls,
varicose balls,
otiose balls,
maggot balls,
faggot balls,
lame balls,
inflamed balls,
torn balls
worn balls
fainting balls,
tainted balls,
cocky balls,
rocky balls,

tramp balls,
poked-up balls,
sun-tanned balls,
gutted balls,
pastry balls,
withered balls,
frayed balls,
foggy balls,
swooning balls,
diluted balls,
hacked balls,
sucked-up balls,
picked balls,
slashed balls,
old fat balls,
skinny balls,
tipsy balls,
fleecy balls,
addled balls,
weak balls,
doleful balls,
spent balls,
confused balls,
crusty balls,
chewed-up balls,
paralyzed balls,
leaky balls,
dim balls,
surly balls,
lip-fart balls,
shriveled balls,
bleary balls,
dazed balls,
stinking balls,
gimpy balls,
jailed balls,
patched balls,
drugged balls,
indifferent balls,
hero balls,
idle balls,
boiling balls,

pampered balls,
smoked-up balls,
un-manned balls,
slutty balls,
tasty balls,
gizzarded balls,
clay balls,
soggy balls,
crooning balls,
disputed balls,
cracked balls,
tucked-up balls,
kicked balls,
bashed balls,
polecat balls,
windy balls,
gypsy balls,
greasy balls,
saddled balls,
bleak balls,
woeful balls,
bent balls,
refused balls,
rusty balls,
glued-up balls,
analyzed balls,
freaky balls,
grim balls,
twirly balls,
dog-cart balls,
sniveled balls,
dreary balls,
crazed balls,
winking balls,
skimpy balls,
impaled balls,
attacked balls,
sluggish balls,
different balls,
zero balls,
tired balls,
toiling balls—

"And the devil with all balls, my good friend Panurge. Since you're going to be cuckolded, and fate's already made up its mind, why should you want to make all the planets go backward? dislocate all the heavenly spheres? blame the High and Mighty Movers for making a mistake? blunt the spindles? criticize the spindle rings? slander the bobbins? scold the spools, say bitter things about the silk thread? try to unstring the Weaving Fates' work? You're out of your mind, fat-head! You'd be even dumber than the Titans, by God. Now, look here, you scumbag. Would you rather be jealous for no reason than be a cuckold without knowing it?"

"I have no interest," answered Panurge, "in either one. But if I do find out about it, I'm going to take care of it, unless the world's run out of good stout sticks. My lord, Brother John, the best thing for me is just not to get married. Listen to these bells: now that we're closer, this is what they're telling me: *Don't get married, don't get married, don't, don't, don't, don't. If you get married (but don't get married, don't get married, don't, don't, don't, don't), you'll regret it, regret it, regret it: cuckold! cuckold!* By all that's holy! I'm starting to get angry. All of you, with your monkish brains, don't you have any cure? Has nature so deprived the human race that a married man can't pass through this world without falling into the abyss of cuckoldry?"

"Let me teach you," said Brother John, "a trick that will keep your wife from ever cuckolding you without your knowledge and consent."

"By all means," said Panurge, "old velvet balls. Tell me, my friend, tell me."

"Get Hans Carvel's ring," said Brother John, "the king of Melinda's great jeweler.

"Hans Carvel was a learned man, and a true professional: his nose was always in a book. And he was a good man, a sensible man, with excellent judgment, good-natured, philanthropic, an almsgiver, a philosopher, but a merry fellow, too, a good drinker—and he told a good joke, if anyone ever did. He was a bit round around the middle; his head shook; and he didn't always seem comfortable. Well, when he was well on in years, he married the bailiff Concordat's daughter—young, pretty, lively, a strapping wench, forthcoming, and distinctly too gracious to both her neighbors and her servants. So, after a couple of weeks, he became as jealous as a tiger and suspected she was getting her ass drummed on by someone else. To prevent that, he told her all sorts of lovely stories about the sad things adultery brought about. He used to read her those fairy tales about modest, virtuous women, and he preached chastity at her all the time. He made a book for her, all about the joys of marital fidelity, and fiercely critical about the wickedness of married rakes. And he also gave her a handsome necklace covered with oriental sapphires. Just the same, she went on being so free and easy with their neighbors that his jealousy just kept on growing and growing.

"Now, one night, lying in bed with her, tormented by these violent emotions, he dreamed that he spoke to the devil and told him all his troubles. The devil cheered him up and put a ring on his middle finger, saying:

" 'I'm giving you this ring. While it's on your finger, your wife will never have carnal knowledge of anyone else without your knowledge and consent.'

" 'Many thanks,' said Hans Carvel, 'My Lord Devil. May I disown Muhammad if I ever take it off my finger.'

"The devil vanished. Hans Carvel, as happy as he could be, woke up and found that he had his finger in his wife's whatchamacallit. I forgot to tell you how his wife, when she felt it, pulled back her ass, as if to say, 'Yes—no—that's not what you're supposed to put in there.' But it seemed to Hans Carvel that someone was trying to steal his ring.

"Now I ask you: is that an infallible cure? You can do the same thing, by God, if you always have your wife's ring on your finger."

And that was all they said, as they went down the road.

Chapter Twenty-nine ⁄⁄ How Pantagruel Brought Together a Theologian, a Medical Man, a Legal Scholar, and a Philosopher, in Order to Deal with Panurge's Problem

When they arrived at Pantagruel's palace, they told him all about their trip and showed him Raminagrobis' poem. Having read and then reread it, Pantagruel said:

"I've seen no response that pleased me more. Bluntly, he means that in marriage everyone is responsible for making up their own minds and must take counsel with themselves alone. That has always been my opinion; it's exactly what I told you, the first time we discussed this subject. You never said it in so many words, but you thought it silly, and I knew that self-love had deceived you. Let's proceed differently. And here's why: everything we are, and that we have, is comprised in three things: the soul, the body, and our property. The preservation of each of these three is assigned, these days, to three different sorts of men: the soul belongs to the theologians, the body to the doctors, and property to the lawyers. It's my opinion that, this Sunday, we have to dinner here a theologian, a medical man, and a legal scholar. And then we can discuss your problem with all three of them together."

"By Saint Picaut!" answered Panurge. "That's not going to accomplish a thing; I can see it already. Consider: this is how the world works. We hand our souls over to theologians, who are for the most part heretics; we consign our bodies to doctors, who dislike medicines and never take them themselves; and our property goes to the lawyers, who wouldn't ever sue one another."

"You talk like Castiglione's courtier," said Pantagruel. "But I deny your first point, since the principal occupation—indeed, the sole and unique occupation—of good theologians is to eliminate heresies and errors, by their deeds, their speech, and their writings (and to that extent, yes, they're necessarily involved in such matters). They work at planting deep in the human heart the true and living Catholic faith.

"Your second point is well taken, since good doctors work so hard at preventing illness, and preserving the good health of their charges, that they have no need of the therapeutic and curative effects of medicines.

"I concede the third point: good lawyers are so absorbed in their pleadings and legal responses that they have neither time nor leisure to attend to their own business.

"And so next Sunday our theologian will be Father Hippothadeus; our medical man will be Maître Rondibilis; and our legal scholar will be our friend Bridlegoose. And since I think we ought to be properly Pythagorean and four-sided, we'll add our faithful philosopher, Wordspooler, especially since the perfect philosopher—and Wordspooler's that, all right—always resolves every doubt you present to him. Carpalim, make sure we're prepared for four guests at next Sunday's dinner."

"It seems to me," said Epistemon, "that in the whole country it would be impossible to make better choices. And I don't mean just the professional excellence of each of them, which is beyond dispute, but even more, because Rondibilis is married, though earlier he wasn't, and Hippothadeus wasn't and isn't, Bridlegoose was, though now he isn't, and Wordspooler was and is. Let me make things a little easier for Carpalim. I'll go and invite Bridlegoose, if you approve, for I've known him a long time and I need to speak to him about the welfare and indeed the future of his honest and learned son, who's studying at Toulouse under the wonderfully learned and virtuous Boissoné."

"As you please," said Pantagruel. "And see if there's anything I can do for his son or for the noble lord Boissoné: I love and admire him as one of the best professors alive today. Anything I can do I will do, and with great willingness."

Chapter Thirty ⁄⁄ How the Theologian Hippothadeus Advises Panurge about Marriage

The next Sunday, all the guests were there when dinner was ready, except Bridlegoose, deputy governor of Fonsbeton.

When they brought in the second course, Panurge said, with profound reverence:

"Gentlemen, all that's involved is a single word. Should I get married or not? If you don't settle the problem for me, I'll have to set it down as insoluble, like the problems in Pierre d'Ailly's *Insolubilia,* Problems No One Can Solve. For each and all of you have been handpicked, selected, and sorted as professionals, like perfect peas on a plate."

At Pantagruel's invitation, and with a bow to all of those present, Father Hippothadeus answered, speaking with incredible modesty:

"My friend, you ask our advice, but first you must advise yourself. Are you feeling the urgings of the flesh?"

"Powerfully," answered Panurge. "I hope that doesn't displease you, Father."

"Not at all, my friend," said Hippothadeus. "But in waging this combat, has God given you His gift and special grace of abstinence?"

"Good God, no," answered Panurge.

"Then get married, my friend," said Hippothadeus, "for it's better to marry than to burn in the flames of lust."

"Spoken gallantly, by God," cried Panurge, "without any dancing around and around the pot. Many thanks, Father! I'll get married all right, and soon. I'll invite you to my wedding. By the holy hen! We'll have a hot time. You'll get one of the wedding ribbons, too—and if we have a goose, by all that's sacred! it won't be my wife who'll roast it! And let me beg you to begin the bridesmaids' first dance, if you don't mind doing me such an honor. There's just one tiny difficulty left to deal with. Tiny, really—less than nothing. Will I be cuckolded?"

"Certainly not, my friend," answered Hippothadeus, "if that's how God wants it to be."

"Oh, may the virtues of God help us!" cried Panurge. "Where are you leading me, good people? Oh yes: to those logical 'maybes' and 'perhaps' where all contradictions and impossibilities are dealt with. If my transalpine jackass flew, my transalpine jackass would have wings. If God so wishes, I won't be a cuckold; if He does wish it, then I'll be a cuckold. Good lord, if this was a hypothetical I could get around, I wouldn't be worried a bit. But you all throw me into the arms of God's privy council, right into the inner sanctum of His everyday pleasures. How do you other Frenchmen find the road that leads there? My good Father, I think it'll be better if you don't come to my wedding. Everyone jumping around and all the noise would give you a headache. What you like is calm—peace, silence, solitude. Anyway, I don't think you'd really come. And then, you dance pretty badly, so you'd be uncomfortable leading them out onto the floor for the first round. I'll send you some nice roasted pork, and some wedding ribbons and bows. Drink our health, if you feel like it."

"My friend," said Hippothadeus, "listen to me, try to understand. When

I say to you, 'If God wishes it,' am I injuring you in some way? Are these malicious words? Is the hypothetical condition a scandalous one—is it blasphemous? Or is it simply honoring our Lord and Creator, our Protector, our Preserver? Isn't it simply a recognition of our one and only source of everything worth having? Isn't it simply to declare that we all of us depend on His kindness, that without Him there is nothing, nothing is worth anything, nothing can happen, if His holy grace isn't instilled in us? Isn't it simply to impose a canonical qualification on everything we do, and to place all our endeavors at the mercy of His sacred will, on earth as in heaven? Isn't it simply to sanctify His blessed name? My friend, you will *not* be cuckolded, if God so wishes. To understand what He wishes there's no need to fall back in despair, as if this were some deep dark secret, something requiring a consultation with His privy council or a journey to the private room of His eternally sacred pleasures. Our gracious Lord has given us the gift of His divine revelation, announcing, declaring, and clearly describing His will in the Holy Bible.

"There you'll find that you'll never be cuckolded, that is to say, that your wife will never be a lewd woman, if she is born of good people, well trained in virtue and honesty; if she has not been the friend, or even frequently in the company, of anyone but people of good manners, people who love and fear their God; if she is someone who pleases God by her faith and her observance of the holy commandments, someone concerned not to offend against Him or to lose His grace by any deficiency in her faith or any transgression against His divine law, according to which adultery is rigorously forbidden; someone who gives all her loyalty to her husband, who cherishes him, who serves him, who loves him second only to God.

"And to reinforce such faith and such practices, you, for your part, must educate her in conjugal affection, and preserve her in her modest ways; you must show her a good example, living in your household modestly, chastely, virtuously, exactly as you wish her to live. For the mirror we admire and call honest and faithful isn't all covered with gilt and gems, but the one that truthfully shows us what it sees: just so the wife we think most highly of is not rich, beautiful, elegant, born to a noble family, but she who tries hardest, with God's help, to shape herself and then to keep herself, with His grace, in conformity to her husband's way of life. See how the moon takes none of its light from Mercury, or Jupiter, or Mars, or from any other planet in the sky: she takes it only from the sun, her husband, according to his various aspects and influences, and even from him takes no more than she gives back. So too should you be a model and example of virtue and honesty for your wife. And never stop praying for God's grace and protection."

"What you want, then," said Panurge, stroking his mustache, "is that I marry the sort of woman Solomon describes—but she's dead, there's not a doubt about it. I've never once seen her, as far as I know. God forgive me! But thank you very much all the same, Father. Try eating a bit of this marzipan biscuit: it'll help your digestion. Then drink a glass of red hippocras: it's very good for the stomach. And let's go on."

Chapter Thirty-one // How Doctor Rondibilis Advised Panurge

Continuing his presentation, Panurge said:

"The first word spoken by the man who was deballing the brown monks, at Saussignac, right after he'd cut the balls off Brother Hothead, was 'Next!' That's what I say: 'Next!' So it's your turn, good Maître Rondibilis: finish me off. Should I get married or not?"

"By the hooves on my jackass!" answered Rondibilis. "I don't know what I ought to say on this subject. You say that you feel the distinct prickings of lust? What we teach at our medical school, having been taught it by the ancient Platonists, is that there are five ways of controlling carnal lust. First, by the use of wine."

"I believe it," said Brother John. "When I'm good and drunk, all I want to do is sleep."

"I mean," said Rondibilis, "by the intemperate use of wine. Because using wine intemperately chills our blood, relaxes our muscles, disperses our generative seed, deadens our senses, and warps our movements, all of which makes the act of generation difficult. Indeed, when you see paintings of Bacchus, the drunkards' god, you see him beardless and dressed like a woman, as if completely effeminate, like a castrated eunuch. But it's a totally different story, when wine is taken temperately. The old proverb emphasizes this side of things, saying that Venus is bored to death without Ceres and Bacchus. And according to Diodorus the Sicilian, it was the ancient view—especially among the Lampsacians, as Pausanias tells us—that Master Priapus was the son of Bacchus and Venus.

"Second, there are certain drugs and herbs that can make a man feel chilled, weak, and absolutely impotent. These include *nymphaea heraclia,* or water lily, willow shoots, hemp seed, woodbine, honeysuckle, tamarisk, Abraham's balm, mandragora, hemlock, the smaller of the two orchid nodules, hippopotamus skin, and others, too. Ingested into the human body, and operating as much by their basic properties as by their specific characteristics, they either freeze and mortify our generative seed, or dispel that vital spirit which is supposed to conduct semen to those places destined by nature to receive it, or block the passageways and conduits through which it can be expelled. So too we have drugs and herbs that warm and excite and prepare a man for the sexual act."

"I don't need them," said Panurge, "thank God. And you, Maître? But let's not be annoyed. I don't bear you any ill will."

"Third," said Rondibilis, "there's hard work. This effectively so sorely decomposes the body that the blood, which is necessarily feeding all parts of the body, has neither time, nor leisure, nor power to effectuate its usual seminal secretion and overflowing abundance. Nature holds that back, finding it more important to keep the individual alive than to permit the multiplication of the human species. Which is why we call Diana chaste: she's always working hard at her hunting. And that's also why camps and arenas used to be known as chaste places, because the athletes and soldiers were continually at work. So Hippocrates, in his *De aere, aqua et locis,* On Vapors, Waters, and Places, writes of certain Scythian tribes which, in his day, were even more impotent than eunuchs, when it came to lovemaking, because they were always up on their horses and at work. And philosophers tell us that laziness is the mother of lust.

"When Ovid was asked why Aegisthus became an adulterer, his only answer was that he was lazy, and that if you took laziness out of the world Cupid's arts would perish: his bow, his quiver, and his arrows would turn into a useless burden, unable to strike down anyone. Because he's not such a fine archer that he can hit cranes in flight or stags dashing through the underbrush (as the Parthian could so readily do). That is, he can't wound human beings while they're busily at work. For him, they have to be easy targets, sitting, lying down, resting. Indeed, Theophrastus, when they asked him what sort of animal or thing sexual passion might be, answered that it was the passion of lazy spirits. Diogenes said, too, that lechery was the occupation of people who didn't have anything else to keep them busy. But when Canachus of Sicyon, the sculptor, wanted to convey the view that laziness and sloth and indifference were what ruled rakes and pimps, he made a statue of Venus seated, not standing, as his predecessors had done.

"Fourth, devote yourself to passionate study. That accomplishes an incredible relaxation of spirit, so there isn't enough energy left to push the generative seed to its destination, thus swelling that spongy nerve which has the task of spurting it forth, for the propagation of the human species. To know this is true, simply consider how a man looks when he's devoted to some scholarly work: you'll see all the brain's arteries bent like the string of a crossbow, so they can swiftly and easily furnish him with a flood of intellectual strength and fill the veins of his common sense, his imagination and perception, his reason and his determination, and his memory, running back and forth from one to the other along those conduits, so clear to the anatomist, which lie under the *plexus mirabilis,* or miraculous network, to which all the arteries lead, those of the left ventricle of the heart indeed beginning there and, after taking their long winding ways through the body, refining the vital spirits into our more animal ones. But in such a studious person you'll see all his natural faculties in suspension, all his exterior senses inactive—in short, he won't seem to you to be alive at all, but to be abstracted out of ordinary existence by his ecstasy. And you'd say that Socrates did not misuse the word when he said that philosophy is nothing but meditation on death. Perhaps this is why Democritus blinded himself, less concerned about losing his sight than about weakening his concentration, which seemed to him interrupted by the wild gyrations of his eyes. That's also why Pallas, goddess of wisdom, guardian and protector of scholars, is said to be a virgin—as are all the muses, and as all the eternal Graces remain forever chaste. And I can recall reading that Cupid, repeatedly asked by his mother, Venus, why he didn't attack the Muses, replied that he found them so beautiful, so spotless, so honest and modest and perpetually busy, one in contemplation of the stars, another in arithmetical calculation, another in measuring geometrical figures, another with rhetorical devices, another with poetic composition, another with the ordering of music, that when he approached them he unbent his bow, closed his quiver, and put out his torch, too ashamed to proceed, and fearful of hurting them. And then he pulled the blindfold away from his eyes so he could more plainly see their faces and listen to their songs and poetic odes. That struck him as the greatest pleasure in the whole world—so much so that, often, he felt himself utterly swept away by their beauty and marvelous grace and fell peacefully asleep. And that was why he had no interest in attacking them or distracting them from their studies.

"On this subject I fully understand what Hippocrates wrote, in the book on the Scythians which I mentioned, and also in his book *De geniture,* On Reproduction, declaring that all human beings become incapable of reproduction if you sever the parotid arteries (which run alongside the ears), for the reasons I explained before, when I spoke of the resolution of spiritual forces and blood in the arteries. And Hippocrates also argued that the largest part of reproduction stemmed from the brain and from the spinal column.

"And the fifth way of controlling lust is by sexual intercourse."

"I was waiting for that," said Panurge. "Now, there's the method I choose. Anyone who wants them is welcome to those other techniques."

"This," said Brother John, "is what Brother Scillino, prior of Saint Victor, near Marseilles, calls mortification of the flesh. And it seems to me (as it did to the hermit of Saint Radegonde, just past Chinon) that the Theban hermits, out in the Egyptian desert, couldn't better mortify their bodies, and subdue this rascal sensuality, and put down the rebellion of the flesh, than by doing it twenty-five or thirty times a day."

"Panurge seems to me," said Rondibilis, "a well-proportioned man, with a sensible disposition, and a good constitution, at the right age and at the right moment, and of a reasonable mind to get married. If he meets a woman of similar temperament, they'll produce children worthy of some far-off royal line. The sooner the better, if he wants to see his children properly provided for."

"My dear maître," said Panurge, "so I will be, without a doubt, and soon. All during your learned discourse this flea, right here in my ear, has been tickling me like never before. I'm keeping you from the banquet. We'll make good cheer, and then some, I promise you. Bring your wife, if you want to, and all her pretty friends, of course. And let's have fun and do no harm!"

Chapter Thirty-two // How Rondibilis Declares Cuckoldry a Natural Accompaniment to Marriage

"There's still one little point to settle," said Panurge. "One very little point—as you've seen displayed on the Roman flag, S.P.Q.R., *Si Peu Que Rien,* So Small That It's Almost Nothing. Am I going to be cuckolded?"

"By the port of heaven!" cried Rondibilis. "What are you asking of me? If you'll be a cuckold? My friend, I'm a married man, and you'll be one too, before long. But write these words in your brain with an iron pen: all married men are in danger of becoming cuckolds. Cuckoldry is a natural accompaniment to marriage. The shadows follow the body no more naturally than cuckoldry follows married people. When you hear it said of someone, 'He's married,' if you say to yourself, 'So he is, or he's been, or he will be, or he might be a cuckold,' no one can call you an unprofessional interpreter of natural consequences."

"By all the devils' leaky bowels!" cried Panurge. "What are you telling me?"

"My friend," answered Rondibilis, "one day, Hippocrates was leaving Lango, in Thrace, to visit the philosopher Democritus, and he wrote a letter to Dionys, his old friend, asking him, in his absence, to bring his wife to her parents' home, they being honorable people with a fine reputation, because he didn't want her to be all alone in her own house. All the same, he asked his friend to keep a close watch on her and to see where she went with her mother, and also to note who came to visit her at her parents' home. 'Not,' he wrote, 'that I doubt her virtue, or her chastity, which I have long since tested and known, but simply that she's a woman, and that's that.' "

"My friend, women's nature is well represented for us by the moon, in these and in other respects: when their husbands are with them, they conceal and restrain themselves, they dissemble. When their husbands are gone, they seize the opportunity, they give themselves a good time, rambling and scampering about, setting all their hypocrisies to the side and truly being themselves. Just so the moon, when it's in conjunction with the sun, can't be seen on heaven or earth, but when it's in opposition and at its farthest distance from the sun, shines her fullest and can be seen everywhere, but especially at night. And that's what all women are like.

"When I say 'woman,' I speak of a sex so brittle, so variable, so changeable, so inconstant and imperfect, that it seems to me (speaking in all honor and reverence) that when nature created woman she was somehow out of her mind and lost the good sense displayed in her other creations. And having thought about this a hundred times, and then five hundred times more, I don't know what to think, except that in making woman nature was more concerned with man's pleasure, and with the perpetuation of the human species, than with the perfection of any individual of the female sex. Plato certainly had no idea at what level he ought to put them: were they reasoning animals or brute beasts? Because nature has hidden away, deep within them, an animal spirit, a secret part, which men do not have, and this sometimes gives rise to certain spicy impulses, nitrous, brackish, bitter, biting, corrosive, throbbing, fiercely provoking, by means of which painful stinging and quivering (for this hidden organ is highly excitable and exquisitely sensitive) their entire bodies are caught up, every sense swept away in rapture, all affective concerns made intensely subjective, and every thought confused. Indeed, if nature hadn't sprinkled their foreheads with a bit of shyness and shame, you'd see them running madly after the male member, wilder and fiercer than Proteus' daughters, who thought themselves cows, or the Mimallonides and Thyades on the day of their Bacchic orgies. For this frightful animal spirit is linked to every part of their bodies, as every anatomist knows.

"I call this spirit animal-like, adhering to both Aristotelian and Platonic views. For if the ability to move is a clear sign of life, as Aristotle writes, and everything which moves of its own accord is called animal, then Plato is perfectly correct to call this spirit animal, recognizing in it independent movements of suffocation, violent haste, contraction, indignation—indeed, movements so violent that, frequently, a woman is deprived of all other sense, all other power of movement, as if she had swooned, or experienced a syncope, an epileptic fit, a stroke of apoplexy, and the true appearance of death. In addition, note that there are palpable odors associated with these symptoms, and women flee from those that repel them, flock to those that attract them. I concede that Claudius Galen tried to prove that these were not voluntary and self-impelled movements, but only accidental, and others of those who adhere to his beliefs have tried to demonstrate that there is no inherent olfactory discrimination involved, but simply a broad spectrum, proceeding naturally from the diversity of odorific substances. But if you study their arguments and all their reasoning with great care, and weigh them in that spiritually attuned balance of

Critolaus, you'll find that—in this as in many other matters—they've spoken out of sheer frivolity and a wish to scold their elders, rather than on the basis of real research into the truth.

"But I won't go into this any further. Let me just say to you that prudent, modest women, who have lived chaste, blameless lives, deserve no small praise, for they have shown the power to restrain this frantic animal spirit and force it to be obedient to reason. Let me end here, adding simply that, if this animal spirit is sated (if it can indeed ever be sated) by the nutritional substance which nature has prepared for it, in the bodies of men, all its unique movements are ended, all its appetites are lulled and quieted, all its furies are appeased. However, don't be at all surprised that we're in perpetual danger of being cuckolded, we who do not always have the wherewithal with which to pay off, with which to completely satisfy this animal spirit."

"O you gods and little fishes!" said Panurge. "Don't you as a doctor have any remedy?"

"Oh, yes, my friend," said Rondibilis, "and a very good one, which I use myself. It was written down by a celebrated author, more than eighteen hundred years ago. Listen."

"You're a good man," said Panurge, "by all that's holy, and I love you with all my benighted soul! Try a little bit of this quince pastry: quince helps get the ventricular orifice properly closed, because there's a sort of happy astringency in it—and it helps with the first stage of digestion, too. But just listen to me! I'm talking Latin to scholars! Now wait, while I get you something to drink in this fine Nestorian mug. Would you like more of the white hippocras? Don't worry about getting a quinsy, not drinking this. There's no rattan in there, and no ginger, and no cardamom seed, either. All it has is good ground cinnamon and good white sugar, blended with white wine grown at La Devinière, right in the garden with the big apple tree, down behind the huge walnut."

Chapter Thirty-three ⁄⁄ How Doctor Rondibilis Cures Cuckoldry

"Back in the days," said Rondibilis, "when Jupiter set up his Olympic household and arranged his gods and goddesses into a regularized calendar, with each of them assigned a day and a season in their honor, and places assigned for oracles and pilgrimages, and sacrifices all regulated . . ."

"Wasn't it done," asked Panurge, "the way Tinteville, bishop of Auxerre, arranged things? That noble pontiff loved good wine, as of course all worthy men do, so he had a special concern for his vines (which after all are Bacchus' own grandfather), and a special curate to care for them. Now, it happened that, several years running, he saw the vines sadly nipped in the bud by frosts, sleet, rain and frozen rain, cold weather, hail, and other disasters, occurring on the feast days of Saints George, Mark, Vitalis, Eutropius, and Philip, as well as on Holy Cross Day, Ascension, and other occasions of churchly celebration, all of which were scheduled during that season when the sun passes into the sign of Taurus. And he began to think that these were saintly sources of hail, frost, and general vine spoilers. So he decided to move their feast days to winter, between Christmas and Epiphany, setting them free, in all honor and reverence, to hail and frost in that season just as much as they wanted to, for at that time of year the frost couldn't damage anything—indeed, it would clearly be good for the vines. In their places he put the feast days of Saint Christopher, Saint John the Beheaded Baptist, Saint Mary Magdalene, Saint Anne, Saint Dominic, and Saint Lawrence—indeed, he determined to have mid-August occur in the middle of May. There's so little danger of frost on all these holy days that no one is so much in demand, at those times, as suppliers of cool drinks, soft-cheese makers, craftsmen who weave branches into shady arbors, and wine coolers."

"But," said Rondibilis, "Jupiter forgot that poor devil Cuckoldry, who was out of town at the time. He was in Paris, at the high-court building, pleading some rascally case for one of his tenants and vassals. I don't know exactly how many days later it was, but Cuckoldry found out about the trick they had played on him and at once broke off his legal pleading, terribly concerned that he might be excluded from the calendar listing, and appeared before the great Jupiter in person, pleading, now, all the many worthy things he had done, the fine and useful services he had rendered, and going on at once to beg that he not be left without a feast day of his own, with no sacrifices, no honors. Jupiter apologized, pointing out that all his gifts had been distributed and that the calendar was completely filled up. All the same, Cuckoldry badgered him so mercilessly that finally he did add him to the list, ordering that he too be given earthly honors, and sacrifices, and a feast day.

"His feast day had to be set (because there was no empty place anywhere in the calendar) at the same time as that of the goddess Jealousy. He was to have dominion over all married men, but especially those with beautiful wives. His sacrifices were to be suspicion, mistrust, complaining and peevishness, husbands sniffing around after their wives, spying, hunting for signs of trouble. Every married person was commanded to revere and honor him, to celebrate his feast day with double rites, and to make the aforementioned sacrifices to him, with due warning being given to those who did not seek his favor, aid, and assistance, those who did not honor him as I have said, that he would pay no attention whatever to them, never enter their homes, never seek out their company, no matter how often they invited him, and so would leave them and their wives to rot forever and ever, without any rivals of any sort. He would always flee from them as heretics, sacrilegious people, just as all the other gods always do to those who should but don't honor them: as Bacchus treats keepers of vineyards, as Ceres treats agricultural laborers, as Pomona treats fruit growers, as Neptune treats sailors, as Vulcan treats blacksmiths, and so on. On the other hand, he also swore that toward anyone who observed his feast day (as it had been decreed by Jupiter), interrupting all their other business in his honor, putting aside their lawful occupations in order to spy on their wives, shutting up and mistreating their wives out of jealousy—thus obeying the regulations for making sacrifices to him—he would always be favorably disposed, loving them, visiting their homes both night and day, never permitting them to be without his loving presence."

"Ha, ha, ha!" laughed Carpalim. "Now there's a cure even more original than Hans Carvel's ring. May the devil carry me off, if I don't believe every word of it. That's exactly how women are. Lightning strikes and burns only hard, solid, resistant substances, paying no attention to anything weak, hollow, and yielding: it will melt a steel sword without harming its velvet scabbard—it will burn up all the bones in a body without breaking the skin that covers them. So women never turn their attention, their subtlety, or their immense powers of contradiction toward anything except what they know perfectly well is prohibited and forbidden to them."

"To be sure," said Hippothadeus, "some of our learned men say that the first woman ever created in this world, called Eve by the Hebrews, would never have been tempted to eat the fruit of all knowledge if it hadn't been forbidden to her. And to understand that this is exactly how it was, consider how the tempter cunningly reminded her of that prohibition, in his very first words on the subject, as if to say, 'It's forbidden to you, so you must eat it or you're not a woman.' "

Chapter Thirty-four ⁄⁄ How Women Usually Long For Forbidden Things

"When I was living like a rake, in Orléans," said Carpalim, "there was no argument I could make that worked better, that was more persuasive and did more to get women in my clutches, ready for playing love games, than to tell them, as emphatically and clearly and scornfully as I could, how their husbands were jealous of them. I didn't have to invent a thing: everyone writes about it, and we have the proof of laws and examples, of reason and daily experience. With that idea in their noggins, they never hesitate to cuckold their husbands, by God! (I don't mean to swear), even if they have to act like Semiramis, Pasiphae, Egesta, or the women of the island of Mendes, in Egypt (about whom Herodotus and Strabo tell us), or any other bitches of that sort."

"It's true," said Powerbrain. "I've heard it said that one day Pope John the Twenty-second, passing the abbey of Corningford, was asked by the abbess and some of the older, wiser nuns to grant them an indulgence, allowing them to confess one another. They declared that religious women have certain minor imperfections, secret but palpable, which they're much too shy and modest to reveal to their male confessors. Under the solemn seal of confession, they would be able to tell these things more freely, and more intimately, to each other.

" 'There is nothing,' answered the pope, 'I wouldn't gladly grant you, but I see one problem: a confession must be kept secret. It will be hard for the rest of you to conceal what you hear.'

" 'We can keep secrets very well," said the nuns, 'and better than men can.'

"That same day, the Holy Father gave them a box to watch over, in which he'd put a small finch, asking them most politely to hide it in some safe, secret place, promising them, on his honor as pope, to grant their request if they faithfully kept this secret, but warning them at the same time that they were strictly forbidden under any circumstances to open the box, under pain of ecclesiastical censure and eternal excommunication. No sooner had they heard this prohibition than they were burning to see what was inside: they could barely wait for the pope to be out the door, so they could get to it. The Holy Father, having given them his blessing, then left them and returned to his lodgings. He hadn't gone three steps past the door when the good ladies, the whole crowd of them, ran to open the forbidden box to see what was in it. Next day, the pope visited them, intending (or so they thought) to grant them the requested dispensation. But before he got to that matter, he directed that they bring him his box. They brought it, but the little bird was no longer there. So he pointed out to them that keeping confessions secret would be far too difficult for them, considering that they hadn't been able to keep the little box in secret, not even for such a short time and in the face of such strong warnings.

"Gracious Maître Rondibilis, you're our most welcome guest. It has been a very great pleasure to listen to you: God be praised for it all. I haven't seen you since Montpellier, when you and the other students put on that moral comedy about a man who married a deaf mute—you and our old friends Antoine Saporta, Guy Bouguier, Balthasar Noyer, Tolet, Jean Quentin, François Robinet, Jean Perdrier, and old François Rabelais."

"I was there, too," said Epistemon. "The good husband wished she could talk. And then she was able to speak, thanks to a doctor and a surgeon, who cut a membrane she had under her tongue. But speech once recovered, she talked so unendingly that her husband went back to the doctor, looking for some medicine that would shut her up. The doctor informed him that he had plenty of cures that would enable women to speak, but none that would silence them. The only possible cure would be for the husband to be deaf, so he couldn't hear his wife's interminable chattering. So they made the idiot deaf, by who knows what magic. His wife, seeing that he'd become deaf and she was talking in vain and he could never hear or understand her, flew into a rage. Then the doctor asked for his fee and the husband answered that, being well and truly deaf, he couldn't hear what he was saying. The doctor then sprinkled some powder down his back, and the poor fellow went mad. So then the crazy husband and the raging wife joined forces and beat both the doctor and the surgeon within an inch of their lives. I've never laughed so much in my entire life."

"Let's get back to our mutton," said Panurge. "What you've said—translated from medical jargon into plain English—means that I should sail right into marriage and not worry about being cuckolded. That's trumping your own ace, all right! My dear maître, I suspect that on my wedding day your practice will call you away, and so you simply won't be able to attend. Well, I excuse you.

> *Stercus et urina medici sunt prandia prima.*
> *Ex alliis paleas, ex istis collige grana.*
>
> Shit and piss are a doctor's first meal.
> He gets straw from one and wheat from the
>   other."

"You're misquoting," said Rondibilis. "The second verse goes like this:

> *Nobis sunt signa, vobis sunt prandia digna.*
> What we see as symptoms, you see as food."

"If my wife fell ill . . ."

"I'd want to examine her urine," said Rondibilis, "take her pulse and see what state her lower belly was in, and also her umbilical region, exactly as Hippocrates prescribes in the second book of his *Aphorisms,* number 35. And only then would I proceed to treat her."

"No, no," said Panurge, "that wouldn't be necessary. That's business for lawyers like me, who understand the subject as it's set out in *De ventre inspiciendo,* Abdominal Examinations. I'd give her a brutal enema. No need for you to break away from more pressing business. I'll send some wedding cutlets over to your house, and you'll always be our friend."

Then Panurge walked over and, without a word, put four gold pieces in his hand. Rondibilis took them handily, but then said, with a start, as if indignant:

"Oh no, sir! This wasn't necessary. But I thank you very much, all the same. I never take anything from wicked people. Nor do I ever refuse anything from good people. I'm always at your service."

"If you're paid," said Panurge.

"That goes without saying," answered Rondibilis.

Chapter Thirty-five // How the Philosopher Wordspooler Dealt with the Difficulties of Marriage

Then Pantagruel said to Wordspooler, the philosopher:

"Our loyal friend, the torch has been passed from hand to hand, and now it comes to you. It's your turn to answer. Should Panurge get married or shouldn't he?"

"Both," answered Wordspooler.

"What are you talking about?" asked Panurge.

"Exactly what you've heard," answered Wordspooler.

"And what have I heard?" asked Panurge.

"What I said," answered Wordspooler.

"Ha, ha! So we've come to that, have we?" said Panurge. "I pass: this isn't the game for me. So: should I get married or not?"

"Neither one nor the other," answered Wordspooler.

"May the devil carry me off," said Panurge, "if you're not driving me crazy—and he will carry me off, if I ever understand you! Just a minute. I'll stick my spectacles right here, on my left ear, so I can hear you better!"

Just then Pantagruel looked toward the door of the room and saw Gargantua's little dog, named Kyné (which is Greek for "dog") because that was what Tobias' dog was called. So he said to them all:

"Our king draws near. Let us rise."

He'd no sooner spoken than Gargantua walked into the room. They all rose and bowed to him. After a good-humored greeting to them all, he said:

"My good friends, please oblige me, I beg you, by not leaving your places or abandoning your conversation. Just set a chair for me, here at the end of the table. Bring me something, so I can drink to your good health. You're all very welcome. Now tell me: what topic are you discussing?"

Pantagruel answered that, after the second course had been served, Panurge had set them a problematical subject, which was: should he get married or not? And he explained that Father Hippothadeus and Maître Rondibilis had completed their responses; as Gargantua had entered, the trusty Wordspooler had been answering. And when at first Panurge had asked him, "Should I get married or not?" he had answered, "Both at the same time," and the second time he'd said, "Neither one nor the other." Panurge had complained that these were such mutually opposed and contradictory responses that there was no way he could understand them.

"But I think I do understand," said Gargantua. "The answer is very like that given by an old philosopher, when he was asked if he had a certain woman, and they gave him her name. 'I have her,' he said, 'as a friend, but she hasn't got me. I possess her; she doesn't possess me.' "

"Exactly the answer," said Pantagruel, "given by a Spartan servant. They asked her if she'd ever had an affair with a man. She answered never—but men had more than once had affairs with her."

"Accordingly," said Rondibilis, "let's call it medically neutral, and philosophically middle-of-the-road, since it swings from one extreme to the other and, neatly divided by time, is first at one extreme and then at the other."

"Blessed Saint Paul," said Hippothadeus, "spoke more plainly, I think, when he said, 'Let those that are married be as if they were not married; let those who have wives be as if they had no wives.' "

"I interpret having a wife and not having one," said Pantagruel, "like this: he who has a wife has her according to the use for which nature intended her, that is, to help the man, for his pleasure and the pleasure of her company. Not to have a wife is not to grow lazy and soft because of her, so that she does not corrupt the unique and supreme affection which man owes to God, and he does not abandon those services which he naturally owes his country, and human kind, and his friends, or become indifferent to his studies and his business, in order to always be with his wife. If you understand not having a wife in this sense, I see no opposition or contradiction in the terms."

Chapter Thirty-six // The Further Responses of Wordspooler, an Ephectic or Uncommitted, and a Pyrrhonian or Skeptical, Philosopher

"You speak like an organ playing," answered Panurge. "But I think I've fallen into a black hole—which is where Heraclitus said you'll find Truth. I can't see a thing, I hear nothing, and my senses are all so dazed that I wouldn't wonder if I'd been bewitched. Let me try a different approach. Our trusty philosopher, stay right where you are. Don't put the money in your pocket—not yet. Let's try throwing the dice again, but this time let's not talk in mutually balanced opposites. I can see that these inadequately phrased explanations confuse and annoy you. All right: by God, should I get married?"

WORDSPOOLER: So it seems.

PANURGE: And if I don't get married?

WORDSPOOLER: I see no problem with that.

PANURGE: No problem at all?

WORDSPOOLER: None, unless I'm not seeing straight.

PANURGE: I think there are more than five hundred problems.

WORDSPOOLER: Enumerate them.

PANURGE: I misspoke myself, taking a number for certain when it was uncertain, taking a number as determined when it was indeterminate: what I should have said was "a lot."

WORDSPOOLER: I'm listening.

PANURGE: By all the devils, I can't manage without a wife!

WORDSPOOLER: Away with all villainous devils!

PANURGE: By God, then, by God! All the Salmagundians tell me that to lie in your bed alone, or without a wife, is to live like a savage, and that's exactly what Dido said in her lamentation.

WORDSPOOLER: I'm at your service.

PANURGE: Lawdy, Lawdy, Lawdy! Let me try it again. So: should I get married?

WORDSPOOLER: Maybe.

PANURGE: Will I like it?

WORDSPOOLER: That depends.

PANURGE: If it goes well, as I hope and trust it will, will I be happy?

WORDSPOOLER: Sufficiently.

PANURGE: Let's try the other side. And if it doesn't go well?

WORDSPOOLER: It won't be my fault.

PANURGE: But let me have your advice, please: what should I do?

WORDSPOOLER: As you please.

PANURGE: Toor-a-loora.

WORDSPOOLER: No magical incantations, if you don't mind.

PANURGE: In the name of God, then! I only want you to advise me. What do you advise me to do?

WORDSPOOLER: Nothing.

PANURGE: Will I get married?

WORDSPOOLER: I wasn't there.

PANURGE: I won't get married at all?

WORDSPOOLER: I'm not a magician. It's out of my hands.

PANURGE: If I don't get married, I'll never be cuckolded.

WORDSPOOLER: I would have thought so.

PANURGE: Let's put it that I do get married.

WORDSPOOLER: Where shall we put it?

PANURGE: I mean, let's suppose I get married.

WORDSPOOLER: Not to me.

PANURGE: Shit up my nose! My God! If I only dared swear some nice fat

little oath up my sleeve, I'd feel a lot better! Now: patience, patience!
So: if I do get married, I'll be cuckolded?

WORDSPOOLER: They've said so.

PANURGE: If my wife is modest and chaste, I won't ever be cuckolded?

WORDSPOOLER: I think you've said that correctly, yes.

PANURGE: Now listen.

WORDSPOOLER: As long as you like.

PANURGE: Will she be modest and chaste? That's the only point I'm after.

WORDSPOOLER: I doubt it.

PANURGE: You've never seen her?

WORDSPOOLER: As far as I know.

PANURGE: Then why do you doubt something about which you know
nothing whatever?

WORDSPOOLER: For a reason.

PANURGE: And if you did know her?

WORDSPOOLER: Then even more.

PANURGE: You, young fellow over there: bring me my hat. Here, let me
give it to you, except for the spectacles. Now, you go outside for a
little half-hour or so, just to swear for me. I'll swear for you, too, if
you'd like. . . . But who will cuckold me?

WORDSPOOLER: Someone.

PANURGE: By the bloody belly of . . . I'll beat the hell out of you, Mister
Someone!

WORDSPOOLER: So you say.

PANURGE: May the devil, who has no white in his eyes, carry me right
off if I don't lock my wife into a chastity belt whenever I leave my
seraglio.

WORDSPOOLER: Please use more appropriate language.

PANURGE: You've shat up this shitty discussion shittily. All right: let's
come to some resolution.

WORDSPOOLER: I won't object.

PANURGE: Wait. Maybe, since I haven't been able to get any blood out of
you here, I should try you on a different vein. Are you married or not?

WORDSPOOLER: Neither one nor the other, and both at the same time.

PANURGE: Dear God, help me! By the holy dead carcass, I'm working like
a galley slave: I feel as if my digestion's been blocked. My whole diaphragm, my thorax even, feel as if everything's suspended, just waiting to be stuffed into the pouch of my understanding, my comprehension
of what you've been saying.

WORDSPOOLER: I won't stop you.

PANURGE: Whoop! Whoop! My trusty one, are you married?

WORDSPOOLER: I seem to be.

PANURGE: You've been married before?

WORDSPOOLER: That's possible.

PANURGE: Was it all right, the first time?

WORDSPOOLER: That's not impossible.

PANURGE: And how is it this second time?

WORDSPOOLER: Exactly as it was intended to be.

PANURGE: But just what, so far as you're aware, strikes you as good about it?

WORDSPOOLER: That's probably it.

PANURGE: Oh, Lord, Lord love you as I love Him—by Saint Christopher's holy burden—I could get a fart out of a dead donkey as easily as I can get anything definite out of you. Try this one on for size. My trusty friend, let's put the devil in hell to shame, let's admit the truth. Have you ever been cuckolded? I'm talking about you—you right here—not the man in the moon.

WORDSPOOLER: Not if I wasn't meant to be.

PANURGE: By the holy flesh, I give up! By the holy blood, I resign! By the holy body, I surrender! He escapes me.

At these words, Gargantua rose, saying:

"May the good Lord be praised in everything. It seems to me the world's gotten itself thoroughly tangled up, since I first became aware of it. Has it come to this? Have our most learned scholars and our wisest philosophers all become Pyrrhonians, professors of uncertainty, skeptics, and ephectics? God be praised! Truly, from now on we'll be able to catch lions and horses by their manes, oxen by the horns, buffaloes by the snout, wolves by the tail, goats by the beard, birds by the feet—but not philosophers like this by their words. Good night, my friends."

And so saying, he left them. Pantagruel and the others wished to follow after him, but he would not permit it.

When Gargantua had left the room, Pantagruel said to his guests:

"Plato's *Timaeus* counted up the guests at the beginning; we, on the contrary, will count them at the end. One, two, three—but where is the fourth? Wasn't that supposed to be our good friend Bridlegoose?"

Epistemon replied that he'd gone to his house, to deliver the invitation, but had not found him. A court bailiff from Mirelingua had come hunting him, to set a date for him to make a personal appearance in front of the judges, to explain a judgment he had handed down. For which reason he had left the day before, so he could be there on the assigned date and not be in default or contempt of court.

"I wish," said Pantagruel, "I knew what that was all about. He's been a judge at Fonsbeton for more than forty years. During that time he has handed down more than four thousand final judgments. Two thousand three hundred and nine of his judgments have been appealed by the losing parties, to the high court at Mirelingua, and every single one of those decrees of his has been ratified, approved, and confirmed, the appeals dismissed as groundless. For him to be personally summoned by the high court, now, in his old age—he who for all these many years has always led such a saintly existence—must mean that something disastrous has happened. I would like to exert all my strength to help him find justice. Evil has become so strong, in this world of ours, that those who deal justly are in sore need of help. Let's think well about this, and take care of it, so nothing untoward happens."

The tables were taken away. Pantagruel gave his guests precious and honorable gifts, rings, and jewels, and vases, gold and silver alike, and after warmly thanking them, retired to his own room.

Chapter Thirty-seven ⁄⁄ How Pantagruel Persuades Panurge to Seek a Fool's Advice

As he was leaving, Pantagruel noticed Panurge in the gallery, rapt in a reverie, slowly nodding his head, and said to him:

"You look like a mouse caught in a trap: the more it tries to get out of the sticky stuff, the more it's smeared with it. So too you, trying to disentangle yourself from your perplexity, get yourself deeper and deeper into it, and I see no possible remedy, except one. Listen. I've often heard the common proverb about a fool teaching a wise man. Now, since the answers of wise men haven't given you any real satisfaction, go seek the advice of a fool—perhaps that will get you better and more satisfying answers. You know how many princes, kings, and republics have been saved by the advice and the prophecies of fools—how many battles won, how many perplexities solved. I don't need to remind you of all the specific examples. You'll agree that this makes sense: like someone who closely supervises his private, domestic affairs, who is watchful and attentive in running his household, whose mind is never distracted, who loses no opportunity to pile up possessions and wealth, who is clever at getting around the difficulties of poverty—well, you call him worldly-wise, even though he may seem like a jackass to the all-seeing, all-knowing eyes of heaven. To seem wise to those celestial intelligences—I mean, wise and capable of accepting divine inspiration and grace—he must learn how to forget himself, to go out of himself, to free his senses of all worldly longing, purge his spirit of all human concern and consider all such matters supremely unimportant. This is commonly thought to be madness.

"Just so, the vulgar herd mocked the great seer Faunus, son of Picus, king of the Latins, by calling him Fatuous.

"Just so, consider the traveling players: when they divide up the roles, the Fool, the Clown, is always played by the most talented and experienced actor in the troupe.

"Just so, the astrologers say that the same horoscope occurs for both

kings and fools. And they give the example of Aeneas and mad Choroe-
bus (Euphorion calls him a fool), who had identical horoscopes.

"It wouldn't be out of the way, either, to remind you of what Giov-
anni Andrea said about one part of a certain papal decree, addressed to
the mayor and citizens of La Rochelle; Nicolas Tedesco, the Panormitan,
criticized the same decree, and so too did Barbatia in his book on Justinian's *Laws,* and so too did, more recently, Jason de Mainus in his *Res-
ponsa,* discussing Lord John, the notorious Parisian fool and great-
grandfather of that other famous fool Caillette. Here's what it was all
about:

"In Paris, at an eating house near the Little Castle, a street porter stood
in front of the shop, flavoring and then eating his bread in the smoke
from the roasting meats, and finding his meal, thus scented, wonderfully
savory. The shopkeeper didn't stop him. But finally, when the bread had
all been guzzled down, the shopkeeper grabbed the porter by the collar
and told him to pay for the smoke from his roasting meat. The porter
replied that he hadn't damaged the shopkeeper's food in any way, nor
taken anything that belonged to him, and therefore was in no way his
debtor. The smoke they were talking about was going to evaporate away
in any event; that was what always happened; no one in all Paris had ever
heard of anyone peddling the smoke from roasting meat. But the shopkeeper answered that the smoke from his roasting meat wasn't meant to
feed porters, and swore that if he wasn't paid he'd take the porter's tools
instead.

"The porter picked up his cudgel and got ready to defend himself. The
argument got heated. Parisian gapers came running from all over to watch
and listen. And among them was Lord John the fool, a Parisian citizen.
And seeing him, the shopkeeper asked the porter, 'Will you take the word
of this noble Lord John, in settling our dispute?' 'Yes, by the holy blood,'
the porter answered.

"So Lord John, after listening to their differing stories, told the porter
to take a coin out of his purse. The porter gave him a gold coin, which
Lord John took and put on his left shoulder, as if testing to see if it weighed
as much as it was supposed to. Then he chinked it against the palm of his
left hand, as if trying to see how pure the gold was. Then he stuck it close
up to his right eye, as if to make sure it had been properly stamped. As
he did all this, the gapers and gawkers were completely silent; the shopkeeper, too, stood in haughty silence, but the porter stood there, sadly
watching. Finally, Lord John clinked the coin against the wall of the shop,
and did this several times. And then, in solemn majesty, he clutched his
fool's stick as if it had been a scepter, jammed down on his head his
monkey-marten cap with paper ears, folded like organ pipes, coughed
two or three times, in suitably preliminary style, and then said in a loud
voice:

" 'The court hereby decrees that the porter who ate his bread in the smoke from the shopkeeper's meat has properly paid therefore by the sound of his money. The said court therefore orders that everyone go home; there will be no costs charged; the suit is hereby dismissed.'

"The judgment of this Parisian fool was so extraordinarily fair that the aforesaid learned legal scholars were convinced that, even had the case been tried before the highest court in France, or before the Rota in Rome, or indeed even before the Areopagites of Athena, it could not have been more justly disposed of. And that's why you should seek the advice of a fool."

Chapter Thirty-eight ⁄⁄ How Pantagruel and Panurge Celebrated the Fool Triboulet

"By my soul," answered Panurge, "I'll do it! It seems to me that my bowels are swelling: until now I've been knotted up and constipated. But just as we chose the fine cream of wisdom to give us advice, so too, now, I'd prefer to consult a truly sovereign fool."

"I think," said Pantagruel, "that Triboulet is a qualified fool."
Panurge replied:
"Perfectly and totally a fool."

PANTAGRUEL
a predestined fool,
a fool of nature,
a heavenly fool,
a jovial fool,
a mercurial fool,
a lunatic fool,
an erratic fool,
an eccentric fool,
an ethereal, Junoesque fool,
an Arctic fool,
a heroic fool,
a genial fool,
a predestined fool,
an august fool,
a Caesar-like fool,
an imperial fool,
a royal fool,
a patriarchal fool,
an original fool,
an honest fool,

PANURGE
a high-toned fool,
a B-sharp and B-flat fool,
an earthly fool,
a happy and frisky fool,
a handsome and lively fool,
a tipsy fool,
a tasseled fool,
a fool with bells,
a laughing and sexual fool,
an abstracted fool,
a fool from the top of the barrel,
a fool of the first barrel,
a foaming fool,
an original fool,
a pope-like fool,
a consistory fool,
a cardinal fool,
a papal-bullish fool,
a synod-like fool,
a bishop-like fool,

a ducal fool,
a flag-waving fool,
a lordly fool,
a palatial fool,
a leading fool,
a magisterial fool,
a total fool,
an elevated fool,
a priestly fool,
a boss fool,
a triumphant fool,
a vulgar fool,
a domesticated fool,
a model fool,
a rare and foreign fool,
a courtly fool,
a polite fool,
a popular fool,
a familiar fool,
a remarkable fool,
a petted fool,
a Latinate fool,
an ordinary fool,
a feared fool,
a transcendent fool,
a sovereign fool,
a special fool,
a metaphysical fool,
an ecstatic fool,
a categorical fool,
a predicated fool,
a violent fool,
an officious fool,
a well-drawn fool,
an algorithmic fool,
an algebraic fool,
a cabalistic fool,
a talmudic fool,
an alchemist's fool,
a compendious fool,
an abridged fool,
a hyperbolic fool,
an Aristotelian fool,
an allegorical fool,
a tropological fool,

a doctoral fool,
a monkish fool,
a fiscal fool,
an extravagant fool,
a puffed-up fool,
a beginning fool,
an oversexed fool,
a fool with a diploma in folly,
a messmate fool,
a licensed fool,
a lickspittle fool,
a superfluous fool,
an echo-like fool,
a faded fool,
a stupid fool,
a fleeting fool,
a well-connected fool,
a wild fool,
a noble fool,
a full-grown fool,
a bone-biting fool,
a recovered fool,
a savage fool,
a driveling fool,
a slack-jawed fool,
a bloated fool,
a coxcomb fool,
a secondary fool,
an oriental fool,
a sublime fool,
a crimson fool,
a born fool,
a middle-class fool,
a feathered fool,
a topmasted fool,
a major fool,
a thought of a thought of a fool,
a scholarly Arab fool,
a queer fool,
an Aquinas fool,
an abridging fool,
a Moorish fool,
a papal-bulled fool,
a proxy fool,
a begging-friar fool,

a pleonasmic fool,
a capital fool,
a cerebral fool,
a cordial fool,
a gutty fool,
a choleric fool,
a splenetic fool,
a lusty fool,
a legitimate fool,
an azimuth fool,
a celestial-circle fool,
an appropriate fool,
an architrave fool,
a pedestal fool,
a perfect fool,
a famous fool,
a happy fool,
a solemn fool,
an annual fool,
a festival fool,
an amusing fool,
a bumpkin fool,
an agreeable fool,
a privileged fool,
a rustic fool,
an ordinary fool,
a constant fool,
a harmonious fool,
a determined fool,
a hieroglyphical fool,
an authentic fool,
a valuable fool,
a precious fool,
a fanatic fool,
a fantastic fool,
a lymphatic fool,
a panicked fool,
an alembic fool,
not a boring fool,

a tenured fool,
a slyboots fool,
a surly fool,
a double-chinned fool,
a high-handed fool,
a well-hung fool,
a scribbling fool,
a giddy fool,
a kitchen fool,
a hardwood fool,
an andiron fool,
a wretched fool,
a rheumy fool,
an elegant fool,
a twenty-four-karat fool,
a bizarre fool,
a transverse fool,
an absurd fool,
a touchy fool,
a cap-and-bells fool,
a well-aimed fool,
an up-to-date fool,
a stumbling fool,
an out-of-date fool,
a boorish fool,
a hard-swotting fool,
a gallant fool,
a luxurious fool,
a quick-footed fool,
a figurative fool,
a protective fool,
a hooded fool,
a full-cut fool,
a Damascus-bladed fool,
an arabesqued fool,
a Persian-pursed fool,
a farting fool,
a speckled fool,
a proven fool.

PANTAGRUEL: If the Romans were right in calling their Quirinalia the "Festival of Fools," here in France we could quite properly start the Tribouletinals.

PANURGE: If fools, like horses, all wore cruppers, their buttocks would be worn bare.

PANTAGRUEL: If Triboulet were the god Fatuous, the prophetess Fatuella's husband, his father would be Goodgod and his grandmother Goodgoddess.

PANURGE: If all the fools went walking, he'd win in a walk, even though his legs are crooked. Let's go to him right away. He'll give us some handsome solution, I know he will.

"I've got to go to Bridlegoose's hearing," said Pantagruel. "But while I go to Mirelingua, on the other side of the Loire, I'll send Carpalim to Blois to fetch Triboulet here."

When Carpalim had gone off on his errand, Pantagruel and his entire establishment—Panurge, Epistemon, Powerbrain, Brother John, Gymnast, Rootgatherer, and others—took the road to Mirelingua.

Chapter Thirty-nine ⁄⁄ How Pantagruel Attended the Hearing of Judge Bridlegoose, Who Decided Cases by Rolling Dice

The next day, at the appointed time, Pantagruel arrived in Mirelingua. The chief judge, magistrates, and other members of the court asked him to join in hearing what Bridlegoose had to say about his rulings, in the matter of a judgment against a certain Toucheronde, a magistrate, which judgment did not seem to the high court to be entirely equitable.

Pantagruel went with them willingly, finding Bridlegoose already seated where, ordinarily, the judges would seat themselves: his only explanation for so placing himself was that he'd grown old and could not see as well as once he could, noting assorted aches and pains that age usually brought with it, as cited in *not. per Archid. D. lxxxvi, C. tanta.* Which was why he could no longer see the points of the dice as clearly as he used to. That might well have been why Isaac, old and shortsighted, mistook Jacob for Esau—and why, in the case at issue, he himself had mistaken a four for a five, especially since in that proceeding he had used his small dice. He reminded them that, by law, natural imperfections could not be considered criminal, as it was plain from *ff. de re milit. l. qui cumuno, ff. de reg. jur. l. fere ff. de edil. ed. per totum, ff. de term. mo. l. Divus Adrianus resolu. per Lud. Ro. in l. si vero, ff. solu. matri.* Anyone who thought differently would not be accusing the man in question, but nature itself, as was clear *in l. maximum vitium. C. de lib. praeter.*

"My friend," asked Trinquamelle, the chief judge, "what dice are you talking about?"

"The decision-making dice," answered Bridlegoose, *"alea judiciorum,* as it is written in *Doct. 26. q. ii. c. Sors l. nec emptio. ff. de contrab. empt. l. quod debetur. ff. de pecul. et ibbi Barthol.,* which you learned gentlemen ordinarily employ here in your right honorable court, as do all other judges, according to D. Henr. Ferrandat, *et no. gl. in c. fin. de sortil. et l. sed cum ambo. ff. de judi.* And *Ubi doct.* notes that chance is very good, respectable, useful, and indeed necessary in making one's way through all the disagreements and disputes involved in any lawsuit. For an even clearer reference, consult Bal., Bart., and Alex. *C. communia de l. Si duo.*"

"Now," said Trinquamelle, "just what is it you do, my friend?"

"I will answer briefly," replied Bridlegoose, "as indicated by *l. ampliorem, sec. in refutatoriis. C. de appella.,* and as stated in *Gl. l. j. ff. quod met cau. Gaudent brevitate moderni,* We moderns are fond of brevity. What I do is exactly what you do, gentlemen, and as judges in general do, to whom our laws require us to defer: *ut no. extra. de consuet. c. ex literis, et ibi Innoc.* First I make sure I have carefully seen, reseen, gleaned, regleaned, combed through and skimmed the complaints, motions for adjournment, summonses, charges, inquiries, pretrial pleadings, factual documentation, legal citations, allegations, defenses, demands, counterdemands, replies, duplicates, triplicates, records, challenges, legal arguments, exceptions, redeterminations, evidentiary statements and restatements, accusations, motions to change venue, official letters, demands for official copies, motions to disqualify, orders to show cause, jurisdictional challenges, allegations of conflict of interest, motions to transfer to another court, statement of conclusions, summaries of motions pending, requests for appointments, appeals, admissions, sheriffs' reports, and all the other sweets and spices emanating from one side or the other, as to be sure the good judge must always do: see *no. Spec. de ordinario sec. iii et tit. de offi. omn. ju. sec. fi. et de rescriptis praesenta, sec. i.*

"Then I push all the defendant's sacks of paper off to one end of my desk and assign him the first throw of my dice, just as you do, gentlemen: as in *not. l. Favorabiliores ff. de reg. jur. et in c. cum sunt eod. tit. lib. vi,* which says: *Cum sunt partium jura obscura, reo favendum est potius quam actori,* When it's not clear what the rights of the parties are, it is necessary to favor the defendant over the plaintiff. Having done this, I also push aside the plaintiff's sacks of paper, just as you gentlemen do, though of course to the opposite end of my desk, *visum visu,* facing each other. Because *opposita juxta se posita magis elucescunt,* When opposing things are set against one another, they become easier to understand, *ut not. in l. i sec. videamus, ff. de his qui sunt sui vel alie. jur. et in l. munerun. i mixta ff. de muner. et honor.* In the same way, and at the same time, I throw the dice for him, too."

"But my friend," asked Trinquamelle, "how do you deal with the vague claims put forward by the parties to the action?"

"Just as you do, gentlemen," answered Bridlegoose, "that is, by determining which of the parties has brought in a larger sack of papers. And then I rely on my small dice, as you do, gentlemen, in observance of the law *Semper in stipulationibus, ff. de reg. jur.,* and that law written out in versified capital letters, *q. eod. tit.:*

> *Semper in obscuris quod minimum est sequimur,*
> In uncertain matters, always strive for minimal consequences,

as accepted into canon law *in c. in obscuris eod. tit. lib. vi.*

"And I have some other nice fat dice, which I use, as you gentlemen do, when the case is clearer—that is, when there's less in the sacks."

"And when you've done that, my friend," asked Trinquamelle, "how do you make your decision?"

"Just as you do, gentlemen," answered Bridlegoose. "I give judgment in favor of whichever party is first awarded it by a throw of the judicial, tribunal, praetorial dice. This is what our laws require: *ff. qui p. in pig. l. potior. leg. creditor. C. de consul., l. i. Et de reg. jur. in vi. Qui prior est tempore potior est jure,* The law is favorable to the person who gets there first."

Chapter Forty // Bridlegoose Explains Why He Reviewed Cases That He Then Decided by Throwing Dice

"Yes, indeed," asked Trinquamelle. "But, my good friend, since you made your decisions by throwing dice, why not let chance make this decision on the very day when the opposing parties appear before you, without any delay? Of what use to you are the pleadings and other documents in the sacks?"

"Just as to you, gentlemen," answered Bridlegoose, "they have three exquisite, requisite, and authentic uses.

"First of all, as a matter of form, since when form is neglected whatever is done is worthless; this is very well proven: *Sec. tit. de instr. edi. et tit. de rescrip. praesent.* Moreover, you know better than I do that, in legal proceedings, form often prevails over content and substance. Because, *forma mutata. mutatur substantia,* change the form and you change the substance. *ff. ad exhib. l. Julianus ff. ad leg. falcid. l. Si is qui quadringenta. Et extra. de deci. c. ad audientiam, et de celebra. miss. c. in quadam.*

"Second, just as they do for you, gentlemen, these papers furnish me with honorable and healthy exercise. The late Maître Othoman Vadare, a great doctor—as you might say, *C. de comit. et archi. lib. xii*—many times told me that lack of bodily exercise is the single greatest cause of ill health and brevity of life span among you other gentlemen and all officers of justice. This was very clearly formulated, even before, by Bart., *in. l. i. C. de senten. quae pro eo quod.* Which is why, for us, too, just as for you gentlemen, *quia accessorium naturam sequitur principalis,* the subordinate should do as his principal does: *de reg. jur. lib. vi. et l. cum principalis, et l. nihil dolo. ff. eod. titu. ff. de fide jusso. l. fidejussor. et extra de offic. de leg. c. i,* and certain honest and recreational games are allowable, *ff. de al. lus. et aleat. l. solent. et autent. ut omnes obediant, in princ. coll. vii et ff. de praescript. verb. l. si gratuitam et l. j. C. de spect. lib. xi.* And this is also the opinion of Saint Thomas Aquinas, *in secunda secundae quaest. clxviii,* very well formulated also by A. Alber. de Ros., who *fuit magnus practicus,* was a great practitioner and an impressive scholar, which is attested by Barbatia *in prin. consil.* The logic is explained *per gl. praemio. ff. sec. ne autem tertii:*

> *Interpone tuis interdum gaudia curis,*
> From time to time, mix some pleasures in with your cares.

"And indeed, one day in the year 1489, having some fiscal business to attend to in the chambers of the excise magistrates, which I entered courtesy the paid permission of the bailiff—for as you gentlemen know, *pecuniae obediunt omnia,* everyone listens when money talks, and as Bald. has said *in l. Singularia ff. si certum pet. et Salic. in l. recepticia. C. de constit. pecun. et Card. in Ble. j. de baptis.*—I found all the judges playing chase-the-fly, a singularly healthy exercise, whether indulged in before or after meals, it doesn't matter to me, provided that *hic no.,* note well, that it's indeed an honest, healthy, old-fashioned, and completely legal game of chase-the-fly, *a Musco inventore de quo. C. de petit. haered. l. si post motam. et Muscarii i.* Players of chase-the-fly are excusable by law: *l. i. C. de excus. artif. lib. x.* And that day the fly was Maître Tielman Piquet, I well remember, who was laughing at all the other judges for ruining their caps, swinging them so hard as they banged them on his shoulders. He warned them that, legal or not, they wouldn't find ruining their caps very readily excused, when they came home from court and presented themselves to their wives, because *c. j. extra de praesump. et ibi gl.* Now, *resolutorie loquendo,* let's speak decisively, and I would say, as surely you would, gentlemen, that there's no exercise, or anything in this lofty legal world we inhabit that makes you more aromatic, than emptying out sacks of pleadings and documents, looking through papers, busying yourself with copybooks, filling baskets, and reviewing cases, *ex Bart. et Jo. de Pra. in l. falsa. de condit. et demon. ff.*

"Third, just as you do, gentlemen, I believe that time ripens everything; time makes everything clear; time is the father of truth, *gl. in l. i. C. de servit. Autent, de restit. et ea quae pa. et Spec. tit. de requis. cons.* Which is why, exactly like you gentlemen, I postpone, delay, and defer my judgment until the case, thoroughly ventilated, winnowed, and debated, over a period of time comes to its maturity, and however the decision of the dice may go, it is more readily endured by those who must suffer its consequences, as *no. glo. ff. de execu. tut. l. Tria onera:*

Portatur leviter, quod portat quisque libenter,
One bears lightly what one bears willingly.

Were I to decide the case when it was unripened, green, and barely begun, there would be a danger of exactly the same problem doctors find when they puncture an abscess before it has ripened, or when they purge the human body of some harmful humor before it has been fully assimilated. Because, as it is written *in Autent, haec constit. in Inno. const. prin.,* and repeated in *gl. in c. Caeterum. extra de jura. calum.:*

Quod medicamenta morbis exhibent, hoc jura negotiis,
What medicines do for the sick, legal judgments do for business.

Besides, nature teaches us to pick and eat fruits when they're ripe, *Instit. de re. di sec. is ad quem, et ff. de acti. empt. l. Julianus,* and to marry off our daughters when they're ripe, *ff. de donat. int. vir. et uxo. l. cum hic status, sec. si quis sponsa. et 27, q. i. c. Sicut,* known as *gl.:*

Jam matura thoris plenis adoleverat annis
Virginitas,

Virginity, already ripe in years, was ready
For the marriage bed,

and nothing should be done before things are well matured, *xxiii q. ii. sec. ult.,* and *xxxiii. d. c. ult."*

Chapter Forty-one // Bridlegoose's Story of the Man Who Settled Lawsuits

"**W**hich reminds me," said Bridlegoose, continuing, "that once, when I was a law student at Poitiers, under Professor Legal Axioms, there lived near Semarve an honorable man named Peter Fat-head, a good worker, who sang quite acceptably in the church choir—a man with a fine reputation and about the age of most of you gentlemen, who was said to have seen with his own eyes that great man Lateran Council, wearing his huge red hat, and also his wife, that grand lady Pragmatic Sanction, with her wide blue-green satin ribbon and her huge jade prayer beads.

"This good man settled more lawsuits than were ever cleared up in all the courts of Poitiers, by the Montmorillon tribunal, or in the town hall at Old Parthenay: he was famous all through the neighborhood. At Chauvigny, Nouaillé, Croutelles, Esgne, Ligugé, La Motte, Lusignan,

Vivonne, Mezeaulx, Estables, and towns around the outskirts, every argument, lawsuit, and dispute was settled by him just as if he'd been a sovereign judge, though he was no judge at all, but simply a good man: *Arg. in l. sed si unius. ff. de jureju. et de verb. oblig. l. continuus.* No one killed a pig anywhere in the neighborhood without him getting some of the chops and the sausages. Almost every single day he was at some banquet, some wedding feast, or a baptism, a woman's churching after she'd had a baby, or at the tavern—settling something, mind you, because he never got the parties together without getting them to have a drink, as a symbol of reconciliation and complete agreement and newfound joy: *ut no. per doct. ff. de peri. et comm. rei vend. l. i.*

"He had a son called Stevie Fat-head, a strapping fellow and a gentleman, so help me God, who also wanted to get involved in settling lawsuits, because as you know

> *Saepe solet similis filius esse patri,*
> *Et sequitur leviter filia matris iter,*

> Sons are often like their fathers,
> And daughters take after their mothers,

ut ait gl. vi. q. i. c.: Si quis; gl. de cons.; d. v., c. i. fi.; et est no. per doct., C. de impu., et aliis. subst., l. ult. et l. legitimae, ff. de stat. hom., gl. in l. quod si nolit., ff. de edit. ed., l. quis, C. ad le. Jul. majest. Excipio filios a moniali susceptos ex monacho, per gl. in c. Impudicas, xxvii q. i. So that was what he called himself: settler of lawsuits.

"And he was so active and watchful in this business, since *vigilantibus jura subveniunt,* the laws help those who are vigilant, *ex. l. pupillus, ff. quae in fraud. cred., et ibid. l. non enim, et Instit. in proaemio,* that as soon as he heard about anything *(ut ff. si quad. pau. fec., l. Agaso. gl. in verbo olfecit, i. nasum ad culum posuit),* and heard anywhere in that region of any sort of argument or lawsuit, he came running to settle things between the parties. It is written:

> *Qui non laborat non manige ducat,*
> He who does not work, won't be in charge of the household,

and it's also said *gl. ff. de dam. infect., l. quamvis,* and *Currere,* at a pace faster than a trot, *vetulam compellit egestas,* need compelling the old woman, *gl. ff. lib. agnos., l. Si quis. Pro qua facit, l. si plures, C. de cond. incer.* But he was so unlucky at the business that he never settled anything, not even the smallest one you could ever think of. Not only didn't he settle these disputes; he stirred things up and made them worse. You understand, gentlemen, that

Sermo datur cunctis, animi sapientia paucis,
Everyone knows how to talk, but not many are wise,

gl. ff. de alie., ju. mu. caus. fa., l. ii. And the tavern keepers of Semarve all said that, under him, they hadn't sold as much settlement wine (which was what they'd come to call the good wine of Ligugé) in a whole year as, under his father, they'd sold in half an hour.

"It happened that he complained to his father, attributing his problems to the corrupt state of his contemporaries, telling him without any hesitation that if, in former times, the world had been as corrupt, litigious, unrestrained, and unappeasable, he—that is, his father—would never have won himself either the honor or the title of unbeatable settler of lawsuits, as he of course had done. In speaking this way, Stevie broke the law, which forbids children to reproach their fathers, *per gl. et Bar., l. iii sec. si quis. ff. de condi. ob caus. et Autent. de nup., sec sed quod sancitum coll. iiii.*

" 'Well,' replied Father Fat-head, 'you've got to do it differently, Stevie, my son. Now,

> Necessity being the royal king,
> You play his game in everything,

gl. C. de appell. l. eos etiam. And that's the gist of the matter, right there. You never settle any disputes: why? You take them up when they're just starting, when they're still green and raw. I settle everything: why? I take them up at the end, when they're nice and ripe, when they're good and mature. Which is what *gl.* says:

> *Dulcior est fructus post multa pericula ductus,*
> Ripe fruit tastes better when it's been risky getting to eat it,

l. non moriturus, C. de contrah. et comit. stip. Don't you know that old proverb about the happiest doctor being the one who gets called when the sickness is at its end? Sickness comes to a head and starts to wind down, whether the doctor's called or not. My litigants did the same thing, winding down toward the end of their case, because they'd emptied their purses; they'd stopped pushing and shoving: they had no more money to push and shove with:

> *Deficiente pecu, deficit omne, nia,*
> When you're short of money, you're short of everything.

" 'All they needed was someone to be their facilitator, their mediator, someone who'd be the first to start talking about settling, to keep both sides from having to suffer that horrible sense of shame, the feeling that goes with: "Oh, him, he was the first to give up; he was the one who started talking about settlement; he was the first to grow weary; the law really wasn't on his side; he felt the shoe really pinching." Stevie, that's right where I came in, Johnny-on-the-spot, just like bacon in peas. That was my hour. That was all the leverage I needed. That, in a word, was my good-luck time. And let me tell you, Stevie, my fine boy, using this method I could make peace, or at least a truce, between the king of France and the Venetians, between the emperor and the Swiss, between the English and the Scots, between the pope and the citizens of Ferrara. Should I venture still further? By God, if He'd help me, I could make peace between the Turks and the Persians—even between the Tartars and the Musco-vites.

" 'Now listen carefully. I'd get them right at the moment when they were both tired of fighting, when they'd emptied their treasure chests, when they'd squeezed every cent they could get out of their subjects, when they'd sold off their kingdom, mortgaged their land, eaten every-thing in their larder, and used up all their war supplies. Then, by God—or by His Mother—whether they like it or not, they have to stop and take a breath, they have to moderate their wickedness. And that's the doctrine taught *in gl. XXXVIII d. c. Si quando:*

> *Odero si potero, si non, invitus amabo,*
> I'll hate if I can, but if I can't, I'll love in spite of myself.' "

Chapter Forty-two ⁄ How Lawsuits Are Born, and How They Reach Perfection

"And that's why," said Bridlegoose, going on, "I temporize, just as you do, gentlemen, waiting for the lawsuit to mature, to be perfect in all its parts: I mean its writings and sacks of documents. *Arg. in l. si major., C. commu. divi. et de cons., d. i., c. Solennitates, et ibi gl.*

"When it's first born, a lawsuit seems to me, as it does to you, gentle-men, shapeless and imperfect. Just as a newborn bear has neither feet nor hands, skin, hair, nor head, but is just a piece of crude and formless flesh. But because of the milk it imbibes, the bear perfects all its parts, *ut no. doct. ff. ad leg. Aquil. l. ii in fi.* And so I watch, as you do, gentlemen, as lawsuits are born, starting off shapeless and without distinct parts. All they have is a document or two, so at that point they're ugly beasts at best. But once they've well and properly piled up, gotten themselves nicely framed and filled their sacks, we can truly speak ·of them as well formed and with proper parts. Because *forma dat esse rei,* Form gives things their existence. *l. si is qui. ff. ad leg. falci in c. cum dilecta extra de rescrip. Barbatia consil. 12 lib. 2,* and before him *Bald., in c. ulti. extra de consue. et l. Julianus. ff. ad exhib. et l. quaestium. ff. de lega. iii.* The procedure is described in *gl. p. q. i. c. Paulus:*

> *Debile principium melior fortuna sequetur,*
> Weak beginnings are followed by better fortune.

"As you do, gentlemen, and also the barristers, bailiffs, underbailiffs, barrators, attorneys, commissioners, advocates, investigators, notaries, notaries public, clerks, and the lower-court judges, *de quibus tit. est lib. iii. Cod.,* we all suck powerfully and unremittingly at the parties' purses, thus creating in their lawsuits heads, feet, claws, noses, teeth, hands, veins, arteries, nerves, muscles, and emotions. These are the sacks of documents, *gl. de cons. d. iiii c. accepisti.*

> *Qualis vestis erit, talia corda gerit,*
> This will be the costume, this the heart.

Hic no., note here, that in this respect the parties are happier than those who administer justice, because

> *Beatius est dare quam accipere,*
> It is more blessed to give than to receive,

ff. comm. l. iii et extra de celebra. Miss. c. cum Martha. et 24. q. i. c. Odi. gl.:

> *Affectum dantis pensat censura tonantis,*
> He who sends forth thunder considers the minds and hearts of
>   those who give.

And so the lawsuit becomes perfected, elegant, well formed, as it is said in *gl. can.:*

> *Accipe, sume, cape sunt verba placentia papae,*
> Receive, accept, take: these are words the pope likes to hear.

Alberic de Rosata says this even more clearly, *in verb. Roma.:*

> *Roma manus rodit, quas rodere non valet, odit.*
> *Dantes custodit, non dantes spernit et odit,*
>
> Rome gnaws on hands, but hates the hands it cannot reach.
> Feed it, and it loves and takes care; ignore it, and it turns away.

And why?

Ad praesens ova, cras pullis sunt meliora,
Today's eggs are better than yesterday's chickens,

ut est glo. in l. quum hi. ff. de transac. The disadvantages of not proceeding in this way are set out *in gl. C. de allu. l. fi.:*

Cum labor in damno est, crescit mortalis egestas,
If your work doesn't work, your needs increase.

"The true etymology of 'lawsuit' lies in its requiring all the work and care that go into filling up those sacks of documents. We have a wonderful legal saying:

Litigando jura crescunt,
Litigando jus acquiritur,

Lawsuits swell the law,
Lawsuits enrich the law.

"*Item gl. in c. Illus ext. de praesumpt. et C. de prob. l. instrumenta. l. non epistolis. l. non nudis,*

Et cum non prosunt singula, multa juvant,
If individual effort won't do it, concerted effort can."

"Indeed," replied Trinquamelle, "but, my friend, how do you proceed in a criminal action, if the guilty party has been caught *flagrante crimine,* in the very act?"

"Just as you gentlemen do," answered Bridlegoose. "I permit, and require, that the complainant have a good sound sleep, before any legal action is taken, then appear before me, bringing me good and sufficient proof of his having slept, according to *gl. 32. q. vii. c. Si quis cum,*

Quandoque bonus dormitat Homerus,
From time to time, even good Homer nods.

"And this act creates another, and from that yet another is born, just as link by link a coat of armor takes shape. And then finally the whole proceeding seems to me to have been sufficiently filled out with documentation so that it has become distinct and perfected in its parts. And then I return to my dice. Nor do I ensure the insertion of that certificate of sleep without good reason, based on sound experience.

"I well remember how, camped just outside of Stockholm, a Gascon named Gratianauld, from Saint-Sever, had gambled away all his money and was in a wild fury about it, as you understand, since *pecunia est alter sanguis,* money is like another bloodstream, *ut ait Anto. de Butrio. in c. accedens. ii extra ut lit. non contest,* and also *Bald. in l. si tuis. C. de op. li. per no. et l. advocati C. de advo, diu jud. Pecunia est vita hominis et optimus fidejussor in necessitatibus,* Money is man's life, and his best surety in need. When he got out of the gambling hall, right there in front of all his companions, he shouted:

" 'By a bull's big head, fellows, may you get so drunk you can't stand up! Now that I've lost every damned cent I had, I ought to beat and kick and bang the devil out of you. Anyone here want to get in the ring with me?'

"No one answered, so he went on to the Germans' camp, and issued the same challenge, inviting them to come out and fight with him. But they just said:

" '*Der Guascongner thut scich usz mitt jedem ze schlagen, aber er ist geneigter zu staelen; darumb, lieben frauuen, hend serg zu inuerm haustrat.*'

(" 'This Gascon fellow thinks he wants to fight with one of us, but he's more interested in stealing; so, my dear ladies, keep your eyes on our baggage.')

"So no one in their group offered to fight with him. Accordingly, the Gascon went on to the French mercenaries' camp, saying the same things and gallantly offering to fight them, decorating his challenge with some typical Gasconesque leaps and flourishes. But no one answered him. And being at the outer edge of the camp, the Gascon lay down near fat Christian's tent, who was a knight from Angevin, and he fell asleep.

"Suddenly one of the mercenaries, who had also lost all his money, came out, sword in hand, determined to fight with the Gascon, since he too was now penniless:

> *Ploratur lachrymis amissa pecunia veris,*
> You weep real tears over money you've lost,

as it is said in *glos. de paenitent. dist. 3, c. sunt plures.* In fact, having looked for the Gascon all over the camp, he finally found him, asleep. So he said to him, 'Hey, you son of all the devils! Wake up. I've lost all my money, too, just the way you did. Let's have ourselves a good fight and really bang at each other. I can see my sword's no longer than yours.'

"Dazed, the Gascon answered, 'By Saint Arnaud's head, who are you, waking me up like this? May you get so drunk you can't stand up! By Saint Sever, patron of all Gascony, I was having such a nice sleep when this came bothering me!' The mercenary offered to fight him, then and there, but the Gascon said, 'Hey, my poor friend, I'll beat the hell out of you, now that I've had a good rest. But come on, you take a little snooze, too, and then we can fight.' He'd forgotten what he'd lost, and so he'd lost all interest in fighting. To make a long story short, instead of fighting, and maybe getting killed, they went off to drink together, both of them having hocked their swords. It was sleep that accomplished this good deed, calming the wild anger of these two good champions. The golden words of *Joan. And.* are applicable, here, *in c. ult. de sent. et re judic. libro sexto:*

> *Sedendo et quiescendo fit anima prudens,*
> Rest and repose make the spirit wise."

Chapter Forty-three ⁄ How Pantagruel Justified Bridlegoose for Deciding Cases by Throwing Dice

And then Bridlegoose fell silent. Trinquamelle directed him to leave the courtroom, and this was done. Then he said to Pantagruel:

"It would be right, O august Prince, that you yourself make the decision in this exceedingly novel matter, so paradoxical and strange, in which Bridlegoose, in your very presence, with you seeing and hearing him, has confessed to judging cases by the throwing of dice. It would be right, I say, not simply because of the debt owed you by this court and indeed by all of Mirelingua, for all the infinite kindnesses shown us, but also because of the good sense, discreet judgment, and admirable views which the Lord almighty, giver of all good things, has reposed in you. Accordingly, we beg you to pass such sentence as may seem to you fair and just."

To which Pantagruel answered:

"Gentlemen, deciding lawsuits is not my profession, as you well know. But since it pleases you to show me this honor, rather than acting like a judge I will assume the role of a suppliant.

"I recognize in Bridlegoose several characteristics which, to my mind, make him worthy of a pardon. First of all, old age; second, simplicity, which as you understand far better than I do, our laws acknowledge as good reason for pardoning and forgiving misdeeds. Third, I recognize yet another circumstance, equally clearly set out in our laws, which favors a pardon for Bridlegoose, and that is that this one failing must be disregarded, extinguished, and subsumed in the vast sea of just decisions which he has rendered in the past—decisions which, for forty years or more, have never once seen him do anything that required that he be reproved. It's as if I threw a drop of seawater into the Loire River: no one would be aware of this unique drop, no one would call the water salty.

"And it strikes me that there is some unknown something here, emanating from God Himself, which has ensured and arranged it that these chance judgments should all have seemed good and proper to your venerable and sovereign court—and God, as you know, often likes to have

His glory appear by means of the confounding of wise men, the abasement of the powerful, and in the elevation of the simple and humble.

"But let me put all these considerations aside. I beg you to grant him a pardon, not because of any obligation to my family, for I do not admit any such obligation, but because of the sincere affection in which your court has for many long years been held by all of us, on both sides of the Loire, for its long-preserved standards and its dignity. I ask this of you on two grounds: first, he must give satisfaction, or promise to give satisfaction, to the party injured by the judgment here in question; on this score, I undertake to guarantee that it will be well and properly done. Second, in order to assist him in his official duties, that you assign him someone younger, more learned, more discreet, more knowing, some virtuous counselor whose advice, in the future, he will be able to depend upon in the execution of his judicial office.

"And in case you decide that he must be suspended from office, I beg you to give him to me, as a gift and present. I will find enough for him to do, in my own realms, in order to keep him employed in my service. And so I pray that our God and Creator, conserver and maker of all good things, keep you all forever in His holy grace."

Having spoken these words, Pantagruel bowed to the entire court and then left the chamber. At the door he found Panurge, Epistemon, Brother John, and the others. They mounted their horses and prepared to ride back to where they had left Gargantua.

Along the way, Pantagruel told them, blow by blow, the whole story of Bridlegoose's trial. Brother John said he had known Peter Fat-head, back in the days when he'd lived at Fontaine-le-Comte, near Poitiers, under the noble abbot Ardillon. Gymnast said he'd been in fat Christian's tent, the knight from Angevin, when the Gascon fellow had replied to the mercenary. Panurge had difficulty understanding how judgments framed by a toss of the dice had been such good ones, especially over so long a time. Epistemon said to Pantagruel:

"A very similar story is told of a provost in Montlhéry. But what can you say about the excellent results of his dice throwing, over so many years? I wouldn't be surprised at one or two judgments, decided by chance, particularly in such ambiguous matters, so full of entanglements, perplexities, and obscurities."

Chapter Forty-four / Pantagruel Tells a Strange Story About the Perplexities of Human Judgment

"So too," said Pantagruel, "the controversy argued in front of Cneius Dolabella, proconsul in Asia. This was the situation:

"A woman in Smyrna had a son, named A.B.C., by her first husband. That husband having died, after a certain time she remarried and had another son, named E.F.G., by her second husband. As it happened (for, as you know, it's rare for stepfathers and stepmothers to have much fondness for the children of deceased fathers and mothers), this second husband and his son secretly, and with clear criminal intent, murdered A.B.C.

"Understanding this treacherous wickedness, the woman refused to permit them to remain unpunished and murdered them both, thus avenging the death of her first son. She was arrested and brought before Cneius Dolabella. And in his presence she confessed, concealing nothing; her only defense was that she had killed them rightfully and with good cause. So: that was where matters stood.

"The proconsul found the case so ambiguous that he did not know which way to lean. The woman's crime was immense, since she had killed her husband and her second son. But her reason for murdering them seemed so completely natural and understandable to him, and so plainly founded in the common law, since they had killed her first son, conspiring together, secretly and feloniously, though that first son had in no way offended against or injured them, and they were motivated solely by a greedy desire to monopolize the entire inheritance, that instead of deciding the case himself he consulted the great court of Areopagus, in Athens, to see what those eminent judges would advise.

"The response came back as follows: the opposing parties were directed to make a personal appearance before the court of Areopagus, but only after an interval of one hundred years, so that they could answer certain questions that were not dealt with in the written record. Which was to say that the case seemed to them so perplexing, so obscure, that they knew neither what to say nor how to decide it.

"Had the case been decided by throwing dice, it would not have been wrongfully handled, no matter what the decision: had it gone against the woman, she certainly deserved punishment, since she had taken vengeance into her own hands, though it was a matter for public justice; and had it been decided for the woman, she had the justification of having suffered horribly.

"All the same, that Bridlegoose could have kept it up over so many years astonishes me."

"I scarcely know," replied Epistemon, "how truly to answer your question. I must admit it. Hypothetically, I might ascribe his good fortune to celestial benevolence and the kindly intentions of the moving forces of the universe. Recognizing Judge Bridlegoose's simplicity, his honest kindness, and his mistrust of his own knowledge and capabilities (knowing full well the oppositions and contradictions of our laws and edicts and customs and rulings), these forces are also keenly aware of Satan's infinite deceitfulness—how he often transforms himself into a minister of light, utilizing his ministers, who are corrupt lawyers, counselors, prosecutors, and other such henchmen—who turn black to white, making one or the other party believe, incredibly, fantastically, that the law is truly on his side (for, as you know, there is no cause so unsupportable that it does not find a lawyer to support it, since otherwise there would be no lawsuits at all). So someone like Bridlegoose, commending himself humbly to that greatest of just judges, God, invoking heavenly grace to assist him, might in a spirit of sanctity, when faced with the risks and perplexities of finding a fixed and final judgment, abandon himself to pure chance, seeking to determine His decree and His wishes (which we call judgment). Those moving forces would then turn and move the dice so they favored whoever, furnished with a just complaint, ought in the name of justice to be sustained in law, for as the talmudic scholars who practiced the same arts used to say, there was nothing wrong with deciding matters strictly by chance, since we might be anxious and uncertain about what humans might decree, but chance would manifest the divine will.

"I wouldn't want to think or claim, and I certainly don't believe, that those who enforce the law in this Mirelinguan high court are so flagrantly evil and corrupt that a case couldn't be worse decided, if determined simply by a throw of the dice, no matter what they decreed, than if it passed through judicial hands stained with blood and perverse states of mind. And remember, in particular, that all their juridical guidance was given them by someone like Tribonian, a thoroughly wicked man, an infidel, a barbarian, so evil, so perverse, so greedy and foul that he sold laws and edicts, decrees, briefs, and rulings, cash down, to whoever offered the highest price. Which was how he chopped it all up for them, in little bits and pieces, and how we came to have the laws we now have, for he suppressed and did away with the rest, which comprised the whole law, being afraid that since that whole and entire law, along with all the books of the ancient jurists, relied on the exposition of the Twelve Laws of Moses and the edicts of its preachers and expounders, if it were ever brought into the open his wickedness would be clearly and unmistakably recognized.

"Which is why it might indeed be better, often (that is to say, at least less bad), for the opposing parties to walk through rows of sharp spikes implanted in the earth than to abandon themselves to the law, in order to preserve their rights. Indeed, Cato suggested that the courts of law of his day might usefully be paved with such spikes."

Chapter Forty-five // How Panurge Consulted Triboulet

Six days later, Pantagruel returned home just as Triboulet, traveling by water, arrived from Blois. To welcome the fool, Panurge gave him a fully inflated pork bladder, which rattled from the dried peas inside it; plus a nicely gilded wooden sword; plus a little turtle-shell purse; plus a demijohn of Breton wine and a basket of Blandureau apples.

"Lord!" said Carpalim. "Is he as crazy as a head of cabbage?"

Triboulet buckled on his new wooden sword, hung his new purse from his belt, snatched up the pork bladder, ate part of the basket of apples, and drank all the wine. Panurge, watching with interest, said:

"I've never yet seen a fool—and I've seen lots of them, more than ten thousand francs' worth—who didn't gulp down his liquor in long swallows."

Then he explained his problem, in lofty and elaborate terms.

Before he'd finished, Triboulet whacked him in the small of his back with his fist, handed him back the empty bottle, rapped him on the nose with the pig's bladder, and—his only verbal response—stood there shaking his head, and said:

"By God, oh, God, you wild fool, watch out for the monk! Hey, Buzançais bagpipes!"

Having said this, he left them and played with the pig's bladder, amusing himself with the melodious sound of the dried peas. They couldn't get another word out of him. When Panurge tried to question him further, Triboulet drew his wooden sword and tried to strike him.

"We've been well and truly hornswoggled!" said Panurge. "What a magnificent response. He's a genuine fool, you can't deny it, but he who brought him to me is a worse fool, and I'm a colossal fool myself, trying to tell him what's on my mind."

"That remark," said Carpalim, "is aimed right at me."

"Let's not get upset," said Pantagruel. "Let's think about exactly what he did and what he said. I find certain mysterious symbols in all of this—so striking, indeed, that I'm not astonished, recalling how the Turks revere these fools as seers and prophets. Did you notice, before he opened his mouth to speak, how his head shook from side to side? According to the beliefs of the ancient philosophers, and the rituals of the magis, and the comments of the legal scholars, we should understand that this movement was created by the onrushing prophetic spirit, sharply breaking over a slender, fragile substance (and, of course, there can't be a large brain, in such a small skull). It's exactly the way doctors tell us that trembling usually overcomes the limbs—that is, in part because of the weight and sudden force of the burden assumed, in part because of the body's inherent weakness, and the feebleness, too, of the organ receiving the blow.

"A clear illustration is those who, while fasting, cannot carry a large glass of wine without their hands trembling. The Pythian prophetess was another plain example: before her oracular responses, she would shake her household laurel. And Lampridius tells us that the emperor Heliogabalus, wanting to be thought a divine prophet, would appear among his devoted eunuchs, at public celebrations of his great idol, shaking his head from side to side. So Plautus says, in his *Asinaria,* that Saurias walked along, shaking his head as if wildly out of his mind, terrifying everyone he met. Moreover, explaining why Charmides shook his head, he says that it was caused by an ecstatic fit.

"So says Catullus, too, in *Berecynthia and Atys,* describing the place where the Maenads, those Bacchic priestesses and powerful prophetesses, carry their ivy branches and shake their heads, like the castrated priests of Cybele, celebrating their rites. At least so the old theologians tell us, for the Greek word they use means to turn and twist, shaking the head while keeping the neck stiff.

"And Livy writes that, at Rome's bacchanals, shaking and other wild movements of the body seemed to make both men and women prophesy. Philosophers all believed, as did the common people, that the heavens would not bestow the gift of divination without an accompanying wildness and shaking of the body, a trembling and quivering all over—and not simply when divine insight was received, but also when it was made known and declared.

"Indeed, that distinguished legal scholar Julian, when asked if a slave could be considered sane, who as a member of a group of wild, fanatic people had probably uttered prophecies but had never exhibited that shaking of his head, answered that yes, he should be considered sane. So nowadays we see teachers shaking the heads of their pupils (like a pot by its handles) by grabbing at their ears and pulling them—for the ears, according to the beliefs of Egypt's wise men, are the part of the body peculiarly sacred to Memory. They're trying to use good, philosophical discipline to restore them to their senses, since their minds are more than likely distracted by strange thoughts and wandering far from the subjects at hand. Virgil admits this was certainly true of him, when he was given a good shaking by Apollo of Cynthius."

Chapter Forty-six ⁄⁄ Pantagruel and Panurge's Differing Interpretations of Triboulet's Words

"He says you're a fool?" continued Pantagruel. "And what kind of fool? A wild one, since in your old age you want to tie yourself, to subject yourself, to marriage. He says to you, 'Watch out for the monk!' On my honor, it will be a monk who cuckholds you. Note: I pledge my honor, the greatest possession I could ever have, even were I the sole, unique, all-powerful, and pacific ruler of Europe, Africa, and Asia.

"Yes: I defer to our wise fool, Triboulet. The other oracles and all the other responses you've gotten have agreed that you'll be quietly cuckolded—but none of them have clearly stated with whom your wife will commit adultery. This the noble Triboulet has done. And that cuckold-ing will be notorious, tremendously scandalous. Can your marriage bed fail to be soiled and stained by monks?

"He also says that you'll be the bagpipe of Buzançais—that is, you'll be well and truly crowned with horns, and deceit, and all the rites of cuckoldry. Just as Triboulet himself, when he wanted to ask King Louis the Twelfth for the salt monopoly in Buzançais, for his brother, made a mistake and asked for a bagpipe, so you, believing you're marrying some fine, upstanding woman, will marry a woman devoid of modesty, full of the rank breath of conceit, shrill, and unpleasant—in short, exactly like a bagpipe.

"Notice, too, how he rapped you on the nose with the pig's bladder, and slapped you on the back: that indicates how you'll be beaten by her, and led around by the nose, and robbed, just as you stole that pig's blad-der from the little children at Vaubreton."

"On the contrary," answered Panurge. "Not that I could arrogantly disclaim allegiance to the kingdom of folly. I'm a loyal subject, I admit it. But the whole world is crazy. In Lorraine, even the village of Fou—or craziness—is quite sensibly located near the town of Tou—or everything. Everyone's crazy; Solomon says that the number of fools is infinite. You can't go any higher than infinity, you can't add anything—Aristotle proved that. And I'd be a wild fool, yes, if being a fool I didn't consider myself one. And that's why the number of maniacs and wild men is infinite. Avicenna says there are an infinite number of different kinds of madmen.

"But as for the rest of what Triboulet said, his other gestures: he says to my wife, not to me, 'Beware of the monk!' And he's talking about a monkey she'll take great pleasure in, as Catullus' Lesbia did—a monkey who'll spend his time catching flies just as happily as Emperor Domitian the flycatcher.

"And he also says she'll be rustic and cheerful, like a beautiful Saulien bagpipe—or perhaps one from Buzançais. That truth-telling Triboulet: he immediately recognized my natural, internal emotions. Because I can swear to you that I take far more pleasure in rumpled shepherdesses, whose asses smell of wild thyme, than I do in any high ladies at court, with their rich finery and their stinking perfumes. I prefer the sound of the rustic bagpipe to the sweet sounds of aristocratic lutes and violins.

"He gave me a good clout on the back? By the love of God, so be it, and may I feel that many fewer such blows in Purgatory! He didn't hurt me. He thought he was whacking some naughty servant. He's a good fool; he's innocent, I swear it; and anyone who thinks evil of him is a sinner. I forgive him from the bottom of my heart.

"He rapped me on the nose: these are just the kinds of little sillinesses my wife and I will practice—the sort of thing all newlyweds do."

Chapter Forty-seven ⁄⁄ How Pantagruel and Panurge Decide to Visit the Oracle of the Holy Bottle

"And here's something else you haven't taken into account. And this is really the crux of the matter. He handed me the bottle. What does that mean? What was he trying to tell me?"

"Perhaps," replied Pantagruel, "he meant that your wife will be a drunkard."

"On the contrary," said Panurge, "because the bottle was *empty*. I swear to you, on the backbone of Saint Fiacre of Brie, that our wise fool, our unique and not at all lunatic Triboulet, is simply sending me back to the bottle. So let me refurbish my original vow and, by the Styx and Acheron, and in your presence, once again swear to wear spectacles on my hat, and not to wear a codpiece on my trousers, until the Holy Bottle has spoken on this business of mine. I have a good and wise friend who knows exactly where to find her, the country and the region where she has her temple and her oracle. He'll certainly take us there. Let's all go together: please, don't abandon me. I'll be an Achates for you, a Damon, and a good friend the whole trip. I've known for a long time how much you like traveling, always wanting to see and understand everything. We'll see some fine sights, believe me!"

"Gladly!" answered Pantagruel. "But before we start on this long voyage, so full of risks and such obvious dangers . . ."

"What dangers?" said Panurge, interrupting him. "Dangers positively avoid me, wherever I am, for at least seven leagues all around—just as the magistrate no longer functions when the king is there, or shadows flee when the sun appears, or sickness runs from the body of Saint Martin of Candes."

"On that subject," said Pantagruel, "before we leave there are still some things you need to clear up for us. First, let's send Triboulet to Blois." (Which was immediately done; Pantagruel gave him a gown all embroidered with gold). "Second, we need the advice and also the consent of the king, my father. And then, we need to find some Sibyl to serve as our guide and interpreter."

Panurge answered that his friend Imported Goods would be all the assistance they'd need; besides, he'd already decided to journey through Lanternland and there find some learned and helpful Lanterner who could do for their journey what the Sibyl had done for Aeneas, when he visited the Elysian Fields. Just then Carpalim, who was going by with Triboulet, heard this and called out:

"Ho, Panurge! you totally-out-of-debt wonder: take My Lord Deputy Debtor of Calais, because he's a good fellow, he is. And don't forget to take our debtors, too—I mean, our lanterns. That way you'll have some truly worthy guides."

"I predict," said Pantagruel, "that this won't be a melancholy trip. I can see that already. The only thing bothering me is that I don't speak good Lanternese."

"But I," answered Panurge, "will speak it for all of us: I know it like my mother tongue. I'm as comfortable with Lanternese as I am with French:

> *Briszmarg d'algotbric nubstzne zos*
> *Isquebfz prusq; alborlz crinqs zacbac.*
> *Misbe dilbarlkz morp nipp stancz bos.*
> *Strombtz, Panrge walmap quost grufz bac.**

"Now just guess, Epistemon, what that means."

"It's the names," said Epistemon, "of fallen devils, crawling devils, awful devils."

"You're right, my good friend," said Panurge, "you're right. That's the high-court form of Lanternese. As we travel along, I'll compose a nice little dictionary for you, which won't last you any longer than a pair of new shoes—you'll learn the whole thing before you see the sun come up, the second day out. What I said, translated from Lanternese into French, goes like this:

> When I was a lover my luck was bad,
> And stuck to me hard. Nothing went right.
> But married men are never sad:
> Panurge is one of them, he's seen the light.

"Now all we need do," said Pantagruel, "is seek out my royal father, hear what his pleasure may be, and ask for his permission."

Chapter Forty-eight // How Gargantua Assured His Son That Marrying without the Knowledge and Consent of Your Mother and Father Was Unlawful

As Pantagruel entered the great hall of the castle, he found our good Gargantua just leaving his council chamber. He gave his father a brief summary of their adventures, told him what they proposed to do, begged him to tell them his opinion, and sought his permission to leave. Gargan-

*Gibberish.

tua was holding two large bundles, which were petitions already dealt with, and requests still to be considered: he handed them over to Ulrich Gallet, his longtime adviser in such matters. Then he drew Pantagruel to the side and, looking even happier than usual, said to him:

"I praise God, my beloved son, who keeps you on the paths of virtue: it pleases me very well that you make this voyage. But I also want you to think about marrying. It seems to me that you're easily of an age. Panurge has worked hard to get over the difficulties that might have kept him from marriage. Tell me what you think."

"My good-hearted father," said Pantagruel, "it's still not something I've thought about. In all such matters I place myself at your disposal, trusting in your goodwill and obeying your paternal commands. I would sooner see myself stone dead at your feet, having displeased you, than to be alive and married but without your consent. I've never heard of any law, sacred or profane and barbarous, which permits children to marry of their own free will, without the consent, the approval, and the active interest of their fathers, their mothers, and their near relatives. All law-makers withdraw this freedom from children and reserve it for their parents."

"O my very dear son," said Gargantua, "I believe you, and praise God for the fact that all you know are good and worthy things; nothing but humane learning has ever entered the windows of your senses and lodged in your soul. It was in my time that we discovered on this continent a country where lived who knows what mole-like priests, hating marriage like the Phrygian eunuchs of Cybele (if they truly were capons, and not in fact cocks full of lewd lustiness), who prescribed marriage laws for the people. It's hard to know which is worse, the presumptuous tyranny of these dreaded mole men, who don't limit themselves to the iron fences of their mysterious temples but intervene in affairs completely out of their knowledge and experience, or the superstitious stupidity of married men, who have sanctioned and sworn obedience to such evil, barbaric laws, not seeing (though it's clearer than the morning star) that these marital regulations work only to the advantage of their priests, neither helping nor profiting married people—and that alone should be sufficient cause for all such laws to be suspect as iniquitous and fraudulent.

"Shouldn't married people, by a reciprocal temerity, establish laws for their priests, governing all their ceremonies and sacrifices, since priests take their tithe out of married people's goods and trim whatever profit they may make from their labor and the sweat of their hands, so priestly folk can live off the fat of the land? To my mind, such regulation of priests wouldn't be nearly as depraved and extravagant as the regulations the priests themselves have imposed. Because (as you have said so well) there is no law in the world according to which children are free to marry without their fathers' knowledge, advice, and consent. According to these laws I've spoken about, there's no lewd, debauched man, no good-for-

nothing, scoundrel, rascal, or rotter, no stinking wretch, leper, thief, rob–
ber, known criminal, who can't violently ravish any girl he pleases, no
matter how noble, beautiful, rich, respectable, and modest she may be,
right out of her father's house, right out of her mother's arms, in spite of
all her relatives, if the rascal has come to an understanding with some
priest, to whom he has given a percentage of the future spoils.

"Did the Goths, the Scythians, or any barbarian people ever do anything worse, or crueler, to their long-besieged enemies, when after hard
fighting they captured their cities by force? So the miserable fathers and
mothers see some unknown stranger, barbarous, some rotten mongrel,
pox-ridden, cadaverous, poor, misfortunate, snatch right out of their houses
their exquisitely beautiful, delicate, rich, and healthy daughters, so dearly
raised in the bosom of every virtue known to man, taught the utmost
respectability—daughters they had hoped, at the proper time, to link in
marriage with the children of their neighbors and dear friends, nourished
and raised with the same care, so they too could find the joys of marriage,
from which happy union the parents would see their lineage and all their
inheritance preserved and extended, no less with respect to their ways
and ideals than to their goods and belongings and everything they could
pass on to subsequent generations. What sort of spectacle might they now
have to confront?

"No, the desolation of the Roman people, and their confederates, when
they heard of the death of Germanicus Drusus, could have been no greater.

"Nor could the sorrow of the Lacedaemonians have been any more
pitiable, when they saw the adulterous Trojan running off with Helen.

"Nor could the sorrow and weeping of Ceres have been any greater,
when her daughter Proserpina was stolen from her—or the sorrow of Isis
at the loss of Osiris—or that of Venus at the death of Adonis—or Hercules for the loss of Hylas—or Hecuba for the abduction of Polyxena.

"But the parents are so terrified by Satan, so trapped by superstition,
that they don't dare raise any opposition, since the mole-man priest was
there and made everything legal. And there in their homes, deprived of
their beloved daughters, the father curses the day and hour he himself got
married, the mother bemoans the fact that this sorrowful and unlucky
child hadn't been aborted in her womb, and so they finish their lives in
tears and lamentations, though they had rightfully expected to end them
in joy and tenderness.

"Others have been so driven out of their senses, turned into maniacs,
that in their pain and sorrow they've drowned, hanged, or in other ways
killed themselves, unable to endure the infamy.

"And others still, of more heroic spirit, filled with the example of the
children of Jacob, who took vengeance for the kidnapping of their sister
Dinah, have sought out the villain and the mole-man monk who worked
with him to secretly win over and seduce their daughters, and they've cut
them into pieces on the spot, murdering them and throwing their corpses

into the fields, for the wolves and the crows to consume. And the brotherhood of psalm-singing mole men has quivered with outrage at such manly, chivalric acts, sending up miserable lamentations, and framing fearsome complaints, clamoring and wailing to the secular arm and all the government agencies, arrogantly demanding and insisting that such things be severely punished and an example made.

"But neither in natural justice nor in the common law of nations, nor in any imperial law, is there any heading, paragraph, subject, or title setting out any punishment or torture for such a deed. Reason itself would oppose any such law; nature would find it disgusting. Because there is no virtuous man anywhere in the world who, by both reason and nature, wouldn't be deeply disturbed of mind, hearing that anyone had so kidnapped, slandered, and dishonored his daughter. Now, anyone finding a murderer in the act of killing his daughter, evilly and premeditatedly, should by reason—and surely must by nature—kill the man on the spot, and never be arrested for any crime. It's hardly miraculous that a father, finding some rascal, aided by a mole man, in the very act of seducing his daughter and stealing her out of his house (no matter that she herself was agreeable), could and indeed would have to butcher the scoundrels then and there, throwing their corpses for brute beasts to rip apart—unworthy to receive that sweet, longed-for, and final embrace of our holy Mother Earth, which goes by our word 'burial.'

"My dearest son, when I am dead make sure that no such laws are ever enacted in our realm. While I remain breathing and alive, I will take very good care of that myself, with the help of my God. And since you leave the matter of your marriage to me, I accept the responsibility and will see to it. Prepare yourself, now, for your voyage with Panurge. Take Epistemon and Brother John with you, and anyone else you choose. Take as much from my treasury as you wish: nothing you can do would displease me. Take from my naval dockyards at Thalasse any ship you like, and any pilots, navigators, interpreters you want—and when the wind is right, set sail, in the name and under the protection of God.

"While you are away, I will see to this question of your wife: there will be a wedding to celebrate, and I will make it a memorable feast, if ever there was one."

Chapter Forty-nine ⁄ How Pantagruel Got Ready to Sail, and about the Herb Called Pantagruelion

Not long after, having taken leave of Gargantua, who prayed that his son might have a safe voyage, Pantagruel arrived at the port of Thalasse, near Saint-Malo, accompanied by Panurge, Epistemon, Brother John

Mincemeat—abbot of Thélème—along with others from the royal household, notably Imported Goods, that great traveler and voyager through
perilous pathways, who had been called to come with them by his good
friend Panurge, since he held some who-knows-what fief in Panurge's
Salmagundian domain.

Once in Thalasse, Pantagruel selected the ships he would need, round-
ing up as many as, long ago, Ajax of Salamis had used to carry the Greeks
to Troy (namely, twelve). He procured and put on board pilots, barge-
men, oarsmen, interpreters, craftsmen, soldiers, provisions, guns, gunpowder, clothing, money, and other assorted baggage, as of course was
required for a long and dangerous voyage. And among other things, I
saw that he loaded on a large quantity of his herb, Pantagruelion, both
green and raw and also in its worked and finished state.

Now, Pantagruelion has a small, tough, roundish root, ending in a
conical tip, white, not very fibrous, which goes no more than about a
foot and a half deep. One single stalk grows from this root, round, somewhat resembling fennel, green on the outside and whitish inside, con-
cave—like the stalk of *smyrnium, olus-atrum,* beans, and gentian. It's a
woody, stringy plant, straight, brittle, notched a bit as if it had lightly
grooved columns, very fibrous—indeed, all the lofty dignity of the herb
consists of these fibers, especially in that part known as *mesa,* or middle,
and in the part called *mylasea.* Generally speaking, the stem grows to a
height of five or six feet. Occasionally it grows to be taller than a knight's
spear, when it finds itself in a mild soil, damp, light, warm, like that of
Les Sables-d'Olonne and that of Rosea, near Praeneste, in Sabinia, where
there's no shortage of rain in the early days of June and the summer solstice. It can grow taller than a tree, under such circumstances (Theophrastus then calls it *dendromalache,* or herb tree), though it remains an annual,
not a rooted tree with an enduring trunk and branches. Large, strong
branches grow from its stem.

Its leaves are three times as long as they are wide, always green, rough
like the leaves of the red alkanet, tough, notched all around like a sickle
or the water betony, ending in points like the Macedonian spear plant or
a surgeon's lancet. These leaves are not shaped very differently from those
of the ash tree or the genus *agrimonia,* and indeed it is so like the *agrimonia*
that more than one botanist, having called Pantagruelion a domestic variety, has labeled *agrimonia* wild Pantagruelion. The leaves grow in rows,
at equal distances around the stem, there being anywhere from five to
seven in each row. And yet another sign that the plant is dear to nature is
this grouping of these two divine, mysterious odd numbers. The scent of
these leaves is strong and not very pleasant to delicate noses.

The seeds grow near the top of the stem—a bit below it. And Pantagruelion has as many seeds as any plant that grows: they are spherical,
oblong, or rhomboid, clear black or brown in color, tough, covered by
a thin skin and much loved by all singing birds—like linnets, goldfinch,

larks, green canaries, the yellow-red finch, and others. But in men they suppress the generative seed, if eaten in quantity and often—though in ancient times, among the Greeks, they were made into fritters, and tarts, and cakes, eaten as dainties after supper and to make wine taste better. But they're not easy to digest, hard on the stomach; they create bad blood, and their excessive heat damages the brain, filling the head with oppressive and painful vapors.

And just as there are two sexes in many plants, both male and female— as we can see in the laurel, the palm, the chestnut, holly oak, asphodel, the mandragora, ferns, toadstools, the birthwort, the cypress, the turpentine tree, pennyroyal, peonies, and others—so too this herb has a male, with no flower but lots of seeds, and a female, which produces tiny white flowers, quite useless, and grows no seed that amounts to anything; like other similar plants, the female has larger leaves, not so tough as the male's, nor does it grow quite so tall.

Planting time for Pantagruelion is marked by the coming of the swallows; it is harvested when grasshoppers begin to go hoarse from too much singing.

Chapter Fifty ⁄⁄ Preparation and Use of the Famous Pantagruelion

Pantagruelion is prepared during the autumnal equinox, and in various ways, according to people's imaginations and differing customs. Pantagruel's first instructions were: strip the stalk of leaves and seeds, soak it in still (never in running) water for five days, if the weather is dry and the water warm, but for nine or even twelve days, if the weather is changeable and the water cold. Then dry it in the sun and afterward, in the shade, peel and separate the fibers (which, as we have noted, constitute the plant's entire worth and value) from the woody part, which is useless, except to burn as luminous torches, to light fires and, in children's games, as a stick to shake an inflated pig's bladder. Sometimes it's also used, on the sly, as a straw to suck new wine out of bung-hole plugs.

Some modern Pantagruelists, to avoid the manual labor necessary to effect this separation, employ certain pounding tools, made in the shape of an angry Juno with her fingers tied together, trying to stop Alcmena from giving birth to Hercules. They bash and break the woody part, making it completely useless, in order to extract the fibers. But the only ones who work in this fashion are those who, flying in the face of the whole world (or operating like paradoxical philosophers), earn their livings by walking backward (as of course rope makers must do). Those who wish to make more profitable use of Pantagruelion work exactly as (according to what we've been told) the three Fates did, or noble Circe in her nocturnal games, or Penelope, with her interminable excuse to her amorous suitors, while her husband Ulysses was away. And thus it can be used as its incalculable virtues permit, which virtues I will now explain to you, at least in part (because for me to tell you everything would be impossible), if first you will allow me to comment on how this herb received its name.

I find that plants are named in a variety of ways. Some take their name from those who first discovered, recognized, demonstrated, cultivated, domesticated, or adapted them—for example, *mercurialis,* from Mercury; *panacea,* from Panace, Aesculapius' daughter; *artemisia,* from Artemis, or Diana; *eupatorium,* from King Eupator; *telephium,* from Telephus, Hercules' son; *euphorbium,* from Euphorbus, King Juba's physician; *clymenos,* from King Clymenus; *alcibiadion,* from Alcibiades; *gentiane,* from Gentius, king of Slavonia. And this privilege of attaching your name to a newly discovered herb was so highly valued, in the old days, that just as Neptune and Pallas argued over whose name to assign to the country they'd jointly discovered, which afterward took its name, Athens, from Athena (or Minerva), so too Lyncus, king of Scythia, plotted to murder young Triptolemus, who had been sent to earth by Ceres, to show men wheat, still at that time unknown—Lyncus hoping that, after Triptolemus' death, he could name the new food after himself and thus acquire the honor and immortal glory of that grain now so necessary and useful for all human existence. For that treachery, Lyncus was turned into a snow leopard or lynx. So too, great long wars were fought, in the old days, by the kings who dwelled near Cappadocia, over a single argument: whose name would be given to an herb—which, because of this dispute, came to be called *polemonia,* meaning warlike.

Other herbs have kept the name of the region from which they were brought—for example, Median apples, which are in fact lemons, named for the land of the Medes, where they were first found; Punic apples, which are pomegranates, brought from Punicia (that is, Carthage); *ligusticum,* or potherb, brought from Liguria, on the coast of Genoa; *rhabarbarum,* or rhubarb, from the barbarian river Rha (now the Volga), as Ammianus tells us; *santonica,* or absinthe, named for Saintonges; fenugreek, named for the Greek fern; *castanea,* or chestnut, from the city of Castanea; *persicaria,* or peach, from Persia; *sabine,* or oleander, from the Italian Sabine; *stoechas,* a lavender from my Hyères Islands, known in the old days as the Stoechades; *spica celtica,* or spikenard, from Celtic Gaul; and others.

Still other plants acquire their name by paradox and irony—for example, *absynthe* as the opposite of *pynthe,* or "good-tasting," because it's hard to drink; or *holosteun,* meaning "full of bone," used in the opposite sense, for an herb as delicate and fragile as anything that grows.

Still others are named after their qualities and effects—for example, *aristolochia,* meaning "good in childbirth," is used for women having labor pains; *lichen,* a blotchy plant, cures skin diseases; *maulve,* or mallow, which mollifies; *callithrichum,* star grass, which makes hair beautiful; *alyssum; ephemerum; bechium; nasturtium,* or nose bender, which is a breath-catching watercress, *hyoscyamus;* and more.

And some plants are named for their fine characteristics—for example, heliotrope, or sun follower, which in fact follows the sun, for when the sun rises, its flowers open; when the sun climbs, it climbs; when the sun declines, it declines, too; when the sun sets, it closes its flowers; and *adiantum,* or never wet, because, though it is born near water, it never keeps moisture, even if you put it in water for long periods; and *hieracium, eryngium,* and more.

And other plants are named for the metamorphosis of men and women with similar names—for example, *daphne,* or laurel, for Daphne; myrtle, or *myrtus,* for Myrrha; pine, or *pytis,* for Pytis; *cynara,* the artichoke, and narcissus, and saffron, and smilax; and more.

Some plants take their names from certain resemblances—for example, *hippuris,* or horsetail, because it looks like a horse's tail; *alopecurus,* or foxtail, which looks like a fox's tail; *psyllium,* or fleabane, which looks like a flea; *delphinium,* from the dolphin; *buglosse,* or oxtongue, from an ox's tongue; iris, for the rainbow (the scarf worn by Iris, Juno's messenger), which its flowers resemble; *myosotis,* or mouse-ear, from the mouse's ear; *coronopus,* or crowfoot, from a crow's foot—and more.

And, reciprocally, men have taken their names from plants, too—for example, the *Fabii,* from *faba,* or bean; the Piso family, from *pisa,* a pea; the *Lentuli,* from *lentes,* or lentils; and Cicero's family, from *cicer,* the chick-pea. And from still more lofty similarities we have Venus' navel, Venushair (also known as maidenhair), venus pot, Jupiter's beard and also Jupiter's eye, which is phlox, Mars' blood, which is bloodwort, Mercury's fingers, hermodactyl (*colchium*), and more.

And other plants have drawn their names from other shapes—for example, trefoil, or clover, which has three leaves; *pentaphyllon,* which has five leaves; *serpoulet,* or wild thyme, because it creeps across the earth like a snake; *helxine,* or clinging plant; *petasites,* or butterbur, whose leaves resemble a parasol; *myrobalans,* or sweet-juice acorn, in fact a plum which the Arabs call *ben,* because it looks like an acorn and is oily.

Chapter Fifty-one ⁄ Why the Herb Is Called Pantagruelion, and Its Splendid Characteristics

And the herb Pantagruelion got its name in all these different ways (except for the fabulous ones, because God would not like mere fables to be employed in this incredibly truthful history). It was Pantagruel who discovered it—not the plant, exactly, but certain ways of using it, which are hated and loathed by thieves, for it is more their opponent and enemy than choke weed or that parasite dodder is to flax, or than reeds are to ferns, or shave grass to the mower's scythe, or than broomweed to chickpeas, or bearded darnel grass to barley, or hatchet weed to lentils, or the deadly antranium weed to beans, or tare weeds to wheat, or ivy to stone walls; or than the water lily, *nymphaea heraclia,* that ancient anti-aphrodisiac, is to lecherous monks; or than the teacher's whipping stick and the birch branch are to the students of Navarre; or than cabbage to vines, garlic to magnets, onions to vision, fern seed to pregnant women, willow seed to depraved nuns, the shade of the yew tree to anyone who sleeps underneath it, dried monkshood roots and wolfsbane to wildcats and wolves, the scent of a fig tree to an angry bull, water hemlock to goslings, purslane weed to the teeth, or oil to trees. For by its use many thieves have come to their ends, hanged high and dropped quickly, as we see by the examples of Queen Phyllis of Thrace; Emperor Bonosus of Rome; Queen Amata, King Latinus's wife; and Iphis, Autolyca, Lycambes, Arachne, Phaedra, Leda, Achaeus (king of Lydia), and others—all of them angry that, though they were not otherwise indisposed, that channel through which witty words emerged and sweet morsels entered was closed, and in a style even uglier and less pleasant than by a heart attack or a quiet choking to death.

We've heard that others, just as Atropos was cutting the thread of their lives, bitterly complained and lamented that Pantagruel had them by the throat. But good Lord! that was hardly Pantagruel: he was never a hangman. No, it was Pantagruelion, doing its gallows work and serving them as a collar. They spoke improperly, and in error, although they can be excused if we take their observation as a synecdoche—that is, taking the invention as the inventor, as one speaks of Ceres in connection with bread, or Bacchus for wine. I swear to you most solemnly, by all the witty words contained in that bottle over there, cooling its heels in that ice bucket, that our noble Pantagruel never ever took them by the throat (except when they carelessly forgot to head off a pressing thirst).

And Pantagruelion also takes its name from similarities. For Pantagruel, as he was being born into this world, was fully as large as this herb we're talking about; nor was it hard to make the measurement, since he was born in a thirsty season, when that herb was being harvested and when Icarus' dog, barking at the sun, turned the whole world into cave dwellers, forcing everyone to live underground.

Pantagruelion also gets its name from its peculiar characteristics. For just as Pantagruel has been the ideal and symbol of all joyous perfection (I don't think any of you other drinkers doubts that for a minute), in Pantagruelion, too, I see such enormous potential, such energy, so many perfections, so many admirable accomplishments, that if its powers had been understood, back in the days when the trees (as Samuel tells us) were choosing who would be king of the woods and rule the whole forest, surely Pantagruelion would have had most of the votes.

Shall I go on? If Oxylus, Orius' son, had spawned it on his sister Hamadryad, he would have valued and taken more delight in it than in all the eight famous children he had by her, so celebrated in our mythology that their names will live forever. The oldest daughter was named Vine; the next was named Fig Tree; then Walnut, Chestnut, Apple Tree, Ash, Poplar; and the last was named Elm and, in her day, was a great surgeon.

I won't stop to tell you how the juice of this marvelous herb, squeezed out and then placed in the ears, kills every manner of putrefied vermin that could possibly have bred in there, as well as all other creatures that might have crawled in. Put this juice in a small pail of water and you'll see the water suddenly coagulate like clotted milk—that's how powerful it is. And this coagulated water is a sovereign remedy for colicky horses, and also those with short breath.

The root of this herb, boiled in water, soothes muscles, stiff joints, gout pains, and rheumatism.

If you want to cure a burn, no matter whether it be from boiling water or burning wood, just rub on raw Pantagruelion, just as it comes out of the earth, without doing anything else. But be careful to change the dressing, when you see it drying out on the wound.

Without Pantagruelion, our kitchens would be unspeakable, our tables disgusting, even if they were covered with all sorts of exquisite delicacies—and our beds would offer no delight, even though they might be liberally adorned with gold, silver, platinum, ivory, and porphyry. Without Pantagruelion, millers could not carry wheat to their mills, or bring back flour. Without Pantagruelion, how would lawyers ever manage to bring their briefs into court? How, without it, would you ever carry plaster into workshops? Or draw water from wells? Without Pantagruelion, what would legal scribes do all day, and copyists, and secretaries, and other scribblers? Their court documents would be destroyed, and landlords' leases, too. And the noble art of printing would surely perish. What would we use to make window coverings? How would we ring our church bells? The priests of Isis are adorned with Pantagruelion, as are statue-bearing priests world round, and all human beings when they first come into this world. All the wool-bearing trees of India, the cotton trees of Tylos, in the Persian Sea, like the cotton plants of Arabia, and the cotton vines of Malta do not adorn as many people as this one herb. It covers armies against rain and cold, and certainly does it more comfortably than, once, skins and hides used to do. It covers theaters and auditoria against heat; it's tied to trees and bushes to make life easier for hunters; it drops down into water, fresh and salt alike, to help fishermen. It shapes and makes possible boots, and half-boots, and sea boots, spats, and laced boots, and shoes, and dancing shoes, slippers, and hob boots. Pantagruelion strings bows, pulls crossbows tight, and makes slings. And just as if it were a sacred herb, like verbena, worshiped by the souls of the dead, corpses are never buried without it.

I'll tell you more. By means of this herb, invisible substances are caught and made visible, captured, held as if locked in prison. Great, huge weights turn easily, when held by Pantagruelion, and human beings' lives are vastly improved. And it stuns me that these mechanical methods were never discovered by the ancient philosophers, over the long centuries, considering their utterly incalculable utility, and the intolerable labor that, without them, used to be endured in ancient mills.

By the use of this herb, which captures and holds the waves of the air, great ships are sent hither and thither, at the will of those who command them—cargo ships, and those that carry passengers, huge galleons, vessels carrying whole armies.

Thanks to this herb, nations which nature seemed to keep hidden away, obscure, impenetrable, unknown, have now come to us, and we to them—something even the birds could not do, no matter how light their feathers or what powers of flight they are given. Ceylon has now seen Lapland; Java has seen the Scythian mountains; the Arabs will see Thélème; Icelanders and Greenlanders will see the Euphrates. Pantagruelion has allowed the north wind to visit the home of the south wind, and the east wind to visit the realm of the west wind. And all of this has terrified the heavenly intelligences, the gods of sea and land, seeing that with the help of this blessed herb the Arctic peoples—with the Antarcticans watching—have leaped over the Atlantic Ocean, swept past both tropics, vaulted down under the torrid zone, and measured the whole zodiac, frisking along under the equinoxes, with both the poles dancing on their horizon. So the frightened Olympic gods cried:

"Using that mighty herb of his, Pantagruel has given us something new and tedious to deal with—worse even than those giants who tried to climb Olympus. Soon he'll be married; his wife will bear him children. And we are powerless to stop his fated progress, because it has been decreed by the hands and the bobbing spindles of those three fatal sisters Necessity's Daughters. Who knows? His children may discover another herb with equal powers, by means of which humans will be able to visit the home of hail, the sluice gates from which rain pours, and the workshop where lightning and thunder are forged. They'll be able to invade the moon, travel to lands owned by the stars of the zodiac, and dwell there—some of them on the Golden Eagle, some on the Ram, some on the Crown, others on the Harp or at the Silver Lion. They will sit at table with us, and take our goddesses as their wives—the only way they can become gods."

And finally they decided to plan ways of stopping this, and called a heavenly council to discuss it.

Chapter Fifty-two ⁄⁄ How One Kind of Pantagruelion Does Not Burn

Everything I've told you is great and wonderful. But if you're pre-pared to believe yet another divine aspect of this sacred Pantagruelion, I'll tell you about it. I don't care whether you believe it or not. It's enough for me to have told you the truth.

And I *will* tell you the truth. But in order to arrive at it, for the road is a rugged and difficult one, I must first ask you: if I had put two bowls of wine and one of water in this bottle, then shaken them exceedingly thor-oughly, how would you have disentangled them? separated them so that you could hand me the water completely distinct from the wine, the wine completely distinct from the water, and in exactly the same proportions as I had at first mixed them?

To put it differently: if your carters and boatmen, bringing a provision of barrels, casks, and half-barrels of wine to stock your wine cellars—wines from Graves, from Orléans, from Beaune, from Mirevaux—had cracked them open en route and drunk them halfway down, then filled them back up with water (the way Limousins do, by the shoeful, when they're transporting Argenton and Saint-Gaultier wines), how would you get all the water out? How would you purify your wine? Oh yes, you'll tell me about an ivory funnel. That's all been written down. It's true; it's been attested a thousand times. You knew that one already. But those who didn't know it, and never saw it done, won't believe it's possible. So: let's proceed.

If we were in the time of Sulla, Marius, Caesar, and other Roman emperors, or back in the days of our old Druids, who burned the dead bodies of their kinsmen and lords, and you wished to drink the ashes of your wives, or your fathers, in a glass of good white wine (as Artemisia drank the ashes of Mausolus, her husband), or perhaps to preserve them in some urn or shrine, how would you preserve those ashes completely separate from those of the funeral prye? Tell me.

By God, you'd have one hell of a time! But let me hurriedly explain to you that, by taking as much of this celestial Pantagruelion as you need, in order to cover the deceased's body, and carefully enclosing that body inside, tied and sewn with the same material, you can throw it on the biggest, hottest fire you like. The flames will leap across the Pantagrue-lion and burn and reduce the corpse, flesh and bones alike, to ashes; but not only won't the Pantagruelion itself be burned, not only won't it lose a single atom of the funeral ashes, you'll take it out of the fire beau-tiful and white and even drier than when you threw it in. And that's why it's called *asbestos*. There's lots of it in Carpasia, on the island of

Cyprus, and it sells for a very reasonable price in the Aswan region of Egypt.

Oh, what a magnificent thing! what a wonderful thing! Fire, which devours everything, ruins and consumes everything, only cleans and whitens this unique Pantagruelion, this Carpasian asbestos. If you refuse to believe this, demanding proof, some acceptable sign, as Jews and other unbelievers do, take a fresh egg and simply tie some of this divine Pantagruelion around it. Then put it in the biggest, hottest fire you choose. Leave it there as long as you like. In the end you'll take out a thoroughly roasted egg, hard and charred, but the sacred Pantagruelion won't be in any way changed, altered, or even heated. You can do the experiment for yourself: it won't cost you fifty thousand dollars, or even the twelfth part of a single dollar.

Don't talk to me about the salamander: that's a fraud. It's true, to be sure, that a brisk little straw fire makes a salamander very active; he likes that. But I assure you that in some great furnace it is suffocated and burned to bits, like all other living things. We've seen it happen. Galen confirmed and demonstrated it many, many years ago: see the third book of his *De temperamentis,* On Humors, and see also the second book of Discorides.

And don't talk to me about feather alum, either, or about that wooden tower in Piraeus that L. Sulla couldn't burn down, because Archelaus, King Mithridates' governor in that city, had completely coated it with alum.

And don't summon up that tree, called *eonem* by Alexander Cornelius, which he said was like the mistletoe oak, but it couldn't be consumed or damaged by water or fire, or the mistletoe either; that famous vessel the *Argo* was supposed to have been built of it. Find people who'll believe such stuff; I'm sorry, not me.

And also don't bother telling me—no matter how miraculous it is— about that special tree you saw up in the mountains of Briançon and Embrun, from the root of which we grow good agaric mushrooms—and from the trunk we get a resin so fine that Galen dares to call it the equal of turpentine—and from its delicate leaves we get that fine celestial honey called manna—and, though it's gummy and full of oil, can't be burned in any fire. In Greek and Latin you call it *larrix,* or larch; the Alpine people call it *melze;* the Paduans and Venetians called it *larege* (which lends its name to *Larignum,* the castle in Piedmont which defeated Julius Caesar as he came back from Gaul).

Now, Julius Caesar had ordered all the landowners and other inhabitants of Piedmont and the Alpine regions to bring food and supplies to assigned stations along the route, for his army as it was passing through. And everyone obeyed, except those from Larignum, who refused to contribute, feeling confident of the natural strength of the location. To punish them for refusing, the emperor ordered his army to march straight to the place. Right in front of the castle gate there was a tower, built of thick larch beams, laid one on top of the other, first this way, then that, like a great wood pile, so tall that from the fortified places on top they could easily drive off attackers with sticks and stones. And when Caesar saw that the defenders had no other weapons than sticks and stones, which they could barely hurl as far as the approaches to the castle, he ordered his soldiers to throw branches and twigs all around and set them on fire. Which was immediately done. The fire roared through the branches; the flames were so high that they covered the entire castle, so they expected first the wooden tower and then the castle itself to burn and be destroyed. But when the branches stopped burning, and were all used up, there was the tower, whole and entire, without having been in any way damaged. And seeing this, Caesar commended them to dig a network of ditches and trenches, well out of the range of thrown stones, and completely encircling the tower.

So the people of Larignum made peace with him. And Caesar learned from their mouths all about the exceptional nature of this wood, which can't be used to make a fire, a flame, or charcoal. And for this it might well be considered at least partially comparable to true Pantagruelion—especially since Pantagruel chose to make all the doors, gates, windows, gutters, moldings, and outer facings of Thélème from this wood. So too he used it to cover the sterns, prows, galleys, decks, gangways, and forecastles of his great ships—brigs, galleys, galleons, brigantines, light galleys, and the other vessels from his dockyards at Thalasse. However, if you place larch in a good-sized furnace, along with other kinds of wood, in the end it does break down and scatter, just the way the stones in a lime kiln will do. But asbestos-Pantagruelion is cleansed and refurbished rather than corrupted or changed. So,

> Arabs—Indians—Sabians—no more
> Loud praise for myrrh, incense, ebony.
> Come see what better things there are
> In this herb of ours, and take its seeds,
> And if you grow this handsome gift
> In your lands, too, give thanks to God
> And royal France, whose happy sod
> Provided you so handsome a gift.

The end of the Third Book
of the heroic words and deeds
of our good
Pantagruel

The Fourth Book
of the Heroic Words
and Deeds of
Our Good Pantagruel

Written by

Maître François Rabelais

Doctor of Medicine

To the Very Illustrious Prince and Most Reverend MONSEIGNEUR ODET Cardinal of Chastillon

YOU are certainly aware, O most noble Prince, just how many high and eminent personages have directed, requested, even begged—not only in the past, but daily—that I continue these Pantagruelian narratives, pointing out that many languishing, ill, or otherwise indisposed and afflicted people have, by reading these volumes, triumphed over their worries, experienced moments of happiness, and been granted a new cheerfulness and comfort. And I have been in the habit of answering that, writing these books as a frolic and sport, I have been totally unconcerned with either glory or praise but thinking only of how these pages might give some small relief to the sick and the afflicted, just as I do when I am able to be with them, gladly and cheerfully, when my knowledge and my services as a doctor are called upon.

And I have sometimes explained to them, at considerable length, how Hippocrates—in several places, but especially in the sixth book of his *On Epidemics*—describes how the doctor educates his disciple. Soranus the Ephesian, Oribasius of Pergamum, Cl. Galen, Hali Abbas, and other later writers have dealt with the same subject, speaking of the doctor's gestures, his bearing, his look, his touch, his face, his charm, his integrity, his cleanliness, his clothes, beard, hair, hands, mouth, even specifying how he should trim his fingernails, how he must play the role of a kind of lover, whether performing in a splendid comedy or invading a well-guarded camp to battle some powerful enemy. Indeed, Hippocrates quite properly compares the practice of medicine to a half-battle, half-farce played out by three characters—the sick person, the doctor, and the disease.

Reading these words of Hippocrates, I'm sometimes reminded of what Julia once said to her father, Octavian Augustus. One day she had appeared in front of him, wearing a stately gown in the height of dissolute lasciviousness, and he had been mightily displeased, though he hadn't uttered a word. The next day, she changed into modest clothing, of the sort then customary among chaste Roman ladies, and dressed in this fashion she came to him. Though he had not said a word, the day before, to express the displeasure he'd felt, seeing her in such immodest garments, he could not conceal the pleasure he now took, seeing her attire so utterly changed, and said to her:

"Oh, how much more appropriate and praiseworthy are these clothes, for Augustus' daughter!"

Her apology ready, she replied at once:

"Today I'm dressed for my father's eyes. Yesterday I was dressed for my husband."

So too must the physician say, similarly disguised in his looks and his dress, and especially wearing that rich, droll robe with four sleeves, as doctors used to do (it was called a *philonium,* as Petrus Alexandrinus tells us, in book six of his commentary on Hippocrates). And to those who may find this disguise strange, he can say:

"I'm not dressed in this fashion in order to make myself elegant or impressive, but to suit the taste of the sick man I'm visiting, for he is the only person I wish to please, and in no way offend or annoy."

And there is more. Reading the aforesaid book by the venerable Hippocrates, what we sweat over, arguing and struggling, is not whether a downcast expression on the physician's face—sour, grim, severe, unpleasant, unhappy, harsh, and sullen—has a depressive effect on the patient, or whether a joyful expression on the physician's face—serene, gracious, open, pleasant—will cheer the sick man. That's been completely proven; there is no doubt whatever about it. But what we try to understand is whether such depressive and encouraging effects stem from the patient's concern at seeing those expressions on his doctor's face, thus imagining how his illness is likely to end—when the physician is happy, ending well, as he wants it to end, and when he is worried, ending in irritation and unpleasantness—or whether those effects are due to some actual transference of the physician's spirits—serene or gloomy, airy or earthbound, joyous or melancholy—directly into the sick man's body, as Plato and Averroës believed.

What all these authors have done, more than anything else, is warn the physician to be careful about the words, statements, intimate comments, and discussions which must take place with their patients, once they've been called into attendance. All such exchanges must have a single goal and keep a single result in mind, which is to cheer up the patient (avoiding any sacred transgressions, of course) and under no circumstances depress him in any way. How roundly Herophilus scolds a certain doctor Callianax, who answered a patient's query "Will I die?" with this sort of insolence:

> Patroclus died, sank into death,
> And of the two of you, he was best.

This same Callianax was queried by another patient, after the fashion of our noble Patelin:

> Doesn't my urine
> Tell you if I'm dying?

And he replied, stupidly:

"No, and it wouldn't tell me if Latona, mother of those beautiful twins Phoebus and Diana, had also borne you."

So too Galen, in the fourth book of his *Comments on Hippocrates' "On Epidemics,"* strongly castigates Quintus, who had instructed him in medicine. After a certain sick man in Rome, an honorable gentleman, said to him, "You have dined, my master: your breath smells of wine," Quintus arrogantly replied, "Your breath smells of fever—and which is the better scent, fever or wine?"

But the slanders and lying insults of certain cannibals, life haters, and deep-dyed scoffers have been so irrational and offensive that they completely overcame my patience and made me decide not to write a word more. For one of the least of their libelous assaults was that my books are stuffed with all sorts of heresies (all the same, they couldn't point to a single one); on the other hand, there certainly is a lot of happy fooling about, offensive neither to God nor to the king, that being the subject and indeed the only point to these books. There are no heresies, except the sort of twisted offense against reason and normal use of language that they perversely wrench out of my words, though—if such a thing were possible—I'd rather die a thousand times over than even to have thought such things. It's like turning bread into stones, fish into snakes, eggs into scorpions. And since you've often enough heard me complaining of all this, in your very presence, I told you straight out that, if I didn't think myself a better Christian than they make me appear, and if I saw anywhere in my life, my writing, my words, even one scintilla of the ideas they attribute to me, there'd be no need for them to fall so disgustingly into the dank pools of the great calumniator himself, lying Satan, who uses them to bring such accusations against me. No, I would imitate the phoenix, collect dry wood and, with no other hand to assist, light the fire that would consume me.

And you replied that the late King Francis, of blessed memory, had been told of those slanders, and after attentively listening to these books of mine, read out to him in the voice and pronunciation of the most learned and faithful reader anywhere in France, had understood my writing—mine, I say, because they have maliciously attributed to me who knows how many false, infamous volumes for which I bear not the slightest responsibility—and found in it not a single doubtful passage, and expressed horror at the foul snake eater who had brought some charge of mortal heresy against me, based solely on a printer's careless, lazy substitution of an *N* for an *M*.

So too his son, our exceedingly good, most virtuous, and heaven-blessed King Henry (may God give him long life), also understood my books, and granted me, through you, his personal protection against these lying slanderers. That cheering document has since, through your extraordinary kindness, been reconfirmed in Paris, and once again, more recently,

when you visited Monseigneur Cardinal du Bellay, who came to Saint-
Maur in order to recover his health after a long and wearisome illness—
Saint-Maur! a place, or should I say more appropriately a paradise of
wholesomeness, goodwill, peace, comfort, delight, and all the honest
pleasures of agriculture and the country life.

And this is why, Monseigneur, I have now, placed as I am beyond the
reach of any intimidation, once again set my pen into the wind, hoping
that your kind favor will make you a second French Hercules for me, in
the face of these slanderers, bringing me knowledge, wisdom, and eloquence, a veritable Alexicacos in virtue, power, and authority—Alexicacos, of whom I can truly say what wise King Solomon said of Moses,
that great captain and leader of Israel (in Ecclesiasticus, 45): he was a man
fearing and loving God, good to all men and beloved by God and man
alike, and forever happily remembered. God made him equal to the brav-
est of the brave, and made him terrible to his enemies; blessed with His
favor, he did prodigious and dreadful things; God honored him in the
presence of kings; through him, God's will was declared to the people
and through him God's light was made manifest. In faith and meekness
he was consecrated and chosen from among all men. Through him He
chose to have His voice heard, and through him those who dwelled in
darkness were taught the laws of life-giving knowledge.

What's more, my lord: if I meet anyone who congratulates me on these
joyous books, I promise you they'll understand that all their gratitude is
owed to you and only to you, and you are the only one to be thanked;
they should pray to our Lord to keep you and magnify you in your high
estate, attributing nothing to me, other than humble subjection and willing obedience to your orders. For it is your lofty urging that has filled me
with the courage and imagination to continue: without you my heart
would surely have failed, and the fountain of my animal spirits would
have remained dry and exhausted. May our Lord keep you in His holy
grace.

At Paris, this twenty-eighth of January 1552,

from your exceedingly humble, very obedient servant,

FRANC. RABELAIS, physician

THE AUTHOR'S PROLOGUE
BY MAÎTRE FRANÇOIS
RABELAIS

For the Fourth Book
Of the Heroic Words and Deeds
Of Pantagruel

To My Kindly Readers

GOOD PEOPLE, may God keep and protect you! But where are you? I can't see you. Just a minute, while I put on my spectacles!

Ha, ha! "How smoothly, how sweetly Lent goes by!" Ah, now I can see you. And so? The wine's been good this year, they tell me. Well, that'll never make me sad. You've found the perfect, inexhaustible cure for every known variety of thirst. That's first-class work. You, and your wife, your children, all your relatives—you're all healthy? That's fine— that's good—that makes me very happy. May God, the good God on high, be eternally praised and (if it's His sacred wish) may you all stay healthy for a long, long time.

As for me, by His holy kindness I'm well, too, and I commend myself to you. Thanks to a touch of Pantagruelism (which you understand means a certain gaiety of spirit, an indifference to all the accidents of daily life), I'm healthy and happy, and ready to drink, if you are. Good people: you ask me why? I have an unbeatable answer: it's God's wish, our great Creator, and I submit myself to Him, I do His bidding, just as I honor the Holy Word of His Good News—that holy Good News which, in Luke, 4, refers to the physician who neglects his own good health in such bitter irony, such biting derision: "Physician, heal thyself."

Claudius Galen took care of his own health, not because of any such sacred reverence—although he had distinct feelings about the Holy Scriptures and knew and was friendly with the Christian saints of his time, as we can see in book two of *De usu partium,* Use of the Limbs, book two, chapter three, and book three, chapter two, of *De differentiis pulsuum,* The Different Kinds of Pulse, and also *De rerum affectibus* (if Galen really wrote it)—but for fear of some such vulgar and satiric joke as this:

> He acts like a doctor, he looks like a doctor, you think:
> But his body's so covered with ulcers and sores that it stinks.

This seems to him such a serious matter that he asserts, grandly, no interest in being valued as a doctor if, from age twenty-eight to ripe old age, he hadn't lived in perfect health, except for a few passing fevers of no great duration, although by nature he was not particularly healthy and had an obviously weak stomach. As he writes in book five of *De sanitate tuenda,* Staying Healthy, "It's difficult to be accepted as a physician, and given the care of others' health, when you're careless of your own."

Asclepiades boasts still more grandly of having been a doctor with whom Fortune had an agreement: he'd never be a physician of any note if, from the time he began his practice until his last years on earth, he ever got sick. And he reached old age sound as a drum, vigorous of limb, and thus won his bet with Fortune. In the end, still without having been ill, he exchanged life for death, by bad luck falling from the top of a badly built and rotting staircase.

If by some disaster, gentlemen, health has escaped you—hiding who knows where: up, down, out front, in back, to the right, to the left, inside, outside, far off, or near—may you quickly and easily find it again, with the help of our blessed Savior! And if you're lucky enough to find it again, seize it without hesitation, whether you claim it by right of possession or by bill of sale. The law gives you that right; the king expects it; and I urge it on you neither more nor less urgently than ancient lawmakers, who allowed a lord to claim his fugitive slave, wherever that slave might be found. Praise the good Lord, and good men, too! Hasn't it always been the rule, here in this noble, ancient, beautiful, flourishing, rich kingdom of France, by ancient custom as much as by written precept, that "the dead give the living their rights"? See the recent comments of the good, learned, wise, deeply humane, mild, and just André Tiraqueau, counselor of the great, victorious, triumphant King Henry, second of that name, at his magnificent parliamentary court, in Paris. Health is our life, as Ariphron of Sicyon has well put it. Without health, life is not life, life is not livable: "A life that is not life, a life no one can live." Without health, life is listlessness—is only an imitation of death. Thus, deprived of life (that is, dead), reach for life, claim life (that is, health).

And I believe that God will hear our prayers, since we make them with such firm faith, and will grant us our wish, it being so moderate. The wise men of old called moderation golden—that is, precious, universally praised, welcome everywhere. Look through the sacred Bible and you'll find that the only prayers never denied are moderate ones. For example: little Zacchaeus, whose body and relics the high and mighty church doctors of Saint-Ayl, near Orléans, boast about having (they call him Saint Sylvanus). What he wanted, simply enough, was to see our blessed Savior as He passed through Jerusalem. This was entirely reasonable, and should have been possible for anyone, but he was too short and, with so many people thronging about, couldn't manage it. He pranced, he jumped, he struggled, he leaped, and then he climbed into a sycamore. Our gracious Lord saw his sincerity, and the simple modesty of what he wanted, and made sure that He was visible to the little man—and not only did He show Himself, but beyond that He made sure He was heard as well, for He visited Zacchaeus' house and blessed his family.

One of the prophets of Israel had a son, who was cutting wood near the river Jordan, and the head of his ax slipped off (as it is written in Kings 2:6) and fell into the river. He prayed that God would return it to him. This is a moderate request. And having firm faith and confidence, he threw—not the axhead after the ax handle, as our theological philosophers stupidly insist—but the ax handle after the axhead, which is how it ought to be said. And suddenly two miracles occurred: the axhead rose up from the bottom of the water, and then it fitted itself to the handle. Now, if his wish had been to rise up to heaven in a flaming chariot, like Elijah, or to sow his seed as widely as old Abraham, or to be as rich as Job, or as strong as Samson, or as handsome as Absalom, would his wish have been granted? That's a good question.

And while we're talking about moderate wishes and axheads (let me know when it's time to stop and have a drink), let me tell you what that wise Frenchman Aesop wrote in his fables—I mean, that wise Phrygian or Trojan, as Maximus Planudes claims—and according to the most reliable chroniclers our noble French race is descended from the Trojans. Of course, Aelian writes that Aesop was a Thracian; Agathias, following Herodotus, says he was a Samian: I frankly don't give a damn.

In Aesop's time there lived a poor villager, a native of Gravot named Bally, a tree chopper and woodcutter who barely managed to eke out a living. And then he lost his ax—and guess who was worried and upset? Everything he had, his entire life, depended on that ax. It was his ax that enabled him to live honorably, and to maintain a decent reputation with all the rich lumbermen: without that ax, he'd die of hunger. If death were to meet up with him, six days later, and he had no ax, death would cut him down with his scythe and weed him right out of this world.

Overwhelmed by his burden, he began to cry, pray, beg, call to Jupiter in the most eloquent language he could think of (and, as you know, necessity is the mother of eloquence), lifting his face to the skies, down on his knees, his head bare, his arms raised high, his fingers spread wide, and after each repetition of his prayer calling out, in a loud voice, over and over and over:

"My ax, Jupiter! my ax, my ax! That's all I want, O Jupiter—either my ax or enough money to buy another! Oh, oh, my poor ax!"

Now, Jupiter was in council just then, dealing with some pretty important business, and listening to old Cybele's opinions—or bright young Phoebus', if you prefer. But Bally was making so much noise that the racket reached right up to the full council and assembly of the gods.

"Who the devil," asked Jupiter, "is howling like that, down there? By all the powers of the Styx, haven't we had enough of that stuff? Aren't we, right now, trying to deal with complex issues, and many, many controversial matters of real importance? We've patched up the quarrel between Prester John, king of Persia, and Sultan Suleiman, emperor of Constantinople. We've smoothed out the difficulties between the Tartars and Ivan the Terrible. We've granted the prince of Morocco's petition. We've even turned Dragut Reis, that Turkish pirate, into a devoted worshiper. Parma's been taken care of, and Magdeburg, and Mirandola, and Africa (which is what human beings call Meheddia, that Tunisian city on the Mediterranean, though we call it Aphrodisium). Unfortunately, Tripoli's changed rulers—but that was already in the cards. And here are the Gascons, swearing and calling for the restoration of their church bells. And over here, in this corner, we have the Saxons, and the Hanseatic cities, the Ostrogoths, and all those Germans—they used to be absolutely invincible, but now they're all washed up, they're under the thumb of some miserable little cripple. They're calling to us for vengeance, for help— they want their old good sense back, and also their old freedom. And what are we supposed to do with Ramus and Pierre Galland, and all their scullions and camp followers and cheerleaders—they're turning the University of Paris upside down! It's puzzlesome; I haven't been able to figure out whose side I'm supposed to be on. They both seem to me good enough fellows, well hung. One of them has a supply of gold pieces, good solid currency; the other would like to have some. One of them knows a thing or two; the other isn't exactly ignorant. One of them likes good people; the other is well liked himself. One of them is a subtle, crafty fox; the other slanders ancient philosophers and orators, by word of mouth and in writing, howling at them like a dog. What's your opinion, eh, you old donkey prick Priapus? I usually find your opinions, and your suggestions, fair and to the point, *et habet tua mentula mentem,* and there's wisdom in that tool of yours."

"King Jupiter," answered Priapus, pulling off his monk's cape, his head erect, red, gaudy, and firm, "since you compare one to a barking dog and the other to a sly, clever fox, it seems to me that, without getting yourself any more irritated or upset, you ought to deal with them exactly as, once upon a time, you dealt with a dog and a fox."

"What?" asked Jupiter. "When? Who were they? Where was all this?"

"Oh, what a wonderful memory!" answered Priapus. "Old father Bacchus—who's right here, his face brick red—wanted vengeance against the Thebans, so he got himself an enchanted fox: the spell on it kept it safe from being captured or hurt by any other animal in the world, no matter what damage or wickedness it might do. Now, noble Vulcan had forged a dog of Monesian brass, and with some ferocious working of his bellows he made it live and breathe. He gave it to you; you gave it to your little sweetheart, Europa; she gave it to Minos; Minos gave it to Procris; and, finally, Procris gave it to Cephalus. And the dog, too, was enchanted: like our lawyers today, he captured every beast he met—none could ever escape him. So it happened that these two animals encountered each other—and what could they do? His immovable destiny dictated that the dog must capture the fox. But the immovable destiny of the fox required that he could not be caught.

"The deadlock was referred to your council. You objected that destiny could not be interfered with. But the two destinies were contradictory: the truth was that the end result, the outcome, of two such contradictions was a natural impossibility. That left you to sweat it out—to the point where, as your sweat dripped onto the ground, it grew row after row of fine white cabbages. And all this noble council, having no logical way to resolve the problem, developed such a magnificent thirst that they guzzled up more than seventy-eight great barrels of nectar. Then, as I suggested, you turned both animals to stone, and that quickly solved all the problems; in a moment, all of high Olympus rang with cries of a truce to thirst. You'll recall that this was the year when balls went droopy, near Teumessus, just between Thebes and Chalcis.

"And it seems to me that's what you ought to do now: turn this dog and fox to stone, too. You're not totally unfamiliar with the art of metamorphosis. And after all, both learned professors already have the name Pierre (which in the French language means stone)—and since, according to the old Limousin proverb, you need three stones for an oven's mouth, you can toss in Maître Pierre du Coignet: you turned him into stone a long time ago, and for the same reasons. Then there'll be a neat equilateral triangle in the great temple of Paris—or, anyway, out in the square in front: three dead stones, and they can all be used to snuff out candles— or torches, tapers, wax lights, candelabra—with their noses, as in the flying-squirrel game, where you have to blow out a candle using just your nose. When they were alive, these two learned rascals had themselves a fine ball-banging time, lighting up the fires of dispute and controversy, creating fat-balled sects and divisions for lazy students to have fun with. As stone monuments, they can bear perpetual witness: such self-enamored little testiculars are more likely to be spat on than condemned by your noble court. And that's what I have to say."

"You're being too nice to them, good Maître Priapus," said Jupiter, "as far as I can see. You're not that well disposed to everyone, by my name. Now, since they're both desperate to have their name and memory last forever, the best thing will be this: once they're dead, we'll turn them into some good hard stone, like marble, instead of putting them back in the ground to rot.

"Now, down there, just behind us, over by the Tyrrhenian Sea and all around the Bolognian Alps, do you see what tragedies the priests are creating? This wild fury will last a long time, like a fire in the enameled ovens of Limoges, and then it'll be over—but not as soon as all that. It'll be a lot of fun for us. I see just one problem, and that's the minor shortage of thunderbolts we've had, ever since all you gods—by my special dispensation, to be sure—had such a fine time throwing them down by the basketful, on the new city of Antioch. Just as, since then—and following your example—those elegant champions, who agreed to defend Dindenrois Castle against all comers, used up their supplies shooting at sparrows, without leaving anything to defend themselves, if they had to. So they courageously surrendered the castle, and themselves, to the enemy, who had already decided to lift their desperate, insane siege and weren't thinking about anything but retreating in shame. Vulcan, my son! Give the orders. Wake up your sleeping Cyclops, and Asterops, and Sterops, and other giants, Polyphemus and Pyracmon and the rest! Set them to work—and make sure they have enough to drink! Fire-workers should never have to worry about getting their fair share of wine. Now: let's get rid of that bawler down there. Mercury: go see what he wants."

Mercury went to the trapdoor in the sky, through which they listened to what was being said on earth. (It looked more like a ship's skylight window, though Icaromenippus said it looked like the mouth of a well.) He saw that it was Bally asking to have his ax back, and came to tell the members of the council what he'd seen.

"Really!" said Jupiter. "How wonderful! Is that all we have to deal with right now—returning lost axes? But he's got to have it back: it's written in the books. That's destiny, right? His ax might as well be worth as much as the duchy of Milan—and, in truth, it is as precious to him as a kingdom to a king. All right! see to it that his ax goes back, and let's be done with him! Now let's deal with the quarrel between the clergy and the mole monks of Landerousse. Where were we?"

Priapus had stayed in the corner near the chimney. But hearing Mercury's report, he said, courteously and with great respect (but also with a grin):

"King Jupiter: in the days when, by your order and special grace, I was in charge of all the gardens on earth, I became aware that this word 'ax' is in many ways ambiguous. It means a certain tool by which trees are cut down and wood is chopped, yes. But it also means (or, at least, it used to mean) a woman well and frequently love whacked. I saw that all good men spoke of their cheerful bed companions as 'my ax.' You see, with that tool"—and here he showed them his own awesome tool, which was nine thumb-lengths long, or close to three feet—"they could bang in their handles so vigorously, so boldly, that they never had to be concerned about that omnipresent female fear: namely, that men's ax handles would just hang down to their heels, for lack of just such a handy fastener. And I remember (because I have a tool—I mean, I've told it, many times, and my memory of it is a handsome one—capacious—a great wide memory, yes), one day during the Roman feasts—the one to brother Vulcan, I think it was, in May—and gathered there in one place were musicians like Josquin des Prez, Johannes Ockeghem, Obrecht, Agricola, Antoine Brumel, Camelin, Vigoris, de la Fage, Bruyer, Prioris, Segni,

Pierre de la Rue, Midy, Moulu, Mouton, Matthew Gascoigne, Loyset Compère, Hilary Penet, Antoine Févin, Ciprano de Rore (called Rousée), Jean Richaford, Francesco Roselli, Jean de Consilion, Constanzo Festa, and Jacquet Berchem and they were singing very prettily:

> Before he lay down
> With his brand-new wife
> Old Tibault put a hammer
> On the floor out of sight.
> "O sweetheart," she said,
> "What's the point to that tool?"
> "The better to bang you."
> "O you silly fool!
> All Johnny does
> Is thump like a mule."

"Nine Olympiads later—or was it ten?—O magnificent tool—I mean, tale! I'm always confusing those two words—I heard others, Adrian Willaert, Nicolas Gombert, Clement Janequin, Jacques Arcadelt, Claudin de Sermisy, Pierre Certon, Pierre de Manchicourt, Auxerre, Villiers, Sandrin, Sohier, Hesdin, Cristóbal Morales, Passereau, Maille, Jean Maillard, Jacotin, Guillaume le Heurteur, Philippe Verdelot, Elzéar Genet Carpentras, Jean Lhéritier, Pierre Cadéac, Doublet, Pierre Vermont, Bouteiller, Lupi, Pagnier, Millet, du Moulin, Alaire, Marault, Morpain, Jean le Gendre de Paris, and many more joyful musicians, all in a hidden garden, under a beautiful arbor, surrounded by a pile of flasks, and hams, and pies, and a flock of juicy female morsels, and they were singing:

> If that's the way it has to go,
> That an ax with no handle is only for show,
> Let's stick your handle into my ax
> And give each other some handsome whacks.

So what we have to find out is this: what sort of ax is our Bally friend crying for?"

At these words, all the venerable gods and goddesses burst into laughter, shaking like a mass of flies. Despite his bad leg, Vulcan—for the sheer love of his dear sweetheart—executed three or four neat little jumps, right up on the front of the dais.

"Well now!" said Jupiter to Mercury. "You go right down there, and throw three axes at this Bally's feet: his own, one of pure gold, and a third of heavy silver, as pure as snow. Give him his choice. If he takes his own and he's happy, give him the other two. But if he takes either of the others, cut off his head with his own ax. And from now on, that's how we'll take care of all these ax losers."

And Jupiter twisted his head around, like a monkey swallowing pills, and screwed his face into such a horrible grimace that all of Olympus trembled.

With his pointed hat, his military cape, his winged heels and wand, Mercury leaped straight out the trapdoor in the skies, dashed down through the empty air and, descending lightly to earth, threw the three axes at Bally's feet, saying:

"You've yelled yourself hoarse. Jupiter hears your prayers, and grants them. See which of these axes is yours, and take it."

Bally picked up the golden ax, considered it, and saw that it was too heavy. So he said to Mercury:

"My, my: this one's certainly not mine. I sure don't want it."

Then he tried the silver ax, and said:

"Not this one, either. You keep it."

Then he picked up the wooden ax, looked at the end of the handle, and, recognizing his own mark, jumped up and down with happiness, like a fox finding lost chickens, and grinning from ear to ear.

"Mother of God!" he exclaimed. "This is my ax! If you'll let me have it back, when the ides of May come—that's the fifteenth of the month, you understand—I'll sacrifice a great big pail of milk to you, all covered with ripe strawberries."

"My good man," said Mercury, "of course you can have it. Take it. And since both your choice and your wishes, in this matter of axes, have been so moderate, it is Jupiter's wish that I also give you these other two. They'll make you rich: be good."

Bally thanked him courteously, bowed his head to great Jupiter, hung his old ax on his belt, and strapped it over his ass, like the bell-ringing gargoyle on the Cambray church tower. Then he hung the two heavier axes around his neck and went strutting around, beaming at all his neighbors and everyone in the whole parish, repeating to them Patelin's brief phrase:

"Have I got it? Have I got it?"

And the next day, wearing a white smock, his two precious axes on his shoulders, he went to Chinon—that magnificent city—noble, ancient— indeed, foremost in the entire world, if you believe what the most learned commentators tell us. And there in Chinon he converted the silver ax into gorgeous ready money, and his gold ax into every kind of handsome gold piece minted anywhere on earth. And then he bought up a slew of small rented farms, and plenty of barns, and more farms, and fields, and meadows, and pastures, and plowland, and vineyards, and woods, and tilled land, and grazing land, and ponds, and mills, and gardens, and grassland, and oxen, and cows, and ewes, and rams, and goats, and sows, and pigs, and donkeys, and horses, and hens, and cocks, and capons, and pullets, and geese, and ganders, and drakes, and ducks, and a bit of this and a bit of that. And pretty soon he was the richest man in the county, even richer than the lame lord of Maulevrier.

All the peasants and Jack Straws in the neighborhood, seeing how well Bally had done for himself, were thoroughly astonished. All the pity and compassion for the poor fellow, which had previously filled their hearts, was now turned into envy of his immense and completely unexpected wealth. They began to scurry and poke about, moaning as they went, trying to find out how, and where, and when, and why this huge treasure had come to him. And then they learned that it was because he'd lost his ax.

"Ho, ho!" they said. "So all we need to do, to get as rich as he is, is to lose our axes? Well, that's an easy road to follow, and it costs precious little. Is that what's in the stars, right now—all the constellations and the planetary aspects mean that whoever loses his ax will suddenly become enormously rich? Ho, ho, ha! By God, my ax, you're going to be well and truly lost, and you won't regret it, either!"

So they all lost their axes. The hell with anyone who kept his ax! No one could be the son of a decent mother who didn't lose his ax. No more trees were cut down, no more wood was chopped, anywhere in the neighborhood, because no one had an ax.

Now Aesop's fable goes on to say that certain scurvy fellows, who thought a lot better of themselves than they deserved, having sold Bally a piece of meadowland or a nice little mill, and used the proceeds to deck themselves out in high elegance, found out that this was the way he'd acquired his treasure—this and no other—and immediately sold their swords and bought axes instead, so they could lose them, too, the way the peasants were doing, and by this simple loss receive in return piles of gold and silver. You could say they were like little pilgrims on their way to Rome, selling everything they had, and borrowing as much as they could, so they could buy indulgences from a newly chosen pope. And then they cried, and prayed, and wept, and called on Jupiter.

"My ax, my ax, O Jupiter! My ax over there, my ax over there, my ax, oh, oh, oh, oh! Jupiter: my ax!"

The air for miles around rang with the cries and yells of all these ax losers.

And Mercury was swift to bring them their axes, offering each of them either the one he'd lost, or another of gold and a third of silver. They all chose the gold one, and snatched it up, thanking the great and generous Jupiter. But the moment they lifted it from the ground, bending down, Mercury cut off their heads, exactly as Jupiter had decreed. And the number of chopped-off heads was precisely equal to the number of lost axes.

And that's how it is, that's what happens to those who, simply, innocently, wish only for moderate things, and make moderate choices. Learn from them, you other lowland humbugs, who say you wouldn't give up your wishes and dreams for ten thousand francs. Don't prattle as shamelessly as I myself have heard you do, "Please God that I might have, here and now, a hundred and seventy-eight million pieces of gold! Ho! How glorious that would be!" May your teeth fall out! What more could a king, or an emperor, or the pope himself, ever wish for?

So you can see the living proof that, having made such immoderate wishes, all you get is whooping cough and sheep pox, and nothing goes into your purse. That way you get no more than the two Parisian good-for-nothings, one of whom wished for as many shining gold pieces as had been spent in Paris, buying and selling, from the time when they'd laid down the foundations for the city's first building, right down to the present moment—basing the calculation on whatever was the most expensive year (wages, prices, and rents) during that whole period. Does he strike you as slightly over particular? Might he have eaten sour plums without peeling them? Could his teeth have been set on edge? The second rascal wished for Notre Dame cathedral stuffed full of steel needles, from the floor right up to the highest vault, and he also asked for as many gold pieces as he could get into as many sacks as each and every one of those needles could sew, until all the needles broke or lost their points. That was some wish, that was! And what do you think? What actually happened? By nightfall they both had frozen feet, nice little canker sores on their chins, croupy coughs deep in their lungs, ratchety coughs in their throats, big fat boils on their rumps, and the devil of a bit of bread to clean their teeth with. So keep your wishes moderate: they'll come true, that way, and better ones, by God, if you keep on struggling and working the whole time.

"But look here," you say. "God would just as soon give me a hundred and seventy-eight thousand pieces of gold as He would the thirtieth part of half a piece, because He's all powerful. A million pieces of gold is like a penny to Him."

Ho, hey, hee! Who taught you poor people to prate and preach about God's power and predestination? Silence! Ssh, ssh, ssh! Humble yourself before His sacred face and be aware of your imperfections.

And *that,* my gouty friends, is where I rest my hopes, believing fervently that, if God so pleases, you will live in good health, since good health will be all you're asking for. Wait, wait a little. Have just half an ounce of patience—as the Genoese don't, because in the morning, after writing at their desks and conferring in their offices, and deciding who they can get money out of that day, and who in their cleverness they can cheat, fleece, deceive, and betray, they go out and, greeting each other, say, *"Sanità et guadain, messer,"* Good health and good profit to you, sir. They're not happy, just having their health: they wish endless profit on themselves—as much money as old Gadaigne himself (that filthy rich banker). So it usually happens that what they get is neither one nor the other.

So cough yourself a good cough, drink down a couple or three good ones, give your ears a happy shake, and then listen to the marvelous doings of our noble, our good Pantagruel.

Chapter One ⁄⁄ How Pantagruel Set Sail, to Visit the Oracle of the Holy Bottle

In the month of June, on the day sacred to the goddess Vesta, the same day on which Brutus conquered Spain and subjected its peoples, and on which day, also, greedy Crassus was defeated and conquered by the Parthians, Pantagruel took leave of his good father, Gargantua—who prayed, as in the days of the primitive church saintly Christians always and most wonderfully did, for his son's safe and prosperous voyage—and set sail from the port of Thalasse, accompanied by Panurge, Brother John Mincemeat, Epistemon, Gymnast, Eusthenes, Rootgatherer, Carpalim, and other trusted members of his household, together with Imported Goods, that great traveler down dangerous roads, who had joined them several days earlier, at Panurge's direction: indeed, it was he who, for good and sufficient reason, had arranged to leave with Gargantua a carefully drawn sea map of the route they would be taking, on their journey to the oracle of the Divine Bottle.

The ships in their party were as I have described them already, in the third book of this tale, plus similar numbers of trireme galleys, rowing barges, great galleons, and Liburnian sailboats, all well equipped, well caulked, and well supplied, and all carrying a good store of Pantagruelion. The officers, interpreters, pilots, assistant pilots, captains, apprentices, chief rowers, and sailors were all summoned to the *Thalamège* (or, in Greek, "Sleeping Ship"), which was Pantagruel's great flagship. On its stern, instead of a flag with Pantagruel's colors, it carried a huge bottle, half of the smoothest, most shining silver, half of gold enameled in rose— which made it easy enough to understand that white and red were the colors of these noble travelers, and that they were seeking wise words from the Holy Bottle.

An old lantern hung high from the stern of the second boat, painstakingly worked in alabaster and clear mica, indicating that they meant to sail by Lanternland.

The insignia of the third boat was a magnificent porcelain drinking mug.

The fourth boat bore a two-handled gold jug, shaped like an antique urn.

The fifth bore a remarkable pitcher, made of bright green emerald.

The sixth had a monk's drinking mug, fashioned of four metals.

The seventh had an ebony funnel, decorated all over in gold wire, interwoven with other metals.

The eighth was a fabulously precious ivy goblet, covered all over with hammered Damascene gold.

The ninth: a toasting glass of delicate pure gold.

The tenth: a cup of fragrant aloe wood (as we call it), with a fringe of Cyprus gold, worked in Damascene style.

The eleventh: a gold market basket, covered with mosaic trim.

The twelfth was a small barrel of gold, in a dull finish, covered with an ornamental border of great fat Indian pearls, fashioned into animal shapes.

And it was all done so that no one, no matter how depressed or angry, no matter how sullen, sour, or sad he might be—indeed, not even Heraclitus the Weeping Pessimist—would not feel a surge of fresh happiness, whose good spleen would not fill and flood with laughter, seeing this noble fleet of ships and their insignia—no one who would not say, simply, that these were all good drinkers, good fellows, and who would not be absolutely convinced that their voyage, both sailing away and then sailing home again, would be conducted in high spirits and in perfect good health.

So it was on the *Thalamège* that everyone assembled. And Pantagruel gave a short, exalted sermon, based on appropriate biblical quotations, on the general subject of sailing off to sea. When that was finished, he spoke a high, clear prayer to God, which could be both heard and understood by all the merchants and other citizens of Thalasse, who had run out on the breakwater to see the fleet sail.

And then, after his sermon, a holy psalm of King David was beautifully sung—the one that begins, "When Israel went out from Egypt." The psalm completed, tables were set out on the deck, and food was served. The Thalassians, who had sung the psalm along with them, sent to their homes for quantities of food and drink. Everyone on board drank to them. They drank to everyone. And this was why no one was the least bit affected by the sea, suffering no disturbance whatever, either of the stomach or in the head. Drinking saltwater for some days before they embarked would not have worked nearly so well, whether they took it straight or mixed it with wine; neither would eating quince, or lemon rind, or drinking bittersweet pomegranate juice, or fasting for a long time, or covering the stomach with paper, or indeed doing any of the things prescribed by foolish physicians, for people going to sea.

After drinking again and again, they all went back to their ships and happily set sail on a good east wind, according to which the chief pilot, whose name was Jamet Brahier, had set their course and fixed the lodestones of their compasses. It was his opinion, and also that of Imported Goods, that since the oracle of the Holy Bottle was near Cathay, in Upper India, they should not take the usual route traveled by the Portuguese, which took them across the equator and around the Cape of Good Hope, at the southern tip of Africa and far beyond the southern equinox, making so immense a voyage that they completely lost any guidance from the northern pole. Rather, they ought to sail nearer the parallel on which lay India, and circle around that pole from the west, so that, turning in a wide arc, they would remain at a latitude roughly equivalent to that of the port of Les Sables-d'Olonne, though never coming closer to the North Pole, for fear of sailing into and then being caught in the Arctic Sea. Then, following this steadily circuitous route along the same parallel, as they approached the Middle East they would have on their right-hand side that which, when they first set sail, had been on their left. Which would be incredibly useful, because without worrying about shipwreck, without any danger, without losing any of their people, they would accomplish the voyage to Upper India in great serenity (except for one day, as they passed the island of the Macraeons) and in no more than four months, while the Portuguese could scarcely sail the same distance in three years, experiencing a thousand worries and dangers too numerous to count. And it seems to me, unless someone who knows better can correct me, that this happy route must have been the same one taken by the Indians who sailed to Germany and were so honorably treated by the king of Sweden, in the days when Quintus Metellus Celer was proconsul in Gaul, all of which was later described by Cornelius Nepos, by Pomponious Mela, and by Pliny, too.

Chapter Two ⁄ How Pantagruel Bought Some Very Nice Things on the Island of Nowhere

That day, and the two following it, they saw no land or anything else of interest. It was a well-plowed route. On the fourth day they sighted an island called Medamothi, or Nowhere, beautiful to look at for all the many lighthouses and high marble towers that decorated its shores—and its coastline was as extensive as that of Canada.

Inquiring as to the ruler of this land, Pantagruel learned that it was King Philophanes (in Greek, "Eager to See and be Seen"), who was just then away, because of the marriage of his brother Philotheamon ("Terribly Curious") to the royal princess of Engys ("Neighboring Lands"). So they disembarked at the harbor, and as their crews took on water and other supplies, they studied all the different spectacles to be found both in the harbor and in its markets—the many carpets and rugs offered for sale, and all the animals, fish, birds, and other strange and exotic merchandise. Indeed, it was the third day of one of that land's largest and most important fairs, regularly attended, every year, by the richest and most celebrated merchants of Africa and Asia. And from them Brother John bought two extraordinary, precious paintings, one of which was a portrait, painted from life, of an anxious litigant, appealing from a judgment against him, and the other depicted a young page hunting for his master, shown with everything necessary for the fullest comprehension—gestures, bearing, facial features and expression, demeanor, and emotions—all painted and imagined by Maître Charles Charmois, royal portraitist to His Majesty Francis the First. And Brother John paid for his purchases in monkey money.

Panurge bought a large painting, copied from the tapestry woven long ago by Philomela, showing her sister Procne how Tereus, Procne's husband, had deflowered her and then cut out her tongue so she could not reveal the crime. Oh, I swear by this lantern handle! but that was an elegant, a miraculous painting. Now, please don't think—please—this was just a picture of a man coupling with a young girl. That would be stupid and vulgar: this was a very different sort of painting, and far more intelligent. You can see it at Thélème, on your left as you enter the main gallery.

Epistemon bought a different painting, a lifelike representation of Plato's philosophy and the atoms of Epicurus.

Rootgatherer bought one, too, showing Echo as she really looked.

Pantagruel had Gymnast buy for him seventy-eight beautifully woven tapestries, showing the life and deeds of Achilles—each tapestry twenty-four feet long and eighteen feet wide, spun of Phrygian silk, and heightened with silver and gold. They began with the wedding of Peleus and Thetis, going on to the birth of Achilles, his youth, as described by Statius Papinius, his heroic deeds, as celebrated by Homer, his death and funeral, as described by Ovid and Quintus of Smyrna. They finished with the appearance of his ghost and the sacrifice of Polyxena, as described by Euripides.

He also bought three fine young unicorns, a male with a chestnut-gold hide, and two dapple-gray females. And from a Scythian, who came from Gelonia, he bought a reindeer.

This reindeer is every bit as big as a young bull, with a head like a stag's, but somewhat larger, with a pair of noble, wide-branching antlers. He has cloven hooves, fur long like a great bear, and skin almost as hard as a suit of armor. The Gelonian told him they were hard to find, in Scythia, because they could change their color to match the places where they lived and grazed: they could look like grass, trees, shrubbery, flowers, meadows, pastureland, rocks, and in general whatever was around them. This is a trait they share with the sea squid, that is, the octopus, and also with certain wolves, as well as with Indian leopards, and with the chameleon, a lizard so remarkable that Democritus devoted an entire book to its appearance and anatomy, as well as to its magical powers and characteristics.

I've seen it change color myself, not simply because things of different color approached it, but all by itself, according to its own fears and emotions. When it was standing on a green cloth, for example, I've seen it turn a deep green. But then, after a moment, it became first yellow, then blue, brown, and violet, just as you can see the color of Indian rooster crests change according to their emotions. But what we found most remarkable about this wonderful reindeer was that not only its face and skin changed color to match its surroundings, but also its fur. When it was near Panurge, and he was wearing his homespun toga, its fur became gray. Near Pantagruel, wearing his scarlet mantle, its skin and fur turned red. Near the pilot, dressed all in white like the Egyptian priests of Isis and Osiris, its skin too turned a snowy white. And these last two colors, red and white, are impossible for the chameleon. The reindeer's natural color, apart from changing fears and feelings, was that of the donkeys of Meung-sur-Loire.

Chapter Three ⁄⁄ How Pantagruel Received a Letter from His Father, Gargantua, and of a Peculiar Way of Rapidly Learning What Was Happening in Strange and Far-off Countries

While buying these strange wild animals, Pantagruel heard ten rounds of shot, fired from small arms out on the breakwater, together with a great and happy shouting from all the ships in his fleet. Turning toward the harbor, he saw that it was one of his father Gargantua's fast messenger boats, named the *Chelidoine* (in Greek, "Swallow") because it bore on its stern a sculpture of a flying fish, or sea swallow, in full flight, executed in Corinthian brass. This is a fish about the size of a Loire minnow, fat, plump, and scaleless, and with cartilaginous wings like a bat's, so long and broad that I've many times seen them flying six feet above the water, and farther than a bow can shoot. (In Marseilles they call it the *exocoetus*, which is Greek for "resting out of its bed.") And this light messenger boat was very like a swallow, often seeming to fly over the sea, rather than sail through it. Malicorne, Gargantua's dining hall page, was on board, dispatched specifically to find out how Pantagruel was, and also to bring him bank letters of credit.

After a formal embrace of greeting, and a gracious bow, and before opening his father's letter or conducting any other business with Malicorne, Pantagruel asked:

"Did you bring a pigeon—a celestial messenger?"

"Yes," was the answer. "It's in the closed basket."

This was a bird taken from Gargantua's pigeon house, who had been in the act of hatching her young when the messenger boat sailed. If Pantagruel had experienced any bad fortune, there would have been black leather straps tied around her legs. But since only good things, and prosperous ones, had come to him, they took the bird out of the basket, tied a strip of white taffeta to her legs, and with no further ado set her free. The pigeon flew up rapidly, beating the air with unbelievable speed, as of course only pigeons do, when they have eggs hatching or just-born little ones, nature having endowed them with a stubborn need to hurry back and take care of their young. Thus it would accomplish in less than two hours, through the air, a journey that the messenger boat, sailing as hard as it could, had taken three days and three nights to complete, sailing through waves and troughs, and with a good swift tail wind always behind it. And when it was seen coming back to the pigeon house, and straight to the nest where its little ones were, brave Gargantua could see at once that it wore a white band on its legs, and could feel happy and secure that all had been going well with his son.

Indeed, this was how noble Gargantua and his son always operated, when they wished immediate news of something that deeply concerned and passionately involved them, as for example the result of a battle, whether at sea or on land, or the capture or defense of some fortified stronghold, the settlement of some important dispute, the successful (or unsuccessful) childbirth labor of some queen or great lady, the death or slow but certain recovery of their sick friends and allies, and the like. A pigeon was transported by post horses, carried from hand to hand all along the route, until it had reached the place from which news was desired. Bearing black or white, depending on what sort of news it bore, the pigeon's return would settle their minds, traveling through the air in a single hour greater distances than could have been crossed by thirty post horses, traveling by land, riding for twenty-four hours. Truly, this was how to save and redeem time. Believe me, for it's true, that in the pigeon houses on their country estates you could find plenty of birds hatching eggs, or tending just-born little ones, in every month and season of the year. It's not hard to manage, using saltpeter and sacred verbena herb.

Once the pigeon had been set free, Pantagruel read the communication sent him by his father, Gargantua, which read as follows:

My very dear child, the affection a father naturally has for a beloved son is vastly increased, for me, by the respect, indeed the warm admiration I feel for the special graces granted you by divine providence, which graces, since your departure, keep commanding my mind, freeing my heart from the single-minded, worrisome fear that your setting out has brought on some misfortune or difficulty—for you know perfectly well how fear keeps creeping into good, honest affection. And because, as Hesiod says, the beginning of anything is at least half the final result— as the common proverb puts it, it's when you bake a bread that you truly find out what it's made of—this anxiety has led me to relieve my concern by dispatching Malicorne on exactly this errand: to inform and assure me how things have gone on the first days of your voyage. If all has gone as I wish, it will be easy for me to imagine, foresee, predict, and evaluate the remainder.

I have had several jolly books rebound, which will be delivered to you by the bearer of this letter. Read them whenever you feel the need to refresh yourself, after your worthier studies. This same bearer will tell you more fully all the news of this court. May the Lord's unending peace be with you. Greet Panurge, Brother John, Epistemon, Imported Goods, Gymnast, and the others of your household, all of whom are my good friends. From your father's home, this thirteenth day of June,
    Your father and friend,

GARGANTUA

Chapter Four ⁄⁄ How Pantagruel Wrote to His Father, Gargantua, and Sent Him Some Rare and Lovely Things

After reading the above letter, Pantagruel discussed several matters with the page, Malicorne, and was with him so long that Panurge interrupted, saying:

"And when do you intend to drink? When will we drink? When will our friend the page drink? Isn't this more than enough palavering to justify a drink?"

"That's well said," replied Pantagruel. "Have a meal put together for us, in this next inn here, which takes as its sign the picture of a satyr on horseback."

And in the meantime, as a formal communication for the page to carry back, he wrote to Gargantua as follows:

My very gracious father, just as our senses and animal faculties suffer larger and more violent perturbations from all the unexpected and unlooked-for accidents which come to us in this transitory life, than from events which we expect and understand are coming (indeed, how often the soul takes leave of the body, even though such unexpected news may be joyful and exactly what is wished for), so the unexpected arrival of your page, Malicorne, has deeply moved and even troubled me. For I had no expectation of seeing any of your servants, or of hearing any news of you, before the end of this voyage of mine. And I was readily accustoming myself to the sweet memory of your august majesty, written—no, truly sculpted and engraved deep in the back portion of my brain, so that it has often re-created for me the very living, authentic image of you.

But now that you have anticipated me, with the goodness of your gracious letter, and your page's reassurances have heightened my spirits with news of your prosperity and good health—you and all of your royal household—it becomes urgently necessary, as in the past it has been simply voluntary, that above all else I praise our blessed Savior, who, by His divine kindness, has so long preserved you in such perfect health. And second, that I render eternal thanks to you for this warm and unchanging affection which you bear for me, your exceedingly humble son and worthless servant. Once, a long time ago, a Roman named Furnius said to Caesar Augustus, after receiving the emperor's favor, and his pardon, for his father, who had been one of Anthony's party, "Having done this for me, today, you have reduced me to such a shameful state that, willy-nilly, I will be thought ungrateful—whether I live or die—for nothing I can possibly do will ever match my gratitude." So too can I claim that your overflowing paternal affection sets me in just such a posture of anguish and necessity, obliged to live and die ungrateful, except that I am freed from such a criminal responsibility by what the Stoics say, when they speak of the three parties involved in any act of kindness: he who gives, he who receives, and the third, he who repays. He who receives amply repays the giver when he voluntarily accepts the proffered kindness, and keeps the giver forever in mind, just as, on the other hand, anyone receiving a kindness is the most ungrateful wretch in the world, if he acts contemptuously toward or forgets what he has received.

And being thus oppressed with an infinity of obligations, all stemming from your enormous kindness, and utterly unable to pay you back so much as the smallest part, I at least preserve myself from blame because the memory of those kindnesses will never pass from my mind, nor will my tongue ever cease both to admit and to assert that to render you any proper return will be forever beyond my strength or power.

For the rest, I remain confident of our Lord's compassion and assistance, and that He will ensure that the end of our journey corresponds to its beginning, and that it will all be experienced in happiness and perfect good health. I will not forget to set down jottings and other regular comments about our entire voyage, so that on our return you may have a truthful logbook account to read.

I have found, here, a Scythian reindeer, a strange and marvelous animal because it varies the color of its skin and fur, depending on its surroundings. You will find it to your liking. Also, it is wonderfully tractable and as easy to feed as a lamb. And I am sending you, similarly, three unicorns, better domesticated and tamed than a trio of little kittens. I have spoken to your squire and explained how they should be treated. They don't graze, because the long horn in front gets in the way. So they necessarily take their food from fruit trees, or from feeding racks, or right out of your hand; you can offer them grass and other plants, corn, apples, pears, barley, wheat—in short, all manner of fruits and vegetables. I have been astonished that our ancient writers made them out to be singularly ferocious, wild, and fierce, without ever having seen a living unicorn. You can, if you like, easily prove the contrary: you will find that they are as gentle as any animals in the world, provided that no one maliciously angers them.

So too, I send you the life and deeds of Achilles, beautifully and most carefully worked in a set of tapestries. And I assure you that whatever new and unknown animals, plants, birds, and rocks we may find and take specimens of, all along our journey, will be brought back to you, with the help of God, our Savior, to whom I pray that in His holy grace He may keep and preserve you.

Written from the island of Nowhere, this fifteenth of June. Panurge, Brother John, Epistemon, Imported Goods, Gymnast, Eusthenes, Rootgatherer, Carpalim, all devoutly kiss your hand and greet you, in return, a hundred times over.

Your humble son and servant,

PANTAGRUEL

While Pantagruel wrote the above letter, Malicorne was feasted, greeted, and embraced on all sides. God alone knows what a time they had, and how many messages from all the travelers he promised to deliver.

Having finished his letter, Pantagruel too feasted with the page. And he gave him a heavy gold chain, weighing as much as eight hundred gold pieces, in which were set, on every seventh link, great diamonds, rubies, emeralds, turquoises, pearls, with no consecutive gems the same. And to each of Malicorne's sailors he gave five hundred gold pieces. To his father, Gargantua, he sent the Scythian reindeer, covered with a satin cape embroidered with gold, along with the tapestries which told the life and deeds of Achilles, and also the three unicorns, decked out in gold-fringed cloth. And so they left the island of Nowhwere, Malicorne to return to Gargantua, Pantagruel to continue his voyage. And when they were on the high seas, Pantagruel had Epistemon read to him from the books which the page had brought, which books they found cheerful and pleasant, and about which I would cheerfully tell you, if you really pressed me to do so.

Chapter Five ⁄⁄ How Pantagruel Met a Ship Returning from Lanternland

On the fifth day, as we were beginning, little by little, to circle about the pole and to move away from the equinox, we saw a merchant ship sailing up on our port side, heading toward us. That was most pleasant for all of us, ourselves and the merchants both—to us, because we could hear news of the sea, and to them, because they could hear news about terra firma.

Meeting up with them, we learned they were French and from Saintonge. As they chatted, Pantagruel realized that they were returning from Lanternland, and the news made him happier still, and so too everyone in the fleet. We proceeded to ask them all about the country and the people, and learned that, toward the end of July (it was now, you will recall, the middle of June), the general council of Lanternland would be meeting, so that if we arrived at that time, as it seemed very likely we would, we would be treated to a fine, honorable, and happy gathering of Lanterners. Indeed, they were already making such extensive preparations for the occasion that, surely, everything was going to be thoroughly Lanternized. And they told us, too, that passing on the way the great kingdom of the Gebarim (in Hebrew, "Warriors"), we would there be honorably welcomed and received by their king, Ohabé the Friendly, lord of that realm. The king and all his subjects, we were informed, likewise spoke French after the fashion of the citizens of Touraine.

Meanwhile, as we were taking in this news, Panurge got into a quarrel with a merchant from Taillebourg, a fellow named Dingdong. It happened like this.

This Dingdong, seeing Panurge without a codpiece, and wearing spectacles on his hat, said to one of his friends:

"Oh, there's a first-class cuckold."

Now, wearing those spectacles kept Panurge's ears more open than usual, and hearing this he turned on the merchant, saying:

"How the devil could I be a cuckold, when I'm not even married? But judging by your sloppy, fat face you know all about it."

"Yes indeed," answered the merchant, "I do, and I wouldn't be anything but married for all the spectacles worn in Europe, or for all the telescopes in Africa, either. Because I've got one of the prettiest, most charming, most respectable, chastest women anyone ever married, anywhere in Saintonge—with all due respect to the others. And what do you think I'm bringing home to her? A handsome branch of red coral, if you know what I mean, a full eleven inches long—her special Christmas present. What's it to you, anyway? Why are you sticking your nose in my business? Who are you? Where do you come from—up there or way down there? O bespectacled Antichrister, tell me if God is really your Father in heaven!"

"What I'm asking you," said Panurge, "is this: if everything went well, and I humpedthumpedpumped your so pretty, so charming, so respectable, so chaste and modest wife, and did the job so well that Priapus, that stiff god of gardens—who lives right here and comes and goes as he pleases, not having to worry about any codpieces—got so far inside her that he couldn't get out and it looked as if he might have to stay there forever, unless you pulled him out with your teeth—well, what I want to know is: what would you do? Would you just let him stay in there? Or would you pull him out with those handsome teeth of yours? Answer me, O you Muhammadan sheep seller, who really does come from all the devils down there in hell."

"I'd give you," answered the merchant, "a whack on that bespectacled ear with my sword, and I'd kill you like a sheep."

And as he spoke, he started to draw his sword. But it stuck in its sheath—which is not hard to understand, for at sea all armor and weapons naturally get rusty, what with the excessive and nitrogenous humidity. Panurge ran back to Pantagruel, for help. Brother John took out his newly sharpened short sword and would have murdered the merchant on the spot, had not the ship's master, and the other passengers, begged Pantagruel not to create any scandal on his boat. So the quarrel was settled and Panurge and the merchant shook hands, and then they drank to one another, to witness their perfect reconciliation.

Chapter Six ⁄ The Quarrel Over, Panurge Haggles with Dingdong for One of His Sheep

The quarrel completely resolved, Panurge whispered to Epistemon and Brother John:

"Just step back a little, out of the way, and have fun watching. This is going to be a nice game, if the string doesn't break."

Then he turned to the merchant and again drank his health, in a full mug of good Lanternish wine. And the merchant answered his toast, courteously and honorably. And then Panurge earnestly begged that he would do him the favor of selling one of his sheep. To which the merchant replied:

"Alas! Alas! My friend, our neighbor—truly, you know how to make fun of poor people like me! Oh, you're a noble client, you are! Ah yes, the brave sheep buyer! My God, you don't look a bit like a sheep buyer— you look like a pickpocket. By Saint Nicholas, my son! but how good it must be to follow you around with a full purse, once the thaw comes! Ho, ho, anyone who doesn't know you—oh, you'd do them in, all right! But look here, ha, my friends, all of you—see how he plays the role—see how important he looks!"

"Hold on!" said Panurge. "Seriously, do me a favor and sell me one of your sheep. How much?"

"What do you expect," answered the merchant, "our good friend, my excellent neighbor? These are first-class sheep—this is where Jason got his golden fleece. This is where the royal house of Burgundy came, to christen their knights of the Golden Fleece. These are Levantine sheep, tremendous sheep, fat, golden sheep."

"Fine," said Panurge. "But sell me one, please: that's all I want. I'll pay you well, and I'll pay you right away, and in good solid Levantine coin, uncropped and heavy. How much?"

"Our neighbor, my friend," answered the merchant, "lend me your other ear for a moment."

PANURGE: At your service.
MERCHANT: You're going to Lanternland?
PAN.: Of course.
MERCH.: To see the world?
PAN.: Of course.
MERCH.: Happily?
PAN.: Of course.
MERCH.: Your name, I believe, is Robin Ram?
PAN.: You seem to think so.
MERCH.: But I don't want to make you angry.
PAN.: I didn't think you did.
MERCH.: And you're the king's fool?
PAN.: Of course.
MERCH.: Put it there! Ha, ha! You're going to see the world, you're the king's fool, your name is Robin Ram. See this sheep here? His name is Robin, too—the same as you. Robin, Robin, Robin.
SHEEP: Baa, baa, baa, baa.
MERCH.: Oh, what a gorgeous voice!
PAN.: Beautiful—and melodic, too.
MERCH.: Now here's the deal we can make, you and me, our friend and neighbor. You—that is, Robin Ram—you climb onto this side of the scale, and my Robin Sheep will go on the other side. I'll bet you a hundred of the best oysters going that in weight, in value, in price, he'll hang you high and tight—just as, some day, you're sure to be hung.

"Hold on," said Panurge. "But it will be a wonderful thing for me, and for your heirs, too, if you'd like to sell him to me. Or some other singer in your bass choir. Please do, my lord, sir, good gentleman."

"Our friend," answered the merchant, "my neighbor, the finest clothes in Rouen will be made from the fleece of these sheep. Compared to these, the finest wool in the finest ball gowns in France is just cotton padding. They'll make the finest, softest morocco leather from their hides, and they'll sell them for genuine Turkish morocco, or morocco from Montélimart, or, at worst, Spanish morocco. Their guts will make strings for violins and harps, which will bring a pretty penny, sold as if they were from Munich or from Abruzzi. So: what do you think?"

"If you'd be so good as to sell me one," said Panurge, "I'll be forever tied to your front door—eternally grateful. Here's all the money you could want. How much?"

And as he spoke, he showed his purse, stuffed full of gold pieces.

Chapter Seven // Panurge and Dingdong Go On Bargaining

"My friend," answered the merchant, "our neighbor, this is food only for kings and princes. The flesh of these sheep is so dainty, so savory, and so sweet, that it's like heavenly balm. I've brought these animals from a country where the pigs—may God save us!—eat nothing but peaches and pears from India: the sows (saving the honor of everyone here) eat only orange flowers."

"Then," said Panurge, "sell me one, and I'll pay you like a king, on my honor. How much?"

"Our friend," answered the merchant, "my neighbor, these are sheep from the very herd that Zeus used, when he had Phrixus and Hellé carried over the Sea of Hellespont on a golden fleece."

"Damnation!" said Panurge. "You're *clericus vel adiscens,* either a priest or a scholar."

"*Ita* are cabbages," answered the merchant, "and *vere* are leeks. But *rr, rrr, rrrr.* Ho, Robin, *rr, rrrrrr.* You don't understand that kind of talk. And just listen to this! In every field where these sheep piss, the wheat comes sprouting up as if God Himself had pissed there: you don't need any other marl or manure. And even more: the chemists get the best saltpeter in the world from their urine. And by using their dung—don't get upset if I mention such things—the doctors in our country cure seventy-eight different kinds of sicknesses, the least serious of them being the dropsy of Saint Eutropius of Saintes—from which may God preserve us! So: what do you think, our neighbor, my friend? I paid through the nose for these sheep, too."

"Who cares what they cost!" answered Panurge. "Just sell me one, and I'll pay you well."

"Our friend," said the merchant, "my neighbor, just think for a minute about what marvels of nature these animals are that you're looking at right now—even in a part of them you probably think is useless. Just take those horns over there, and grind them up with an iron mortar and pestle or an andiron—it doesn't matter which. Then spread as much as you like out in the sun, and keep it moist. In a couple of months you'll have the best asparagus in the world sprouting right up—and I don't even concede that they grow better stuff in Ravenna. Hah! Now just tell me that the horns on you other cuckolds have such incredible powers, such marvelous properties!"

"Hold on—patience," answered Panurge.

"Now I don't know," said the merchant, "if you're a scholar. I've seen lots of scholars cuckolded—I mean really big, important scholars. Oh yes! And by the way, if you are a scholar, then you know that the lowest parts of these divine animals—I mean, their feet—have a bone, the heel, or strictly speaking the ankle bone, with which in the old days they used to play at knucklebones—and they never used the bones of any other animal in the world, not even the Indian donkey or the Libyan gazelle. One night, Emperor Octavian Augustus won more than fifty thousand gold pieces, playing knucklebones. Now, you other cuckolds, you don't have to worry about winning that much!"

"Patience—hold on," answered Panurge. "But let's get this over with."

"But how," said the merchant, "how, our friend, my neighbor, will I ever be able to properly praise for you the internal organs of these animals? The shoulders, the fat haunches, the hindquarters, the prime ribs, the chest, the liver, the spleen, the tripes, the guts, the bladder—with which they play ball—the mutton cutlets, which in fact they use in Pygmy Land, and make little bows for shooting cherry pits at cranes—and the head, from which, with just a touch of sulfur, you can make a miraculous concoction, sovereign for easing the bowels of constipated dogs."

"Oh, shit, shit!" said the master of the boat, speaking to the merchant. "This is too damned much salesmanship. Sell him a sheep, if you want to. And if you don't want to, stop playing games."

"I'll sell him a sheep," answered the merchant, "out of my affection for you, dear captain. But he's going to pay me three pounds in good Turnois gold for each one he wants."

"That's steep," said Panurge. "Where I come from, I could have five—no, six, for that price. Make sure you're not asking too much. You're not the first man I've met who wanted to get rich too fast and finally fell into poverty—yes, and often broke his neck in the process."

"Forty thousand fevers!" said the merchant. "Oh, you thick-skulled fool! By the bit of Christ's holy foreskin, in the abbey of Charroux, the smallest, scrawniest of these sheep is worth four times as much as any the Coraxians sold in Tuditania, in the old days—that's in Spain—and got a gold talent for every one of them. And just what do you think, you prize fool, a single gold talent was worth?"

"Blessed sir," said Panurge, "you're getting hot under the collar—I can see it—I understand. Fine! Take it—here, here's your money."

Having paid the merchant, Panurge looked through the flock and picked out a splendid big ram, and carried him off, bleating and baaing. Hearing which, all the other sheep began to bleat, watching to see where their companion was being taken. And the merchant said to his shepherds:

"Oh, what a buyer he is—just see which one he picked! He knows his sheep, the rascal! Really and truly, I was saving that one for the lord of Cancale, because I know just what he likes. The way he is, he gets deliriously happy when he's got a leg of mutton in hand, cooked just right—like a left-handed tennis racket, so he can do his work with the knife in his right hand. Oh, he wields a wicked knife!"

Chapter Eight ⁄⁄ How Panurge Drowns the Merchant and His Sheep

Suddenly, I have no idea how (everything was so unexpected that I had no time to think about it), Panurge simply went to the side of the boat and pitched his ram, bleating and bellowing, right into the sea. All the other sheep, bleating and bellowing at the same pitch, began one after the other to jump and leap into the sea after him: they pushed and shoved to see who would be the first to follow their companion. It was impossible to stop them, since as you know sheep always follow the leader, wherever he goes. So says Aristotle, in the ninth book of his *Animal History:* the sheep is the stupidest, most foolish animal in the world.

The merchant, terrified that right under his very eyes he was about to see all his sheep die of drowning, struggled with all his might to stop them, to hold them back. But it was useless. One after the other they jumped into the sea and were gone. At last, he grabbed a great, strong ram by the fleece, at the edge of the deck, thinking he could thus hold back and save the rest of the flock. But the ram was so powerful that he carried the merchant into the sea with him, just as Polyphemus' sheep—the one-eyed Cyclops' flock—carried Ulysses and his companions out of the cave. And along with their master, Dingdong, went all the shepherds and other herdsmen, too, some of them trying to hold on to horns, some to legs, some clutching at a fleece. But all of them were swept into the sea and miserably drowned.

Standing just outside the galley kitchen, Panurge picked up an oar—not to help the shepherds, but to keep them from climbing up onto the boat and escaping the general shipwreck. And he was preaching to them most eloquently, as if he were a junior Friar Olivier Maillard or a second Friar John Bourgeois—demonstrating to them, according to proper rhetorical argument, the world's infinite miseries, the good and the happiness of the other life, asserting that in this valley of misery those who had passed on were happier than those still living, and promising each of them that he would put up a fine tombstone for them, an honorable grave site, high on Mount Cenis, when he returned from his trip to Lanternland. But if they were in truth not yet weary of this mortal life, and uninterested in drowning, he wished them all good luck in finding some whale which, perhaps on the third day following, might set them ashore, safe and sound, in some sweet land, after the example of Jonah.

And with the boat swept clean of the merchant, his sheep, and his shepherds:

"Have we still," said Panurge, "any sheepish souls among us? Where are those who follow Thibault the Lamb and Reginald the Ram, who sleep while others graze? I don't know of any. Well, Brother John, that was an old military maneuver: what do you think of it?"

"I like everything you do," answered Brother John. "I don't find anything wrong—except it seems to me that, just as in wartime we used to promise double pay for the whole day, right on the eve of the battle or the assault: if the battle's won, then there's plenty to pay it with; and if the battle's lost, they're ashamed to ask for it—not the way those Swiss runaways did, after the battle of Cerisoles. Anyway, you ought to promise the money but not actually pay it: let it stay in your purse."

"I," said Panurge, "have had one hell of a good time for my money! Mother of God, I've had enough fun for fifty thousand francs. Let's go in: the wind's blowing in the right direction. Brother John, just listen to me. No one amuses me for free, or at least without some acknowledgment. I'm not as ungrateful as all that: I never was, and I never will be. And no man does me dirty without being sorry for it, whether in this world or the next one. I'm not as conceited as all that!"

"You," said Brother John, "damn yourself like an old devil. It's written: *Mihi vindictam,* etc., etc., Vengeance is mine. Well, that's all in the prayer book."

Chapter Nine ⁄⁄ How Pantagruel Came to the Island of Ennasin, and Its Strange Kinship System

The wind kept blowing to us from the southwest; it had been an entire day since we'd seen land. On the third day, just when the flies were beginning to stir themselves (or a little before noon), we saw a triangular island which, in shape and location, looked very like Sicily. It was called Alliance Land.

Both the men and women resembled the bloody red Poitevins, except they all—men, women, and little children—had a nose shaped like the ace of clubs. Which was why the old name for the island was Ennasin, or Noseless. Every one of them was related to all the rest, as they themselves boasted: the mayor told us quite openly:

"You people from another world, you think it was wonderful that, from a single Roman family (that is, the Fabians), on a single day (that is, the thirteenth of February), there sallied forth through a single gate (that is, the Carmental Gate, which used to stand at the foot of the Capitol, between the Tarpeian Rock and the river Tiber), to fight against certain enemies of Rome (that is, the Etrurian Veientes), three hundred and six soldiers of the same blood, together with five thousand other fighting men who served them, and all of them destined to die (that is, near the Cremera River, which flows from Lake Baccano). But this land, if need be, could send out more than three hundred thousand fighting men, all related, all of a single family."

Their familial relationships were exceedingly strange. Indeed, since everyone was related to everyone else, we found that no one was either father or mother, brother or sister, uncle or aunt, cousin or nephew, son-in-law or daughter-in-law, godfather or godmother, or anything else. Except that I really saw one very old man, who had no nose, call a little girl of three or four "my father," and the little girl called him "my daughter."

The relationships between them were such that I heard a man call a woman "my beanpole," and the woman call him "my porpoise."

"Those two," said Brother John, "must really feel the tide coming up, when they rub their bellies together."

One of them, laughing, called to a pretty girl, "Good morning, my curry comb!" And she greeted him back: "Good day to you, my sorrel nag!"

"Hey, hey, hey!" cried Panurge. "Come see a curry comb, a hot little horse, and a calf. Hasn't that comb got a nice sorrel tint? That black-striped nag must certainly get himself well curried."

Another one greeted his sweetheart, "Good-bye, my desk." And she answered, "The same to you, my lawsuit."

"By Saint Trinian," said Gymnast, "that's a lawsuit that must spend a lot of time lying around on that desk."

One of them called another woman "my worm" and got called, in return, "my rascal."

"That worm," said Eusthenes, "must really get wriggled around."

Another man greeted a female relative, "Good day, my ax," and she answered, "The same to you, my handle!"

"God's belly!" cried Carpalim. "How do they ever get that handle off that ax? How does that handle get axed? Is this really the splendid handle all the Italian whores go hunting? Or just a Franciscan friar with a big fat handle of his own?"

Walking past, I saw a rake who, greeting a woman relative, called her "my mattress." She answered, "My quilt." And indeed, he looked a lot like a good thick quilt.

One called a woman "my crumb," and she called him "my crust." Another man addressed a woman as his fence post, and she called him her poker. One called a woman "my good old shoe," and she called him slipper. Another called a woman his high-heeled boot, and she called him her sandal. One called a woman his mitten, and she called him her glove. One called a woman his pork rind, and she called him her bacon— and they were like bacon and rind to each other. So too, one of them called a woman "my omelet," and she called him "my egg"—and they were every bit as close as eggs in an omelet. In the same way, one of them called a woman "my bundle," and she called him "my stick." But you couldn't for the life of you figure out what kinship, or relationship, or connection, or degree of bloodline lineage they had, according to our way of looking at things, except that someone told us he was a stick from her bundle. Another fellow, greeting a woman, said, "Hello there, my shell," and she answered, "And the same to you, my oyster."

"That's an oyster," said Carpalim, "on the half shell."

And another one greeted a woman, "Long life to you, my pea pod!" To which she replied, "Long life to you, my pea!"

"And that," said Gymnast, "is surely a pea in a pod."

One miserable fellow, wearing big, thick wooden clogs, met up with a great, fat, squatty wench, and said to her, "May God keep you, my old wooden shoe, my toy top, my old water pump!" And she answered him, stoutly, "And the same to you, you birch-rod whip!"

"By Saint Francis!" said Imported Goods. "Is he a good enough whip to set that top spinning?"

A high and mighty professor, in full academic wig and robes, after chatting for a while with a certain aristocratic young lady, took leave of her, saying, "Thank you, thank you, O lovely lady!" "But," said she, "even more so to you, unlucky roll of the dice!"

"From a lovely lady to an unlucky roll of the dice," said Pantagruel, "is hardly an irrelevant linkage."

A ripe old rake went by and said to a young girl, "Hey, hey, hey! Long time no see, old bag!" "But I'm always glad to see you," she answered, "my hornpipe!"

"Put them together," said Panurge, "and blow up their assholes: that'll be a bagpipe."

One man called his woman "my sow," and she called him her hay. It occurred to me that this was one sow who was glad to be put out to pasture.

I saw, near us, a slightly humpbacked fop, greeting a woman, "Bye-bye, my hole!" And she returned his greeting in the same fashion: "May God keep you, my peg!" To which Brother John said:

"Now she, it seems to me, is all hole, and he, in the same way, is all peg. The question is, then: can this hole be completely stopped up by this peg."

Another man greeted a woman, saying, "Good-bye, my bird coop!" She answered, "Hello, my goose!"

"I think," said Powerbrain, "that goose spends a lot of time in his coop."

One good drinker, chatting with a lively girl, said to her: "Now don't forget, fart face!" "You neither, shit-head!" she answered.

"Are those two really relatives?" Pantagruel asked the mayor. "They seem like enemies to me, not people of the same blood, because he called her a fart face. Where we come from, you can't imagine a greater insult than that."

"My good friends from another world," answered the mayor, "you won't find closer or better kinsmen than this Shit-head and that Fart Face. They popped out into this world invisibly, the two of them together, at the same time and from the same hole."

"Ah," said Panurge, "the same northwest wind blew up their mother's skirts?"

"What 'mother,' " said the mayor, "do you mean? That's a word from your world. But they have neither father nor mother. All that is for people from over the water—provincials with hay in their boots."

Our good Pantagruel saw everything and heard everything, but hearing these statements he seemed distinctly upset.

And then, after a thorough look at the land and the customs of the Ennasin people, we went to an inn for a bit of refreshment. We found a wedding going on, and everyone having a high time. With us looking on, they made a happy union between a pear—a juicy young woman, as far as we could see (although those who had felt her said she was over-ripe)—and a fuzzy young cheese, a bit on the reddish side. I'd heard of such marriages before, and I knew several that had been celebrated. And they do say that in our cow country there's no marriage like that between pears and cheese.

In another room I saw them marrying an old lady boot to a lithe young shoe. And Pantagruel was told the young shoe was taking her as his wife because she was in wonderful shape, extremely well made and heavily greased for household use, which was of course especially good for a fisherman.

And in yet another room I saw a young dancing shoe marry an old slipper. And they told us that the young shoe was motivated neither by her beauty nor her charm, but by pure avarice and covetousness for the gold pieces she had sewn into her.

Chapter Ten ⁄ How Pantagruel Disembarked on the Island of Peace, Whose King Was Saint Bread Roll

The southwest wind blew on from behind us; leaving those unpleasant Relatives, with their ace-of-clubs noses, we took to the high seas. As the sun was setting, we reached the island of Peace, a large island, fertile, rich, and populous, where the king was Saint Bread Roll. Accompanied by his children, and by the princes of his court, the king came to the harbor to receive Pantagruel and to lead him to his castle. The queen, together with her daughters and the ladies of the court, greeted us as we entered. It being the courtesy and custom of the country, the king directed the queen and all her following to kiss Pantagruel and all his people, and so it was done—except for Brother John, who stayed away, slipping in among the king's officers.

The king tried as hard as he could to keep Pantagruel with him for that day and the next, but Pantagruel excused himself, maintaining that such fair weather and such a good wind could not be neglected: travelers more often wish for than find such opportunities, and when they were available they had to be exploited. You could not always have them, though you often wished you did. With this reminder, and after each of us had drunk twenty-five or thirty toasts, the king gave us permission to leave.

But returning to the harbor and not seeing Brother John, Pantagruel asked where he'd gotten to and why he wasn't with the rest of us. Not knowing how to excuse him, Panurge wished to go back to the castle and call him, but just then Brother John came running up, all smiles, and shouting with immense and heartfelt delight, saying:

"Long live noble Bread Roll! By God's own belly, he knows how to eat! I've just come from there: everything gets ladled out hand over fist. I thought I'd just get myself well stuffed, right up to the top of my cloak, in good monkish style."

"There you go, my friend," said Pantagruel, "always in the kitchen!"

"By the body and blood of chickens!" answered Brother John. "I know how to behave in a kitchen a lot better than I know how to crap around with women—*magni, magna, chiabrena,* creepery, crappery, oh, a double bow, and then another, and all that hugging and squeezing and kissing hands, if you please, oh, thank you, Your Grace, Your Majesty, you're so welcome, tiddle-taddle, fiddle-faddle. Shit—it's all Rouen piddle, it's all piss and crap! Lord! I'm not saying I never take a shot at it, when I've got the chance—when I can get my name on a lady's list. But this shitting and shatting and bowing and scraping gets me angry faster than a young devil—I mean, a young double. Saint Benedict never lies about stuff like this. You talk about kissing ladies? By the noble, the sacred habit I wear,

I'm delighted to leave it alone, because I'm afraid that what happened to the lord of Guerche might happen to me."

"What?" asked Pantagruel. "I know him, he's one of my best friends."

"Once," said Brother John, "he was invited to a sumptuous, a magnificent banquet, given by his neighbor and relative, to which were also invited all the gentlemen, ladies, and noble girls in the neighborhood. Now, all these other guests, while awaiting his arrival, dressed up the host's young pages as elegant, fine young ladies. And then these decked-out pages greeted him as he entered, as if they really were young women. He kissed them all, with great courtesy and a lot of magnificent bowing and scraping. But finally the ladies, who were waiting for him in the gallery, burst out laughing and signaled to the pages to take off their fancy clothes. And when the good man saw this, in sheer shame and anger he refused to kiss these genuine women and girls. He said that since they'd disguised the pages so well, by the body and blood of God! the women and girls might be servants, too, even more elaborately disguised.

"By the Lord on high! *da jurandi,* forgive me for swearing, but why aren't we more anxious to bring our souls into God's fine kitchen? And there why don't we contemplate His spits turning, the lovely harmony of the jacks that keep them turning, how the flavoring pork and bacon have been placed, how hot the soup is, how the desserts are being prepared, how the wine is being served? *Beati immaculati in via,* Blessed are those who remain undefiled along the way. That's prayer-book stuff, that is."

Chapter Eleven ⁄ Why Monks Like Being in Kitchens

"That, said Epistemon, "is spoken like a true monk. I say a monk showing how to be truly monkish; I do not say a monk who's simply been monked. Indeed, I'm reminded of what I saw and heard in Florence, perhaps twenty years ago. We were a great fine company of scholarly folk, lovers of travel and anxious to visit Italy's ancient sites, and her special wonders, and her learned men. But when we looked very closely at Florence—its location, its beauties, the structure of the cathedral, the magnificence of the splendid churches and palaces—and began to compete with one another, to see who could best praise this glorious city, a monk from Amiens, Bernard Lardon, said to us, all puzzled and annoyed:

" 'I can't see what deviltry makes you fall all over yourselves, praising this place. I've looked as hard as you have, and my eyes are every bit as good as yours. So? What does this place have? These are nice houses. That's that. But by God and our master Saint Bernard, may our good patron protect us in our need! Nowhere in this entire city have I seen a single eating house—and I've looked hard and anxiously. I tell you I've had my eyes open in every direction, ready to count them up and number them, on this side or that—how many I'd find, and on which side of the road there'd be more ovens cooking away. Now, back in Amiens, in less than a fourth of the distance we've covered—but let's say a third of all we've been looking at so closely—I could have shown you more than fourteen good old eating houses, and blessedly aromatic ones. I can't understand the pleasure you've obviously taken, seeing all these lions and— well, you call them Africans, but I call them tigers—anyway, staring at them, near the belfrey, or the porcupines and ostriches at Lord Philip Strozzi's palace. By my faith, fellows, I'd rather see a good fat goose roasting on a spit! All this porphyry and marble is pretty: I don't say a thing against it. But the sweet cakes in Amiens are more to my taste. These old statues are very well put together, I agree, But by Saint Ferreol of Abbeville, who beat us all at tending geese, the pretty girls back home are a thousand times better-looking!' "

"What's the significance," asked Brother John, "what does it mean, that you always find monks in kitchens, but never kings, popes, or emperors?"

"Is it," answered Rootgatherer, "something intrinsic, some special property in the cooking pots and roasting spits, which draws the monk to them, as a magnet pulls in iron? and yet a special culinary quality which has no effect on emperors, or popes, or kings? Or is it some more subtle tendency, an attraction natural to monkish habits and cowls, which inevitably draws and pushes our good monks right into kitchens, as if they had no volition whatever in the matter?"

"I refer," answered Epistemon, "to the fact that form imitates substance. Or so says Averroës."

"Yes, yes!" said Brother John.

"Let me speak to that," replied Pantagruel, "though I won't even try to solve the problem you raise, because it's a bit prickly—you barely need to get near it and you'll get stung. I remember reading that Antigonus, king of Macedonia, went into his camp kitchen one day and found the poet Antagoras, who was frying an eel and tending to the sauce pan himself. So he asked him, gaily, 'Did Homer fry eels, when he described Agamemnon's heroic deeds?' 'Ah,' answered Antagoras, 'my king, do you think that Agamemnon, when he was doing such noble deeds, was interested in whether anyone in his camp was frying eels?' The king thought it was wrong for a poet to be up to such things in his kitchen. But the poet showed him that it was far worse for a king to be found in the kitchen at all."

"I can beat that one," said Panurge. "Let me tell you what Claude Breton, lord of Villandry, told my lord the duke of Guise. They were discussing a battle between King Francis and Emperor Charles the Fifth, on which occasion Breton had been brilliantly armored, with gleaming leg plates and steel shoes, and with a splendid horse, although he'd never been seen in the actual fighting. 'But I was there, by my faith,' said Breton, 'and it's easy enough to prove it, because, My Lord Guise, I was in a place where you yourself would never dare be found!' The royal duke was annoyed at this remark, which struck him as distinctly too bold and reckless, so he broke off the discussion. But Breton had no trouble smoothing it all over with a joke, adding, 'Yes, I was with the baggage, a place your honor would not likely hide, as I was doing.' "

And chatting in this way, they came to their ships and set sail, remaining no longer on the island of Peace.

Chapter Twelve ⁄⁄ How Pantagruel Passed through Proxyland, and the Strange Ways of Shysters

Continuing on, the next day we passed Proxyland, a dirty, botched-up place. I couldn't make head or tails of it. There we saw lawyers and Shysters—people plainly capable of absolutely anything. No one asked us to have a drink, or to take a bite of food. But with an infinity of learned compliments they did tell us they were eternally ready to serve us—provided we paid them. One of our interpreters explained to Pantagruel what a strange way of earning their bread these people had—it was exactly the opposite of life in present-day Rome. In Rome, countless numbers of people earn their living by poisoning, clubbing, and killing, but the Shysters live by being beaten. It's gotten to the point where, if they have to go for too long without being beaten, they necessarily die of starvation, and their wives and children with them.

"It's just," said Panurge, "like those people, according to Galen, who can't lift their tools up to their belt buckles unless they're soundly whipped. By holy Saint Thibault, if anyone whipped me like that it would knock me down, not stand me up—by all the devils!"

"It happens," said the interpreter, "like this. In this country, if a monk, or a preacher, or a moneylender, or a lawyer wants to injure some nobleman, he sends one of these Shysters. The Shyster hands him a summons, setting a day and time, and insults him, annoys him, slanders him outrageously, as he's been hired and instructed to do, until the nobleman—if he isn't paralyzed from the neck up, and dumber than a tadpole—has no choice but to whip him, and beat him on the head with a sword, or else on the legs—or, better still, to throw him off the walls or out the windows of his castle. Once that's done, voilà! the Shyster's rich for four months, as if getting beaten up were the way he naturally makes his harvest. The monk, or the usurer, or the lawyer will pay him handsomely—and then he'll get such extravagant compensation from the nobleman, that that gentleman's likely to go bankrupt and perhaps even to languish and die in prison, as if the person he'd beaten had been the king himself."

"I know a splendid remedy for such nastiness," said Panurge. "The lord of Basché uses it."

"What?" asked Pantagruel.

"The lord of Basché," said Panurge, "is a brave, virtuous, magnanimous, chivalric gentleman. Coming home from a certain long war, in which the duke of Ferrara, helped by the French, had valiantly defended himself against the furies of Pope Julius the Second, he found himself, day after day, summoned, subpoenaed, and generally shystered, all according to the will and the leisure time of the fat prior of Saint Louant.

"One day, dining with his household (for he was both affable and charming), he sent for his baker, a man named Loire, and his wife, together with the curate of the parish, whose name was Oudart, and who served him as wine steward (which was then the custom in France), and in the presence of his gentlemen and the other domestics said to them:

" 'My children, you see what profound distress these villainous Shysters are causing me, day after day. I have made up my mind that, if you won't help me, I'm going to abandon this country and go fight for the sultan, devil take me if I don't. Now, from this day on, when any of these Shysters come to this house, I want you to be ready—you, Loire, and your wife—to present yourselves in my great hall, wearing your beautiful wedding clothes, exactly as if you were newly engaged and were about to be married. Take this: here are a hundred gold pieces, so you can keep those beautiful clothes in good condition. Now, you, my dear Oudart, must be certain to also appear, wearing your best surplice and stole, and carrying holy water, as if you were going to perform the ceremony. Now you, Trudon' (that being his drummer's name), 'you have to be there, too, with your flute and your drum. Once the marriage vows have been exchanged, and the bride's been kissed (to the sound of your drum), I want all of you to give one another something to remember the wedding by—using your fists, but just gentle taps. This will only make your dinner taste better. But when you get to the Shyster, hit him as if you were threshing green rye—don't hold back: smack him, whack him, beat him—please! Wait: in a minute I'm going to give you some good heavy jousting gloves, covered in kid leather. Hit him anywhere and everywhere—don't count the blows. Whoever beats him best will prove he best loves me. Don't be afraid of any legal reprisals: I'll stand guarantee for every one of you. Hit him, of course, as you're laughing, in the traditional style—the way it always is at our weddings.'

" 'Of course,' asked Oudart, 'but how will we know just who is the Shyster? In this great house of yours, there are always lots of visitors from all over.'

" 'I've taken care of that,' answered Basché. 'When a man comes to this door, either on foot or on some scraggly nag, with a great fat silver ring on his thumb, that will be the Shyster. After introducing him courteously, the porter will ring a bell. Be ready, come right into the hall, and play out the tragicomedy I've explained to you.'

"That same day, as God would have it, an old, fat, red-faced Shyster arrived. When he knocked on the door, the porter recognized him by his thick, heavy gaiters, his miserable horse, by a linen bag stuffed with legal papers, hanging from his belt—and most especially by the great silver ring he wore on his left thumb. The porter greeted him courteously, introduced him respectfully, and then gaily rang the bell. At that sound, Loire and his wife, dressed in their beautiful clothes and looking very handsome, appeared in the great hall. Oudart had put on his surplice and stole. Coming out of his private room, he met the Shyster, and took him back into his room, where he made sure he had plenty to drink, and took enough time doing it for all of them to put on their heavy gloves. And then he said to the Shyster:

" 'You couldn't have come at a happier moment. Our lord is in a splendid humor. Pretty soon we'll all be celebrating—and they'll be ladling it out by the bucketful, because we're just about to have a wedding. Here, drink up, enjoy yourself.'

"While the Shyster drank, Basché saw that everyone was gathered in the great hall, all their equipment ready, so he sent for Oudart, who came, carrying the holy water. The Shyster followed him, being careful, as he entered the hall, to bow humbly in all directions. And then he served Basché with a summons. But Basché only embraced him warmly, gave him a gold piece, and begged him to remain for the wedding ceremony, which he did.

"When it was done, they began to exchange light blows on the arms and shoulders. But when they got to the Shyster, they treated him to great whacks with their heavy gloves, pounding him so thoroughly that he stood there dazed and bruised, one eye as black as burned butter, eight ribs broken, his breastbone cracked, both shoulder plates smashed, his lower jaw hanging down in three pieces, and everyone laughing wildly. God knows what Oudart did to him, covering the steel-lined gloves with the sleeve of his surplice, trimmed with ermine, for he was a powerful rascal.

"And so the Shyster went back to L'Ile-Bouchard, striped black and blue like a tiger, but all the same happy and well satisfied with My Lord Basché. After the good surgeons of the place had finished with him, he lived as long as anyone could want. But no one ever said a word about the whole affair. The very memory of it died with the sound of the bells ringing out at his funeral."

Chapter Thirteen // How, after the Example of Maître François Villon, My Lord Basché Praised His People

"The Shyster emerged from the castle and climbed back on his one-eyed steed (which was what he called his half-blind horse). Basché, who was in the arbor of his private garden, sent for his wife and daughters, and for all the rest of his household, had them bring wine and all sorts of good things to eat—hams and fruit and cheese—and drank with them most happily. Then he said:

" 'When he was an old man, Maître François Villon retired to Saint-Maixent, in Poitou, under the protection of the good abbot of the place. There, to entertain the people, he gave a performance of the Passion, using Poitevin dialect and in the local style. When the roles had been assigned, the actors rehearsed, the theater prepared, he told the mayor and his underlings that the play would be ready after the Niort Fair; all he still had to do was find appropriate costumes. The mayor and his subordinates agreed, and the date was set. Now, to costume an old peasant who had the role of God the Father, he asked Brother Etienne Bungtail, sacristan for the local Franciscans, to lend him a robe and a stole. But Bungtail refused, arguing that according to the rules and regulations of his order it was completely forbidden either to give or lend anything for mere theatrical entertainments. Villon replied that those rules and regulations concerned only secular farces and other such mummery; in Brussels, and elsewhere too, he himself had seen such arrangements made. But Bungtail told him flatly to get his costumes anywhere he liked, if it pleased him and anyone else would help him, but there'd be nothing from the Franciscans—and that was definite. So Villon had to report all this to his actors, in great annoyance—but he added that God Himself would take suitable revenge on Bungtail, and make an example of him—and very soon.

" 'The next Saturday, Villon got word that Bungtail, riding the convent's virgin mare, would be out making collections in Saint-Ligaire, and that he would be coming back at two that afternoon. So he staged a devil show all through the town and the marketplace. His devils were all wearing wolfskins, and cow and sheep skins, decorated with sheep heads and ox horns and great kitchen pots. They wore heavy straps hung with heavy cowbells and mule bells, and made an incredible racket. Some carried black rods covered with firecrackers; others carried burning brands, and at every crossroad they threw handfuls of powdered wax onto these flaming sticks, which made them flare horribly and give off a ghastly smell. Having pleased the townspeople immensely, and frightened all sorts of small children, they took everyone to a farmhouse, just outside the gate on the Saint-Ligaire road, and fed them handsomely. Shortly thereafter, Maître Villon saw Bungtail in the distance, coming back after his collecting, and recited the following doggerel:

> Here comes a local fellow, good for nothing,
> Carrying holy scraps in his worn-out wallet.

" ' "By all that's holy!" said some of the devils. "He wouldn't even lend God the Father a tattered cloak. Let's give him a scare." '

" ' "A fine idea," answered Villon. "But let's hide until he gets here—and make sure your firecrackers and those flaming brands are ready." '

" 'Bungtail arrived, and they all leaped out onto the road right in front of him, making a huge racket, flinging fire at him and his horse from all sides, banging on their bells and screaming and shouting in devil talk, "Ho, ho, ho, ho, brour-our, rrours, rrourss! Hoo, hoo, hoo! Ho, ho, ho! Brother Etienne, aren't we splendid devils?"

" 'Frightened silly, the horse farted and leaped into the air, then broke into a trot, and a gallop, bucking and kicking, snorting and twisting and farting like mad, so that Bungtail was thrown out of the saddle, though he clung to the pommel horn as hard as he could. He had rope stirrups, and his right sandal was so twined around in them that he simply couldn't pull his foot free. So the horse dragged him along on his ass, still bucking and kicking out at him, pounding wildly down hedgerows, through bushes and ditches. And pretty soon the crazed animals had smashed in his head, his brain tumbling out near the Holy Hosanna Cross. His arms came off in pieces, a bit here, a bit there. So too his legs. Then his guts wound out in a long bloody trail, so that by the time the horse got back to the convent all that was left of Bungtail was his right foot, still entwined in the stirrup ropes.

" 'Seeing that it had all gone exactly as he'd expected, Villon said to his devils:

" ' "Oh, you'll be great actors, my devilish friends—great actors—I swear it. How well you'll play your parts! Don't tell me about the devils of Saumur, or Douay, or Montmorillon, or Langeais, or Saint-Espin, or Angers—no, by God! not even those fellows from Poitiers with their wonderful rehearsal room—they can't any of them be compared to models of perfection like you. Oh, you'll do your parts beautifully!" '

" 'So,' said My Lord Basché, 'I too have arranged for you to be good actors in this tragic farce, my friends, since in this your first performance you gave this Shyster such an eloquent rapping, tapping, and tickling. I hereby double all your wages. And you, my love" (he said to his wife), "offer whatever honors you think fit. My treasury is in your hands: do with it as you think best. As for me, first let me drink to all of you, my good friends. Ah! that's a good fresh drink! Second, you, my steward, take this silver bowl: it's yours. And you, my squires, take these two gold-plated silver cups. Pages: for three months you're to be exempted from all whipping. My love, give them my beautiful white plumes, with the gold frills. My dear Oudart, let me give you this silver flask. Give this other one to the cooks. Let the room servants have this silver basket—the grooms and stableboys get this silver vase, trimmed in gold— the porters are to have these two serving dishes—and the coachmen get these ten spoons. Trudon, you shall have all these other silver spoons and also this engraved box. You, the rest of you, this great saltcellar is for you. Serve me well, friends, and I'll acknowledge you—for by all that's holy I'd rather take a hundred sledgehammer blows right on my helmet, fighting for our good king, than be summoned just once by these hounddog Shysters, only for the amusement of such a fat priest.' "

Chapter Fourteen ⁄ The Shysters Go On Being Beaten in Lord Basché's House

"Four days later, another young, tall, lean Shyster came to issue My Lord Basché a summons, on behalf of the fat prior. He was immediately recognized by the porter, and the bell was sounded—a signal to everyone in the castle that the farce was to be played yet again. Loire was kneading his dough; his wife was sifting flour. Oudart was working on his wine steward's accounts. The gentlemen of the household were playing tennis. My Lord Basché himself was playing cards with his wife. The ladies were playing knucklebones. The officers had a good game going; the pages were guessing at how many fingers were being held up. And then everyone heard that a Shyster had arrived. So Oudart got dressed up, Loire and his wife put on their beautiful wedding clothes, Trudon played his flute and beat his drums—everyone laughed and got themselves ready— and this time they put on their heavy gloves well in advance.

"Basché came downstairs. Meeting him, the Shyster fell to his knees, begged him not to be offended if, on behalf of the fat prior, he served him with a summons, reminding the lord in a fluent speech that he was no more than a public figure, a monkish servant, a man who was obliged to carry the abbot's miter, but adding that he was always ready and eager to do quite as much for Lord Basché—indeed, for the lowest personage in all his household—whenever it might please them to employ and command him.

" 'Come now,' said Lord Basché, 'surely you're not going to serve me with a summons before you've drunk some of my fine Quinquenays wine and taken part in the wedding we're about to have. Oudart, be sure that he drinks well, and is well refreshed. Then bring him into the high hall. You're very welcome, my friend—very welcome!'

"Well fed and watered, the Shyster was led into the great hall by Ou-dart, and found there all the characters in the farce, all in their proper places and ready. As he entered, they all began to laugh. To be sociable, the Shyster laughed with them, as Oudart pronounced some hocus-pocus Latin, and joined the woman's hands to the man's, and bade the bride be kissed, then sprinkled them all with holy water. Then, as they began to bring in wine and gingerbread, the blows began to fall. The Shyster hit Oudart. Oudart had his steel-lined gloves under his surplice. Slipping them on like mittens he began to clobber the Shyster, and pepper him properly. And then the steel-gloved blows began to rain down on the Shyster from all sides.

" 'Wedding time,' they all cried, 'wedding time, wedding time! And you'll remember it!'

"They beat him up so thoroughly that blood was running out of his mouth, out his nose, out his ears, out of his eyes. They beat him every-where, cracked his shoulder blades, banged his head, his neck, his back, his chest, his arms—everywhere. Not even in Avignon, at carnival time, have the young men ever done such a job: oh, they played on him so melodiously! And finally he fell to the ground. They threw pitchers of wine in his face, pinned a handsome yellow and green ribbon to his jacket sleeve, and set him up on his half-dead horse. Once he got back to L'Ile-Bouchard, I have no idea if he was properly bandaged up and taken care of, either by his wife or by the local doctors. But I do know that no one ever said another word about him.

"The next day the same thing happened, because they hadn't found the acknowledgment of service in the skinny Shyster's briefcase. So the fat prior had another Shyster sent to serve a summons on the lord of Basché, and with two bailiffs to protect him. The porter's bell made everyone in the household happy, since they realized that another Shyster had come. Basché himself was at table, dining with his wife and his gentlemen. Sending for the Shyster, he made him sit next to him, placing the bailiffs near the young ladies, and they all had a fine and jolly dinner. When dessert was served, the Shyster rose and, in the presence and hearing of the bailiffs, served the summons on Basché. Basché asked, most politely, for a copy of his warrant, which was given him; Basché then accepted service and directed that four pieces of gold be given to the Shyster and his bailiffs, after which everyone retired to get ready for the farce. Trudon began to beat his drum. Basché begged the Shyster to assist at the nuptials of one of his officers—indeed, to record the wedding contract—for which he would be well and sufficiently paid. The Shyster courteously took out his writing desk, quickly got paper ready; his bailiffs stood beside him. Loire entered the great hall by one door, his wife and the young ladies by another, all dressed as for a wedding. Oudart, wearing full priestly robes, took the bride and groom by the hand, queried them as to whether they were marrying of their own free will, then gave them his blessing—not sparing the sprinkling on of holy water. The wedding contract was signed and witnessed. Wine and spices were brought in from one door, and from another a host of white and tan ribbons, while through a third door, secretly, they brought in the heavy leather gloves."

Chapter Fifteen ⁄⁄ How the Shysters Revived an Ancient Wedding Custom

"Having guzzled down a great glass of good Brittany wine, the Shyster said to Lord Basché:

" 'My good sir, what's going on here? Don't you still have real weddings? By our holy sainted mother's blood, we've lost all our good old customs—there are lots of holes in the ground, but you can't find a rabbit in any of 'em. Friendship's all gone—vanished. See how many churches have stopped us from drinking Christmas toasts in the names of the blessed saints—O, O, O Noel! The world's just slipping away, it's only daydreaming, it's coming to an end. So, now: the wedding, the wedding, the wedding!'

"And then he whacked Basché, and Basché's wife, and then the young ladies, and then Oudart.

"At which the heavy gloves were set free and did their work so well that the Shyster's head was broken in nine places, one of the bailiffs had his right arm cracked, and the other's upper jaw was pulled so far down that it hung halfway to his chin and you could see right through his throat, all the way to his uvula: he coughed out most of his molars and incisors and canines.

"Then the drum changed its beat, the leather gloves were hidden away so deftly that no one noticed a thing, and sweets and treats were handed around once again, and everyone went back to laughing. They were all toasting one another, and toasting the Shyster and his bailiffs. But Oudart swore and grumbled about the wedding, claiming that one of the bailiffs had thoroughly discombobulated his shoulder. All the same, he drank the fellow's health gaily enough. The split-jawed bailiff prayerfully joined his hands and, dumbly, begged Oudart's pardon, because of course he couldn't talk. Loire complained that the cracked-arm bailiff had hit him on the elbow so hard that that he was halfdeadandburiedandotherwise discomfited all the way down to his toenails.

" 'Hey,' said Trudon, covering his left eye with his handkerchief, and exhibiting a drum bashed in on one side, 'what harm have I ever done you? It wasn't enough for them, brashamumblepeggingallthewaytotown my poor eye, look! they've even punched in my drum. You always beat drums, at weddings. Drummers beat drums, but you don't ever beat drummers. Now, all it's good for is a hat for the devil's head!'

" 'Brother,' said the one-armed bailiff, 'I'll give you a beautiful—really magnificent—ever so ancient royal letter—I've got it right here in my wallet—so you can use the parchment to fix your drum—and by God! forgive us! By our lady of the river, our lovely, lovely lady, I meant no harm!'

"One of the squires came over, limping and hobbling like the good noble lord of La Roche-Posay. He spoke to the split-jawed bailiff:

" 'Are you one of those Banging monks—those Bangers, those Bang-Bangers? Wasn't it enough that you kicked Jesusandmaryandalltheblessedsaintsinheaven out of us, bashing away with your damned boots? Did you also have to beatthebloodyhellanddamnation into us with those sharp, pointy-toed monstrosities of yours? You call that playful? By God, there's no fun in that!'

"The bailiff joined his hands, as if begging pardon, but all he could do was mumble his tongue like a monkey:

" 'Mon, mon, mon, vrelon, mon, mon, mon.'

"The new bride was crying while she laughed, and laughing while she cried, because—she said—the Shyster hadn't just clobbered her all over, here and there and everywhere, but he'd loutishly rumpled her up by secretly tickleteasingsqueezing her private parts.

" 'May the devil take him!' said Basché. 'It was obviously required that these king's men, as all Shysters and their bailiffs like to call themselves, had to beat both me and my good wife on our poor old backs. But I don't hold that against them: these are just little wedding caresses. Yet now I see perfectly well that he served me my summons like an angel but beat me like a devil. There really is something of Brother Banger about him: it's true. Still, I drink to him with all my heart—and to you too, my bailiff friends.'

" 'But,' said his wife, 'what reason could he have had, what dispute could possibly have provoked him to beat me as hard as he did? May the devil carry me off if I appreciate that! By God, I don't appreciate it one little bit! But I'll say this about him: he has the hardest hands I've ever felt on my shoulders.'

"The steward had his left arm in a sling, as if it were all bashedsmashedcracked.

" 'The devil himself,' he said, 'must have helped officiate at this wedding. By all that's holy, both my arms are strummeddrummedthummed! You call this a wedding celebration? I call it a shit celebration. That's exactly what it is, by God!—a wild Lapithian orgy, just the way Lucian describes it.'

"The Shyster didn't say another word. The bailiffs insisted that they hadn't hit anyone with the slightest ill will, and begged that for the love of God their excesses would be pardoned.

"And so they left. Half a mile on their road, the Shyster found himself a bit sick to his stomach. The bailiffs got to L'Ile-Bouchard, and announced publicly that never in all their lives had they seen a man as good as My Lord Basché, nor ever visited so honorable a house, nor ever attended such a wedding feast. Anything that had gone wrong was entirely their own fault, they proclaimed, because it was they who had begun the whole beating business. I have no idea how long they lived, after that.

"But from that time forward it was well known and certain that Basché's money was deadlier, more fatal, more dangerous to Shysters and bailiffs than ever was, in the old days, the golden treasure of Toulouse or Sejanus' horse. And from then on the lord of Basché lived in peace—and a Basché wedding became a proverbial saying."

Chapter Sixteen ⁄⁄ How Brother John Tested the Shysters' Dispositions

"This tale," said Pantagruel, "would be a merry one, if we didn't have to keep the fear of God forever in front of our eyes."

"It would be a better story," said Epistemon, "if that hailstorm of leather gloves had fallen on the fat prior. He amused himself, spending his money partly to anger Basché, partly so he could see the Shysters beaten. All those blows really should have fallen on that shaved head of his, especially when you think about all those circuit judges, some of them priors just like him, riding around the country in search of bribes. What were those poor Shysters guilty of?"

"I'm reminded," said Pantagruel, "of an old Roman nobleman named L. Neratius.

"He came from an aristocratic family, and a very rich one. But he had a tyrannical quirk: he'd fill his servants' wallets with gold and silver, then go out into the streets and, whenever he met any bright young fellows, dressed to the nines, he would—just for the pleasure of it, without their giving him the slightest cause for offense—punch them hard in the face. And then immediately, to pacify them and keep them from taking him to court, he'd give them enough money to keep them smiling and silent, all exactly as the laws of the Twelve Tablets required. And so he spent all his money, buying himself the right to go around beating people."

"By Saint Benedict's holy boot!" said Brother John. "I'm going to find out if this is true!"

So he dismounted, stuck his hand in his purse, and pulled out twenty gold pieces. Then, speaking in a loud voice, and in the presence of a whole mob of Shyster folk:

"Who wants to earn twenty gold pieces, in return for being beaten like the devil?"

"Me, me, me!" they all answered. "You'll knock us silly, sir—that's for sure. But at a good price."

And they thronged around him, trying to be the first to get beaten up at such a good price. Brother John chose one of them, with a red snout, who wore on the thumb of his right hand a big, thick silver ring, set with a great toadstone.

Once he'd been chosen, I saw the others were mumbling and grumbling, and I heard a tall, thin young Shyster, a good, clever scholar who was said to be an honest canon lawyer, complaining that this red-nose fellow grabbed up all the business, and that if there were only thirty good hard blows to earn anything from, he'd pick up twenty-eight and a half of them. But all this complaining and grumbling was simple jealousy.

Brother John gave him such a good drubbing, front and back, arms and legs, with such powerful blows of his stick, that I expected him to fall down dead. But the rascal got his twenty gold pieces and stood right there, as relaxed as a king—or two kings. And the others said to Brother John:

"Sir Brother Devil, if you'd like to beat some of us, at a lower rate, we're at your disposal, Sir Devil. We're completely at your service— purses, papers, pens, and all."

Red Nose protested in a loud voice:

"In the name of God! Pigs! Stay away from my business! Are you trying to steal my customer—seduce him away? I'll have you in front of the judge next week, my fine fellows-o. I'll shyster you like a Vauvert devil!"

Then, turning to Brother John, smiling and happy, he said:

"Reverend Father in the devil, sir: if you've had fun beating me, and you'd like to beat me some more, I'd settle for just half the price, and gladly. You needn't hold back, either: please. I'm completely at your service, Sir Devil—my head, my chest, my guts—everything. I speak the simple truth."

But Brother John cut him off and turned away. The other Shysters went over to Panurge, Epistemon, Gymnast, and the others, begging them most earnestly to beat them, and for just pennies. Otherwise, they'd be in danger of not eating for a long, long time. But none of them wanted to listen.

Then, hunting fresh water for the galley rowers, we met two old Shyster women, crying and weeping pitifully. Pantagruel had stayed on his ship, however, and was already calling us back. Wondering if these were relatives of the Shyster who'd been beaten, we asked them why they were so unhappy. They told us that they had more than enough reason to mourn and weep, since two of the best men in the whole land had just been obliged to drop off the gallows with a rope around their necks.

"My pages," said Gymnast, "often tie up their sleeping friends, with a rope from their feet to their necks. But if you start with the rope around your neck, you can get hanged—you can strangle yourself."

"How true, how true," said Brother John. "You sound exactly like Saint John of the Apocalypse."

When we asked them why there'd been this hanging, they told us that the two Shysters had stolen what in Poitevian parlance are called "mass irons" (meaning gold ornaments used in the mass) and hidden them under "the parish broom handle" (meaning the church bell tower).

"Now that," said Epistemon, "is a pretty awful way of talking around the truth."

Chapter Seventeen ⁄⁄ How Pantagruel Sailed by the Formless and Wordless Islands, and the Strange Death of Splitnose the Windmill Eater

That same day, Pantagruel went past the two islands of Formless and Wordless, where nothing at all could be done: the great giant Splitnose had eaten every frying pan, saucepan, kettle, pot, drip pan, and double boiler in the entire country, since he'd run out of the windmills he usually ate. And so it happened that, just before dawn, when it was time for his intestines to go to work, he'd fallen very ill of a definite hard indigestibility, caused (said the doctors) by the inability of his gut, so accustomed to digesting windmills and their sweeping vanes, to satisfactorily process frying pans and kettles. Saucepans and double boilers, however, had been handled quite well, as they could tell from the sediment and albumin found in the four fat barrels of urine he had filled, that very morning, on two separate occasions.

They tried all sorts of well-tested remedies, trying to help him. But the sickness was stronger than their cures. And so the noble Splitnose departed this mortal life, that very morning, in a manner so strange that no one need ever again be startled by Aeschylus' death. Aeschylus, you will recall, had been given a mortal warning by the soothsayers, who said that on a specified day he would die from something falling on him. When that day came, he left the city, went away from all houses, trees, crags and hills, and everything that towered on high, all things that could fall and cause his death. So he stayed in the middle of a great meadow, trusting in the broad, open sky, confident, or so he thought, that he would be safe unless the skies themselves fell, which he considered out of the question.

Nevertheless, it is said that larks are terribly afraid of the sky falling, because if they ever did fall, every single one of them could be caught. In the old days, too, the Celts who lived near the Rhine experienced the same fear: these are the noble, valiant, chivalrous, warlike, and triumphant people of France who, when asked by Alexander the Great what they most feared in the whole world, hoping and expecting they would say him and only him, after all his great deeds and victories, all his conquests and triumphs, answered that they were afraid of nothing, except that the sky would fall. However, they did not decline to enter into an alliance and confederation, and into friendship, with such a brave and magnanimous king—if you believe what Strabo wrote, in his seventh book, and Arrian in his first. Plutarch, too, in the book he entitled *The Face of the Man in the Moon,* says that one Pharnaces, who was terrified that the moon would fall onto the earth, was full of an immense pity for those who were obliged to live under its shadow, like the Ethiopians and the Ceylonese, since so huge a mass might fall on them. He would have been just as afraid of the sky falling on the earth, if they hadn't been held up and supported by the columns of Atlas, as the ancients believed, according to the evidence cited by Aristotle in book five of his *Metaphysics.*

But Aeschylus, in any case, was in fact killed by a falling tortoise shell, which was dropped from the claws of an eagle flying high in the air and fell on his head, splitting his skull.

And then there was the poet Anacreon, strangled to death by a grape seed. And Fabius, the Roman praetor, who choked to death on a goat hair, drinking a bowl of milk. And that shamefaced fellow, holding back his wind for fear of emitting a wicked fart in the presence of Claudius, emperor of Rome, who suddenly dropped dead. And the man who's buried on Rome's Flaminian Way, whose epitaph complains that he died because a cat bit his little finger. And Q. Lecanius Bassus, who dropped dead of pinprick on his left thumb, a mark so tiny that it was almost impossible to see it. And Quenelaut, the Norman doctor, who died so suddenly at Montpellier after digging a tiny worm out of his hand with a penknife. And Philomenes, whose servant had prepared fresh figs for the first course of his dinner, but who had then gone to fetch the wine, and while he was gone a jackass had wandered in and set devotedly to work eating the figs off the plate. Philomenes came in and stood watching how delicately the ass chewed up his figs, then said to his servant, as he came back with the wine:

"It makes sense, since you've set out figs for this pious ass, that you also give him some of that good wine you're carrying."

And, so saying, he fell into such a fit of laughter, and laughed so long and so hard, that he burst his spleen and could not breathe, and died on the spot. And Spurius Saufeius, who died eating a soft-boiled egg, after he emerged from his bath. And that man Boccaccio writes of, who dropped dead after picking his teeth with a twig of bitter sage. And Philippot Placut, healthy and strong, who paid off an old debt and suddenly, without the slightest sign of sickness, fell down dead. And Zeusis, the painter, who died after a fit of laughter, brought on by contemplating the face of an old woman he himself had painted. And all the others, by the thousand, recorded for us by Verrius, Pliny, Valerius Maximus, Baptiste Fulgose, and old Backaberry the Elder.

But our good Splitnose—alas!—died of suffocation, after his doctors had him eat a wedge of fresh butter set in the mouth of a hot oven.

We were also told that, in Wordless, the king of Cullan had defeated the minions of King Affliction and sacked the fortress of Nothingness.

Afterward, we sailed past the Angry and Defiant islands, and also the exceedingly beautiful islands of Manna and Honey, which were overflowing with the makings of first-rate suppositories. We also passed the islands of Any and Forever, which caused so much trouble for the duke of Hesse when Charles the Fifth imprisoned him "not *forever*," though a change of only two letters in a single German word (*einige* instead of *ewige*) would have granted him freedom without *any* imprisonment.

Chapter Eighteen ⁄⁄ How Pantagruel Escaped a Wild Storm at Sea

The next day, on our starboard side, we met up with nine old tub boats full of monks—Dominicans, Jesuits, Capuchins, Hermits, Augustinians, Bernardines, Celestines, Theatines, Egnatins, Amadeans, Franciscans, Carmelites, Minims, and monks named for all the other holy saints—who were on their way to the Crazy Council, where they were going to polish up the articles of faith so they could deal with new styles of heretics. Seeing them, Panurge half swooned in rapturous joy, as if convinced now, that this would surely be a lucky day—and many more would follow. Having courteously greeted the good fathers, and commended his soul to their devoted prayers, he had seventy-eight dozen hams thrown onto their ships, plus a heap of caviar, cases of smoked pork sausages, hundreds of pots of Mediterranean caviar, and two thousand shining gold pieces, for the sake of all sinful souls.

But Pantagruel stood there, thoughtful and rather sad. Brother John noticed him, and was just asking why he'd fallen into such an unusual state when the ship's pilot, watching how the wind-flag on the stern was flapping about, and seeing that a fierce squall was blowing up, with a savage storm to follow, ordered a sharp watch to be kept, by the sailors, apprentices, and cabin boys, as well as by the passengers. He had the sails lowered—square foresails, fore and aft, crossjack, mainsail, mizzen sail, bowsprit; he had them haul down the fore-topmast staysail, the main topsail and the topsail aft, and lower the main mizzen sail and all the yardarms, leaving only the ratlines and shrouds.

Then suddenly the sea began to swell and heave; immense waves beat against the sides of our vessel; the fierce wind whistled through the yardarms, swirling frightfully in a black squall, a howling blizzard, with gusts of deadly snow; thunder roared in the sky, lightning crackled, blazed, and rain poured down, and hail; the air darkened, thickened, until all was shadowy and obscure and you could have seen nothing except for the flashes of lightning which lit up the heavens, splitting them in flaming streaks; violent winds, whipping in powerful gusts, swirled and soared all around us, and thunderstorms, along with flaring lights, gleaming and jagged, and all manner of other celestial emanations: we no longer knew where we were; the ghastly storm threw up huge wave after wave. It seemed to us like Ancient Chaos itself: fire, air, sea, and land—all the elements—in rebellious confusion.

Having fed the shit-eating fish with the contents of his stomach, Panurge crouched down on the deck, overcome, miserable, woeful, and half dead. He called on all the blessed saints of both sexes to come to his aid, vowing that he'd go to confession the moment he had the opportunity, and the time, then cried out in great fright:

"Steward, hey, my friend, my father, my uncle, bring me a bit of salt fish: pretty soon we're going to have too much to drink, as far as I can see! From now on, eat a little and drink a lot will be my motto. Oh, if only God and the saints in heaven and the holy blessed Virgin had me back on solid ground, safe and sound—and now, I mean this minute!

"Oh, those who plant cabbages are three times blessed—no, four times! O you Fates: why didn't you make me a planter of cabbages? Oh, how small is the number of those so favored by Jupiter that they were born to be planters of cabbages! One of their feet is always planted right on the ground—and the other foot isn't far from it. Let anyone who feels like it go around arguing about happiness and eternal bliss, but I swear right here and now that those who plant cabbages are truly fortunate, and I have better reason for saying this than Pyrrho ever did, when he was in the kind of danger we're in and saw a pig, near the shore, eating scattered barley and swore that that pig was doubly happy—first, because he had lots of barley, and besides, because he was on solid ground.

"Ha! If you want a noble, a heavenly country house, just walk where the cows walk! Oh, that wave's going to carry us off—Lord save us! Friends: a little vinegar, for the love of God! How I'm panting—how I'm sweating! Alas! The sails are ripped, the anchor cable's in pieces, the pulleys are broken, the main topsail just fell into the sea, the keel's turning upside down, all our ropes are tearing apart. Alas, alas! what happened to our bowlines? By God, it's all up with us! Our mast's falling to pieces. Alas! Who cares about this damned, lost ship? My friends, stow me away behind one of these thick gates! Children, children: your towrope just fell off. Alas! Don't let go of the helm—keep that rope tied on. I hear the rudder cracking. Is it broken, is it? O Lord, hold that wheel together—don't worry about those ropes! Oh beh, beh, beh, boo, boo boo! Keep an eye on your compass needle, please, please, Master Star-Steerer, and find out where this storm's coming from. By my faith, I'm scared! Boo, boo, boo boo, boo! I'm done for! I'm so crazy afraid that I'm shitting in my pants. Boo boo, boo boo! At-tow, tow, tow, tow, tow, tiy! At-tow, tow, tow, tow, tiy! Boo boo boo, oo oo oo boo boo boo boo boo! I'm drowning, I'm drowning! I'm dying! Good people, I'm dying!"

Chapter Nineteen // How Panurge and Brother John Behaved during the Storm

Having thus begged the aid of God the eternal Savior, and made a public declaration of his intense faith and devotion, Panurge was holding on to the mast as hard as he could, at the pilot's suggestion. Brother John had thrown off his cassock and was helping the sailors, as were Epistemon, Powerbrain, and the others. But Panurge crouched down on his ass, on the deck, crying and weeping. As he went by on the gangway, Brother John saw him, and said:

"By God, Panurge you baby calf, Panurge you crybaby, Panurge you blubbermouth, you'd do a lot better helping us up here than bawling like a cow, squatting down on your balls like a baboon."

"Beh, beh, beh boo, boo, boo," answered Panurge. "Brother John—my friend—I'm drowning, I'm drowning, my friend—I'm drowning! I'm all done for, O my father in Christ, my friend—I'm done for! You can't save me now, with your good stout sword! Alas, alas! We've gone as high as the waves can take us—we're right off the scale. Beh beh beh boo boo! Alas! And now we're right down at the bottom of the scale! I'm drowning! Ha! My father—my uncle—my everything! The water's running down my neck right into my shoes. Boo boo boo, poosh, hoo hoo hoo, ha ha ha ha ha. I'm drowning! Alas, alas, hoo hoo hoo hoo hoo hoo! Beh beh boo, boo boo hoo, boo hoo, ho ho ho ho ho! Alas, alas! Right now I'm like a cleft tree, my feet up over my head, my head down. Oh, if only God would see fit to drop me, right this minute, into that tub boat with the holy blessed fathers, headed for their holy council, the ones we met this morning—so holy, so fat, so happy, so soft and nice—such charming fellows. Oh, oh, oh! Alas, alas! This wave straight out of hell (*Mea culpa,* Forgive me, *Deus*)—no, this holy wave will squash our ship. Alas! Brother John, my father, my friend—confess me! See me here on my knees! *Confiteor!* Confess me! Give me your blessed benediction!"

"Get over here, may the devil hang you!" said Brother John. "Come

here and help us! By thirty legions of devils, get over here, come on! . . .
Are you coming?"

"Let's not swear," said Panurge, "my father, my friend—not now!
Tomorrow, yes—as much as you like. Ho, ho! Alas! The ship's taking
water. I'm drowning! Alas, alas! Beh beh beh beh, boo boo boo boo!
Now we're right at the bottom! Alas, alas! I'd give eighteen thousand a
year in rents to anyone who'd set me down on solid ground, all shit-
covered and leaking shit as I am—as shitty as any man ever was in my
shitty country. *Confiteor!* Hear my confession! Alas! Let me give you one
little word of a will—or at least a codicil!"

"May a thousand devils," said Brother John, "jump onto this cuckold!
By all that's holy! You're talking about a will—when we're in danger and
we can help ourselves if ever we could? Are you coming over here, hey—
you devil? Sergeant, my dear sergeant, you good-natured whip swinger—
over here! Gymnast, come here, up on this post. By God, we'll be finished
when this next wave hits! Our lantern's about to go out. Here we go,
down to a million devils."

"Alas, alas," said Panurge, "alas! Boo, boo, boo, boo, boo-hoo! Alas,
alas! Is this where we're fated to die? Oh, good people, I'm drowning,
I'm dying! *Consummatum est,* It's done—I'm done for!"

"Lord, ord, ord," said Brother John. "Fagh! What a mess he is, the
shitty crybaby! Boy, over here! By all the devils, take over the pump! Are
you wounded? By all that's holy, tie it around with this rope—here, right
there—by the devil—hey! That way, my child, that way."

"Ha, Brother John," said Panurge, "my father in Christ, my friend,
let's not swear. It's sinful. Alas, alas! Beh beh beh boo, boo boo, I'm
drowning, I'm dying—my friends! I pardon all of you—everyone! Adieu,
in manus, into Your hands! Boo boo boo-hoo boo-hoo. O Saint Michael
of Aure, O Saint Nicholas, help me this once and never again! I swear to
you, in the name of our Lord, that if you help me now, if you get me out
of this danger and set me down on dry land, I'll build you a beautiful big
chapel—or two chapels,

> Between old Candes and Monsarrat,
> Where cows and calves won't ever get fat.

Alas, alas! I've swallowed at least eighteen buckets of water—at least two.
Boo boo, boo-hoo! How bitter and salty it is!"

"By our good Lord," said Brother John, "by His blood, His flesh, His
belly, His head! If you go on whimpering like that, you hell-bound cuckold, I'll make you dance like an old sea dog! By all that's holy! Why don't
we just throw you to the bottom of the sea? Rowers, rowers, hey there,
my good friends, that's the way to do it, keep it up! Hold steady up there!
I've never seen such lightning or heard such thunder. They must have

taken the chains off all the devils—or maybe Proserpina's in childbirth. All the devils are dancing on the bells."

Chapter Twenty ⁄ How at the Height of the Storm the Sailors Abandoned Their Ships

"Ha!" said Panurge. "You're sinning again, Brother John, my one-time friend! I say 'onetime,' you see, because right now we're as good as nothing, you and I both. I'm sorry to have to say it, because I think swearing does wonders for your spleen—the way a woodcutter feels a lot better if someone standing right next to him yells out, at each stroke, and in a loud voice, 'Han!' Or the way a bowler feels incredibly better, when he hasn't rolled the ball straight, if some lively fellow standing nearby turns and twists both body and head half around, following where a well-thrown ball would have hit the pins. But all the same, it's a sin, my sweet friend. Still, do you think we'd be safe from this wild storm if we ate just a bit of roast goat? I've read that when there's a storm on the high seas, the worshipers of the goat gods have nothing to worry about—they're always safe—like Orpheus, Apollonius, Pherecydes, Strabo, Pausanias, Herodotus."

"He's gibbering," said Brother John, "the poor devil. Let a thousand—millions—hundreds of millions of devils carry this crowned cuckold off to hell! Hey, tiger! give us a hand over here! Is he coming? Here, on the larboard side! By God's holy head all stuffed with relics! What kind of monkey's paternoster are you muttering between your teeth? This crazy devil of a seagoing idiot brought the storm down on us, and he's the only one who isn't lending us a hand! By God, if I could get over to you, I'd whip you like a stormy devil! Over here, lad, there's a good boy—hold on, while I get this tied. Oh you good child! May God make you the abbot of Talemont, and send the old abbot over to Croulay! Powerbrain, my brother, you'll get hurt over there. Epistemon, watch out for those railings—I saw lightning strike right there."

"Up it goes!"

"That's well said. Run it up, run it up, run it up! I see a boat coming! Run it up! By all that's holy, what's that? The prow's cracked. Oh roll your balls, you devils—fart away—belch it out—let it roar! Shit to the sea! By all that's holy, you didn't get me down under the waves! Damn, if all the millions of devils aren't holding their annual meeting right here—or maybe they're fighting over who's to be the next president."

"To larboard!"

"That's well said. Watch out for the pulley block! Hey, boy, by the devil—hey! Larboard, larboard!"

"Beh beh beh boo boo," said Panurge. "Boo boo beh beh beh boo boo-hoo, I'm drowning. I can't see the sky, I can't see the ground. Alas, alas! Of the four elements, all we've got left is fire and water. Boo-hoo boo-hoo boo boo! May it please God the Almighty Mighty One that right now I were in the cathedral close at Seuilly—or in Innocent the baker's shop, right in front of those cellars dug into the hill at Chinon—lord, even if I had to strip down and bake the pies myself! Good man, do you know how to throw me onto land? You know so many many things, they tell me! I'll let you have Salmagundi—all of it—and every penny I get from my snail farm, if you can just get me back onto solid ground. Alas, alas! I'm drowning! Oh God, my sweet friend, if we can't find any good port, just let us dock somewhere—anywhere—I don't care. Drop all the anchors over. Let's escape this storm, I beg you. Our good friend, sound the depths with your lead! Let's find out how far down we might have to go! Sound it, sound it, our good friend, my friend, by our Lord on high! Let's find out if maybe we're not close enough in—maybe we could stop and get a drink here. I'll believe anything."

"Helm hard over, hey!" cried the pilot. "Hard over! All hands to the halyards! Up she goes! Shake it out up there, hard over, watch that sail! Heave ho, haul away! Heave her hard over, let her ease around! Swing her into it, out with the sails!"

"Are we there?" said Pantagruel. "O God, God, help us!"

"Up with the sails, hey!" cried Jamet Brahier, master pilot. "Up they go! All of you think of your souls and pray—only a miracle of heaven will save us now!"

"Swear," said Panurge, "some good and holy vow. Alas, alas, alas! Boo boo beh beh beh boo boo-hoo boo-hoo. Alas, alas! Let's all chip in and send a pilgrim to the Holy Land! Yes, yes! Everybody chips in a penny, yes!"

"Over here, hey!" said Brother John. "By all the devils! Starboard! Haul away, in the name of God! Let the rudder go free, hey! Haul away, haul away! And now let's have a drink! The best we've got, I say, and the best for the stomach. Listen to me, up there! Steward: bring it up, bring it out! Otherwise it's just going down to all those millions of devils. Bring it here, hey! boy! Fetch me my flask!" (which is what he called his prayer book). "Hold on! Pull, my friend—that's the way! By all that's holy, this is real hail, it is, and damned good thunder! Keep it up there, please! When is All Saints' Day? I think today's All Devils' Day for millions of devils."

"Alas!" said Panurge. "Brother John's going to hell in a handbasket. Oh, such a good friend I've lost! Alas, alas, it's even worse than it was before! We're going right between Scylla and Charybdis—oh, oh, I'm drowning! *Confiteor!* Hear my confession! Just a tiny word of my will, Brother John, my good father—my extractor of essences—my friend, my Achates—O you—my Imported Goods—my everything. Alas! I'm drowning! Just two words for my will. Here, write them here on this mattress."

Chapter Twenty-one // The Storm Goes On; Some Brief Words on Wills Made at Sea

"To make a will," said Epistemon, "right now, when you ought to be doing everything you can to help us and our crew avoid shipwreck, seems to me as unpleasant and inappropriate as the behavior of those dismounted cavalrymen, Caesar's favorites, who when they were entering Gaul amused themselves with wills and codicils, lamenting their ill fortune, weeping and wailing over the absence of their wives and their Roman friends, when what they ought to have been doing was rushing to fight as hard as they could against their enemy, Arovistus. This is stupidity equal to that of the cart-horse driver who, when his cart turned over in a newly harvested field, fell down on his knees and begged for Hercules' help, instead of spurring on his oxen or trying to set his wheels right. What good will it do you, here and now, to make a will? We'll either escape from this danger, or else we'll all be drowned. If we escape, a will won't be of any use to you. Wills have neither value nor authority, absent the death of their testators. And if we're drowned, won't Brother John drown along with all the rest of us? Who do you suppose would bring your will to your executors, eh?"

"But some good wave," answered Panurge, "will throw it up on the shore, as it did for Ulysses, and some king's daughter, walking out in the lovely weather, will find it and make sure it's carried out to the letter. And she'll build a magnificent monument to my memory, as Dido did for her dead husband, Sichaeus; as Aeneas did for Deiphobus, on the banks of Troy, near Rhoeteum; as Andromaché did for Hector, in the city of Buthrotum; as Aristotle did for Hermias, at Eubulus; as the Athenians did for the poet Euripides; as the Romans did for Drusus, in Germany, and for their emperor Alexander Severus, in Gaul; as Argentarius did for Callaischrus; as Xenocrates did for Lysidice; as Timares did for his son Teleutagoras; as Eupolis and Aristodicia did for their son, Theotimus; as Callimachus did for Sopolis, Diocledés' son; as Catullus did for his brother; as Statius did for his father; as Germain de Brie did for Hervé, the Breton sailor."

"Are you out of your mind?" said Brother John. "Help us, here and now—do your share, in the name of five hundred thousand million wagonloads of devils—help us! May you get a canker on your mustache—may three rows of great fat cankers make you a pair of high-pocket breeches and a new codpiece! Our boat hasn't run aground, has it? In the name of all that's holy, how could we ever pull it off again? All the devils are whipping up this sea! We'll never get out of it, may I hand myself over to all the devils if we do."

And then Pantagruel was heard, exclaiming woefully, in a loud voice:

"Lord God, save us: we are dying! And yet, let it not happen according to our wishes, but Your holy will be done!"

"May God and the Blessed Virgin," said Panurge, "be with us! Alas, alas, I'm drowning! Beh beh beh boo beh beh boo boo. *In manus*, into Your hands. O one and only God, send me a dolphin to carry me safely to land, as if I were some good little Arion. I'll play my harp beautifully, if it hasn't been ruined."

"May all the devils take me," said Brother John, . . .

("Oh God be with us!" said Panurge between clenched teeth)

". . . and if I come down there, I'll show you, by God, that your balls hang down from a calf-assed cuckold, a crowned cuckold, a horned cuckold. Mgnan, mgnan, mgnan! Come and help us, you great bawling calf, or may thirty million devils jump on you! Are you coming, O you sea calf? Agh: how disgusting he is, the whimpering baby!"

"That's all you ever say."

"Ah, now for a good quick pull: little prayer-book flask, I'll empty you out a bit. *Beatus vir qui non abiit,* Blessed is the man that walketh not in the counsel of the ungodly. Hey: I know all that by heart. Let's have a look at the story of good Saint Nicholas:

> *Horrida tempestas montem turbavit acutum,*
> The ghastly storm broke over the mountain peaks.

Mountain peaks? No, Montagu! That storm was a magnificent whipper of schoolboys, at Montagu School. If teachers go to hell just because they whip poor little children, innocent schoolchildren, then by my honor he'd be on Ixion's wheel, whipping the docked puppy that pulls it around and around. But if those whippings saved some innocent children's souls, ah, then without doubt he's high above . . ."

Chapter Twenty-two ⁊ The End of the Storm

"Land, land!" cried Pantagruel. "I see land! Be as brave as sheep, boys! We're not far from port. I can see the sky starting to clear, off to the north. Get ready for a south wind."

"Courage, my children," said the pilot, "the sea's going down. All hands up the foremast! Haul it, haul it! Close-haul the trysail! Get the rope on that windlass! Pull, pull, pull! Now heave those halyards! Haul, haul, haul! Hold her steady! Tighten those pulleys! Ready to tack! Ready sails! Ready the bowlines! Steer her into the wind! Lower the trysail, you whore-son bastard!"

"It must make you feel good," said Brother John to the sailor, "to hear news of your mother."

"Into the wind! Keep her steady! Hard over!"

"Hard over she goes," answered the sailors.

"Straight on! Right into the harbor! Stud sails, ho! Haul them, there—haul, haul!"

"Very well said," commented Brother John. "Exactly the right thing. On, on, on, children—keep it up! Good! Heave, heave!"

"Starboard!"

"Very well said, exactly the right thing. I think the storm's dying down—it'll soon be over. But God be praised all the same. All our devils are starting to leave us."

"Easy, easy!"

"Ah, that's well—that's learnedly said. Easy, easy! Over here, by God, my good friend Powerbrain, you great rascal! He'll plant nothing but male children, the scoundrel. Eusthenes, you gay dog, grab the forward mast!"

"Pull, pull!"

"Oh, that's well said. Pull! By God, pull, pull!"

> "Hey, there's nothing to fear today,
> For today's a holiday—
> Noel, Noel, Noel!"

"Now that chanty," said Epistemon, "is just exactly right, and I like it, because it is a holiday."

"Pull, pull—good!"

"Ah!" cried Epistemon. "You'd better be happy. I can see Castor, off to the right."

"Beh beh boo boo boo!" said Panurge. "I'm scared silly it'll be that great bitch Helen."

"Indeed," answered Epistemon, "if you want to talk like the old Greeks, you can call it Mixarchagevas. Hey, hey! I see land, I see the harbor, I see all kinds of people out on the pier! I see the light in the lighthouse."

"Hey, hey!" said the pilot. "Weather around the cape and the jetties!"

"Weather she goes," answered the sailors.

"Now she's going," said the pilot. "And the other ships, too. Skies broke just in time."

"Saint John!" said Panurge. "Now that's well spoken! Oh, that lovely word!"

"Mgna, mgna, mgna," said Brother John, as he gulped. "If you get a single drop of this, may the devil drink me down! You hear me, you devil's dangling ball? Here, good friend pilot, is a great full mug of the best. Hey, bring up your bottles, Gymnast, and that great fat iambic pie—or ham pie: I don't care which. Now careful, pilot: bring her in straight."

"Courage!" cried Pantagruel. "Courage, my children! Let's be polite. There are two rowboats pulling alongside, and three little sailboats, and five small ships, and eight sloops, and four gondolas, and six frigates, all sent to help us by the good folk who live on this next island. But who is that Ucalegon down there, that good for nothing, crying and whimpering? Isn't the mast solidly in my hands, and held straighter than two hundred cables could make it?"

"This," answered Brother John, "is that poor devil Panurge, who has a bad stomach ache. He's shaking with fear because he's a sot."

"If he was afraid," said Pantagruel, "during that ghastly storm, that dangerous tempest, I don't think any the worse of him, provided he did his best the rest of the time. To be afraid of getting hurt is the sign of a coward (as Agamemnon was, which is why Achilles mocked him for his dog eyes and his deer's heart), but not to be afraid when you're clearly in mortal danger is the sign of little or no common sense. Now, if there's anything to be afraid of in this life of ours, other than offending against God, it may not be death. I have no interest in arguing with Socrates and the Platonists: death is hardly intrinsically bad, and there's nothing to be afraid of about it. But if death by drowning isn't something to be afraid of, then nothing is. As Homer says, it's a sad, loathsome, unnatural thing to die in the ocean. And Aeneas, when his fleet was caught by a tempest near Sicily, was sorry he hadn't died at Diomedes' hand: those who died at the burning of Troy, he said, were three and four times happier. But no one died, here: may God our protector be eternally praised! But this ship of ours is truly in terrible disorder. Fine: we've got to repair all this damage. Watch out! Don't run us aground!"

Chapter Twenty-three // Once the Storm Is Over, Panurge Becomes a Fine Fellow

"Ha, ha!" cried Panurge. "Everything's fine. The storm's over. Please, I beg you: let me disembark first. I've got urgent business to take care of. Can I do anything for you? Let me roll up that rope. Oh, I've got courage and to spare. I'm really not afraid. Let me have that, my friend. No, no, I'm not a bit afraid. But I will admit that biggest wave, the one that smashed down on us from stem to stern, did make my heart beat a little faster."

"Down with the sails!"

"Oh, that's well said. What? How come you're not doing anything,

Brother John? Is this really the time for drinking? How do we know the devil isn't brewing up another storm for us? Would you like me to help you over there? For the love of God! I'm really sorry, though it's of course too late, that I didn't listen to the good philosophers, who agree that to walk near the sea and sail near the land is a lot safer and more comfortable—rather like walking along next to your horse, holding on to his bridle. Ha, ha, ha, by God, everything's all right! Should I help you over there? Let me have it—surely—I'll do it, all right, or the devil must be in it."

Epistemon had kept a firm grip on one of the ship's ropes, in spite of the violent storm, and his hand was all ripped up and bloody. Hearing what Panurge was saying, he observed:

"Believe me, my lord, I was just as frightened and afraid as Panurge. But so what? It didn't keep me from helping. It seems to me that if we're all inevitably fated to die (as we are), then just when or how we die is up to God's holy will. And certainly we need to implore, and invoke, and pray to, and call on, and supplicate Him. But we can't stop at that: we have to do everything we can for ourselves, and as the holy Apostle says, we must cooperate with Him. You remember what Caius Flaminius, the consul, said, when wily Hannibal had him pinned against Thrasymenus, that Perugian lake: 'My children,' he said to his officers, 'don't think that prayers to God, or sacred vows, are going to get us out of here. We must escape by strength and ability: our sword blades will have to cut us a road right through our enemy's ranks.' Sallust tells us the same thing. You don't get the gods' help, says M. Portius Cato, by casual vows and lady-like weeping. You have to be eternally vigilant, ready to work as hard as you can, to make things work out as you want them to and bring yourself safely home to port. If a man is careless, womanish, and lazy in times of necessity and danger, imploring the gods won't do him a bit of good: they're just irritated and angry."

"Well, may the devil take me," said Brother John, . . .

("Me, I'll take the other half," said Panurge)

". . . if the abbey at Seuilly wouldn't have been looted and destroyed if all I'd done was sing *'Contra hostium insidias,* Against the attacking enemy' (it's all in the prayer book), as those other monkish devils were doing, without saving the vineyards, swinging that heavy cross against those thieves from Lerné."

"Let's give it a try!" said Panurge. "Everything's going well. But Brother John is still doing nothing. He's called Brother John Do-nothing, and he stands there, watching me sweat and strain to help this good man. Best sailor of sailors, our friend, ho! Two words, please, if that wouldn't bother you? How thick are this vessel's planks?"

"They're two good fingers thick," answered the pilot, "so there's nothing to worry about."

"Mother of God," said Panurge. "So we're always just two fingers from death. Is that one of the nine joys of marriage?

"Ha! Our friend, that's very good, measuring danger by the degree of fear!

"But as for me, I'll have none of it: my name is William the Fearless. Courage enough, and to spare! And I don't mean sheep's courage, either: I mean wolf's courage, confident, murderous. I'm afraid of nothing except danger."

Chapter Twenty-four ⁄ Brother John Proves That Panurge Was Senselessly Terrified during the Storm

"Good day to you, gentlemen," said Panurge, "good day to you all! Is everything well with you? Thanks be to God, and you? You're most welcome—you've come at just the right time. Let's go down. Rowers, hey! Toss down the ladder! This skiff is coming right up to us. Should I still help you, over there? I'm hungry and starved, ready and eager to work like four oxen. This is really a beautiful place, and these are truly good people. Children, do you still need my help? Don't spare my sweat, for the love of God! Like all men, Adam was born to work and labor, the way a bird is born to fly. It's our Lord's wish, if you know what I mean, that we eat our bread from the sweat of our bodies—not by doing nothing, like this rag doll of a monk, the one you see right there, Brother John, who drinks and dies of fear. This is gorgeous weather. Here and now I understand how true and well founded was the answer given by Anacharsis, that noble philosopher, when he was asked which ship seemed to him the safest, and he replied, 'The one that's in port.' "

"Still better," said Pantagruel, "is his reply when they asked him whether there were more men dead or living, and he asked, 'And in which class do you put those who sail the sea?' Thus he subtly indicated that sailors are continually so close to death that they live dying and die alive. So too Portius Cato said there are only three things to regret: remembering that he'd ever told a secret to a woman, having spent a day doing absolutely nothing, and going anywhere by sea if he could have gotten there by land."

"By the sacred garment I wear," said Brother John to Panurge, "my bally friend: during the entire storm you were in a senseless, irrational panic. Your fatal destiny is not to die at sea: you know that. You'll hang high in the air, or you'll burn bright, like a holy martyr. My Lord Panurge, would you like a fine raincoat? Never mind wolf-skin cloaks, or badger coats. Have this Panurge skinned and cover yourself with his skin. Of course, don't go too near the fire, and—by God!—don't walk in front of a blacksmith's forge, because it will turn to ashes in an instant. But you can go out in the rain as much as you like, or snow, or hail. Indeed, by God! dive right down to the bottom of the water: you'll never even get damp. Turn him into winter boots: they'll never leak. Turn him into bobbing buoys, to teach children how to swim: they'll learn in absolute safety."

"So," said Panurge, "his skin will be like that tight-woven grass we call Venushair, which never gets damp or wet. It's always dry, even if you hold it under water as much as you like. That's why it's also called *adiantum,* or maidenhair."

"Panurge, my friend," said Brother John, "don't worry about water, please: your life will be ended by an element exactly the opposite of water."

"Yes," answered Panurge, "but sometimes the cooks in hell daydream and don't do their jobs right, so they put someone on to boil when they were supposed to roast him—the way our own cooks often grease up partridges, ringdoves, and pigeons, intending (perfectly likely) to roast them, but then it somehow happens that the partridges are in with the cabbage, the ringdoves with leeks—and the pigeons get boiled with turnips. Now listen, my good friends: I want to make it clear, right in front of the entire noble company, that when I swore to build a chapel to Saint Nicholas, out there between Candes and Monsarrat, what I meant to say was a little chest of rosewood, and that no cow or calf would ever graze there, because I'd throw it to the bottom of the ocean."

"Ah!" said Eusthenes. "There's our gallant friend! Gallant—gallant and a half! This just proves the Italian proverb:

> *Passato el pericolo, gabato el santo,*
> When the danger's over, cheat the saint."

Chapter Twenty-five ⁄⁄ After the Storm, Pantagruel Goes Ashore on the Island of the Macraeons

Just then we made port at the island of the Macraeons ("Long-lived People").

The good people of that place received us honorably. An old Macrobe (which is what they called their high magistrate) wanted to lead Pantagruel to the city hall, there to refresh himself, relax, and take some food. But Pantagruel was reluctant to leave the harbor until all his people had disembarked. Having made sure they were all ashore, he ordered them to change their clothes and to lay out all the ships' supplies, so all the galley rowers could eat and drink their fill. This was immediately done. And God only knows how they drank and guzzled. The local people brought in loads of food and drink, too, and the Pantagruelists gave as good as they got, their provisions having been absolutely undamaged by the storm they'd just passed through. Their meal over, Pantagruel asked them to go to work and dutifully repair the damage. This was done, and gladly. The repairs were simple, since all the people of that island were carpenters and artisans of the sort you see at the dockyards in Venice. (It was a large island, but had only three ports and ten parishes: all the rest was covered with tall, dense forests, and as uninhabited as the forest of Ardennes.)

At our request, the old Macrobe showed us everything that was notable and worth seeing on the island. And in the wild, unpopulated forest he pointed out several ruined old temples, a number of obelisks, pyramids, monuments, and ancient burial sites, bearing a variety of inscriptions and epitaphs, some in hieroglyphics, others in Greek, Arabic, Moorish, Slavonic, and the like. With great interest, Epistemon took copies. But Pantagruel said to Brother John:

"This is the island of the Macraeons. Now, 'Macraeon,' in Greek, means a very old man, a man who has lived a very long time."

"What would you like me to do about it?" said Brother John. "Should I pull all this down? I wasn't here when they gave the place its name."

"On that same subject," answered Panurge, "I think the word 'mackerel' comes from here. Because pimping—which is what 'being a mackerel' means—is only appropriate for old men. Young men are too busy chasing ass. Which is why this must be *the* Mackerel Island—the original and prototype of the one in Paris. So let's go catch some oysters in their shells."

Speaking in Greek, the old Macrobe asked Pantagruel how they had managed to make port that day, by what ingenuity and hard work, for it had been singularly windy and there had been a terrible storm out at sea. Pantagruel told him that our Lord on high had taken into account the simplicity and honest affection of his people, who were not voyaging for any monetary reward and carried on no commercial traffic. The one and only cause of their having put to sea was a deep scholarly desire to see, learn, and understand, and to visit the oracle of the Holy Bottle and hear the divine words of the Bottle on certain difficult problems concerning one of their company. Nevertheless, this voyage had not been undertaken without great difficulty and the obvious danger of travel by sea. Then Pantagruel asked him why this horrible storm had blown up, and whether the seas near this island were usually subject to such tempests as afflicted the Straits of Saint Mathieu and Maumusson, in the Atlantic, and, in the Mediterranean, the Gulf of Adalia, Porto di Telamone in Tuscany, Cape Melea in southern Laconia, the Straits of Gibraltar, the Straits of Messina, and others.

Chapter Twenty-six // The Good Macrobe Tells Pantagruel How Heroes Live and Die

To which the good Macrobe replied:

"My voyaging friends, this is one of the Sporades Islands—not your Sporades, which are in the Carpathian Sea, but the oceanic Sporades, which in the old days were well off, even wealthy, much visited, a trading center, densely populated, and ruled by Britain—now, after the lapse of time and in the general decline of the world, poor and uninhabited, as you see.

"This dark forest, more than seventy-eight thousand parasangs in length and breadth, is the home of daemons and heroes who have grown old. We believe—the comet we saw for three days is no longer visible—that yesterday one of them died, and at his passing the horrible storm you endured was created. When these daemons and heroes are alive, nature is overflowing, both on this island and on those near us, and at sea everything is perpetually calm and serene. But when one of them dies, we hear immense and sorrowful weeping from the great forest, and our land is infested with plagues and storms and all manner of afflictions—the air dark and wildly blowing, the sea heaving with squalls and tempests."

"It does indeed seem," said Pantagruel, "to be much as you have described it. Just as a torch or a candle lights up those near it, while it's burning and hot, shedding light all around it, delighting everyone and offering everyone its useful clarity, and neither offending nor injuring anyone—but the moment it's snuffed out its smoke and fumes infect the air, bothering those close by and annoying everyone: so too that's how it is with these noble, distinguished souls. While they inhabit their bodies, the places where they dwell are calm, thriving, pleasant, honorable; but the moment their souls leave their bodies it's perfectly usual for whatever islands and continents they inhabit to be visited by great whirling winds, darkness, thunder, hail, and shaking, trembling, and cracking of the ground, and tempests and storms out at sea, with everyone in mourning, religions in immense upheavals, kingdoms passing from one hand to another, and republics overthrown."

"Recently," said Epistemon, "we've had exactly that experience, when that brave and learned knight Guillaume du Bellay died. When he was alive, France was such a happy country that the whole world envied her, followed her, feared her. And suddenly, once he was dead, the world turned and began to scorn her, and now this has gone on for a long time."

"And so too," said Pantagruel, "when Anchises died at Trapani, in Sicily, a storm made lots of trouble for Aeneas. Perhaps this is also why Herod, the cruel and tyrannical king of Judea, seeing himself close to a horrible death, and being of an appallingly horrible disposition (indeed, he died of an infestation of lice, consumed by worms and bugs, just as, before him, Lucius Sulla died, and Pherecydes the Syrian, Pythagoras' teacher, and the Greek poet Alkman, and others), and knowing, too, that at his death the Jews would be lighting joyous bonfires, invented a totally fraudulent excuse to summon to his castle all the nobles and magistrates from all over the country—saying he had important matters to communicate to them about the governance and protection of the land. And then, when they appeared, he had them locked into the great castle arena. After which he told his sister Salome, and her husband, Alexander, 'I know that the Jews will rejoice at my death. But if you'll listen and do exactly as I tell you, my burial rites will be honorable and there will be public mourning. The moment I'm dead, have the archers of my guard, who have already had my express commands on this subject, kill every one of these nobles and magistrates, locked up here. Then, in spite of itself, all Judea will fall into sorrow and lamentation, and strangers will think this was caused by my death, exactly as if some heroic soul had passed away.'

"The same pretense was made by another desperate tyrant, when he claimed, 'After my death, the earth will be afflicted by fire,' meaning that the whole world would perish. That scoundrel Nero changed this to 'While I live,' as Suetonius tells us. That disgusting remark, which Cicero speaks of in *De finibus,* On Death, book three, and Seneca deals with in *De clementia,* On Mercy, book two, is attributed by Dion Nicaeus and Suidas to Emperor Tiberius."

Chapter Twenty-seven ⁄⁄ Pantagruel's Discourse on the Death of Heroic Souls and the Hair-raising Wonders Which Preceded the Death of Guillaume du Bellay, Lord of Langey

"I would not have wanted," said Pantagruel, going on, "to avoid that horrible storm, which so much troubled and taxed us, for it is because of that experience that we have heard what this good Macrobe has to say. Indeed, it's easy for me to believe what he has told us of the comet they saw in the air, during those days before the death. For some souls are so noble, precious, and heroic that their departure and fall is foretold to us by the heavens, before the event itself. And just as the prudent physician, seeing by all the prognostic signs that his patient is nearing death, warns his wife, children, relatives, and friends some days in advance of the imminent death of their husband, father, or next of kin, so that during whatever time he has left he can put his house in order, spur on and bless his children, give his wife advice about her widowhood, take care of what he knows to be necessary for the maintenance and upkeep of his wards, and not be taken unawares by death, without having had the opportunity to provide for both his soul and his household, so too the benevolent heavens, as if happy to be soon receiving such blessed souls, seem to emit joyous fires before their actual deaths, comets and meteors which they intend as definite signs and truthful predictions for human beings, informing them that in not too many days such venerable souls will leave both their bodies and our earth.

"Once, in Athens, it was exactly the same: in voting on the guilt or innocence of criminal prisoners, the judges would use certain marks, according to the sentence being imposed. *TH* (or *thanatos,* "death") indicated a vote for condemnation by death; *T* indicated acquittal; *A* indicated a need to study the case further. Publicly exhibited, these signs freed the relatives and friends, and others, of their excitement and worry, naturally concerned as they were to learn what had been decided as to the offenders held in prison. So too such comets, like ethereal markings, allow the heavens to say, without words, 'Mortal men, if of these happy souls there is anything you wish to know, learn, understand, become acquainted with, or foresee—anything touching public or private good or utility— be careful to present yourselves to them and have their response, because the end and climax of the comedy is drawing near. Once they have gone, you will regret them in vain.'

"And these heavenly signs do still more. They declare that neither the earth nor those who live upon it are worthy of the presence, the company, and the great joy of such remarkable souls; they astonish and overwhelm us by wonders, marvels, monsters, and other portents formed against every one of nature's laws. We saw all of this for days before the departure of that infinitely illustrious, generous, and heroic soul belonging to the learned and brave knight of Langey, of whom we have spoken."

"I remember it well," said Epistemon, "and my heart still shivers and shakes in my chest when I think of the incredible, hair-raising wonders which began to take place five and six days before his departure. It happened in such a fashion that Lord d'Assier, Lord Chemant, Lord Mailly the one-eyed, Lord Saint-Ayl, Lord Villeneuve-la-Guyart, Maître Gabriel Taphenon, the Italian physician, as well as Rabelais, Cohuau, Claude Massuau (lord of Belle-Croix), Maiorici, Bullou, Cercu (known as the mayor), François Proust, Ferron, Charles Girard, François Bourré, and many, many others, friends, members of the household, and servants of the deceased—all of us were terrified, staring at one another in silence, no one saying a single word, but all of us thinking, understanding that very soon France would be deprived of a perfect knight, desperately needed for her glory and her protection, and all of us well aware that the heavens were calling him back, as if by natural right he was owed to them."

"By the tassel on this robe of mine!" said Brother John. "I'd like to be a learned man, too, when I grow older! And I think I've got a good enough head for it. Now let me ask you a question—

> The way a king speaks to his tribe
> And a queen addresses her child:

Can these heroes and demigods you've been talking about really be killed by death? By our Lady's Ladyness! I thought (as I ought to have thought) they were as immortal as the lovely angels—may God forgive me. But this wonderfully noble Macrobe tells us they die and then they're dead forever."

"Not all of them," answered Pantagruel. "Even the Stoics said that, while all human beings are mortal, there is one exception, one only who is immortal, immutable, unseeable.

"Pindar tells us very plainly that the hard-hearted Fates don't spin out any more thread—that is, any more life—for wood-nymph demigoddesses than they do for the trees the wood nymphs take care of. And those trees are oaks: according to Callimachus, it's oaks that give birth to the wood nymphs, and Pausanias agrees, as does Martianus Capella. As for the demigods—pans, satyrs, wood genies, sprites, pixies, nymphs, heroes, and daemons—some have calculated their lives, using the sum total of all the different life spans computed by Hesiod, to last nine thousand seven hundred and twenty years—this being a number attained by transforming unity into quadrinity, and then doubling quadrinity four times, after which you multiply the resultant five times by solid triangles—that is, 4 times 20 plus 1, which is first multiplied by 3, and then by 8, and then by 5. Consult Plutarch, in his *On Terminating Oracles*."

"That," said Brother John, "is definitely not prayer-book stuff. I'll believe only as much of it as you tell me to."

"I believe," said Pantagruel, "that all intellectual souls are immune to Fate's scissors. They're all immortal, whether angels, daemons, or humans. On which subject, indeed, let me tell you an exceedingly strange tale, and yet one recorded and vouched for by many learned and knowing historians."

Chapter Twenty-eight ⁄⁄ Pantagruel Tells a Sad Story about the Death of Heroes

"Epitherses, father of the orator Aemilian, was sailing from Greece to Italy in a ship carrying an assortment of merchandise and a number of passengers, when one night the wind died down near the Echinades Islands (between Morea and Tunis) and their vessel was carried close to Paxos.

Anchoring there, some of the passengers asleep, some awake, others eating and drinking, they heard a loud voice calling, from the island of Paxos, 'Thamous!' This terrified them. Thamous was in fact their pilot, a native of Egypt, but only a few of the passengers knew him by name. Then they heard the voice a second time, shrieking most horribly, 'Thamous!' No one answered; they all remained silent and fearful; and then the voice was heard a third time, crying out even more horribly than before. And then Thamous replied, 'I'm here, what do you want of me? what do you want me to do?' At which the voice spoke again, even more loudly, and commanded him, when he came to Paloda, to publicly announce that the great god Pan was dead.

"Epitherses tells us that, hearing this, all the sailors and passengers were stunned and terribly frightened. Debating among themselves whether it was better to keep silent or to make the public pronouncement that had been commanded, Thamous told them that he thought they should stay silent, if a wind blew up behind them and swept them along on their way, but if the sea remained calm they ought to speak as the voice had commanded. When they were near Paloda, it happened that the wind was not blowing. So Thamous, climbing up on the prow, his face turned toward land, announced as he had been commanded to that the great god Pan was dead. He had not spoken the last word when deep sighs were heard on land, great lamentations and startled cries not from just one person but from many, all together.

"The news (because many people had by then heard it) was soon revealed in Rome. And Tiberius Caesar, then the emperor, sent for Thamous. Having heard him speak, he believed Thamous' tale. And when he consulted the learned men, then present in great numbers at his court in Rome, to find out just who this Pan was, he was informed that Pan had been the son of Mercury and Penelope.

"Herodotus had long since recorded this fact; so too had Cicero, in the third book of his *On the Nature of the Gods*. Nevertheless, I would interpret this story to concern the great Savior of the faithful, ignominiously put to death in Judea because of the jealousy and the unrighteousness of the high priests, scholars, preachers, and monks of the Mosaic law. Nor does this seem to me an impossible interpretation, for He can quite properly be called Pan, in Greek, since He is our All, and all that we are, all that we live, all that we have, all that we hope for is Him—in Him, from Him, by Him. It is the good god Pan, a noble shepherd, who—as that ardent shepherd Corydon testifies—has the love and affection not only of his flock but also of his shepherds. And on His death, certainly, there were moans, sighs, cries, and lamentations in every part of the universe—heavens, earth, sea, hell itself. And the chronology, too, supports my interpretation, because when that infinitely good, infinitely great Pan who was our one and only Savior died near Jerusalem, it was Tiberius Caesar who ruled in Rome."

Having stated his case, Pantagruel fell into silence and profound contemplation. Not long after, we saw tears as large as ostrich eggs rolling down his cheeks. May I be taken from this earth if I lie in one single word of all this.

Chapter Twenty-nine // How Pantagruel Sailed by the Island of Rigorous Bigots, Where King Lent-Observance Ruled

The happy boats of our fleet were refitted and repaired, our supplies replaced, and the Macraeons were more than satisfied with what Pantagruel had spent, just as our people were smiling even more broadly than usual when, the next day, in great gaiety we spread our sails to the calm and delightful north wind. At high noon Imported Goods pointed out to us, from a distance, the island of Rigorous Bigots, in which land Lent-Observance was king. Pantagruel had previously heard of him and would have liked to meet him in person, but Imported Goods discouraged this, as much because it would take us far from our proper route as, he explained, because of the meager pleasures to be experienced anywhere on the island, including at the ruler's court.

"All told," he said, "what you'll see there is a great guzzler of dried peas, a great imbiber of snails, a great monkish rat-catching dreamer, a great cheapskate, a hairless half-giant with a shaved head, born of Lanternish blood and empty-headed like all his relatives, a flag-waving fish eater, a mustard tyrant, a child beater, an ash cooker, father and nurse of physicians, stuffed with pardons, indulgences, and church tickets, but an honest man, a good Catholic, and terribly devout. He spends three-quarters of the day crying. He never goes to weddings. And he's the best roasting skewer and spit maker you'll see for forty kingdoms around. About six years ago, going by this island, I bought a gross of them, which I gave to the butchers in Candes, near Chinon. They were delighted, and with good reason. When we get back, I'll show you two of them hanging from the church doors.

"He feeds on dry mail shirts and helmets (sometimes with plumes, sometimes well salted), and sometimes this diet gives him a good painful hot piss. But he wears gay clothes, fashionable and brightly colored: everything gray and cold, nothing in front and nothing behind, and sleeves to match."

"Just as you've told me about his clothes," said Pantagruel, "his diet, his lifestyle and amusements, it would be good to hear exactly what he looks like and the shape of each and every part."

"Yes, please, my bally friend," said Brother John, "because I've found him in my prayer book, right after the movable feasts."

"Gladly," answered Imported Goods. "We may hear more said about King Lent-Observance, when we pass Savage Island, ruled by the Fat Sausages, who are his mortal enemies and against whom he wars perpetually. Indeed, if it weren't for the help they get from the noble Mardigras, their protector and good neighbor, this great sniveling Lent-Observance would long since have exterminated them."

"But," asked Brother John, "are they male or female? Angels or mortal? Women or virgins?"

"Their sex is female," said Imported Goods, "and their state is mortal. Some of them are virgins, some aren't."

"May the devil take me," said Brother John, "if I'm not on their side! What sort of natural chaos is this—making war against women? Let's sail back there. Let's beat the hell out of that great rascal."

"Fighting against Lent-Observance?" said Panurge. "By all the devils, I'm not *that* stupid! *Quid juris,* What would the courts say if we got ourselves involved between Fat Sausages and Lent-Observance—between the hammer and the anvil? Damn! Just forget about that! Let's go on! Bye-bye, King Lent-Observance. My best to the Fat Sausages—and don't forget the Black Puddings, either."

Chapter Thirty // Imported Goods Analyzes and Describes King Lent-Observance

The internal organs of King Lent-Observance," said Imported Goods, "include—or at least used to, in my time—a brain about the size, color, substance, and power of the left testicle of a male cheese mite, and

the cerebellum of a screw spike,
the cerebral lobes of a carpenter's mallet,
the cranial membranes of a monk's cowl,
the optical nerves of a bricklayer's hod,
the cerebral fornix of a lady's bonnet,
the pineal gland of a bagpipe,
the circulatory system of a horse's head armor,
the jaw nodes of a pair of heavy shoes,
the eardrums of a yardarm winch,
the forehead of a feather duster,
the backbone of a stable lamp,
the nerve channels of a spigot,
the uvula of a blowpipe,

the palate of a mitten,
the saliva of an incense holder,
the tonsils of a monocle,
the gullet of a two-handed wicker basket,
the stomach of a money belt,
the stomach tube of a pitchfork,
the trachea of a small pocketknife,
the throat of a ball of yarn,
the lungs of a flapping cape,
the heart of a cassock,
the pulmonary septum of a beer mug,
the pulmonary membranes of a pair of forceps,
the arteries of a sleeveless cloak,
the diaphragm of a paper hat,
the liver of a glazier's hammer,
the veins of a weaver's loom,
the spleen of a bird whistle,
the bowels of a fishnet,
the gallbladder of a carpenter's ax,
the guts of a leather glove,
the peritoneum of an abbot's staff,
the small intestine of a dentist's tongs,
the large intestine of a brass breastplate,
the colon of a wineglass,
the rectum of a drinker's ox horn,
the kidneys of a trowel,
the loins of a padlock,
the pissing pores of a chimney hook,
the renal veins of a pair of water guns,
the sperm glands of a puffy pastry,
the prostate of an inkpot,
the bladder of a catapult,
(fitted with a neck like a bell clapper),
the abdomen of an Albanian hat,
the stomach wall of a suit of armor,
the muscles of a blacksmith's bellows,
the tendons of a falconer's glove,
the ligaments of a wallet,
the bones of a dried cracker,
the marrow of a beggar's bag,
the cartilage of a turtle,
the lymph glands of a billhook,
the animal spirits of a punch in the face,
the vital spirits of a flick of the finger,
the boiling blood of repeated raps on the nose,

the urine of a heretic burning at the stake,

the sperm of a hundred plasterer's nails (and his nurse told me that, having married the Middle of Lent, all he could spawn was a number of locative adverbs and a few two-day wonders),

the memory of a waving scarf,

the common sense of a bug,

the imagination of bells chiming,

the thoughts of flapping crows,

the awareness of flying herons,

the determination of a pile of barley,

the repentance of a cannon's undercarriage,

the vim and vigor of a ship's ballast,

the comprehension of a prayer book with half its pages ripped out,

the understanding of a slug crawling off a strawberry bush,

the willpower of three nuts in a bowl,

the desire of six bales of hay,

the judgment of a shoehorn,

the discretion of a mitten,

the rationality of a tiny toy drum."

Chapter Thirty-one // King Lent Observance's External Anatomy

"As far as his external anatomy is concerned," said Imported Goods, continuing his analysis, "King Lent-Observance is a bit better proportioned, except that he has seven ribs more than ordinary humans, and

toes like the feathers on an old harpsichord,

nails like a corkscrew,

feet like a guitar,

heels like a club,

soles like the bottom of a hanging lamp,

legs like bird trainer's leather,

knees like a wooden stool,

thighs like a crossbow,

hips like swivel sticks,

a potbelly, buttoned up in the old style and buckled to his jacket,

a belly button like an old lady's,

pubic hair like a whipped-cream tart,

a penis like an old slipper,

balls like a double leather bottle,

seminal vesicles like a turnip,

testicle muscles like the strings of a tennis racket,
a perineum like a small flute,
an asshole like a crystal mirror,
buttocks like a farmer's harrow,
kidneys like a butter pot,
a sacrum like a billiard cue,
a back like a machine-wound crossbow,
a spinal column like a bagpipe,
ribs like a spinning wheel,
a sternum like a stone canopy,
shoulder blades like mortars and pestles,
a chest like a panpipe,
pectorals like a trumpet mouthpiece,
armpits like a chessboard,
shoulders like a wheelbarrow,
arms like a monk's hood,
fingers like a monastery's andirons,
wrist bones like a pair of stilts,
arm bones like sickles,
elbows like rattraps,
hands like currycombs,
a neck like a beggar's cup,
a throat like a funnel,
an Adam's apple like a keg with two beautiful brass warts hanging
    from it, shaped like hourglasses,
a beard like a woman's twat,
a chin like a toadstool,
ears like a pair of mittens,
a nose like a coat of arms pasted on a velvet shoe,
nostrils like a baby's bonnet, tied with a string,
eyebrows like a roaster's drip pans,
(and under the left eyebrow, a birthmark shaped like, and every bit as
    big as, a pisspot),
eyelids like the strings on a violin,
eyes like running streams,
optical nerves like a flintstone,
a forehead like a turret vase,
temples like a gutter spout,
cheeks like two wooden shoes,
jaws like a dinner goblet,
teeth like steel spears (one of his baby teeth can be found, today, at
    Coulonges-sur-l'Autize, and two more at La Brosse, in Saintonge,
    at the mouth of the cave),
a tongue like a harp,
a mouth like a monk's cowl,

a face slashed like a mule's packsaddle,
a head shaped like a distiller's pot,
a skull like a game bag,
(scarred like the pope's signet ring),
skin like a peasant's loose robe,
an epidermis like a sieve,
hair like a dirty doormat,
and whiskers—exactly as already described."

Chapter Thirty-two // More about How King Lent-Observance Looked

"It's truly extraordinary," said Imported Goods, going on, "to see and understand what King Lent-Observance is like:

"If he spits, it's basketfuls of wild artichokes,
If he blows his nose, it's pickled eels,
If he weeps, it's duck in white sauce,
If he shivers, it's great rabbit pies,
If he sweats, it's cod in fresh butter,
If he belches, it's oysters on the half shell,
If he sneezes, it's barrels and barrels of mustard,
If he coughs, it's boxes of quince marmalade,
If he sobs, it's bunches of watercress,
If he yawns, it's pots and pots of ground peas,
If he sighs, it's smoked tongues of beef,
If he whistles, it's baskets of green monkeys,
If he snores, it's buckets of shelled beans,
If he scowls, it's pig's feet in lard,
If he speaks, it's rough Auvergne homespun, not those words of
    crimson silk to which Queen Parysatis compared the speech of her
    son, the Persian king Cyrus,
If he snorts, it's church collection boxes, for indulgences,
If he winks, it's waffles and wafers,
If he snarls, it's the cats of March,
If he nods his head, it's carts with iron wheels,
If he pouts, it's broken sticks,
If he mutters, it's law clerks' games,
If he jumps up and down, it's debt-forgiveness time,
If he steps back, it's seashells down by the seashore,
If he slobbers, it's public ovens,
If he's hoarse, it's time for the Morris dancers,

If he farts, it's brown-cow leggings,
(or else it's leather stockings),
If he scratches himself, it's new rules and regulations,
If he sings, it's peas in the pod,
If he shits, it's mushrooms and toadstools,
If he gets angry, it's cabbage in oil (better known, in Languedoc, as
   cabbages in oil),
If he preaches, it's the snows of yesteryear,
If he worries, it's for the bald and the close-cropped,
If he gives nothing, then that's all they get,
If he daydreams, it's about penises climbing and flying up walls,
If he dreams, it's about landlords' rent rolls.

"A strange case: when he works, he makes nothing; he makes nothing when he's working. He has his eyes open when he sleeps, and sleeps with his eyes open—like the hares in Champagne: he's afraid of a surprise attack from the Fat Sausages, his ancient enemies. He laughs as he chews, and chews as he's laughing. He eats nothing when he's fasting, and when he's fasting eats nothing. He eats with absolute indifference, and drinks only in his imagination. He takes his baths way up over the highest steeples, and dries himself in rivers and ponds. He fishes in the air, where he catches lots of crawfish. He hunts at the bottom of the sea, where he finds antelope, ibex, and deer. He usually pokes out the eyes of all the crows he traps. The only things he's afraid of are his shadow and fat young goats bleating. There are days when he just loafs. He fools around with holy things. He uses his fist as a hammer. He writes out predictions and calendars on hairy parchment, using the big fat pen he carries around in his pants."

"Oh, he's a real rascal," said Brother John. "That's my man. He's the one I'm looking for. I'll challenge him, I will."

"What a strange and monstrous sort of man," said Pantagruel, "if we have to call him a man. You make me think of the faces and the bodies of Immoderation and Discord."

"And what sort of bodies," asked Brother John, "did they have? I've never heard them mentioned. May the good Lord pardon me."

"I'll tell you what I've read about them," answered Pantagruel, "in ancient fables. Physis (that is, Nature) first gave birth to Beauty and Harmony, without having had sexual intercourse, being in and of herself immensely fecund and fertile. But Antiphysis, the opposite of Nature in every way, was immediately jealous of this fine and honorable childbirth and, setting herself up in direct opposition, copulated with Tellumon and gave birth to Immoderation and Discord.

"They had spherical heads, round as a balloon, not gently pressed in on the sides like the human form. They had big donkey ears that stuck way up; their tough, cockroach eyes, framed by heel-like bones, and with no eyebrows, protruded right out of their heads; their feet were round, like tennis balls; their arms and hands were turned backward, toward their shoulders; and indeed they walked on their heads, flipping over in continual cartwheels, ass over head, their legs up in the air. And just as monkeys think their little ones are the prettiest in the world, so Antiphysis boasted about their good looks, trying to prove that her children were infinitely better shaped and more pleasing than Physis', claiming that to have such beautifully spherical feet and heads, and thus to roll along doing cartwheels, was both the ideal shape and the perfect way to move, partaking indeed of the divine, since it was of course the way in which the heavens themselves rotated, and all other eternal things. Having their feet in the air, and their heads down, was to imitate the Creator of the universe, since after all men's hair was like roots and their legs were like branches: tree roots were far more appropriately planted in the earth than tree branches—thus demonstrating, to her own satisfaction, that her children were a great deal better, as well as better equipped, than those of Physis, being just like upright trees rather than upside-down ones. And as for their hands and arms, she proved how much more rational it was to have them turned back toward the shoulders, so that part of the body would not be defenseless, the front side being well taken care of by the teeth, useful not only for chewing (without any help from the hands) but also for protecting themselves against harmful assaults.

"And thus, citing evidence from the brute beasts, in her wisdom she gathered around herself all the idiots and madmen, and was much admired by all those without brains, all those stripped of good judgment and common sense. Later she gave birth to Monkey Scholars, Skunky Scholars, and Popish Hypocrites, Wild Monks, Daemoniacal Calvins (Genevan Fakers), raving Puy Herbaults, gluttonous Monk Stuffers, Bigots, Hypocrites, Cannibals, and other deformed and unnatural monsters."

Chapter Thirty-three ⁄⁄ How Pantagruel Saw a Monstrous Whale near Wildmen's Island

At midday, approaching Wildmen's Island, Pantagruel saw from far off a monstrously huge whale, puffed up taller than the top of the ships' masts, swimming right toward us, snorting, booming, and spouting out water from its throat into the air in front of it, like a great river swirling down a mountain. Pantagruel pointed it out to the pilot and to Imported Goods. The pilot advised that the trumpeters on board the *Thalamège* sound out the war call! To arms!

Hearing this, all the ships, galleys, warships, and light attack vessels (according to their standing orders) set themselves in a formation like the

Greek letter Y (sacred to Pythagoras), like cranes in flight, sailing in an acute angle, at the center of which was the aforesaid *Thalamège,* ready to do gallant battle. Brother John climbed up on the quarterdeck, gallant and determined, along with the bombardiers. But Panurge began to weep and wail louder than ever.

"Ba-ba-bi-boo," he said, "this is worse than before. Let's run! By God, this whale is the Leviathan described by the noble prophet Moses, in his life of that sainted man Job. He'll swallow us all, people and boats alike, as if we were so many pills. In that great infernal throat of his we won't bulk any larger than a grain of musk swallowed by a donkey. Here it comes! Run—let's get back to shore! I swear this is that sea monster meant, in the old days, to gobble up Andromeda. We're all lost! Oh, if only some valiant Perseus was here, right now, to kill him!"

"I'll be his Perseus!" answered Pantagruel. "Don't be afraid."

"Mother of God!" said Panurge. "Just get rid of the reason for being afraid. When would you have me feel fear, if not when danger is obvious?"

"If your fatal destiny," said Pantagruel, "is what Brother John recently said it was, you ought to be afraid of Pyroeis, Heous, Aethon, Phlegon— the famous fire-breathing horses of the sun, breathing flames through their nostrils. But whales, who only spout water through their blowholes and their throats, shouldn't make you afraid at all. It's clear that the water they spout up can't possibly threaten you. Indeed, you're more likely to be saved and protected by water than saddened or hurt."

"That's different!" said Panurge. "How well you put these things, my lord! Oh Lord! Haven't I carefully explained the transmutation of elements, and the close connections between roast beef and boiled beef, between boiled beef and roast beef? Alas! Here it comes! I'm going down there and hide! We're all of us dead men, as soon as he reaches us! I see Atropos, the goddess of death, up there on the quarterdeck—the traitor— with her freshly sharpened scissors, ready to snip the cords of our lives. Watch out! Here it comes! Oh, what a horrible, disgusting sight you are! You've drowned so many others who never even had a chance to boast about it. God! If only he spouted up good wine—white, red, fresh, delicious—instead of this bitter water—stinking, salty—it would be a little easier to bear, and we'd have some decent excuse to be long-suffering, like that English nobleman who was ordered, for the crimes he'd been convicted of, to die any way he chose, and decided to die by drowning in a great barrel of Malmsey wine. Here it comes! Ho! Ho! You hellish devil, you Leviathan! I can't look at you—you're too hideous and awful! Go bother the lawyers and judges—go after the bailiffs!"

Chapter Thirty-four // How Pantagruel Defeated the Monstrous Whale

Coming to the bulwarks formed by the ships and galleys, the whale threw tons of water on the first ones it met, with a roar like the waterfalls of the Nile, in Ethiopia. Javelins, short spears, darts, hunting spears, Corsican javelins, and pikes flew at him from all sides. Brother John did not spare him. Panurge was dying with fear. The cannons roared and thundered like the devil himself, trying their best to get at him. But nothing worked, because the heavy cannon shells, iron and brass, seemed to just melt into his skin, like tiles in the sun, seen from a distance. So Pantagruel, seeing that it was time to intervene, rolled up his sleeves and showed what he could do.

Talk about that good-for-nothing Commodus, emperor of Rome, of whom it is written that he could handle a bow so skillfully that, from far, far off he could shoot arrows between the upraised fingers of little children, never touching one of them.

Tell us about that Indian archer, in the days when Alexander the Great conquered that country, who could wield his bow so beautifully that, from far, far away, he could shoot arrows inside the circle of a man's ring, although his arrows were a full yard in length and were so heavily covered with iron they could pierce thick steel shields, steel breastplates—indeed, pretty much anything they hit, so hard were they, so strong and unbreakable, so perfectly made.

Or talk about the marvelous skills of the ancient French, who stood highest of all in the bowman's art: hunting animals black or brown, they rubbed the heads of their arrows with deadly hellebore, because that made the meat tenderer, sweeter, healthier, and more delicious, even though they had to draw a circle around the part where the arrow had entered and cut the meat away.

Or tell us, if you like, about the Parthians, who could shoot backward better than other people could, facing forward. Or celebrate the Scythians and their skillfullness—tell us how, once, they sent an ambassador to Darius, king of the Persians, who offered him a bird, a frog, a mouse, and five arrows, not saying a single word. Asked what these presents meant, and if he had orders to say anything, the ambassador said no. Which astonished and dazed Darius, until one of the seven captains who had killed the false magi, and thus made Darius king (his name was Gobrias), explained it to him:

"The implicit meaning of these gifts is as follows: the Scythians say that unless the Persians are like birds, and can fly up in the sky, or are like mice that can hide themselves deep in the earth, or are like frogs that can hide themselves in ponds and swamps, they'll be swept into hell by the power and wisdom of the Scythians."

But our noble Pantagruel was incomparably better than any of them, in all the arts of throwing spears and other weapons. With his deadly javelins and darts (which in truth were, in length, size, weight, and the amount of iron they contained, more like the great beams holding up the bridges at Nantes, Saumur, and Bergerac, and the Change and Meuniers bridges in Paris) he could open oyster shells from a thousand paces, without touching the edges. He could hit a candle flame without snuffing it out; or hit a magpie in the eye; or peel the shoes off a pair of boots without ripping them; or strip the fur lining out of a helmet without spoiling it; or turn the pages of Brother John's prayer book, one after the other, without tearing a thing.

Using such darts (of which there was a plentiful supply on board), he sent his first throw right through the whale's forehead, piercing both jaws and the tongue and ensuring that he could no longer open his throat, no longer suck up water, and no longer spout it forth. His second throw put out the monster's right eye; his third put out the left one. And everyone saw, with immense joy, that the whale was now wearing three horns on his forehead, like an equilateral triangle leaning slightly forward. He was turning from one side to the other, staggering and blundering about as if stupefied—blind and already close to death.

Not satisfied, Pantagruel threw another dart into his tail, which (like the others) stuck in his flesh with its end sloping backward, and then threw three more in a perpendicular line down his spine, which they cut into three equal parts (measuring from his tail to his nose).

And then, finally, he threw fifty darts into one side of the beast and fifty into the other, so that the whale's body began to look like a three-masted galleon's keel, when the carpenters have measured out and nailed up her beams, and all the iron rings and chains are laid out along the hull. And this was a most pleasant sight to see.

And then, as it died, the whale rolled over, belly up, as dead fish always do, and with all the great wooden handles of Pantagruel's darts jutting down into the sea it looked like some great hundred-legged sea monster, a giant centipede out of the pages of that ancient wise man Nicander's book about snakes and other poisonous creatures.

Chapter Thirty-five ⁄⁄ Pantagruel Disembarks on Wildmen's Island, the Ancestral Home of the Fat Sausages

The chief oarsmen from the ship *Lanternland* tied up the whale and towed it to the next island, which was Wildmen's Island, in order to dissect it and collect the oil from its kidneys, said to be very useful and even necessary for curing a certain disease which they called lack of money.

Pantagruel paid no attention, because he had seen other whales, indeed many much larger, in French waters. But he graciously agreed to their stopping on Wildmen's Island, to restore and refresh—at a small unused harbor near the middle of the island—those of his people who had been soaked through and befouled by the villainous whale. The harbor was located near a stand of tall trees, well shaped and attractive, from which ran a delightful stream of clear, sweet water, bright and sparkling. Setting up their kitchens under good tents, they lit great fires. Everyone who cared to changed his clothes. Brother John rang the bell, and at that sound the tables were made ready and the food quickly served.

Dining happily with his people, Pantagruel noticed, as the second course was being served, some small, tame Fat Sausages scrambling and climbing, not making a sound, up a tall tree that stood right near the tables on which their wine was set out. So he asked Imported Goods, "What sort of animals are those?" They seemed to him to be like squirrels, or weasels, or marten, or ermine.

"They're Fat Sausages," answered Imported Goods. "This is Wildmen's Island, which we talked about this morning. Between them and King Lent-Observance—their evil, ancient enemy—there is a long-standing, deadly war. Do understand that the cannon we fired at the whale have made them frightened and concerned that their enemy might have landed here with all his armies, intending to surprise them or to burn and pillage this island of theirs, as he has several times before tried to do, though most unsuccessfully, having to confront such careful, vigilant opponents as the Sausages, who (as did Dido: recall her explanation to those companions of Aeneas who had sought to make port in Carthage without her knowledge or permission) were constrained by the viciousness of their enemy, and the close proximity of his realm, to be continually watchful and on their guard."

"Indeed, my good friend," said Pantagruel, "if there is any decent way we can end this war, and reconcile both sides, please tell me how to do it. I'll engage myself in the task most cheerfully; nor will I spare anything if I can draw up a treaty of peace and soothe the antagonisms now dividing the two parties."

"Right now that's impossible," answered Imported Goods. "About four years ago, journeying through this place and the island of Rigorous Bigots, I tried to make peace between them, or at least some significant truce—and they would have been good friends and neighbors, had either side been able to put aside their passions in any respect whatever. King Lent-Observance did not want any treaty of peace to include the savage Black Puddings, or the Mountain Sausages, both of whom have long been his people's good comrades and allies. The Sausages demanded that Herring-Barrel Castle be handed over to their rule and dominion, as Salty

Castle already is, and that it be scrubbed clean of all the God knows what stinking, villainous assassins and thieves who currently occupy it. They could not come to any agreement: everything seemed iniquitous to one or the other party.

"So nothing could be done. Nevertheless, they were not quite such bitter enemies as they had been in the past. But now, since the proclamations of the Crazy Council, in which they were analyzed, harassed, and given many solemn warnings—and in which, furthermore, King Lent-Observance was declared a filthy, stinking, dried-up fish if he made any agreement or alliance whatever with the Sausages—things have gone from bad to worse, and they've been quarrelsome, righteous, and stubborn, and there's nothing to be done about it. It would be easier to bring about a peace between cats and rats, or dogs and hares."

Chapter Thirty-six // How the Wild Sausages Set an Ambush for Pantagruel

As Imported Goods was speaking, Brother John noticed twenty-five or thirty slender young Sausages in the harbor area, proceeding rapidly back toward their city, stronghold, castle, and fort, known as Chimney. So he said to Pantagruel:

"I predict there's going to be a rumpus here. Maybe these old Sausages will confuse you and King Lent-Observance, although you don't look a bit alike. Let's stop eating and get ready to fight back."

"Now that," said Imported Goods, "would not be a bad idea. Sausages are Sausages—always two-faced and traitorous."

So Pantagruel rose from the table, to have a look around the wood; he came back quickly, telling us he'd seen, off to the left, an ambush of truly fat Sausages, while to the right, half a league farther, he'd spotted a large battalion of great, powerful Sausages, all along a small hill, marching rapidly toward us in full battle gear, to the sound of bagpipes and flutes, black-pudding wrappers and sheeps' bladders, joyous fifes and drums, trumpets and bugles.

Using the seventy-eight flags and banners we counted, we calculated that there couldn't be any fewer than forty-two thousand of them. Judging by their excellent military discipline, their proud way of marching, and their confident looks, we realized these were no fresh-ground meatballs, but battle-hardened old Sausage warriors. From the front ranks to the flag carriers, they were wearing full armor and carrying pikes that were rather short, as far as we could tell from a distance, but which nevertheless seemed to have steel points and to be well sharpened. The two flanks of this army were accompanied by crowds of wild Blood Puddings, huge Pâtés, and Sausage Cavalry, all of good size, plus local men, brigands, and a host of wild people of all sorts.

Pantagruel was much concerned, and with good cause, although Epistemon pointed out that it might be the custom, in this land of Sausages, to welcome friendly strangers with a military display, as the kings of France are welcomed in the principal cities of their realm, thus received and greeted on their first tour of the country after the sacred ceremonies of coronation and the new ascent to the throne.

"Perhaps," said Epistemon, "this is simply the ordinary royal guard—the local queen, warned by the young Sausage lookouts we saw under the trees that our fine, rich fleet had come into the harbor, realized that their visitor had to be some rich and powerful prince and now comes to visit you in person."

Not convinced, Pantagruel called his chief officers into council to quickly learn what, in their opinion, had to be done in this doubtful situation, full of fearful uncertainty.

Accordingly, he tersely reminded them that such military displays had often heralded deadly injury, under the color of a friendly welcome.

"Thus," he said, "Emperor Antoninus Caracalla killed the Alexandrians, once, and another time destroyed the troops of the Persian king Artabanus, pretending that he'd come to marry off his daughter. But he did not escape unpunished for such deceits: not long afterward, he too was killed. And thus, too, the children of Jacob avenged the rape of their sister Dinah, massacring the Shechemites. It was in this deceitful fashion that Gallienus, emperor of Rome, crushed the fighting men of Constantinople. Thus, pretending friendship, Antonius lured Artavasdes, king of Armenia, then bound him in heavy chains, and finally had him killed. The ancient records reveal a thousand other such cases for us. And we still rightly praise, to this day, the great wisdom of Charles, the sixth of that name to rule France, who as he was returning to his capital city of Paris, after victories over the Flemish and the people of Ghent, reached Bourget and was informed that the Parisians, carrying their wooden mallets (on which account they were known as Malleteers), had come out of that city in battle array—twenty thousand of them. He promptly declared that he would not go to the city (though they reminded him that the people had armed themselves the better to greet him—quite without evil intent or any attempt to deceive) until they had returned to their homes and disarmed themselves."

Chapter Thirty-seven ⁄⁄ How Pantagruel Sent for Colonels Scrapesausage and Chopupbloodpudding, with a Wise Discourse on the Proper Names of Places and Persons

The council decided that, whatever happened, they must be watchful. Then Pantagruel commanded Carpalim and Gymnast to summon the soldiers from the good ships *Toasting Glass* (commanded by Colonel Scrapesausage) and *Market Basket* (commanded by Colonel Chopup-bloodpudding, junior).

"I'll take over from Gymnast," said Panurge, "at this point. And besides, he's needed here."

"By this habit I'm wearing," said Brother John, "you want to get away from the fighting, you fat-head. On my honor, you'll never come back! Not that it would be any great loss. All you'll do is weep and wail and cry and generally discourage our good soldiers."

"I'll most certainly come back, Brother John," said Panurge, "my spiritual father—and as soon as possible. But you make sure these irritating Sausages don't climb on board our boats. And while you're fighting, I'll pray to God for your victory, just like noble Moses, leader of the Israelites."

"The very names of these two colonels of yours," said Epistemon to Pantagruel, "Scrapesausage and Chopupbloodpudding, seem to be an assurance of victory in this combat, if by any chance these Sausages intend to attack us."

"You understand such things," said Pantagruel. "I'm glad that their names enable you to foresee and predict our victory. This sort of prediction by names is nothing new. The Pythagoreans praised and religiously followed it, long ago. And many noble lords and emperors have employed it, much to their profit. One day, Octavian Augustus, second emperor of Rome, met a peasant named Euthyche—that is, in Greek, 'Fortunate'—who was leading a donkey named Nicon—or 'Victorious.' The meaning of these names, both the donkey driver's and the donkey's, made him feel confident of complete prosperity, happiness, and victory. Vespasian, another Roman emperor, was all alone, one day, praying in the temple at Serapis, when he suddenly saw his servant, Basilides—that is, 'Son of Kings'—who had been sick and long since left behind. This gave him new hope and confidence that he would indeed rule the Roman Empire. And Regilian—that is, 'Royal'—received the crown from his soldiers for no other reason than his name. See the divine Plato's *Cratylus* . . ."

"By my thirst!" said Rootgatherer. "I want to read him: I've heard you mention him so often."

". . . See how the Pythagoreans, using names and numbers, calculated that Patroclus had to be killed by Hector, Hector by Achilles, Achilles by Paris, and Paris by Philoctetes. Just thinking of Pythagoras' wonderful discovery makes my head whirl: whether a proper name had an *even* or an *odd* number of syllables revealed to him, for example, on which side a man would be lame, humpbacked, blind, gouty, paralyzed, weak lunged, as well as many other natural deformities. The trick is to assign the *even* number to the left side of the body, and the *odd* to the right."

"Indeed," said Epistemon, "I've seen this done at Saintes, during a general procession, in the presence of that exceedingly good, exceedingly virtuous, exceedingly learned and fair-minded presiding judge Brian Vallée, lord of Douhet. As each person went by—male or female, lame, blind, humpbacked—he was informed of their proper name. And if the syllables of that name were *odd,* at once, without seeing the person, he would declare that they were misshapen, blind, lame, or humpbacked on the right side. If the number of syllables was *even,* it was the left side. And he was correct, without exception."

"Using this discovery," said Pantagruel, "learned men have established that Achilles, being down on his knees, was wounded by Paris' arrow in his right heel—since his name contains an *odd* number of syllables (and note, too, that the ancients always knelt on the right side). They have established that Diomedes wounded Venus, in front of Troy, on the right hand, since in Greek his name has four syllables. Vulcan was lame in the left foot, for the same reason, and Philip, king of Macedonia, and also Hannibal, were blind in the right eye. Using this Pythagorean method, we could give the same details for people with back pains, with hernias, or with migraines.

"But, to return to names: consider how Alexander the Great, King Philip's son (about whom we've already spoken), managed to succeed by interpreting just one name. He was besieging the strong, fortified city of Tyre, and for several weeks threw his entire army into the attempt, but in vain. His siege machines were useless: everything they demolished was immediately repaired by the Tyrians. So he thought he might as well abandon the siege, though it made him extremely unhappy to make such a decision, for it might well ruin his reputation. And while in this agitated, troubled state, he fell asleep. He dreamed that there was a satyr in his tent, dancing and jumping about on his goat legs. Alexander tried to capture him, but the satyr kept slipping away from him. But finally the king, chasing him into a narrow passage, seized him. At this point, Alexander awoke and, when he told his dream to the philosophers and learned men of his court, was informed that the gods had promised him victory and Tyre would soon be taken, since the word *Satyros,* divided in two, was *Sa Tyros,* meaning 'Tyre is captured.' And, indeed, the next assault his armies made, they swept away all resistance and, magnificently victorious, subjugated that rebellious people.

"And on the other hand, consider how the meaning of a name reduced Pompey to despair. Having been vanquished by Caesar, at the battle of Pharsalia, the only way he could save himself was to flee. Traveling by sea, he arrived at the island of Cyprus. Near the city of Paphos, he saw a rich and beautiful palace built on the beach. When he asked the pilot its name, he was told it was Kachobasiléa, or 'Evil King.' The name filled him with such fear and loathing that he fell into the blackest despair, as if certain that escape was impossible and he would soon lose his life. Everyone on the ship, passengers and sailors alike, heard his cries, his sighs and moans. And in truth, not long after, an unknown peasant named Achillas cut off his head.

"And we could still add the story of Lucius Paulus Aemilius, when the Roman senate chose him to be emperor—that is, general of the army they were sending against Perses, king of Macedonia. That very night, returning home to get ready for his departure, he kissed his little daughter, Tratia, having observed that she was distinctly unhappy. 'What's wrong,' he said, 'my Tratia? Why are you so sad and upset?' 'My father,' she replied, 'Persa is dead.' This was the name of a pretty little bitch of which she was very fond. But at this Paulus knew he would be victorious against Perses.

"And if time permitted, we could also discuss the sacred Bible of the Hebrews, where we would find a hundred notable passages showing us without any doubt how faithfully, even devoutly, they understood proper names and their meanings."

As they finished this discussion, the two colonels arrived, accompanied by their troops, all well armed and ready. Pantagruel made a short speech, urging them to show their valor in combat, if combat should become necessary (for he himself could still not believe that the Sausages were so treacherous), but warning them not to begin hostilities. And he gave them *Mardi Gras* as their watchword.

Chapter Thirty-eight ⁄⁄ Why Men Should Not Look Down at Sausages

You're laughing, all you good drinkers; you don't think there's a word of truth in what I'm telling you. I don't know what to do with you. Believe me, if you want to, and if you don't want to, go see for yourselves. But I know perfectly well what I myself saw. All this happened on Wildmen's Island. I've given you the exact name. And remember, if you please, how strong the ancient giants were, who took on the task of

piling Mount Pelion on top of Mount Ossa, and then lifting Ossa until it
shadowed Olympus, so they could fight the gods and capture the heavens. Now, this is a strength you can hardly call common or ordinary. But
still, half the bodies of these giants were no more than Sausages—or snakes,
to be strictly accurate.

The serpent who tempted Eve was sausage-like, and yet it is written
of him that he was cunning and clever beyond any of the other animals.
And so too the Sausages. In certain universities it is still argued that the
tempter was a Sausage named Penis, and that our good Master Priapus
was afterward transformed into that same shape, he who was a great
tempter of women in what the Greeks call paradise but which, in French,
we call gardens. The Swiss, who are now such a strong and belligerent
people, may very well have been Sausages, once upon a time. (I should
hate to have to put my finger into the fire on that subject!) The Himantopodes, a notable Ethiopian race, are quite simply Sausages, according
to Pliny's description.

And if this discussion does not satisfy your lordships' doubts, go and
visit (that is, after you've all had a good stiff drink) Lusignan, Parthenay,
Vouvent, Mervent, and Pouzauges, in Poitou. There you'll find solid old
witnesses ready to swear by Saint Rigomer's arm that Melusine, their
original founder, was a woman down to the cockpit but all the rest, lower
down, was a Sausage snake or else, in truth, a snake Sausage. In any case,
she swung her hips like a brave and gallant woman, and the Breton clowns
still to this day imitate her when they do their singing hop-and-dance
step.

Why did Erichthonius decide to invent coaches, litters, and chariots?
Because Vulcan conceived him with Sausage legs and, to hide them, he
chose to go about in a litter rather than on horseback. In his day, Sausages
still didn't have much of a reputation. Ora, the Scythian nymph, was
similarly formed—half woman and half Sausage. Nevertheless, she seemed
beautiful to Jupiter, who slept with her and got out of it a handsome son
named Colaxes.

So stop poking fun and start believing that there's nothing truer than
this tale of mine, except the Bible.

Chapter Thirty-nine // How Brother John and the Cooks Teamed Up to Fight the Sausages

Watching the furious Sausages march boldly toward them, Brother
John said to Pantagruel:

"This is going to be a fun fight: I can see it. Ho! What honor our victory will bring us—what magnificent praise! I just wish there was an audience, back in our boat, and I wish you'd just let me and my men handle this."

"What men?" asked Pantagruel.

"Prayer-book stuff," answered Brother John. "Why was Potiphar, Pharaoh's main kitchen man—the one who bought Joseph, and whom Joseph could have cuckolded if he'd wanted to—put in charge of the whole Egyptian cavalry? Why was Nebuzardan, Nebuchadnezzar's chief cook, selected over all his other generals to lead the siege and assault against Jerusalem?"

"I'm listening," answered Pantagruel.

"By our Lady's holy slit!" said Brother John, "I'll bet this isn't the first time they've had to fight with Sausages—or folk as poorly regarded as Sausages—and for that kind of slaughtering and slashing, conquering and massacring, cooks are incomparably better and more skilled than any other warriors, horsemen, mercenaries, or foot soldiers in the world."

"You remind me," said Pantagruel, "of one of Cicero's lovely witty remarks. During the Roman civil war, Caesar on one side and Pompey on the other, he was naturally more inclined to side with Pompey, although Caesar was widely favored to win. One day, hearing that in a certain battle the Pompeians had lost a significant number of their men, he decided to visit their camp, where he saw little strength, less courage, and a great deal of disorder. Seeing perfectly clearly that it was all going to rack and ruin, as he had warned, he began to scold and mock them, first this one, then that, with bitter, sharp gibes, as he knew very well how to do. Some of the generals, sitting and drinking like calm and completely composed gentlemen, said to him:

" 'See how many eagle banners we still have?'

"At the time, this was the Roman insignia of war.

" 'That would be all fine and good,' answered Cicero, 'if you were fighting against magpies.'

"But seeing that our battle must be against Sausages, it strikes you as culinary warfare and you want to ally yourself with cooks. By all means. I'll remain here and await the result of all this swaggering talk."

So Brother John went to the cooks' tents and said to them, in all polite cheerfulness:

"Fellows, I want this day to bring all of you honor and triumph. You will perform feats of arms no one has ever seen before. Belly to belly! Is that all they think brave cooks are worth? Let's go fight these rascally Sausages. I'll be your general. Drink up, my friends. Now, courage!"

"General," answered the cooks, "you're absolutely right. We place ourselves in your good hands. We'll live and die at your command."

"Living," said Brother John, "yes. But dying, no. That's the Sausages' job. Now let's get ready. Your battle slogan will be *Nebuzardan*."

Chapter Forty ⁄⁄ How Brother John Got the Sow Ready, and the Brave Cooks Who Climbed inside Her

Then, at Brother John's order, the master engineers readied the great sow stored in the ship *Monk's Drinking Mug*. This was a marvelous machine, fitted up so it could hurl great rocks and steel-feathered stones from rows and rows of cannon mouths, while in the center there was room and shelter for at least two hundred men, and even more. It was built on the model of the Reole sow, which had made it possible to capture Bergerac from the English, during the time when young King Charles the Sixth was on the throne of France.

And here are how many brave and valiant cooks, and the names of each of them, who climbed into the sow, just as men once climbed into the Trojan horse:

Sour Sauce	Salt Master
Handy Andy	Thick Guts
Fat Belly	Mortar Pestle
Slack Guts	Watered Wine
Fat Pork	Salt-and-Butter Peas
Filthy Face	Roast Goat
May Apple	Roast Anything
Bread Pudding	Sheep Guts
Weary Way	Beef Pot
Spatula Face	Pork Patties
Codfish Paste	Cut Face
Piled-up Crepes	Hash Face

The coats of arms of all these noble cooks bore a green roasting skewer on a crimson field, striped in silver, and tilted to the left.

Bacon Strips	Bacon Fat
Bacon Lard	Antibacon
Fragrant Bacon	Crispy Bacon
Twisted Bacon	Tied-up Bacon
Fatty Bacon	Layered Bacon
Life-saving Bacon	

plus one Gabacon, who came from a little town near Rambouillet: the true name of this doctor of culinary science was Gay Bacon (just as we shorten "holy day" to "holiday"); plus, additionally,

Soiled Bacon
Baconness
Sweet Bacon
Chewed-up Bacon
Lumpy Bacon
Enough Bacon
Sliced Bacon
Fly Bacon

Beautiful Bacon
New Bacon
Sour Bacon
Rolled-up Bacon
Bad Bacon
Heavy Bacon
Shit Bacon
Basic Bacon

—none of these names, of course, being used by Jews (whether converted or not). Plus

Fat-head
Salad Bowl
Watercress Bowl
Scraping Knife
Pig Pot
Rabbit Skin
Pepper Pot
Pastry Pot
Full Pot
Free Fritters
Mustard Maker
Berry Masher
Swill Pot
Happy Rascal
Booby

Green Sauce
Double Boiler
Trivet
Beef Pot
Crackpot
Scraping Pot
Shaking Pot
Thirsty Throat
Snail Pot
Dry Soup
Soup Maker
Rib Picker
Custard Maker
Cookie Cutter
Pot Licker

plus Crumbly, who was later withdrawn from kitchen duty and sent to serve our noble Cardinal Veneur-Carrouges. Plus

Burned Roast
Oven Mop
Cook's Cap
Coal Raker
Prick Head
Big Prick
Empty Prick
Pretty Prick
New Prick
Feather Prick
Triumphant Prick
Old Prick
Hairy Prick

Hastyman
Beef Sirloin
Beef Shoulder
Sour Milk
Mountain Hopper
Gut Wheezer
Ray Fish
Gibeonite
Lump Head
Crocodile Tears
Readiwell
Scarface
Smutty Face

—plus Mondam, who invented *Madame* sauce (our Lady's sauce), and on that account got himself named according to Scottish-French usage, plus

Chatterbox	Waffle Maker
Monkey Mouth	Saffron Boiler
Wonder Tongue	Dirty Cleaner
Woodcock	Antitus Watercress
Pot Cleaner	Turnip Boiler
Hot Lips	Radish Eater
Filthy Face	Pudding Stuffer
Fish Cleaner	Pig Face

—plus Robert, who invented *Robert* sauce—so healthy, so necessary for roasting rabbits, ducks, and fresh pork, and for poached eggs, salted codfish, and a thousand other similar dishes—plus

Cold Eel	Quink Qunk
Red Ray Fish	Salmagundian
Fishy Face	Horse Face
Idiot Face	Pickled Herring
Bread Bag	Cake Nose
Swaggerer Braggerer	Big Nose
Squirrel Face	Blubber Lips
Cow Belly	Shit Pants
Donkey Tongs	Slimy Paws
Saltpeter	Bully Boy
French Fryman	Quick Grill
Lazybones	Fish Stuffing
Wop Cook	Prick Brain
Chuckle Head	Rubberneck
Loose Bowels	Calf Face
Pig Foot	Dandy Boy

And so these noble cooks climbed into the sow—these beaming, gallant cooks, marching briskly, ready to do battle. Carrying his great scimitar, Brother John was the last one in, and he swung the doors shut behind him.

Chapter Forty-one ⁄⁄ How Pantagruel Snapped Off Sausages at the Knees

The Sausage armies had come so close that Pantagruel could see how they carried their weapons, and that they were already deploying their lances. So he sent Gymnast to find out their intentions and what sort of pretext they had for going to war—utterly without provocation—against their old friends, who had in fact neither said nor done a thing to precipitate such a state of affairs.

Standing in front of their front ranks, Gymnast made a deep, respectful bow and called out, as loud as he could:

"We're at your service—yours, yours—all of us. Whatever you tell us to do, we will do. We're all on the side of Mardi Gras, your old ally."

But I've been told by some who were there that what he actually said was Gardi Mars, not Mardi Gras. Anyway, as soon as he'd said whatever it was he did say, a huge Brain Sausage, savage, hugely plump, jumped out from the front rank and tried to grab him by the throat.

"By God," said Gymnast, "I couldn't eat you, except in slices: you're so big I could never get you all down."

So he swung his sword, Kiss-My-Ass (that was the name he'd given it), with both hands, and cut the Brain Sausage in two. My God, but that was a fat one! It reminded me of the fellow they called the Bull of Berne, who was killed at Marignan when the Swiss were defeated. Let me tell you, that Brain Sausage had at least four inches of fat on his belly.

After the Brain Sausage was debrained, all the Sausages attacked Gymnast, and they would have knocked him roughly to the ground if Pantagruel and all his men hadn't run to his assistance. Then a real rumble-tumble fight began. Scrapesausage sliced up Sausages, Chopupbloodpudding cut up Blood Puddings. Pantagruel snapped off Sausages at the knees. Brother John was staying quietly in the sow, watching everything and planning what to do next, when the Pâtés (who had been hidden in ambush), came leaping out, with a horrible racket, and attacked Pantagruel.

Seeing this wild fracas, Brother John threw open the doors of the sow and emerged, together with his good old troopers, some of them wielding roasting skewers, others armed with andirons (large and small), frying pans, shovels, pots, grills, pokers, tongs, grease pans, brooms, double boilers, mortars, pounding rams—and they came charging out like a pack of disciplined housebreakers, screaming and shouting horribly as they came, "Nabuzardan! Nabuzardan! Nabuzardan!" With such cries, and making all the noise they could, they threw themselves at the Pâtés and overran the ranks of the Cold Sausages. Seeing these fresh reinforcements, the Sausages suddenly began to run like mad, as if they'd been attacked by all the devils in hell. Firing his cannon, Brother John mashed them like flies, nor did his troops give any more quarter than he did. It was pitiful. The whole battlefield was covered with dead and wounded Sausages. And according to the story, if God had not intervened the entire Sausage race would have been exterminated by these kitchen troops. But a miracle happened. Believe it or not, as you please.

There came flying out of the north a huge, heavy-fatted, heavenly gray pig, with great, flapping wings like the vanes of a windmill. It had bright red feathers, like a flamingo (the Greek name for which is phoenicopter). Its eyes burned red, too, like flaming gemstones; its ears were green, like an emerald; its teeth were yellow, like a topaz; it had a long tail, black as the Egyptian marble Lucullus brought to Rome; its feet were white, clear and transparent as diamonds, webbed like geese or like Queen Pedauque, in the old days at Toulouse. There was a gold collar around his neck, with Ionic writing on it, of which I could read only two words: YS ATH-ENAN, meaning "A Pig Teaching Minerva."

It was a fine, clear day. But when this monster appeared, there was such a clap of thunder from the left that we were all stunned. As soon as the Sausages saw it, they threw down all their weapons, and knelt on the ground, raising their clasped hands high in the air, saying nothing, as if in worship.

Brother John and his men went on stabbing and spitting Sausages. But then Pantagruel ordered retreat to be sounded, and all military action ceased. Having flown several times around and around the two armies, the monster threw more than twenty-seven barrels of mustard to the ground, then flew off through the air, screaming over and over:

"Mardi Gras! Mardi Gras! Mardi Gras!"

Chapter Forty-two // How Pantagruel Parleyed with Niphleseth, Queen of the Sausages

The monster did not return; the two armies remained silent; and Pantagruel sought a parley with Lady Niphleseth (for that was the queen of the Sausages' name, meaning "Penis" in Hebrew), who was in her coach, near her army's banners. This was readily granted.

The queen descended from her coach and greeted Pantagruel graciously, indicating her pleasure at meeting him. Pantagruel at once complained to her about the war. She offered him courteous excuses, explaining that the error had come about because of faulty information: her spies had declared that their old enemy, King Lent-Observance, had landed on their island and was busy examining whale urine. Then she begged him to pardon their offense, explaining that Sausages had more shit in them than they did bile, and declaring that she and all the Niphleseths who held the throne after her would ensure that the whole land paid him homage, obeying any and all his commands, eternally the friend of his friends and the enemy of his enemies, and each year, in acknowledgment of this fealty, sending him seventy-eight thousand Royal Sausages and constituting the first course at his table for six months of the year.

And indeed she did as she promised, the very next day dispatching to our good Gargantua, in six large boatloads, exactly the aforesaid number of Sausages, under the command of the crown princess of the island, the young Niphleseth. Noble Gargantua, in his turn, sent them as a present to the great king in Paris. But the changed climate, and also the lack of mustard (natural balm and restorant of all Sausages), caused the death of virtually all of them. By the king's decree and command, they were buried in a great heap, in Paris—a neighborhood that to this day is called Sausage Street.

The ladies of the royal court interceded for young Niphleseth, and she was well and honorably treated. Later she made a good, rich marriage and had several handsome children, for which may God be praised.

Pantagruel gave the queen his gracious thanks, forgave any and all offenses, refused the offer she had made, and gave her a beautiful little pocketknife. Then, distinctly curious, he asked her about the appearance of the monster mentioned earlier. She answered that it was the Symbol of Mardi Gras, their tutelary god in time of war, original founder and first member of the race of Sausages. Which was why he looked like a pig: Sausages were made from pork. Pantagruel asked her why, and for what medicinal purpose, the monster had thrown so much mustard to the ground. The queen answered that mustard was their Holy Grail, their heavenly balm: just a little placed on the wounds of any injured Sausage, and in no time at all those wounds would be entirely healed and he would be returned from the dead.

Pantagruel had no further discussion with the queen; he left her and returned to his ship, he and all his jolly companions, along with their weapons and their sow.

Chapter Forty-three ⁄⁄ How Pantagruel Landed on the Island of the Wind

Two days later we arrived at the island of the Wind—and let me swear by the starry Pleiades that I found the people's way of life stranger than I can say. They live just on wind. They drink nothing, eat nothing—only wind. Their only dwellings are weather vanes. All they grow in their gardens is three kinds of windflowers (or anemones); they also carefully cultivate evergreen and other herbs causing windy guts. To feed themselves, the common people employ fans made of feathers, paper, or linen, according to their standing and capability. The rich live off windmills. When they have a feast or a banquet, they set up their tables under a windmill or two. And there they dine, as comfortable as at a wedding, and as they eat they discuss the goodness, excellence, healthfulness, and rarity of these winds, just as, at your banquets, my drinking friends, you philosophize about wines. One praises the southeast wind; another, the southwestern; another, a slightly sweeter southwestern; another, the northeast wind; another, the northwestern Zephyr; another, the north-eastern Galerne; and so on. One celebrates, for flirting and lovemaking, the breeze of a chemise. Sick people are treated with drafty winds, just as we nourish our sick with meat jellies and custards.

"Oh!" a little balloon face said to me. "If I could just get a bladderful of that good Languedoc wind—the one they call the Circius. Your great and wonderful doctor Schyron, passing through our country, told us it's strong enough to tip over loaded wagons. Oh, how it would help my puffed-up leg! The biggest aren't always the best."

"Ah," said Panurge, "how about a great barrel of that good Languedoc wine from Mirevaux, Canteperdrix, and Frontignan!"

I saw a most proper man with a great swollen belly furiously angry at his big fat servant, and his small page, and beating them like the devil, kicking them savagely. Not knowing just why he was so angry, I thought this was something his doctors had prescribed—a healthy activity for the master, getting angry and beating, and useful for the servants, to be beaten. But I heard him scolding both of them for having robbed him of a good half a bag of Garbin wind, a rare delicacy he'd been hoarding for the end of the season.

The people of that island neither shit nor piss nor spit. In exchange, they burp and fart and belch like mad. They suffer from a wide variety of illnesses. Of course, for them all illness comes from flatulence, as Hippocrates understood and wrote about in his *Liber de flatibus,* Book of Gassiness. Their most contagious disease is windy colic. To cure it, they use great ventilating cupping glasses, through which they suck out strong currents of air. They all die of dropsical swelling, their bellies immensely puffed up; the men die farting, the women pooping. So their souls always leave the body via their assholes.

Later, walking around the island, we met three great windbags, who were going to have fun watching the sea plovers, who are all over and live on the same diet as the people do. I noticed that just as you, my good drinking friends, always carry flasks and canteens and bottles when you go out for a walk, so too each of them had a nice little bellows hanging from his belt. Should they be short of wind, with these pretty bellows they can make it for themselves, all nice and fresh, using the principle of reciprocal attraction and repulsion—since as you know the basic definition of "wind" is nothing more than moving, flowing air.

Just then their king ordered us, for the next three hours, not to allow any man or woman of the country onto our ships. For he had been robbed of a full fart out of that bag of winds which, many years ago, that great snorer Aeolus had given Ulysses, to steer his ship through becalmed waters, which bag he had always guarded religiously, like some Holy Grail, using it to cure several major illnesses simply by loosening it and allowing as much out as the sick people required to deliver themselves of a virginal fart—what the nuns call ringing the backdoor bell.

Chapter Forty-four ⁄⁄ How a Gentle Rain Can Kill a High Wind

Pantagruel praised their form of government and way of life, and said to their governor, Hypenemien (in Greek, "Windy"):

"If you agree with Epicurus, who says that the best thing of all is pleasure (calm pleasure, mind you—not the laborious sort), I consider you happy. Because your way of life, which is windswept, costs you nothing—or very little. All you have to do is blow."

"Exactly!" answered the governor. "But in this mortal life, nothing can be completely fortunate. Often, when we're at table, we dine off some good strong wind, blown to us by God like some celestial manna, happy and relaxed like monks—and then it starts to rain a bit, which kills off the wind for us. And we lose a lot of our meals in just that way, for lack of available food."

"It's like," said Panurge, "our Jenin from Quinquenays, pissing on his wife Quelot's ass, to dampen the stinking wind that poured out as if from some mighty Aeolian cavity. I made a nice little poem about it, not long ago:

> One night, guzzling his own fresh wine
> (Still murky, boiling and bubbling and strong),
> Jenin decided they could dine
> On turnips. 'So, Quelot, hurry along
> And get it ready.' She did, they ate,
> Fell into bed, screwed, then slept.
> But Jenin found himself wide awake,
> For Quelot lay there and farted, and kept
> On farting. So he pissed, then cried, 'You'll find
> A gentle rain can kill a high wind.'

"In addition," said the governor, "every year we're obliged to experience a serious and deeply injurious calamity. A giant named Splitnose, who lives on Wordless Island, comes here every spring, on his doctors' advice, in order to clean out his system. He devours many of our windmills as medicinal pills, and he also gobbles up bellows, which he thinks are a real delicacy. Which makes us thoroughly miserable, creating three or even four Lents a year for us, not to mention all the special processionals and extraordinary prayers."

"And," asked Pantagruel, "you know no way to stop this?"

"Acting on the advice of our chief physicians," said the governor, "when it got to be the time of year that usually brings him here, we put as many cocks and hens in the windmills as we could. Indeed, the first time he swallowed them, they very nearly killed him. Because they sing inside him and fly around in his stomach, which set him on the road to heart failure—terrible cardiac pains and a ghastly convulsion, as if snakes had crawled into his mouth and gone down into his stomach."

"Now *that*," said Brother John, "is a thoroughly ridiculous comparison. I've often heard it said that a snake getting into your stomach won't bother you a bit, and indeed it'll come right out again if you hang the patient up by his heels and put a basin of warm milk right next to his mouth."

"Well," said Pantagruel, "you've heard that said, and so have those who put it into writing, and whose books you read. But that cure has never actually been witnessed or authenticated. In book five of his *Of Epidemics,* Hippocrates writes about a case that happened in his time: the patient was dead before he knew it, of spasms and a convulsion."

"And there's more," said the governor. "All the foxes in the country ran into his mouth and down his throat, chasing after the chickens. He could have dropped dead in another minute, except that, having consulted a sly magician, as soon as the fit began he made himself vomit, which served as an antidote and counterpoison. He's had better advice, since then, and cures himself with a suppository they concocted for him, made of grains of wheat and millet, which of course attract the chickens, together with goose livers, which of course attract the foxes. And there are pills, too, that he takes by mouth, made of greyhounds and hunting terriers. And so you see how unlucky we are."

"Don't be afraid, good people," said Pantagruel, "not any more. This huge Splitnose, gobbler of windmills and swallower of winds, is dead. It's true, I assure you. He died of suffocation and strangulation, after eating a wedge of fresh butter set in the mouth of a hot oven, on his doctors' orders."

Chapter Forty-five ⁄⁄ How Pantagruel Landed on Popefigs' Island

The next morning, we reached Popefigs' Island, once rich and free and in those days called Happyland, but now poor, miserable, and ruled by the Papalmaniacs. It happened like this.

One day, at the annual parade in honor of the saints (whose images were carried aloft like a great banner), the mayor, the aldermen, and the high rabbis of Happyland had all gone to pass the time watching the festival in Papalmaniac, the island next to theirs. One of them, seeing the pope's portrait (which it was the worthy custom to carry aloft on a pair of tall poles), gave it the obscene sign of the fig, signifying open derision and contempt. To revenge that insult, some days later the Papalmaniacs, without a word of warning, mobilized their entire army and, catching the Happylanders completely by surprise, burned and pillaged their way across the whole island, putting to the sword every man old enough to wear a beard. They pardoned women and children, on terms much like those once imposed on the Milanese by Emperor Frederick Barbarossa.

He being away, the Milanese had revolted against him and ignominiously driven his wife, the empress, out of the city, mounted backward on an old mule named Thacor (in Greek, "Fig")—her ass turned forward, her head facing the beast's tail.

On his return, Frederick put down their revolt and took control once again, moving so quickly that he recaptured Thacor, the famous mule. And then, right in the middle of the great hall of the city, he had the hangman put a fig in the private parts of this old mule—with all the captive citizens present and watching. Then, to the sound of trumpets, the hangman declared that, at the emperor's orders, any of them who wished to stay alive would have to publicly pull that fig out with their teeth, then—still not using their hands—put it back once more. Whoever refused would be immediately strung up and strangled to death. Some of them were so shocked and horrified by this awful punishment that they thought it worse than death, and were promptly hanged. For others, the fear of death prevailed. And having drawn out the fig with their teeth, they displayed it to the hangman, saying, "*Ecco lo fico,* Here is the fig."

The remainder of these poor, desolate Happylanders were saved from death by just such an indignity. They were made slaves, forced to pay tribute, and the name *Popefigs* was imposed on them, since they had given the sign of the fig—that is, sticking your thumb between your first two fingers—at the pope's portrait. And from that time on, these poor people had known no prosperity. They had lived through constant hail, storms, disease, famine, and every manner of bad luck, as if they were being eternally punished for the sins of their parents and ancestors.

Seeing how miserable and unfortunate the people were, we did not wish to go any farther into their land. Only to be blessed by holy water, and to commend ourselves to God, we went into a small chapel near the harbor, half destroyed, deserted, roofless, like the church of Saint Peter in Rome. As we entered the chapel, and took the holy water, we saw in the font itself a man, all dressed in ecclesiastical garments: he was completely immersed in the water, like some kind of diving duck, with just the tip of his nose sticking out, so he could breathe. Around him were three close-cropped, tonsured priests, reading out of magical books and exorcising demons.

This seemed exceedingly strange to Pantagruel, so he asked what kind of comedy they were staging, and was informed that for the last three years the island had been afflicted with a pestilence so horrible that at least half the country was now abandoned, the earth uncultivated and owner-less. Once the plague was ended, this man, buried in the font, had farmed a great field, fertile all the year round, and at just the exact moment when he was sowing his wheat a small devil (too small, still, to be able to manage thunder and hail, except over parsley and cabbage, and also too small to know how to read or write) had gotten permission from Lucifer to visit this Popefigs' Island, to have fun and entertain himself, for devils like to take liberties with men and women, and often spend their leisure time among them.

Arriving there, this devil spoke to the farmer and asked him what he was doing. The poor man replied that he was sowing wheat in his field, so he and his family would have something to eat the next year.

"Well, yes, of course," said the devil, "but this isn't your field: it's mine. From the moment you people made the sign of the fig at the pope, everything in this country has been handed over to us, made completely our own, to do with as we will. But sowing wheat, nevertheless, isn't my business. So I'll lease this field to you, but only on condition that we share the profit."

"Agreed," said the farmer.

"I propose," said the devil, "that we divide our profit into two por-tions. One will be whatever grows on the earth, and the other will be whatever the earth covers. I get to choose which I want, since I'm a devil of noble and ancient lineage, and you're nothing but a common clod. So I choose what's in the earth; you'll have what grows up out of it. When will the harvest be?"

"In the middle of July," answered the farmer.

"Now mark me," said the devil. "I won't fail to be here. For the rest, do what you're supposed to do: work, you clod, work! I'm going to go tempt the noble nuns of Dryfart with the merry sin of lust—and those hypocrite priests, too, not to mention the begging monks. I feel more than confident of their cooperation. And then, when I get them together, the battles of love can begin."

Chapter Forty-six // How the Little Devil Was Tricked by a Popefig Farmer

When the middle of July arrived, so did the little devil, accompanied by a squadron of little devilish choirboys. Coming up to the farmer, he said:

"So, you clod, how's it been going since I left? This looks like a good time to share things up."

"Right," said the farmer. "Right."

Then the farmer and his men began to cut up the wheat, and all the little devils began to pull the stubble out of the ground. The farmer threshed his wheat, winnowed it, put it in sacks, and carried it off to the market, to sell it. The little devils did the same, and took up their place in the market right near the farmer, intending to sell their stubble. The farmer's wheat sold so well that he quite filled the old leather boot hanging on his belt. But the devils sold nothing; indeed, right out in public the other peasants laughed and jeered at them.

When the market had closed, the devil said to the farmer:

"Clod, maybe you got away with tricking me, this time. But you won't do it again."

"My dear Sir Devil," answered the farmer, "how could I possibly have tricked you, when you were the first to choose shares? In fact, you thought you'd pretty nicely tricked me. You didn't think there'd be anything growing out of the ground for my share, and all the grain I'd planted would still be in the ground. You thought you'd use it to tempt needy people, and hypocrites, and misers, and that way get them to fall into your traps. But you're very new at this business. The grain in the ground is dead and rotten, but its rotting has given birth to that other substance which you've seen me sell. So you made the worse choice. And that's why you've earned the Bible's curse."

"Enough of that," said the devil. "What are you going to plant in our field this coming year?"

"It seems to me," said the farmer, "that a good, profitable choice would be turnips."

"Ah!" said the little devil. "You're a good old clod, you are! Well, plant a lot of turnips: I'll make sure there'll be no storms and no hail falling—not on our field. But get this straight: my share is whatever grows above ground, and yours is everything below. So work, clod, work! I'll go off and tempt heretics: oh, such juicy, delicious souls, when they're properly grilled. Lord Lucifer has a bit of a stomach ache, so they'll make him a marvelous snack."

When harvest time came, the little devil appeared once more, this time with a squadron of devilish lackeys. Coming up to the farmer and his men, they began to cut and stack the turnip leaves. When they were done, the farmer dug up the big, thick turnips, and put them into sacks. And again they went off to the market together. The farmer sold his turnips for a good price. The devil didn't sell a thing—worse still, everyone made fun of him, right out in the market square.

"Clod," said the little devil, "I see perfectly clearly you've tricked me again. All right: that's the end of trying to share this field. Here's what we're going to do: we'll have a scratching contest, and whoever ends up by running away will also give up his half of the field. This is winner-take-all. We'll have our contest a week from today. You'd better run, clod, because I'm going to scratch the devil out of you! I'd meant to go tempt some thieving bailiffs, pretend process servers, false notaries, and lying lawyers, but one of my go-betweens tells me I've already got them all. And anyway, Lucifer's pretty disgusted with their souls: he usually sends them to the dirty kitchen help, unless they're really well spiced. Don't you have a saying that scholars have the best breakfast, lawyers have the best lunch, wine dealers have the best snacks, merchants serve the best suppers, chambermaids have the best midnight suppers, and monks eat the best all the time? It's true—and in fact Lord Lucifer prefers to have monks as the entree at all his meals. He always used to have scholars for breakfast, too. But—alas!—I don't know by what ill fortune, for the last few years they've added the Holy Bible to their studies, and on that account we just can't pull them down to the devil any more. I suppose that if the churchly hypocrites don't help us, yanking their Bibles out of their hands by threats, insults, force, or violence, and making their Saint Pauls burn in their hands, down below we won't have them to nibble on.

"He usually dines on corrupt lawyers and those who steal from poor men—and he dines well. But it annoys him to have to eat the same thing all the time. Not long ago he said to us, with everyone assembled, that he'd be glad to eat the soul of any religious hypocrite who might forget, in his sermon, to commend himself to the prayers and especially to the charity of the faithful, and he promised double pay and rapid advancement to any of us who could get one for him lickety-split. So we've all been trying, but none of us have been able to pull it off. They're always soliciting highborn ladies for gifts to their convents.

"And he's completely given up snacking, which has been giving him bad stomach pains ever since the northern countries started to mistreat all his suppliers, his butchers and bakers and candlestick makers. But he makes a very good supper on usurious merchants, cheating druggists, dealers in counterfeit coins, and those who adulterate what they sell. And sometimes, when he's in a good mood, he makes a supper of chambermaids who, after drinking their masters' good wine, fill the barrel back up with stinking water.

"Work, clod, work! I'm going to go tempt the scholars of Trebizond to leave their fathers and mothers, renounce their usual way of life, ignore their king's decrees, and live a free, underground existence, scorning everyone, making fun of everyone and, sticking the pretty little cap of poetic innocence on their heads, make themselves into perfect noble monks."

Chapter Forty-seven // How an Old Popefig Woman Tricked the Devil

Going back home, the farmer was sad and thoughtful. His wife, seeing him, thought he had been robbed at the market. But hearing the cause of his melancholy, and also seeing his purse full of money, she sweetly comforted him, assuring him that nothing bad would come of this scratching contest, if only he would just relax and leave it to her: she had already thought out a fine plan.

"At the worst," said the farmer, "I'll have just one scratch: I'll surrender at the first blow and let him have the field."

"Don't be silly!" said the old woman. "Just leave it to me, and relax: let me take care of it. You said this is a young devil: I'll make him surrender to you, all in a flash, and the field will be ours. Now, had it been a full-grown devil, I'd have had to think a little harder."

The appointed day was the day we arrived on the island. Early that morning, the farmer went and made a very full confession, and took communion like a good Catholic—and at the priest's advice, he had hidden himself in the font of sacred water, just as we had found him.

And just as we heard this story, we got word that the old woman had tricked the devil and won the field. It happened like this. The devil came to the farmer's door and, ringing the bell, called out:

"O clod, clod! Let's see what sharp claws you have!"

Then, going into the house, bright-eyed and determined, he couldn't find the farmer, but only his wife, lying on the floor, weeping and crying.

"What's this?" asked the devil. "Where is he? What's he up to?"

"Ha!" said the old woman. "Where is he—that wicked fellow, that executioner, that highwayman? He's ripped me all apart—I'm done for—I'm dying, after what he's done to me."

"But," said the devil, "what has he done? I'll make him dance for you, I will, just as soon as I can."

"Ha!" said the old woman. "He told me—that hangman, that monster, that scratcher of devils—that he had an appointment for a scratching contest with you. Just to test his nails, he just scratched me once, with his little finger, here between the legs—and he's ripped me to shreds. I'm done for! I'll never recover! Just look! And he's still gone off to the blacksmith, to have steel tips put on his claws, and to have them well sharpened. You're done for, my dear devil, my friend! Save yourself! He'll stop at nothing. Get yourself out of here, I beg you."

Then she pulled her clothes up to her chin, as in the old days Persian women would show themselves to their sons, running from the battlefield, showing them their whatdoyoucallits. The devil, seeing the enormous wound, extending in all directions, cried out:

"Muhammad—Demigorgon—Megaera—Alecto—Persephone—he won't get me! I'm getting out of here right now! That's it: I'm giving him the field."

Having heard the final outcome of the story, we went back to our ship. Nor did we go back ashore again. Pantagruel dropped eighteen thousand gold pieces into the collection box in the church vestry, in consideration of the people's poverty and the general misery of the island.

Chapter Forty-eight // Pantagruel Goes Ashore on Papalmaniac Island

Leaving the desolate island of Popefigs, we sailed on for a day, through calm waters and with great pleasure, until we saw the blessed island of Papalmaniac. As soon as we'd thrown down our anchors, and even before we'd tied the boat up, we saw a skiff coming toward us, bearing four people, all dressed differently. One was a monk in full habit, dirty, wearing boots; another was a falconer, wearing his heavy leather glove and carrying a feathered bird lure; the third was a lawyer, with a briefcase full of briefs, summons, legal tricks, and motions for adjournment; and the fourth was an Orléans wine merchant, wearing linen leggings and carrying a basket and a billhook hanging from his belt. As soon as they were aboard our boat, they began to shout, all at once and in loud voices:

"Have you seen him, O honest passengers? Have you seen him?"

"Who?" asked Pantagruel.

"Him," they answered.

"Who?" asked Brother John. "By all that's holy, I'll beat his brains in!"—thinking they were complaining about some thief, or a murderer, or some singularly sacrilegious person.

"What?" they said. "O honest strangers, don't you know the One-and-Only?"

"Gentlemen," said Epistemon, "we don't understand such terms. Please tell us what you mean, and we'll tell you the truth, without any concealment."

"He is," they said, "he that is. Have you ever seen him?"

"He that is," answered Pantagruel, "according to our theology, is God.

Those were the words He used, in showing Himself to Moses. Most certainly we've never seen Him, nor is He visible to earthly eyes."

"We're not talking about that high God," they said, "who rules in heaven. We're talking about God on earth. Have you ever seen him?"

"On my honor," said Carpalim, "they mean the pope!"

"Oh yes, yes," answered Panurge, "most certainly, gentlemen. I've seen three popes, but the sight didn't do much for me."

"What?" they said. "Our sacred edicts sing that only one pope is alive at a time."

"I mean," said Panurge, "three, but each right after the other. I've seen only one at a time."

"Oh," they said, "you good people are three and four times happy— you're welcome here, and far more than welcome!"

Then they knelt in front of us and tried to kiss our feet. We wouldn't allow it, explaining to them that even if some great good fortune brought the pope himself to them, in person, that was all he'd allow, too.

"Oh no, no!" they answered. "We've long since decided all that. We'd kiss his bare ass, and his balls too. Because he really does have balls, our Holy Father—we've read about it in the papal edicts: he couldn't be pope, otherwise. And it follows, in our subtle edictal philosophy, that since he is pope, he necessarily has balls. If there weren't any balls left in the world, the world couldn't have a pope any more."

While all this was going on, Pantagruel asked a cabin boy from their skiff who these persons were. He was told, in reply, that they were consuls representing the four classes of people who lived on the island, adding that we would be very well received and treated, since we had seen the pope. Pantagruel told this to Panurge, who whispered:

"I swear to God, that's it! All things come to him who waits. Seeing the pope never did me any good—but now, by all the devils! We'll do very well indeed, it seems to me."

Then we disembarked, and in front of us there was a veritable procession of all the people in that country—men, women, little children. Our four consuls said to them, in loud voices:

"They have seen him! They have seen him! They have seen him!"

At this proclamation, all the people knelt in front of us, joining their hands in prayer and raising them toward the heavens, shouting:

"O happy people! O happy happy people!"

And they shouted on and on, for a good quarter of an hour. Then the schoolmaster came running up, with all his teachers, his ushers, and his pupils, and whipped the devil out of them, as we used to whip little children in our country, when we hanged some evildoer, so all of them would remember the occasion. At this, Pantagruel got angry and said:

"Gentlemen, if you don't stop whipping those children, I'm leaving!"

They were stunned, hearing his stentorian voice; we saw a tiny hump-back with long fingers asking the schoolmaster:

"By the holy edicts! Do all those who get to see the pope become as large as this one who's threatening us? Oh how incredibly I long to see him, so I can grow and become as big as he is!"

Their exclamations were so extravagant that Big Dumbman came hurrying up (that was their bishop's name), riding a mule with no bridle, all decked out in green; he was accompanied by his servant-apostles (as they put it) and also by his servant-supporters, carrying crosses, banners, streamers, canopies, torches, and vessels of holy water. And he, too, wanted desperately to kiss our feet (as Christian Valfinières did to Pope Clement the Good), informing us that one of their historical interpreters, men who scoured and annotated their sacred edicts, had written an account certifying that just as the Messiah, so longed for and awaited by the Jews, had finally come to them, so too the pope would one day come to this island. While they waited for that happy day, he had written, should anyone come who had actually seen the pope, at Rome or anywhere else, they must be welcomed as honored guests and treated reverentially. All of which we gently declined.

Chapter Forty-nine // How Dumbman, Papalmaniacal Bishop, Showed Us Their Heavenly Edicts

Then Dumbman said to us:

"Our holy edicts urge and command that we first go to church and then go to taverns. This being a gracious custom we should not fail to observe, let us now go to church, and then, afterward, we can have our banquet."

"My good man," said Brother John, "you go first, and we'll follow. You've spoken well and like a good Christian: it's been a long time since we've seen one. This pleases me immensely: I'm sure it will enable me to eat better. What a fine thing to meet up with good men."

Coming to the door of the church, we saw a great golden book, all covered with beautiful precious stones—rubies, emeralds, diamonds, and pearls, all better than, or at least as good as, those that Emperor Octavian consecrated to Jupiter Capitolinus. It hung by two great golden chains, suspended from the frieze of stone animals over the doorway. We looked at it with admiration. Pantagruel could touch and turn it as he pleased, since he could easily reach it. And he assured us that at the very touch of it he felt a kind of sweet itching in his fingernails, a quickening in his arms, which taken together made him sorely tempted to thrash a lawyer or two, provided they weren't in holy orders.

And Dumbman said to us:

"In the old days, Moses gave the law to the Jews, as written by God's own hand. In Delphi, in front of the gate of Apollo's temple, they found this sentence, written in a divine hand: GNŌTHI SEAYTON, 'Know thyself.' And not long after they also saw written there 'You are,' once again in a divine hand, and clearly of heavenly origin. Cybele's image was sent down from heaven to a Phrygian field, called Pessinonte. According to Euripides, the image of Diana was sent down to Taurus. The orange-red flag of the kings of France was sent to those noble and Christian rulers from heaven, so they could fight against infidels. During the reign of Numa Pompilius, second king of Rome, the bright shield called Ancile was seen to descend from heaven. Long ago, the statue of Minerva fell from heaven into the Acropolis, at Athens. So too, here, you can see the sacred edicts, written by the hand of an angelic cherub. Perhaps you people from across the sea may not believe this—"

"Not a bit of it," answered Panurge.

"—but these, too, were transmitted to us from heaven, miraculously, just as Homer, the father of all philosophy (excepting, to be sure, that contained in these divine edicts), calls the river Nile *Diipetes,* or 'Sent from Jupiter.' And because you have seen the pope, our eternal protector, who has himself divulged these edicts, we will permit you to look into this book, and kiss its pages, should you so choose. But before so doing, you would have to fast for three days and make a punctilious confession, carefully reviewing and cataloguing your manifold sins so that not a single incident is allowed to slip by—as, with divine inspiration, these sacred edicts that you see here have directed must be done. That will of course take some time."

"My good man," answered Panurge, "sheepdips—I mean, edicts are something we have seen by the ton—inscribed on paper, on Lanternland parchment, on vellum, and written by hand or printed on a printing press. So we don't need to trouble you with showing us these: we'll be glad to take the wish for the deed, and say thank you in any case."

"Good God!" said Dumbman. "But you've never seen these angelic productions. What you have in your country are only transcriptions of ours, according to the critical writings of one of our ancient edictan scholars. Nor do I want you to worry about causing me trouble. Just let me know if you would like to make your confessions and fast for three short, blessed days."

"Cuntfessing," answered Panurge, "is something we most cheerfully agree to. But not the fasting, not right now, since we've had to fast so much, and so long, while we've been at sea, that spiders have spun webs on our teeth. You see our good Brother John Mincemeat—"

Dumbman courteously embraced Brother John.

"—Well, moss has grown in his throat, for lack of moving and exercising his teeth and jaws."

"It's the truth!" answered Brother John. "I've been fasting so much that I've become a hunchback."

"Then,'said Dumbman, "let's go into the church, and you'll forgive us if we don't immediately sing you a holy mass. It's past midday, and our sacred edicts forbid us to sing a mass after that time—a full, high mass, that is. But I could sing you a low, dry mass."

"I'd prefer," said Panurge, "the dampness of some good Anjou wine. But do it—do it low and hard."

"By all that's green and blue!" said Brother John. "I don't like it a bit, having my stomach still empty. Because if I'd had a good solid breakfast, and eaten the way monks like to eat, he could sing us a whole Requiem and I'd fetch him bread and wine for the benefit of the dead and buried. But patience! Get it under way, do it, proceed—but let it go trippingly, and keep it short, so there's no danger of dragging it in the dirt—and for other reasons, too—please, I beg you!"

Chapter Fifty ⁄ How Dumbman Showed Us What an Ideal Pope Would Look Like

Once the mass had been said, Bishop Dumbman took a whole jumble of keys out of a chest, near the great altar, with which he proceeded to open the thirty-two locks and fourteen padlocks on an iron window, heavily barred, located just above that altar; then, with an air of high mystery, he draped himself in a damp sackcloth and, drawing back a red satin curtain, showed us a picture—terribly badly painted, in my judgment—which he touched with a long, slender stick and had each of us kiss the spot he had touched. Then he asked us:

"Who do you think this picture looks like?"

"This," said Pantagruel, "is the painting of a pope. I recognize the tiara, the papal cape, the surplice, and the slippers."

"You speak well," said Dumbman. "This is the ideal image of that good God on earth, whose coming we devoutly await and whom we expect and hope to see here in our country. O happy and long-desired day! And you, happy and more than happy, whom the heavens have so favored that you have actually seen this living God on earth, face-to-face—for simply seeing his picture earns us full remission of all the sins we can remember, not to mention a third plus eighteen-fortieths of the sins we may have forgotten! Mind you, we're allowed to see him only at our great annual festival."

Pantagruel observed that this was a work very much in the tradition of Daedalus. And though it had been done crookedly and on the whole badly, nevertheless there definitely was some latent, secret divine energy in the portrait, which could very well engender some pardoning.

"Just the way it was," said Brother John, "in my religious house at

Seuilly. One fine festival day the beggars were having their dinner at our poorhouse, and boasting: one said he'd gotten six pennies that day; another two sous; another seven dimes; and one fat tramp declared that he'd gotten three whole shillings. 'Sure,' answered his companions, 'but you've got God's lucky leg.' As if there really was some divinity hidden in a rotting, festering leg."

"My friend," said Pantagruel, "when you tell us such stories, try to remember to fetch a basin: a little more and I'd be throwing up. To employ the sacred name of God for such dirty and disgusting things! Fagh! I say: fagh! If your religious house does indeed contain such misuse of words, please leave it there—don't take it outside those cloistered walls."

"So too," answered Epistemon, "physicians say there's a definite divine content in certain illnesses. Which is why Nero extolled mushrooms, and why a Greek proverb calls them 'God's food,' since he used them to poison his predecessor, the Roman emperor Claudius."

"It seems to me," said Panurge, "that this portrait isn't much like our last popes: I've seen them without a cape, but wearing a battle helmet on their heads, and crowned with a Persian tiara—and it was a time when the entire Christian world was peaceful and quiet, except for the cruel and vicious wars they'd started."

"Wars," said Bishop Dumbman, "against rebels, heretics, hopeless Protestants, people who refuse to obey the holy God on earth: that's not only permitted, and entirely lawful, but approved by our sacred edicts. He is obliged to put to the fire and sword, and without delay, all emperors, kings, dukes, princes, and republics who transgress one single iota from his decrees. He must deprive them of their possessions, take away their kingdoms, and proscribe and anathematize them. And not only must he kill them, and their children, and all their relatives, but he must damn their souls to the deepest, hottest levels in hell."

"Now here," said Panurge, "by all the devils! You don't have any heretics like Raminagrobis, and of the sort there used to be among the Germans, and in England. You're all proven and tried Christians."

"Oh, indeed," said Dumbman. "And we're all destined for eternal salvation, too. So let's take the blessed water, and go in to dinner."

Chapter Fifty-one ⁄⁄ Dinner Conversation in Praise of the Edicts

Please note, my good drinking friends, that while Dumbman was singing his dry mass, three ecclesiastical bell ringers, each carrying a large basin in his hands, went around among the people, saying in loud voices,

"Don't forget the happy people who have actually seen him, face-to-face!"

As we were leaving the church, they brought Dumbman their basins, all filled with Papalmaniac money. Dumbman explained that this was for our hospitality, and that this contribution and tax would be used in part for good wine, in part for good food, all according to a marvelous commentary buried in a certain obscure corner of their sacred edicts.

And this was done, in a handsome tavern very like that run by Guillot in Amiens. I assure you the food was abundant and the wine flowed freely. Two noteworthy things struck me, about that dinner: first, that not a single dish was brought in which did not feature official church-style stuffing—whether it was roast kid, capons, pork (there are lots of pigs in Papalmania), pigeons, rabbits, hares, turkeys, or anything else; and second, that every course was served by intensely nubile Papalmaniac virgins—pretty girls, let me tell you, dainty morsels, fair haired, sweet, and wonderfully graceful, wearing long, white, delicate robes, double belted, their heads bare, their hair braided with fine, narrow bands and silk ribbons, violet colored, covered with roses, carnations, sweet marjoram, yellow dill, orange blossoms, and other fragrant flowers, and who as they served each course invited us to drink, with charming, well-schooled curtsies. They were obviously pleased to be seen by everyone there. Brother John stared at them sidelong like a dog carrying off a chicken.

After serving the first course, they sang, and quite beautifully, a hymn in praise of their sacred edicts.

When they had brought in the second course, Bishop Dumbman, singularly bright and cheerful, spoke to the wine stewards:

"Gentlemen: let there be light."

At these words, one of the girls quickly brought him a great beaker brimming with wine. Taking it, with a profound sigh, he said to Pantagruel:

"My lord, and you, my good friends, I drink to you with all my heart. You are very welcome here!"

After drinking it down, and handing the beaker back to the noble maiden, he exclaimed ponderously:

"O divine edicts! Like everything else that's good, this good wine comes from you!"

"It's not the worst I've ever tasted!" said Panurge.

"But it would be better still," said Pantagruel, "if those edicts could turn bad wine into good."

"O seraphic sixth edict!" Dumbman went on. "How necessary you are for the salvation of all poor human beings! O heavenly edicts from Pope Clement's hand! How in you we find described, as nowhere else, the perfect governance of the true Christian! O angelic appendices! How all poor souls would perish, without you, for here below in this valley of misery our mere mortal lives go astray! Alas! When will all human beings be given the special grace to desist from all other studies, and all other business, and read only you—understand only you—know only you—employ you, practice you, ingest you, transsubstantiate you, and incorporate you in the deepest recesses of their brains, in the inner marrow of their bones, in the complex networks of their arteries? Oh then, then, the world will be made happy—for it cannot come unless it comes through you."

Hearing this, Epistemon rose and quietly said to Panurge:

"There's no shit stool here: I have to go outside. All this ecclesiastical stuffing has given me diarrhea. I won't be long."

"Oh then," went on Dumbman, "there'll be no more hail, or ice, or frost, or storms! Oh then earth will see an abundance of all good things! Oh then peace will endure, inviolable in all the universe—no more war, looting, forced military service, thievery, assassinations—except against heretics and cursed rebels! Oh then all human nature will experience joy, happiness, gaiety, entertainment, and all manner of fun, pleasure, and delight! What magnificent theology, what utterly invaluable erudition, what godly instruction is immortalized in the divine chapters of these eternal edicts! Oh, reading no more than half a section, a small paragraph, even a single sentence of these sacred edicts, how you feel your heart flaring in the fiery furnace of divine love—overwhelmed by charity for your neighbor (provided that he's not a heretic)—filled with firm contempt for all earthly, transitory matters, and an ecstatic elevation of your spirit, even to the third ring of heaven, happy, certain in your every emotion!"

Chapter Fifty-two ⁄⁄ More about Miracles Wrought by the Edicts

"Now that," said Panurge, "was sheer music—but I'm inclined to believe as little of it as I can. Because once, when I was at Poitiers, with the Scots fellows, a professor of edictology read a chapter of the stuff: may the devil carry me off if, after listening to him, I wasn't so constipated that for more than four—no, five—days I couldn't shit anything but a little drop of dung. You know what kind of turd it was? I swear, it was like the shit shat by Furius, Catullus' neighbor:

> Ten turds a year: that's all you shit:
> Rub the stuff between your palms
> And your hands will hardly be dirty: it's
> Harder than beans, harder than stones."

"Ha ha!" said Dumbman. "My little saint, my friend, you may be in a state of mortal sin."

"That," said Panurge, "is a horse of a different color."

"One day," said Brother John, "at Seuilly, I was wiping my ass with a page from one of Pope Clement's wicked edicts, which our house steward, Jean Gruymard, had tossed into the courtyard, and may I hand myself over to the devils in hell if I didn't get such horrible hemorrhoids that my poor asshole was all deranged."

"My saint," said Dumbman, "that was clearly God's punishment on you, vengeance for the sin of shitting up these sacred books, which you have a duty to kiss and adore—as much as you do God or the saints, if not more. Panormitanus never lies."

"At Montpellier," said Powerbrain, "John Barnowl bought a beautiful set of the edicts from the monks at Saint Olary, beautifully enscribed on Lamballe parchment, so he could hammer out his gold on those nice heavy sheets. But somehow he could never get a single piece to come out right. They were all ripped and ragged."

"Again," said Dumbman, "punishment, and divine vengeance."

"At Le Mans," said Epistemon, "the apothecary François Cornu used to use a banged-up set of the appendices to wrap things in—and may I disbelieve in the devil if everything he put inside them wasn't poisoned right on the spot—gone all rotten and ruined: incense, pepper, cloves, cinammon, saffron, wax, ginger, cassia, rhubarb, tamarind—everything, all his drugs and herbs and medicinals."

"Vengeance," said Dumbman, "and divine punishment. To use such sacred writings for such profane purposes!"

"At Paris," said Carpalim, "the tailor Groignet used an old set of Pope Clement's edicts for making patterns and taking measurements. What a strange business! Everything he made from those patterns and those measurements was ruined—worthless: robes, capes, mantles, cassocks, skirts, ruffs, coats, jackets, cloaks, monks' habits, petticoats. Once, trying to make a cape, Groignet found himself cutting out a codpiece. Instead of a skirt, he found himself cutting out an ornamental cap. Instead of a cassock, he cut out a surplice. After his workmen sewed it together, and put a scalloped edging at the bottom, it looked more like a stove for frying chestnuts. Instead of a collar, he made a pair of boots. Using the pattern for a petticoat, he cut out a cassock. Thinking he was making a cape, he made a Swiss soldier's hat. It went on like that, until the poor man was ordered to give back their materials to all his customers, and now he's bankrupt."

"Punishment," said Dumbman, "and divine vengeance!"

"At Cahusac," said Gymnast, "an archery match was held between Lord Etissac and the count of Lausanne. Perotus had ripped up half a set of edicts, which he'd gotten from good Canon La Carte, and cut the blank parts of the pages to use for the white in the targets. Let me hand myself over—let me sell myself—to all the devils in hell, if any archer in the whole country (and the archers in Guienne are the best you'll ever find) could get an arrow into one of them! Every one of them shot off to the side. Not one bit of that sanctified soiled whiteness lost its virginity or got the least little hole made in it. And Sansornin the Elder, who was in charge of the targets, swore to us by the golden figs (that was his highest oath) that he'd plainly seen—visibly, manifestly—Carquelin's arrow about to go right into the center, just about to hit and drive in, when it was pushed six feet away, off to the side, toward the laundry house."

"A miracle!" shouted Dumbman. "A miracle, a miracle! Let there be light over here—light, light, bring me light! I'll drink to all of you! Oh, you seem like real Christians to me!"

Hearing him, the girls began to giggle. Brother John puckered up the end of his nose, as if ready to jump on them and play stallion—like famine or my old friend Herbault attacking the poor.

"It seems to me," said Pantagruel, "you'd be in even less danger, near those targets, than Diogenes was, once upon a time."

"Who?" asked Dumbman. "Who? Was he an edictarian?"

"Now that," said Epistemon, coming back after doing his business, "that's a splendiferous way to play your cards!"

"One day," Pantagruel answered, "Diogenes wanted to amuse himself, so he went to see the archers at practice. There was one of them who was shooting very badly indeed, really incompetent, so that when he was getting ready to shoot, all the spectators stepped back, for fear he'd hit them. Having seen one arrow shot so crazily that it fell more than a pole length from the target, Diogenes ran up and stood right at its center— everyone else was running off to one side or the other—exclaiming that this was surely the safest place to be, for this archer was more likely to hit anything but the target, and the dead center was surely the safest possible place to be."

"One of my lord Etissac's pages," said Gymnast, "whose name was Chamouillac, finally figured out the spell. He got Perotus to change the target paper and use, instead, sheets from Pouillac's lawsuit. Then every one of them began to shoot extremely well."

"At Landerousse," said Rootgatherer, "at Jan Delif's wedding, there was a fine, sumptuous banquet, as was then the custom. After they'd eaten there were funny plays, comedies—all different kinds of pleasant nonsense, masques, and mummeries. My schoolmates and I, wanting to do whatever we could to do the party justice (that morning we'd all been given bolts of handsome white and violet cloth), made up a costumed masquerade, and we did it merrily by decorating ourselves with all sorts of shells and things. Since we didn't have any nice broad leaves (like burdock or Nile weed) or any handy supply of paper, we made our false faces out of the pages from an abandoned old sixth book of edicts, cutting them out for the eyes, the nose, and the mouth. What a wonder! When we'd finished our little dances and our youthful games, we took off our false faces—and we looked uglier and more villainous than the devils in the passion play at Douay: everywhere those pages had touched our faces, they were ruined. One fellow had smallpox, another had whooping cough, another had syphilis, another had measles, and still another had broken out in huge boils. In short, our friend who simply lost all his teeth was the least damaged of us all."

"A miracle," cried Dumbman, "a miracle!"

"It's still not funny," said Rootgatherer. "My sisters, Catherine and Renée, put their wimples and cuffs and collars in a big volume of the sixth book of edicts, as if it were a clothes press (it was covered with heavy boards, and it shut with iron locks). And they were all fresh and snowy white and starched. But by the virtues of God . . ."

"Wait!" said Dumbman. "What God do you mean?"

"There's only one," said Rootgatherer.

"Indeed," said Dumbman, "as far as heaven is concerned. But don't we have another one here on earth?"

"Giddy up!" said Rootgatherer. "By my soul, I don't think we do! Anyway, by the virtues of this earthly God–pope, their wimples and collars, their dickeys and neckerchiefs, and all their other linen turned blacker than a sack of charcoal."

"A miracle!" cried Dumbman. "Gentlemen stewards: let there be light over here—and pay close attention to these fine tales."

"Why then?" asked Brother John, "so people say:

> Since edicts have grown their doctrinal wings
> And soldiers have carried their heavy packs,
> Monks have traveled on horses' backs
> And the world's been full of awful things."

"I hear you," said Dumbman. "This is the kind of song sung by our new heretics."

Chapter Fifty-three // How the Power of the Edicts Craftily Sneaks Gold Out of France and Sends It to Rome

"I'd be glad," said Epistemon, "to pay for a bucket of tripes, if we could collate some of those horrific chapters with their originals—*Execrabilis, De multa, Si plures, De annatis per totum, Nisi essent, Cum ad monaster-*

ium, Quod dilectio, Mandatum, and a few others, which take four hundred thousand ducats a year, and maybe more, out of France and send it off to Rome."

"That isn't nothing, no," said Dumbman. "But all the same, it seems to me nothing at all, when you consider how your Very Christian France is Rome's sole and special wet nurse. Can you find any other books, anywhere in the world—philosophy, medicine, law, mathematics, humane letters, even (by God!) the Holy Bible—which have such pulling power? None! Piddle, paddle! Let me tell you, you'll never find any books with such gold-sucking energy. And still those diabolical heretics don't want to read and learn from them. Burn them—tear them apart with red-hot tongs—slit them open—drown them—hang them—impale them—rip off their shoulders—cut them up—disembowel them—cut off their heads— fry them—grill them—chop them up—crucify them—boil them—char them—pull them apart—grind them into dust—pull off their legs—roast them—those evil, wicked edict haters, edict killers—worse than murderers, worse than father killers—devilish edict slayers.

"You other good men: if you wish to be called, and thought, good Christians, I beg you with clasped hands to believe nothing else, to think of nothing else, say nothing else, do nothing else, nothing at all, but only what's contained in our sacred edicts and their supplements: our fine sixth book, these lovely edicts of Pope Clement, this beautiful set of appendices. O godlike books! Thus may you be in glory, honor, exaltation, riches, dignity, privileged and favored in this world, revered by everyone, feared by everyone, bowed to by everyone, everyone's chosen and elect. Nowhere under heaven's broad roof will you find men better able to perform all manner of deeds than those who, through divine prescience and holy predestination, have dedicated themselves to the study of these sainted edicts.

"Do you want to choose a brave emperor, a good general, a worthy chief and wartime leader of an army, who knows how to foresee everything which might be inappropriate, who understands how to avoid all danger, and can lead his men into assault and combat with an easy joy, risking nothing, always a conqueror but losing none of his soldiers and making superb use of his victories? Listen to me and pick an edict maker. No—no: I mean to say, a student of the edicts."

"Oh, you really missed that one!" said Epistemon.

"In time of peace, do you want to find a man capable of governing well—whether a republic, a kingdom, an empire, a limited monarchy— someone who can maintain the church, the nobility, the senate, and the people in prosperity, friendship, harmony, obedience, virtue, and honesty? Choose a student of the edicts.

"Do you want to find a man who, because of his exemplary life, his fluent speech, his holy teachings, can quickly, and without any human blood flowing, conquer the holy earth and convert to the true faith the wicked Turks, the Jews, the Tartars, the Muscovites, the Egyptian Mamelukes and Sarrabovites? Choose a student of the edicts.

"What makes the people of so many countries rebellious and deranged, their young serving men greedy and wicked, their students stupid and lazy? Their governors, their leading men, their teachers aren't edictalists.

"But what is it that, in good conscience, has established, confirmed, and put true authority in the hands of these fine religious orders, which you can see everywhere embodying a Christianity ornamented, decorated, illustrated, as the heavens are by the bright, clear stars? Our holy edicts.

"What founded, set on their feet, gave a solid foundation for—what maintains—what gives substance and weight to—what nourishes the holy monks and nuns and their convents, monasteries, and abbeys—those devoted religious folk without whose unceasing daily (and nightly) prayers the world would be in plain danger of falling back into its ancient chaos? Sanctified edicts.

"What has created and every day increases the temporal, corporeal, and spiritual prosperity of the famous and justly celebrated patrimony of Saint Peter? The holy edicts.

"What has created the eternal Holy See in Rome, today so formidable throughout the entire universe that, willy-nilly, all kings, emperors, potentates, and lords are obliged to depend on it, do homage to it: it is the Holy See that crowns them, confirms them, and empowers them, and they prostrate themselves in front of, and press their lips against, its miraculously holy slipper, of which you yourselves have seen the portrait? God's beautiful edicts.

"Let me tell you a wonderful secret. On the crests and seals of the universities of your world there's a book, sometimes shown open, sometimes closed. Now what book do you think that is?"

"I'm not sure," said Pantagruel. "I've never read any of it."

"The sacred edicts," said Dumbman, "without which the powers and privileges of all universities would perish. You have to hand me that one! Ha, ha, ha, ha, ha!"

And Dumbman began to belch, fart, laugh, slobber, and sweat, and he pulled off his huge, four-cornered ecclesiastical hat and handed it to one of the girls, who happily clapped it on her pretty head, after having lovingly kissed it for a guarantee that she would be the first to get married.

"Vivat!" shouted Epistemon. "Vivat! Fifat! Pipat! Bibat! Long life! Long life! Wrong wrife! Dong dife! And drink up! Oh, what an apocalyptic secret!"

"Gentlemen," said Dumbman, "Gentlemen: light—double lanterns over here. Bring us fruit, my little chickadees! Let me tell you, my friends: in this world you'll be rich and honored in exact proportion to your study of the sacred edicts. And let me tell you, too, that you'll infallibly be granted salvation in the blessed realm of heaven, the keys of which have been given to our sovereign papal author of edicts. O my good Roman lord, whom I adore and have never seen, at the hour of our death at least open to us, by your special grace, the infinitely sacred treasure of our mother, holy church, of which you are the protector, conservator, guardian, administrator, and dispenser! And command that these precious prayerful books, these lovely pardons, do not fail us when we need them, so the devils cannot sink their teeth into our poor immortal souls, and so the horrible gaping mouth of hell cannot swallow us down! And if we chance to come to purgatory, patience! In your capacity as judge you can deliver us whenever you choose to."

And Dumbman began to weep great hot tears, and to beat his chest, and to cross his thumbs and kiss them fervently.

Chapter Fifty-four ⁄ Dumbman Gives Pantagruel Good Christian Pears

Seeing things come to this irritating pass, Epistemon, Brother John, and Panurge began to hide their faces behind their napkins, crying, "Meow, meow, meow!" and at the same time wiping their eyes as if in tears. The well-trained girls brought everyone full mugs of Clementine wine and plenty of sweets. And so the banquet was restored to jolliness.

When the meal was over, Dumbman gave us a lot of fine, juicy pears, saying:

"Take them, my friends: they're unusual pears, which you won't find anywhere else. You can't grow everything everywhere. Black ebony grows only in India. Good incense comes from Saba. The island of Lemnos has apothecary soil. And only here on this island can you find these fine pears. Try to grow them, if you like, in your own country."

"What do you call them?" asked Pantagruel. "They seem to me very good and very juicy. Cut in quarters, and baked with a little wine and some sugar, I suspect they'd be just as good for sick people as for healthy ones."

"Exactly," said Dumbman. "We're simple people, here, since that's how God wishes it. We call figs, figs; plums, plums; and pears, pears."

"Indeed," said Pantagruel, "when I'm back home (which, God willing, will be soon), I'll try both planting them and grafting them in my garden at Touraine, on the banks of the Loire, and they'll be called good Christian pears. For surely you can't find better Christians then these good Papalmaniacs."

"And I'd like it," said Brother John, "if he'd also give us two or three wagonloads of his girls."

"What for?" asked Dumbman.

"We'd bleed them," answered Brother John, "straight between their two big toes, with certain handy sword tools. And what we'd graft onto *them* would be good Christian children, and in our country that would be a fast-multiplying race, because we don't have many."

"In the name of God!" answered Dumbman. "We're not going to do that, because you'd play boy games with them: I can tell it from your nose, though I've never seen you before. Alas! alas! You're a good young fellow! Do you want to damn your eternal soul? Our edicts won't permit it. I only wish you knew them as you should."

"Just a minute!" said Brother John. *"Si tu non vis dare, praesta, quesumus,* If you won't give them to us, please lend them. That's prayer-book stuff. I'm not afraid of anyone who wears a beard, even if he is a doctor of sheep dipping—I mean, of edicts—in his three-cornered doctoral hat."

When dinner was done, we took leave of Bishop Dumbman and all his good people, humbly thanking them for many, many good things and, in return, promising that when we were next in Rome we would do everything we could to persuade the Holy Father to visit them in person. Then we went back to our ship. In recognition of the sacred papal portrait, and also out of generosity of spirit, Pantagruel gave Dumbman nine lengths of heavily embroidered gold cloth, which could be hung in front of the barred window; he also filled the church collection box with gold, and sent to each of the girls who had waited on us, during dinner, nine hundred and fourteen gold pieces, so they could marry when the time was right.

Chapter Fifty-five ⁄⁄ Out on the High Seas, Pantagruel Hears Thawed-out Words

Back out at sea, as we feasted, sang, gossiped, and talked pleasantly, but briefly, on various serious subjects, Pantagruel jumped up and stood looking around. Then he said to us:

"My friends, do you hear anything? It seems to me I can hear people talking out of the air, though I can't see anyone. Listen!"

As he had ordered, we were attentive: with our ears wide open, we scanned the air like oysters in their shells, trying to hear if there was a voice or any other sound—and, so we would miss nothing (like Emperor Antoninus with his spies), some of us set our hands behind our ears. But we had to admit that we heard no voices.

Pantagruel stayed where he was, declaring he did indeed hear voices in the air, though he could not say whether it was men or women speaking, and we realized that we could hear them, too, or else our ears were ringing. The more carefully we listened, the more we could indeed make out the voices, until we were hearing whole words. This frightened us terribly, and not without reason—seeing no one and yet hearing all these voices and other sounds—men, women, children, horses—and hearing them so clearly that Panurge shouted:

"By God! What kind of game is this? We're lost. Let's run! This is an ambush. Brother John, are you there, my good old friend? Stay near me, I beg you! Are you wearing your sword? Make sure it doesn't just lie around in its scabbard! You don't keep it half as polished as you ought to. We're lost! Listen, listen: by God! that's cannon firing. Let's run! I'm not talking about fleeing by hand and foot, the way Brutus did at the battle of Pharsalia—I'm talking about sails and oars. Let's run! I'm an absolute coward, out at sea; down in a wine cellar, or anywhere else, I've got courage to spare. Let's run! Let's save ourselves! I'm not speaking because I'm afraid: as I always say, I'm afraid of nothing except danger. That's what the militiaman of Bagnolet said, too. But let's not take any chances, so we don't get our noses bashed in. Let's run! The other way! Hard over the helm, you whore son over there! I wish to God I was in Quinquenays right now, even if it means I never get married! Let's run! We can't handle them. It'll be ten against one, let me tell you. And besides, they're on home ground and we don't know a thing about this place. They'll kill us. Let's run! There's no dishonor in that. Didn't Demosthenes say that when you run away you just go to fight at the other end of the battlefield? Let's step back a little, at least. Starboard! Port! Up the foremast! Man the bowlines! We're dead men! Let's run! By all the devils, let's run, run!"

Hearing the racket Panurge was making, Pantagruel said:

"Who's that sniveler down there? Let's first find out who these people are. Maybe they're Frenchmen. I still can't see anyone, even though I can see all around us for a hundred miles. But let's listen. I've read in Plutarch that a philosopher named Petron believed there were other worlds adjacent to ours, like an equilateral triangle, the bottom and center of which, he said, was where Truth dwells, and where you'd find Words, Ideas, Forms and Structures, and images of all things, past and future. What lies around them is Time and the World. And in some years, at long intervals, parts of all these things come falling down on human beings like misty vapors, as the dew fell on Gideon's fleece—and some stays there for the future, waiting for the end of time.

"And I also remember how Aristotle claims that Homer's words flutter and fly, alive and moving.

"And Antiphanes, too, said that Plato's teaching about words is very probably true, namely, that in certain countries, in the dead of winter, words freeze as you send them out into the frigid air, and no one can hear them. He also said that what Plato taught to little children was just barely understood by the time they'd grown up and become old men.

"Now, let's be philosophical ourselves and find out if, perhaps, this might be the place where such frozen words thaw out. Wouldn't it be astonishing if this was Orpheus' head, and his lyre? You'll remember that, after the Thracian women tore him apart, they threw his head and his lyre into the Hebrus River, and they floated downstream to the Black Sea, all the way to the island of Lesbos, swimming together across the water. And all the time the head kept on singing a sad song, as if lamenting Orpheus' death, and the lyre, as the winds blew across it, sounded out chords in harmony with that song. Let's see if that's what's lying around us, here."

Chapter Fifty-six / How Pantagruel Finds Bright Red Words among Those That Thaw Out

The ship's pilot explained:

"My lord, there's nothing to be afraid of! This is the region of the Arctic Sea, and at the beginning of last winter there was a fierce and savage battle fought here, between the Arimaspians of Scythia and the Cloud Dwellers. Men's and women's words and cries, clattering and jangling swords and spears and shields, crashing armor (men and animals alike), whinnying horses, and all the other sounds and noises of combat—it all froze in the air. Now that winter's gone, and it's pleasant warm weather, everything's melting and is heard."

"By God!" said Panurge, "I believe he's right! But why can't we see anyone? I recall having read that, all along the mountain where Moses received the law of the Jews, his people could see a palpable voice."

"Wait, wait!" said Pantagruel. "See? There are more that still haven't thawed out."

Then he threw on the deck in front of us handfuls of frozen words, which might have been sugared almonds, like so many pearls of different colors. We saw bright red words, green words, blue words, black words, golden words. And after they had been warmed for a bit, between our hands, they melted like snow and we actually heard them, but without understanding a word, for they were in a barbarous language—except that one fat word, which Brother John had warmed between his hands, made a sound like chestnuts bursting, after they've been thrown into the fire without being cut open, and we all shivered with fear.

"Now that," said Brother John, "was once a cannon firing."

Panurge asked Pantagruel to give him more. Pantagruel observed that giving words was like making love.

"Then sell me some!" said Panurge.

"Selling words," said Pantagruel, "is more like what lawyers do. I'd prefer to sell you silence, and make you pay more for it, just as Demosthenes once sold his silence to the senate."

But still, he threw three or four handfuls onto the deck. And we could see sharp words, bloody words (which, according to the pilot, sometimes went back to the place where they'd been spoken, only to find the throat that uttered them had been slit open), horrible words, and many others equally unpleasant to see. And when they'd melted, we heard: *hin, hin, hin, hin, hiss, tick, tock, whizz, gibber, jabber, frr, frrr, frrr, boo, boo, boo, boo, boo, boo, boo, boo, crack, track, trr, trr, trr, trrr, trrrrr, on, on, on, on, wooawooawoooon, gog, magog,* and God only knows what other barbarian words. The pilot explained that these were the sounds of combat, and the whinnying of horses as the armies met. And we heard some large words turning into sound as they thawed, some like fifes and drums, others like bugles and trumpets. We had a great time, believe me. I wanted to save some bright red words by putting them in oil, as you preserve snow and ice, storing them under good clean straw. But Pantagruel didn't want to, saying that it was folly to save something we never ran out of and always had ready to hand—like the bright red words always exchanged between good, happy Pantagruelists.

At this point, Panurge rather annoyed Brother John, and made him sulk, taking him right at his word just when he never expected it, and Brother John threatened to make him sorry just the way William Jousseaume was sorry for selling cloth to our noble Patelin, and getting back only his word to pay for it. If Panurge did get married, said Brother John, he'd grab him by the horns like a calf, for "words bind men as ropes bind bulls' horns," and Panurge had taken him by the word like a man. Panurge lip-farted at him, then cried out:

"I wish to God I had the Divine Bottle right here and right now, without taking another step!"

Chapter Fifty-seven // Pantagruel Goes Ashore on Maître Gaster's Island and Meets the World's First University Graduate

That day, Pantagruel went ashore on an island wonderful beyond all other islands, both because of its location and because of its ruler. To begin with, it was rugged, rocky, mountainous, and non-arable all around, unpleasant to look at, hard on the feet, and not much less inaccessible than that mountain in the Vercors range, shaped like a pumpkin, which as far back as memory goes has hardly ever been climbed, other than by

Doyac, commander of King Charles the Eighth's artillery, who used his marvelous equipment to climb up there—and on the peak found an old ram. He couldn't figure out how it had ever gotten up there by itself, so they told him that, when it was just a lamb, some eagle or great horned owl must have carried him and he then escaped into the bushes.

After making our way in, which we did with great difficulty and not without sweating, we found ourselves on the peak of a mountain so pleasant, fertile, healthful, and delightful that I thought this must have been the true Garden of Eden, the earthly paradise (the exact location of which is so hotly disputed among our good theologians). But Pantagruel assured us that this was the seat of Areté (or Virtue), which Hesiod describes, though he made the claim without disparaging any sounder judgment.

The govⁿ or of the place was named Maître Gaster, or Belly, the first master of arts graduate in the world. Now, should you believe, as Cicero writes, that fire is the great master of all the arts, you're quite simply wrong, because Cicero never believed any such thing. If you believe that Mercury was the first practitioner of the arts, as the old Druids used to think, then you're really on the wrong track. The *Satyricon* is absolutely right, asserting that Master Belly is the true master of all the arts.

And with him, most peacefully, there lives our good lady Poverty, otherwise known as Indigence, mother of the nine Muses, from whose ancient union with Resourcefulness, lord of Abundance, Love was born— that noble child, mediator of heaven and earth, as Plato claims in his *Symposium*.

We of course paid our respects to this chivalric king, swearing to obey and honor him. And indeed he is haughty, hard, blunt, inflexible, difficult, and unyielding. You can't convince him of anything, or show him anything, or persuade him: he doesn't hear you at all. And just as the Egyptians said that Harpocras, god of silence (called in Greek Sigalion), is mouthless, so Belly was created without ears—like the likeness of Jupiter in Candia. Belly speaks only through signs. But the whole world is quicker to obey his signs than the policemen and laws of any king. His summons allows for no delay of any kind. It's said that when a lion roars all the animals for miles around tremble, for as far as his voice can be heard. It's written. And it's true. I've seen it myself. But I can tell you that at Master Belly's command the very sky trembles and the whole world shakes. The name of his command is: do as I say, and at once, or die.

The pilot told us how, one day, just as the limbs once conspired against the stomach (according to Aesop), so too the whole Somatic realm conspired against Master Belly, plotting to free themselves from obedience to him. But pretty soon they felt the pangs and were sorry and, in all humility, returned to his service. If they hadn't, they'd all have died of hunger.

Whatever society he enters, no one needs to talk about superiority or precedence: he always goes first, whether it's among kings, emperors, or even the pope. Even at the Council of Basel he went first, although we hear that that was a rebellious council, scrabbling and fighting over just who was to take precedence.

The whole world is busy serving him, everyone working. And in return he brings all sorts of good things to the world, inventing all the arts, every engine known, all trades and crafts, all machines and subtleties. He even teaches the brute animals arts denied them by nature. He turns crows, jackdaws, parrots, and starlings into poets; he makes magpies into poets, too, teaching them to jabber and speak and sing in human language. And all of this just to stuff their guts!

Eagles, hawks, falcons, Eurasian falcons, African falcons, goshawks, sparrow hawks, pigeon hawks, and all wild-eyed birds, peregrine falcons, every bird that flies, or steals, or hunts—he tames and domesticates them all, leaving it to him when they are to be permitted that freedom of the sky which they love, leaving it to him to determine how high they fly, how much they fly, keeping them high aloft, swooping, flying, hovering, flirting with him, paying him court there up above the clouds, then suddenly dropping down out of the sky and down to the earth. And all just to stuff their guts!

Elephants, lions, the rhinoceros, bears, horses, dogs—he makes them dance, hop, fly, fight, swim, play dead, fetch exactly as he pleases, carry anything he pleases. And all just to stuff their guts!

Fish, from salty and fresh seas, whales and sea monsters, he draws out of the depths; he pulls wolves out of the woods, bears off the high cliffs, foxes out of their lairs; he makes snakes crawl out of the ground. And all to stuff their guts!

In short, he is so enormously powerful that, in his anger, he consumes everything, beasts and men alike, as he did the Basques when Quintus Metellus besieged them, during the Sertorian wars—as he did the Saguntins when Hannibal besieged them—as he did the Jews when they were besieged by the Romans—and there are six hundred other examples. And all to stuff their guts!

When his regent, Poverty, is seen abroad, everywhere she goes parliaments are closed, all laws struck dumb, all order useless. She is subject to no law, exempt from all of them. They run from her everywhere she comes, preferring to risk themselves in ships on the sea, preferring to go through fire, to climb mountains, to cross great chasms, rather than be caught by her.

Chapter Fifty-eight // At This Ingenious Master's Court, Pantagruel Despises Both the Ventriloquists and the Belly Worshipers

Pantagruel found two kinds of people at this great ingenious master's court, all of them oppressive, officious bureaucrats and utterly loathsome to him. One sort were called Engastrimythes, or Ventriloquists; the others were Gastrolaters, or Belly Worshipers.

The Ventriloquists were said to be descended from the ancient race of Eurycles, which claim they based on the testimony of Aristophanes in his comedy *The Wasps.* In the old days, accordingly, they were called Eurycleans, as in Plato and also in Plutarch's *On the Disappearance of Oracles.* In the sacred edicts they're called ventriloquists, which is what Hippocrates calls them, in Greek, in book five of his *Epidemics,* meaning "men who speak from the belly." Sophocles calls them *Sternomantes,* or magicians using the sternum (or chest). They were in fact magicians, men who bewitched and took advantage of simple people, appearing to answer questions not with their mouths but with their bellies.

Jacoba Rhodogina, a lowborn Italian woman, was one of them, in the year of our blessed Savior 1513. We and many, many others, both in Ferrara and elsewhere, have frequently heard an unclean, evil voice, deep and weak and low, coming from her belly, but clearly articulated, distinct and perfectly intelligible. Curious princes and rich lords of northern Italy used to summon her to perform for them, and to prevent any suspicion of pretense or hidden fraud, she would be stripped completely naked and both her mouth and her nose stopped up. The evil spirit which spoke from her was called Curly Head, or Cincinnatus, and seemed to like hearing its name: when thus spoken to, it would answer questions at once. Asked questions about present or past matters, it answered so aptly that the audience was thrilled. But as to future matters it always lied, never once telling the truth. It often appeared to confess its ignorance by responding, not with a word, but with a fat fart, or else by murmuring some unintelligible words in a barbaric accent.

The Belly Worshipers, on the other hand, lived in troops and bands and kept to themselves, happy, simpering, some of them mollycoddlers, others sad, serious, severe, sour, but all of them lazy do-nothings, never working, a heavy weight and burden on the land, as Hesiod says, always afraid (as far as anyone could tell) of doing anything to offend or shrink their bellies. For the rest, they were so strangely masked, disguised, and dressed that they were really something to see.

You may say—and indeed it's been written by more than one of the ancient sages and philosophers—that nature's ingenuity is marvelously well reflected in the delight she seems to have taken, shaping all the different seashells: they're so various, with so many shapes, so many colors, so many characteristics and forms art simply cannot imitate. Let me tell you that you could see no less diversity, no less elaboration and complexity, in the clothing worn by these belly-worshiping monk shells. They all considered Master Belly the greatest god of all, adoring him, sacrificing to him exactly as they would to an omnipotent god, serving him, loving him in everything, honoring him as their one and only deity. You might say of them what the holy Apostle wrote, in his Epistle to the Philippians, chapter three:

"For many walk, of whom I have told you often, and now tell you even weeping, that they are the enemies of the cross of Christ: Whose end is destruction, whose God is their belly."

Pantagruel compared them to the Cyclops Polyphemus, in whose mouth Euripides put the following words:

"I sacrifice only to myself (not to the gods), and to this my belly, which is the greatest of all the gods."

Chapter Fifty-nine ⁄⁄ The Ridiculous Statue Called Manducus, and How, and What Things, the Belly Worshipers Sacrifice to Their Belly-Potent God

As we were staring, astonished, at the faces and gestures of these milksop, lazy-livered Belly Worshipers, we heard a great bell ringing, at the sound of which they all drew themselves up as for a battle, each according to his post, rank, and age.

And in this formation they marched before Master Belly, led by a young, heavy, powerful belly, holding aloft, by means of a long gilded stick, a wooden statue (badly executed and roughly painted) of a sort described by Plautus, Juvenal, and Pompeius Festus. In Lyons, at carnival time, they call it *Maschecroute,* or Boogyman; on this island, it was called *Manducus,* or Gobble-up. It was a monstrous effigy—ridiculous, hideous, and terrible to little children, with eyes bigger than its stomach and its head bigger than all the rest of its body, and with broad, wide, horrible jaws filled with teeth both above and below; a little rope running down into the gilt stick allowed them to click-clack those horrible jaws to immense effect, just as, in Metz, they do with the dragon in the Saint Clement's Day parade.

When the Belly Worshipers drew close, I saw that they were followed by a host of fat servants loaded with breadbaskets, hampers, parcels, pots, sacks, and cooking pans. Thus, with Gobble-up conducting, they sang

God knows what wild hymns, lazy songs, and drunken songs in honor
of their god, opening for him their baskets and pans, and offering him:

> white hippocras wine
> tender dry toast
> white bread
> breakfast rolls
> sugared bread
> plain ordinary bread
> six kinds of grilled meat
> roast goat
> cold roasts of veal loin, seasoned with mustard and powdered ginger
> couscous
> sheep hearts and liver
> nine kinds of fricasseed meat
> meat pies
> heavy supper soup
> rabbit stew
> lyonnaise soup
> young cabbages in beef marrow
> beef stew
> mutton stew

plus an endless supply of good things to drink, starting with excellent,
delicate white wine, and followed by claret and fresh ruby red wine—
cold as ice, let me tell you, served and offered in great silver glasses.
And then they offered:

> sausages in fine mustard
> beef sausages
> smoked beef tongues
> pigs' feet
> beef with peas
> veal stew
> blood puddings
> smoked pork sausage
> dry sausage
> hams
> boars' heads
> salt venison with turnips
> roast sliced liver
> pickled olives

And more and more drinks were served.
And then they shoveled down his throat:

shoulder of mutton in garlic
meat pies in hot sauce
pork chops with onions
roast capons in gravy
chickens
ducks
goats
fawns and bucks
rabbits and hares
partridges and chicks
pheasants and chicks
peacocks and peahens
storks and storklings
woodcock and snipe
ortolans
Indian cocks, hens, and chicks
pigeons and doves
pigs in wine sauce
duck with onions
blackbirds and marsh quail
waterfowl
wild ducks
egrets
river ducks
loons
bittern and spoonbills
curlews
hazel grouse
coots in pear sauce
robins and kids
shoulder of mutton with capers
beef royale, sliced
breast of veal
boiled chicken and fat capons with blancmange
grouse
pullets
rabbits and young rabbits
quail and young quail
pigeons and young pigeons
heron and young heron
bustards and young bustards
warblers
guinea fowl
plover
geese and goslings

wild pigeons
young wild ducks
larks
flamingos and swans
broad-billed ducks
snipe and cranes
sandpipers
great plovers
francolin quail
turtledoves
rabbits
spiced pork
brook ouzel

—all with a good supply of vinegar.
   —And then they served him lots of

venison pie
lark pie
mouse pie
alpine goat pie
goat pie
pigeon pie
chamois pie
capon pie
lard pie
pork pie in lard
fricasseed pie crusts
black-fried capons
cheese
corbeil peaches
artichokes
puffed pastry cakes
Swiss beets
butter-and-egg tarts
fritters
sixteen other kinds of tarts
pancakes and wafers
quince pastries
clotted milk
floating islands
plum jam
ices
mulled wine (red and ruby red)
Angevin cakes and macaroons

twenty more kinds of tarts
cream
seventy-eight kinds of dry and liquid sweets
sugared almonds, in a hundred different colors
cream cakes
sugared Parisian pastries

—all followed by vinegar, to avoid a sore throat, and toast, to drop into wineglasses.

Chapter Sixty // How the Belly Worshipers Sacrificed to Their God on Fish and Fasting Days

Seeing this rabble of sacrificers, and the ridiculous number of their sacrifices, Pantagruel grew angry and would have left, but Epistemon asked him to stay and see how the comedy finally ended.

"What," he said, "will these rascals sacrifice to their belly-potent god, on fish and fasting days?"

"I'll tell you," said the pilot. "For the first course, they serve him:

caviar
pressed caviar
fresh butter
thick pea soup
spinach
sweet white herring
assorted other herring
sardines
anchovies
salted tuna
cabbage in oil
bean and onion salad

—and a hundred other different salads: watercress, hops, wild watercress, rampion, Judas-ear mushroom (a kind of fungus growing on old elder trees), asparagus, mushroom, and many others—plus

salt salmon
pickled eels
oysters on the half shell.

"And then he needed to drink, or the devil would have carried him off. But they take good care of that, and he gets everything he needs, after which they serve him:

lampreys in wine sauce	smelt
mullet	fish *du jour*
barb fish	trout
gray mullet	Bourget lake fish
striped mullet	cod
skate	octopus
cuttlefish	humped flounder
sturgeon	flatfish
whale	striped bass
mackerel	Mediterranean fish
flounder	gudgeon
plaice	brill
fried oysters	bastard smelt
scallops	carp
crayfish	pike
bonito	spotted dogfish
squid	sea urchin
stickleback	tench
sea anemone	torpedo fish
black goby	Mediterranean mollusks
bullhead	lumpfish
crawfish	swordfish
clams	dogfish
Provençal lobster	lamprey eel larvae
lamprey eels	young pike
conger eels	pickerel
dolphin	speckled trout
sea perch	young carp
shad	salmon
moray eels	young salmon
mudminnow	grampus
freshwater minnow	porpoise
sand eels	turbot
small pickled eels	white skate fish
turtle	sole
pipefish	lemon sole
mussel	dorado
lobster	sea sole
shrimp	perch
fallfish	southern sturgeon
bleak fish	loach

young tench	crab
spotted trout	snails
fresh eels	frogs

"After he'd eaten all this, death would have been just two steps behind him if he hadn't done some drinking. So he was well provided with liquid refreshment.

"And then they also sacrificed to him:

dried salted codfish
dried moray eel
eggs—which they served fried, sunk, suffocated, steamed, cooked in
   hot embers, tossed around the chimney, daubed and smeared, and
   tarred, etc.
mussels
young thornback skate fish
haddock
pickled young pike,

—to which was added, for good cooking and easy digestion, a plenitude of good wine. And to complete the meal, they offered up:

rice	caraway
millet	millet porridge
oatmeal	wheat porridge
almond butter	prune paste
whipped butter	dates
pistachio nuts	walnuts
more pistachio nuts	hazelnuts
figs	parsnips
grapes	artichokes

—all of which were well washed down.

"You couldn't blame them, believe me, if this god of theirs, Master Belly, wasn't properly, carefully, and copiously served by all these sacrifices, more emphatically than the statue of Heliogabalus, more even than the statue of Baal in Babylonia, under the reign of King Balshazzar. All the same, Master Belly would not admit that he was indeed a god, but only a poor, lowly, weak creature. And just as King Antigonus the First replied to a man named Hermodotus, who in his poems had called the king a god, the sun's own son, and so on, saying, 'The Keeper of my Bedpan denies it' (this bedpan being an earthenware pan used to receive the stomach's excrement), so Belly sent all these Monkey Scholars to go examine, consider, philosophize about, and generally contemplate the contents of his privy, to see what divinity they could find in his feces."

Chapter Sixty-one ⁄⁄ How Master Belly Invented Assorted Methods for Getting and Keeping Grain

When those devilish Belly Worshipers had gone, Pantagruel made a close study of that noble master of arts Master Belly. You of course realize that nature herself has provided him with bread, and all that naturally comes from bread, as his rightful food, with an additional heavenly blessing which ensures that the getting and keeping of bread will never be denied him.

At the very beginning he invented the arts of blacksmithing and agriculture, in order to cultivate and draw forth his grain from the earth. He invented the martial arts in order to defend grain; the arts of medicine and of astrology, along with their necessary mathematics, so that grain could be safely stored over time, and kept from the dangers of the air, the damage caused by brute animals, thieves, and robbers. He invented water mills, windmills, and windmill vanes, and a thousand other machines, in order to grind grain and turn it into flour; he invented leavening in order to make dough rise; he invented salt in order to give it savor (for he knew that nothing in the world makes men more subject to illnesses of all sorts than unfermented bread, or bread made without salt); he invented fire in order to bake it, and clocks and sundials in order to understand and control the time it took to bake bread, that substance which is created out of grain.

It would happen that a country lacked grain: he invented the art of taking it from one country to another. With immense inventiveness, he crossed two kinds of animals, mares and donkeys, to produce yet a third kind, which we call mules, the strongest, least delicate, most durable and hardworking of all animals known. He invented wagons and carts to carry grain more readily. If seas or rivers blocked the way, he invented boats, galleys, and ships (creations which astonished the four elements) to navigate over seas, over rivers and streams, and to carry grain to barbarous nations, unknown and far distant.

It happened that, in some years, it would not rain at the right time and in the right season, and for lack of water the grain which had been planted stayed dead and inert in the ground. Sometimes it rained too much, and the grain was drowned. Sometimes hail would destroy it, or winds would shred it, or storms would tumble it down. Long before we came to his island, he invented the art and practice of rainmaking, which he accomplished simply by cutting up a certain herb, common in meadows and fields but not often known by men, and he showed it to us. It seemed to me that it must have been that same herb, one branch of which, long ago, was put in the fountain of Agno by the high priest of Jupiter, high on

Mount Lycaeus, in Arcady, and which in a dry and parched season created mists, from which mists great clouds formed, which clouds then dissolved in rain, watering the entire region as much as anyone could have wanted. And he invented the art, and perfected the practice, of making the rain stop in midair, and then fall out at sea. He invented arts for destroying hail, suppressing wind, and turning away storms, as was commonly done by the Methanians of Troezen.

Other disasters occurred. Robbers and thieves stole grain out of the fields. He invented the art of building cities, fortresses, and castles, in order to keep it stored safely away. Sometimes it happened that there was no grain in the fields, although there was grain stored away in the cities, fortresses, and castles, where it was more closely guarded and defended than dragons ever guarded the golden apples of Hesperides. So he invented the art of smashing and destroying fortresses and castles, using engines and machines of war—battering rams, stone hurlers, catapults, the drawings for which he showed us, which were not well understood even by ingenious architects and engineers, disciples of Vitruvius (as the great architect and engineer of that great king Francis the First of France, Master Philbert de l'Orme, once admitted to us). But when these heavy weapons were no longer of use, because of the wicked subtlety and subtle wickedness of those who designed fortifications, he'd recently invented cannons of every imaginable weight and bore, heavy, medium, and light, as well as mortars and great pieces of artillery that hurled flaming bullets, both lead and bronze, weighing more than large anvils, all of them impelled by that ghastly powder which astonished even nature herself, for in it she was obliged to admit herself beaten by mortal art, which could thus look down on that Oxydraquian race which, utilizing the power of thunderbolts, hail, lightning, and storms, conquered and swiftly put its enemies to death out on the open battlefield. For this powder was more horrible, more frightening, more diabolic than a hundred thunderbolts, murdering more men, shattering and breaking and killing them, devastating humankind more effectively, and demolishing more castle walls than the blows of any battering ram or catapult.

Chapter Sixty-two // How Master Belly Invented the Art and Practice of Escaping Untouched and Unharmed by Cannonballs

It happened that, as Master Belly withdrew into his fortresses, he found himself attacked by his enemies, those fortifications demolished by such triply wicked men and their hellish engines, their titanic strength carrying off his grain and his bread. So what he invented was a way of protecting his castles and fortresses and bastion walls from such cannonading—a method of ensuring that the bullets never touched them, remaining unexploded in the air, falling short of their targets, neither touching nor harming anything, neither the defenses nor the citizen defenders.

He'd managed to get rid of these inconveniences very nicely, long before we came, and he showed us his method, which has since then been employed by Fronton, and is at this very moment commonly used in the games and honest exercises held at Thélème. Here's how it worked—and after reading this, you'll find it easier to believe what Plutarch tells you he has done: for example, that if a flock of goats starts to run away, galloping as hard as they can, all you have to do is put a sprig of thistle into the mouth of one of the laggards, and they'll all come right to a stop.

Taking a small cannon, charged with carefully prepared gunpowder (all the sulfur removed, and neatly balanced with exactly the right amount of pure camphor), he inserted a small, well-calibrated iron ball and twenty-four iron pellets, some completely round, some tear-shaped. Then he aimed the cannon at one of his young pages, as if intending to hit him right in the stomach, and from a distance of only sixty paces—but midway between the page and the cannon, on a straight line, he hung from a rope, tied to a T-shaped wooden structure, a large magnetic stone (sometimes called siderite, sometimes ironstone or Hercules stone; once upon a time a man named Magnus found it at Ida, in the land of the Phrygians, as Nicander bears witness—but we just call it lodestone, or magnet). Then, using the cannon's touch hole, he set fire to the gunpowder. Burned up by the fire, the gunpowder strove to avoid the vacuum that would otherwise have been left by this sudden combustion (nature naturally abhorring vacuums: it would be easier to reduce the whole functioning universe—heavens, air, earth, sea—to primeval chaos than it would be to substitute a vacuum for this world of ours), which caused the ball and the pellets to be forced violently out of the cannon's mouth, to let the air come rushing in. Thrown so forcibly forward, the ball and pellets seemed sure to strike the page—but as they reached the magnetic stone they lost all their force and simply stayed in the air, floating, turning slowly around the magnet and, for all their original violence, never going past it.

He also invented a way of making bullets turn around and head back toward his enemies, just as strongly and dangerously as they'd been fired, and on the same trajectory. It was not a difficult art to create and perfect, considering that the herb we call æthiopis opens any and all locks it encounters, and the echeneis—a singularly feeble fish—can stop all the winds from blowing and, even in a hurricane, make even the most powerful ships at sea come to a halt, and the flesh of this same fish, pickled in salt, can draw gold out of wells, no matter how deep they may be dug.

And considering what Democritus wrote, and Theophrastus believed and tested, namely, that there is an herb which, just touching a wedge of iron driven with great violence deep into a thick, hard block of wood, causes it to leap right out again—an herb used by green magpies (you call them French woodpeckers) if the entrance to their nests, which they usually work hard to carve in the trunks of strong trees, is blocked by a mighty iron wedge.

And considering that stags and does, if deeply wounded by spears, arrows, or crossbow bolts, will eat, if they can, a bit of that herb we call dictamnus, or dittany, very common in Candia, and it immediately makes the arrows fall out and causes all wounds to be cured—the same herb used by Venus to cure her beloved son, Aeneas, when he was wounded in the right thigh by an arrow shot by Juturna, Turnus' sister.

And considering that the only fragrance emanating from laurels, figs, and old seal bulls deflects lightning, which never ever strikes them.

And considering that just looking at a ram turns crazed elephants sane again; that wild mad bulls are tamed, turned as motionless as if frozen into place, simply by coming near wild fig trees; that angry vipers are calmed by the touch of a beechwood branch.

And considering, also, that on the island of Samos, before the temple of Juno was built there, Euphorion records having seen animals called neads, at the mere sound of which the earth cracked and split open in chasms and abysses.

And considering, too, that the best, most resonant elder wood for making flutes always grows in countries where the cock is never heard to crow, as the ancient wise men wrote and Theophrastus tells us—as if the cocks' song deadened, softened, cracked, and splintered the elder wood—just as the lion, hearing the same song, though an animal of immense strength and toughness, becomes confused and dazed.

I am aware that some people have thought this proverbial saying applied, instead, to the wild elder tree, growing so far from towns and cities that no cocks' crows could be heard. To be sure, this is the wood to be chosen for making flutes and other musical instruments—not the domestic elder, which grows around houses and cottages.

Still others have taken this in a higher sense—not according to the letter, but allegorically, like the Pythagoreans: so that when it's said that a statue of Mercury should not be made of just any wood, they explain the statement to mean that God ought to be worshiped not in common, vulgar ways but in a fashion properly pious and elevated.

In which style, they argue that this maxim teaches us how wise and learned men ought to give themselves up not to common, trivial music but to music which is heavenly, divine, and angelic, music more esoteric and learned in distant places—that is, places where the cock's crow is not heard. And indeed, when we wish to speak of an out-of-the-way spot, where men seldom come, we too speak of it as a place where the cock's song is never heard.

Chapter Sixty-three // Passing Near the Island of Hypocrites Pantagruel Has a Dream, and the Problems Set for Him When He Awoke

The next day, as we sailed along, indulging ourselves in small talk, we arrived near the island of Hypocrites, where the wind failed us and the sea went completely calm, preventing Pantagruel's ship from making land. We made headway only by tacking this way and that, swinging from starboard to port and then from port to starboard; even rigging up the wind-catching bonnet sails didn't pull us along. So we lay around and thought, and chased empty ideas, stupefied and irritated, no one saying a word to anyone else.

Pantagruel slept on a mattress, near a hatchway, holding a Greek text of Heliodorus in his hands. That was his usual way, for he slept better by book than by heart.

Epistemon, using his astrolabe, was measuring the elevation of the pole, to calculate what latitude we were in.

Brother John had gone to the kitchen, where he was using the ascendant of the spits and the horoscope of the frying pans to calculate the time.

Panurge was blowing bubbles with a reed stalk of hemp.

Gymnast was fixing toothpicks for Lent.

Powerbrain was dreamily dreaming, tickling himself to make himself laugh, and scratching his head with one finger.

Carpalim was making a pretty little windmill, a pleasant, gay toy, out of a fat walnut shell: it had four delicate little vanes, cut from an alder stick.

Eusthenes sat on a cannon barrel, moving his fingers as if he were playing on a keyboard.

Rootgatherer was turning a tortoise shell into a purse (later to be covered with velvet).

Imported Goods was repairing an old lantern, using falconers' thongs.

And our pilot was pulling worms out of his sailors' noses when Brother John, returning to the cabin, saw that Pantagruel had woken up. So he shattered that stubborn silence, shouting with great gaiety and in a very loud voice:

"How do you amuse yourself, and blow up good weather, when the wind's gone down?"

Panurge quickly seconded him, insisting:

"How do you deal with boredom?"

Epistemon tossed in, gaily:

"How do you piss, when there's no piss to piss?"

Gymnast stood up and asked:

"How do you cure dizziness?"

Powerbrain, after rubbing his forehead and flapping his ears, asked:

"How can you keep from sleeping like a dog?"

"Hold on!" said Pantagruel. "Our subtle peripatetic philosophers have taught us that all problems—all questions—all formulated uncertainties, must be definite, clear, and comprehensible. Just what do you mean by 'sleeping like a dog'?"

"That means," said Powerbrain, "sleeping in the midday sun, with your belly empty—as dogs do."

Rootgatherer, squatting on the gangway, lifted his head and yawned most profoundly—so profoundly, indeed, that natural sympathy made everyone else yawn, too. Then he said:

"What's a cure for yawning?"

Imported Goods, busy with his broken lantern, asked:

"How do you calibrate and balance out the stomach's bagpipe, so it doesn't lean more to one side than to the other?"

Carpalim, playing with his toy mill, asked:

"What has to happen inside a man's body before you can say he's hungry?"

Eusthenes, hearing all the racket, came running out on the deck and, standing near the capstan, called out:

"Why is a hungry man in greater danger of death from a hungry snake, when after both have eaten there's no danger for either? And why is a hungry man's saliva poisonous to snakes and all other poisonous animals?"

"My friends," answered Pantagruel, "there's only one solution to all the questions and problems you've posed, just as for all of you suffering from these symptoms and ailments there's only one medicine. You'll have the answer shortly, but not by great windy speeches and lots of words: the hungry stomach has no ears and hears nothing whatever. You'll be satisfied, you'll be satisfied and made entirely content, by means of signs, gestures, and results. Just as in Rome, long ago, Tarquin the Proud, last king of Rome" (as he said this, Pantagruel gave the bell rope a pull, and Brother John ran toward the kitchen), "replied to his son Sextus Tarquinius by signs. Sextus was among the Gabini and had sent a man to his father, expressly to ask how he ought to completely subjugate the Gabini, reducing them to perfect obedience. The king, suspicious of the messenger's loyalty, said not a word to him, but simply led him to his private garden and there, as the man watched, drew out his short sword and chopped the heads off the tall poppy flowers growing there. The messenger then returned to the king's son, carrying no verbal message, but recounting what he had seen the king do, after which it was easy for the son to understand that, by these signs, he had been advised to cut off the heads of the leading men among the Gabini, so as to be sure of the total cooperation and obedience of the rest of the population."

Chapter Sixty-four ⁄⁄ Pantagruel Is Unable to Answer Their Questions

Then Pantagruel asked:

"Who lives on this lovely Hypocrites Island?"

"In fact," answered Imported Goods, "they're all hypocrites, bloated bellies, prayer mumblers, religious liars, saint worshipers, bigots, and hermits. And they're all poor, living (like the hermit of Lormont, between Blaye and Bordeaux) on whatever alms travelers give them."

"I'm not going ashore," said Panurge, "I assure you: may the devil blow up my asshole if I do! Hermits, saint worshipers, religious liars, bigots, hypocrites—they're all devils: get away, all of you! I'm reminded of our fat council-goers, headed for the Crazy Council: if only Beelzebub and Astaroth had set them counciling with Proserpina, for all the storms and assorted deviltries we had to deal with after meeting them. Now see here, Imported Goods—my little fat man, my drum corporal: all of these hypocrites, and hermits, and prayer mumblers, are they virgins or married? Are there any women? And is it possible, hypocritically, to do a little hypocritical business with them?"

"Now that," said Pantagruel, "is a bright and happy question!"

"Indeed!" answered Imported Goods. "These hypocrites have women who are beautiful and gay—and they also have lovely religious liars, handsome female hermits, dazzling women of immense piety—and, of course, they've got lots of little hypocrites, small-sized religious liars, tiny hermits."

"Keep them away!" said Brother John, breaking in. "A young hermit is an old devil. That's an authentic proverb: bear it in mind."

". . . If they didn't," Imported Goods continued, "and there was no propagation, Hypocrites Island would long since have become an empty desert."

Pantagruel sent them his alms, via Gymnast in the skiff: seventy-eight thousand handsome gold pieces. Then he asked:

"What time is it?"

"Nine and a little over," answered Epistemon.

"That," said Pantagruel, "is exactly the right time to have dinner. The shadow on the sundial is approaching that sacred line so celebrated by Aristophanes in his comedy *The Preachers,* falling on the tenth point in a quadrant. Long ago, among the Persians, the time for eating dinner was prescribed only for the king: everyone else used his appetite and his belly as clocks. In Plautus, indeed, a certain hanger-on complains about the invention of clocks and sundials, which he hates and loathes, since (as he argues) it's plain that no clock is ever as accurate as the belly. When Diogenes was asked at what time a man ought to eat, he answered, 'The rich, when they're hungry; the poor, when there's something on the table.' Doctors say, more appropriately, that the approved hour is:

> Wake up at five, dine at nine;
> Have lunch at five, go to bed at nine.

"The famous king Petosiris practiced a different sort of magic."

But at these words, the guardians of men's gullets set up tables and sideboards, covering them with scented tablecloths, plates, napkins, and saltcellars, and fetching tankards, bottles, flasks, cups, mugs, bowls, and pitchers. Brother John, together with maîtres d'hôtel, waiters, butlers, stewards, carvers, cupbearers, food tasters, brought in four huge ham pies, so huge that to me they looked like the four towers at Turin. My God, how we drank, and how we ate, and what a splendid time we had! Nor had we reached dessert when, suddenly, the northwest wind began to fill our sails—jibs and moorish lateens and square foresails and all. At which everyone sang hymns in praise of our noble Lord on high.

And when the fruit was brought in, Pantagruel asked:

"Tell me, my friends, if your doubts have been fully resolved."

"I'm not yawning any more, thank God," said Rootgatherer.

"I'm not sleeping like a dog," said Powerbrain.

"Now I can see perfectly well," said Gymnast.

"I'm not fasting any more," said Eusthenes. "And so, the rest of this whole day, my saliva won't be able to injure an

asp	ant	arachnid	alligator
anteater	auk	adder	aardvark
antelope	agouti	Airedale	albatross
alpaca	amoeba	angelfish	angora
anole	avocet	ass	armadillo
bull	baboon	bear	beagle
canary	caribou	cow	crow
crustacean	caracara	canvasback	camel
cacomistle	curlew	caddis fly	curassow
crocodile	cricket	crane	crab
coyote	cowbird	copperhead	coral
dragon	dodo	dalmatian	dove
elephant	egret	eagle	eland
fox	falcon	flounder	flea
gar	gopher	gorilla	grouse

hare	hen	hummingbird	horse
ichneumon	ibis	ichthyosaur	itch mite
kraken	koala	kookaburra	kiwi
lamb	lark	lamprey	lemur
muskrat	mouse	mule	mastiff
musk-ox	macaw	mallard	mosquito
newt	narwhal	nightjar	nuthatch
ostrich	ox	orangutan	opossum
platypus	parrot	partridge	peacock
quail	quagga	quarter horse	quahog
raven	ray	rattlesnake	rabbit
robin	rhea	rhinoceros	rhesus
scallop	skunk	swordfish	skate
snake	shrike	silverfish	sheep
seal	sea gull	screech owl	schnauzer
shark	saluki	salamander	skimmer
snipe	snail	snow goose	sow
tinamou	tiger	tit	toad
unicorn	otter	umbrella bird	uncinaria
viper	vireo	vulture	vampire
wallaby	wasp	warthog	wagtail
xancidae	xiphias	xiphosura	xylophaga
yellowtail	yapok	yak	yellowhammer
zebra	zebu	zoril	zyzzyva."

Chapter Sixty-five // How Pantagruel and the Members of His Household Blew Up Good Weather and Amused Themselves

"At what level on that animal scale," asked Brother John, "do you put Panurge's future wife? Among the venomous ones?"

"Are you criticizing women," answered Panurge, "my gallant young fellow, O error-filled monk?"

"By the ancient bladder of Mans," said Epistemon, "Euripides wrote, and put into Andromaché's mouth, that there are useful remedies against all venomous creatures, thanks to human ingenuity and some helpful hints from the gods. But against evil women, alas, there are still no remedies at all."

"This gay blade, Euripides," said Panurge, "always had nasty things to say about women. And divine vengeance made sure that he himself was eaten by dogs, as Aristophanes warned him. But let's go on. Whose turn is it?"

"I'm about to piss," said Epistemon, "as much as a man can."

"My stomach," said Imported Goods, "is now about as nicely ballasted as it ought to be. I won't lean either to one side or the other."

"And I," said Carpalim, "have suffered no insufficiency of either wine or bread. As the song says, 'No more thirst, for a while, no more hunger.'"

"I'm not upset any more," said Panurge, "thanks to God—and to you, my lord. I'm as happy as a parakeet, gay as a hawk, light as a butterfly. Your fine Euripides once put truthful words into Silenus' mouth—that notable tippler:

> He's got to be mad, who gets no sense from his glass,
> But drinks, and never relishes what he has.

"Without the slightest doubt in the world, we owe infinite praise to the good Lord, our Creator, our Savior, our Protector, who by means of this good bread, and this good fresh wine, and all this fine food, cures us of our agitation (both physical and mental)—not to mention the delight and pleasure we get from having eaten and drunk. But you've still not answered our blessed venerable Brother John's question, who wanted to know how we amused ourselves and blew up good weather."

"But," said Pantagruel, "if you're happy with this frivolous solution to all the questions you asked, then I am, too. Anyway, perhaps we'll have another chance to say more of these things, if you care to. Let's just settle the matter raised by Brother John: how do we amuse ourselves and blow up good weather? But haven't we done exactly that? Just look at the pennant up on the mast. Look at those whistling sails. Look at the taut stays, and ropes, and the sails themselves. We blew up good weather by raising our cups: the weather and our drinking were linked by some hidden natural sympathy. So too the raising up of Atlas and of Hercules, if you believe the wise old mythmakers. But they raised it just a little too much: Atlas, because he wanted to better carouse with Hercules, his host, and Hercules, because of the immense thirst he'd just had to endure, off in the Libyan desert . . ."

"Well said!" said Brother John, interrupting. "More than one learned man has told me that Tirelupin, your good father's wine steward, saves more than eighteen hundred barrels of wine a year, making unexpected guests and servants drink before they're thirsty."

". . . because," said Pantagruel, going on, "just as camels and dromedaries in a caravan drink for thirsts past, present, and future, so too did Hercules—who raised everything too high and caused sudden oscillations and tremors in heaven—and the crazy astrologers have been arguing about it ever since."

"There's a common proverb," said Panurge, "which speaks to this matter:

Bad weather passes, and good returns,
If you sit and drink while a ham fire burns."

"And it's not just good weather," said Pantagruel, "that our eating and drinking raised: we also lifted away a lot of the stores that our ship had to carry—and not simply the way Aesop emptied out his basket. We've gotten rid of the supplies, yes, but we've also gotten rid of our hunger and thirst. For just as the body weighs more dead than alive, so too a man who's hungry and thirsty is earthier and thus heavier than a man who's eaten and drunk his fill. People going off on a long voyage, who eat a good breakfast and drink all they need, often say—and rightly—'Our horses will ride better for it.' Remember the Amyclaeans who, long ago, revered and worshiped our noble father Bacchus above all other gods, and called him by that fitting and proper name *Psila*? That means 'Wings,' in Greek. And just as birds fly lightly through the air, using their wings, so with Bacchus' help (that is, by means of good fresh wine) human spirits are elevated, too—and their bodies plainly lightened—and all that's earthly about them is quieted and worn away."

Chapter Sixty-six // How Pantagruel Ordered the Muses Saluted, near the Island of Thieves

The fair wind blew on, and they went on talking until, in the distance, Pantagruel perceived a mountainous land, which he pointed out to Imported Goods, asking him:

"Do you see, over there on the port side, that tall crag with two ridges, looking rather like Mount Parnassus, in Phocis?"

"I see it perfectly," answered Imported Goods. "It's the island of Thieves. Would you like to go ashore there?"

"No," said Pantagruel.

"You're right," said Imported Goods. "There's nothing worth seeing: the people are all thieves and robbers. Still, toward that right-hand ridge there's the most beautiful fountain in the world, and a fine forest all around it. Your rowers could draw water and gather wood."

"Well and learnedly spoken," said Panurge. "Hey ho ho! Let's never disembark on any island of thieves and robbers. I can tell you that's what this land is, for I've several times seen the islands of Sark and Herm, near Guernsey, between Brittany and England, which are very like Philip's island of Scoundrels, in Thrace—criminals, thieves, brigands, murderers, and assassins, all of them drawn, appropriately, from the best ratholes of Paris' Conciergerie prison. Please, let's not go ashore! If you won't listen to me, at least listen to the advice of our good, wise guide, Imported

Goods. By God's own head! they're worse than cannibals. They'd eat us all alive. Please, let's not go ashore! We'd be better off, even in Avernus, at the very gates of hell. Listen: by God, I can hear a ghastly banging— they're sounding alarms, the way the Gascons in Bordeaux used to do, years ago, when the revenue men came to collect the salt tax. If it isn't that, then my ears are ringing for nothing. Let's just sail by! Ha! Keep going, keep going!"

"Let's go ashore," said Brother John, "let's go ashore! Let's go, let's go, let's go! That way we won't have to pay for our lodgings. Let's go! We'll lay waste to them, every one of them. Let's go!"

"The devil can take my share!" said Panurge. "This devil of a monk, this wild devil of a monk, isn't afraid of anything! He's as reckless as all the other devils, and like all the others he doesn't give a damn. And he thinks everyone in the whole world is a monk."

"You spotted green leper," answered Brother John, "may a million devils take you and carve your brain into slices! This devil of a fool is such a wicked coward that he's always beshitting himself with crazed fear! Well, if you're really that afraid, don't come ashore, stay here with the luggage—or else go hide under Proserpina's petticoat, along with a million other devils."

At these words Panurge left the others and hid himself below, in the storeroom, among the crusts and crumbs and scraps of bread.

"I feel," said Pantagruel, "a fierce contraction in my soul, as if some dim far-off voice were telling me not to go ashore. And every time I've felt that sort of thing, I've been right, and done well, to avoid what it tells me to avoid—but at the same time, whenever I've done what I've felt impelled to do, I've never regretted a thing."

"Just like Socrates' daemon," said Epistemon, "so famous among Plato's pupils."

"Listen to me," said Brother John. "While the rowers get their supplies, Panurge will be down there, burrowing like a wolf in the straw. Do you want to have some fun? See this cannon over here, near the fo'c-'sle? Set it off. That'll be a way of saluting the Muses on this Mount Antiparnassus. And the powder in there will spoil, otherwise."

"Very well said," answered Pantagruel. "Bring me our master gunner."

The man came at once. Pantagruel ordered him to set off the cannon, and in any case to recharge all the pieces of artillery with fresh powder. This was done promptly. The gunners on all the other ships, warships, galleys, and Venetian-style boats, hearing the first volley from the cannon on Pantagruel's ship, similarly fired off their biggest and heaviest guns. And you'd better believe there was an incredible racket.

Chapter Sixty-seven / Panurge in Great Fear Thoroughly Beshat Himself, Thinking the Great Cat Bacon-Eater Was a Devil

Like a dazed goat, Panurge came up from the storeroom, wearing only his shirt and one stocking that was half falling off, his beard all speckled with bread crumbs, and in his hand a fat sable cat, tied up with his other stocking. His jaws were shaking and trembling like a monkey hunting lice on his skull, his teeth were clattering, and he headed straight for Brother John, who was sitting on the starboard gunwales, devoutly begging him to show compassion and protect him with his short sword, swearing that by his share of Papalmania he had just seen all the devils in hell set loose.

"Just see here, my friend!" he said, "my brother, O my spiritual father: today the devils are celebrating a wedding! You've never seen such preparations for an infernal banquet! Don't you see the smoke from their hellish kitchens?" (And he gestured toward the black smoke drifting up from all the just-fired ships' cannon.) "You've never seen so many damned souls. And do you know what? Just see, my friend! They're all so soft, so fair haired, so tender, that you'd be tempted to call them Stygian ambrosia. I thought (may God forgive me) they were English souls, and that Horse Island, off Scotland, had been invaded and sacked by the noble lords of Thermes and Dessay just this morning, with the death of all their English defenders."

As he approached, Brother John smelled God knows what—but it wasn't cannon powder. So he swung Panurge around, and saw that his shirt was all freshly beshatten. The retentive faculty of the nerve which restrains the muscle we call the sphincter (that is, the asshole) had been loosened by the strength of the fear caused by his phantasmic visions, plus the thundering of the cannon, which had sounded even more horrific down in the rooms under the deck. Indeed, one of the usual symptoms and consequences of fear is that it opens the gate to the chamber where, for the time being, fecal matter is stored.

Consider, for example, Maître Pandolfo de la Cassina, of Siena, who was traveling by post chaise and, happening to pass through Chambéry, stopped at wise Vinet's inn. Picking up a pitchfork in the stable, he said to Vinet, *Da Roma in qua io non andato del corpo. Di gratia, piglia in mano questa forcha et fa mi paura*, "I haven't had a bowel movement since I left Rome. Please: take this pitchfork and scare the shit out of me." So Vinet made several passes at him, as if intending really to hit him. Then Master Pandolfo said, *Se tu non fai altramente, tu non fai nulla. Pero sforzati di adoperarli più guagliardamente*, "If you don't do it differently, you won't do a bit of good. So try to do it with more dash—please." At which point Vinet hit him so hard with the pitchfork, right between his ass and his collar, that he knocked him over, feet up over his head. And then, laughing wildly, Vinet said, "By God's feast! That's what we call, around here, *datum Camberiaci,* a deed done in Chambèry." Master Pandolfo had luckily let down his pants, because then and there he shat more copiously than nine buffaloes and fourteen archpriests from Ostia. And then he thanked Vinet most graciously, saying, *Io ti ringratio, bel messere. Cosi facendo tu m'hai esparmiata la speza d'un servitiale,* "Many thanks, dear sir. You've just saved me the expense of a suppository."

And as another example consider Edward the Fifth, king of England. Maître François Villon, banished from France, had taken refuge at the English court. He'd been received so warmly that nothing in the household, not the smallest thing, was concealed from him. One day, when the king was sitting on his shit stool, he showed Villon a painting of the French coat of arms, and said:

"Do you see what deep respect I have for the kings of France? I keep their coat of arms here, only here near my shit stool."

"Dear God!" answered Villon. "How wise you are, how sensible, how careful and attentive to your health, and how well served you are by your learned physician, Thomas Linacre. Seeing how naturally, in your old age, you'll become constipated and need to stuff a suppository up your ass every day, or else you won't be able to produce a thing, he has very properly had you paint the coat of arms of France here, and nowhere else—a remarkable and wise bit of foresight, for simply at the sight of this coat of arms you feel such flaming, horrible fear that, on the spot, you shit like eighteen wild Paeonian bulls. Had you placed this painting anywhere else in your palace—your bedroom, say, or your dining room, your private chapel, your galleries—anywhere at all—dear God! you'd be shitting in all directions the moment you saw it. And if you'd had the great banner of Saint Denis portrayed with equal richness and abandon, at the sight of it you'd shit your bowels right out your asshole. But, hey, ho, *atque iterum,* ho, hey once more!

> I'm just a lazy Paris bum,
> From Paris where the river flows,
> And a rope reaching from head to toes
> Will weigh my ass for my neck—ho, hum.

"A bum, I say, always acting on bad advice, misunderstood, misunderstanding—because when I came in here with you, I was astonished to see you pull your pants down right here in your bedroom. Really—I thought maybe you'd set your shit stool behind a curtain, or between the bed and the wall. It seemed powerfully strange to me, this way, pulling down your pants in your bedroom and then having to go so far to attend to your family business. Isn't that just the way a bum might think? But clearly you've worked it out according to a different theology, for which God be praised! Take your time, and go as far as you like before you drop your pants—because when you come in here, and your pants aren't down, and you see this coat of arms, and think about what it means, and by God! the seat of your pants would be doing the job of a shit house, a shit carrier, a slop bucket, and a shit stool."

Brother John, holding his nose with his left hand, pointed the index finger of his right hand at Panurge's shirt, showing it to Pantagruel. But seeing Panurge thus shaken, half dead, trembling with fear, unable to speak, beshatten, and all scratched up by the claws of that notable cat Bacon-Eater, couldn't stop laughing, and said:

"What are you going to do with that cat?"

"This cat?" answered Panurge. "Devil take me if I didn't think it was a furry little devil, which I'd snatched out of the great bread bin of hell down there, just as it was sneaking away, and using my stocking like a glove. Let the damned thing go to the devil! He's ripped up my skin like fancy lacework."

And then he threw the cat down.

"Go," said Pantagruel, "go, for God's sake, and get a hot bath, clean yourself, get a grip on yourself, find a clean shirt and make yourself presentable!"

"Are you saying," answered Panurge, "that I was afraid? Not a bit of it. By all that's holy, I'm braver than if I'd swallowed all the flies ever put into pies in Paris, from Saint John's Day in June to All Saints' Day in November. Ha, ha, ha! Hooray! What devil is this, anyway? Do you call this stuff right here diarrhea, crap, dung, shit, turds, bowel leavings, fecal matter, excrement, ordure, droppings, bird lime, slop, offal, dried-up diarrhea, or goat shit? Ho, ho, hey! It's Spanish saffron, by God! Damned right! So let's drink!"

End of the Fourth Book
of the heroic words and deeds
of our noble Pantagruel

The Fifth and Last Book
of the Heroic Deeds
and Words of
Our Good Pantagruel

Composed by

Maître François Rabelais

Doctor of Medicine

Containing the Visit to the Oracle of
the Divine Bottle, and What the
Bottle Said, Which Prophetic
Utterance Was the Entire Purpose of
This Long Journey

MAÎTRE FRANÇOIS RABELAIS' PROLOGUE

for the Fifth Book of Pantagruel's Heroic Words and Deeds

To My Kindly Readers

HIGH AND MIGHTY GUZZLERS, and you, O all you precious pox-ridden—while you have the leisure and I have nothing else more important to do, let me ask you a question: why does everybody say, as if it were proverbially true, that the world is no longer flat? Understand, please, that "flat" here means "without zest, unsalted, insipid, washed-out": taking it metaphorically, it signifies "crazy, foolish, senseless, rot-brained." Would you argue, as indeed one might logically infer, that if we say that the world has been flat, now we have to say that it's become wise? What was it that made it flat? Why was it flat? Why should it be wise? What do you think ancient stupidity was? What do you think constitutes our present wisdom? What made it flat? What has made it wise? Are there more lovers of flatness or more lovers of wisdom? Just exactly when was it flat? Just exactly when was it wise? Who's responsible for that earlier flatness? Who's responsible for that later wisdom? Why did that ancient flatness end right now, and not at some other time? Why did our present wisdom begin right now, and not sooner? What harm did our earlier flatness do us? What good is this new wisdom? How did we get rid of our ancient flatness? How was our present wisdom brought about?

Answer me, if you want to: I'll make no more urgent appeal to Your Reverences, for fear of making Your Holinesses angry (or thirsty). But don't be shy, let's make my lord the devil, eternal enemy of heaven, and of truth, confess everything. Courage, my boys! If you're really with me, take three drinks, or five, for the first part of the sermon, and then answer my question. If you're on the other side, get thee behind me, Satan! Because I swear my warmest oath: if you won't help me solve this problem, pretty soon I'm going to be sorry I asked you in the first place. Indeed, I'm already sorry. Anyway, I'm in the same difficulty as a man who has a wolf by the ears, and knows no one will help him.

What's that? I quite understand: you don't feel like answering. Well, by my beard, I won't, either—but I will quote to you what a terribly

learned old pedant foresaw, with his prophetic spirit—namely, the author
of *The Bishops' Bagpipes*. What does he say, the rascal? Listen, you donkey
pricks, listen:

> The year of the Jubilee, when they all go wild
> And shave their heads, has now arrived
> For the thirtieth time. These churchmen glow
> With prayers, which only *seem* unknowing
> And flat: their panting psalms will pluck
> Spring fruit that spring was afraid of, but luck
> And determined greed will get to suck.

Ah, you've heard it—but have you really understood? Our author is a
very old philosopher, his language is spare, his meaning medieval and
obscure. Although he deals with intrinsically profound and difficult matters, the best commentators have read our good father's words to mean
that the thirtieth time will now yield to the thirty-first, and in this year
of our Lord one thousand five hundred and fifty the pope will bless us
with another Jubilee. And we won't have to worry about these springtime flowers. The world will never be flat again, but forever vernal. Fools,
whose number is infinite (as Solomon assures us), will die of their folly,
and all foolishness will disappear—and there are infinite fashions of foolishness, as Avicenna declares: *maniae infinitae sunt species*. Harsh winter
made folly shrink, but when sap ascends in trees, folly too blossoms forth.
But you see all this in action: you know it, you understand it. And it was
all treated by that great and good man Hippocrates, in his *Aphorisms:
Verae etenim maniae*, Truly in the spring, etc. As the world thus grows
wiser, it will have less and less fear of bean flowers bursting out in the
spring—that is (as you, with a glass in your hand and tears in your eyes,
will of course with due piety readily credit), in Lent, when a pile of books
may seem to be blossoming, blooming, bloomed like lovely butterflies,
but is really as boring, irritating, dangerous—prickly, impossible to
understand—as Heraclitus—as obscure as Pythagoras and his numbers
(he who was king of beans, according to Horace). Those kinds of books
will disappear, no one will ever see them again, or read them. Such was
their destiny, such their predestined end.

Instead, we'll have beans in the pod—that is, joyous, fruitful Pantagruelistic books, since the word has gotten around that they sell well
(while we're waiting for the coming Jubilee), and everyone is poring over
them, which is how the world got to be called wise. So there's your
problem, all solved and resolved—there's the highroad to true importance. So clear your throat and let's do some serious drinking, since the
vines are thick with grapes and the usurers are hanging themselves: I'll
lose a lot of rope, if the good weather lasts, because I swear I'll give them
all the rope they need, and free of charge, just as long as they feel like

hanging themselves: just think of how much gets saved in executioner's fees.

But to participate in this coming wisdom, and free yourself of all old folly, you've got to do this for me, and right now: erase from the pages of ancient philosophical law all mention of Pythagoras and his golden thigh, he who forbade you to use and consume beans. All good fellows and drinkers are to hold it as an undoubted article of truth that his interdiction was meant just as the late Amer (nephew of the lawyer lord of Camelotière), that freshwater doctor, meant his forbidding his patients to dine on partridge wings, chicken tails, and pigeon necks, saying, *Ala mala, croppium dubium, colum bonum pelle remota,* Wings are bad, tails are doubtful, but the neck is all right if you remove the skin—by which proscription he saved those delicacies for himself and left his patients only the bones to gnaw on. And there are monks walking in his footsteps, forbidding us eat beans—that is, to read Pantagruelistic books—just as Philoxenus and Gnatho, the ancient founders of their monastic and belly-oriented orgies, whenever they were at table and served some delicious morsel, would spit on their food, so that others might be too revolted to eat it. These hideous, snot-nosed, mucous-filled, worm-eaten hypocrites loathe fresh new books, both in public and in private, and in their impudence spit disgustingly all over them. And although we now read many excellent books in our Gallic language, written both in verse and in prose, and few relics of the hypocritical Gothic age remain, I've still chosen to cackle and hiss like a goose among swans (as the proverb says), rather than be silent in the midst of so many noble poets and fine orators, just as I'd rather play the part of a country bumpkin among all the high-spoken actors who strut this noble stage of ours, rather than be set among those who only serve in the shadows, mere ciphers, fit just to gape at flies, pricking up their ears like Arcadian asses when the music begins, indicating simply by their silence that they agree with everything being said.

Having made that choice, I thought it wouldn't be particularly shameful to roll my Diogenic barrel along, just so you wouldn't be tempted to say I conducted myself without any reliable guides.

Indeed, I've considered a huge pile of literary exemplars—like Colinet, Morot, Drouet, Saint-Gelais, Salel, Massuau, and a whole long century of such Gallic poets and orators. And I see that, after years spent on Mount Parnassus, in the school of Apollo, drinking deep at the Caballine fountain along with the joyous Muses, all they bring to the eternal fabric of this vulgar tongue of ours is Paros marble, and alabaster, and porphyry, and good royal cement, just as all they ever write about is heroic deeds, great doings, and complex, serious, and difficult subjects, all written about in a polished, subtle silk style; all their writings ever produce is divine nectar, precious wine—delicious, sparkling, flavorful, delicate, delightful. Nor is this glory confined to male writers, for women, too, have shared in it, one of whom also shares the royal blood of France, and whose name cannot be mentioned here without insult—a woman who has astonished this entire century, quite as much by her imaginative invention as by her decorative language, her miraculous style. Write like them, if you know how to; as for me, I know I can't: it isn't granted to everyone to dwell in Corinth. When Solomon built his temple, it wasn't possible for everyone to donate a gold shekel. Since we cannot design buildings as beautiful as theirs, I've decided to imitate Renaud de Montauban and do what I can to help the masons—keep their cooking pot boiling—and if I cannot be their equal, at least they'll have me as an audience, and an indefatigable audience, for their heavenly writings.

Go die of fear, you carping, jealous critics: go hang yourselves—and pick your own trees, for there'll be no shortage of rope. I hereby declare, right in front of my Mount Helicon, and in the presence of all the divine Muses, that if I live to be an old dog, plus the span of three crows, and in the kind of good health enjoyed by Moses (that saintly Jewish general), or by the musician Xenophilus, or the philosopher Demonax, I will prove by pointed, irrefutable arguments, and right in the face of all the hopeless copying hacks, bottlers of vintages reworked a hundred hundred times before, hiccoughers of old Latin scraps, patchers and mongers of mildewed, half-incomprehensible old Latin phrases, that our French language is neither so vile, so incompetent, so beggarly, nor so contemptible as they think it. And just as, once, Phoebus Apollo divided all his treasures among the great poets, leaving Aesop the task of creating his fables, so too I beg in all humility for just that special grace, for like Aesop I aspire to nothing higher: let me be granted, like Pyricus, the post of journeyman painter of common objects. Our great poets will be that gracious, I know they will, for they're as kind, and humane, and generous, and good-natured as anyone could be. Which is why, my drinking friends— and why, all you guzzlers—you like to enjoy books like this to the very last drop. You can quote them to each other, whenever you meet, honoring the deep mysteries to be found in these pages, and come to participate in their high and remarkable reputation—just as, very similarly, Alexander the Great drew on the books of that primal philosopher Aristotle.

Belly to belly! What guzzling swizzlers! What rascals, what lechers!

But all the same, my drinking friends, let me warn you, while the time is right: lay in a good supply of them as fast as you can, and just as soon as you find them on sale in the shops—and don't just turn the pages, but devour them like some heart-warming draught, and incorporate them bodily: that's how you'll learn what goodness is waiting, here, for all noble bean shellers. Here it is: I offer you a fine basketful, picked in the same garden as those I brought you before, begging you most courteously to accept my gift with a smile, while you wait for the better beans the swallows are sure to bring, the next time they appear.

Chapter One // How Pantagruel Came to Ringing Island, and the Noise We Heard There

Continuing on our way, we sailed for three days without finding anything. But on the fourth we sighted land, and were told by our pilot that this was Ringing Island. From a great distance we could hear a noise, frequent and loud, which to our ears sounded like bells—small, large, and in-between—all ringing together, as on feast days at Paris, Tours, Jargeau, Medon, and other cities, and the closer we drew, the louder this ringing became.

We wondered if this might be Dodona, with its holy kettles, or the seven-echoed portal of Olympus, or perhaps the perpetual din of the Colossus built over Memnon's tomb, at Thebes, in Egypt, or the unholy racket that at one time could be heard around a certain tomb on the island of Lipara, in the Aeolides, but the geography was all wrong.

"I wonder," said Pantagruel, "if some swarm of bees suddenly decided to take to the air, and to bring them back everyone in the neighborhood began this banging on pots, kettles, basins, this corybantic, Cybelian bashing worthy of the mother of all the gods. Listen."

Coming closer still, we could make out, amid the perpetual din of the bells, an unending chant that seemed to us to be coming from the residents of the place. And so, before we reached Ringing Island, Pantagruel was of the opinion that we ought to get into our little skiff and disembark on a small rock, on which we could make out a hermit's hut, surrounded by a little garden.

There we found a small old man, a hermit named Dandyboy, from Glenay, who explained to us in detail what all the bell ringing was about, and entertained us in a very strange fashion. He made us fast for four consecutive days, insisting that otherwise we would not be allowed onto Ringing Island, this being their feast of the Four Seasons.

"Now this," said Panurge, "is a puzzle I simply don't understand. It looks more like the season of the four winds, because when we fast, that's all we'll have in our bellies. Is fasting your only entertainment? It strikes me as pretty feeble amusement: we could do very nicely without such fast feasting."

"In my Latin grammar," said Brother John, "there are only three seasons, or temporal periods: past, present, and future. This fourth one must be the waiter's tip."

"It's the aorist, or uncertain, tense," said Epistemon, "drawn from the past highly imperfect, used by the Greeks and the Romans to deal with war and other strange times. But patience cures all things, as the lepers say."

"As I've told you," said the hermit, "it's a mortal matter: anyone who opposes it is a heretic, and there's nothing for him but the fire."

"When I'm at sea, father," said Panurge, "I'm always more afraid of getting wet than hot, and of being drowned rather than burned. So let's fast, then, by God! But I've already been fasting for so long that it's eaten off all my flesh: I'm worried that, pretty soon, the whole structure of my body's going to collapse. And another thing that worries me is that my fasting might offend you, because I don't know anything about it, and many people have told me I don't do it very well, and I think they're right. Not that fasting bothers me: it's easy enough to do, God knows! I worry a lot more about having to fast some time again, because you can't make clothes without cloth, and when you go to the mill you've got to bring grain with you. So let's fast, by God, since we got here at a fast season: it's been long enough since I've seen anything like it."

"If we have to fast," said Pantagruel, "and there's no help for it, let's get it over with—like a stretch of rough road. I wouldn't mind spending some time with my papers, to see if studying at sea is as good as studying on land. When Plato wanted to describe a fool—someone incompetent, ignorant—he'd say he was like a man brought up at sea, on board ship, just as we speak of a man brought up in a barrel, who's seen the world only through a bunghole."

Our fasting was terrible, frightful: the first day we fasted on broken sticks; the second, on cracked swords; the third, on sharp steel; and the fourth day, on fire and blood. That was how fate and destiny had decreed it.

Chapter Two ⁄⁄ How Ringing Island Had Once Been Inhabited by Funereal Singers, Who Turned Into Birds

When our fasting was done, the hermit gave us a letter of introduction, addressed to a man named Abihen Camar, or Pagan Preacher, who was the sexton of Ringing Island, but Panurge, as he greeted him, called him Maître Antitus (or Fool). He was a little old man, bald, with a bright red nose and a crimson complexion. We were pleasantly received, on the hermit's recommendation, he having explained that we had done our fasting. After we had dined extremely well, the sexton carefully explained the island's peculiarities for us, noting that the first inhabitants had been Funereal Singers, but since it is nature's law that everything changes, these original inhabitants had become birds. At which point I was abundantly enlightened about everything written about these Funereal Singers, whether by Ateius Capito, Julius Pollux, Marcellus, Aulus Gellius,

Athenaeus, Suidas, Ammonius, or by others, nor did it seem to us hard to believe in the transformations experienced by Nyctimeme, Procne, Itys, Halcyone, Antigone, Tereus, and other bird folk. Nor had we any doubts about Matabrune's children, who were changed into swans, or the men of Pallene, in Thrace, who, after they had bathed nine times in the Tritonic lake, were suddenly transformed into birds.

But after this he was only interested in talking about cages and birds. The cages were large, rich, gorgeously designed and crafted. The birds themselves were big, beautiful, and elegant, very like the men of my country, eating and drinking like men, shitting like men; they farted and slept and screwed like men—in short, at first sight you'd have had to say they were men, and yet, according to the sexton, they weren't men at all, for he insisted they were neither secular nor in any way worldly. And their plumage made us wonder, some of them being entirely white, others completely black, or gray, or half white and half black, or bright red, or part white and part blue: indeed, they were exceedingly good to look at. He called the males clergyhawks, monkhawks, preacherhawks, abbothawks, bishophawks, cardinalhawks, and popehawks—the last-named being a rare and unique animal. He called the females clergytits, monktits, preachertits, abbesstits, bishoptits, cardinaltits, and popetits. Just as among the bees, he told us, the drones do nothing but eat and ruin everything in sight, so too for three hundred years these joyous birds— for who knows what reason—had been afflicted by an immense influx of winged hypocrites, who regularly flew in every fifth month, disgracing and shitting up the whole island—hypocrite birds so hideous, so monstrous, that everyone tried to get away from them. They all had twisted necks, hairy paws, claws and bellies like harpies, shit-covered asses—and it's impossible to get rid of them, since for each one you kill, twenty-four more come flying in. I found myself longing for some second Hercules; Brother John was half out of his mind with violent thoughts; and as for Pantagruel, the same thing happened to him as happened to My Lord Priapus, watching Ceres' naked devotees sacrificing to their goddess—he half choked with laughter.

Chapter Three // Why Ringing Island Has Only One Popehawk

Then we asked the sexton why, considering how these venerable birds multiplied and flourished, there was only one popehawk. He answered that this was the primal law, predestined by fate. He told us that the preacherhawks and monkhawks were born of the clergyhawks, but without any carnal mingling, just as Aristaeus' magic arts produced bees from a young bull. The preacherhawks gave birth to the bishophawks; the bishophawks spawned the lovely cardinalhawks; and unless they died first, the cardinalhawks ended by becoming the popehawk—of which, ordinarily, there is only one, just as in beehives there is only one king, and the world has just one sun. When the popehawk dies, another one is born from among the whole brood of cardinalhawks, but of course without any carnal copulation. Thus this species is composed of one unique individual, perpetually constituted, exactly like the Arabian phoenix. It must be admitted that, around the time of the two thousand seven hundred and sixtieth moon, nature did produce two popehawks, but this was the greatest disaster they'd ever seen on the island.

"You see," said the sexton, "all of these birds are forever stealing from each other, and during that time they fought so long and so hard that the island was in real danger of depopulation. Some of them followed one popehawk, and gave him all their support; some followed the other popehawk, and defended him; some of them became as silent as fish and never sang a note, and some of the bells might as well have been forbidden to ring, for they never made a sound. During this time of high treason they called for help from all the emperors, kings, dukes, monarchs, counts, barons, and all the republics everywhere in the world, and until one of the popehawks left this life there was no end to the schism and the treason, and plurality could not be returned to unity."

Then we asked why these birds sang so incessantly. The sexton answered that this was because of the bells hung above their cages. Then he said:

"You see those monkhawks, draped with hoods that look like wine strainers—those savage larks over there? Would you like me to make them sing?"

"Please," we replied.

Then he rang a bell exactly six times, and the monkhawks came running up and began to sing.

"Now suppose," said Panurge, "I rang this bell over here; would I make those birds sing—the ones with plumage like red herrings?"

"Indeed," answered the sexton.

Panurge rang the bell, and the well-smoked birds came running right up and began to sing, but they had harsh voices that sounded terrible. The sexton also told us that they lived exclusively on fish, like ravens and herons in our world, mentioning that they were a fifth variety of hypocrite bird, newly printed. And he added, moreover, that he had heard from Robert Valbringue, newly returned from a voyage to Africa, that soon a sixth variety would be flying in, called capuchinhawks, and these were grimmer, more maniacal, and altogether fiercer than anything the island had yet seen.

"Africa," said Pantagruel, "always produces new and monstrous things."

Chapter Four // Why the Birds on Ringing Island Are All Migrants

"Now," said Pantagruel, "since you've told us how the popehawk is born from among the cardinalhawks, and the cardinalhawks from the bishophawks, and the bishophawks from the preacherhawks, and the preacherhawks from the clergyhawks, I should like to know where the clergyhawks come from."

"They're all birds of passage," said the sexton, "and come to us from the other world. Some come from a great and wonderful country, called Breadless; some come from another land, toward the west, called Just-toomany. These clergyhawks come to us, year after year, from these two countries, leaving their fathers and mothers, and all their friends and relations. It's exactly like what happens in some noble house, when there are too many children, no matter whether male or female: if all of them had a share of the family heritage (as reason requires, nature directs, and God commands) there would soon be nothing left and the family line would come to an end. Which is why their families unload them onto Boussard—that is, Humpback—Island."

"I beg your pardon," said Pantagruel, "but don't you mean Bouchard Island, near Chinon?"

"I said Boussard, or Humpback Island," said the sexton, "because that's usually what they are: humpbacked, one-eyed, lame, one-armed, gout-ridden, deformed, and ugly—just heavy weights lying across the land."

"But this," said Pantagruel, "is a total departure from the rules and regulations that, once upon a time, governed the process of admitting vestal virgins. As Labeo Antistius tells us, it was forbidden to select a girl for this honor if there was any corruption in her soul, or if any of her senses were deficient, or if her body had the slightest blemish of any sort, no matter how small or how well hidden."

"I'm surprised," said the sexton, "that the mothers of that country carry them in their wombs for nine months, because they can't stand having them in their houses for nine years, and more often not even seven. They just put a white robe on them, and then they chop I don't know how much hair from their heads and mumble some magically protective words—the way the Egyptians consecrated the priests of Isis, using white robes and cutting their hair, in a visible, perceptible, manifest Phythago-rean metempsychosis: not cutting or breaking the skin in any way, but turning them into the sort of birds you can see right here in front of you. All the same, my good friends, I don't really know how it happens, or if it ought to happen, that the females (whether they're clergytits, monktits, or abbesstits) don't sing the kind of pleasant, grateful hymns that used to be sung, at Zoroaster's own orders, to the good spirit Ormazd. No, instead they sing curses and laments to the daemon Ahriman, and—no matter how young or how old they are—they rain imprecations down on the heads of their family and friends, who had them transformed into birds.

"Most of them come to us from Breadless, which is extraordinarily large, and immensely crowded. And when the inhabitants of that country are in danger of starving to death, having nothing whatever to eat, they neither know how to do anything nor wish to—no working away at some decent trade or profession, no swearing faithful service to some wealthy and powerful man. Some of them, too, have been disappointed in love; some have failed in business and are desperate; and there are some who have wickedly committed crimes and are being hunted down, so they can be put to death—and they all come flying here, all of them: here they find a place made for them, here they suddenly become as fat as dormice, though they used to be as skinny as magpies: here they enjoy perfect safety, security, and freedom."

"But," asked Pantagruel, "once these handsome birds have flown here, do they ever return to the world where they were hatched?"

"Some of them," answered the sexton. "It used to be only a very few, and they flew back only very late in life, and with great reluctance. But certain eclipses have lately occurred, and since then a whole flock of them has flown back, motivated by these celestial reconfigurations. Nor does their going make us particularly unhappy: it just leaves more for those who remain. Before they fly back, they all shed their plumage, leaving it in the nettles and thornbushes."

We actually found some of these discarded feathers, and as we hunted about we also turned up a pot of roses and solved some mysteries.

Chapter Five ⁄⁄ On Ringing Island, Greedy Bird Knights Don't Sing

He had just finished speaking, when twenty-five or thirty birds flew up to us, their color and plumage unlike any we had yet seen on the island. Indeed, their plumage was continually changing, like a chameleon's skin or the tripolium and teucicum flowers. And under the left wing they all had a mark, like either a pair of diameters crisscrossing a circle or one straight line perpendicularly intersecting another. They were all shaped alike, and of one size, but not of one color, some being white, some green, others red, violet, or blue.

"Who are these," asked Pantagruel, "and what are their names?"

"They're hybrids," answered the sexton. "We call them greedy bird knights, and in your world they have a lot of splendid greedy houses."

"Please," I said, "make them sing a bit, so we can hear their voices."

"They don't sing," he answered, "ever. But to make up for that, they eat twice as much."

"But where are the females?" I asked.

"They have none," he replied.

"Then why," wondered Panurge, "are they all scabby and mangy with the pox?"

"That," he said, "is the way this species looks, because sometimes they go to sea."

And then he told us why they'd come over to us.

"This one, right near you, wants to see if he can find among you a certain species of hawk, fearsome birds of prey, but not the kind of hawk that will be seduced by a falconer's lure or fly to his glove, as they're said to do in your world. Some of those hawks wear, strapped to their legs, a rare and precious leather band, on which is inscribed *Qui mal y pensera,* Whoever may think evil of this—the punishment for which thinking is to be swiftly and thoroughly covered with shit. And there are other such hawks who carry on their breasts a sign of their great victory over the devil; and some wear a ram's fleece."

"That may be," said Panurge, "but we don't know anything about them."

"But that's enough talk," said the sexton. "Now let's drink."

"And eat," said Panurge.

"Eat," said the sexton, "and drink well, too—double or nothing, half on credit, for nothing is so expensive, or so precious, as time. So let's use it for good works."

Then he wanted to take us, first, to bathe in the cardinalhawks' luxurious, supremely delightful baths, after which the bath slaves would anoint us with precious balms. Pantagruel told him, however, that he'd drink too much even without such ceremonies. So he led us directly to a sumptuous, delicious meal, saying:

"The hermit Dandyboy made you fast for four days, so to balance that out we'll spend the next four days here, eating and drinking without ever stopping."

"Will we stop to sleep?" said Panurge.

"As you please," answered the sexton, "for sleepers are drinking, too."

My God, what a time we had! Oh, what a magnificent fellow!

Chapter Six // How the Birds on Ringing Island Are Fed

Pantagruel made a long face, obviously not happy to spend the four days prescribed for us by the sexton, and the sexton, seeing this, said:

"My lord, you know that, for seven days before the shortest day of the year, and for seven days afterward, there are never any storms at sea. This is a kindness which the elements show to the Halcyons, birds sacred to Thetis, who lay their eggs at just this season and hatch them right along the shore. And then the sea makes up for this long calm and, whenever voyagers arrive, is furiously stormy for four days without interruption. We think these outbursts occur because travelers are thus obliged to stay here and be wined and dined, courtesy the moneys we make from ringing our bells. So don't think your time here is wasted. It is superior force which detains you on our island. Unless you'd like to fight Juno, Neptune, Doris, Aeolus, and all the gods who warred against Jupiter, just make up your minds to have a jolly time."

After the first course, Brother John asked the sexton:

"All you have on this island are cages and birds. No one works, no one cultivates the earth. All they do is amuse themselves, and chirp and sing. How did you acquire this magical horn of plenty—all the things you own, all the delicious food you eat?"

"It comes to us," answered the sexton, "from the whole rest of the world, except for a few northern countries which some years ago made the mistake of stirring up their cesspools. Hey,

> But they'll be sorry, they will,
> They'll be sorry, they will, they will.

"Drink up, my friends!

"But tell me: where do you come from?"

"From Touraine," answered Panurge.

"Ah," said the sexton, "you were never hatched by an evil magpie, since you're from that blessed land of Touraine. We get so many good things from Touraine, year after year, that some of your people, happening to pass through here, once told us that, for all his income, the duke of Touraine didn't have enough left to fill his belly with bacon, because of the tremendous bounty his predecessors bestowed on these sacrosanct birds, so we on this island can stuff ourselves with partridges, grouse, pheasants, fat Loudunoys capons, all kinds of venison, and other game. Drink up, my friends! See the birds on this perch, how plump and fine they are, and all from the moneys Touraine sends us—and they sing beautifully for them, too. You'll never find nightingales warbling any better than these birds—oh, what a clamor they make—when they see those two gold staffs."

"A regular saints' parade," said Brother John.

"Or when I ring these big bells, which you can see hanging around their cages. Drink up, my friends! It's a lovely day for drinking—but every day's a lovely day for drinking. Drink. I drink to you with a good heart: you're very welcome. Don't worry for a moment that food and wine will ever run out—not here: let the heavens turn to brass, and the earth to iron, but we'll never lack for anything, even for seven years— even for eight! And the famine in Egypt never lasted that long. Let's drink together, in sincere friendship."

"By all the devils!" exclaimed Panurge. "What an easy time you have of it in this world."

"And in the other," replied the sexton, "we'll have it still better. For us, it'll be the Elysian Fields, at least. Drink up, my friends: I drink to you."

"What a divine, not to say a perfect, idea," I said, "your founders had, to imagine a life like this, a life which lets you have what all human beings naturally want and few—or none, strictly speaking—ever enjoy. And that is paradise in this life and also in the next one.

> O happy people! Half divine!
> I would to God that this were mine."

Chapter Seven ⁄ Panurge Tells the Sexton the Fable of the Horse and the Donkey

After we had eaten and drunk exceedingly well, the sexton brought us to a handsomely furnished room, beautifully tapestried, elaborately gilded. He had them bring us plums, balm, and green ginger sweets, with cordials and all the delicious wine we could drink, and invited us, by means of these medicinal measures, as if we had drunk of the waters of Lethe, to forget all the weariness and boredom we had suffered at sea. And he also had an abundance of food sent to our ships, which had by then sailed into the harbor. So we rested there, that night, but the endless tintinnabulation of the bells kept me from sleeping.

The sexton came to wake us at midnight, so we could drink, and he himself took the first cup, saying:

"You people from the other world say that ignorance is the mother of all evil, and you're right, but you never get her out of your heads: you'll live in her, with her, by her. And that's why so many misfortunes afflict you, day after day. You're always complaining, always lamenting; you're never satisfied. I can see it right now. It's ignorance which ties you down in your beds, as Vulcan's metal-making art once tied down the god of war; nor do you understand that your duty was to hold back from sleep but not to hold back from the good things available on this glorious island. You should already have eaten three meals—and take it from me, you have to get up early in the morning, to eat here on Ringing Island. If you eat, there's always more; if you don't, there's less. Mow your meadow when it's ready: the grass will grow back even thicker, and you'll make better use of it. If you don't mow it, before very long you'll just have a field full of moss. Drink up, my friends, let's all drink up. The very leanest of our birds are singing just for you: let's drink to them. Let's drink once, twice, thrice nine times, *non zelus, sed charitas,* not out of zeal, but out of charity."

At daybreak, once again he woke us, so we could make a hearty breakfast of hearty soup. It was really all one continuous meal, lasting the entire day, nor did we know what was dinner, or supper, or whether we were snacking or helping to bring in the New Year. Simply to amuse ourselves, we took walks around the island, to see the sights and hear the happy singing of those blessed birds.

That night, Panurge said to the sexton:

"You won't be annoyed, my lord, if I tell you a happy story, one that took place in Poitou some twenty-three months ago. One April morning, a gentleman's stableman was walking his master's great battle horse through the fields. He chanced to meet a gay shepherdess, who

> was watching over her lambs,
> deep in the shade of a bush

—and with the lambs, she had a donkey and some goats. After a little chat, he talked her into climbing up behind him, to visit his stable for a rustic snack. While they were discussing these matters, the horse spoke to the donkey, whispering in his ear—because that year, all over the world, animals talked:

" 'You poor, miserable donkey, I feel intensely sorry for you. You work hard every day—I can tell by how worn your ass harness has gotten. But that's all right, since God created you to work for human beings. You're an honest donkey. But not to be better rubbed down than I can see you are, and better curried, and better fed, and with a better harness—that seems to me a bit tyrannical, not to say unreasonable. You're as spiky as a hedgehog, you're quite exhausted, your hide's half peeled away, and all you get to eat is reeds and thorns and tough thistles. Which is why, my donkey friend, I advise you to trot along behind me and see how we others, meant by nature for war, are treated and fed. You'll get a taste of what I have every single day.'

" 'Oh yes,' answered the donkey, 'I'll be glad to go with you, Mister Horse.'

" 'Donkey,' said the battle horse, 'I'm *Mister* Battle Horse, to the likes of you.'

" 'Please excuse me,' replied the donkey, 'Mister Battle Horse. We rural, rustic animals don't always speak properly, I know; we're not very well educated. But believe me, I'm glad to do exactly as you say, and I'll stay most respectfully a few steps behind you, since you've done me the honor to invite me. I don't want any more beatings—my hide's all striped from them as it is.'

"So the shepherdess climbed up, and the donkey trotted along behind the horse, intending to eat well when they got to his stable. But seeing the donkey, the stableman ordered the grooms to take a pitchfork to him and give him a good sound beating. Understanding what they said, the donkey said a prayer to Neptune and scampered out of there as fast as he could, thinking to himself, 'He's perfectly right: I've got no business with these great lords. Nature meant me just to help poor people. In one of his fables, Aesop gave me fair warning. This was presumptuous, and the only cure for it is to get away with a smile, and faster than they can cook asparagus.' And the donkey trotted, and farted, and jumped, and kicked, and galloped, and then farted some more.

"Seeing the donkey chased away, the shepherdess told the stableman that the animal was hers and asked that he be well treated, or else she'd leave without even entering his quarters. So the stableman exclaimed that he'd rather see every one of the horses go for eight days without oats, then not let the donkey stuff his belly. The hardest part, however, was to get the donkey to come back, though the stableboys coaxed him, calling, 'Hey, donkey, donkey, come here, donkey.'

" 'I'm not coming,' said the donkey. 'I'm too shy.'

"The nicer they called to him, the more he skittered away, kicking and jumping and farting up a storm. And they'd still be at it, if the shepherdess hadn't told them to sieve some oats high up in the air, as they were calling him, which they did, and just as quickly the donkey wheeled around, saying, 'Ah ha—now it's oats they owe me, instead of a pitchfork. Well, I'm not *that* shy: you won't catch me passing.' So he ran back to them, singing melodiously as he came—and you know how good it is to hear the music of Arcadian animals.

"As soon as he got there, they led him into the stable, next to the horse, and he was rubbed down, dried, curried; they gave him fresh litter up to his belly, filled the hayrack to the brim, stuffed his feedbag full of oats—but as the stableboys sieved it out, he pricked up his ears at them, as if to say he'd eat perfectly well without any sieving and he didn't deserve too much fussing over.

"When they'd eaten their fill, the horse questioned the donkey:

" 'And now, my poor donkey, how do you feel, eh? What do you think of treatment like this? And you didn't want to come! What do you say now?'

" 'By the fig,' answered the donkey, 'that one of my ancestors ate, at the sight of which Philomenes died of laughter, this is sheer heaven, Mister Battle Horse. But still, it's only half what I want. Don't you ever do any frisking around here, you and the other horsey gentlemen?'

" 'What kind of frisking are you talking about, donkey?' asked the horse. 'May your long ears drop off, you ass! Do you think I'm at all like you?'

" 'Ha, ha!' the donkey replied. 'It's a little hard for me to learn the courteous language you horses use. What I asked was this: Don't you ever do horse battle, you dignified battle horses?'

" 'Be quiet, you donkey,' said the horse. 'If the stableboys hear you, they'll give you such whacks with the pitchfork that you'll lose all interest in frisking around. We don't dare stiffen even the tip of it, just to urinate, for fear of being beaten—but except for that, we live like kings.'

" 'By the packsaddle I wear on my back,' said the donkey, 'I disown you, and I say fie on your straw litter! fie on your hay! and fie on your oats, too! Long live the thistles in the fields—because out there you can at least have fun frisking around: eat less and frisk every chance you get, that's what I always say. For us, that's all the hay and oats we need. O Mister Battle Horse, my friend, if we'd just run into you at a fair, when we hold our regular meetings, how we'd have set about frisking, while our mistresses were busy selling their fish and onions!'

"And so they separated. And that's my story."

At which Panurge stopped talking and didn't say another word. Pantagruel urged him to finish his argument, but the sexton answered:

"A word to the wise: I understand perfectly what you mean by this fable about donkeys and horses—but how shy *you* are. But understand, please, that there's nothing here for you—and let's not say another word about it."

"All the same," said Panurge, "I just saw an abbesstit with white feathers, who'd be a lot better for riding than for leading by the hand. And if all the others are good game birds, then by God she seems to me a good bird for games. She's a plump, pleasant pheasant, well worth a sin or two. But God forgive me—I'm not thinking of any deviltry: I just like that kind of wickedness."

Chapter Eight // How Hard It Was, Getting to See the Popehawk

The third day, we went on feasting just exactly as we had the two days before. That day, Pantagruel made an urgent request to see the popehawk, but the sexton answered that it wasn't easy to get to see him.

"Why?" said Pantagruel. "Does he have Pluto's invisibility helmet on his head, or on his claws the ring that made Gyges unseeable, or does he carry a chameleon on his breast, to keep himself unseen?"

"No," answered the sexton, "but in the nature of things he's rather hard to see. But perhaps I can arrange it."

Having said this, he left us to our dining. He came back fifteen minutes later, saying that at that hour the popehawk would indeed be visible. Then he led us, softly and silently, directly to the cage where, along with two little cardinalhawks and six great big bishophawks, the popehawk was crouching. Panurge stood carefully considering his body, his gestures, and his bearing. Then he said in a very loud voice:

"The devil take him, with that tiara he looks like a hoopoe."

"Speak softly, by God," said the sexton. "He has ears—as Michel de Macon has wisely observed."

"So has a hoopoe," said Panurge.

"If he ever hears you blaspheming like that, good people, you're lost. Do you see that bowl, there in his cage? From that he makes lightning flash, and thunder, too, and devils and storms, all of which will in an instant bury you a hundred feet under the ground."

"Eating and drinking," said Brother John, "would be better."

Panurge continued his fierce contemplation of the popehawk and those around him, and suddenly saw, above the cage, a screech owl. He exclaimed:

"By all that's holy, we're up the creek, now, without a paddle. By God, there's paddling and addling and saddling going on, and more. Just look at that screech owl: by God, we're dead men, all of us."

"More softly, please!" said the sexton. "That's no screech owl. It's a male bird, and a noble treasure guardian."

"Let the popehawk sing to us a little," said Pantagruel, "so we can hear his harmonies."

"He sings," said the sexton, "only according to his own schedule, just as he eats only according to his own schedule."

"Not me," said Panurge. "I'm good for it anytime. So let's go have a drink."

"Ah," said the sexton, "now you're saying the right thing at the right time: that sort of talk will never be heretical. Let's have a drink: I agree.'

As we went back, we saw an old bishophawk with a green head, who was in a cage with three ecclesiastical pelicans—happy birds, all of them sitting and snoring in the shade of an arbor. There was a pretty abbesstit nearby, singing gaily, who pleased us so much that we would have liked to be transformed bodily into living ears, so that we'd lose nothing whatever of her song, being emptied of everything else. Said Panurge:

"That lovely abbesstit's likely to break her head, singing so hard, but that fat, disgusting bishophawk just keeps on snoring. I'll make him sing, too, by the devil."

So he rang a bell that was hanging on the cage, but the harder he rang, the harder the bishophawk snored, and didn't sing a note.

"By God," said Panurge, "you old buzzard, I'll make you sing, one way or another."

So he picked up a big stone, intending to hit him right on the head. But the sexton called out to him:

"My good man, you can beat, strike, kill, even murder all the kings in the world—betray them, poison them, or whatever you please. You can drive the angels out of heaven—and the popehawk will pardon you every bit of it. But don't touch these sacred birds, if you love your lives and all the pleasure and satisfaction you get from them, not to mention the lives of your families and friends, the living and the dead—and those still to be born, for disaster will pursue them, too. Remember that magical bowl."

"I think it would be better," said Panurge, "to go back to eating and drinking."

"He's right," said Brother John. "Seeing these devilish birds just makes us blaspheme, but emptying your bottles and pots just makes us praise God. So let's go drink. Oh, what a lovely word!"

At the end of the third day, having as I've said done our share of drinking, we bade farewell to the sexton. We presented him with a beautiful little Norman knife, which made him happier than Artaxerxes when a peasant gave him a glass of cold water. And he thanked us courteously, sending fresh supplies of all sorts to our ships. He wished us a good voyage and a safe return home, and the success of all we undertook, making us swear, by Holy Father Jupiter, that we'd return by way of his lands. And finally he said to us:

"My friends, be well advised that the world has a lot more balls than it has men. Keep that fact in mind."

Chapter Nine ⁄⁄ How We Landed on Toolmaking Island

After we'd properly stuffed our stomachs, the wind began to blow from behind us, so we raised our main mizzen sail and in less than two days reached Toolmaking Island, which was deserted and without any inhabitants, and there we saw an immense array of trees hung with hoes, axes, tilling forks, scythes, sickles, spades, trowels, hatchets, billhooks, saws, adzes, clipping shears, chisels, tongs, shovels, gimlets, and bitbraces.

And there were also short daggers, daggers, hunting swords, knives, marlinespikes, rapiers, long swords, short swords, scimitars, dueling swords, square swords, and clasp knives.

If you wanted one, all you had to do was shake the tree: they'd drop right down like plums—and what's more, in tumbling to the ground they'd fall into hollow stalks of a reed known as *scabbard,* and there sheathe themselves. You had to be very careful, when they came down, that they didn't fall on your head, or your feet, or any other part of the body, because they fell point first (so they could properly sheathe themselves) and might have inflicted serious wounds. Underneath many other trees I saw other varieties of plants, which grew like spears, pikes, javelins, lances, boar spears, spiked spears, triple-pointed spears, pitchforks, hunting spears—and they grew tall, which allowed them to intersect the trees above them, which is where they found their blades and points, each according to its particular need. And the trees kept the blades ready for their coming, when they would grow tall enough, just as you prepare little children's garments when you plan to take them out of swaddling clothes.

And to keep you, from now on, more respectful of the opinions of Plato, Anaxagoras, and Democritus (no trivial philosophers), note that we thought these trees very like earthly animals, no different from those we knew, having skin, flesh, fat, veins, arteries, ligaments, muscles, cartilage, glands, bones, marrow, body fluids, wombs, brains, and easily recognizable joints, exactly as Theophrastus said they did, but since their heads (that is, their trunks) are underneath them, and their hair (that is, their roots) is in the ground, and their feet (that is, their branches) are up above, they're like a man doing a handstand.

And like you, my poxy friends, whose rheumatic legs and shoulder blades sense the rain and the wind, and clear skies, and all changes in the weather, so too their roots, stalks, saps, and marrow can feel what kind of staff is growing underneath them and prepare proper blades and points. Naturally, everything can make a mistake (except God). Nor is nature herself immune, since even she is capable of producing monstrosities and deformed animals. So too I noted flaws here: one short spear, for example, grew up toward these iron-bearing trees but, in touching the branches, found a broom head instead of an iron point (though it would still do perfectly well for sweeping out chimneys). One pike staff grew onto a pair of scissors, but that would be fine, too, for getting rid of garden caterpillars. One spear staff grew onto a pitchfork, and looked rather hermaphroditic—but who cares? Some harvester will make perfectly good use of it. How splendid it is to believe in God!

As we were returning to our ships, I saw some people or other, behind some sort of bush, doing I don't know what, nor do I know how or why, sharpening some sort of tools, which they kept who knows where and with which they did who knows what.

Chapter Ten ⁄⁄ Pantagruel Reaches the Island of Lying Illusions

Leaving Toolmaking Island, we continued on our way. The next day we arrived at the island of Lying Illusions—really, a kind of ideal re-creation of the wild forest of Fontainebleau, because the soil was so lean that its bones (that is, rocks) stuck right through its skin: sandy, sterile, unhealthy, unpleasant. Our pilot pointed out two small rocks, each carved into cubes with eight equal faces, and so dazzling white that to me they seemed like alabaster, or perhaps snow covered, but he assured us they were dice. Each of them, he said, held six black storeys inhabited by the twenty gambling devils so dreaded in our own country, the largest pairs and combinations among whom he called Box Cars, the smallest Snake Eyes, and those in between Double Five, Double Four, Double Three, and Double Two, with others called Six and Five, Six and Four, Six and Three, Six and Two, Six and One, Five and Four, Five and Three, and so on. Which made me aware that there aren't many gamblers who don't constantly invoke devils. Because as they throw their dice on the table, they call out, with great piety, "Box Cars, my friends" (that is, the largest devil), or "Snake Eyes, baby" (that is, the smallest devil), or "Four and Two, come on, buddies," and so on, invoking the devils by both their first and their last names. And not only invoking them but describing them as their friends and using the most intimate language. Now, it's true these devils don't always come as soon as they're called, but is it their fault? They had to be somewhere else, according to the date and priority of those invoking them. However, it can't be said that they have neither senses nor ears. They've got them, and good ones, let me tell you.

Then he told us that on and around these rocks there have been more smashups, shipwrecks, and lost lives and possessions than have ever been caused by the Syrtes, in Africa, or Scylla and Charybdis, or the Sirens, or Scyllas, or the Harpy Islands, or by all of the whirlpools and chasms in all the seas in the world—indeed, all of them added together. And I had no trouble believing him, remembering as I did that even among the ancient Egyptians the first cube was designated as Neptune, in hiero-glyphic letters, and the number one was assigned to Apollo, two to Diana, seven to Minerva, and so on. And he also told us that on this island there was a flask of Christ's blood, a truly divine thing and most uncommon. When we went ashore, Panurge so devoutly begged it of the rulers of the place that they showed it to us, and with more high ceremony and three times the solemnity exhibited, in Florence, to the manuscript of Justini-an's *Pandects,* or Veronica's holy veil, in Rome. I've never seen so many costly silk wrappings, so many flaming torches and tapers, so many smoking oil lamps, and so many rituals. What they finally showed us was the face of a broiled rabbit.

We saw nothing else that was memorable, there, except Bad Luck's wife, Happy Face, and the shells of two eggs which Leda had long ago laid and hatched, from which shells came Castor and Pollux, the beautiful Helen's brothers. We traded a bit of bread for a piece of these shells. As we were leaving, we bought a bundle of Lying Illusion hats and bonnets, on the resale of which I don't expect we'll make much profit. I suspect those who buy them from us will profit still less.

Chapter Eleven ⁄⁄ How We Passed Spy Hole Island, Home of Grabby Puss, Archduke of Furry Lawcats

After we passed Judgment, yet another deserted island, we also passed Spy Hole Island, where Pantagruel thought we ought not to land, and he was right, for we were arrested there, and made prisoners by the express command of Grabby Puss, archduke of Furry Lawcats, because one of our people tried to sell some of our Lying Illusion hats to a local bailiff.

The Furry Lawcats are singularly horrible, frightening animals. They eat little children and feast on marble stones. Now, you tell me, drinkers, whether or not lying face down on marble doesn't give them snub noses! Their fur doesn't grow outward, but inward. Their symbol is an open purse, but they don't all wear it in the same way: some tie it to a scarf, around their necks; others wear it on their tails; some have it hanging across their bellies, or along their sides—and they all have their reasons, but none of them ever tell what it is. They also have such long, fierce, steel-tipped claws that nothing ever escapes them, once it's in their grip. Some of them wear square-shaped hats, with four spouts or four cod-pieces; others wear their hats backward, or wear black mortar caps, or mortarboard capes.

As we entered their den, a street beggar to whom we'd given a coin said:

"Good people, may God grant that you come right out of there, safe and sound. Take a good hard look at the faces of these bold robbers, flying buttresses of Grabby Pussish justice. And keep in mind that if you live another six Olympiads, plus the ages of two dogs, you'll find these Furry Lawcats the lords of all Europe and peaceful possessors of all its property, real and personal, unless this unjustly acquired money and wealth simply wastes away for their heirs. Listen to an honest beggar's words. For these hypersubtle creatures, the ruling principle is the Sixth Essence, according to which they grab everything, devour everything, and shit on everything: they burn, smash, decapitate, murder, imprison, ruin, and undermine everything, without the slightest discrimination between good and evil. Among them, "vice" is known as "virtue," "wickedness" is called "goodness," and "treason" is their word for "loyalty"; they call "thievery" "liberality," and robbery is both their slogan and what they do, and everyone except heretics approves—and they always act with sovereign and irrefutable authority.

"As proof of my prediction, notice, please, that the feed troughs, here, have been placed above rather than below the stable racks. Some day you'll remember this. And if ever the world experiences epidemics, famine, or wars, whirlwinds, cataclysms, conflagrations, or any other disasters, don't blame it simply on unfortunate astral conjunctions, or the abuse of the Roman court, or the tyranny of earthly kings and princes, or false zealots, heretics, pretend prophets, or the wickedness of usurers, counterfeiters, coin clippers, or the ignorance, impudence, and imprudence of doctors, surgeons, and druggists, or the perversity of adulterous women, poisoners, baby killers—no, blame it all on their unspeakable, incredible, incalculable wickedness, constantly wrought and carried forward in the Furry Lawcats' dens. The world knows no more about it than it does about the Jews' Cabala—which is why it is neither hated, corrected, nor punished, as reason would dictate. But if someday it is known, and the people learn all about it, there neither is nor ever has been an orator so eloquent that his art will restrain them; there is no law however rigorous, even draconic, which would be fearsome enough to hold them back; no ruler or judge so powerful that he'd be strong enough to stop them—and these creatures would all be driven down into their holes and burned alive. Their own children, the Furry Lawkittens, and all their other relatives, would find them objects of horror and disgust.

"Which is why, just as Hannibal's father, Hamilcar, made him swear a solemn, holy oath, that as long as he lived he would harass the Romans, so too my late father commanded me to remain out here, waiting for the thunder of heaven to fall on these Lawcats, burning them to ashes exactly like those other profane, God-hating Titans. For men have such tough hides that all the evil done to them, and being done, and still to be done, goes unnoticed, unsuspected, and unhindered—or if it is noticed, they neither dare nor wish (or perhaps are able) to wipe it out."

"That's what it's like?" said Panurge. "Ha—no, no, I'm not going in there, no, by God. Let's go back. Let's go back, I say, for God's sake.

> This noble beggar's frightened me more
> Than calm autumn skies that suddenly roar."

Returning, we found the gate closed, and they told us it was as easy to get in here as in through Avernus, the gates of hell. It was getting out again which was difficult, and we'd be allowed to leave only if we had a certificate of discharge from the authorities—for the simple reason that you can't walk away from a fair the way you can from a marketplace, and also because our dusty feet made us seem to be vagrants.

The worst of it came when we tried to get our certificate of discharge, for which purpose we were obliged to present ourselves before the most hideous monster imaginable. His name was Grabby Puss. The best comparison I can think of is to the Chimaera, or to the Sphinx or Cerberus, or perhaps to the image of Osiris, as portrayed by the Egyptians, in which he is shown with three heads, all joined together, one a lion roaring, another a flattering dog, and the third a yawning wolf, all three wound around by a dragon biting his own tail, encircled in gleaming rays of light. His hands were drenched in blood; he had claws like a harpy, a snout like a crow's beak, the teeth of a grown boar, eyes that flamed like hell's own throat. He was covered from head to foot in legal symbolism, through which only his claws could be seen.

He and all the wild Furry Lawcats who followed him were seated at a brand-new stable rack, long and ample, above which (as the beggar had warned us) usual stable practice was reversed and there were great, handsome feeding troughs. Just to the right of the principal seat there hung the portrait of an old woman, holding a sheathed sickle in her right hand, and a scale in her left, with spectacles perched at the end of her nose. The trays of the scale were a pair of velvet-covered purses, one full of gold bullion, which hung down, the other completely empty and raised high in the air. And it seems to me that this was a portrait of Grabby Pussish justice, thoroughly repulsive to justice, as the ancient Thebans had pictured her—the Thebans, who erected statues of their judges, after their deaths, worked either in gold or silver or marble, depending on their merits, but all of the statues having no hands.

When we appeared before him, a strange group of men, all dressed in purses and bags, covered with great flapping strips of parchment, directed us to sit on church repentance stools. Panurge said:

"O you rascals, my friends: I can stand very well—and those stools are too low for a man with new shoes—and besides, they're too small."

"You sit right down!" they answered. "We don't want to tell you again. The earth will open up right under you, and swallow you alive, if you don't tell the truth, the whole truth, and nothing but the truth."

Chapter Twelve ⁄⁄ Grabby Puss Asks Us a Riddle

When we were seated, Grabby Puss spoke to us from the middle of his Furry Lawcat circle, his voice angry and hoarse:

"All right, all right, all right!"

"A drink, a drink, a drink," muttered Panurge between his teeth. Grabby Puss went right on:

> "A fair young girl, a good enough lass,
> Gave birth to a black-skinned baby, a bastard.
> She dropped him, the sweet young thing, like a calf,
> But he bit his way from her womb like an adder.
> It was wrong, quite wrong, but he chewed away
> At her side, impatient to be out in the air,
> Then barreled off on his merry way,
> Flying here, and walking there:
> All of which stunned Wisdom's good friend,
> Who'd thought the child a humanoid blend.

"All right, answer me," said Grabby Puss. "Solve this riddle; tell us, here and now, what it's all about. All right!"

"By God," I replied, "I could easily solve your riddle, if I happened to have the Sphinx at my side, or even, by God, the silver Sphinx that Verres had (and his way of life paved the way for yours). But by God I don't, and I am, by God, absolutely innocent."

"All right!" said Grabby Puss. "By the river Styx, since you have nothing else to say—all right!—I'll show you—all right! that you'd have done better to fall into Lucifer's own claws—all right!—and all the other devils—all right!—than into our claws—all right! You see that perfectly clearly, don't you—all right!—you vulgar rascal? You plead innocent—all right!—as if that were the way to avoid our tortures. All right! Our laws are like a spider's web—all right!—foolish flies and little butterflies get caught in them—all right!—big horseflies break them—all right!—and go through—all right! So that's why we don't go hunting big-time thieves and tyrants—all right! They're too hard to digest—all right!—and they make us sick—all right!—but you others, you nice little innocents—all right!—you're perfectly harmless—all right! The devil in hell himself—all right!—will sing a mass for you, down there—all right!"

Annoyed at Grabby Puss' litany, Brother John said:

"Hah, you devil in petticoats—how can you ask him to reply to a proposition he doesn't know anything about? Isn't the truth enough for you?"

"All right!" said Grabby Puss. "Now this is the first time—all right!—since I came to power here that anyone, ever—all right!—has dared to speak before being asked a question. Who untied this crazy fool?"

"You're a liar," said Brother John without moving his lips.

"All right—when it's your turn to answer—all right!—you'll have more than enough to deal with—all right!"

"Scoundrel, you're lying," said Brother John under his breath.

"Do you think you're in the groves of academe—all right!—with all those lazy hunters chasing after truth? All right! We're up to a very different sort of thing, here—all right!—here, you answer—listen to me—all right!—I speak categorically—you answer questions about which you know nothing. All right! And you admit to having done—all right!—what in fact you've never done. All right! Here you say you know what you've never heard a word about. All right! Here you have to be patient, even when you're wild with anger. All right! Here you pull feathers out of a goose, and he never lets out a peep. All right! You speak without a proper power of attorney—all right!—I see that perfectly clearly—all right!—oh, there's a damned pestilence—all right!—will it be able to marry you? All right!"

"You devils!" cried Brother John. "No, archdevils, perfect devils, complete devils—you want to marry off monks, do you? Ho, ho, ho, hoo! I'll get you for heresy!"

Chapter Thirteen ⁄⁄ Panurge Solves Grabby Puss' Riddle

Pretending not to understand Brother John's remarks, Grabby Puss turned to Panurge, saying:

"All right—all right—all right! And you, you happy clown, haven't *you* got anything to say?"

Panurge answered:

"Now, by the devil, I see perfectly clearly that the plague's gotten in here, so now, by the devil, since innocence is no guarantee of safety, here, and since the devil himself is singing a mass for us, now, by the devil, please, kind sir, allow me to pay him for all of us, by the devil, and then let us go. That's the best I can do, now, by the devil!"

"Let you go?" said Grabby Puss. "All right! It's been more than three hundred years—all right!—since anyone got out of here without leaving us a piece of his fur—all right!—and more often, a piece of his hide—all right! Because otherwise—all right!—that would amount to saying that someone was unjustly summoned here before us—all right!—and that we treated him unjustly. All right!—you're unlucky—all right!—but you'll be even more unlucky—all right!—if you don't solve the riddle I set for you. All right! So what do you say—all right!"

"Now that, by the devil," replied Panurge, "is a black boll weevil, born of a dried white bean, now by the devil, by means of the hole he gnawed in it, now by the devil, and sometimes he flies, and sometimes he walks, which is why Pythagoras, who was Wisdom's good friend (which would be, in Greek, 'Philosopher,' now by the devil), thought it had somehow gotten a human soul, by metempsychosis, now by the devil. If

you others were human, now by the devil, after you'd met your miserable deaths, according to Pythagoras' way of thinking, your souls would
go into the bodies of black weevils, now by the devil. Because in this life
you gnaw and consume everything. In the other,

> You gnaw and chew like adders
> Consuming their mothers' bodies—
> Now by the devil."

"By God's holy heart," said Brother John, "I wish from the bottom of
my heart that my asshole would turn into a white bean, so these weevils
could gnaw on it."

Having spoken these words, Panurge threw down a large, gold-filled
purse, right in the middle of the courtroom floor. At the sound of its
clinking, all the Furry Lawcats began to flex their claws, as if they were
tuning their violins. And they all began to cry, in loud voices:

"Our bribes, our bribes! It's been a fine lawsuit, thoroughly delicious,
nicely sweetened. These are good people."

"It's gold," said Panurge. "Let me tell you: twenty-four karat."

"The court," said Grabby Puss, "understands—oh yes, oh yes, oh yes!
You may go, my children—oh yes!—with our leave—oh yes!—for we're
not such devils—oh yes!—we're not so black as all that—oh yes, oh yes,
oh yes!"

When we finally went through the gate, we were escorted to the harbor by Swiss legal eagles. Before we boarded our ships, they advised us
not to set sail without paying proper tribute to Lady Grabby Puss and
also to all the Furry Lawkittens. Otherwise, they explained, it would be
their duty to escort us right back through the gate.

"Shit," answered Brother John. "We'd have to dive right down to the
bottom of our purses, to pay all of them off!"

"And also," they went on, "don't forget to tip the lesser devils."

"Lesser devils," replied Brother John. "Oh, we never forget them.
They're always well remembered, in every country on earth—always."

Chapter Fourteen // How the Furry Lawcats Live Off Corruption

Brother John had not finished speaking when he saw seventy-eight
galleys and frigates making port, so he ran right off and asked for news,
and also what merchandise the vessels were carrying. He saw they were
all loaded with game: hares, capons, pigeons, pigs, goats, plover, chick-

ens, ducks, wild ducks, geese, and many other edible varieties. He also saw bolts of velvet, satin, and damask silk. So he asked the sailors from where and to whom they were bringing these delicious morsels. They replied that all this was for Grabby Puss, the Furry Lawcats, and the Furry Lawkittens.

"What," said Brother John, "do you call this stuff?"

"Corruption," answered the sailors.

"Those who live by corruption," said Brother John, "will die in pro-creation. By all that's holy, that's exactly right: their fathers swallowed up the good gentlemen who, on account of their station in life, practiced hawking and hunting, to keep themselves ready for war, whenever it might come. For hunting is indeed a warlike exercise, and Xenophon did no more than tell the truth when he wrote that all good generals come from the hunting field, just as they come from the Trojan horse. I'm no learned man, but I've been told that, and I believe it. The way Grabby Puss sees it, after the death of such men, their souls passed into the wild boar, stags, goats, herons, partridges, and other such animals that, during their first lives, they loved and hunted. And now these Furry Lawcats, having devoured and destroyed their castles and lands, all their realms and domains, their possessions, rents, and revenues, go on hunting after their blood and their souls in their new lives as well. Oh, that good beg-gar warned us about these creatures, and their feed troughs set up above the stable racks!"

"Indeed," Panurge said to the sailors, "but the king has proclaimed that no one, under pain of hanging, is to hunt stags, or does, or boar, or goats."

"That's true," said one of them, speaking for all the rest. "But the king is so good, so kind, and these Furry Lawcats are so wild and starved for Christian blood, that we're not as concerned about offending the king as we would be about not bringing these Furry Lawcats the corruption they expect—and especially right now, since tomorrow Lord Grabby Puss is marrying one of his Furry Lawkittens to a great Tomcat, a truly well-furred animal. In the old days, his kind were called hay eaters, but alas! That's not what they eat any more. Today, we call them hare eaters, partridge eaters, pheasant eaters, woodcock eaters, pig eaters, goat eaters, rabbit eaters—because that's all they'll eat."

"Shit, shit!" said Brother John. "Next year you'll be calling them turd eaters, dung eaters, shit eaters. Will you listen to me?"

"Oh yes," they all answered.

"Let's do two things," he said. "First, let's grab all this game that you see here, because I'm tired of salted provisions, too: they heat up my intestines. But I'll pay what's due. And second, let's go back and stamp out these devilish Furry Lawcats."

"Not me," said Panurge. "I'm not coming. I'm naturally a coward."

Chapter Fifteen ⁄⁄ Brother John Plans to Stamp Out the Furry Lawcats

"By all that's holy," said Brother John, "what kind of voyage is this? It's a shitty voyage: all we do is fart and shit and shit and daydream, and we never do a thing. By God's heart, that's not the way I am! If I don't keep on doing some heroic deed or other, I can't sleep at night. Did you take me along on this voyage so I could say mass and hear confession? By God, the first man to give me his confession—oh, he'll have his penitence all right! He'll be thrown to the bottom of the sea, as a good-for-nothing coward—that'll be deducted from the pains of purgatory. And he'll go in head first, I say!

"What gave Hercules his eternal fame? Isn't it because he traveled around the world, liberating people from tyranny, from folly, from perils, from oppression? He killed all the robbers and monsters and poisonous snakes and evil beasts. Why don't we follow his example, doing as he did in all the countries we pass through? He attacked and destroyed those harpy birds, the Stymphalides, and the Lernean Hydra, and three-headed Cacus, and Antaeus, as well as the Centaurs. Now I'm no scholar, but this is what the scholars tell us. Let's imitate him—let's attack and destroy these Furry Lawcats: all they are is devil hawks. Let's free this country from their tyranny. By God, if I were as strong and as powerful as he was, I wouldn't ask you for any help, and I wouldn't ask for your advice, either. Now, what do you say? Are we going to do it? I can tell you, it won't be hard to kill them; they won't put up much of a fight—I'm not worried, seeing how they've already tolerated all sorts of insults from us, more than ten fat sows can drink out of washtubs. Let's go."

"They don't care about insults and dishonor," I told him, "as long as their purses are full—it doesn't matter how shit-smeared, just so it's gold. And they can be destroyed, all right, just the way Hercules did—but he was acting under orders from Eurysthenes, king of Argos, and we're not. That's all we need, right now, though I could wish for Jupiter to stroll among them for a couple of hours, in the same thunderous shape he took on when he visited his girlfriend Semele, our good Bacchus' noble mother."

"God showed us His great grace," said Panurge, "letting us escape their claws. Me, I'm not going back: I'm still shaken, still suffering from that torment. I'm deeply upset, and for three reasons: first, because I was so upset; second, because I was so upset; and third, because I'm still upset. Brother John, you just put your right ear to my left ball, and listen: anytime you want to go down there with all the devils, and appear before those deadful judges Minos, Aeacus, Rhadamanthus, and Dis, I'm ready to stay right at your side. I'm ready to cross the Acheron, the Styx, the Cocytus, and drink deep from the river Lethe; I'm prepared to pay Charon for my fare and yours, too. But for going back through that gate, if you're not interested in going alone, find someone else: I'm not going back—and consider my words framed in bronze and mounted on a wall! Unless someone uses force and violence to bring me there, I won't go near the place, any more than one of the Herculean columns at Gibraltar will cross the strait to the other one, not as long as I live. Did Odysseus go back into the Cyclops' cave, hunting for his sword? By Jupiter, no! Anyway, I haven't left anything in there, and I'm not going back."

"Oh," said Brother John, "what a fine open heart you have, and what paralyzed hands! But let's look at this more closely, after the fashion of that learned jackass Duns Scotus. Why did you toss them that full purse? Who compelled you? Have we so much money as all that? Wouldn't it have worked just as well if you'd thrown them less?"

"Because," answered Panurge, "all the time he was talking, Grabby Puss kept opening that velvet purse of his, yelling, 'All right, all right, all right.' That made me think we could get clean away if we gave them gold—gold, by God, gold! by all the devils in hell. You don't keep copper coins in a velvet purse, nor small change. Fat gold pieces are what goes in there—don't you understand that, Brother John, my little shriveled ball brain? When you've been held in the fire as long as I have, and well roasted, you'll talk differently, let me tell you. But now, as we were warned, we ought to sail away from here."

All the harbor rascals were waiting for us, expecting a juicy bribe. Seeing us getting ready to sail, they spoke to Brother John, warning him that we could not leave unless we'd paid off the bailiffs, in accord with the provisions of the spice tax.

"By Saint Hurlyburly," said Brother John, "are you still hanging around, you devil claws? Haven't you bothered me enough, without more badgering? By God's holy heart, you'll be paid off, and right now: I'll promise you that!"

Then, drawing his short sword, he left the ship, fully determined to murder them all. But they ran away as fast as they could, and we never saw them again.

But we still weren't out of our difficulties, because while we'd been dealing with Grabby Puss, some of our sailors, with Pantagruel's permission, had gone to an inn near the harbor and had themselves a banquet and then rested a bit. I don't know if they'd actually paid or not, but an old hag of an innkeeper, seeing Brother John back on dry land, complained bitterly; she had a bailiff with her, a son-in-law of one of the Furry Cats, and two underbailiffs as witnesses. Annoyed and impatient, Brother John turned on them:

"O you rascals, my dear friends: are you trying to tell me our sailors aren't worthy men? I say just the opposite, and if you'll just step in front of the judge I'll prove it to you—and I mean this Judge Short Sword, right here."

So saying, he flourished his sword. The rascals ran off. Only the old hag remained, who assured Brother John that the sailors were indeed worthy men, but hadn't paid her for the bed they'd slept in, after their dinner, and complained that she had a right to be paid five gold pieces for her bed.

"Indeed," said Brother John, "that's a good bargain, and they're lucky to have gotten it at that price. I'll be glad to pay you myself, but I need to see the bed."

So the old woman led him to her inn and showed him the bed and, after having carefully explained all its good qualities, assured him she wasn't asking too much when she'd asked for five gold pieces. Brother John gave her the money and then, with his sword, cut the quilt and pillows in half, and tossed the feathers out the windows, to flutter away on the wind, at which the old woman ran down the stairs, shouting Help! Murder! and desperately trying to gather up her feathers. Paying no attention, Brother John carried off the bedclothes, the mattress, and a pair of sheets and brought them back to our ship, unobserved—because the air was dark with feathers, thick as snow. He gave them to the sailors. Then he observed to Pantagruel that beds were a lot cheaper here than in Chinon, even though back home we had the famous Pautillé geese. The old woman had asked only five gold pieces for the bed, but in Chinon it would have been worth at least twelve.

As soon as Brother John and the others were back on board, Pantagruel ordered the sails set, but a sirocco blew up so violently that we lost our way and pretty much retraced our route to the land of the Furry Lawcats. The ships were blown into a great gulf from which, the sea being terribly high, a boy at the top of the mast called out that he could still see the unpleasant realm of the Furry Lawcats. At which, half mad with fear, Panurge cried:

"Captain, my friend, never mind the wind or the waves—just turn her around! O my friend, let's never go back to that wicked land, where I left my purse."

Then the wind blew us near an island where, at first, we did not dare make land, but hove to about a mile offshore, near some large rocks.

Chapter Sixteen ⁄ How Pantagruel Landed on the Island of the Ignorant, Men with Long Fingers and Greedy Hands, and the Terrible Adventures and Monsters He Met There

As soon as the anchors had been dropped and the vessel made fast, the skiff was lowered. After our good Pantagruel had said his prayers, thanking the Lord for having saved him from such great danger, he and all his associates climbed down into the little boat, in order to row ashore—and this was very easily done, the sea being calm and the winds having died away, so that in a short time they reached the great rocks.

When they were on dry land, Epistemon, who was admiring the lay of the land and the strangeness of the rocks, noticed some local people. The first he spoke to was dressed in a short robe, blue as the king's, the sleeves of which were decorated with English lace at the cuffs and, above, with soft chamois leather. He wore a cocked hat and seemed a very presentable fellow; as we later learned, his name was Getalot.

Epistemon asked him the name of these strange rocks and valleys. Getalot told him that this rocky country, originally a colony of Lawyerland, was called Accountbooks, and that beyond the rocks, after passing a small ford, we would find the island of the Ignorant.

"By all the holy decrees!" said Brother John. "You and all your countrymen, what do you live on? Will we know how to drink out of glasses like yours? Because all I see here are parchments, inkhorns, and pens."

"That's exactly what we live on," said Getalot, "because everyone who has any business on this island has to pass through our hands."

"Why?" said Panurge. "Are you barbers, and they have to be clipped?"

"Yes," said Getalot—"at least, if you're talking about their purses."

"By God!" said Panurge. "You're not going to get a penny out of me! But I beg you, my dear sir, to lead us to these Ignorants, because we've just come from the land of the Learned, where I didn't do too well."

Chatting, they walked over to the island of the Ignorant, for the ford was soon crossed. Pantagruel greatly admired the architecture of the buildings: these people lived in a huge winepress, to which you ascended by almost fifty staircases, and before you entered the main press (because they had little ones, big ones, hidden ones, midsize ones—presses of every variety) you came through a large cloister in which you could see paintings of virtually all the ruins in the entire world, with gallows and gibbets and torture racks everywhere, so many that it made us all shudder with fear. Seeing how fascinated Pantagruel was, Getalot said to him:

"Sir, let's go on. This is nothing."

"What?" said Brother John. "This is nothing? By the soul of my red-hot codpiece! Panurge and I are shaking with hunger. I'd far rather be drinking than looking at these ruins."

"Come," said Getalot.

Then he led us to a little press, concealed in the back, which in the language of that island was called Ultra. Don't bother asking if our masterly John (and Panurge) did properly by it: Milanese sausages, Indian pheasants, capons, turkeys, Malmsey wine, and all manner of good things to eat and drink, all ready and waiting.

A little waiter, seeing Brother John casting loving looks at a bottle, standing on a sideboard, set apart from the horde of other bottles, said to Pantagruel:

"Sir, I see that one of your people is lusting after that bottle. Let me beg you not to let him touch it, because it's for their lordships."

"What?" said Panurge. "There are lordships here? You do a lot of harvesting in this place, as far as I can see."

Then Getalot took us higher, by a small, hidden staircase, to a room from which he showed us their lordships, who were in the great winepress, into which (he told us) it was illegal for anyone to enter without their permission. But we could see them clearly through the narrow little window, without their seeing us.

What we saw in the great winepress were twenty or twenty-five fat rascals, gathered around a huge gallows desk all covered in green cloth, staring at each other, their hands as long as cranes' legs, their fingernails at least two feet in length—because they were forbidden ever to clip them, so they'd become as crooked as boat hooks or grappling irons. Just then, they were brought a fat bunch of the grapes they harvest in that country, grown on the Extraordinary vine that often hangs in public squares. The bunch had no sooner been brought in than they shoved it into the winepress, and every bit of it was squeezed into golden oil, and the poor bunch was carried out so dried up and plucked clean that there wasn't another drop of liquid left in it. Getalot told us they didn't often get bunches quite as juicy as that, but there were always others in the winepress.

"But, my dear fellow," said Panurge, "do they work with many varieties?"

"Yes," said Getalot. "Take a look at that little one, which they're just now putting back in the winepress. That comes from Church Tithe stock. They squeezed it almost dry, the other day, but the oil had too much whiff of priestly treasure box to it, and their lordships didn't find it particularly flavorful."

"Then why," said Pantagruel, "are they putting it back in the winepress?"

"To find out," said Getalot, "if there isn't a little more juice, or something, still left in the grapes."

"By all that's holy!" said Brother John. "Do you call these people igno-rant? Like Satan himself! They could get oil out of a stone wall."

"They do that, too," said Getalot, "because quite frequently what they put in the winepress are castles and meadows and forests—and they get potable gold from all of it."

"You mean to say *portable* gold," said Epistemon.

"I say potable," said Getalot, "for they drink lots more bottles of it, here, than they ought to be able to. They have so many different varieties that no one has any idea how many there are. Come over here and look down into the courtyard. You see? There are more than a thousand, just waiting for their time to be squeezed. Some are from public stock; some are private—stemming from fortifications, loans, gifts, judicial decisions, crown real estate, pocket moneys, the post office, offerings, and the king's personal household."

"And what's that great fat one over there, with all the little ones around it?"

"Ah, that," said Getalot, "is the Treasury, and it's the best stock in the whole country. When they squeeze that growth, for six months after-ward there isn't one of their lordships who isn't still drawing on it."

When their lordships finally rose, Pantagruel begged Getalot to con-duct them into the great winepress, to which Getalot readily agreed. As soon as they were inside, Epistemon, who understood every language in the world, began to point out to Pantagruel what was written, in large, handsome letters, on all the parts of the winepress, which had been made, as Getalot informed us, of the wood of the true cross. Each part was inscribed, in the language of the country, with its proper name. The great main screw was called *Receipts;* the bowl, *Expenses;* the female screw, *The State;* the shaft, *Moneys Accounted For But Not Yet Received;* the drum, *Outstanding Bills;* the pile drivers, *Forgivenesses;* the guide poles, *To Be Collected;* the vat, *Values Higher Than Par;* the eyebolts, *Court Rolls;* the treading troughs, *Paid in Full;* the feeding hoppers, *Ratifications;* the har-vest baskets, *Authenticated Orders;* the buckets, *Powers of Attorney;* the fun-nels, *Releases.*

"By the noble queen of the Sausages!" said Panurge. "Egyptian hiero-glyphics never came close to this jargon! The devil! These words don't fit together any better than goat shit. But tell me, old friend, old buddy: why do you call these people ignorant?"

"Because," said Getalot, "they neither are nor ever can be scholars, and because here, by their orders, everything must be dealt with by ignorance and never by reason or right. It's all: 'Their lordships say, their lordships wish, their lordships command.' "

"By the true God!" said Pantagruel, "since they get so much out of bunches, they must tie everything up with vines and oaths."

"How could you doubt it?" said Getalot. "They use them all the time.

"It's not the way it is in your country, where neither vines nor oaths are worth anything to you except once a year."

From there he led us past a thousand smaller winepresses, and in leaving we became aware of another small bureau, around which there were four or five of these Ignorants, filthy, as bad-tempered as donkeys with firecrackers tied to their tails. They had a little winepress, through which they were running the pulpy residue of one squeezed-out bunch after another. In the language of the country, they were known as *Auditors*.

"I think these are the grimmest rascals," said Brother John, "I have ever set eyes on."

After leaving the great winepress, we passed an infinite number of smaller ones, all full of harvesters picking over the grapes with tools they called *Bills of Account,* until at last we arrived in a low room, where we saw a huge watchdog with two heads, a wolf's belly, and the claws of the devils on the walls at Lamballe, who was fed on the milk of *Fines,* a delicacy expressly ordered for him by their lordships, because there wasn't one of them to whom he wasn't worth more than the income from a good farm. In the language of Ignorance, his name was *Double Fines.* His mother was there, too, and she looked very like him, except that she had four heads, two male and two female, and her name was *Quadruple Fines:* she was the wildest and most dangerous animal ever seen, except for her grandmother, whom we saw locked up in a dungeon they called *Fees Refused.*

Brother John, who always had twenty yards of empty guts, ready to swallow down a fricassee of lawyers, began to get irritable and asked Pantagruel to think about having dinner and taking Getalot with us. As we left there by the rear door, we saw an old man chained up, half an Ignorant, half a scholar, like some hermaphroditic devil: he was decked out with spectacles, like a kind of tortoise with shells, and all he lived on was something they called, in their local dialect, either *Appeals* or *Audits.*

Seeing him, Pantagruel asked Getalot what race of men this clerk came from, and what his name was. Getalot explained to us that, many, many years ago, to the great regret of their lordships, he had been chained there, that he was very nearly dead of hunger, and that he was known by the name of *Look Again.*

"By the pope's holy balls!" said Brother John. "That's a handsome dancer, nor would I be surprised if their Ignorant lordships made a great fuss about this canting idiot. By God! It seems to me, my friend Panurge, that if you look at him carefully, you'll see a resemblance to Grabby Puss. These fellows may be Ignorants, but they understand quite as much as other people do. I'd send him back where he came from, after a good whipping with an eel skin."

"By these oriental spectacles of mine!" said Panurge. "Brother John, my good friend, you're dead right! Just look at the face on this cheating rascal: he's even more of an Ignorant, and more wicked, too, than these other poor Ignorants all around us here, who grab whatever they can but do as little damage as they know how, and don't drag out the proceedings—all it takes them is three little words and they've closed out the harvest and sold off the grapes. They don't worry about interlocutories or re-interlocutories, and of course that irritates the Furry Lawcats."

Chapter Seventeen ⁄⁄ How We Came to the Land of Too Much and Panurge Just Missed Getting Killed

We immediately set out toward the land of Too Much and told everything that had happened to Pantagruel (who had refused to go ashore on Spy Hole Island, and so had not himself encountered the Furry Lawcats); he commiserated deeply and even composed several elegies, to pass the time.

When we arrived, we ate a bit and drank some fresh water, then collected wood for our supplies. The local people struck us as decent, companionable fellows.

They were all as round and full as wineskins, farting with fat, and it seemed to us (something we had never seen in any other country) as if they had slashed their skin in order to let the fat come swelling out, just as modish folk in my own country slash the tops of their trousers, to let the taffeta lining show through. They claimed there was nothing vainglorious or ostentatious about this, but that it simply allowed them to stay in their skins. Having so perforated themselves, they became larger and larger, just as gardeners cut the skin of young trees so they will grow faster.

Near the harbor there was a fine-looking inn, toward which we saw a great number of the people of Too Much hurrying—people of all sexes, ages, and social status—and we thought they were staging some special feast or banquet. But we were told that the innkeeper had issued an invitation to come to his bursting, and all his neighbors and relatives and friends were rushing to do just that. Not understanding what they meant, we thought that in this country feasts were referred to as "burstings" (just as we refer to weddings, betrothings, churchings, sheepshearings, harvestings), but we were told that in his day the innkeeper had been a fine fellow, always stuffing it in, guzzling up Lyonnaise soups, watching the clock for his next meal, forever eating (like the innkeeper at Rouillac), and having for the last ten years farted away a ton of fat, he had finally come to the point of bursting, which was how, according to the custom of the country, he proposed to end his days, since neither his stomach wall nor his skin, after so many years of being slashed, could close in and contain his guts, keeping them from flopping out, like a bashed-in barrel.

"But," said Panurge, "good people, don't you know how to bind up his belly with good stout webbing, or strong tree bands—even iron ones, if necessary? If you bind him up like that, it won't be easy for him to pop out his guts and he won't be as likely to burst."

He hadn't finished speaking when we heard a sound so loud and strident that it seemed as if a chain had snapped. His neighbors told us that he had indeed burst and that the noise was his death fart.

It made me think of the venerable abbot of Chastelliers (who would not condescend to screw his servants *nisi in pontificalibus,* unless he was wearing full churchly regalia): in his latter days he was urged by his relatives and friends to give up his abbotship, but answered that he never got undressed when he got into bed and that the last fart his holiness would ever blow out would be an abbot's fart.

Chapter Eighteen ⁄⁄ How Our Ship Ran Aground, and We Were Aided by Travelers Who Came from the Land of the Fifth Essence

Having raised our anchors and untied our ropes, we set sail in a sweet zephyr. After we had gone about two hundred and twenty-two miles, we ran into a wild whirlwind, gusting from here and there and everywhere; using only our foresail and proceeding close-hauled, we moved cautiously along, carefully heeding our pilot, who assured us that since these were pleasant winds, gently pulling and tugging at one another, and the air and the sea remained calm and peaceful, we should neither expect any great forward impetus nor worry about any huge disaster: like the philosopher who counseled that one should both bear and forbear— that is, temporize. All the same, this whirlwind lasted so long that, at our urgent request, the pilot tried to break through it and resume our prior course. And indeed, by raising the great mizzen sail and steering hard-right by the compass, he did break through, but only at the cost of finding ourselves in a stiff hurricane, which blew in on the whirlwind's heels. But this was just as bad, like someone escaping Charybdis only to fall into Scylla, and two miles farther on our ships were driven aground on sand flats like those at Saint-Mathieu.

All the sailors and rowers were unhappy; the winds blew across our foresails; but Brother John, who never let himself be depressed, consoled first this one and then that with gentle words, assuring them that we would soon have the assistance of heaven and that he had personally seen Saint Elmo's fire running across the yardarms.

"Would to God," said Panurge, "we were on dry land right now—just exactly that—and that all the rest of you, who love the sea so much, were granted two hundred thousand gold pieces each; I'd keep a calf in a chicken coop for when you came back, and cool down a hundred bundles of firewood. All right: I agree never to get married: just fix it so I'm back on dry land and I have a horse to carry me home; I can manage without a servant. I'm never treated as well when I travel with a servant. Plautus isn't telling any lies when he says that the number of crosses we have to bear—all the afflictions, boredoms, irritations—is exactly proportional to the number of servants we have, and even if they have no tongues, because of course that's the most dangerous, evil part of a servant's body, on account of which—that and that alone—tortures have been devised for them—inquisitorial racks and all sorts of hellish machines. There's no other reason for such things, although our legal eagles—but not the ones in this kingdom—have derived thoroughly illogical—that is, unreasonable—deductions from them."

Just then we saw coming straight toward us a boat loaded with drums and tambourines, and I recognized several passengers of good families, Henry Cotiral among others, an old friend and drinking companion, who had a huge donkey dong hanging from his belt (the way women wear rosary beads) and carried in his left hand a big, greasy, dirty old hat (the kind people wear when they have itchy heads), and in his right a fat head of cabbage. As soon as he saw me he cried out happily, saying:

"Have I got it? Well, just look at this" (showing me the donkey prick): "it's the true amalgam, mercury fused with another metal—and this doctoral cap is our unique mercurial elixir—and this (showing me the head of cabbage) is *Lunaria major,* papal herbs. We'll make the Fifth Essence, the philosopher's stone, out of it, when you get home."

"But," I said, "where are you coming from? Where are you going? What are you carrying? Have you had a good taste of the sea?"

He answered me:

"From the Fifth Essence—to Touraine—alchemy—up to our asses."

"And who are those people," I said, "on the deck with you?"

"Singers," he answered, "musicians, poets, astrologers, would-be poets, mathematical prognosticators, alchemists, loafers, watchmakers: they all come from the land of the Fifth Essence; they all have handsome, fulsome letters to prove it."

He had barely finished when Panurge, angry and indignant, said:

"You people who can do everything, including making good weather and little children, why don't you take hold of the bow of our boat and, with no further ado, just put us right back on the high seas again?"

"Just what I was going to do," said Henry Cotiral. "Right now, immediately, in just a moment, I'll have you off these sands."

Then he cut one side off 7,532,810 drums and tambourines, turned that side toward the forward end of our ship, and tied the ropes tight, all up and down; then he set the stern of his ship against the bow of ours, and lashed us to his mooring posts. And then, at the first pull, he pulled us easily off the sands—and gaily, to boot, since the sound of the drums and tambourines, together with the sweet murmur of the gravel and the rowers' chanting, produced harmonies not much inferior to that celestial music which the sleeping Plato is said sometimes to have heard at night.

Not wanting them to think us ungrateful for this kindness, we shared our sausages with them, filling their drums and tambourines, and we had just set out on the deck sixty-two jugs of wine, when two immense whales came splashing up to their ship, throwing more water up on them than you could find in the whole river Vienne, from Chinon to Saumur, which flooded all their drums and tambourines, sprinkled all their yardarms, and washed their trousers for them (starting at the neck). Panurge fell into fits of laughter, seeing this, pumping up his spleen so hard that he suffered from colic for more than two hours after.

"I wanted to give them their wine," he said, "but they've been more fittingly granted water, instead. They're not much concerned about fresh water, anyway: they only use it to wash their hands. This nicely salted water should serve them as borax, and saltpeter and sal ammoniac, too, for their alchemical kitchens."

Nor did we have any further opportunity for conversation with them, since the original whirlwind had jammed our tiller. And our pilot urged us, from now on, just to let the sea guide us, and not worry about anything except having a good time: for the time being it was better for us to just coast along the edges of the whirlwind, letting the current take us, if we hoped to make it safely to the land of the Fifth Essence.

Chapter Nineteen ⁄⁄ We Arrive in the Land of the Fifth Essence, Also Known as Entelechy (or Complete Self-Realization)

Having prudently spent half a day skirting the whirlwind, on the third day after that it seemed to us that the air was purer than usual, and we arrived at the port of Mateotechnie, or Useless Knowledge, in perfect safety. It was very near the palace of the land of the Fifth Essence. Disembarking at the port, we found a whole horde of archers and other soldiers drawn up in front of us, guarding the arsenal. They rather frightened us, when we first arrived, making us set down our weapons and quite arrogantly interrogating us.

"Gentlemen, what country have you come from?"

"My dear cousins," answered Panurge, "we're men of Touraine. We've come from France, anxious to present our respects to the lady of Fifth Essence and to visit this celebrated kingdom of Entelechy."

"What?" they asked bluntly. "What are you saying—Entelechy or Endelechy?"

"My dear cousins," answered Panurge, "we're simple people—fools, really. Please excuse our rustic language because, at bottom, our hearts are both frank and loyal."

"We haven't asked you about this," they said, "without good reason, because a great many people from Touraine have come this way, and they seemed decent enough clods who bespoke themselves nicely, but some who've come here from other countries have been pretty well puffed-up, as proud as Scotchmen, and as soon as they got here they launched into stubborn argument with us. We gave them a good hiding, for all their angry faces. Do you have so much time you don't know what to do with, in your world, so you can come here and talk and argue with our queen, and impudently write against her? It must have been singularly important, eh, for Cicero to abandon his book on the republic and spend all his time on the subject. And not only him, but Diogenes Laërtius, and Theodorus Gaza, and Argyropoulos, and Bessarion, and Politian, and Budé, and Jean Lascaris, and all those wise-fool devils, though their number wouldn't be terribly large if they hadn't recently been joined by Scaliger, Bigot, Chambrier, François Fleury, and who knows what other poor young hairless fops. May the croup strike them, and constrict their throats and their epiglottises too! We'll . . ."

"I'll be damned if he doesn't flatter the devils," said Panurge between his teeth.

"You people haven't come here to support them in their madness: you have no powers of attorney from the likes of them—so let's say nothing more about them. That paragon of all philosophy, and first among men, Aristotle, was our queen's godfather; it was he who well and properly named her Entelechy. And Entelechy is her real name—and anyone who calls her anything else can go beshit himself! Indeed, anyone who calls her by a different name is wrong, by all that's holy. You are very welcome here."

At which he warmly embraced us. We were all delighted. Panurge whispered in my ear:

"Brother, weren't you afraid during this business?"

"A little," I answered.

"Me," he said, "I was more frightened than Ephraim's soldiers, once upon a time, when the Gileadites butchered them for saying 'Sibboleth' instead of 'Shibboleth.' To tell the truth, there isn't a man in all Beauce who wouldn't have been welcome, with a wagonload of hay to stop up my asshole."

Then, silently, and with great ceremony, the captain of the guard led us to the queen's palace. Pantagruel wished to discuss several matters with him, but since he could not reach Pantagruel's level, he wished he'd had a ladder, or at least a big pair of stilts. Then the captain said:

"Enough! If our queen so desired it, we'd be as tall as you—and when she wants us to, we will be."

In the first galleries of the palace we saw a great mob of sick people, all arranged according to the nature of their illness: the lepers to one side, those who'd been poisoned in one place, the plague-stricken in another, the pox-ridden in the very front ranks, and so on.

Chapter Twenty // How the Fifth Essence Cured the Sick with Songs

In the second gallery, the captain of the guard pointed out the young lady queen (she was at least eighteen hundred years old)—beautiful, dainty, gorgeously dressed—surrounded by her ladies and gentlemen in waiting. And he said to us:

"It isn't yet time for an audience with her; simply be attentive spectators and see what she does. In your kingdom you have a number of kings who can magically cure certain illnesses, as for example scrofula, epilepsy, and malaria, just by a laying on of their hands. But our queen can cure any and all illnesses without touching anyone, simply by playing the sick an appropriate song."

Then he pointed out to us the organ on which she played, in order to effect her wonderful cures. It was exceedingly strangely fashioned, for its pipes were made of cassia sticks, its sounding board of resin gumwood, the keys of rhubarb, the pedals of turpeth vine roots, the manuals of scammony.

As we were examining this wonderful and novel organ, the lepers were introduced by her majesty's essence abstractors, metal oxidizers, kneaders and molders, food tasters, cooks, wise men, vassals, notables, men of enlightenment, princes, nobles, servants, satraps, chiefs, strongmen, scholars, scribes, doctors, bishops, prefects, professors, giants, as well as by others of her officers; she played a song for them, I have no idea what; and all of a sudden they were completely cured. Then those who'd been poisoned were brought in; she played them another song, and there they were, perfectly upright. Then the blind, the deaf, the mute, all of whom she treated in the same fashion. All of this astonished us, and quite properly: we fell to the ground, prostrating ourselves like men swept up in an ecstasy, ravished to the highest degree with an intense, overwhelming admiration for the powers we had seen the lady exercise, and it would not have been in our power to utter a single word.

And we remained prostrated until the lady, touching Pantagruel with a bouquet of white roses which she carried in her hand, brought us to our senses and back on our feet. Then she spoke soft-linen words to us, of the sort Parysatis wished men to use toward her son Cyrus, or at least words as silken as crimson taffeta:

"The decency gleaming through your individual circumferences makes me absolutely certain of the virtues latent in the center of your spirits; and seeing Your Eloquent Reverences' honeyed sweetness, I am readily persuaded that your hearts suffer from no vices of any sort whatever, or from any deficiency of lofty humane learning, but instead are overflowing with far-flown and rare knowledge of all kinds—knowledge which at the moment it is far easier (because of the common practices of the vulgarly incompetent) to long for than actually to encounter. Which is precisely why I, who in the past have successfully subdued all personal emotions, cannot keep myself from saying to you the most trivial words in the world, namely, that you are very—no, more than very—no, most, most welcome."

"I'm no scholar," Panurge whispered secretly to me. "You answer her, if you want to."

But I did not respond, nor did Pantagruel; we all remained silent. So the queen then said:

"In this taciturnity of yours I recognize that you not only come from the school of Pythagoras, from which my own progenitors spring, in an ancient and direct line, but that many moons ago you also bit your nails and scratched your heads in Egypt, that famous dispensary of lofty philosophies. For Pythagoreans, silence was the symbol of knowledge, and for the Egyptians taciturnity merited sanctified praise, and at Hierapolis the priests sacrificed to the great god in absolute silence, neither making a sound nor speaking a word. It is not my intention to deal with you via any deprivation of gratitude, but by the use of living formality—and no matter if thereby matter abstracts itself out of me—to whirl my thoughts from my center toward yours."

Having finished this statement, she turned to her officers and, speaking directly to them, said:

"Cooks, a panacea!"

The cooks immediately told us that the queen graciously excused us from dining with her, for she hardly ate anything at all, taking only a few categories, abstractions, truths, images, formulations, concepts, dreams, abstractions of abstractions, nightmares, entities, antitheses, metempsychoses, and transcendent prolepses (or anticipations of ideas as yet unthought of). Then he took us to a small room lined with alarm bells, where we were treated, God alone could possibly say how well. They say that Jupiter writes everything that happens, anywhere in the world, on the skin of the goat which suckled him, in Candia, and which he used as a shield when he was fighting the Titans, from which usage it derived its name of Aegiochus, or Shield Bearer. But by my faith, drinkers, O my friends, you couldn't describe even on eighteen goatskins the good food served to us, not even if you wrote in letters as small as those which

Cicero says he once saw used for a copy of Homer's *Iliad*, which was so tiny that you could put it into a walnut shell. For myself, even if I had a hundred tongues, a hundred mouths, a voice of iron, and Plato's eloquence, I couldn't in four whole volumes tell you one-third of one instant of it. Pantagruel told me that in speaking the words "a panacea" to her cooks, the queen had used their symbolic expression for "sovereign good food and drink," just as Lucullus would say, "In Apollo," when he wanted to give his friends an especially fine banquet, even when they'd taken him by surprise, as Cicero and Hortensius sometimes did.

Chapter Twenty-one ⁄⁄ How the Queen Passed the Time after Dinner

Dinner over, one of the wise men led us to the lady's rooms, and we saw how after the meal, according to her custom, she and her ladies and gentlemen in waiting passed the time: they sifted and sieved it with a large silk sieve, colored white and blue. Then we saw that, following truly ancient ways, they all danced

the wild Cordace	the frenzied Calabrime
the tragic Emmelia	the corybantic Molossia
the satiric Sicinnia	the corybantic Cernophore
the lively Iambic	the savage Mongas
the Persica	the Thermanstry
the Phrygian	the Florula
the Nicatime	the Spartan Pyrrhic
the Thracian	

and a thousand others.

Afterward, at her command, we visited the palace and saw such novel, wonderful, and strange things that just thinking of them I am still ravished right out of my senses. But all the same, nothing was more wonderfully overwhelming than the feats performed by the gentlemen of her household, essence abstractors, noblemen, leaders, metal oxidizers, and others, who frankly and simply explained to us that everything truly impossible (like curing those who were incurably ill) was done strictly and solely by their royal lady; they, who were just her officers, accomplished everything else, including the curing of the lesser sick.

I saw one aristocratic alchemist cure the pox—and I mean the worst cases you'll ever see, the kind you get on the docks at Rouen—simply by touching the dentiform vertebra three times with the stump of a wooden shoe.

I saw another cure all manner of dropsies—tympanic, ascitic, and hyposargic—by striking the patients' bellies nine times with the double-bladed ax of justice, never breaking the skin.

One instantly cured malarial fevers simply by hanging a fox tail from the sick man's belt, on the left side.

Another cured toothache simply by bathing the root of the afflicted tooth three times with elderberry vinegar, then letting it dry in the sun for half an hour.

Another cured all kinds of gout—whether hot, or cold, natural, or accidental—simply by making the sick man close his mouth and open his eyes.

I saw another one cure nine good gentlemen of Saint Francis' disease (which is, of course, poverty), all in less than an hour: he paid off all their debts and hung, from a cord around their necks, a purse holding ten thousand gold pieces.

Another, using a miraculous invention, threw houses out their own windows, thus cleansing them of pestilent air.

Another cured all three varieties of tuberculosis—atrophic, tabetic, and emaciative—without using any baths, any Tabian milk, any balms compounded of peas and oil, or any made of peas, oil, pepper, and salt—indeed, without using any medicine whatever, but just by making the sick men be monks for three months. And he assured me that if they didn't fatten up when they were monks, neither art nor nature would ever put any flesh on their bones.

I saw another one accompanied by a great many women, in two groups: one was composed of young, lively girls, tender, fair-haired, gracious and—or so I thought—good-tempered; the other made up of toothless hags, rheumy eyed, wrinkled, swarthy, cadaverous. It was explained to Pantagruel that he melted down and recast these old hags, rejuvenating them, artfully turning them into the young girls we saw with him, who had that very day been utterly transformed, turned into creatures of the beauty, elegance, shape, size, and with the gracious limbs they had had when they were fifteen and sixteen years old—excepting only for their heels, which remained somewhat shorter than they had been in their first youth. And this was why, thereafter, in all their encounters with men, they were much more inclined (and much easier) to tumble onto their backs.

The band of old hags were waiting for the next baking with great piety but also with great impatience, insisting that it was a totally unnatural and intolerable situation for such willing cunts to be so deficient in beauty. This alchemist practiced his art without interruption; nor were his profits small. Pantagruel asked him if, by a similar melting process, he could rejuvenate old men, but he answered that he could not—but they could be rejuvenated if they cohabited with a melted-down woman, thus impregnating themselves with that fifth variety of pox, known as alopecia, or skinlessness (in Greek, *Ophiasis*), by means of which they sloughed off their hair and skin, the way snakes do every year, and thus were rejuvenated, like the Arabian phoenix. This is the true Fountain of Youth, in which, just like that, the old and decrepit become young again, bright and cheerful, just as Euripides says happened to Iolaus, and as happened also, to Sappho's beloved Phaon, by Venus' kindness, and to Tithonus, by the intervention of Aurora, and to Aeson, by Medea's art, and also to Jason, who, according to Pherecydes and Simonides, was also rejuvenated by her, and as it happened, finally (according to Aeschylus), to our good Bacchus' nurses—and to their husbands, too.

Chapter Twenty-two ⁄⁄ The Different Feats Performed by the Queen's Officers, and How She Employed Us as Essence Abstractors

I later saw a great number of these officers whitening the skins of Ethiopians (it didn't take them long) simply by rubbing their bellies with the bottom of a basket.

Others were using three yoked pairs of foxes to plow the sandy shore, without losing any of their seeds.

Others were turning roof tiles white by washing them.

Others were drawing water from powdered rock, which you call pumice stone, grinding it for a long time in a marble mortar and thus changing its substance.

Others were shearing donkeys and finding an excellent fleece of first-rate wool.

Others were picking grapes from thornbushes and figs from thistles.

Others were milking billy goats and collecting it in a sieve, which helped the household enormously.

Others were washing donkeys' heads without losing their soap (which worked quite as well as washing black men white).

Others were chasing the wind with nets and catching huge crawfish.

I saw a young metal oxidizer ingeniously pulling farts out of a dead donkey and selling them for five cents a yard.

Another was decaying ideas and images. Now, that made for good eating!

But Panurge threw up most violently, seeing a prefect fermenting a huge vat of human piss with horse shit, adding in large quantities of Christian crap. Shame on the disgusting fellow! All the same, he assured us that this sacred distillation was drunk by their kings and royal princes, and prolonged their lives a good fathom or two.

Others were snapping sausages over their knees.

Others were skinning eels, tail first; nor did these eels scream before they were skinned, as Melun eels always do.

Others were making a great deal out of nothing, and then turning great things back into nothing again.

Others were cutting fires with a knife and drawing water with a net.

Others were making lanterns out of bladders, and shaggy clouds out of brass.

We saw twelve of them feasting in an arbor and guzzling four kinds of fresh and delicious wine out of huge tumblers, toasting each other all around, and they told us they were clearing up the weather according to local custom, this having been the method by which Hercules and Atlas, too, raised the weather by its heels.

Others were making a virtue of necessity, which seemed to me a handsome and appropriate occupation.

Others were performing alchemical feats with their teeth, picking at them for their dinners, a process which didn't do much toward filling up the latrines.

Others, on a great lawn, were carefully measuring how far fleas jumped, and told me this was highly essential for the proper governance of kingdoms, the conduct of wars, and the administration of republics, arguing that Socrates, who had been the first to bring philosophy out of the heavens and down to earth, and the first, also, to have turned an idle and persnickety pursuit into something useful and profitable, had spent at least half his time measuring flea jumps, as Aristophanes the Quintessential attests.

I saw two giants, off to one side, high up on a tower, who were standing guard, we were told, to protect the moon from wolves.

In one corner of the garden I met four others, arguing so bitterly that they were ready to pull out each other's hair. When I asked them what the argument was about, I learned that for four solid days they had been disputing three lofty and metaphysical propositions, for resolving which they fully expected mountains of gold. The first concerned a well-hung donkey's shadow; the second, the smoke from a lantern; and the third, whether a goat's fur was made of wool. Then they told us it did not seem at all strange to them that two contradictory statements could both be true, in mode, form, figure, and time. That was something the sophists of Paris would sooner see themselves unbaptized than admit.

We were watching the wonderful operations of these gentlemen with close attention, when the lady returned, together with her noble retinue, and Hesperus, the clear evening star, was already shining. Her return once again deprived us of our senses and dazzled our eyes. She immediately noted our awe, and said:

"What makes human thought wander, lost, in the abysses of wonder, is not these masterful effects, which, as they plainly see, stem from completely natural causes, assisted by the labors of knowing artisans. Rather, it is the novelty of the experiences which their senses must confront, being unable to foresee how simple and easy the work truly is, since a calm judgment is necessarily associated with diligent study. So stay alert, and put all fear aside, if fear should seize you as you contemplate what my officers are doing. Watch, listen, and consider everything in my household exactly as you please, bit by bit freeing yourselves from the bondage of Ignorance. This is precisely how I would have it be. And to give you sincere proof of that fact, and in testimony to those studious longings of which, it seems to me, you have given large and sufficient evidence, I hereby appoint you official royal essence abstractors. My chief cook will inscribe your names on the rolls when you leave here."

We thanked her humbly but silently, accepting the offer of the handsome appointment she had given us.

Chapter Twenty-three // How the Queen's Dinner Was Served, and What She Ate

Having made this declaration, the lady turned toward the gentlemen of her court and said:

"The orifice of the stomach, which is a common ambassador for the nourishment of the entire body—its inferior as well as its superior organs—urges us to restore to them, by means of proper foods, that which is taken away by the continuous process of natural heat affecting the basic humors, and nature, my own queen, makes it painful if we do not satisfy our animal spirits. My strongmen, my faithful followers, my noblemen: make it your only concern to promptly to see to it that tables are set out, adorned to profusion with every variety of legitimate restoratives. And you, too, my noble food tasters, together with my gracious molders and kneaders: knowing your skills, ornamented with care and diligence, I have no need to order that you do your work, now, any differently from how you did it before or how, clearly, you will always do it. I ask only that you proceed to do what you do."

Her speech done, she left us for a little while, together with some of her waiting women, and we were told this was to bathe herself, which was as common a custom among the ancients as is, now, washing one's hands before dining. The tables were set out at once, then draped with singularly precious cloths. Food was served according to the following arrangements: the lady ate nothing but celestial ambrosia, and drank only divine nectar, but the lords and ladies of the household, and we along with them, were served dishes as rare, dainty, and costly as any that Apicius ever dreamed of.

When the meal was done, they brought in a huge platter of assorted foods, just in case hunger had not declared a truce—so large, and filled so high, that the golden plane tree Pythius Bithinus gave King Darius would barely have covered it. There were pots of meat and vegetables and soups, salads, fricassees, stews, grilled goat meat, roast beef, boiled beef, grilled beef, great chunks of salt beef, legs of ham (cured in the old-fashioned way), heavenly salt bacon, pastries, tarts, a veritable mountain of Moorish couscous, cheeses, clotted cream, jellies, and all kinds of fruits. It all seemed to me both good and delicious, though I didn't eat any, being already nicely stuffed.

But I should mention that I saw pastries in pastry, really a rare sight, and these pastries in pastry were potted pastries, at the bottom of which I saw lots of dice, cards, tarot packs (of several kinds), chess pieces and boards, and cups full of gold pieces for those who wanted to gamble.

Finally, still farther down, I noticed a number of mules with well-decorated saddles, and velvet cloths, and gentle palfreys for use by either men or women, and I don't know how many velvet litters, plus Ferrara coaches for those who might want to take the air.

None of this seemed strange, but I did find the lady's way of eating very odd indeed. She chewed nothing, although she had good strong teeth and the food certainly needed chewing, but just because that was her custom. First the tasters tried all the dishes, and then the molders and kneaders thoroughly chewed them, their throats lined with red satin, with little gold stripes and braids, and their teeth like beautiful white ivory, by means of which, after they had thoroughly chewed her food, they poured it down into her stomach, through a fine gold funnel. For the same reason, the only way she ever shat was by proxy.

Chapter Twenty-four ⁄⁄ A Joyous Ball, in the Style of a Tourney, and in the Queen's Presence

Supper over, a ball in the style of a tourney was held, and in the lady's presence—worthy not only of being seen but of being forever remembered. To begin with, the hall floor was covered with a great velvet tapestry, fashioned like a chessboard—that is, in squares, half of them white, half yellow, each square three handbreadths across and perfectly evenly shaped. Then thirty-two young people entered the hall, sixteen of whom were dressed in golden cloth—that is, eight as young nymphs (looking just as the ancients painted them, in Diana's company), one king, one queen, two tower guardians, two knights, and two archers. The other sixteen were arranged in the same categories, but were wearing silver cloth. They were arranged on the tapestry in the following order: the kings kept to the back line, on the fourth square, with the golden king on a white square and the silver king on a yellow one; the queens were alongside their husbands, the golden queen on a yellow square, the silver on a white; the two archers, one on each side, were like guardians of their kings and queens. After the archers came the two knights, and after the knights the two tower guardians. In the front rank, in front of all the others, were the eight nymphs: between the two lines of nymphs four rows of squares remained empty.

Each of the two bands had its own musicians, eight to a side, dressed in similar costumes, one in orange damask, the other in white; they played with bright inventiveness on various instruments, most wonderfully in harmony and marvelously melodic—and as the progress of the ball required, they varied the tone, tempo, and measure of their performance, which particularly impressed me, considering the immense diversity of stances, steps, leaps, jumps, turns, escapes, ambushes, retreats, and unexpected encounters.

It seemed to me even further beyond ordinary human judgment that the personages in the ball immediately understood the sounds signaling their advance or retreat: no sooner was the music heard than they put themselves in the designated spot, although each of them moved differently. The nymphs, who were in the first rows, marched directly at their enemies (as if ready to provoke combat), one square after the other, except for their first move, when they had the option to go two squares. And they alone never retreated. And if one of them succeeded in getting to their enemy's last row, where the king ruled, she was crowned a queen—but to her own king—and thereafter moved in all respects and with the same privileges as the queen herself. But unless she became a queen, she could attack her enemies only on a diagonal line, and only an enemy in front of her. Neither the nymphs nor any other could lawfully capture any of their enemies if, in seizing him, they left their own king open to capture.

The kings moved and captured their enemies from any direction, moving always from the white squares to the yellow and then back again, except for their first move, when, if there were no other officers in their row but the tower guardians, they could exchange places with one of the guardians, and withdraw to their side.

The queens could move and capture more freely than anyone else—that is, everywhere and anywhere, and in every lawful manner, moving as far as they pleased across unoccupied space, either in a direct line or on a diagonal, provided only that in the latter case they remained on whatever color square they began on.

The archers could go forward or back, as far as they chose to. They too could never vary the color from which they started.

The knights moved and captured at right angles, first jumping across any space, whether occupied or not, and whether occupied by one of his own or by his enemies, and then dropping down either to the right or the left, going from one color to another—a leap capable of causing great damage to the adverse party, and so one that has to be watched for most carefully, since they never capture in a straight line.

The tower guardians move and capture directly, either to the right or the left, and can go backward as well as forward, like the kings, but also can travel as far as they like in any unoccupied direction, which the kings cannot do.

The basic law governing both sides was that, at the end of the combat, they were to try to lay siege to and shut away the other party's king, so that there was no escape. Once the king was thus shut in, unable to escape or to be helped by any of his people, the battle was over and the besieged king had been defeated. To try to keep him from such an unpleasant end, each and all of his troops is ready and willing to sacrifice his or her own life; they are all constantly attacking and capturing each other in all directions, all to the sound of the appropriate music. Anyone capturing a prisoner would first bow, then strike him lightly on the right hand, removing him from the board and taking his place. But if one of the kings was exposed to capture, it was unlawful for either side simply to make him prisoner. It was absolutely and inflexibly required that whoever thus put him or kept him in jeopardy make the king a profound bow and explicitly warn him, saying, "May the Lord protect you!"—so that his officers could help and protect him, or at least change places with him if, unhappily, he could not be assisted. So the king was never captured, but always greeted on bended knee (the left knee touching the ground) with the words "Good day to you, my lord." And that would be the end of the tourney.

Chapter Twenty-five ⁄⁄ The Fighting among the Ball's Thirty-two Participants

When the two companies were all in their places, the musicians began to play martial airs, quite as frightening as the signal for real battle to begin. We could see the two sides quiver and then settle down, ready to fight as soon as the moment arrived and they would be called from their camps. Then, suddenly, the silver company's musicians stopped, and only the gold company's could be heard, which signified to us that the gold company was about to attack. Which soon did indeed happen, because as a new tone was sounded we saw that the nymph stationed in front of the queen turned completely around and to her left, toward her king, as if asking his permission to begin the combat; she also bowed toward the whole company. Then, with admirable modesty, she moved two squares forward, bowing low to the opposite company, which she was attacking. When the gold musicians stopped, the silver ones began. I should not fail to mention that when the gold nymph had saluted first her king and then the rest of her company, they had not remained motionless, but all saluted her as well, turning to their left—except the queen, who turned to the right, toward her king. Indeed, this was the procedure followed at every move thereafter, through the entire course of the ball, by both companies alike.

As the silver musicians struck up, the silver nymph who had been stationed in front of her queen moved forward, saluting her king and her entire company most graciously, and they in turn saluting her, just as the gold band had done, except that they turned to their right and their queen to the left. The silver nymph went forward two squares, and bowing toward her adversaries stood face to face with the first gold nymph, with no distance whatever between them, each of them ready for battle, but unable to strike except to the side. Their companies then followed them, gold and silver alike, each in turn, acting as if they meant to skirmish, for the gold nymph—she who had arrived first—struck the silver nymph on her left hand, sent her off the board, and took her place. But to a new tune from the musicians, the silver archer did the same thing to the gold nymph. Another gold nymph made him move away; the silver knight came sallying forth; the gold queen moved in front of her king.

Then the silver king changed places, wary of the gold queen's fury, hiding himself where his right-hand tower guardian had been—a location which seemed to him very well supplied and defended.

The two left-hand knights, both the gold and the silver, came riding out, capturing many opposing nymphs, who were of course unable to retreat. The gold knight was especially active, devoting all his efforts to the taking of nymphs. But the silver knight had more important things on his mind, though he disguised what he was up to, and more than once when he could have captured a nymph he left her where she was and pressed forward, and ended close to his enemies and in a spot from which he greeted the enemy king with the words "May the Lord protect you!" Being thus warned to help their king, the gold company trembled—not because they were unable quickly to help their king, but because, in saving the king, they were inevitably going to lose their right-hand tower guardian. So the gold king moved away, to his left, and the silver knight captured the gold tower guardian—a very heavy loss indeed. At which point the gold company considered how best to avenge themselves on the knight, surrounding him on all sides so he could neither run away nor escape from their hands: he made a thousand attempts to flee, but they used a thousand tricks to detain him, until finally he was captured by the gold queen.

Deprived, now, of one of their important members, the gold company did everything they could to avenge themselves, striking out at random and most incautiously, and wreaking much havoc among the hosts of

their enemies. The silver company pretended to be deeply injured, waiting for their time to come, and handed over one of their nymphs to the
gold queen's nymphs, having set up a hidden ambush, but capturing the
nymph almost allowed the gold archer to capture the silver queen. The
gold knight meant to capture both the silver queen and king, saying to
them, "Good day, my lords." The silver knight saved them; he was captured by a gold nymph, who was taken, in turn, by a silver nymph.

The battle was intense. The tower guardians left their places to join in.
It was all a dangerous melee: the goddess of war had not yet declared
herself. Sometimes the silver forces swept right up to the gold king's tent,
and were suddenly repulsed. The gold queen in particular performed many
heroic deeds, in one sally capturing the silver archer and then, skirting
around, taking a tower guardian as well. Seeing this, the silver queen
came forward and hurled thunderbolts equally well, capturing the last
gold tower guardian and several nymphs, too.

The two queens fought long and hard, trying now to surprise one
another, now to protect and save their kings. In the end, the gold queen
captured the silver one, but was herself taken, immediately afterward, by
the silver knight. All that was left to the gold king were three nymphs,
an archer, and a tower guardian. The silver king had three nymphs and
the right-hand knight—and these reduced forces made them fight, from
that point on, more slowly and cautiously.

The two kings seemed melancholy, having lost their well-beloved royal
ladies, and gave all their study and effort to raising others to that dignity
and a new marriage, if they could, to one of their nymphs, who were
solemnly assured they would reach that exalted station if they could pen-
etrate to the last row of their enemy's territory. The gold company got
there first and turned one of their nymphs into a new queen, on whose
head they placed a crown and to whom they gave new garments to wear.

The silver company followed suit, and were just one row from creating a new queen as well, but the gold tower guardian was guarding that
line and the silver nymph was stopped where she was.

The new gold queen wished to show herself strong, brave, and warlike. She performed great feats of arms on the battlefield. But meanwhile
the silver knight captured the gold tower guardian, who was protecting
the camp's outskirts, which allowed the crowning of a new silver queen,
who also wished to show her courage in her new role. Fighting was
renewed, more fierce than ever. A thousand tricks, a thousand attacks, a
thousand moves were made by both sides, until the silver queen sneaked
into the gold king's tent, saying, "May the Lord protect you!" And only
his new queen could save him, which she made no trouble about doing.

Then the silver knight, leaping from all sides, joined up with his queen
and so disarranged the gold king that, when the knight greeted the king,
he was obliged to surrender his new queen. Nevertheless, the gold archer

and the two remaining nymphs defended their king with all their might. But in the end they were all captured and taken off the field, leaving the gold king entirely alone.

Then the whole silver company said to him, bowing most profoundly, "Good day to you, my lord," thus making the silver king the conqueror. At which words both companies of musicians began to play together, as a sign of victory. And thus this first ball ended in such great good cheer, such wonderfully decorous steps and bows, such honest, upright bearing, and such rare grace, that we were all as happy as people in an ecstasy, thinking—not inaccurately—that we had been transported to the sovereign delights and ultimate felicity of Olympus itself.

With the first tourney finished, the two companies returned to their original places and, just as they had fought before, so too they began their combat for the second time, except that the music was half a beat faster than it had been earlier—and the combat proceeded entirely differently, this time. I saw that the gold queen, as if upset at the rout of her army, was aroused by the music and put herself among the first in the field, along with an archer and a knight, coming very close to surprising the silver king in his tent, along with his officers. Then, seeing her plan had been discovered, she threw herself among the silver troops, causing so much difficulty for the nymphs and other officers that it was pitiable to see. You would have said this was another Amazonian Penthesilea, thundering through the Greek camp, but the scandal lasted only a very short time, because the silver company, shuddering at the loss of their comrades, nevertheless hid their grief and secretly arranged an ambush for her, placing an archer at a distant angle, as well as a roaming knight, who captured her and sent her off the battlefield. It didn't take long to defeat the remainder of the gold army. The queen would have been far better off to stay near her king, rather than to go so far away from him, and to venture out only when it was necessary, and even then to go properly accompanied. Thus the silver company prevailed, as they had the first time.

For the third and final ball, the two companies took their positions, as before, but they seemed to me more cheerful, more thoughtful than the first two times. And the music, too, was more than a fifth faster, and in a warlike Phrygian mode of the kind Marsyas pioneered, so long ago. And they began to turn and fight so nimbly that, in one beat of the music, they made four moves, including the turning and bowing we have already described, so that the combat was just a series of leaping jumps and capers and somersaults, one right after the other. And seeing them make their bow and then turn swiftly on one foot, we thought their movements were like a child's whirling top, whipped along as fast as it can go and spinning so rapidly that it doesn't seem to be moving at all, appearing to be at rest, not in motion, or to sleep (as they call it). And if you put a point of color on such a top, it seems to our eyes to be simply a continuous line, as Nicholas of Cusa has wisely noted in his divine book.

All we heard were hand claps and exclamations from both sides, repeated at every move. Cato was never so severe, or Grandfather Crassus so grim, or Timon of Athens such a misanthrope, or Heraclitus so alienated from that which is truly human—that is, laughter—that they would not have dissolved in gaiety, seeing (to the sound of such brisk music) these young men and their queens and nymphs moving, stepping, leaping, tumbling, capering, spinning in five hundred different ways, so agilely that one never blocked another. As the number of those on the battlefield diminished, it was even more marvelous to see the tricks and turnings which they used to surprise each other, following the lead of the music. And let me say more: if this superhuman spectacle confused our senses, astonished our spirits, and drew us right out of ourselves, we felt our hearts even more moved and frightened by the music. I can easily believe that it was by means of such harmonies, such melodies, that Ismenias drove Alexander the Great, though he was at table and quietly dining, to leap up and seize his weapons. The gold king was the victor in this third tourney.

During these dances, the lady quietly disappeared, and we never saw her again. Her chief cook and his men took us and duly enrolled us in the high rank and estate she had ordered. Then we went down to the port of Mateotechnie and on board our boats, having heard there was a wind at our stern and, should we neglect to take the opportunity when it was offered, we might well not have another such chance for three weeks or more.

Chapter Twenty-six ⁄⁄ How We Arrived at the Island of Roads, in Which the Roads Roaded

After we had sailed for two days, the island of Roads came into sight, and there we saw something truly memorable. The roads there are animals and alive, thus proving Aristotle's argument that the unmistakable sign of animal existence is a creature that can move by itself. Because these roads in fact moved exactly like animals, some of them even being wandering roads, after the fashion of the planets; others were passing roads, crossing roads, crisscrossing roads. And we saw that travelers often asked the natives:

"Where's this road going? And that one?"

And they were told:

"Between Midi and Faverolles . . . To the parish church . . . Into the city . . . To the river."

Then, taking the proper road, without any further fuss or bother, they'd find the way to their destination, just as people do who take a boat on the Rhône, to journey from Lyons to Avignon and Arles. But just as there's always something wrong with everything, and nothing is uniformly good, so they told us they were afflicted with a species of men called road enemies and street beaters, of whom the poor roads were terrified, shrinking and recoiling from them as we do from thieves and robbers. These men lay in wait for the roads, as one hunts wolves with traps, and ducks with nets. I saw one of these men arrested because, contrary to all reason, he'd taken the school road, which was clearly a much longer way. Another boasted that, acting absolutely fairly, he'd taken the shortcut, and claimed he'd done very well indeed, being the first one to finish.

So too Carpalim once said to Epistemon, meeting him one day, his pisser in his hand, pissing against a wall, that he wouldn't be surprised, now, seeing Epistemon always the first to rise with Pantagruel, because what he held in his hand was both the shortest and the least ridden on.

I recognized the great Bourges highway and saw it strutting slowly and solemnly, then running as fast as it could when some carters came along, threatening to trample it under their horses' hooves and run their carts right over its belly, as Tullia ran her chariot over the belly of her father, Servius Tullius, the sixth king of the Romans.

I also recognized the old green Peronne highway, heading for Saint-Quentin, and no road ever seemed tidier or more decent.

And I recognized, there among the rocks, the good old Ferrata road, winding up over Great Bear Mountain. It reminded me of a painting of Saint Jerome—at least, it would have looked like him, if his lion had been a bear, because it was completely mortified, with a long, white, scraggly beard (you'd have thought they were icicles). It had a lot of big sea-pine rosaries, rough and unkempt, and seemed to be down on its knees, not standing upright, or lying down, beating on its chest with fat, coarse stones. It made us feel both pity and fear.

As we stood watching it, a young bachelor, a native of the place, showed us a beautifully smooth road, all white and more or less padded with straw, and said:

"In the future, don't look down on Thales the Milesian, who asserts that everything begins with water, or the judgment of Homer, in the *Iliad,* that everything is born of the ocean. This ice road which you see was born of water and will return to water: two months ago boats journeyed down this road; now carts roll along it."

"Indeed," said Pantagruel, "how sad a tale. In our world we see this all the time, five hundred or more of these transformations every year."

Then, as we stood watching the motion of these moving roads, he told us that in his opinion Philolaus and Aristarchus had philosophized on this island, that Seleucus had here concluded that the earth in fact moved around on its poles, rather than the sky turning (though we still feel as if the contrary is true—just as, when we're traveling along the Loire River, the trees near us seem to be moving, although it's we who are moving, in our boat, and they're not moving at all).

Returning to our ships, we saw, near the shore, three road enemies who'd been caught trying to ambush a road being racked on the wheel, and one great rascal was being burned in a slow fire, who had beaten a road and broken one of its ribs; they told us the injured road was the one which followed the banks of the river Nile, in Egypt.

Chapter Twenty-seven ⁄ How We Passed the Island of Wooden Shoes and the Order of Trilling Friars

Later we passed the island of Wooden Shoes, where they eat only codfish soup. Nevertheless, we were well received and treated by the king of the island, named Benius the Third, who after drinking took us to see a new monastery entirely founded, erected, and built for the Order of Trilling Friars, according to his own plan. "Trilling Friars" is what he called his monks, explaining that in our world we had Friars Minor, or Augustinians, Little Servants and Beloved of our Blessed Lady, as well as the glorious and handsome Franciscans, who by papal order were a sort of half-men; there were also Friars Minim, Saint Francis of Paola's order, and enormously fond of smoked herrings, and also the Half-Minim Friars— and, in short, with all those musically modest names having already been appropriated, the best he could do was "trill."

The statute of the order, obtained from the lady queen of the Fifth Essence (for whom all things are harmonious), required that all the monks be dressed like licensed house burners (otherwise known as soldiers), except that just as roofers in Anjou wear quilted kneepads, so these monks wore belly pads, so that belly-pad makers enjoyed a splendid reputation among them.

The codpiece of their breeches was shaped like a slipper, and each of them wore two, one in front and one stitched behind, thus asserting, via this bit of codpiecetic double-dealing, that some terrible mysteries were being fully and properly represented. Their shoes were round like pots and pans, in imitation of those who lived along the Dead Sea, in Arabia. They also wore their beards close-cropped and shoes with hobnails. And to demonstrate that they cared nothing for Fortune, the backs of their heads were shaved and plucked like pigs, from the top of the head down to the shoulder blades. In front, the hair grew as it pleased, from the parietal bones on down. Thus they defied Fortune, like men who did not even think about all the good things which exist in the world. And in order to defy wayward and shifting Fortune still further, each of them wore a well-sharpened razor, nor did they carry it in their hands, as Fortune does, but in their belts, as if it were a rosary. And they ground it still sharper twice a day, and stropped and honed it three times a night.

Each of them wore a round ball under his feet, because Fortune is said to have one under hers. Their hoods had flaps in front, rather than in back: thus their faces were concealed and they were free to scoff as much as they pleased, both at Fortune and at the fortunate—neither more nor less than our young ladies do when they're wearing a half-mask, which you call a nose mask (though the ancients called it "charity," since it covered a multitude of sins). And they always have the back of the head uncovered, as we do our faces: which is why they can go either belly first or ass first, as they please. When they went ass first, you'd think it their natural way of walking, as much because of their round shoes as because of the codpiece they wear back there, and also because they shaved the backs of their heads and painted them, crudely, with two eyes and a mouth (like those you see painted on coconuts). When they went belly first, you'd think they were playing blind man's buff. It was a fine sight to see.

And that was how they lived. When the clear morning star began to rise over the earth, they began to charitably kick each other with booted feet, spurring one another on. And thus booted and spurred they slept— or at least snored, and as they slept they wore spectacles on their noses, or opera glasses, anyway.

This seemed to us very strange, but their response was very much to the point. They assured us that, when the Final Judgment came, human beings would rest and sleep. In order to show quite obviously that they had no inclination to refuse that last call, as the fortunate do, they keep themselves booted, spurred, and ready to leap onto their horses when the trumpets sound.

When the noon bells rang (note that all their bells—church bells, watch bells, dinner bells—were made according to Pontano's plan, meaning they were quilted over with down, and the clapper was a fox tail), it was midday and they woke up and took off their boots. Anyone who wanted to piss, pissed, and anyone who wanted to shit, shat, and anyone who wanted to sneeze, sneezed. But by strict law, and a rigorous statute, everyone yawned like crazy, and breakfasted while yawning. It struck me as a pleasant spectacle: hanging their boots and spurs on a rack, they went down to the cloister, where they carefully washed their hands and mouth, then seated themselves on tall stools and picked their teeth until the provost gave them a sign by whistling into his cupped hands—and then they opened their gullets as wide as they could and yawned, sometimes for half an hour, sometimes more, sometimes less, until the prior thought their breakfast was appropriate for that particular day on the ecclesiastical calendar. After that they marched in a handsome procession, carrying two banners, one a handsomely painted portrait of Virtue, the other a portrait of Fortune. One of the Trilling Friars came first, carrying Fortune's banner; another came after him, with Virtue's, and in his other hand a sprinkling can containing holy water, exactly as Ovid describes it in his *Fasti,* or Poetical Calendar, with which he continually whipped the Trilling Friar just in front of him, who was carrying Fortune's banner.

"This ordering," said Panurge, "runs directly contrary to Cicero's judgment, and that of Plato and Aristotle, according to whom Virtue should precede and Fortune follow."

But they reminded us that it did indeed make sense, since their purpose was to thrash Fortune.

During the procession, they trilled between their teeth (but melodiously) I don't know what devotional songs: I didn't understand their mumbo jumbo. But listening most attentively, I became aware that they sang only with their ears. Oh, what lovely harmony, and how beautifully consonant with the sound of their bells! You'll never find *them* out of tune.

Pantagruel made a wonderful observation about their procession, saying to us:

"Have you seen, and duly noted, the remarkable shrewd subtlety of these Trilling Friars? To make their procession absolutely perfect, they left by one church door and they're going back by another. Thus, they're being scrupulously careful not to go in where they originally came out. On my honor, these are people of fine discrimination—fine enough to be gilded, as fine as elephants, fine without fineness, but in essence fine (if you run them through a fine filter)."

"That kind of subtlety," said Brother John, "comes from superfine philosophy, and I don't understand it one bit—damned if I do!"

"But," answered Pantagruel, "it's even more remarkable because we can't understand it. Because subtlety understood, subtlety anticipated, subtlety uncovered, loses its subtlety, and its essence, and its very name: we call it heavy lumpishness. On my honor, these people know a thing or two!"

Once the procession had ended, which served them as a walk and healthy exercise, they retired to their dining hall and stuck their knees under the tables, each of them leaning his stomach and chest on a lantern. Seated thus, they awaited the entrance of a great wooden shoe, with a fork in his hand, who gave them all a taste of it. Then they began their meal with cheese and ended it with mustard and lettuce, as Martial tells us was the ancients' habit. Each of them indeed got a dish of mustard and, at the end of the meal, each was served with mustard once again.

This was how they ate. On Sundays they dined on blood puddings, sausages, chitterlings, veal stew, roast liver (nicely sliced), and quail, but always with cheese at the beginning and mustard at the end. Mondays, beautiful peas and bacon, with more than enough commentary and interlinear glosses—that is to say, sauces and everything else necessary. Tuesdays, heaps of holy bread, flatcakes, pancakes, griddle cakes, plain cakes, and biscuits. Wednesdays, sheep's heads—beautiful sheep's heads, and calf's heads, too, and badger heads, all of which are abundant in that country. Thursdays, seven sorts of soups and—as ever—mustard in between. Fridays, nothing but sorb apples—although as far as I could judge, from their color, they weren't very ripe. Saturdays, they gnawed on the bones. Not that they were poor or needy, because they'd all been given excellent stomachs. They drank antifortunal wine, which was what they called God-only-knows-what country brew. When they wanted to eat or drink, they pulled down the hoods of their capes, which did very well as either a visor or a bib.

Dinner done with, they uttered very fine prayers to God, all by way of trills. The rest of the day, while waiting for the Final Judgment, they devoted themselves to charitable works: on Sundays, they thrashed each other; Mondays, they scoffed; Tuesdays, they scratched each other's backs; Wednesdays, everyone blew everyone else's nose; Thursdays, they pulled the snot out of each other's noses; Fridays, they all tickled each other; Saturdays, they whipped each other.

That was their regimen when they were living in their monastery. If the prior directed them to go out into the world, they were strictly forbidden, under the threat of ghastly punishment, to eat or even touch fish, if they were traveling on the sea or down a river, nor were they allowed to eat, when they were on dry land, the idea being to clearly demonstrate that enjoying an object was not, for them, the same as enjoying power over it, nor was it the result of any strong or overwhelming desire, for they could no more be shaken by such feelings than could the rock of Marpesus. They did everything to the sound of proper, appropriate hymns and chants, always however sung through their ears, as we have said. When the sun lay down in the ocean, they booted and spurred each other, just as they always did, and readied themselves for sleep, their spectacles on their noses. At midnight, the wooden shoe entered, and they rose; they would sharpen and whet their razors, and having conducted their procession, would put the tables on top of them and eat all exactly as they always did.

Brother John Mincemeat, seeing these happy Trilling Friars, and listening to the nature of their governing rule, completely lost himself and, crying in a loud voice, said:

"Oh, a fat church rat sitting at table! I'll tear him apart, I will, or tell me another, by God! Oh, if only Priapus were here, as he was when Canidia and old Sagana were staging their rites in the dark, so he could see them farting and counterfarting, trilling back and forth! Now I know we're really on the underside of the earth. Over in Germany they're tearing down monasteries and defrocking monks. Here, they're turning them upside down and backward."

Chapter Twenty-eight ⁄⁄ Panurge, Questioning One of the Trilling Friars, Gets Only Monosyllables Out of Him

Ever since our arrival, Panurge had done nothing but stare hard at the faces of these royal Trillers. Then, taking one of them by the sleeve (a monk as lean as a dried devil), he asked:

"Brother Triller, Thriller, Killer-Diller, where're the sluts?"

THE FRIAR answered him:

"Down there."

PANURGE: Got a lot of them here?

F.: No.

P.: How many?—tell me the truth.

F.: Twenty.

P.: How many do you want?

F.: Hundred.

P.: Where're you hiding them?

F.: There.

P.: I guess they're not all the same age—but how do they look?

F.: Good.

P.: What kind of complexions, eh?

F.: Smooth.

P.: Their hair?

F.: Blond.

P.: And their eyes?

F.: Black.

P.: Their tits?

F.: Round.

P.: Their face?

F.: Pretty.

P.: Their eyebrows?

F.: Long.

P.: Their charms?

F.: Ripe.

P.: Their glance?

F.: Frank.

P.: What about their feet?

F.: Flat.

P.: Their heels?

F.: Short.

P.: And their arms?

F.: Long.

P.: What do they wear on their hands?

F.: Gloves.

P.: What kind of rings on their fingers?

F.: Gold.

P.: What do you dress them in?

F.: Cloth.

P.: What kind of cloth?

F.: New.

P.: What color?

F.: Green.

P.: And their headdress?

F.: Blue.

P.: What kind of shoes?

F.: Brown.

P.: Now all this cloth, what sort is it?

F.: Fine.

P.: What are their shoes made of?

F.: Leather.

P.: And what shape are they in, usually?

F.: Filthy.

P.: But do they do the job?

F.: Fast.

P.: Let's get to the kitchen—I mean, your wenches' kitchens. Let's run down the menu, slow but sure. What's in their kitchens?

F.: Fire.

P.: What keeps this fire going?

F.: Wood.

P.: This wood, what kind is it?

F.: Dry.

P.: What kind of trees do you get it from?

F.: Yews.

P.: The little pieces? the sticks?

F.: Alder.

P.: What do you burn in your own rooms?

F.: Pine.

P.: And what else?

F.: Elm.

P.: Now these sluts, I'll take half of them—but how do you feed them?

F.: Well.

P.: What do they eat?

F.: Bread.

P.: What kind?

F.: Brown.

P.: And anything else?

F.: Meat.

P.: What kind of meat?

F.: Roast.

P.: Do they eat any soups?

F.: No.

P.: And pastries?

F.: Tons.

P.: I'm with them. Don't they eat any fish?

F.: Yes.

P.: Really? But what else?

F.: Eggs.

P.: And how do they like them?

F.: Cooked.

P.: I mean, cooked how?

F.: Hard.

P.: Is that all they eat?

F.: No.

P.: All right, what else?

F.: Beef.

P.: Anything else?

F.: Pork.

P.: And anything else?

F.: Goose.

P.: Besides that?

F.: Gander.

P.: Plus?

F.: Cocks.

P.: What's their sauce made of?

F.: Salt.

P.: And if they have a sweet tooth?

F.: Grape-mash.

P.: At the end of the meal?

F.: Rice.

P.: Anything else?

F.: Milk.

P.: Anything more than that?

F.: Peas.

P.: What kind of peas do you mean?

F.: Green.

P.: What do you mix with them?

F.: Bacon.

P.: And fruit?

F.: Good.

P.: How do you eat it?

F.: Raw.

P.: Plus?
F.: Nuts.
P.: How do they drink?
F.: Straight.
P.: But what?
F.: Wine.
P.: What sort?
F.: White.
P.: And in the winter?
F.: Healthy.
P.: In spring?
F.: Sharp.
P.: And in summer?
F.: Fresh.
P.: In the fall, when they're bringing in the grapes?
F.: Sweet.

"By all the holy whores!" cried Brother John. "How fat these trilling bitches must get, and how they must have to keep moving, if they eat so much and so well!"

"Please wait," said Panurge, "until I'm finished. Now, what time do they go to bed?"

F.: Night.
P.: And when do they get up?
F.: Day.

"Now here," said Panurge, "is the easiest Triller I've ridden on all year. I wish to God, and to blessed Saint Triller, and the blessed and most sanctified Saintess Trillerine, that this fellow was Lord High Justice in Paris! By all that's holy, my friend, how he'd hurry those lawsuits along, and shorten all the pleadings and counterpleadings, and run down the hearings, and clean out the briefcases, and rip through the papers—oh, what a documentary paraphraser he'd be! But now, let's turn back to their way of life and have some clear, sensible, sober conversation about our aforementioned sisters in charity.

"What kind of shape is it in?"

F.: Big.
P.: At the entrance?
F.: Fresh.
P.: At the bottom?
F.: Hollow.
P.: I meant, what's the weather like in there?
F.: Hot.

P.: What's at the edges?

F.: Hair.

P.: What color?

F.: Red.

P.: But on the oldest ones?

F.: Gray.

P.: How are their leaps?

F.: Prompt.

P.: How well do they move their asses?

F.: Hard.

P.: They all know how to jump?

F.: Too much.

P.: But what kind of tools do you have?

F.: Large.

P.: How are they, around the ends?

F.: Round.

P.: What color are the tips?

F.: Red. Brown.

P.: When they've done the job, what are they like?

F.: Limp.

P.: And your ball bags?

F.: Heavy.

P.: How are they tucked up?

F.: Close.

P.: What're they like, when you're done?

F.: Dead.

P.: Now, by the holy oath you've sworn, tell me: when you're ready to screw, how do you spread them out?

F.: Flat.

P.: What do they say when they're screwing?

F.: Words.

P.: But they do you right, eh? They really work at it?

F.: True.

P.: Do you give them children?

F.: Never.

P.: How do you sleep together?

F.: Nude.

P.: Now, by that same oath you've sworn, how many times a day do you usually do it?

F.: Six.

P.: And at night?

F.: Ten.

"By the holy pox!" said Brother John. "The rascal can't be bothered going past sixteen. He's shy."

P.: Yes, but could you do as well, Brother John? By God, he's a green leper! And is this how all the others do it?

F.: All.

P.: Who's the very best?

F.: Me.

P.: Do you ever come up wanting?

F.: Never.

P.: Now, that's just too much for me. When you've emptied and exhausted your spermatic vessels, one day, can there be much left the next?

F.: More.

P.: Either I'm dreaming, or they've gotten hold of that Indian herb Theophrastus talks about. But now, while you're having your fun, just suppose that by some lawful impediment—or for any reason at all—your tool gets smaller, how would it be for you then?

F.: Bad.

P.: And what would the sluts do?

F.: Yell.

P.: And if it lasts all day?

F.: Worse.

P.: What do you give them then?

F.: Trouble.

P.: And what do they give you?

F.: Shit.

P.: So what do you say?

F.: Fart.

P.: How does it sound?

F.: Rough.

P.: How do you punish them?

F.: Hard.

P.: And what's the result?

F.: Blood.

P.: What does that do to their complexion?

F.: Flushed.

P.: How would you like it better?

F.: Painted.

P.: What do you always remain?

F.: Feared.

P.: And what do they think of you, afterward?

F.: Sainted.

P.: By that same holy oath, what time of year do you do the job worst?

F.: August.

P.: And when do you do it best?

F.: March.

P.: And how is it the rest of the year?

F.: Fun.

Then Panurge, smiling, said:

"Here's the poorest Triller in the world. Have you heard how emphatic he is, how concise and yet complete in all his replies? All he gives me are one-word answers. I'll bet he'd make three bites of a cherry."

"By God's heart," said Brother John, "I'll bet he doesn't talk like that with his sluts: he's pretty polysyllabic with them. And you talk about taking a cherry in three bites: by holy Saint Francis, I swear he'd make only two bites of a leg of mutton, and he'd handle a quart of wine in one gulp. Just see how drag tailed he is."

"These wicked monastic orders," said Epistemon, "are all the same, always scrabbling for food—and then they tell us that's all they have in this earthly life. What the devil more do kings and great princes have?"

Chapter Twenty-nine ⁄⁄ Epistemon's Dislike of Lent

"Have you noted," said Epistemon, "how this wicked, uncouth Triller cites March as the most ribald of months?"

"Yes," answered Pantagruel. "Yet it's always in Lent, which was created to mortify the flesh, mortify the sensual appetites, and subdue sexual excitement."

"And from that," said Epistemon, "you can tell how smart the pope was—the first one to create Lent: this worn-out rascal of a Triller admits he's never more of a filthy lecher than in Lenten season. You can also consider the obvious proofs, brought forward by all good, learned doctors, that the whole rest of the year people don't eat as much aphrodisiac food as, plainly, they eat during Lent: beans, peas, kidney beans, chickpeas, onions, nuts, oysters, herring and other salted meats, pickling brine, and salads made up of aphrodisiac herbs—like dame's violet, garden cress, tarragon, watercress, river cress, rampion, horned poppy, hops, figs, rice, raisins."

"You'll be flabbergasted," said Pantagruel, "to hear that the good pope who created Lent specifically commanded those exact foods, in order to assist in the propagation of the human race, knowing it to be the season of the year when natural warmth leaves the center of the body (where it has been confined by winter's cold) and, just as sap does in trees, is dispersed to its outer limbs. I was reminded of that, seeing the baptismal register at Thouars, where the number of children born during October and November is greater than during all the other ten months of the year—and, when you calculate backward, you find that all these children were made, conceived, and engendered during Lent."

"I've been listening to all this," said Brother John, "with great pleasure. But the late curate of Jonvert didn't credit this copious impregnating of women to Lenten foods, but rather to those little round-shouldered alms collectors, those little preachers in their shiny boots, those filthy little confessors, who at this season in their holy roaming empire damn all wandering husbands to the third level in hell, down under Lucifer's very claws. And the husbands are so terrified that they stop screwing their chambermaids and come back to their wives. I have spoken."

"Ah," said Epistemon. "You interpret the institution of Lent according to your private fantasy: we're all overflowing with our own ideas. But though I think we're coming to the total suppression of Lent, all the medical men are going to fight the ban—I'm sure of it, I've heard them say so. Because, you see, without Lent their art will be scorned, they'll earn nothing, no one will ever be sick. All illness begins with Lent: it's the true nursery, the original seedbed and storehouse of all sicknesses. Worse still, Lent not only rots the body, it also drives the soul wild. That's when devils really work at their trade; hypocrites come out into the sunlight; bigots enjoy their finest hours, full of solemn meetings, stations of the cross, pardons, confessions, whippings, and condemnations. I don't mean, of course, that in these matters the northern peoples are any better than we are: I'm just reciting facts."

"All right," said Panurge, turning to the Trilling Friar, "my ball-shaking friend, what do you think of this fellow, eh? Is he a heretic or is he a heretic?"

P.: Very.
P.: Should he be burned?
F.: Should.
P.: And as soon as possible?
F.: Right.
P.: Without being parboiled?
F.: Without.
P.: Then how?
F.: Alive.
P.: Until what happens?
F.: Death.
P.: Because he's made you very angry?
F.: Skunk!
P.: So what would you like him to do?
F.: Burn.
P.: As you've burned many others?
F.: Many.
P.: Who were heretics?
F.: Less.
P.: But you've burned them anyway?
F.: Lots.
P.: Do you redeem any of them?
F.: Hardly.

P.: They all have to be burned?

F.: All.

"It escapes me," said Epistemon, "what pleasure you can get, reasoning with this wicked rag-barrel monk, but if I didn't already know you, you'd give me an impression something less than honorable."

"By God, let's go, then!" said Panurge. "I like him so much, I'll bring him straight to Gargantua. When I'm married, he can serve me as my wife's fool."

"Indeed," said Epistemon, "he'll serve her, all right!"

"And now," said Brother John, laughing, "you've gotten what's coming to you, my poor Panurge. You'll never get away from the fact that, once you're married, you're going to be cuckolded, ass-high."

Chapter Thirty // How We Visited the Land of Sweetness

We sailed on for two days, happy to have had the chance to see the new Order of Trilling Friars. On the third day, our pilot brought us to the most beautiful and delightful island in the world, called Frieze Island, because all the roads were made of that coarse woolen cloth. Here we came upon the land of Sweetness, so famous at court, since its likeness is embroidered on all the pages' uniforms—a land where neither trees nor flowers ever lose leaves or petals, for they are made of damask and velvet. And all the birds and beasts are made of woven tapestry.

We saw a number of animals, birds, and trees very like those we have here, in shape, size, girth, and color, except that none of them ate anything, or sang, or ever bit anyone, as ours do.

But we saw some, there, that we had never seen before. Among others, we saw a number of elephants of different sorts, especially six males and six females which their trainer had exhibited in the theater at Rome, in the days of Germanicus, Emperor Tiberius's nephew—learned elephants, musical elephants, philosophers, dancers, ballroom dancers, buffoons—and which sat at table, in good order, silently eating and drinking like so many good monks in a monastery dining hall. Their snouts (which we call "proboscises") were two yards long, and they use them to get water for drinking, and to take palm leaves, apples, plums, and all sorts of foods; they can defend themselves or attack with their noses, exactly as if they were hands, and in battle they throw people high in the air, and when they fall split their sides with laughter. Their ears, shaped like a windmill vane, are very large and beautiful. Their legs have joints and are articulated: anyone who has written to the contrary has never seen the animals except in paintings. They have two huge horns between their teeth—at least, Juba called them horns rather than teeth, and Pausanias, too, but Philostratus says they're teeth and not horns. It's all the same to me, so long as you understand that they're the true ivory—three or four yards long—and grow out of the upper and not the lower jaw. If you believe those who have written anything different, you'll be in trouble, like that flying liar Aelian. It was there and nowhere else that Pliny saw them, dancing on ropes hung with little bells, and doing all sorts of fantastic things, passing back and forth above tables laden with food and drink, without bothering those who were drinking.

I saw a rhinoceros who looked very like one that Hans Kleberg showed me, and not much different from a boar I saw, once, in Limoges, except that it had a horn on its snout, a yard long and pointed, which it was not afraid to use against an elephant in combat. Striking under the belly (the softest and most vulnerable spot on an elephant's body), it laid him dead on the ground.

And I saw thirty-two unicorns, wonderfully vicious beasts which strikingly resemble a good horse, except that they have staglike heads, the feet of an elephant, a tail like a wild boar, and a sharp black horn in the middle of their foreheads, six or seven feet long, which ordinarily hangs down like a turkey's crest, but when needed for fighting or anything else can be raised stiff and straight. I saw one unicorn, accompanied by a number of other wild animals, purifying a fountain with its horn. Panurge informed me that his horn (not, however, located on his forehead) was very like the unicorn's, not in overall length but in its powers and capacities, for just as the unicorn cleansed stagnant ponds and fountains of any muck or poison that might have been in them, so that any animal who wanted to drink after he had been drinking could do so in perfect safety, so too you could grope around after him without any danger of cankers, or the pox, or hot piss, or syphilitic sores, and other minor improvements of that sort, because if there was any kind of sickness lurking in the noxious slit, his sensitive horn would completely cleanse it away.

"When you're married," said Brother John, "we'll test that out on your wife. Let's do try it, for the love of God, for you're giving us most helpful information."

"Fine!" answered Panurge. "And immediately afterward your stomach will take in that holy little pill which brings you to God, made up of twenty-two blows from a dagger (swallowed once upon a time by Julius Caesar)."

"I'd prefer," said Brother John, "a glass of some good fresh wine."

I also saw the golden fleece, won by Jason. Those who have said it was not a fleece, but a golden apple, since the Greek *melon* means both "apple" and "sheep," haven't made good use of their visit to the land of Sweetness.

I saw a chameleon like the one Aristotle describes, and very like the one shown me by Charles Marais, distinguished physician in that noble city of Lyons, on the Rhône River—and this animal lived on air alone, just as the other one did.

I saw three hydras, though I'd seen this creature before. They're snakes with seven different heads.

I saw fourteen phoenixes. I have read in various authors that, at any one time, there is only one of these beasts in the world. But, so far as my puny brain can understand, those who have written such things have never seen the phoenix except in a tapestry—like the one in Lactance, near Firmium.

I saw the skin of Apuleius' golden ass.

I saw three hundred and nine pelicans, six thousand and sixteen Jovian Seleucid birds, marching along in good military style and devouring grasshoppers in wheat fields; and cynamolgi, argathyles, caprimulges, thynnuncules, crotenotaires—no, I mean, onocrotales, with their gaping gullets, stymphalides (or harpies), panthers, gazelles, antelopes, cenocephals, satyrs, sea unicorns, narwhals, reindeer, wild oxen, buffalo, pegasus steeds, monkeys, earth-splitting neades, serpents, cercopithecus apes, bison, musk-oxen, byturi, ophyr snakes, vampires, and griffins.

I saw the Middle of Lent on horseback (the Middle of August and the Middle of March held his stirrups), and werewolves, centaurs, tigers, leopards, hyenas, giraffes, and orygian unicorns.

I saw a remora, or sucking fish, tiny, called *echeneis* by the Greeks, near a great ship which, though all its sails were set and there was a brisk wind, could not move. I'm sure it was the boat in which the tyrant Periander sailed, which was stopped, in the teeth of the wind, by just such a small fish. It was surely in the land of Sweetness, and nowhere else, that Mutianus saw the remora. Brother John told us there used to be two kinds of ruling fish, in the parliamentary courts, both of which rotted the bodies and ruined the minds of all litigants—noblemen and commoners, poor and rich, great and small. One was the April fish, also known as mackerel or pimps. The other was the poisonous remora, who would keep a lawsuit going forever, with no hope of a final judgment.

I saw sphynxes, jackals, lynx, cephi (which have forelegs like hands, plus hind legs like a man's feet), crocutes, eales (which are as big as hippopotamuses and have a tail like an elephant, jaws like a wild boar, and movable horns like donkey's ears), and cucrocutes, light-footed beasts as big as Mirebalais donkeys, which have the chest, neck, and tail of a lion, legs like a stag, a mouth that opens right up to their ears, and just two teeth, one above and one below: they are said to speak with a human voice, though when we were there they never said a word.

You may say that no one gets to see a hawk's nest; frankly, I saw eleven of them, and examined them with care.

I saw left-handed halberd spears, which I'd never seen before.

I saw manticores, exceedingly strange animals: they have the body of a lion, red fur, a human face and ears, and three rows of teeth, interlaced, much the way you can fit the fingers of one hand into the fingers of the other. They have a stinger in their tail, which they use much like scorpions, and their voices are soft and melodious.

I saw catobleppes, small, savage animals with immensely big heads—so big, indeed, they can scarcely lift them. Their eyes are so venomous that whoever looks into them dies at once, as if they'd seen a basilisk dragon.

And I saw some beasts with two backs, who seemed to me wonderfully happy and even better ass wigglers than the wagtail itself: their asses were perpetually in motion.

And I saw crawfish being milked, which I'd never seen before; they marched in very good order and were a fine sight.

Chapter Thirty-one ⁄⁄ How We Saw Hearsay, in the Land of Sweetness, and His School for Legal Witnesses

We did a bit of exploring in this tapestry land, and saw the Mediterranean Sea opened right down to its farthest depths, just as, once, the Red Sea parted, at the Gulf of Arabia, to create a road for the Jews fleeing out of Egypt.

I recognized Triton blowing his great conch horn, Glaucus, Proteus, Nereus, and a thousand other gods and sea monsters. We also saw an infinite number of fish, in all sorts of species, dancing, gliding, leaping, fighting, eating, breathing, screwing, hunting, setting ambushes and springing them, making peace, buying and selling, swearing, and generally amusing themselves.

In one nearby corner we saw Aristotle holding a lantern, looking very like the hermit in the picture who lighted the way for Saint Christopher, watching, examining, and writing everything down. Walking behind him, like briefcase carriers for lawyers, were several other philosophers: Appian, Heliodorus, Athenaeus, Porphyry, Pancrates the Arcadian, Numenius, Posidonius, Ovid, Oppian, Olympius, Seleucus, Leonides, Agathocles, Theophrastus, Demostratus, Mutianus, Nymphodorus, Aelian, plus five hundred other gentlemen of leisure, like Chrysippus or Aristarchus of Soli, who spent fifty-eight years contemplating the life of the bee, and did nothing else. Among them I noticed Pierre Gilles, who held a urinal in his hand and was examining, with the most profound care, the urine of these beautiful fish.

After long consideration of this land of Sweetness, Pantagruel said:

"I've feasted my eyes for a long time, here, but I can't get my fill: my stomach's screaming with hunger."

"Let's eat, let's eat, " I said. "Let's try some of those aphrodisiac anacampserotes hanging over there."

"Fagh! It's worthless."

So I plucked some mirobalan plums, hanging from one end of a tapestry, but I couldn't chew them, or swallow them—and if you'd tasted them you'd have said (indeed, you'd have sworn) absolutely correctly, that they were just twisted-up silk threads, without any flavor at all. You'd have thought Heliogabalus had modeled his banquets on them, and copied them as closely as one copies a papal bull—those sumptuous, abundant, imperial feasts he promised to those on whom he'd enforced strict, long fasts, but which turned out to be food made of wax, and marble, and pottery, and painted or woven on cloth.

While looking through that country, trying to find ourselves something to eat, we heard a shrill noise of the sort women make when they're washing clothes or like the click-clacking of Bazacle's mills, at Toulouse. We rushed toward the sound and saw a tiny old man, a hunchback, deformed and monstrous. His name was *Hearsay:* his mouth opened right up to his ears, and he had seven tongues, each of which was divided into seven parts. However he managed it, all seven tongues talked at the same time, on different subjects and in different languages. His head, and the rest of his body, too, had as many ears as Argus once had eyes. He was blind, and his legs were paralyzed.

I saw endless numbers of men and women all around him, listening most carefully, and among them I recognized some who were handsome and plainly wellborn, one of whom had a map of the world and was briskly explaining it to the others, using well-turned little aphorisms. Thus they quickly became scholars and learned folk, and spoke authoritatively and elegantly on all sorts of tremendously important subjects, drawing on their fine memories—though a man's life would not be enough to learn a hundredth part of what they discoursed on: the pyramids, the Nile, Babylonia, Troglodytes, the Himantopodes, the Blemmians, pygmies, cannibals, the Hyperborean mountains, the aegipans, all the devils in hell—and all from *Hearsay*.

I saw there, so far as I can tell, Herodotus, Pliny, Caius Julius Solinus, Berosus, Philostratus, Pomponius Mela, Strabo, and many other ancients, in addition to Albertus Magnus, Peter the Martyr, Pope Pius the Second, Raphael Maffei of Volterra, the valiant Paulus Jovius, Jacques Cartier, Chaiton the Armenian, Marco Polo the Venetian, Ludovico Romano, Pedro Alvarez, and I don't know how many other modern historians, hidden behind a piece of tapestry and sneakily scribbling down some great stuff, and all from *Hearsay*.

Behind a piece of velvet, worked with mint leaves and right near *Hearsay* himself, I saw a horde of men from Perche and Maine, good students and young enough, and when we asked them in what faculty they were studying, we learned that from childhood on they had been studying to become witnesses, and did so well practicing that art that, when they left to return home to their provinces, they would earn a most respectable living as professional witnesses, giving their testimony, on any and all subjects, to those who paid them best, and all from *Hearsay*. Say what you will, but they shared their bread with us and let us drink their wine in good cheer. Then they advised us, most cordially, to try as hard as we could not to be too liberal with the truth, if we wished to become great lords at court.

Chapter Thirty-two ⁄⁄ How We Located Lanternland

Badly treated, and badly fed, in the land of Sweetness, we sailed for three days and, on the fourth, most luckily, we approached Lanternland.

As we drew closer, we saw some little fires hovering on the water. Myself, I thought they were lantern fish, which with their flaming tongues drew fire out of the sea, or perhaps lampyrides (which you call glowworms), shining as they shine in my own country at night, when the grain has ripened. But the pilot informed us that these were warning lanterns, which the people of that country set around their borders as an escort for foreign lanterns coming, like good Franciscans and Dominicans, to a meeting of their orders. Although we were worried that this might be some indication of a storm, he assured us that it was as he had said.

Chapter Thirty-three ⁄⁄ We Disembark at the Port of Those Who Burn the Midnight Oil, and Enter Lanternland

We sailed right into the Lanternese port.

Pantagruel at once recognized, on a high tower, the lantern of La Rochelle, which gave us very good light. We also saw the lanterns of Pharos, Nauplion, and that of the Acropolis, in Athens, sacred to Pallas Athena.

Near the port there is a small village inhabited by Those Who Burn the Midnight Oil, people who live by lanterns (as, in our country, certain lay brothers live by young nuns)—good folk, and studious. Demosthenes had done some lanterning, here. Three obelisk lanterns (port guards with high hats, like Albanians) brought us from this village to the palace, and we told them why we were making our voyage and what we hoped to accomplish, which was to obtain from the queen of Lanternland a lantern lady who would light our way and guide us on our journey to the oracle of the Divine Bottle. They assured us they would do that, and gladly, adding that we'd arrived at a most opportune time and would have an excellent choice of lanterns, since they were holding their annual meetings.

Coming to the royal palace, two lanterns of honor (namely, Aristophanes the grammarian's, and the philosopher Cleanthes') presented us to the queen, to whom Panurge briefly explained, in Lanternese, the reasons for our voyage. She welcomed us generously, and directed us to sit down to supper with her, so that we would be better able to choose whom we wanted as our guide. This pleased us immensely; nor were we slow to take note of and consider everything about us, from their gestures, clothing, and bearing to the order in which food was served.

The queen was dressed in virgin crystal, overlayered with Damascus embroidery and ornamented with large diamonds. Some of the noble lanterns were decorated with paste jewelry, others with clear stones, and the remainder with horn, paper, or oilcloth. The hanging lanterns were similarly adorned, depending on the age and status of their families. Among the ranks of the truly elegant I noted only one of clay, for all the world like an ordinary pot, which astonished me, until I learned that this was Epictetus' lantern, for which he was once offered three thousand drachmas.

I examined with great care the construction and fittings of Martial's many-spouted lantern, and considered with even closer attention the twenty-wick lantern of Icosymix, consecrated to Canope, many years ago, by Tysias' daughter. I noted with much interest that hanging lantern, which Alexander the Great once took from the temple of Apollo in Thebes, and brought to the city of Cyme, in Aeolia. I also took note of another, distinguished by the handsome red silk tassel it wore on its head. I was told this was Bartolus, lantern of the law. I further noted two more, distinguished by the enema bags hanging from their waists, and I was told one was the great and the other the lesser light of pharmacists.

Supper time having come, the queen took the first place, and after her all the others, according to their titles and stations. As soon as we were all seated, we were all served fat molded candles, except that the queen was served a huge, straight flaming torch of white wax, a bit red at the tip, and the noble lanterns, too, were served somewhat differently from the rest of us, as was the governor lantern of Mirebalais, who was brought a walnut oil candle, and the governor of Lower Poitou, who received a candle covered with heraldic emblazonings—and God alone knows how brightly they burned, once they'd been lit, except for a number of young lanterns, in charge of a certain large, fat lantern. They didn't light up like the others, and seemed to me to have a distinctly pallid look.

After supper, we retired to bed. The next morning the queen had us choose one of the most distinguished of her lanterns, to guide us on our way. And then we took our leave.

Chapter Thirty-four ⁄⁄ How We Reached the Oracle of the Bottle

With our noble lantern lighting our way, guiding us in great happiness, we arrived at our longed-for island and its oracle of the Bottle.

Stepping down, Panurge leaped gaily in the air, saying to Pantagruel:

"Today we have what we've been searching for—after all sorts of work and struggle!"

Then he commended himself courteously to our lantern, who told us all to hope for the best and, whatever might come and show itself to us, not to be at all frightened.

Approaching the temple of the Divine Bottle, we had to pass through an exceedingly large vineyard, containing all species of wines, like Falernian, Malmsey, Muscadine, Taggia, Beaune, Mirevaux, Orléans, Picardent, Arbois, Coussy, Anjou, Graves, Corsican, Verron, Nérac, and others. Bacchus himself had planted this vineyard, blessing it so that in all weathers and all seasons it would bud and flower and bear fruit, like the orange trees of San Remo. Our magnificent lantern ordered us to eat exactly three grapes per man, to put a vine tendril in our shoes, and to take a green branch in our left hands.

As we left the vineyard, we passed under an ancient arch, which was a beautifully carved memorial to a drinker: that is, in one place there was a long row of flasks, leather wine sacks, bottles, metal gourds, casks, barrels, jugs, mugs, amphora, all hanging from a leafy trellis; in another, a vast quantity of garlic, onions, shallots, hams, salted mullet-roe relish, cheese cakes, salted beef tongues, well-ripened cheeses, and the like, all interlaced with vine tendrils and very cleverly joined to young vine shoots; in another, a hundred kinds of glasses—glasses shaped like feet and like horses, cups, round drinking bowls, tankards, simple kitchen bowls, German mugs, tin mugs, goblets, and a whole Bacchic artillery. On the face of the arch, below the frieze, these two lines were carved:

> To pass here, under this arch,
> Get a good lantern to keep off the dark.

"And that," said Pantagruel, "we've provided. In all of Lanternland, there's no better or more divine lantern than ours."

This magnificent arch ended in a large and beautiful arbor, made entirely of young vine shoots, ornamented with five hundred differently colored grapes, in five hundred artful designs shaped by uncommonly clever agriculture: yellow grapes, and blue, tan, azure, white, black, green, violet, parti-colored, streaked with red—long, round, triangular, testicular, fat as cabbages, thick as an unshaven beard, lush as unmown grass. Three ancient ivy vines grew at the end of the arbor, thick with leaves and heavy with berries. Our most illustrious lantern directed each of us to make an Albanian hat of this ivy and completely cover our heads, which we did without any objection.

"In the old days," said Pantagruel, "Jupiter's priest wouldn't have dared walk under this arch."

"The explanation," declared our illuminating lantern, "is mystical. Passing through here, he'd have wine (that is, grapes) over his head and would seem to be dominated and controlled by wine, thus signifying that priests and everyone who gives and dedicates himself to the contemplation of divine matters must keep their spirits calm and free from any sensual perturbation—which perturbation is more marked in drunkenness than in any other passion of any sort.

"So too the Divine Bottle would not receive you in the temple, once you've passed through here, unless the noble Bottle priestess saw your shoes full of vine shoots, for this is demonstrably the complete and diametrical opposite of such perturbation and plain proof that you despise wine, and disdain it, and have freed yourselves from its bonds."

"I'm no scholar," said Brother John, "and I regret that fact. But I find in my prayer book that in Revelation it is said to be a fine thing for a woman to have the moon under her feet—that is, as the philosophical Guillaume Bigot has explained it to me, this means that she's not of the same stock, or the same sort as other women, who—exactly the reverse—have the moon in their heads and, as a result, always have loony brains. This makes me very inclined to believe what you've said, my dear Madame Lantern."

Chapter Thirty-five // How We Descended Underground, in Order to Enter the Bottle's Temple, and Why Chinon Is the Oldest City in the World

Then we went underground, following a plastered archway, crudely painted on the outside with a depiction of women and satyrs dancing, together with old Silenus on his donkey, laughing. There, I said to Pantagruel:

"This entrance reminds me of the painted caverns, in the oldest city in the world, for there you'll find similar paintings, just as fresh as these."

"Where," said Pantagruel, "is this oldest city you're talking about?"

"Chinon," I said, "in Touraine, also known as Cainyon."

"I know where Chinon is," said Pantagruel, "and the painted caverns, too; I've drunk many a glass of fresh wine, there, and I haven't the faintest doubt that Chinon is an old city. Its coat of arms attests to it, reading:

> Chinon, two times, three times Chinon,
> Small city of great renown,
> Set on ancient rocks, and then,
> Below its woods, the winding Vienne.

"But how could it be the oldest city in the world? Where do you find that written? What are you assuming?"

"I find it written in the Holy Bible that Cain was the first builder of cities. It seems very likely that he named the very first one after himself: Cainyon—for ever since then, in imitation of him, all other founders and builders of cities have imposed their names on their creations, as Athena (in Greek, Minerva) did with Athens; Alexander with Alexandria; Constantine with Constantinople; Pompey with Pompeiopolis, in Cilicia; Adrian with Adrianople; Cana (Noah's grandson) with the Canaanites; Saba with the Sabians; Assur with the Assyrians; and then there are Ptolemais, Caesaria, Tiberias, and Herodium in Judea."

As we chatted like this, the Great Flask came out (our lantern called him Phlosque, or Flame): he was the Divine Bottle's governor, and was accompanied by the temple guard, who were all French carafes. And seeing that we were carrying vine leaves, as I've said, and were crowned with ivy, and also recognizing our distinguished lantern, the Great Flask allowed us to enter in peace, ordering that we were to be led directly into the presence of the princess Baqbuc (in Hebrew, "bottle"), lady in waiting to the Bottle herself and priestess of all the mysteries. And this was done.

Chapter Thirty-six ⁄⁄ How We Experienced the Tetradic Stages, and Panurge's Fear

Then we went down an underground marble staircase, and came to a landing; turning to the left, we went down two more, and there again was a landing; then there were three more to the right, and another landing, and then four more to the left. Then Panurge asked:

"Is it here?"

"How many stairs," said our magnificent lantern, "have you counted?"

"One, two, three, and four," answered Pantagruel.

"How many is that?" she asked.

"Ten," answered Pantagruel.

"Multiply this result by the same Pythagorean tetrad," she said.

"That," said Pantagruel, "would be ten, twenty, thirty, and forty."

"Which makes how many in all?" she said.

"A hundred," answered Pantagruel.

"Add the first cube," she said, "which is eight. When you reach that preordained number, you will find the door to the temple. And be wise: note that this is Plato's true Psychogonie, or birth of the soul, so famous among the Greek philosophers, and yet so little understood: one-half of it is unity, the first two plain numbers, their squares and also their cubes."

As we went down all these underground stairs, our primary task was to be careful of our legs, for without them the only way we could go down would be like barrels rolling into a deep cellar; and our secondary task was to watch out for our illuminative lantern, since in this descent we were granted no other light, any more than we would have had we gone down into Saint Patrick's Hole, in Ireland, or into Trophonius' Pit, in Boeotia.

After we'd gone down about seventy-eight stairs, Panurge cried out to our luminous lantern:

"O wonderful lady, I beg you with a contrite heart, let's turn back. By the death of God, I'm dying of fear. I agree never to marry; you've gone to such great lengths and so much trouble for me, but God will repay you, at His Final Judgment; I won't be an ingrate, if I run from this cave of Troglodytes. Please, let's go back. I'm worried sick that this is Taenarus, through which you get to hell—and I think I already hear Cerberus barking. Listen: that's him—or else my ears are ringing. I have no love for him, because there's no toothache as painful as when a dog bites you in the leg. If this is Trophonius' Pit, the lemurs and goblins will eat us alive, the same way, once, they ate one of Demetrius' soldiers, because he didn't bring them a bite of sacred honey cake. Are you there, Brother John? I beg you, my glorious kettledrum, keep me near you: I'm dying of fear. Have you got your short sword? Me, I have no weapons at all, neither to attack nor to defend myself. Let's go back."

"I'm here," said Brother John, "I'm here, don't be afraid: I'll hold you by the collar. Eighteen devils won't pull you out of my hands, even if I have no weapons. You're never short of weapons, in a pinch, if you've got a good heart and a pair of strong arms: weapons would sooner come flying down out of heaven, as they did, once, on the field at La Crau, near the Marian pits, in Provence, when boulders came raining down (they're still there) to help Hercules, because he had no other weapons with which to fight Neptune's two children. But what's happening? Are we going down into the limbo of little children (by God, they'll shit all over us!), or even right into hell and all its devils? By God's holy heart,

I'd make them hop around, I would, now that I've got vine leaves in my shoes. Oh, I'll fight like the devil, I will! Where are we? Where are they? All I'm afraid of is their horns. But the two horns Panurge is going to wear, when he's married—they'll completely protect me. I can see him already (I'm in a prophetic mood): a new Actaeon, but horned, horny, and horning in."

"Make sure, Brother John," said Panurge, "if they ever let monks marry, that you don't get a wife with a fourfold fever. Because if you do, and I get home safe and sound from this underground tomb, I'll ram her for you, just to get you wearing horns, you horn-farter. Anyway, I think the fourfold fever's bad stuff. Didn't Grabby Puss want you to marry one who had it, but you called him a heretic?"

At this point the conversation was interrupted by our splendid lantern, warning us that this was a place where we had to be silent, both by holding back words and by keeping our tongues quiet. For the rest, she informed us brusquely that there was no way of going back without some word from the Bottle, now that our shoes were filled with vine leaves.

"So let's go on," said Panurge. "Let's lower our heads and butt right through all those devils. You only die once. All the same, I've been saving my life for some glorious battle. Let's go, let's go, go on. I have enough courage and to spare: it's true my heart is trembling, but that's just because it's cold and musty here in this cavern. It's not fear, no, and it isn't fever, either. Let's go, let's go, move on, shove on—oh, shove it: they call me William the Fearless."

Chapter Thirty-seven // How the Temple Doors Opened by Themselves, Wonderfully

When we reached the bottom of the stairs, we found a gate of fine jasper, beautifully made in Doric style, on the face of which was written, in Greek letters fashioned of pure gold, this sentence: ἐν οἴνῳ ἀϑλχθεια, meaning, "In wine there is truth." The doors were of a Corinthian-like brass, massive and decorated with little ornaments representing vine leaves, in bas-relief and carefully enameled according to the lines of the sculpture, and the doors were shaped and balanced so perfectly that they swung smoothly shut, needing neither lock nor key nor any chain. A great magnetic stone from India hung between them, as large as an Egyptian bean, set at two points in fine gold, and hexagonal in shape, its lines straight and true. On each side of the doors, near the wall, there hung cloves of garlic.

And here our noble lantern told us she could guide us no farther, hoping we would understand that her excuse was a legitimate one: she was not allowed to enter the temple, for reasons about which, in speaking to living, mortal beings, it was better to be silent, and all we had to do now was follow the instructions of the priestess Baqbuc. In any event, she told us to be alert, not to be afraid of anything, and to rely on her when it was time to go back. Then she drew down the magnetic stone hanging at the juncture of the two doors and with her right hand tossed it into a silver box, placed there for that exact purpose; she also drew out of the hinges on each side a red silk rope, a yard and a half long, from which the garlic hung; she tied it to two gold buckles, fastened there for that purpose, and then left us.

Suddenly, and without anyone touching them, the doors opened all by themselves, not making a shrill noise as they swung back, not shaking horribly as heavy, rough brass doors usually do, but emitting only a sweet, gracious murmur, which reverberated through the temple vault. And Pantagruel immediately saw why they swung open so quietly, for he spied under each door a small roller, affixed under the hinge, so that when the door moved outward toward the wall it moved on a stone as hard as porphyry, polished smooth by this movement, and thus creating the sweet, harmonious murmur we had heard.

I was startled to see two heavy doors thus opening of their own accord, without anyone pushing on them. The better to understand this marvel, once we were all inside, I stared as hard as I could at the space between the doors and the wall, anxious to understand by what force and what device they had thus moved, and I wondered if our friendly lantern might not have employed the herb we call ethiopis, which enables one to open every closed door. But then I noticed that, just at the point where the doors came together, there was a strip of fine steel, set into the Corinthian brass.

And I also saw two slabs of magnetic stone from India, each half a hand wide and of the same thickness, cerulean blue and smoothly polished, set into the wall to their full thickness and just at the point where, when they were entirely open, the doors would meet the walls.

Thus, the strong pull of these powerful magnets on the steel strips, according to the wonderful, secret laws of nature, was what drove this movement: the doors were slowly pulled and carried outward—not necessarily every time, however, but only when the great magnetic stone that had held them was itself removed, and the steel was thereby freed and absolved from the obedience which it naturally owed to a magnet placed so close to it, and only when the cloves of garlic were also removed, as our joyous lantern had done, for garlic overpowers magnets and deprives them of their ability to attract.

On the right-hand magnetic stone we could see carved, in exquisitely sculpted old Latin letters, the following iambic hexameter line:

Ducunt volentum fata, nolentum trahunt,
Fate leads the obedient, but drags those who resist.

And on the left-hand stone, in capital letters, the following line was carved:

EVERYTHING MOVES TO ITS DESTINED END

Chapter Thirty-eight // How the Temple Floor Was Made of a Wonderful Mosaic

After reading these inscriptions, I gazed around me, contemplating the magnificent temple, and I examined its unbelievable tiled floor—to which nothing that is or ever was on this earth can possibly compare, neither the temple of Fortune in Praeneste, in Sulla's time, nor that Greek floor, called Asserotum, which Sosistratus built in Pergamum. This was all inlaid with small squares of fine, polished stone, set on the diagonal and each in its natural color—red jasper, with delicately variegated spots; porphyry, and also a rare green porphyry, stippled with white; four-colored licotalmy, red, white, brown, and black, flecked with bits of gleaming gold, tiny as atoms; agate shot through with irregular wave-like milky ripples in no observable pattern; costly chalcedony; and green jasper, veined with red and yellow.

Under the portal, the tiling was a mosaic shaped by myriad small stones, again in natural colors but, here, blended into the design, and it seemed as if someone had strewn the floor with vine leaves and not given a thought to their arrangement. In one place they were thick and tangled; in another, sparse. And anywhere and everywhere you looked, this leafy foliage was remarkable, because in the half-light you could see, here, a few snails crawling on the grapes, and there, small lizards running across the vines, and in yet another place half-ripe grapes, and fully ripened grapes, all so wonderfully planned and executed that they could have fooled the crows and other small birds just as easily as Zeuxis Heraclis' painting. And indeed they fooled us extremely well, because at the place where the designer had tangled the vines with particular lushness, we were afraid to hurt our feet, and found ourselves lifting our legs high in the air, as if we were walking on some rocky, irregular surface.

And then, looking up at the temple vault and its high walls, encrusted from one end to the other with marvelously worked marble and porphyry mosaics, I saw—beginning just to the left of the entrance and spread across the entire vault—Bacchus' victorious battle against the men of India, spread out in all its detail, as follows in the next chapter.

Chapter Thirty-nine ⁄⁄ The Temple Mosaic, Showing Bacchus' Victorious Battle against the Men of India

It began with cities, villages, castles, fortresses, fields, and forests all consumed by fire. It also showed frenzied, wild women tearing apart live calves and sheep and ewes, and gorging on their flesh. This indicated how, when he invaded India, Bacchus burned and slaughtered right and left.

Nevertheless, the Indians thought him so insignificant that they didn't bother sending troops against him, having been informed by their spies that there were no soldiers in his armies, but only a little old man, effeminate and always drunk, accompanied by naked young peasants who were constantly dancing and jumping, wearing tails and horns like half-grown billy goats, plus a horde of drunken women. So they made up their minds to just let Bacchus and his armies pass by, without any fighting, as if it would be disgraceful rather than glorious to win a victory over such people, and dishonor and ignominy would be their reward, rather than honor and heroism.

Taking advantage of their contempt, Bacchus went on conquering the country, burning everything he found, since fire and thunder were his familial weapons, and indeed before his birth Jupiter had greeted him with thunder and blood (his mother Semele and her maternal home were burned and destroyed in the resulting fire), so it was natural for him to quicken the blood in times of peace and draw it forth in times of war. Proof of this is the fields on the island of Samos called Panaima, meaning "blood-drenched," where Bacchus caught the Amazons, who were fleeing from Ephesus, and put them all to death by bleeding, so that the field was soaked and covered with blood. Which should allow you to understand more clearly than you could from Aristotle's account, in his *Problems,* why in ancient times there was a proverbial saying: "In wartime, neither eat nor plant mint." And this is the reason: in war one strikes out in all directions, and if a man is wounded it's impossible—or at least exceedingly difficult—to control his bleeding.

And then the mosaic showed how Bacchus marched into battle, drawn in his magnificent chariot by three pairs of yoked leopards. His face was like that of a young child, in order to show that good drinkers never grow old—red as a cherub, without any trace of a beard. He wore pointed horns on his head, and on top of these a handsome crown made of grapes and vine leaves; in his hand he carried a bright red staff, and on his feet he wore gold-embroidered boots.

There wasn't a single grown man in his entire army: his bodyguard and all his forces were composed of Bacchantic women—Bassarides,

Evantes, Euhyades, Edonides, Trieterides, Ogygies, Mimallonides, Maenads, Thyades, and Bacchae—all frenzied, furious, raging, their gowns belted with dragons and live snakes, their hair flying into the air, and vines as their headbands, dressed in stag and goat skins, and carrying in their hands small axes, staffs tipped with pinecones and wound around with ivy, pikes, spears shaped like fir trees, and light shields which rang out when they were touched, which was not often, for they were used, when necessary, as tambourines and drums. Of these women there were seventy-nine thousand, two hundred and twenty-seven.

The vanguard was led by Silenus, a man in whom Bacchus had total confidence, having on more than one occasion seen his capabilities, noble courage, and wisdom. He was a tremulous old man, small, bent, fat, pot-bellied, with large, straight ears, a pointed, aquiline nose, and coarse, heavy eyebrows. He rode a jackass and held in his fist the stick that supported him when he walked, and which he also used in gallant combat, if he happened to dismount; he wore a yellow woman's gown. His troops, as I have said, were young country fellows, horned like goats and as cruel as lions, all of them naked, constantly singing and dancing like lascivious clowns: they were called satyrs and, in the Dorian tongue, tityrs, and there were eighty-five thousand one hundred and thirty-three of them.

The rearguard was brought up by Pan, a ghastly, monstrous man, the lower part of his body like a billy goat, with hairy thighs, and with stiff, straight horns on his head. His face was red and glowing, his beard extremely long—a bold man, courageous, who took risks and got angry easily. He carried a flute in his left hand, and a bent staff in his right. His troops, too, were composed of satyrs, hemipans, aegipans, sylvans, fauns, lemurs, lares, elves, and goblins, of whom there were seventy-eight thousand one hundred and fourteen.

Their common battle cry was *Evohé*.

Chapter Forty // How the Mosaic Portrayed Our Good Bacchus Attacking the Men of India

And next we could see our good Bacchus attacking the men of India. We could see how Silenus, leading the vanguard, was dripping with sweat, and how restlessly he worried his jackass, which, in turn, made its mouth gape horribly, swatted its tail back and forth, pranced, danced, and capered frightfully, as if it had a wasp up its ass.

The satyrs, captains, sergeants, squadron leaders, and corporals sounded the charge on their trumpets, whirling wildly through the army, leaping and jumping and farting and bucking and kicking, whipping up their comrades' fighting spirits. Everyone in the picture was shouting *Evohé!*

The lead Maenads charged at the Indians with horrible cries, making ghastly noises with their cymbals and shields: all of heaven echoed with it, as the mosaic clearly showed—so clearly, indeed, that you've no need to be so fond of Apelles' art, or Aristides the Theban, or others who paint lightning, thunder, thunderbolts, winds, words, manners, and spirits.

Next came the Indian army, warned that Bacchus was devastating their country. First came the elephants, carrying fortified towers on their backs, followed by an infinite number of soldiers. But the whole army was running wildly for its life: their elephants had turned on them, stamping and crushing them, because the Bacchantes' ghastly uproar, and the terror of Pan, had deprived them of their senses. You could see Silenus sharply spurring his jackass and fencing away with his stick, after the old fashion, and his jackass leaping after the elephants, his jaws wide as if braying, his braying sounding the assault in military style (just as bravely as, once, he woke the nymph Lotis, at the height of Bacchic revels, when Priapus, at the full height of his Priapism, was about to Priapize her as she slept, without bothering to seek her consent).

You could see Pan, with his twisted legs, leaping around and around the Maenads, his rustic flute exciting them to courageous combat. And you could also see a young satyr coming behind them, leading seventeen captured kings, and a Bacchante pulling along forty-two captains with her snakes, a little faun carrying twelve banners taken from the enemy, and our good man Bacchus, in his chariot, parading comfortably all around the battlefield, laughing, rejoicing, and exchanging toasts with everyone he met. And, finally, there was an allegorical representation of the victorious trophy, and good Bacchus' complete triumph.

His triumphant chariot was entirely covered with ivy, plucked and gathered on Mount Meros, since ivy was exceedingly rare (and, like all things, costly because of its rarity) in India. Alexander the Great later imitated this, when he too conquered India. The chariot—with noble Bacchus riding in it, drinking from a great festive bowl—was drawn by yoked elephants, which Pompey the Great later imitated, in Rome, on the occasion of his African triumph. Caius Marius later imitated Bacchus drinking as he rode in triumph, after his victory over the Cymbri, which he won near Aix-en-Provence. The whole army was crowned with ivy; even their spears and shields and cymbals were covered with it, including Silenus' jackass.

By the sides of the chariot were the Indian kings, captives bound in great golden chains. The whole army marched in divine pomp, inexpressibly happy and rejoicing, carrying endless numbers of trophies stripped away from their enemies, sounding out joyous victory songs, and gay village songs, and passionate dithyrambs.

At the end we could see the land of Egypt, with its Nile and its crocodiles, its monkeys, apes, ibises, gold-crested wrens, Pharaoh's rats, hippopotamuses, and other animals native to that country. And Bacchus marched across the land, led by two oxen, on one of which was written, in letters of gold, *Apis,* and on the other, *Osyris,* since before Bacchus' coming no Egyptian had ever seen either an ox or a cow.

Chapter Forty-one // How the Temple Was Lit by a Wonderful Lamp

Before I get to the Divine Bottle's prophecy, let me describe for you the marvelous lamp by which the entire temple was brightly illuminated—so bright that, even though it was underground, you could see as well there as you can, above ground, at high noon, with the sun shining clear and calm.

In the middle of the vault hung a massive gold ring, as large around as a fist, and from this there were suspended three silver chains, two and a half feet long, beautifully fashioned, and not much lighter in weight than the ring. They formed a triangle around a thin, round gold plate, so large that its diameter was more than four feet across. This plate had four loops or rings, each of which held an empty bowl, hollow, open at the top and looking much like a small oil lamp about two handbreadths wide, and all made of precious stones, one of amethyst, another of Libyan diamonds, the third of opals, and the fourth of red topaz. Each was filled with alcoholic spirits, a liquid distilled five times over in a coiled still, and like the oil which Callimachus long ago put in Pallas Athena's golden lamp, on the Acropolis, in Athens, inexhaustible. Each had a flaming wick, in part made of asbestos (once used in the temple of Jupiter at Ammon, where it was seen by Cleombrotus, that very studious philosopher), in part made of Carpasian linen, and both of which are sooner renewed than consumed by fire.

About two and a half feet below the gold plate, the three silver chains were attached to the three handles of a great, round lamp of exceedingly pure crystal, more than a yard in diameter and with an opening about two handbreadths wide. In the middle of this opening there was a gourd-shaped vessel (it also resembled a urinal) of the same pure crystal, which hung all the way to the bottom of the great lamp, and contained enough of the alcoholic spirits so that the flame of the asbestos wick was exactly in the center of the great lamp. This ensured that the whole crystalline sphere seemed to be lit and burning, since the fire was thus perfectly centered.

It was hard to keep looking, just as one cannot look steadily right into the sun, for the whole lamp was so wonderfully transparent, so diaphanous and delicate, because of the reflection of all the different colors (caused by the natural properties of precious stones) from the four smaller lamps up above to the great lamp below: the brightness of these four lamps hung tremblingly, flickeringly, all through the temple. Further, this hazy light struck the high polish of the marble inlaid through the entire temple, creating colors like those we see in the rainbow, when the clear sun strikes rain-filled clouds.

The invention was marvelous—but it seemed even more wonderful, to me, that around the width of this crystalline lamp the sculptor had engraved a gay and lively battle of little naked boys, riding little wooden horses, with little windmill lances and shields made of bunches of grapes, layered with vine leaves, their childlike gestures and movements so ingeniously expressed by his chiseled art that nature herself could not have done it better. Nor did they seem carved at all, but to stand in bas-relief, or perhaps in full relief like cathedral grotesques, thanks to the varying, cheerful light which shone through the carving.

Chapter Forty-two ⁄⁄ The Priestess Baqbuc Shows Us, inside the Temple, a Fantastic Fountain

As we were staring ecstatically at this wonderful temple and unforgettable lamp, the holy priestess Baqbuc came to us, all happy and laughing, together with her retainers, and, seeing us garbed as has been described, without any objection brought us right into the temple, where, under the light of that lamp, we saw a fantastic fountain, made of the most precious materials, most beautifully worked—rarer and more wonderful than anything Daedalus ever dreamed of.

The fountain's rim, column, and base were of singularly pure, translucent alabaster, over a yard high, or even a bit more, heptagonally shaped, marked on the outside into equal parts, and with many coping supports, small ornamental altars, curved moldings, and waved, Doric-style decorations all along its periphery. The inside was a perfect circle. There was a ventriculated column at the midpoint of each of the seven angles along the edge, shaped like a round log of boxwood (modern architects call this a *portri*); there were seven in all, one at each angle. From the base to the architrave, each of these columns was about seven handbreadths long, or perhaps a little less, which was neatly and exactly the length of a diameter passing through the center of the fountain's interior circle.

The columns were so placed that, looking out at the other columns from behind any of them, no matter from what point, we found that the pyramidal cone of our visual line ended precisely in that same center and, starting at that same point and proceeding to the two opposite columns, shaped an equilateral triangle, two sides of which exactly divided the column we were trying to measure, and further, passing on either side of the two columns parallel to the first, formed one-third of the distance which constituted their basic, fundamental line, which in turn, according to an imaginary line drawn straight to the universal center, and equally divided, made an exact division of the seven opposing columns. Nor could you proceed to the opposite column by a direct line drawn at an obtuse angle to the edge, since, as you know, anytime you have an odd number of angles one always has to be inserted between two others.

Which is tacit proof that, in geometry, seven half-diameters are somewhat less than the circumference of the circular figure from which they are drawn, meaning three whole diameters plus one-eighth and a half, or a bit more, or perhaps one-seventh and a half, according to the ancient calculations of Euclid, Aristotle, Archimedes, and others.*

The first column, meaning the one nearest the temple entrance, and the first we saw, was made of blue sapphire.

The second was jacinth, in its natural color, and with the Greek letters *A* and *I* in a number of places, representing the hyacinth, into which flower the blood of that choleric man Ajax was transformed.

The third was anachite diamond, gleaming as bright as lightning.

The fourth was Persian ruby, a masculine stone with a trace of amethyst coloring as well, so that its gleam and glow seemed to fade into purple and violet.

The fifth was emerald, more than five hundred times as magnificent as Serapis' stone, in the labyrinth of Egypt—gleaming more vividly, more brightly, than the emerald eyes of the marble lion lying on King Hermias' tomb.

The sixth was agate, more brightly and gaily marked and colored than that so beloved of Pyrrhus, king of the Epirotes.

The seventh was transparent crystalline selenite, or moonstone, as white as beryl, gleaming like Hymettian honey, inside of which appeared the image of the moon exactly as it moved through the skies, full, silent, waxing and waning.

All of these are precious stones which the ancient Chaldean astronomers and wise men assigned to the seven planets in the heavens. And so even the crudest, dullest brain could understand:

—on the first, or sapphire column, just below the capital at the very top, along the central perpendicular line, there hung a pure and precious lead image of Saturn, scythe in hand, a golden crane at his feet, beautifully enameled in the colors proper to this saturnine bird;

—on the second, or jacinth column, in black lead, hung Jupiter, facing to his left, an eagle enameled in gold on his breast;

—on the third, there was Phoebus Apollo, in purified gold, a white cock in his right hand;

---

*The translation is approximate: the original is both textually corrupt and exceedingly difficult to follow.

—on the fourth, in Corinthian brass, there was Mars, with a lion at his feet;

—on the fifth, there was Venus in copper, the same material Ariston-ides used for the statue of Athamas, the pale redness expressing the shame he had felt, seeing his son Learchus dead at her feet, after a fall;

—on the sixth, there was Mercury in fixed mercurial metal, flexible and yet unmovable, a stork at his feet;

—on the seventh, there was Luna in silver, a greyhound at her feet.

These statues were large enough to cover a third of the columns, per-haps a bit more, so beautifully and mathematically accurate in their por-trayals that even the canon of Polycletus, according to which he was said to have produced art artfully, could not compare.

The columnar bases, the lofty capitals, the architraves, the friezes and cornices, were in the Phrygian style, massive, of gold purer and finer than anything mined from the river Lez, near Montpellier, or the Ganges in India, the Po in Italy, the Hebrus in Thrace, the Tagus in Spain, or the Pactolus in Lydia.

The arches thrusting between the columns were each fashioned of the same stone as the column they left, until they reached the next one, so that the arch connected to the sapphire column was sapphire until it reached the jacinth column, the next arch was jacinth, and so on.

Along the interior facing above these arches and the capitals of the columns was a cupola, placed there to cover the fountain. Beginning behind the planets in heptagonal shape, it gradually became spherical, and was made of crystal so pure, so diaphanous, so beautifully and evenly pol-ished at each and every point—without streaks or murkiness or flaws or scratches or ridges—that Xenocrates never saw anything to compare with it.

Exquisitely carved into the bulk of this cupola were the twelve signs of the zodiac, properly represented and arranged in good order, plus the twelve months of the year and their particular qualities, the two solstices, the two equinoxes, and the ecliptic line, with certain of the most notable fixed stars around the Antarctic pole, all done with such deft art and wonderful expressiveness that they seemed to me the work of King Nechepso, or of Petosiris, the great mathematician of antiquity.

At the top of the cupola, exactly above the center of the fountain, were three identical pearls, perfectly tear-shaped, joined in a marvelously clear representation of a fleur-de-lis, so large that the flower was more than a handbreadth wide. A diamond as large as an ostrich's eye projected from the calyx of this flower, cut in heptagonal form (the number seven being dearly loved by nature), so enormous and impressive that, raising our eyes to stare at it, we were very nearly blinded. Neither the sun's fire nor that of lightning can flame any more brilliantly, or swell any more pow-erfully. Indeed, for any fair judges it would be easy to see that in the fountain and lamp just described there is greater wealth, and more that is remarkable, than in the continents of Asia, Africa, and Europe all taken together. The fiery red magnetic jewel of Iarchus, the great Indian magician, would have been as easily obscured by these wonders as the sun at midday obscures the stars.

Now go boast, Cleopatra, queen of Egypt, about the two great pearls hanging from your ears, one of which, in the very presence of the noble Anthony, you dissolved in vinegar, though it was said to be worth ten million sesterces.

Now go strut, Pompey Paulinus, over your robe covered with pearls and emeralds, woven in alternate rows, which everyone in Rome admired— a city said to be the cesspool and storehouse of all the victorious thieves in the world.

Everything that flowed and spouted from the fountain was led away by three pipes made of fine pearls, placed on the outside of the three equilateral angles already described, which pipes were shaped in the form of a double spiral.

Having thoroughly examined these wonders, we were turning our attention elsewhere when Baqbuc directed us to listen to the water: we heard a marvelously harmonious sound, though not fully clear and somewhat intermittent, as if it came from some distant, subterranean source. All the same, to us it seemed more delightful than if it had been nearer and could be heard more clearly: as much as the windows of our eyes had charmed our senses, now our ears too enraptured us with these harmonies.

Then Baqbuc said to us:

"Your philosophers deny that the mathematical relationships of a form can inspire movement, but here you see and hear the contrary. This sacred fountain runs only because of the double spiral, which you can see is divided into two (with five inward-folded parts that move at every internal contact, as the hollow vein does at the point where it enters the heart's right ventricle): it is this which makes that harmony you hear, and lifts the water right up to the sea in your world."

Chapter Forty-three ⁄⁄ How the Fountain's Water Tasted like Wine, According to the Drinker's Imagination

Then she ordered goblets, cups, and tankards to be brought—gold ones, and silver, crystal and porcelain—and graciously invited us to drink of the liquid springing from that fountain, which we very willingly did. For, to tell the truth, we're not like a herd of calves who, like sparrows (that eat only when you hit them on the tail), won't eat or drink until thrashed with a stick. We never say no to anyone who politely offers us a drink.

Then Baqbuc queried us, asking what we thought. We replied that it seemed to us good fresh springwater, more silvery clear than the Argirontes in Italy, the Peneus in Thessaly, the Axius in Macedonia, or the Cydnus in Cilicia—which in the very heart of summer seemed to Alexander the Great so lovely and clear and cold that he gave himself the sensual delight of bathing in it, though he had a premonition of the harm that would come to him from so transitory a pleasure.

"Ha!" said Baqbuc. "This is what comes of not understanding how the muscles of your tongue move when your drink comes rolling over, descending—not into the lungs, via the trachial artery, as good old Plato, Plutarch, Macrobius, and others thought—directly into the stomach, via the esophagus. Strangers, are your gullets plastered and tarred—paved—enameled, like Pythillus' (they called him Theutes), so you can't taste this godlike liquid and recognize its flavor? Now," she said to her ladies in waiting, "bring me my pallet scrapers, you know which I mean, so we can get their pallets rinsed off and cleansed."

So they brought in splendid, great hams, gorgeous even to see, fat and lovely smoked beef tongues, good salt fish, dry Milanese sausage, Mediterranean caviar, fine fat venison sausages, and such other throat sweepers. As she directed, we ate until we had to admit that our stomachs had been thoroughly cleaned and thirst was beginning to clamor at us. And then she said:

"Once upon a time there was a Jewish leader, Moses, learned and chivalrous, who was guiding his people through the desert. Their hunger being intense, he begged heaven for manna, which to their imaginations had the taste of real food. And this is just the same: as you drink this miraculous liquid, you will have the taste sensations of any wine you have ever imagined. Now: imagine—and drink."

We did. And Panurge cried out:

"By God, either this is vintage Beaune, the best I've ever drunk, or I'll hand myself over to a hundred and six devils! Oh, to hold on to that taste, if only I had a throat three yards long, such as Philoxenus wanted—or the length of a crane's, as Malanthius wished for!"

"Now, by my faith," cried Brother John, "it's Greek wine, bright and sparkling. Oh, for the sake of God, lady, teach me how you make this!"

"To me," said Pantagruel, "it seems like Mirevaux wine, since that's what I was thinking of before I drank. There's only one thing wrong with it, which is that it's fresh—but more than fresh, it's cold, colder than ice, colder than the water of Nonacris or of Dirce, colder than the fountain of Cantoporeia in Corinth, which freezes the stomachs and intestines of anyone who drinks it."

"Drink," said Baqbuc, "drink once, or twice, or three times. And each time, if you change what's in your mind, that's what you'll taste—exactly the flavor, exactly the liquid you've imagined. And now admit that, to God, nothing is impossible."

"We'd never say anything else," I said. "We would argue that He is all-powerful."

Chapter Forty-four ⁄⁄ The Garments Baqbuc Put on Panurge, So He Could Hear the Divine Bottle's Prophecy

When we were done drinking, and the words I have here set down had been spoken, Baqbuc asked:

"Which of you wishes to hear the Divine Bottle's prophecy?"

"Me," said Panurge, "your insignificant, humble funnel."

"My friend," she said, "I have only one piece of advice for you, and that is, when you get to the oracle, be careful to listen to its words with only one ear."

"Now that," said Brother John, "is very good wine indeed."

Then she put a green smock on Panurge, and on his head a handsome white hood and a wine strainer, at the end of which, instead of a tassel, she hung three meat skewers; gloved him in a pair of old codpieces; belted his nun-like smock with three bagpipes tied in a row; washed his face three times in the sacred fountain; and finally threw a handful of flour in his face, set three cock feathers on the lower right side of the wine strainer, made him walk around the fountain nine times and make three nice little leaps in the air, then bang his bottom seven times on the ground, and all the time she was incanting God only knows what incantations in the Etruscan language and sometimes reading aloud from a book of rituals, carried by one of her mystical collaborators.

In short, I doubt that that famous cultist Numa Pompilius, the second king of Rome, or the religious Etruscans of Caere, in Tuscany, or that sacred leader of the Jews, Moses himself, ever performed ceremonies like the one I saw, nor did the ancient prophets of Memphis celebrate for Apis, or the Euboeans for their god Nemesis Rhamnusia, in their city of Rhamnus, nor were ever celebrated for Jupiter Ammon, or for his goddess Feronia, such wonderfully sacred observances as those I witnessed.

When she had thus dressed and prepared him, the priestess Baqbuc drew Panurge apart from the rest of us and, taking him by the right hand, led him out of the temple, through a golden door, into a circular chapel made of translucent stones. The sun penetrated to that chapel through a crack in the rock covering the temple proper, entering without any need of a window or any other opening, and pouring down so easily and in such abundance that the light seemed to emanate from inside, rather than to make its way in. The chapel was no less magnificent than, long ago, the sacred temple of Apollo, at Ravenna, or that in Egypt, on the island of Chemnis: I must not forget to mention that this circular chapel had been built with such perfect symmetry that its height and diameter were exactly equal.

In its middle there was a fountain of fine alabaster, once again heptagonal, remarkably constructed and ornamented, full of water so utterly clear that it seemed positively elemental in its simplicity. In that water there stood, half immersed, the sacred Bottle, in its garb of pure crystal, oval shaped, but with a lip slightly more open and emphatic than an oval required.

Chapter Forty-five ⁄⁄ How the Priestess Baqbuc Brought Panurge into the Divine Bottle's Presence

That noble priestess Baqbuc made Panurge kneel and kiss the edge of the fountain, then stand and dance three Bacchic dances around it. That done, she ordered him to sit down between two stools that were waiting for him, with his ass on the ground. After which she opened her sacred book of rituals and, whispering the words into his left ear, made him sing an ancient Greek wine song, as follows:

O
Bottle
So full
Of mysteries,
I listen to you
With just one ear:
Don't keep me waiting,
Speak the words my heart
Hangs by!
That sacred liquid
Your crystal body holds,
O Bacchus, who conquered India,
Contains all truth.
That holy wine can't know
Lies or pretense.
May Noah's days be spent
In joy, who taught us temperance.
Speak kind words, I beg you,
Which surely will end my misery,
But cost you not a single drop,

> Whether you're white or red.
> O Bottle
> So full
> Of wonders!

The song finished, Baqbuc threw I have no idea what into the fountain, and all at once the water began to boil like the great monastic cooking pots at Bourgueil, when they celebrate high holidays with feasting and processions. Panurge sat silently, listening with one ear. Baqbuc knelt down beside him—and then the sacred Bottle gave forth a sound like that made by bees bred in the flesh of a young bull, sacrificed and dressed by Aristaeus' artful hands—or like the roar of a crossbow shot out at full tension—or like a strong summer rain, falling without warning. And then a single word sounded:

"*Trink!*"

"By all that's holy!" shouted Panurge. "That bottle's broken, or else it's cracked—and I mean it: that's how crystal bottles always sound, in my country, when they split from being too near the fire."

But Baqbuc rose and, taking Panurge gently under the arm, said:

"My friend, give thanks to heaven: it's the only reasonable thing, for you have heard the unhesitating word of the sacred Bottle. And it is the happiest, most divine, most certain message I have heard her give to anyone in all the time I have served, here, as minister to this sacred oracle. Rise: let's go to the chapter, where that lovely word will be properly glossed for you."

"Let's go," said Panurge, "by God! I'm just as wise as I was. Enlighten me: where's that book—where's that chapter? Let's have a look at this joyous gloss."

Chapter Forty-six // Baqbuc Explains the Bottle's Prophecy

Baqbuc threw who knows what into the water, which immediately stopped boiling, then led Panurge back into the center of the temple proper, to the marvelous fountain. There, taking down a great silver book shaped like a half-barrel (or the fourth volume of Peter Lombard's *Maxims*), she dipped it into the fountain, and said to him:

"The philosophers, preachers, and learned men of your world stuff fine words into you, through your ears. Here, we actually incorporate our teachings through our mouths. So instead of saying to you, 'Read this chapter, look at this explanation,' I say, 'Taste this chapter, swallow this fine gloss.' Once, an old Jewish prophet ate a book and became a scholar to the teeth; now you're going to drink one and become a scholar right up to the liver. Come on, open your jaws."

Once Panurge had his gullet gaping, Baqbuc took the silver book—which we thought was really a book, because of its shape: it closely resembled a prayer book, but was in fact a flask, full of Falernian wine, and she made Panurge swallow it all.

"Now that," said Panurge, "was truly a notable chapter, and a powerfully authentic gloss. Is that all the triply magical Bottle wanted to tell me? It went down very well, believe me."

"No more than that," replied Baqbuc, "because *Trink* is an oracular word, celebrated and understood everywhere on earth, and says to us: Drink. In your world you say (or at least Gropius does) that *sac,* or bag, is common to all languages, and to all good legal systems, and is understood by all nations—just as in Aesop's *Fables* all human beings are born with a bag under their necks, half starved by nature and all begging from each other. No king on earth is so powerful that he can manage without others' help; no poor man is so arrogant that he can manage without the rich—not even the philosopher Hippias, who (he said) could do everything. And if no one can manage without his begging bag, certainly no one can manage without drinking. And here we would argue that it is drinking, not laughter, which makes men human. Not that I mean simply imbibing fluids, because even animals do that: I mean drinking good, fresh wine. And note, my friends, that in drinking wine you find yourself divine: no argument is more accurate, no prophetic art is less fallacious. Your own academicians affirm this, in their etymology for the word "wine," saying it comes from the Greek *oinos,* which is the Latin *vis,* and means "force" or "power." And wine indeed has the power to fill the soul with truth—with all truth, all learning, all philosophy. If you took note of the words written in Greek, over the door to this temple, you should have known that truth is hidden in wine. The Divine Bottle sends you to it: for the rest, you just be your own interpreters in this business."

"No one," said Pantagruel, "could speak more cogently than this venerable priestess. That's exactly what I said, the first time you broached the subject. So *Trink!* What does your heart say to you, swept up in Bacchic passion?"

"Let's have a drink," said Panurge. "In the name of good Bacchus,

> Ho, ho: I see some dangling ass
> Taking on a proper mass
> Of banging balls, well enough stuffed
> With my little pointed genital tuft.
> What's this? I feel my heart predicting
> Marriage problems won't need fixing
> As soon as I've got a wife in bed:
> She'll take the lead once I've led.

Ah, God! What wondrous debates we'll make,
On who shall give and who shall take,
And I'll stuff it in, again and again,
Proving myself the best of men.
It's me, it's me, husband supreme,
Every hungry woman's dream:
Apollo, Apollo! Victory, victory,
Hail to marriage! Hail to my dickory!
And now, my friendly Brother John,
I'll swear an oath (and you know what on):
This oracle never makes a mistake:
It speaks true words, its words are fate."

Chapter Forty-seven ⁄⁄ Panurge and His Friends Rhyme Furiously

"Have you gone crazy," said Brother John, "or are you bewitched? Look at him foaming at the mouth! Just listen to him rhyming! Have all the devils in hell swallowed him down? He's turning his eyes in his head like a dying goat! Shouldn't he go off by himself? Shouldn't he go shit someplace else? Maybe he ought to eat grass, the way dogs do, to empty out his stomach? Or—the way monks do—maybe he ought to shove his fist down his throat, all the way up to his elbow, so he can get his colon cleaned out? Or is he going to take more of the hair of the dog that bit him?"

Pantagruel took hold of him, and said:

"Poetic fury like this comes
  From Bacchus: that wine he drank has stunned
  His senses and made the rhymes come running:
     There's nothing wrong
     With singing songs
     In a liquid throat,
     But all his notes
     His laughs, his cries,
     His rolling eyes,
     Are alcohol born;
     His heart beats along
     To a hazy tune,
     And he thinks he's strong
     When he howls at the moon—
  And since his brain's gone slightly frantic,

And made his mood triumphant, antic,
To make fun of this drunk would be worse than pedantic."

"What?" said Brother John. "Are you rhyming, too? By all that's holy, we're all infected! Oh, I wish Gargantua could see us like this! God— what am I supposed to do? Should I rhyme, too, or shouldn't I? I don't know anything about it, but this seems to be rhyming land, so by Saint John! I'll rhyme with the rest of you, by God I know I will! Now wait: remember, excuse me if my verse isn't the best handmade stuff:

> O God in heaven, eternal Father,
> Who once turned water into wine,
> Let my ass like a lantern shine,
> To light the way for my stumbling brother."

Panurge returned to the charge:

> "The Pythian prophet, writhing on high,
> Gave no better answers than I
> Have had right here, more certain, more sure:
> This fountain spirit speaks so pure
> A voice, it must have drawn its breath
> From Delphos, stolen those sacred depths.
> Had Plutarch drunk these waters, as we
> Have done, he'd have no doubts, seeing
> Delphos mute, gone pale and dumb,
> For Delphos is here, the spirit has come
> To stay, leaving silence behind:
> The piercing, penetrating mind
> Of the god is here, and nothing's there.
> And Athenaeus (who was there)
> Confesses the truth: even in Greece,
> Even in Delphos, the voice wheezed
> From inside a bottle, full of wine—
> But a wine of truth, and spirits divine.
> No prophet's voice has ever spoken
> More honest, truer words than croaked
> Up out of that Bottle; it cannot lie.
> Therefore, Brother John, I
> Suggest you seek its magic wording
> Before your feet go homeward turning,
> And learn if marriage sails across
> Your bow, or not. You too can toss
> Your head and prance a Bacchic caper:

Throw some flour, light a taper,
And hear the truth. It's now or later."

Wildly angry, Brother John answered:

"Marry! By Benedict's boots and gaiters,
Anyone who knows me knows this, too:
I'd rather they shaved my head and blew
The habit off my back than ship me
Anywhere where marriage might trip me.
What! Let them put chains on my wrists?
Tie me to a woman? And not resist?
By all that's holy, they'll never wed me
To Alexander, or Caesar, bed me
As an emperor's son-in-law: no wife
Could ever be worth ruining my life."

But Panurge threw off his green robe and all his mystical garb, and answered:

"And that's what you'll be, you filthy beast—
Damned for a dirty snake. While I feast
In paradise, playing my harp, and pissing
Down on you (and never missing).
But listen: when the time arrives and you visit
Hell and the grand old devil (is it
Likely you won't?), and his dried-up wife,
Old Proserpina, decides there's life
Left in the front of your pants, and she's hot
To try it, and she gives you a chance (why not?),
But before you play the game (the beast
With a pair of backs) I'll bet the least
You'll do is send for a bottle of wine
And some oats from the best little joint you can find
In hell, to make sure that tired old dreamer
Lucifer won't get in your way while you cream her.
They tell me she's crazy for fat old monks,
Even the kind that smell like skunks."

"Go to the devil, you old fool!" said Brother John. "I can't rhyme any more: all this rhyming has dried out my throat. Let's pay our bill and go home."

Chapter Forty-eight ⁄⁄ They Take Their Leave of Baqbuc and Leave the Oracle of the Divine Bottle

"No one pays, here," said Baqbuc. "We're completely satisfied if you are. Down here, in these circoncentric regions, we consider the supreme good to be giving, not taking and receiving, and we don't call people happy if they've taken and received a lot from others (as perhaps the sects of your world do), but if they're always giving a great deal. All we ask is that you leave your names and countries inscribed in our ritual book."

Then she opened a big, beautiful book in which, as we dictated, one of her mystical assistants seemed to be writing, with a golden pen, but we could see nothing appearing on the page.

That done, she filled three leather bottles with water from the fantastic fountain and handed them to us, saying:

"Go, my friends, under the protection of this intellectual sphere, the center of which is everywhere and the circumference of which is nowhere to be found (we call it God), and return to your own world bearing witness that here underground there are vast treasures and wonderful things. Truly, Ceres—worshiped across the entire universe, to which she demonstrated and taught the art of agriculture, and by inventing grain abolished among men the beast-like eating of acorns—did not wrongly lament the ravishing of her daughter to our subterranean regions, for she surely foresaw that here underground the daughter would find more good things, more excellent things, than the mother had created above it.

"What has become of the art of summoning heavenly thunder and lightning, invented long ago by wise Prometheus? You've certainly lost it; your hemisphere sees it no longer, but here underground we still employ it. And it's wrong of you to be so astonished, seeing your cities burned and charred by thunder and ethereal fire, not understanding from whom, and by whom, and why this ghastly scene comes to you, though to us it is both familiar and useful. Your philosophers love to tell you that the ancients have already described everything, that there's nothing new left to invent, but they're obviously wrong. That which appears to you out of the sky, and which you call natural phenomena, and that which the earth shows you, and that which the sea and the rivers contain—all that is nothing, compared to what is hidden underground.

"It is just and proper, therefore, that in almost all languages the subterranean ruler has been described in terms of riches. When your philosophers dedicate themselves to the study, and the zealous exhortation, of that sovereign Goddess the Egyptians used to call, in their language, Isis, meaning She Who Is Secret, Hidden, Concealed, and invoke Her by that name, and beg Her to come to them, and show Herself to them, She will open out their understanding both of Herself and of Her creatures, and will provide them, too, with a good lantern. For all the ancient philosophers and sages, in order to more confidently and pleasantly travel the road of divine understanding and the pursuit of knowledge, thought there were two absolutely necessary things, namely, the guidance of God and the fellowship of men.

"Thus, among the Persians, Zoroaster took Arimaspe as his companion on all his philosophical wanderings; Hermes Trismegistus, among the Egyptians, had Aesculapius; Orpheus in Thrace had Musaeus, and in that same place Aglaophemus had Pythagoras; among the Athenians, Plato first had Dion of Syracuse, in Sicily, and after he died took Xenocrates; and Apollonius had Damis.

"So when your philosophers, guided by God and accompanied by some clear lantern, wholly dedicate themselves to research and investigation (which is natural among humans, and is the quality which both Hesiod and Homer call *alphestes,* that is, researchers and inventors), they will learn that wise King Thales at Amasis, king of Egypt, spoke truly when he was asked where the greatest wisdom was to be found, and he answered, 'In Time.' Because in time, and by time, all hidden things always have been and always will be discovered, which is why the ancients called Saturn: Time, Father of Truth, and Truth the Daughter of Time. Your philosophers will also find, infallibly, that everything they and their predecessors know is scarcely a minute fraction of all there is to be known.

"From these three leather bottles, which I now give you, you will draw wisdom and knowledge, as the proverb says: *By his claws, you will know the lion.* The rarefaction of our water, enclosed in these containers, interacting with the warmth of the heavenly bodies and the ardor of the salt sea, according to the natural transmutation of the elements, will produce for you a most salubrious air, which will serve you as a clear, calm, and delightful wind—for what is wind but moving, flowing air? By means of this wind you will follow a direct route, if you so desire, straight to the port of Les Sables-d'Olonne, in Salmondais. Use this little gold vent, which you can see has been placed here as on a flute, to allow as much wind to blow across your sails as you wish, so you can sail as slowly as you like, and always pleasantly and safely, free from danger and from storms.

"Have faith in this, and do not believe that storms emanate from wind: wind is born of storms as they come up out of the bottom of the abyss. Nor should you believe that rain is caused because the heavens are unable to hold it back and because the clouds are hanging heavy and low. No, it is caused by the command of the subterranean regions, just as the heavenly bodies have imperceptibly drawn it up out of the depths. You have the testimony of your prophet king, David, who has sung and said that the abyss calls to the abyss.

"Of these three leather bottles, two are filled with the magic water; the third has been drawn from the well of the wise men of India, known as the Brahman Barrel.

"Further: you will find your ships properly and very well provisioned with everything that might be useful or necessary for your maintenance; while you have been here, I have made sure to arrange all that extremely well.

"So go, my friends, with joyous spirits, and carry this letter to your king, Gargantua. Greet him for us, and also all the princes and the other officers of his noble court."

Having said this, she gave us a sealed envelope and, after acknowledging our eternal thanks, we were shown out by a door next to the chapel, this being the spot where the priestess Baqbuc summoned people, in order to ask questions twice as tall as Mount Olympus.

Passing through a countryside full of every delight—pleasant, more temperate than Tempe in Thessaly, more salubrious than that part of Egypt which faces Libya, better irrigated and greener than Themiscyra, more fertile than that part of Mount Taurus which faces toward Aquilonia, or than the Hyperborean Island in the Red Sea, or than Caliges on Mount Caspius—a sweet-smelling countryside, as serene and gracious as Touraine itself, we finally came to our ships, waiting for us in port.

End of the Fifth Book
of the heroic deeds and words
of noble Pantagruel